DESCENSION

Layla Reddoch

First Printing: August, 2015
Printed in the United States of America

First Edition: August, 2015

This book is humbly dedicated to the wonderful men, women and children of my life, that have left this world to become angels, themselves. Without you, your guidance and continuous support, I would not be the woman that I am today.

For those who have lost their lives in the line of duty, both foreign and domestic; I thank you, from the bottom of my heart, for your selfless commitment. This world is a better place, because of you. I'll take it from here.

Most importantly, this book is for my dad. Daddy, you gave me the world. You opened my eyes to reality, with a beautiful twist and fairy tale approach. You taught me that life is what you make of it, and an adventure can happen at any moment. I see life in a different light because of you, and that light shines brighter because of your soul. I love you with every ounce of my being.

PREFACE

Everything is red. Different shades and saturations, but the same foreboding feeling every direction that I turn. I can see for miles. Miles of crimson swept with wisps of loneliness, black and grey. The shadows are darting on the ground below me. Scurrying. Hiding. But what could they be running from? Shadows are untouchable, broken only by light.

As I glance out in the distance, the clouds dance to lilting only heard by the gods. Below me, the trees are all black and twisted. They look as if they are screaming in pure agony. I struggle to raise my feet, to push forward. It feels as if I'm walking through freshly poured cement. As I look down, I see the ledge ahead of me. It is three feet away and I instantly feel the surge of panic in the pit of my stomach.

While keeping my eyes trained on the rocky edge, I scramble backwards, praying to find a miraculously well placed foothold. To my dismay, I find myself only six feet further backwards and splayed across a stone wall. I take in a deep breath, and decide to venture closer to the edge to see if there is a hidden escape. *What was that sound?*

Every sense is piqued. Every thought is crystal clear. I'm not a fan of heights, so why am I so close to a cliff? This isn't like me. Why the hell is everything red? The sky itself is glowing the same shade as squirting arterial blood.

The air is stagnant and smells of death; decay. My hands feel like they are statically charged. They feel numb, like they have fallen asleep. Pins and needles stab at my feet, then my calves, slowly moving up my legs. The sensation makes me look down, terrified of what I could find touching me. As I glance toward my feet to assure myself nothing is stabbing me, I notice my chest. I'm breathing four times what I should be. I'm hyperventilating. That explains the numbness and tingling. I have to slow down. The last thing I want is to pass out this close to a cliff. I take a deep breath, close my eyes, calming myself and my senses.

This will all be over soon. Someone will find me, standing on the precipice. Someone will swoop in and save this little damsel in distress and ride off on a valiant steed into the rich, vibrant colors of a fairy tale.

Leaving this blood red world miles behind sounds like a plan. A goal. How did I even get here? What am I doing here? My breathing finally slows down. It's safe to open my eyes again.

I feel a shift in my balance and see rocks falling into the darkness below. I try to step back to stable ground, but feel my footing slip on the rolling rocks. I turn to right my stance, to make a run for it. Facing away from the edge, I see a mass of black, shifting, shrinking, coalescing into the form of a crouching human. As I watch, the figure slowly stands upright. It's ominous and terrifying. I feel a wave of panic rush down my spine and jolt me. I don't know what it is, but I know what it is not. It isn't the knight in shining armor on his valiant steed coming to save me from my precipice.

I stare intently at the figure, waiting. It shifts again, faster than my eyes normally would have caught. It's now in a liquid smooth sprint, almost feline; shadows and light morphing and lapping at its heels as it charges directly at me. I take a step back and feel the ledge crumbling beneath my foot. I turn my head to the side and scan behind me. There's nowhere to go.

My choices are: a) stand my ground and brace for the impending impact I'm sure to receive; b) curl into a fetal position and beg for mercy, that I'm fairly certain I won't be granted; c) okay, I can't think of a third option and it's closing in.

As I deliberate, I catch a glimpse of its face as it stares up from the ground. A face, if that's what you want to call it. There is nothing. No landmarks to grant symmetry. No bloodthirsty grin, as I half expected. No frenzied eyes. No nose to inhale deeply and fill the lungs with more motivation from the stinging air. There is nothing but black. Black as pitch. Black as its heart, if it even has a heart. There's no sign of stopping. My two options seem less and less likely as I stare at my impending doom. I suddenly know exactly what to do, my wild card, my third option.

Being the hardheaded creature that I am, I decide to do the one thing my newfound attacker wouldn't predict. Granted, I don't know what it is, what it wants, or why I'm even in this situation, but I trust my instincts at this point. I trust my sight, my hearing, my self-preservation that is screaming to move.

I turn to glance behind me. My heel's still teetering on the edge, teasing the darkness below. With a wild smirk I bow my head, pretending to roll a hat in front of me like I had seen in movies countless times. I close my eyes, raise my arms into a horizontal embrace of the wind and step back for the last time.

A wave of confidence rushes through my veins. Maybe confidence isn't the correct word. Cockiness is more like it. I feel my smile stretch from ear to ear. *Boom! Checkmate.* Wait a second, what am I thinking?

I turn my head to the side and glance over my shoulder. The wind created by my free fall stings my eyes, choking my senses. I can't breathe. *Oh, my God! What have I done?* My eyes dart back up to the cliff and I see the being coming to an abrupt stop on the edge. It peers down at me, head bowed in defeat. I close my eyes and sigh, "Shit."

Chapter One
Screw You, Mr. Sandman!

I shot awake, startled by the sound of breaking glass. My head was spinning, my breathing uneven. My throat ached and my ears were ringing, like I had been at a decibel inducing concert all night, shrieking out the lyrics with the band on stage. I tried to familiarize myself with my surroundings. I was in my bedroom. I was in my bed. I tried to rub the sleep from my eyes. My body felt like I had just gotten out of a swimming pool. I was drenched. The sheets felt like damp, clammy hands wrapped around me, squeezing the life out of me. I kicked my legs like a toddler having a temper tantrum to break the hold of the overaggressive sheets, then flung myself back into my pillow, face down.

I got out of bed and opened the bedroom door. Scratching my head and looking bewildered, I walked into the dark living room. There he was, the knight in shining armor I had been waiting to save me. By armor, I meant plaid pajama pants and a faded t-shirt that was once a colorful masterpiece, depicting one of the greatest cartoons in TV history. He was standing in front of our 70 inch TV, with the word "paused" framing his figure on the oversized television screen. He had a look of horror on his face. At his feet was what I could only assume had once been an intact glass holding his beverage of choice. Whiskey and Coke, I presume.

"What the hell was that about?" he asked as I rounded the corner of the kitchen counter.

The look of confusion I was wearing must not have helped him figure out the details. Controller still in hand, he walked to where I stood. He rubbed my arm and had a genuine look of concern on his face. "Again with the screaming? I thought I was about to walk into a massacre or something." he cocked his head to the side and studied my expression.

"Yeah, sorry. Not sure what the hell is going on lately. Just another bad dream. At least, I think it was bad? I can't really figure out what's going on anymore." I looked down at my feet, ashamed.

He knows exactly what I go through on a regular basis. My dreams have tormented me long before I began trying to become accustomed to them. They've been a burden ever since I can remember. Constantly eating at me, even during my waking hours.

"You didn't *scare* me. I was 'in the zone'." he gestured with quotation marks. "It caught me off guard. I was about to come in there and tear some shit up." he was motioning his arms like he wielded a sword.

He was all I needed to feel at ease, to feel safe. For years, he had protected me from everything, including myself. I smiled and his eyes narrowed cynically.

"Whatever." he rolled his eyes and did an about-face. He started picking up the pieces of glass on the floor. Piece by piece, he carefully set them on the end table. I grabbed a trashcan, walking it over to him.

"I knocked a glass off of the table in my hurry to *save* you. Again." he was examining the wet spot on the rug when he noticed me with the trashcan at his side. He stood with his hands on his hips, staring at the floor.

"Do you think this is ever going to stop? I mean, dozens of glasses have met their fate the same way. When are we gonna invest in some plastic? It's getting expensive." he shook his head then looked at me.

I shrugged and set the trashcan down, turning to get a broom and dustpan. It was true. We had gone through more sets of glasses In the past year than most families with children do from birth to graduation. I felt horrible. If I could just learn to keep myself quiet, if I could just learn to suffer in silence, he wouldn't have to deal with our constant lack of glassware. That was now number three, this month alone.

When he was finished cleaning up the glass, I took the trashcan back to its rightful place in the kitchen and lifted the bag out. I carried the bag of trash to the bedroom, slid my feet into my fluffy Boston Bruins slippers and walked back to the patio door. He had already returned to his zombie killing spree when I stepped into the night.

Once outside I took a deep breath. I realized that I hadn't even looked at a clock. I had no idea what time it was, but I assumed it was later than I probably wanted it to be. When was all of this going to end? When was I going to get to sleep through the night? Why was that so much to ask? Screw you, Mr. Sandman!

I walked down the street of our cute little neighborhood to the dumpster. I heaved the heavy trash bag up and into its new home and listened as it hit the bottom. The glass shards shattered even more with a dull clinking; the sound was somehow satisfying.

I turned and walked back towards our house, cigarette in hand. I blew out heavily with a sigh and turned my face to the sky. I was thankful to look to the heavens and see the familiar midnight blue with twinkling stars and satellites, instead of the unnerving red I had so clearly seen just a few short moments ago. I was home; I was safe. I wish it could be this way forever, but it seems like every night that I sleep, I end up somewhere very far from my humble abode.

It's always too familiar. It's always different. Twisted and distorted, but a place I've spent my unconscious life, since I was at least four. I've read countless books, hundreds of forums and blogs, thousands of opinions. Some of it made sense, though it was increasingly rare. Most of the time it sounded more like insane rants from an asylum patient. Imagine that, a *crazy* person claiming to know the truth.

I've heard that I travel to another dimension, a time rift of sorts. I've read that it's an alien world; that I'm seeing out of Martian eyes. Or maybe it was explained accurately in that article I read about transcendence and the out of body experience. Was this some sort of travel to the spirit world? The thought scared me more than the thought of little green men. The thought that my family and friends that have left this life were somewhere stuck in that hell hole, scared me beyond belief. It was so desolate. So alone. So... dead.

As for what I put myself through with these dreams, I have no explanation other than my mind is very twisted. My imagination is very sadistic. The only excuse I have is years of fascination with the macabre, horror movies and the darker 'arts' that this world hides in its ugly corners. But in all honesty, I'm not sure which came first, the dreams or the lifestyle. I was so young when it all started. Surely I wasn't a fan of the concept often referred to as "Death" when I was four years old?

Then again, I spent my Saturday mornings running through the house, cereal sloshing over the sides of my bowl, as I raced to the TV to make sure I didn't miss the opening sequence of my favorite cartoon. I loved the dog and his friends, but I especially loved the villains. The ghosts that I later found out were only projections. *Bastards.*

There was always trickery afoot. Heaven forbid, for once, it was actually something paranormal. There was always a logical explanation. The baddies wanted the house because there was something buried beneath it. The "big bad ghost" ran off all of the townsfolk and they would've gotten away with it, too, if it hadn't been for those damn meddling kids.

Was that the reality of life? Was there really something so complex behind the scenes? Every time something happens that isn't right, there's just some asshole behind the curtain with a projector and a smoke machine? That gives me so much hope. People are always to blame.

I was back to the house. The warm glow of the TV radiated through the curtains, sending a sigh of comfort out of my lungs. The neighborhood was asleep, other than the street lamps that stood guard until dawn. Their only company was the light that billowed from our windows. The bright flashes that indicated rapid fire told me that my knight was in the middle of an epic battle with a horde of angry, flesh crazed zombies. He was our savior. All hail Riley, scourge of the undead.

As I walked back inside from the patio, I saw him standing, controller in hands, deep in thought and dedication to his mission. This was his release. This was his way of escaping reality. I never blamed him for his 'other' love. I can't always be entertaining, I'm not always in the best of moods and I definitely don't like to hover. He spends his time protecting people in all realities. Cop by day, zombie poacher by night and every form of hero in between.

He's the kind of guy that little boys want to be when they grow up; charming, smart, overly sarcastic to the point of pain. He's the kind of guy that every girl wants to have; charming, smart, overly sarcastic to the point of a challenge. I've been proud to have him on my arm, on my mind and in my life. But none of that changes the fact that, this man, my soul mate, drives me absolutely crazy. In a good way, of course. I think. But I digress.

I glanced into the kitchen and noticed the little clock on the stove. 2:15. Lovely. Once again, I wasn't able to sleep through the night and it left me with a horrible feeling. There would be no comfort in unconsciousness tonight. At least it was Saturday and I was off work to drag-ass around the house and get absolutely nothing done in my state of vegetation. I'd get some rest at some point, but my mind was currently far from relaxed.

I walked into the kitchen and opened the cupboard. The dwindling of the glasses reminded me that we needed to go shopping, but walking around a 24-hour store was not what I had in mind right now. I didn't want to be alone at the moment, but mixing with a crowd of drunken college kids beating each other with those foam pool noodles and wearing neon pink plastic cowboy hats wasn't exactly my definition of adventure or the fulfillment of a dream.

I clutched one of the lone survivors and filled it to the brim with tea. I looked at the ice swimming around and thought maybe I should go ahead and write out a speech for the funeral this glass was sure to have in the upcoming weeks.

...he was a brave soul. He was always half full when his comrades were half empty. He stood for justice. He stood with orange juice in the face of adversity. He was created by the best, the Chinese, woven from the finest of glass particles and duly appointed with the words 'douche bag' on his exterior. We mourn his loss.

We mourn the $8.00 we paid to giggle at his namesake. We mourn the fact that we can no longer hand his glory to a friend, nonchalantly, pretending as if we didn't notice the proclamation they held. We will deeply miss you, my dear douche bag. Although you will be replaced, you will never be forgotten...

And on that note, I bowed my head for a moment of silence and knew, deep in my soul, that I had officially lost it. I snickered to myself and walked to the living room, never to speak of my douche bag glass dirge, ever. It was for the best.

I sat down on the couch and watched as my zombie slayer did his nightly business. Head shot. Head shot. Knee shot, head shot. He was a master of his craft. The big screen flashed to a cinema scene and he turned to face me. He wore the smug grin of a flashy superhero. He knew he was untouchable in his pixilated world. I couldn't help but smile back. To put it mildly, I sucked at shooting games. I dabbled in the arts of video games, but I enjoyed my time watching him play, more than anything.

My mind wasn't in the room with us as I curled up to his side and stared at the seizure-inducing brilliant screen. What did finally get my attention were the splashes and splatters of blood that eventually covered the screen as he hacked and slashed the undead in first person combat.

I shuddered and stood up. I turned to Riley and pressed pause on his controller, mid-button mashing.

"Food. Gimme," I said, as I held out my arms like Frankenstein's monster did in the movies.

I didn't want brains, kidneys, hearts or dismembered appendages. I wanted breakfast. He laughed as he saved and turned off his game with a stiff stumble from his seat. Once he sat up, I noticed the furry orange blob that was tucked under his arm unroll and crash to the center of the couch with confusion. Riley didn't even notice and walked to the bedroom to change clothes.

Rufio opened his eyes, yawned and stretched. He looked at me in the middle of waking. He instantly began purring and meowing as he always did. He's always so excited to see us. What a bizarre little animal. He's our child.

He doesn't need fancy food, extravagant toys or sparkling spring water, found in the Alps, to sip from a wine glass. He wants attention and red straws. He's obsessed with them. No, not the white ones with the red stripes down the sides that we could buy at any grocery store. It has to be the red ones from certain fast food places. He has forced us, many times, to feel guilty because we shoved a hand full of straws into my purse. He's the little devil on my shoulder. *'Steal them. Steal the straws. I require reparation.'* It never fails.

I hope I don't end up in prison some day for all the stolen straws I've brought home. I'm not a kleptomaniac; I'm the guardian of an insane cat whose only joy in life comes in the form of little tubes of red plastic.

I scratched behind his ears and ruffled the fur on his back. I knew what pisses him off and gets him off of my lap, as it did this time with a dejected look over his shoulder as he left the room.

I got up and changed, sad to take off my overly comfortable pajamas. I refuse to be one of *those* people. You know the ones I'm talking about. The ladies who wear their nightgown and curlers into stores, carrying themselves like they're wearing formal attire. The guy who wears his torn up 80's band t-shirt, sweat pants resembling Swiss cheese, with his gut protruding between the two. There's a time and place to make yourself look like a complete ass, but in public while others are still semiconscious is not it.

Welcome to my mind and my voice of reason. I never said there was a proper method to my madness or motivation.

Once changed, I met Riley in the living room and we stepped out into the night. I felt the cool breeze blow through my messy hair as it sent a chill through me. We got in the car and backed out into the silent streets of our neighborhood.

I stared out of the passenger window as the neon lights of the hospital and surrounding businesses blurred by. We live in the heart of our city. What city you ask? It doesn't matter. It's the same thing, cookie cut across the country. There's crime. There's political corruption. There's homelessness. There's godlessness, godliness, or was that god-fearing-ness? I live in your city, their city, the city. It doesn't sleep, it just turns its head and closes its eyes, pretending not to see people getting robbed and murdered over shoes or car stereos.

I love it here. This is raw humanity, the core of our beings. If we are what we eat, then we're definitely weak humans. We devour ourselves daily.

I stared out of the window for the entire drive. I was only half listening to the music blaring from the speakers as we drove to the 24-hour diner. I was thinking about the dream I had. Normally, I can make sense of them, or at least can write them off as tainted by my day's activities. But this one was different. It was lucid. I fully knew what I was doing at all times. I thought I was really there, even though I didn't know how or why.

The reasons were inconsequential. What mattered to me was how I reacted. I'm not one to hurt myself intentionally. I've dedicated my life to helping people who have been hurt. I don't condone suicide, I'm not the type of person to give in and be taken down the easy way.

Easy? A black mass barreling towards me is easy now? I shook my head and snapped back to reality when I heard the music and engine turn off. Riley was staring at me with an eyebrow raised.

"Am I supposed to bring you your food? I'm not your butler, Edie, as much as you tried with your little voodoo curses and hexes." He unbuckled his seatbelt and closed the door.

I sat there for a second wondering if this early morning breakfast was going to be as filled with bickering as usual. "It wasn't hexes, it was vows, you dick," I mumbled as I got out of the door and sulked after him.

We were *escorted* to a dimly lit back corner of the diner by your typical southern beauty. She had fried, bleached blonde hair with grey and muddy brown roots, crow's feet around her eyes that looked like the damned bird must've weighed forty-five pounds, and her smile reminded me of checkers. She slapped our menus down and mumbled something about our waitress coming.

I smiled my fakest of smiles and upped my voice two octaves with a pleasant "why, thank you!"

Riley smirked and rolled his eyes. He's more accustomed to my sarcasm than most. I blame his immunity on years of exposure, although he's the one who taught me a majority of it. Our waitress appeared out of thin air, mid-conversation, like a magician. She offered us countless options that we reluctantly turned down.

"I'll take some coffee, eggs over medium, bacon and French toast," I said, with my nose crammed in the menu staring at the pictures.
Riley just said, "Same".

He was a man of few words when we were outside of our domicile. He was never rude, unless provoked, but he never felt the need to say more than necessary. I, on the other hand, spoke more than I should have and spent many moments choking on my shoes.

Our waitress smiled politely and took the menus, stating that our food would "be right up". Those of us that venture into public for sustenance know that our food will *never* be right up, at least not as we ordered it. I turned away from the drunken patrons and smiled at Riley.

"So. How was the killing spree? Successful, I presume." I had my fingers locked together on top of the table in a professional, interview type of manner.

He shrugged. "Success only goes so far with a never ending supply of undead. Could you imagine what this place would be like if there were zombies? I mean really, we could hole up at the house for a couple days, at max. We'd have to eventually bunker down at the station or something," he trailed off.

"That's not a bad idea, though. There's at least riot gear and guns and shit. I can't guarantee edible food, so we might want to grab some from home…" he was now looking out of the window next to us, more than likely picturing the onslaught in a play by play. He turned back to me. "…and maybe I should start bringing the assault rifle in when I get home. You know, just 'in case'." He made the little quotation marks with his fingers again and smiled.

I started shaking my head instantly. He was on a roll tonight. "Oh yeah, now that's a *good* idea. Something tells me an Irish man with a combustible temper, and halfcocked schemes doesn't need to have a cocked rifle in his hands at any time. I'm sure the cat, the walls and the neighbors would be more than bullet riddled by the time you got your point across," I jabbed.

He just grinned and began to spin his fork on the table.

I could see the cogs turning and his grin turned into a full-fledged smile. He laughed to himself and I could easily recognize the spark in his eyes. He thought it was a *great* idea. I suddenly wished I hadn't mentioned the cat or the neighbors. I instantly thought of the countless nights waking up to him yelling at Rufio and threatening him with every ounce of wrath possible, before rolling over only to resume the cycle in twenty minutes like two old men in a nursing home. I thought about the mounds of crap we've stepped in thanks to the neighbor's massive dog. I swear, it seems like that beast eats whole villages or small communes then defecates on our lawn, with the most unholy of smells. You don't need a poop scoop, you need a priest or two to excommunicate the grass.

He was deep in thought, spinning the fork, grinning wickedly. I could've sworn I saw little horns burst from his forehead. He was more dedicated to this idea than I would've thought possible. Suddenly, our waitress appeared again.

She had plates, bottles of syrup and mugs of hot coffee so strategically placed on her arms and hands that I was dumbfounded. Do they send wait staff to school for this or was it a natural talent? I held my breath as she set everything down.

Allow me to set the scene. She'd accidentally drop the plates and coffee, glass shattering and scalding liquid exploding into our unexpected faces. And there, my poor bacon would lay, helpless, hopeless, lifeless and ruined. I almost shed a tear before I realized my plate and coffee mug were set perfectly in front of me, without a drop spilled. I sighed with relief and thanked her. And by "thanks" I really meant: "I appreciate your graceful ascendance to my table without brutally maiming me or my husband with molten coffee and egg yolks."

I was so thankful for her timing and the short attention span of my other half. I knew he had finally given up the thought of bringing said rifle into the house and figured it was probably best if I stopped thinking about it, as well. I stabbed at the butter mote in my toast and drowned my powdery friends with syrup.

We sat in silence, for the most part, until we were finished eating. We then spent several hours talking about unrealistic events, conspiracy theories, religious propaganda and old cartoons. We drank gallons of coffee, until we finally felt jittery enough to shamble home.

We walked to the front door and were once again greeted by our loyal pet. I'm sure he was delighted to see us, but I couldn't help but wonder if he was looking for "presents" in our hands.

CHAPTER TWO
HOPELESSLY DEVOTED TO EWE

It was so rare to sleep and not dream, or at least not remember them. I couldn't recall getting into bed, but I pulled the sheets away from my face and was immediately blinded. The sun was invading my space. I slid closer to my side of the bed to try and avoid the beam of light encroaching on my personal bubble, then hissed and guarded my eyes like a vampire would. I glanced over at the alarm clock. 7:23am.

I decided more sleep was in order. I pulled the comforter back over my head to block the sunlight and closed my eyes, listening to the sound that was pouring out of Riley's throat. It had to be painful. It sounded as if a lumberjack had finally met his match. Riley's vocal cords and tongue had been replaced by prehistoric trees, larger than life and impervious to chain saws. The sawing was loud, then louder, then quieted by a fart and a sigh.

Riley rolled over and wrapped his heavy arms around me. I snickered and continued to misconstrue the sounds around me, picturing something obscure that could be making them happen. I closed my eyes again and listened to Rufio snore with a light sighing.

I know people supposedly count sheep to fall asleep, so I pictured a vast meadow. As I looked into the distance, I could see a herd of sheep feeding on grass and frolicking around. I wonder why I haven't thought about this before.

My mind is always in the darker spots. My visions are under the trampled rocks, behind the creepy shed, hanging by a noose from the tree in the meadow. I had replaced Rufio's breathing with the whispers in the grass, the chewing of the ewes. I saw the scampering sheep and I finally understood why people decide to count them instead of rabid dogs or pages of a trigonometry textbook to pass on to dreamland. They're peaceful and carefree. I could feel the smile on my face as I stared off into the beautiful meadow. The clouds were rolling by with graceful speed. The breeze was so warm, it felt like mid-August. I sat down on the side of a hill to watch the animals play and munch on their vivid green breakfast.

One of the sheep's head snapped up, suddenly alert, staring at a distant hill. I couldn't see what it was looking at, but it stiffened, frightened. I watched as all of the sheep turned to face the same spot. Suddenly, they scattered. They ran in every direction, except for the direction of the knoll, bleating as they did.

As I stared, confused, I saw a black shape starting to surface at the top. Behind it, the sky began to turn red, like blood being dripped into water, spreading upward like water colors. I gasped, afraid to keep watching but powerless to turn away. I was petrified. The shape came into focus. It was humanoid. And now there were two. The same pitch black I saw on the cliff.

Baa baa black sheep, have you any ghouls?
Yes, sir. Yes, sir.
Two graves full...

I watched as they slowly walked down the hill. The sky continued to expand into a crimson wall. How could something so serene become so bleak? I rose to my feet and started to back away. I didn't want to turn and be caught off guard.

Assuming this is the same blackness from my prior encounter, now with a "friend", he may be more reluctant to allow my escape. I stepped back and felt my heel crumble the ground. I glanced behind me and saw the same edge, the same distance below me I had seen previously. I turned around to face the blackness.

He was now running at me, full speed, with his companion along the cliff side. Where the hell did my meadow go? At that moment I stopped, closed my eyes and raised my arms again in defeat. I took my final step backwards and grinned.

"See you tonight, asshole," I snarled as I watched him skid to a stop at the top of the ledge.

I fell further than I had originally, but shot up from my slumber just as alarmingly.

When I sat up, I noticed that the bed was empty beside me. I could hear Riley in the kitchen, more than likely concocting a makeshift breakfast. Rufio was going on about something, with his typical talking. He was just like a kid, constantly telling stories however his little cat mind and mouth could.

I sat up and tried to rub the stress from my eyes. I got up and slipped on some pants, combing out my tangled locks with my quivering fingers and then walked into the kitchen, groggy and annoyed.

"Good morning, sunshine!" Riley spun around.

"Ugh," I moaned and laid my head down on the counter.

He was standing at the toaster in his boxers and equipped with oven mitts. I was afraid to ask, or to even show concern. I grabbed the last clean and unbroken glass from the cupboard and filled it with water, leaning against the counter and glancing at the stove. 8:07am. So much for rest.

"How did you sleep? You were out cold all morning." he turned to extricate his breakfast.

I stood silently, perched next the edge of the counter for a few moments while I planned my strategy.

"No rest for the wicked." I smiled.

After so many years, I learned that we both have skeletons in our closets. Sometimes it's best if we just pile more shit on top of them and pretend they're coat racks, instead of allowing them free roam of the house. It could get pretty crowded in here if we were more passive. We're never *dishonest*, but we omit the things that would stir up unneeded fears and anxiety.

We're both preoccupied with civil service, including the wellbeing of each other. We put up our armor, throw on our masks and help each other along like we're steel crutches. It's a strength. It's also a weakness. It's not that we don't talk about what's bothering us; we just don't drag each other down when it's unnecessary.

I know he worries about me. I know he wonders what I see in my sleep and why he can't protect me from it. I know it hurts him to see me covered in sweat and panic stricken. And I can see the pain on his face every time he asks me if I'm okay. My lips say I'm fine, while my mind is screaming "NO!", but I smile and shrug it off like it's nothing at all.

It's getting harder to brush off. That's two dreams in a row that blindsided me. I'm used to the horror, but I've never seen my dreams like this. In all my years of dreaming, I feel like I've become an expert of my experiences. I've learned to interpret my dreams on my own, without a "dream dictionary" written by some quack with a mail-order doctorate in psychobabble bullshit. I know how I think, I know what stresses me out or what makes me laugh. I don't need some outside source to tell me what I'm "truly thinking".

I shook my head to stop the thoughts again. I hopped off of the counter and walked out to the patio. I pulled the curtains aside and was once again blinded by my intruding nemesis. I raised both hands in the air and threw up my middle fingers like a rock star to the media. The sun seems to have held a grudge against me and my fair complexion all of my life. We've been mortal enemies ever since I was old enough to run around naked in the spray of the garden hose. Not that I still *do* that…often.

But mocking a yellow dwarf that was once referred to as a god, with numerous antics over the past few decades hasn't exactly been my brightest idea. Oh well, what is it going to do? Burn me? I'm not going to spontaneously combust anytime soon. Can it say the same thing? I watch the science channels on TV. I'm not sure that's a safe assumption for it to make.

I've always been fascinated with science, philosophy and theology. From the beginning of mankind, people have always tried to spiritually tie the celestial heavens to the Earth. People have always needed a structure, a belief to fall back on and why not take something so powerful, so mysterious and claim it to be God, gods or some supernatural phenomenon. I'm not sure what I believe, or where I stand on the subject, but I do know that the universe and the elements can easily be explained without the mention of pious mumbo jumbo. Neutrons, atoms and isotopes are not characters from the Bible, by the way.

I leaned back in the chair on the patio and propped my feet up on the stool. I threw my head back and smiled, taunting my adversary in the sky, again. I closed my eyes and thought about the way only Saturdays made me feel. Content. At peace with my inner slacker. I listened as the birds chirped back and forth like the bickering couples on those ridiculous "who's the baby-daddy" talk shows on TV. I could hear the willows and magnolias swaying in the breeze, the soft melody of the wind chimes, and the traffic in the distance. I thought about the things that had gotten me here and about my life, as a whole.

Cue Intermission music…

I was once Eden McDowell, born in a little city in Southeast Texas. My parents got married and combined their boys to form my family. My Mom always described it as "his, mine and ours". I was the only ours, the baby. The only girl. I was raised by four older brothers and it showed. We moved around a lot, due to work and religious "pioneering". I had my first steps on the white sands of the Micronesian islands. I spent my first birthday (or two) rampaging the villages in my tiny grass skirt. I was a golden-locked menace. My pout was Earth-shattering. My smile was suspicious. Not much has changed in thirty years.

We moved all across the South Pacific and eventually made it back to the United States before my fourteenth birthday. I spent so much time living on the islands, raised alongside people who lived their life governed by tradition and superstition. It was a culture shock to return to the land of the dead, emotionally disconnected and otherwise discontented. We moved from Texas to Louisiana and back a few times. I spent a few of my teen years as a chameleon. I gave into peer pressure and slowly slipped into the spiral that is commonly known as the American teen way. I didn't know who I was, who I wanted to be or why I even gave a shit.

By the time I was adjusted to being a teen, I snapped back to reality and realized what I was doing to myself. I started to detach myself from my bad influences and became an individual again. As time progressed, with a clear mind and clean conscience, I found my counterpart and eventually tied the knot. The wild one had actually managed to settle down. I surprised a lot of people with that.

We spent years struggling in a dying city. It was a ghost town. The smart people found their escape plans and ran, the rich people bought their way out or ruled the city with a greedy iron fist and the less fortunate suffered silently, trapped. The auto city once operated like a well-oiled machine, but was now broken down, rusting and corroding from the inside out.

Corruption, murder, rape and neglect headlined the papers and newscasts on a daily basis. The city was the epitome of hell on Earth. We both knew it, but didn't know how to save ourselves. We jumped from dead end job to dead end job, taking what we could when it was available and as the economic wells dried up, we decided that education was our only option. We struggled to get me through school first and I finally began doing something with myself.

I became an EMT, while I went to school to get my paramedic license. I knew ever since I was fifteen, due to a close call with my mother, someday I wanted to help people. I knew deep down that fear and raw human emotion was dangerous, but I would face it to help others. I was cool at times of awkwardness. I was collected when chaos reigned. I knew that I was meant to put my life on the line to attempt to bring peace to those I helped. After a while of working on the road, I realized it was monkey's work. But I loved it nonetheless.

Once I finished school, I was offered an opportunity we couldn't refuse and we moved to Louisiana. Riley was a transplant, but I was at home. I was in the land that held my heart. We moved to the tumultuous city, cradled by the arms of the Mississippi river and shadowed by the stifling bayou. Baton Rouge. Home, at long last. There were other cities, other options, of course, but something drew us here. Something we didn't understand, but we also didn't fight. We found our new home very welcoming. It didn't take us long to find our place and become acclimated to the changes. New life. Rebirth. That was the plan and so far, it had been successful.

And here we are. The story of my life thus far. Granted, there's far more to it than I mentioned, but I'd prefer not to delve too deeply into my past. Some things are better left unspoken, or thought of, for that matter. My history has darkness, but it also has so much joy entwined. My personality and mental stability are an entirely different story all together. It's hard to pinpoint who I am, but insight never hurts.

I'm surrounded by death, even in reality. I've become so used to seeing death and pestilence in my dreams, that I've become intrigued by it. I've always loved Halloween and all things associated with it, but that's different. Luckily, I found someone else, who appreciates the same things, but for different reasons.

The truth is I'm not anything special. I imagine that I'm pretty average. I think I've lived through crazy times, with a vibrant history. I'm sure everyone has in their own way. But the difference between me and the rest of society is, I don't mind talking about my dark side. I've embraced it. I don't hide behind it and pretend to be someone that I'm not. I *know* I have problems. I'll be the first to admit it. I am who I am, accept it or don't. The only thing that matters to me is that the people that I love have accepted my flaws and faults.

I'm a typical girl; I'm just cloaked in a different suit. I don't hide who I am behind expensive clothes and designer tags. I hide behind my colorful Halloween tattoos. My skin is my armor.

I love shiny things, flowers, baby animals, poetry, unicorns, fairies and happy endings... (ha ha). But I also love bats, skulls, zombies, vampires, thunderstorms and the things that go bump in the night. I love mythology. I love tarot. I love the infallible truth that we aren't the greatest creature to inhabit the universe. It's a scary thought. It's intimidating. It's even more disturbing when you see it firsthand.

CHAPTER THREE
BROKEN MORAL COMPASSES

I sat on the patio for hours, it seemed. I could feel the twinge of pain that shot across the bridge of my nose. I knew it. That son of a bitch got me. I got up and walked into the house and caught my reflection in the hallway mirror. I had definitely been kissed by the sun, as they say. I knew I was playing with fire when I decided to reflect on the patio. It was a small price to pay to replenish my supply of vitamin D.

Riley walked into the hallway behind me and glanced at the mirror. I watched as his cheeks puffed up. He threw his hand to his mouth to stifle a chuckle. He cleared his throat and grinned. I walked to the bathroom, where I would commence the healing ritual. I slathered my face with lotion as I winced and groaned.

Riley leaned against the bathroom door. I could see the restlessness coiled in his stance. "I need to get the hell out of here. I don't know what you want to do, but I think it's time we headed out. I just want to go... somewhere." He was already out of the doorway and changing his clothes by the time I answered.

"Well. Where do you wanna go?"

"Out."

I raised a brow. "To?"

"I don't care. I just think we both need a healthy dose of fresh air, society and shitty traffic to remind us that we're still alive." He flopped on the bed in an overdramatic manner and turned on the TV.

He sat up with a heavy sigh, turned the TV off and put on his shoes. I knew it was pointless to argue. I wanted to get out of the house just as much as he did. I was tired of thinking. Tired of being stuck in my own mind. Maybe getting out and seeing the world around me would help. I pulled off my pajama shirt and threw it at him. It landed on his face and he grinned, knowing he had won.

We pulled onto our street and I silently watched as two boys from our neighborhood chased each other with foam swords and plastic shields. What I would give to be a kid again, carefree, open minded, innocent and naive. I smiled at the thought. Riley was singing along with the music blaring from the stereo. He always seems just as carefree and innocent as the children from our block. It was refreshing.

We made our way through the dense traffic to the interstate and took the exit for College Drive. As we exited, I saw a man standing at the corner holding a sign to his chest. We were more than accustomed to seeing the homeless and hungry at the intersections, but something caught my attention.

He was dressed far more sophisticated than the typical "domestically challenged". He wore the pea coat of a sailor, with very minimal wear and tear. His face was shrouded by the hood of his jacket worn under his coat. The only skin left visible was his hands, delicately placed on the sides of his sign. They almost seemed to glow, impossibly white and unblemished. Not workers hands or the hands of the homeless. He never looked up.

As we approached the stop light, I was able to read his sign. "Will save your souls for food? Ha ha, that's awesome."

I heard Riley snicker as he began fumbling through his pockets. "Our souls could use a little saving, but I don't think he wants the half eaten bag of chips that's been in the back seat for a week. I gotta have some cash somewhere. Maybe he could spend it on a t-shirt or something, its eighty-fuckin'-six degrees out here today! What the hell is he thinking?" Riley started to roll down his window.

"He's gonna have a heatstroke."

The man turned away from us as if he had heard what Riley was saying. He began to cross the street in front of the car. I stared at him as he passed in front of me and darted across the rest of the way. The light had turned green and people honked and threw up their hands, yelling at the man to move faster.

I turned to look in the direction he had run, but couldn't see him anywhere. It was bizarre, to say the least. Riley sped around the corner and took off, like the entire event had never happened. For some reason, I was reading more into it than I probably needed to.

We spent a couple of hours walking around the grocery store, trying to stock up on the essentials. We attempted to survive at home as long as we could, without having to make a trip to the store. It wasn't that we didn't like to be in public. We simply tried to avoid the massive amount of morons who, for whatever reason, seem to lack social skills and volume control when in groups.

They were like wild herds of stoned frat boys who prided themselves on being the "coolest" guy, from their high school of two hundred students. The only talent they had was determining the trajectory of the perfect wedgies. I never understood them.

We made it out of the store alive and headed home to unload our new stock of food and accoutrements. The trip home was filled with the typical small talk, never mentioning my dreams or crazy street people. Spending time with Riley was like spending time with a game show host. He was constantly equipped with smarmy jokes and one-liners.

We carried everything inside, put it all away and escaped to our patio with beer and cigarettes in tow. It was dusk. The sky was beyond beautiful with vibrant shades of pink and orange peeking around the dark, fast moving clouds. We sat outside for a while, until a storm began to roll in and we felt the delicate sprinkles of rain began to fall. We grabbed our stuff and bolted for the door just as the flood gates opened and the sky spewed massive amounts of rain onto our city.

We made it inside before everything was blanketed in rain. Riley walked into the living room, grabbed the TV remote and began flipping between channels. I strolled to the kitchen to get dinner ready. He stopped on the weather forecast and read the scrolling text aloud, "A severe thunderstorm warning is in affect for our area. This storm is capable of producing large hail and strong damaging winds in excess of 50 miles per hour. You are advised to seek shelter… ha! I'm so scared."

He continued his channel surfing, occasionally stopping to laugh at commercials or mock the over acting of a low budget, made-for-TV movie. He eventually stopped on the news channel when he saw the "Breaking News" message at the bottom of the screen.

"...the meteor shower wasn't expected. Astrologists assume that some of the ice and debris has broken through the atmosphere just south of Rome. Witnesses stated that the phenomenon was awe inspiring and believed it to be a sign from God in these depressing times," a female anchor was saying. "One woman said she had chills as she stared at the Vatican, softly silhouetted by the multicolored light show behind it. The shower began around ten o' clock, Central European Time, and continued for approximately an hour and a half. Local news stations broadcasted these amateur videos sent in shortly after midnight." The woman shuffled her papers and waited for the video footage to begin.

I stepped around the counter and sat on the arm of the couch.

The screen flashed from the News anchor's face to the video mentioned. The footage was shaky and slightly out of focus as it panned from the enormous Trevi Fountain to the brightly lit night behind it. The lights sparkled and shimmered as they shot across the European sky with amazing speed and grace. In the background of the video, you could hear people cheering, and speaking in multiple languages. The video ended and the news report continued.

"Astrologists say they were unaware of the cosmic event. Meteor showers occur annually or in a set amount of years, based on when the Earth passes it's 'parent' comet or constellation in orbit. The next anticipated meteor shower wasn't due until August, with the approach of Perseids, associated with the comet Swift–Tuttle."

I returned to the kitchen, never breaking my gaze.

"No comet was noted to have passed through our solar system recently and the event has left many observers baffled. The star storm was compared to the noted Leonids, also known as the king of meteor shows, which occur annually and peaks around the middle of November."

I was completely enraptured by the story and noticed I had been staring at the TV screen. A knife was still balanced in my hand and my vegetable prey was cowering beneath me, waiting for the cut.

Riley lost interest in the news when they began talking about the economy and the debt our country is in. I listened to him as he flipped through the channels with record speed and laughed. He was not intrigued by reality.

After dinner was ready, I walked out on the patio to smoke and clear my head. The rain had temporarily let up, leaving the city much cooler than it had been before the storm. I wasn't sure why the news report of the meteor shower intrigued me so much. I had a gut feeling something odd was going on. But what was going on, I couldn't decipher.

I sat down on the damp chair and listened as the wind whipped through the trees. The rain drops left on the leaves splattered heavily as they fell and hit the ground. Thunder crashed in the distance, shaking the ground around me. It was getting closer, coming in for another round.

"..A sign of God, my ass…" I thought out loud, as I looked to the thundering sky.

I can't explain why I get so frustrated with people's futile attempt to connect themselves with spirituality. I guess I've just lost hope in humanity. Yes, I believe in God. Well, I believe in *a* God. God to me is subatomic. It's the fabric of our lives, the foundation of every organism in the universe, of our existence.

What I don't believe is that there's this supernatural, divine being sitting in his rocking chair in the heavens that mystically guides us and sets us up like pawns on a chess board of life. That contradicts free will. That goes against everything we've been taught to recognize as individuality and human nature.

I believe in science. I believe in evolution. I believe what is placed in front of me, seen with my own eyes. Truth. Evidence. Undeniable. I respect the prophets of religion. They did a wonderful service for humanity. But I mainly view them as historical figures. *Men* who were gifted. They were outspoken, human or self-appointed, talented debaters who had a tendency to win people over, or outwit them.

These men, these *human beings*, broke down the defenses of countless people by speaking the words they wanted to hear. They promoted wonderful philosophies that organized religion picked apart and twisted, to form fit the lifestyle they thought was proper. But what happened in the long run? Most of the prophets of religion were murdered, martyred for their beliefs and opinions. That sure says a lot for humanity.

We let murderers and rapists live long lives in prison where they're given an excellent education most of us can't afford. We provide free food, cable TV, books and art classes, while hard working people struggle to survive. We allow people to rule with tyranny, but we kill someone who gives guidance and claims to be the Son of God? *That* seems more blasphemous than being a false prophet, a made up messiah. Human beings are hypocrites.

And what about the shamans and mystics of the more secluded societies? They're looked at as magicians. Apparently, a "little sleight of hand" performance has saved generations of tribes without proper medical supplies and technology. *What's happened to our world? When did we stray from reality and honor?*

People are driven by faith that isn't even what it was intended to be. Don't get me wrong. I think faith is of the essence. *Any faith.* Be it faith in a prophet, a god, an atom, or even yourself. You must have faith in *something* to push forward in life. It's what guides us; Our moral compass. But some people, suffice it to say, have a broken moral compass. It always points south, or it spins faster than it can be controlled.

The "rulers" of religion now, the leaders of these *sects*, have turned our faith against us to force us into submission. If you don't act accordingly, if you don't follow *their* doctrine, you are a sinner and will be going to Hell. When Nordic mythology, the ancient Egyptians, or any other form of pagan belief is mentioned, they're primitive. They believe in "false idols". Yet in modern Christianity, much is based on paganism, although they refuse to admit it. I'm not pointing fingers, I'm stating facts and explaining why I feel the way I do.

What is organized religion anyway? Nowadays it's a group of power hungry politicians and con artists telling us to live our lives by an outdated book that wasn't even written by a prophet of God. We still believed the Earth was flat and that the sun revolved around us at that point in history. We were the biggest fish in the sea of importance. Does the Bible mention anything about how to live as a single parent, raising three kids, with two part time jobs in a failing economy? If it does, it only states that you, sinner, screwed the pooch. We're hiding behind the unseen, the unapproachable, the invisible and thanks to modern society, the unforgiving.

What will the future civilizations have to say about us? If we still even exist, if we haven't blown ourselves to pieces in the midst of another world war. We will be lumped in with our "primitive" predecessors, when science and technology have filled the gaps and holes left by religion. We will be "old school", when they've mastered the arts of immortality and resurrection through education and intelligence, not miracles.

They will look back on our religious wars, which never brought answers by the way, and wonder how we managed to sleep at night after killing our brothers. Religion as a whole has been smeared with shame and tainted by more death than any other circumstance in our history. No one that I've ever heard of has died because of their belief of photosynthesis or the binding of carbons. Oh, the naiveté of man.

We have to be our own saviors. We have to be our own messiahs. We have to help each other and stop hiding behind a mythical idol. We are God. The trees, the wind, the dog that takes a crap on my lawn, the mother that smothered her baby to death, thanks to postpartum depression… it's there, in our fabric. In our DNA. We have to recognize what we are doing and own up to our misguided mistakes. We have to take control of our actions and correct it, before it's too late. Or is it already too late?

The thunder cracked and startled me from my reveries. I walked back inside to my now cold dinner, and began picking and poking at my food while my mind was still trying to piece together what I'd seen on TV. I still couldn't figure out why it wasn't making sense to me. It bothered me that something had just "slipped" by scientists across the globe. I could understand one or two "oops", but everyone? And of course, this was just another reason for the religious to give God credit. *It's a sign!* I guess, for once, I agree. It is. But what does it mean?

Riley made small talk over dinner and I tried my best to answer as if my mind wasn't elsewhere. He'd think I was once again, reading too much into it. Or he'd develop a conspiracy theory about how the government was trying to cover up some crash landing debris of extraterrestrials. I hate not having answers.

"I don't really see what the big deal is. The media can blow *anything* out of proportion." He picked up his plate and headed to the kitchen.

"Yeah." I took that as my cue. "I don't know. I don't really see the symbolism that they're reaching for. I mean, it's kind of surprising, but," I trailed off before I began to delve too deeply into the discussion. I didn't want to bore him, again, with my inner monologue. He knew how I felt about things.

"Ugh, back to work tomorrow," he said as he loudly smacked his forehead into the freezer door.

"Hooray," I replied sarcastically, waving my fists in the air like a child. I was glad he changed the subject. Sort of.

We finished up in the kitchen and then walked outside to watch the storm. We sat quietly for a while, listening to the city shaking and buckling under the heavy rain and thunder. Lightening shot across the sky, leaving trails of light burned into my vision. *This* is what we lived for.

The breeze picked up and turned towards us as if answering our wishes. A wave of rain sprayed us. I shrieked and squealed with laughter as we ran towards the door. Standing behind me, Riley wrapped his arms around my waist and laid his head on my shoulder.

"Let's get in bed," he said with a smile, grabbing my hand and spinning me.

"Okay." I sighed dramatically. "I really don't feel like going to work. Maybe we should both call out. Our weekends are never long enough."

"Yeah, I know." He hung his head in defeat and squeezed my hand.

We walked to the bathroom to perform our nightly rituals, preparing for sleep. Rufio had wandered into the room and splashed in the sink as we tried to finish brushing our teeth. We could hear the storm picking up outside. Thunder crashed and shook the windows in their frames.

We curled up in bed and talked for a few minutes. Riley turned off the TV, gave Rufio his nightly bedtime treats and kissed me good night. I laid there, listening to the storm. I was at peace.

CHAPTER FOUR
I DIG TRAUMA, NOT DRAMA.

When the alarm sounded, I awoke more surprised than usual. I felt tranquility. I felt rested. I rolled over to see the empty, cold pillow lying next to mine. Riley had already gotten up and slinked to work and I didn't even notice. Did I even dream? I slept through the night so soundly.

I stretched and smiled, then got out of bed and sauntered to the kitchen. I fixed myself a glass of water and turned towards the stove. 6:05am. I saw my lunch bag on the counter with a note attached to the top.

Edie-
  Didn't wanna wake you up.
  Made your lunch, PB&J as usual.
  And how about this time, you actually eat it?
  See you around dinner. Have a good day at work!
  Don't get covered in blood, that shit is gross.

The bottom of his note had a crudely drawn stick figure flexing and smiling, with another stick figure, which I can only assume was me *swooning*, with little floating hearts around it. I shook my head and laughed. I stared at the drawing at the bottom of the note and realized how much of a dork Riley truly was. It was going to be a good day, I could feel it.

I got ready for work and grabbed all of my things as I headed out. I unlocked the car door and set my stuff in the passenger seat. While the windows defogged, I silently watched my sleepy neighborhood. Every day that I worked I watched the routine of everyone around me. I've always been a people watcher. I'm fascinated by humans.

Flipping through my iPod, I found some music to mirror my enthusiasm. I was feeling bouncy, so I cranked the volume up and raced through the neighborhood, a fast paced Irish punk morning revelry blaring. I smiled as an elderly couple scowled at me on their early morning walk. I was feeling feistier than usual.

As I drove, I noticed all the people around me in their cars. Some looked half asleep, blinking and leaning forward, as if trying to get the road to come into focus. Some were accustomed to the dawn life; eating, drinking, putting on their makeup, talking on their cell phones or texting with both hands off the wheel. These were the people that ensured my job security. I loved them for it.

Besides the hands free drivers, there were also the average Americans, focusing and avoiding those maniacs. Truly focusing on it, there was such an odd mix of people around here. It brought balance.

Even though everyone in our city is different, it still reminds me of a hive. The morning commute is equivalent to the flight of the worker bees. Our wings and exoskeletons have been replaced with three piece suits and briefcases, or uniform and clipboard in my case. We're slaves to routine. Ruled by our queen, capitalism. The drones stay home, sleeping until 3pm, watching cartoons or porn and eating all of their cheese puffs. Mindless. Stingless; idle. We're all creatures of habit, so why not mix it up a little?

Crossing the bridge, I watched the sun rising over the Mississippi River. There were parts of Baton Rouge that weren't very "pretty". I still couldn't help but love this place. The river was a prime example. I've seen crystal clear oceans in my lifetime, but I still preferred to look down and see the buoys tumbling in the muddy waters.

I pulled into my base and walked to the ambulance, tossing my stuff onto the front seat. Crew change is always an exciting event, at least when you're the one leaving. Although we all took an oath to serve society to the best of our ability and do no harm, we all preferred a quiet day (or night). No one *wants* for someone to get hurt, right?

The previous crew passed on the pagers and radio and gave us a report of our truck, then ran off to their cars as quickly as humanly possible. I checked all of my gear then sat on the stretcher in the back. I often reflected there, thinking of what I do and why I do it.

For anyone who doesn't understand our job, it may be difficult to see the significance. Most people don't realize that in the event of a sudden injury or illness, the first hour is critical. In military and medical circles this is referred to as the Golden Hour, for obvious reasons. Sometimes, the interventions we do in the twenty to thirty minutes that we're with a patient determine whether someone will live or die.

We aren't specialized in a certain age group or situation. We're educated and trained to handle neonates to geriatrics, in all stages of development and under all circumstances. We're faced with death, disease, pain and suffering. We work in environments that most people run from screaming, thriving on the challenge. We never know what we're going to walk in to, so we're never fully prepared or know what to expect. The job is not routine by any means. Every patient or condition is different. It's a matter of learning how to cope, learning how to think quickly on your toes and do the best you can, with whatever you have at the time.

We've been trained to hang upside down in rolled over cars, with no light but the little bulb of a laryngoscope to intubate and keep someone breathing. We've been trained to start an IV while going 70mph down bumpy roads. We do things that even doctors will admit they maybe couldn't or wouldn't do. Our work settings are never controlled. But we've adapted.

There will always be innocent people at the wrong place, at the wrong time. There will always be stupid people doing ridiculous things when they shouldn't. There will always be accidents. There will always be a loss of control and feeling of dread that forces people to attempt to end it for themselves or others. It would be a fantastic world, if we weren't needed. But we are, and probably always will be.

There are upsides and downsides to EMS, just like every other job out there. There are those people who get into this field for the bragging right or to "pick up chicks". Some people get into EMS for money, actually thinking it pays well. Well let me tell you, it doesn't. Not like you'd expect it to. So if that's someone's motivation, it won't last. You have to have your heart in the right place.

Much like any other career choice, you also have drama. It's like high school. I think it's because crews spend so much time together. We're stuck with our partners for twelve or twenty four hours at a time. It's like a second marriage. We all get to know each other, from bad habits, to thoughts and opinions. Once you've had a partner for so long, you don't have to communicate. You can anticipate what the other person is going to do and help accordingly. You become unbelievably close with your partner, whether you want to or not. And that's why there are always rumors or emotions that come in to play.

My job isn't perfect, but it's as close to it as it can be for the time being. I've tried working in retail, serving food, manual labor. I never found my place in the world until I became a paramedic and started to make a difference. Of course, I have bad days, it's inevitable. But for the most part, I'm happy with what I do. Hearing a "thank you" every once in a while, or being able to comfort a little old lady who's scared, really gives me pride. I'm proud of who I am and what I do. I can't save everyone. I don't work miracles. But I do make an impact. If I only get the chance to help one person, that's good enough for me. That feeling should be good enough for anyone.

It's hard to tell someone that you're sorry for their loss when you've pronounced their loved one as deceased. But when you can tell someone that their loved one is going to be just fine, it makes up for it. It's hard to separate yourself from everything and everyone, but it's a job requirement. It comes with experience.

Although I can't help but wonder sometimes; if there *is* a benevolent God, will he appreciate what we do? Or will he feel like we were trying to do his job and smite us? Anytime I find someone in cardiac arrest, anytime I've reversed death, I wonder. Would I spend an eternity in damnation for my services? Am I doing a public service, or stepping in the way of a higher power, "playing God" as they say. Would I be made to suffer for interjecting? It kind of makes me question things.

I hopped out of the back of the ambulance and shambled inside. I found my partner crashed out on a couch. We've all become narcoleptic. We sleep when the seconds are available and never a moment too soon.

Melanie was the best partner I ever had. I respected her, looked up to her and was proud to call her my *work wife*. She was my partner in crime, good cop to my bad cop and an inspiration to be a better person. Now she did drive me crazy sometimes, especially because of her bad habit of being nice all the damned time. You gotta mix it up sometimes. Or maybe that was just my Irish side talking, with my love for shenanigans-a-plenty.

Mel was a couple of years older than me. She was beautiful, strong and my conscience, more often than not. She was a black American, and proud of that fact. That was what she claimed and showed true by her actions. She had never been to

Africa. Her parents hadn't, either. She was smart and independent. She was everything you could love and admire in another human being, let alone a complex woman in the prime of her life. She was openly gay and advocated for the civil rights of others, without being pushy or condescending. I loved that woman. And I'd proudly stand by her side.

I threw myself onto the couch across the room and picked up the TV remote. Flipping through the channels, I tried desperately to find something somewhat entertaining to watch. It was still early morning, so my choices were limited to infomercials, early development programs about sharing and learning letters, or the news. Sadly, the hockey channel was not available at base (no budget for cable I suppose). Who'd have guessed?

I stopped on a national news channel, while the commercials were still playing, hoping that they'd discuss the meteor shower from Rome again, maybe this time with a plausible explanation. I waited patiently as the news room flashed back into view.

The reporter smiled and greeted the nation with a smarmy "welcome back," then nonchalantly began talking about stocks and the crumbling market. I slid deeper into my slouch and made myself comfortable, preparing for a nap. Nothing bored me more, than seeing this country pissing away its money.

A few minutes later, the reporter began talking about a *phenomenon* occurring in the Pacific. My curiosity piqued and I sat up slightly to see the TV screen better, perching on my elbow.

"Marine biologists from across the globe are gathering today to discuss strange events occurring in the Pacific Ocean. The phenomenon is known as the 'red tide', or 'algae bloom'. The red discoloration is caused by a bloom of dinoflagellates, or phytoplankton."

"It's unclear what causes this marvel, whether it's natural or result from human influence, but the ramifications are clear; the tide has stretched from as far west as the coasts of Australia, to French Polynesia, the farthest known span of any red tide to date."

The screen cut to an overhead view of the ocean, a blood-red swirl twisted through it.

"The growing berth of the algae bloom has also stirred growing concerns. Marine wildlife has begun to pay the price. Along the coasts of Oceania, thousands of reports have been made of cetaceans found beached, or dead. Scientists have been observing many animals, migrating away from the tide, towards a specific location in the Indian Ocean."

"Today's meeting is expected to help formulate a plan to protect the aquatic wildlife, before any more harm is done. These dinoflagellates produce neurotoxins, Saxitoxin and Brevetoxin, capable of causing paralysis, respiratory distress or even death. People are being urged not to consume shellfish or any other type of seafood, until it has been tested and verified as safe to eat. For future updates and more coverage on the matter, please stay tuned, or visit our website, provided at the bottom of your screen." the anchor stared forward as if waiting for his next cue.

I changed the channel before I caught something else on the news to make me panic. I'm not sure what's going on exactly, but something clearly is. Unexpected meteor showers? A red tide killing sea life? What's next, a plague or swarms of locusts devouring the Earth?

I'm not saying this was prophecies of biblical proportions or that Nostradamus was right, but give me a break! *Something* was very wrong and the media was either covering this up, pretending to be naive to keep the masses from going hysterical or they were being forced. I for one, don't like being lied to. I'm a big girl, I can handle it.

The phone rang. Mel sprung up in a flash and answered. It appeared that it wasn't going to be a quiet day after all. We grabbed our radio and keys and ran out the door to the ambulance.

"So, what do we have?" I asked as I fastened my seatbelt.

"Supposedly a jumper, not sure if I believe it." Mel began pushing buttons, and turning on the lights.

"Mondays..." I growled, flipping the screen of the laptop open.

"Someone actually looked at their pay stub and saw how much taxes the government takes out for social security which we'll never see," she said as she turned on the sirens, revved the engine and sped out of the gravel driveway, stirring up a cloud of dust, like a smoke screen covering our escape.

"Maybe the dude's wife left him; took his dog and his truck. You know the drill... tear in his beer." I wiped away fake tears and continued pulling up information on the laptop.

Most people would assume that we don't care, or that we're harsh. Sometimes the only way to deal with something is with humor. And sometimes that humor is at someone else's expense. The reality is, laughing and joking are the only ways we can make it through our day sane.

We aren't coldhearted. We're pessimistic. We're half empty.

"I don't care what the reason is, honestly. Whoever it is, is screwing up traffic. Rush hour, bridge, nosey assholes who would rather point and take blurry cell phone pictures of a guy having an emotional breakdown than drive on the opposite side... it's going to be a mess. It's gonna be impossible to get up there."

"Do we have PD on scene? Do we know it's safe?" Melanie turned to me concerned.

"The call notes don't give us much info. I'd assume they are, but I guess we'll find out."

We began our ascent up the bridge, slowly. Traffic was backed up on both sides, naturally. We honked, gestured with our hands and yelled over the microphone for people to "moooooo-ve ooooo-ver".

The sides of the bridge were lined with flashing lights, blinking and strobing like a rave. Police cars and fire trucks blocked off the top of the bridge. As we approached the scene, I saw the familiar numbers 19 on the back of one of the police cars. Riley was here. I was filled with a mixture of panic and relief. I was safe, but that also meant he may not be.

We pulled up as close as we could to the scene and put the ambulance in park.

I loaded my pockets with gloves and hopped out of the passenger seat. I walked to the back of the ambulance and saw Riley walking towards me with a grin on his face. As usual, I was sure he was going to give me a hard time on scene. We had a routine to maintain.

"Ah, the vultures have descended! I was wondering if you guys were going to park or just circle overhead all day and wait for home-dude to take us all out so you could feast," he said, gesturing to the man standing on the railing.

"Oh, hardy-har-har, smart guy. What's your hurry? I don't have any donuts in my lunch bag. You should know that, you packed it." I smiled.

We heard honking and yelling from the cars. He put his hand on his gun. Turning towards the nearest car in sight, he narrowed his eyes and shook his head slowly, threateningly.

"This isn't the place for target practice."

"These douche bags in their fancy cars don't give a shit why we're up here; they just want us to move out of their way. We're wasting their fourteen miles per gallon premium gas with our shenanigans. *We're* holding up tee time. I swear, if it was legal," he cut his thought short.

I grabbed his arm and pulled him around the back side of the ambulance. "So what's going on? Why are you down here with me, instead of 'negotiating'?"

"Meh, Jere's on it. We played a match of rock, paper, scissors when we pulled up and he lost. Honestly, I don't even know what the dude's deal is." he shrugged.

"This doesn't seem normal." my brow furrowed.

"Wanna go check it out?" he motioned towards the top of the bridge. I nodded in reply and walked beside him.

Melanie was already walking towards the top. There was an obvious sense of urgency in her step. As we approached the scene, we could hear the man yelling, frantically. He didn't look like the typical person losing their mind. He appeared to be in his mid-thirties, well kempt, average.

"Sir, I understand you're upset. If you would just step back, away from the edge, we could talk this over. We have people here to help. That's the only reason we're *all* here. We just want to help you." Jeremiah had his hands held out, palms up, pleading.

"Help? How the hell can you help me?! No one can help. It's too late!" the man said.

"Sir, what's your name?" Riley stepped up, putting his hand on Jeremiah's shoulder.

"What, are you the bad cop? Are we playing *that* game? My name's Matt. What difference does it make?" the man replied, turning outwards, facing the water.

"Look, Matt, I don't know what's going through your head, but I can tell you this; *nothing* is going to be solved if you don't step back. There's a bus full of kids stuck in this traffic, do you really want them to see you do something stupid?" Riley was getting impatient.

"Oh officer, I'm so sorry!" the crazed man mused. "Really? The world is coming to a flaming end and you think I give a shit about a handful of snot-nosed kids? Fuck off."

"I'm not going down with the ship. I'll go on my own terms if it's all the same." he stepped over the rail, onto the small platform running along the water side of the railing.

"Okay look, let's start over. Matt, what's going on? We can get you help. We can take you somewhere, anywhere. Let's just get you off the bridge and talk about this like civilized adults." Riley slowly walked towards the man.

"What's the point? Civilization is about to crumble, there's no need to be civilized any more. Everything we've worked to accomplish, everything I've worked for. My life is over. All of our lives are over! We've been damned. Haven't you seen the signs? They're everywhere. We're fucked, man. Completely!" he returned his gaze to the muddy waters below.

"The Apocalypse is coming, the end is here. The skies will glow red with the blood of man. Your blood. Not my blood. Not my family's blood. They're sleeping peacefully now. I'm sorry Anne, I had to. I'll see you soon," he spoke quietly, almost as if to himself.

My heart climbed into my throat, turning on my gag reflex and sending a shockwave of nausea and pain through my body. What did he mean? Oh, God, tell me he didn't kill someone. I was trying to process everything he had said logically.

"The skies will glow red…" I whispered to myself, looking at my feet. I took a step past Riley and walked towards the railing.

"What are you doing? Get back! I'm not afraid to take you with me!" the man was now hysterical.

"Hi, I'm Eden. I'm a paramedic. I just want to talk with you. Please," I took a tentative step towards Matt. "What happened with your family? Where are they?" I didn't want to know the answers.

"I shot them. All three of them. My wife, my kids."

"Oh, my God. Don't judge me! I was saving them. I was protecting them. I didn't want my little girls to see what happens next. It's bad. So bad." he shook his head back and forth mechanically.

My heart tore farther up my throat. I felt like I was choking on it. "Matt, where do you live? We can send an ambulance there. Please, let us help." I was fighting the urge to kill him myself.

"I'm sorry. Anne, I'm so very sorry. It was for the best. I'm coming. I can't stay here without you." he closed his eyes, turning his face towards the sky and began slowly leaning back.

"Wait! Wait! No! Don't do it! Please, just… please, don't do this. You can talk to me, what did you see?" I leaned forward, arm outstretched to him.

"If you'd seen what I saw, you'd be standing right next to me. I'm not sticking around to see the end of the world." he took one step back.

"NO!" I reached for him. My fingers brushed his shirt as he slipped away.

He was gone. We all ran to the edge, grabbed the railing, and watched as he fell to the mighty Mississippi below. He hit the water with a hard slapping sound and was quickly moved by the current, down the river and out of sight.

Jeremiah was already on the radio, calling for someone to retrieve the body from the river. Riley and I both stood at the edge of the bridge, staring below. His gaze shot up quickly.

"Shit! We need to get to his house. We have to check on the kids! Maybe they're still alive." he sprinted away frantically, searching for the man's vehicle. "Anyone know if he drove up here? Is there an abandoned car around?"

"Nix, down here!" Jeremiah was running towards a midsize truck parked on the edge of the bridge, facing southbound.

We tried the doors, while Riley decided to skip that process and bust through the driver's side window with his pistol. He reached inside to the handle, opening the truck door. He reached across to the passenger side and unlocked the door for Jeremiah. They fumbled through a pile of paperwork, to no avail. Riley popped the glove compartment open and found the insurance and registration.

"Got it!"

A few minutes pass and Riley returned from a private phone call. "Eden, call your dispatch. Get a crew over to this address. I'm gonna get a few cars to head over with them. Let's get those kids out of there." Riley handed me a piece of paper and ran off to his car.

I stared down at the name on the paper, reaching for my cell phone in my pocket. I dialed the number of dispatch and waited while it rang through.

"Hey, it's Eden on 88," I paused. "We're gonna need a crew to head to an address and do a welfare check. We have three possible DOA's." I rubbed my temples, attempting to force the images out of my mind.

The line was silent for a few seconds. "88? Wait, what? What happened? Repeat your message." the dispatcher was obviously confused.

"He jumped. But not before shooting his wife and two girls at home. We found his home address on his registration. Get someone on their way to check on them." I didn't want to waste the time explaining the circumstances. I gave him the address.

"10-4, I'm sending someone out now. Are you two okay?" he asked, concerned.

"Peachy. I'll chat with you later. We need to get this shit cleaned up. We won't be clear for a while. Sorry." I hung up and looked out at the water.

Storm clouds were rolling in from the west, blanketing the land with an ominous shroud. Lightning flashed in the center of the system, the thunder muffled by the thick clouds.

I stared out at the storm and drew in a deep breath. "I really, really, *hate* Mondays."

CHAPTER FIVE
FINDING PNEUMO

I felt my body rocking, back and forth, side to side. It was making me nauseated. I could smell salt and something else. I recognized the other smell, but couldn't put my finger on it. It was pungent, harsh.

Ah, the smell of death and decay. Lovely!

I could hear knocking, the sound of water splashing, moving. The ebb and flow of... *the ocean?* The constant movement sent my head and stomach spinning. I took a slow, deep breath in through my nose and exhaled slowly through my mouth.

The water's wake was getting violent. I opened my eyes to see the wide open sky above me. Crystal clear blue skies, without a cloud in sight. I sat up and took in my surroundings. I was in a small boat, devoid of paddles or a motor. How the hell did I end up in the middle of... *Where the hell am I?*

I looked out into the vast ocean, a sea of red. The top of the water was covered with a sheet of foliage and carcasses. The bloated body of a small whale bounced against the side of the boat. My stomach turned and twisted with a sharp stabbing pain.

In my peripheral vision, I could see the shape of someone sitting to the side of me. I turned to face my company. It was Matt, the man from the bridge. I instantly felt very uneasy, more so than I had simply seeing my environment. His face was calm, serene. His eyes were glowing. They looked like two miniature suns, blindingly intense.

"Where are we?" I nervously asked.

"Jump," Matt looked up and met my gaze. He took a deep breath.

"Uh, no thank you. I think I'll stay in." I grabbed the side of the boat.

"Jump," Matt was pushing himself up into a crouch.

"Shit. I, uh. Look, I'm not sure what you're doing here, or what I'm doing here for that matter." I backed myself against the side of the boat and grabbed onto the side with both hands.

"JUMP!" Matt lunged forward, capsizing the two of us and the small craft.

I fell backwards into the red water, with Matt on top of me, forcing me under. I couldn't breathe. The water stung in my lungs as the salt licked and bit into the sides of my bronchioles. I closed my eyes and let go. I opened my mouth and let out the last of my oxygen reserve followed by one deep intake of water. I opened my eyes for the last time. I was enveloped in red.

I gasped heavily. I could breathe again. The salt water in my lungs had been replaced with hot, stagnant air. I looked around me. There was a vast skyline, black clouds on a bright red backdrop. The wind tore past my face with breathtaking speed.

I'm falling. Oh God, I'm falling!

I glanced behind me and saw the ground inching closer with every second. My eyes flashed back up and I saw someone following after me. *That son of a bitch!* It was the same shadowy form from the previous dreams.

He descended faster than I'd expect of a free fall. As he caught up to my own descent, he held his hand out to grab me. I looked behind. The ground was only a couple hundred feet away and coming fast. I held my arms across my face and closed my eyes tightly, bracing for the impact.

I spiraled to the ground below me, like autumn leaves caught in a whirlwind. I hit the ground with unmistakable inertia. I laid there, with my dead eyes open, staring. The shadow was hovering above me, now a bright, glowing being with gigantic flapping wings and dull glowing eyes. He looked down at me and let out a blood curdling roar.

The sound of his scream rang in my ears, startling me awake. I couldn't catch my breath. I felt like I was drowning again, flailing my arm frantically for something to grab onto. Riley shot up and grabbed my shoulders.

"Holy shit! Are you okay?" he had fear in his voice that I could see reflected in his eyes.

"I… can't… breathe!" I tried to slow down my heart rate and find my breath.

Riley jumped out of bed and ran to the overhead fan. He pulled the cord and turned the light on. I watched him as he instantly lost color in his face, his jaw dropped.

"What the? What happened to you?" he ran to my side.

"I… can't… breathe! Help!" I clawed at my throat.

The collar of my shirt felt like a noose. I tried to stand up, but felt light headed and dizzy. I felt soaked. I looked at my hand and saw red.

Blood. My blood? What happened?

"Eden, are you okay? Please answer me! What's wrong? What the hell is going on?" Riley was frantic.

I shook my head, terrified. "Can't… breathe… help!" I forced the words out, and fell backwards.

I was no longer in bed. The air smelled sweet. The light breeze tickled my skin as it danced past me. Wherever I am, where ever I have been for the past couple of days, beats the pants off of my last little mental field trip. I stood up and walked, looking at my surroundings. I held my hand out at my side and lightly touched the ferns as I passed.

The ground felt cold on my bare feet, the soft grass was damp with dew. The trees around me formed a canopy over the lightly tread path. I leaned down slightly to see past the ferns. There was a clearing ahead of me. I grabbed the sides of my dress and began to run for the meadow.

I'm in no hurry. It's so peaceful here, so very tranquil.

I slowed my pace. As I approached the edge of the clearing, the birds began to sing. The cute woodland creatures from the surrounding forest entered the meadow as I did. I watched as they scampered and pranced in the wildflowers and gentle sunshine. I couldn't help but smile.

In the center of the beautiful meadow was a large oak tree. White and soft pink petals danced in the breeze, spinning and twirling. Everywhere I stepped, the ground seemed to embrace my feet. I noticed small, delicate flowers and clovers springing to life in my footprints.

As happy as I am here, I can't help but feel as if something is wrong. Something is not as it should be. I looked to the sky, half expecting it to swirl into the macabre crimson I've become so accustomed to. It was a beautiful shade of blue. The clouds were gigantic, bright, fluffy, almost animated. The sun shone so brightly, yet I was able to look directly at it without my retinas burning. It appeared to be smiling.

I heard a soft giggle coming from the forest. I cocked my head to the side, turning my ear to the last place I heard the little chuckle. When I heard it again, I turned and began to walk towards the tree line. I crouched down and silently crept towards the forest.

I peeked through the bushes and saw a collection of animals standing in a small circle. A squirrel broke ranks and pranced towards me. Watching silently as it approached, the tiny rodent bowed and giggled. I snickered to myself, both amused and confused. His tail twitched and flickered like a furry flame. He turned and frolicked off towards the other animals. I followed my new friend as he returned to his companions.

I sat a few feet from them, bewildered. I was definitely dreaming. How else could I sit so close to a wolf or deer, without them dashing to the trees for cover and protection? The animals faced me and stepped towards me tentatively. The young wolf sniffed at the air and let out a yelp. The squirrel returned to me and sat on my lap. I gently stroked its fur.

I leaned my head back and closed my eyes, taking in a deep breath. I felt the warm sunshine on my face and smiled. I felt a gentle shift in weight on my lap and opened my eyes to see the squirrel running away from me. The wolf rose off his haunches and slowly backed away, snarling and growling. The deer had already sprinted off into the trees.

I looked around, trying to figure out why they ran from me after allowing me to be part of their collective. Then I saw the reason. The brightly lit forest began to darken as a figure approached. The being seemed to consume the light, folding it into its shadows. And as quickly as the shadows arrived, they dissipated.

I tried to stand, but felt a sharp pain in my chest, buckling me to my knees. It was so painful to breathe. I stared at the ground, trying to catch my breath. The form was now blindingly bright and less than ten feet from me. I averted my eyes, trying to see an escape route. The closer it walked towards me, the more I realized that I no longer had the strength or energy to run from it. For once, it won, I forfeit.

"This is it," I whispered. I felt like a trapped animal.

"It is time for your return, Eden," the being said calmly.

"What? Return where? Who the hell are you?"

"Now is not the time for questions. The time will come when I will be allowed to assist you further. You must return to your husband. You must return to reality."

he offered me his hand.

I reluctantly took it and rose to my feet, holding my chest. It was so unbearably painful to move or breathe.

"They're weaning you from the anesthesia. They're ready for you to awaken. I tried to catch you, to help. I feel horrible that this has happened. I am truly sorry." he leaned down to help me to my feet.

"Seeing as how I'm unable to fight you, both physically and mentally, apology accepted. However, I expect some answers. Why the hell have you been following me?" I braced against his arm to hold myself up. The pain was excruciating.

"I'm sorry I can't explain any more to you, but we will discuss things soon." he turned to me, opening his brightly glowing eyes wide.

"How soon?"

"Goodbye, for now." he touched my forehead gently with his hand. I felt a burning pain in my chest and took a deep cleansing breath. I closed my eyes. The sounds of the forest morphed into the beeping of a heart monitor.

Reality was coming back into focus and I wasn't ready for it. I opened my eyes and saw Riley sitting on the edge of my bed looking at me, with a soft smile. He shoved a beautiful bouquet of flowers into my face. I pulled my face aside, wiping the pollen from my nose.

"Welcome back." his gentle smile widened.

"My chest hurts."

"Yeah, they said it will for a while. They turned your meds down a few hours ago." he pointed to the left side of my rib cage, wrapped in bandages.

"What the hell happened?" I asked, completely confused.
A man in a white coat walked into the room, holding a chart.

"We were hoping you'd be able to answer that yourself, Eden. Hi, I'm Doctor Jones. I've been your attending physician." He offered me his hand to shake.

"I really don't remember much. I remember being asleep and having a crazy dream, then waking up unable to breathe. I told Riley what was going on, and then I think I passed out. I remember seeing the ceiling, then the roof of the car, and that's it." I searched through my memory bank, leaving out the parts they would call me crazy for.

"Well, Eden. It appears you had a pneumothorax. Basically your left lung had collapsed and we were forced to re-inflate it," he attempted to explain.

"I know what that means Doc, I'm a paramedic. I know what decompressions do." I was in pain and feeling rather testy.

The doctor chuckled to himself, flipping through my chart. "I'm sorry. It wasn't my intention to talk down to you. I forgot Riley had said you were a medic. I'm so used to having to explain everything."

"Anyway, we had to keep you sedated. You were waking up occasionally, screaming and trying to take out your chest tube. We figured it was best to keep you out until we knew your lung was fine." he flipped more pages, looking down.

"I understand," I replied, feeling slightly guilty for my tone.

"So, you're saying there was no trauma involved? You didn't get hit in the ribs or do anything that could've caused this?"

"No, no way. Spontaneous pneumo, maybe. Nothing happened that could've done this. I know what you're insinuating and *it didn't happen*. I know I don't fit the typical profile for spontaneous pneumothorax, but this wasn't traumatic."

"Plausible. I guess we'll leave it at that. But, I'd like to keep you for observations," he replied, scribbling in my chart.

"No, I'm fine, I just want to go home."

"I really insist that you stay. Since the drainage tube just came out last night, I recommend staying for another 24 hours, or so."

"Doc, I know. I'm choosing to go against medical advice. I'd like to be discharged. Please." I closed my eyes and sighed, trying to remain calm.

He asked me a round of questions, guaranteeing that I was of sound mind and capable of making such a bad decision. I was. And I did.

"Then I guess we're going to go ahead and discharge you. You'll need to follow up with your doctor in a couple of days. I'll send you home with a prescription, but you need to rest. I'm sure you'll be sore for a little while. I'll give you a note for work, and I recommend you stop smoking." he handed Riley a few small pieces of paper and left the room.

"Thank God you woke up when you did. They've been driving me crazy. The bastards were acting like I beat you." Riley's eyes narrowed.

"Yeah well, it feels like someone did. And I can't imagine I look much better." I grabbed the rails of the bed, trying to sit up.

"Let's get the hell out of here before I give them a reason to have me arrested," Riley said.

A few *hours* later, a nurse walked in with some papers and handed them to Riley. I unhooked the electrodes from my chest as she put on gloves and walked to my bedside. Riley laid some clothes next to me while the nurse started pulling the tape back, away from my IV site.

"How are you feeling, honey?" she asked as she ripped the catheter out of my arm and held some gauze on the site.

"Ouch!" I flinched. "I'm fine. I just wanna go home," I replied, pulling my arm away from her and holding the gauze down myself.

"Well, you need to be really careful. Your chest tube hasn't been out very long. We'd much rather you stay, so we can confirm your lung's healing properly," she lectured me.

"I know what to watch for, thanks."

"Make sure you come back in if you're feeling short of breath again or have any other *problems*." she shot an accusatory glare at Riley, who returned the gaze.

"Yeah, I will. Thanks." I smiled, politely. "Can I get dressed now?" I picked up my clothes.

The nurse took off her gloves, turned and walked out of the room. Riley followed behind her. I got dressed in my pajamas, and then sat back down on the edge of the hospital bed. Riley returned a few minutes later with a wheelchair. I stood up and grabbed his outstretched hand, allowing him to help me into the seat.

"Your throne, *madam*." he smiled and twirled his hand, presenting my transportation.

"Thank you, sir."

"Anything else I can get for you, ma'am?" he asked sarcastically.

"Just get me home. You know I hate hospitals." I buried my face in my bag. He wheeled me through the emergency room, towards the double exit doors.

"As you wish."

Chapter Six
Does Your Cult Have Kool-aid?

A few days had passed since my trip to the emergency room. I had to admit, I'd enjoyed my time at home, regardless of the pain in my chest. I'd had a lot of time to think and reflect. I'd also had more time with Riley. He decided it would be "in my best interests" to stay home and help. So, he took some time off of work to lounge around with me and play video games.

I hadn't spent a ton of time awake, but my dreams had also been relatively peaceful. I hadn't seen the shadow/bright guy since we made amends. Normally, I would've been happy to state that. Since our last conversation, however, my fear of the unusual being had turned to a heightened curiosity. I know that's strange, but he managed to pique my interest and I knew it was going to drive me insane unless I knew the whole story.

I still hadn't really talked to Riley about that night, or my dreams in the hospital. As far as he'd be concerned, you can't be hurt in a dream world existing only in your head, and as for the dreams at the hospital? Well, I was doped up on God only knows what. At the moment, I felt it was necessary to say as little as possible. Who would believe my ramblings anyway?

They say you can't die in your dreams, because the brain can't comprehend something it has never experienced. Instead the human brain adlibs, filling in the blanks or just changing course once it's too overwhelmed or confused. I still can't explain what happened, but I feel the obvious is true. I died in my dream. The physical damage I sustained was directly related to my fall. I'm thankful it wasn't any worse, which it very well might have been, I'd imagine.

I asked Riley what exactly had happened the night of my *accident*. He told me that after waking up and asking for help, I was in and out of consciousness. He called 911, put me in some pajama pants, and cleaned the blood off of my face. After waiting almost ten minutes and realizing no sirens were within earshot, he carried me out to the car and drove to the nearest hospital. Thankfully, our home is safely nestled between two prominent, able hospitals.

I don't remember anything from that night. I can barely remember the dream I had prior to my hospital trip. It's all a mixture of blurry flashes and broken sounds. Maybe it was all the drugs, or maybe my brain had finally had enough traumatic experiences and decided to shut it out. Either way, it may be for the best.

I can still remember the crazy dream I had in the hospital, though. Friendly woodland creatures, the perfect meadow, the flowers springing to life with every step I took? Yeah, that was definitely drug induced. I've never had much of a green thumb. I can't even keep cacti alive.

I slowly got up from the bed and walked to the bathroom. I stopped to look at myself in the mirror. I looked like absolute shit. My skin was paler than usual, almost translucent. Even my tattoos looked sadly pale, the normally vibrant colors appeared faded. My auburn rat-nest was now an untamable mane, resembling Medusa's reptile tresses. My hazel eyes have become a lifeless grey from lack of sunlight. I still had some fading bruises on my face and arms. I lifted my shirt and poked at my rib cage, grunting and yelping as I touched my side. I pulled the bandage aside and examined the wound that remained as a reminder of that night. The bruises surrounding the spot the chest tube had been were black, blue and painful. I reapplied the dressing to my wound, wrapping my chest tightly with a bandage and swallowed more pain medication.

I walked back to the living room and sat on the couch next to Rufio's sleeping body, stroking his soft fur. I loved my kitty companion. He was the best child any mother could ask for. Luckily, he appreciates affection. I slowly lowered myself next to him, curling my body around his. His heavy purr vibrated in my chest, luring me into a restful trance.

Shortly after getting comfortable, there was a knock on the door. I reluctantly eased myself off of the couch and walked to the front door. It seemed that I had gained some popularity after my injury; everyone had begun to stop by with flowers or alcohol. I glanced through the peephole and saw two men I didn't recognize, standing on our doorstep.

"It's 9am. Who the hell is it?" Riley popped his head out of the pantry doorway.

"Um, not sure exactly," I unlatched the chain on the door.

Riley gently pushed me aside and looked through the peephole. "Ha, missionaries!" he snarled.

"Uh oh, poor guys."

The two men knocked again, impatiently. I stepped behind Riley, rose to my toes and set my head on his shoulder. He opened the front door to expose two well-dressed young men. They had matching iron pressed shirts, black ties, combed over short hair and name tags. They were holding books at their sides.

"Hello sir! My name is Steve, and this is Brian. We're local missionaries here to talk to you about our savior, Jesus Christ," the taller one proclaimed.

Riley stepped back and raised an eyebrow. "Your savior... who?" he asked with inquisitive, narrowed eyes.

"Je...Jesus Christ," Steve replied, fumbling over his words, bewildered at Riley's aggressive response.

I poked my head around Riley's side. "No, I'm sorry. There's no Jesus here. Did you try next door?" I interjected with a serious expression.

"Yeah, sorry, *Steve*. I'm afraid I haven't heard of your friend. He doesn't live in this house." Riley began to close the door.

"Wait! No, it's a misunderstanding. I meant I was here to speak to you about our savior, Jesus Christ, *the prophet*," he held up a book and pointed to it. The cover was a copy of a gaudy painting.

"Wait, so you're from a cult?" Riley asked, accusingly.

"No, we're from a *church*. We're not a cult," Brian, the shorter of the two clarified.

"So, does your cult have Kool-Aid? Preferably grape. The last guys only had the blue stuff. I wasn't a fan. Tasted like fertilizer," Riley continued, ignoring their previous answer.

"We're NOT a cult!" Brian retorted with a twinge of annoyance in his voice.

Steve put a hand on Brian's arm, calmingly.

"So you don't have Kool-Aid? Hmm, I don't know then. Sorry boys." Riley began to close the door again.

I was having a hard time muffling my laughter.

"Wait, sir! Can we at least give you a business card, or some reading material?" Steve was sticking his head in the door, fishing for a card in his pocket.

"I read comics or hockey magazines. And to clarify, that's only when I'm using the can. How about you come back when you have something to offer? You aren't very good at bartering for souls, when you have nothing for trade. You need to work on your haggling, Steve. Jesus would be ashamed!" Riley put his hands on his hips and shook his head with disapproval.

"I can see that you aren't interested. Have a nice day." Steve surrendered.

"Good luck on judgment day," Brian flouted smugly.

"You too, douche! I bet God's real proud of your fantastic social skills!" Riley closed the door and began to laugh maniacally.

I had to brace myself against the doorjamb. I was laughing so hard, it felt as if my chest was going to explode, or implode. I wasn't sure which one.

"Is it sacrilegious to call missionaries douche bags? I mean, they are trying to spread God's word," I asked with a grin.

"First off, I didn't hear God mentioned in any of their door to door propaganda. Secondly, Jesus isn't the only prophet. What if we had been Muslim? That would've been insulting, not just entertaining. And thirdly, don't show up on my doorstep when I'm still in my jammies and expect a friendly welcome," Riley ranted.

"Unless you come bearing donuts."

"Damn, I should've told'em to return when they had donuts." Riley hung his head in shame.

"We're boned." I leaned on the counter with my elbows, resting my head on my palms.

"Yeah, we're going to hell, if there is one." Riley was making little horns next to his forehead with his fingers.

"I'm pretty sure we were going there long before we picked on a couple of missionaries. Even so, I'm sure God has a sense of humor and chuckled a little. C'mon, it was hysterical." I giggled as I thought about the exchange that just took place.

"True. Very true," Riley nodded.

I walked back to the couch and laid my head down on the arm rest, snuggling with my couch companion once again, who had not moved an inch since we parted ways. Riley returned to the kitchen pantry to continue his hunt for breakfast. I became drowsy and listened to him preparing his food as I drifted off to sleep.

I awoke four hours later to the sounds of a massacre. Riley was hard at work, killing zombies. I blinked heavily, trying to clear my vision. I watched as Riley sat on the edge of the couch, moving and bending his body to mirror his character on screen as he methodically pushed buttons. I closed my eyes.

When I opened them again, Riley had disappeared. I stretched and yawned, then grabbed my left side as a wave of pain shot through my chest. I sat up, groggy and hurting, stumbled to my feet and turned to face the kitchen. Riley was standing by the stove, concocting some sort of semi-edible experiment. The clock on the oven read 6:43pm.

I walked to the bathroom and grabbed more pain pills. Apparently, the last ones had worn off. I stared at myself in the mirror again. I looked even more disheveled than the last time I saw myself a few short hours ago.

Was I turning into a zombie? Riley would kill me. We've already had that conversation before. When asked, "If I were a zombie, would you kill me?" He duly replied with, "Fuck yeah! You wouldn't be *you* anymore. It wouldn't count," then paused, and asked me if I would be a fast or slow zombie and how freshly dead I would be. The questions disturbed me slightly. I had hoped for a 'no'.

As far as I was concerned, I *could* be turning into a zombie, or some other form of monster. No one is able to give a straight answer of how they become what they are. What if it all started with an 'accident' and then 'poof'?
What the hell am I talking about? My mind is getting lost inside itself.

I felt like I'd been losing myself altogether, not just my mind. That's three days now that I'd slept the majority of the waking hours. I knew I needed my rest, but this was ridiculous. I wasn't sure I'd had a single dream within the past few days.

I felt like something was missing, like I lost a part of myself when I hit the ground. If I could just go back to where it all happened and look around, maybe I'd find something vital lying on the ground. The thought is farfetched, but I had the feeling it was true.

I walked into the kitchen to survey the damage left by Riley's "cooking". I smiled to myself as I watched him reading instructions. He looked confused, like he had just been given a life altering mathematical equation or turned his meal into a blitzing time bomb. If he answers wrong, or measures incorrectly, his food would self-destruct and kill us both.
Green wire? Red wire? Green wire?

"More milk will neutralize the blast." I grinned and grabbed the milk from the fridge.

"I don't really know what I'm doing with this shit." he held up a spoon and inspected it, perplexed.

"I've noticed. Just add some milk to soften the potatoes." I started to pour in the lactose diffuser. Riley handed me the spoon and stared at the bowl of mashed potatoes.

"Are you okay? I mean, *really*. You've seemed different the past couple of days. Something on your mind?" Riley didn't make eye contact with me.

"I'm alright, just sore and really tired." I answered nonchalantly.

"Is that all? You know you can talk to me, Edie. If something's bothering you, or if something happened. You should know I wouldn't judge you." He frowned, concerned.

"Thanks," was all I could say. The timing wasn't right for much more.

Riley wrapped his arms around my waist and pulled me close. He hugged me tightly and gently kissed me on the lips. As he pulled away from me and returned to fixing our dinner, I realized how afraid I was to let him go. I had a deep seated fear that things were changing. The world around us was changing. Life as we knew it was changing. And if we weren't prepared, it was going to blindside us. I stayed close by, staring at Riley as he messily piled food onto plates. He was one of the most handsome creatures I'd ever seen. Always has been, always will be. His features are so masculine, yet warm and welcoming. His smile melts my heart, which always gets him out of trouble. His hair was short, dark brown, which is hard to tell, always hidden under a hat turned backwards. His eyes are like two ferocious storm clouds, a mixture of gray, green, blue and gold. When I look into them, I feel like I did when we first began dating. I instantly turn bashful and nervous. There's only one other set of eyes in this world that have made me lose focus, or fumble.
Wherever those eyes are now...

I've always said I believe everyone has soul mates. Dozens of them, even hundreds maybe. Everyone you can connect with, everyone you can share emotions and dreams with, is a soul mate. But there's only one person out there who is your other half. There's only one person who completes you, filling in the gaps you've been missing. The one who can complete your sentences, complete your thoughts. Riley filled that void.

He handed me a plate and opened the patio door for me. I walked outside and sat my food down on the patio table. I looked up and saw the soft glow of the full moon, shining on the surrounding clouds. The stars were muted by the overcast ceiling and street lights, but the moon glowed unhindered. The dark clouds moved hastily towards the east. As usual for this time of year, a thunderstorm was on the horizon. The darting clouds stirred a sweet breeze; the smell of rain was in the air. I kicked my feet up on the seat across from me and settled in for our version of a romantic dinner filled with poop jokes and sarcastic remarks. I wouldn't trade this for the world.

"Hope it tastes okay, you know damned well I don't know what I'm doing." he poked at his food with his fork, his face full of apprehension.

"Well it hasn't bitten me back yet, so you did a good job. Thanks," I shoved a spoonful of potatoes into my mouth.

We both sat quietly for a few minutes as we ate. The sound of thunder rumbled in the distance, shaking the ground. It was going to be a good storm. When we were finished eating, Riley gathered the dishes and walked them inside. The sound of sirens in the distance rang through the neighborhood. Riley slid the door open to see me staring at the sky.

"So what happened that night? Did you drug me and sneak out to a bar? Did you get into a brawl or something?"

We both knew nothing of the sort had happened. I decided if he was going to finally come out and ask, I'd come right out and tell him the truth.

"I fell," I answered, taking a sip of my tea.

"You *fell*? Where did you fall? You didn't fall out of the bed, you weren't on the floor. What the hell do you mean?" he leaned forward.

"I've been having some excessively crazy dreams for the past few weeks, at least. I mean, way crazier than the ones I normally have. I don't know where I am, but there's a cliff and someone chasing me. I've always woken up before I hit the ground. Monday night, I didn't."

"*What?* Wait. You lost me."

"I normally wake up before hitting the ground in my dream. I didn't wake up in time on Monday night. I hit the ground and laid there for a moment before I woke up," I explained.

"That's it. You've gone fucking nuts." he shook his head dubiously.

"You asked what happened, I'm telling you the truth! As farfetched as it may seem." I hung my head, dejected.

"So you're saying you blew out a lung like a cheap tire, by face planting into the ground that was completely created in your twisted mind?" he mocked cynically.

"Yeah, basically."

"Look, I didn't ask you to believe me. I didn't ask you to tell me it was logical. You asked what happened and I gave you the only answer I had. Why do you think I didn't tell the doc or talk to you about it sooner? Ever think that maybe I *feel* crazy for saying it?" I got up and began to walk to the patio door.

Riley caught my arm and turned me around to face him. "Edie, it's just hard to believe. I dream about zombies and stupid shit. It's hard for me to think that if I was bitten in my dreams, that I'd wake up and maul half of Baton Rouge, or eat your pretty little face off. You know I believe you when you tell me things, this is just *crazy*. I'm sorry. I didn't mean to hurt your feelings." He had both of his hands on my cheeks, turning my face towards him so he could look me in the eyes.

I fought his hands and turned my face away.

"Holy shit, you're serious. You... you're actually serious for once?" he stepped back, startled.

"I'm not lying to you, Riley." I sat back down.

"How is that possible? You didn't move. We've gotta talk to someone about this." he sat back down next to me, wrapping his arm around my shoulder.

"Like who?"

"I don't know." he looked to the sky, as if expecting an answer.

The thunder cracked in reply. We sat outside while the storm rolled in around us. Neither of us spoke. We were both searching for answers and explanations in our minds. I pulled myself close against his chest and rested my head on his shoulder. I closed my eyes and listened to his heartbeat as it kept pace with the heavy rain. Thunder rumbled, reverberating through his torso. It was so peaceful. I fell asleep in his arms and awoke to him carrying me to the bedroom. He gently laid me down on the bed and pulled the sheet and comforter over me. He kissed me on the forehead and took off my glasses.

"I'm not crazy." I yawned and closed my eyes again.

"I know. Get some rest. You need it." he kissed my lips softly.

"I love you," I mumbled.

"I love you, too." he turned off the light and walked out of the room.

I closed my eyes and settled in for sleep. My dreams were very confusing, flashes and unintelligible sounds. I can't recall what was going on, just that I felt so out of place. It was as if I was sitting in on someone else's dreams. I was watching someone else's mind flail about.

When I woke up, I tried to remember what I had dreamt but couldn't. I stirred in bed for a few minutes. I could hear laughter coming from the living room. The sounds were too muffled to identify, but it was obvious there were multiple voices. I sat up and put my glasses on. Was Riley harassing more missionaries? I wouldn't have been surprised to walk into the living room and see a room full of angry villagers with torches and pitchforks. We *are* 'Godless monsters' after all. I slipped on some pajama pants and opened the bedroom door, pulling my messy hair back into a ponytail. I walked into the living room to see our usual party of friends sitting on the couches, laughing and joking.

Oh, God. Tell me this isn't an intervention.

"Mornin', Edie, nice of you to join us, *finally.* I was wondering if you were going to sleep all day," the bubbly blonde, Lana, said as she ran and hugged me.

"Ouch. Hey," I mumbled, as I pulled away from her. I looked at my friends and turned to look at the clock on the stove. 1:09pm. How long had I slept? I had lost most of my day. Had I slipped into a coma?

"Good afternoon, Llama, Lord Fartleroy," I greeted my guests with a slight curtsey.

They both laughed.

Mike was also known to me as Beauregard Fartleroy. Don't ask me why, either. I think the name just amused me. It suited him well. He had been a friend of ours for years, prior to us moving to Baton Rouge. The others had become friends through our acquaintance with Mike.

Since meeting Lamar, aka Llama, he had proven to be more than just a casual, occasional acquaintance. He had become my best friend. Well, basically our best friend. Riley, Lamar and I spent a lot of time together. Having him around was great. It was like he was a part of our family.

"Edie, Jere and Mel are coming over, too. Sounds like we're all going out for dinner and drinks if you're up for it." Riley gave me the awkward smile, the 'I had no idea' look.

"I don't wanna hang out with these ass-hats. Are you kidding me?" I taunted, pointing to Mike.

Lana pouted and put her hands on her hips like she was about to scold me.

"I'm kidding, woman! Sounds good. I'm gonna go hop in the shower and get ready." I turned and headed back to the bedroom.

I heard a knock on the front door and the commotion in the living room grew louder as I entered my bedroom. Rufio was hiding in the adjoining bathroom when I walked in. He wasn't afraid of people, per se. He was terrified of Lana. He chirped as usual, content that it was just the two of us in his safe haven.

I hurried through my shower, tenderly caring for my wounds and attempting to unravel the tangled chaos known as my hair. I got dressed and put on some make up, striving to make myself slightly presentable.

Like that'll ever happen...

I walked out into the living room and instantly let go of everything that was bothering me. I was always content to be with my group of friends. They were my extended family, although I felt closer to these people than I did with some of my blood relatives.

Mel and Lana were sitting on the couch, apparently in the middle of *girl talk*. Mike had put his arm around Riley's shoulder, rubbing his arm softly. Riley turned to Mike and belted him in the stomach, laughing. Lamar and Jeremiah were shooting zombies. This was a typical occurrence for our group of dorks. I sat down on the couch next to Lana and watched all of my friends as they interacted with each other.

Lana, the bubbly blonde, was the youngest of the bunch, in her mid-twenties. She was still untamed, but fun. She laughed and talked, keeping her eyes trained on Mike. They had been dating about a year now and were still in the 'honeymoon' stages. They both admired each other like love struck teens. It was sweet, almost sickeningly so.

Jeremiah and Riley were almost like a married couple themselves. They'd been friends since they were kids. Jeremiah followed us to Louisiana, realizing just as we had that the state was in much better shape than Michigan had been.

Lamar is quiet, when he's being shy; which is never when he's with us. He's kind of the mysterious one of our dysfunctional family. His sense of humor is profound, very highbrow, I believe it's called. He's realistic. When he speaks, we listen.

The afternoon continued with 'your momma' jokes and zombie headshots. After a few hours of business as usual we left the house, loaded into our respective vehicles and went out for dinner.

We arrived at the sushi bar and walked inside, where we were escorted to our tables and handed menus. Typical conversation resumed where it had left off. As we ate, the TV screen over the bar caught my attention. The sound was turned off, so I read the captions as they scrolled across the screen. Apparently, the 'meteor shower' that occurred in Rome was now known as an 'astral anomaly' and had also been seen in Shanghai and Haifa, Israel this week. The appearance was the same, witnessed by hundreds and recorded by amateurs. They still didn't have any insight on how or why the meteor showers occurred. Big surprise.

"What's going on?" Riley leaned over and whispered into my ear.

"That meteor shit happened again. Shanghai and Israel now," I said, never breaking my gaze from the TV.

"They didn't see these coming either?" he asked.

"Nope."

I peeled my attention off of the TV and decided I wasn't going to let more world events ruin my night with my friends. Conversation continued and the evening got out of hand, as usual.

When we were finished eating, Jeremiah and Mel had to go. Lana and Mike also decided to head home early. Lamar, Riley and I shrugged and decided we were going to continue with our night.

We ran across the street, picked up a few six packs of beer and returned to our home for a night of cold drinks, video games and laughter on the patio. Somehow, we always managed to migrate outside for hours on end. Though Lamar didn't smoke cigarettes like Riley and I did, he frequently enjoyed a cigar with us. I opted to call him a 'professional turd smoker'. They looked and smelled like turds to me.

CHAPTER SEVEN
PRIDE AND PESTILENCE

A warm wind swept across the land, carrying a plume of smoke and the sound of screams. My eyes stung as the breeze passed. I pulled my hood down to shroud my face and grabbed the scarf from my bag, making a makeshift mask to protect my mouth and nose from the burning smoke and tied a secure knot at the nape of my neck.

I looked to the south, where I remembered the village being. I saw nothing but burnt rubble and bodies crawling from where the church once stood. I looked to the north and saw two horses standing at the top of the hill, with riders pointing towards the village. One began descending the hill towards me swiftly. I stood in place, awestruck. What had happened here?

As one the horseman advanced towards me I noticed his armor was black, with specks of light radiating beneath. His steed was black as well, with bright glowing eyes. He stopped at my side and extended his arm to me. I took his hand and climbed onto the back of his horse, wrapping my arms around his waist as we rode off hastily to the west. I was glad to be headed away from the other horseman. His flaming steed spread more than just flames, he spread panic. The horseman stood in place on the hill ominously, marveling at the disease and destruction he had created below. He was malice, pain, anguish incarnate.

I laid my head against my rider's back and watched silently as we passed the farm I once called home. The fields I had spent years tending were now a crop of flame. I saw bodies lying in the fields. Crows circled above, waiting for a break in the smoke to swoop in and pick at the bodies.

We rode silently for miles, escaping into the forest. The sound of screams and crying eventually disappeared in the distance, replaced by the chirping of crickets in the woods. When the horseman slowed, I eased my grip on his sides. The horse halted and we both jumped off. The horseman pulled his hood back and exposed his eyes; I instantly recognized them, though his face was still covered with a mask.

"Gabriel, what are you doing here?" I asked, baffled.

"I came to get you. The question that should be asked is what are *you* doing here?" his tone was low, agitated.

I looked at my rescuer and gasped. How did I know his name now? He had never told me what it was. Why did I think of the village as home?

"What the hell's going on?" I sat down on the ground, pulled back my hood and removed my mask.

"I'm not sure what you're doing here, but until you wake, I'm not leaving your side. You should not be here, Eden. This place is dangerous." He stood over me, locking eyes with a penetrating gaze.

"How do I know your name... that is your name, isn't it? Gabriel?" I began my interrogation.

"Yes it is."

"What was going on back there? How did I know that village? And where the hell am I?"

"You're in Drogheda, Ireland. The plague struck. We're trying to *clean* up the mess, so to speak." he sat down next to me.

"*The* plague? As in, the *bubonic* plague?" my jaw dropped.

"Yes. Welcome to pestilence."

"I'm so confused. How do I get back? Oh shit, Riley's going to freak."

"You aren't in *actual* Ireland. Well, you are and you aren't. You haven't time traveled. You're dreaming. Consider this memory retrieval," he chortled.

"But *who's* memories?" I asked. I laid down, suddenly overcome by all that was happening around me. I closed my eyes, took a deep breath and began counting backwards from ten. I slowed my breathing to match the timing of my count. *Breathe in, two seconds, breathe out.*

I pictured my bed, my husband, my crazy cat and told myself when I reached 'one', I'd wake up. I had trained myself to do this when the nightmares first began. This was my way of exiting. I coached myself along.
Ten, you're in bed.
Nine, you're safe at home.
Eight, this is just a dream.
Seven, you have to wake up.
Six, you're lying in bed.
Five, you have to wake up.
Four, wake up now.
Three, wake up now.
Two, now, NOW!

"One!" I opened my eyes.

"It didn't work. You're still here." Gabriel shook his head slowly.

"Well, shit." I sat back up.
Back to square one.

"Come." he rose to his feet and offered me his hand.

I accepted his help and pulled myself to my feet. We climbed onto the back of his horse and rode back towards the village. The sun was setting, casting a red glow across the smoldering land. We stopped at the edge of the forest and stared down towards the fields. The screaming had been silenced in our absence. There was no more crying.

"So, this is it. It's over now?" I frowned, staring out at what was once a beautiful, peaceful village, now a ruined shell of its former self.

Three women stood in the middle of the field. They wore long, flowing black dresses. I watched as they knelt down over bodies and laid their hands on the chests of the fallen. After they had spent time with each body in turn, there was a bright flash and the women were gone. Three crows hovered low over the field, with bright glowing orbs in their beaks. They turned towards the sky and were gone in a blur of light. I was dumbfounded.

"Mórrígna," Gabriel pointed towards the three streaks of light.

"What was that?" I asked, a bit startled.

"Mórrígna, as they say in Gaelic."

"The *Morrigan*; the war *goddess*. The 'three sisters'. She's saving the souls; she came to help us. Don't be afraid. She's here as a personal favor, to aid me," he attempted to comfort me.

"*War* goddesses? What are they doing here? I thought the plague had killed these people?"

"*Goddess*. They are one. And as I said, she came to help. We're here to gather souls, to protect them so they aren't lost. And as I'm sure you've seen, this entire village has been lost to the Black Death. We had our hands full and time was running short," he spoke with confidence.

"Can I ask you something?" I turned and faced him.

"Perhaps," he answered reluctantly.

"Who... *What* are you?"

"You'll remember soon enough. Don't rush things. Have some patience." he sat down on the ground, and I followed suit.

"That's not one of my more admirable traits."

We sat and watched as the Morrigan returned, swooping out of the smoke towards the field. The smoke trailed behind them, swirling in the current created by their wings. I watched as they transformed back into three women. The black mist wrapped around their bodies, forming gentle coverings against their pale, glowing skin. Their long black hair whipped in the air like dark flames.

I glanced over at Gabriel. He was sitting with his elbows on his crossed knees, his chin rested on his arms, staring out at the beautiful women in the field. He sighed deeply.

I had seen him in my dreams as a solid black figure, then as a brightly glowing being. I didn't realize how odd it was to see him differently, until now. He had taken off his mask and had his hood down. His face was dazzling, aglow, like a halogen bulb. His features were masculine, but still very boyish. He stared at the women with a brilliantly bright smile stretching across his face. His eyes dimmed to grey while his face was exposed.

"Can I meet them?" I asked.

"No." his smile vanished.

"It's time to wake up. We're done here, I have to leave."

"No, I'm not ready," I replied, pulling away from his touch.

"You have no choice in the matter. I must leave." he placed both of his hands on my temples.

I opened my eyes with a loud gasp and rolled out of bed in one fluid motion. I awoke with a mission and a new morbid curiosity. I opened the bedroom door and walked into the living room. Riley and Lamar were lounging on the couch, watching TV. They were watching some kind of talk show, obviously bored and hung over.

"Oh, I love my men like I love my coffee; strong and black," Lamar jokingly said, snapping his fingers in the air, mocking the people on the television.

"That's funny. I love my women like I love my coffee. Ground up in bags and shoved in the freezer," Riley retorted, changing the channel. The three of us laughed.

"Guess he doesn't love you much, Edie." Lamar shrugged and raised an eyebrow.

"I suppose not." I slapped Riley in the shoulder. "I'm not surprised."

"She's growing on me. Soon enough," Riley winked at me.

I tore the foot rest out from under Riley's feet, grabbed my laptop and settled in for some research in the papasan. I had so many questions and I knew they wouldn't be answered easily. I'm too impatient for the 'wait and see' answer I seem to receive much too often recently. I tapped on the side of my laptop as I waited for it to load up. I honestly had no idea how I would find information. The screen loaded and I typed in my password.

"You ok?" Riley asked me.

"Yeah, yeah. Fine," I answered, short.

"You sure?" he peeked at me, over the top if my laptop.

"*Finally!*" I shouted as the screen changed.

I clicked on the Internet icon and began my expedition. I growled to myself as my mind went blank. I realized I didn't even know where to start, so I went to a search engine and typed in *morrigan*. Thousands of entries popped up. They were in the order of how many views they had. A popularity contest, of a sort. I clicked on the first link, then the second, the third, the fourth, all to no avail. Did I mean *Morgan*? Nooo, I didn't. Stupid computers, always trying to make you second guess yourself. I read the descriptions further down the list, until finally, a hit that appeared to be right.

The Mórrígna, as Gabriel had called them, were mentioned throughout Celtic mythology. Led by Naimen the war goddess, or Lamia, as she was known in other cultures. They had changed the course of history by manipulating or counseling leaders through wars. The three sisters appeared as beautiful women who could change their forms; they were most known to change the outcome of events with their influence. In some stories, they were a bad omen. In some, they were good. Maybe they were just misunderstood, like teenagers. Women, full of angst and jealousy. If lonely men could start stories about seducing mermaids, how was this any different?

The more I read, the more it seemed the Celtic stories were in line with the Norse mythology. I followed links and changed my search phrase. The Mórrígna resembled the three witches from Norse myths. They controlled the past, present and future. They presented themselves how they wished and influenced decisions, as well. It seemed that the Mórrígna had been mentioned throughout history as many different women. They had been referred to as Valkyrie, or banshees. Their connotations were always linked to war, death and the souls of humans. Whatever their part in my dream, it left me with great unease. And nowhere in my search did I find anything about the three being a single entity. They were distinctly three. The "three sisters".

I continued my research, moving on to the bubonic plague. I searched through pages of historical accounts and documentaries. The plague swept across Ireland, Scotland and Wales in 1349, leaving hundreds of thousands dead in its wake. I remembered discussing the plague in school, briefly, but never knew to what extent it had influenced history. I read about plagues and epidemics for hours. I didn't realize how long I had been wrapped up in my research until Riley brought it to my attention. I hadn't even noticed that Lamar had left.

"So, whatcha doing?" he asked, leaning against the arm of the couch next to me.

"Reading," I answered, without looking away.

"Reading what?" he asked, placing his balled fist under his chin.

"Stuff."

"What kind of stuff?" he continued, like a child playing the questions game.

"Bubonic plague kind of stuff," I looked up.

"Oh, that's uh, nice. Um, why are you reading about the bubonic plague? Planning a comeback?" he jabbed.

"I don't know, bored I guess." I was playing coy.

"Ah, yes. Because when I'm bored I spend three hours reading about millions of people dying in disturbing, grotesque, undignified ways. Lovely way to spend a Saturday afternoon," Riley mused.

"You, too?! O-M-G! We really do have so much in common! Eerie."

"Come on." Riley stood up and offered me his hand.

I shut down the laptop and set it on the couch. I took Riley's hand and walked with him to the patio.

"You need to get out of the house," he stated.

"Very observant, Nancy Drew."

"Seriously. Let's go grab some food. Go to the park or something," he continued.

"That actually sounds kinda good." I smiled.

We walked in the house and changed clothes. We debated our endless food options until we finally reached an agreement and left. Arriving at the chosen destination we pulled through the drive-thru, ordered our food and continued our journey to find peace.

Arriving at the park, we walked to a quiet spot by the lake and stuffed our faces with chicken fingers and Texas toast. There were a ton of people at the park. There were old guys fishing in the lake, hippie-stoner kids playing Frisbee and giggling, dorks on bikes, bums and birdwatchers. We passed the time pointing out people and laughing about how they looked or mimicking what we thought they were saying. It seemed to be a hobby of ours. Rude? Maybe. Funny? Definitely. Possibly going to burn in hell for it? It was worth it. We finished our lunch and walked towards the lake.

There was a man standing on a bench near the lake, yelling at people as they passed by. Riley and I tried to ignore him to the best of our ability. He continuously shouted verses from the Bible and how we were all living in sin and doomed to damnation. Riley eventually had heard more than he could handle and started walking towards the preacher.

"You sheep are wandering blindly through this world, sinful and misled. You must repent. You must atone for your sins and cast out the demons that have led you astray. The end is nigh," The man continued on his spiel.

"Hey, asshole!" Riley was walking towards the man, fists balled angrily.
  The man ignored Riley's insult and continued his tirade.

"Hey, why don't you hop off your soap box and peddle push your evangelical propaganda elsewhere. We're not interested." Riley was standing beneath the man, irate.

"Don't confuse your guilt with anger, son. The Lord will forgive your transgressions." the man smiled.

"I'm not your fucking son. And it's not guilt; it's pure, unadulterated annoyance. Religion isn't the answer to everything. We have the right to believe what we want, without being forced to hear your God-fearing gibberish." Riley wasn't going to be swayed.

"As you feel you have the right to choose what you believe, I have the right to offer my message wherever I choose to do so. I believe it's known as the *first amendment*." The man smirked and turned away from Riley.

"Oh wow, you went there. Nice," Riley scoffed. He was pissed.

"Come on, Riley. Please. It's not worth it." I grabbed Riley's hand and pulled him back.

"No, I'm not finished." Riley shrugged off my grip.

I stepped in front of him and placed my hands on his chest, looking up at his obviously distressed face.

"Please," I pleaded.

"Whatever. You're lucky dude! Really lucky. I wouldn't want to beat your ass in front of all these *witnesses*." Riley grinned wickedly and turned away.

He threw his arm around my shoulder and walked with me towards the lake. He glanced over his shoulder frequently and laughed when he noticed the speaker had retreated. We walked around the east side of the lake and found a spot that wasn't encompassed with fishermen or stoners and relaxed on the shore. I had kicked off my shoes and was dipping my feet in the water. Riley was leaning back on his elbows, watching the sunset.

"I had a dream last night that I was in Ireland when the bubonic plague hit," I stated nonchalantly.

"Hmm. Weird."

"You asked why I was looking up the plague, there's your answer."

"Well, I had kind of let that go. I figured you didn't want to discuss your diabolical plan to destroy mankind. I don't think I want to be an accomplice to something that shitty," he mused.

"It was really dark. Everyone was dead. I don't know where it came from."

"Edie, I really think we should find you someone to talk to. I think something is going on in your head that needs some sorting. I don't think you're *crazy*, but I think you're overstressed or something." he sat up and rubbed my back.

"It wasn't like that. It wasn't stress. When you get stressed out, do you dream about people lying everywhere? Children screaming as they find their dead parents, only to join them in death within a couple of minutes?" I continued defensively.

"No, but I also don't dream about stuff like that, regardless. I dream about work, videogames, things that actually occurred throughout the day," he replied.

"Well, I can't control what I dream."

"You think there's more to it than just *dreaming*, don't you? You think something's going on?"

"I don't know. I'm scared. Scared to ask too many questions. Scared to find out the answers," I rubbed my crossed arms for security.

"Don't be *scared*, it's just a part of who you are. So you have fucked up dreams. Big deal." he tried to comfort me.

"What if I'm becoming schizophrenic? What if something is wrong with my brain? You said yourself, there could be something going on in my head. Something off. I'm going crazy, Riley. I don't want to jump off a bridge. I don't want to shoot you." I was feeling panicked.

"Calm down, you're afraid of heights and I don't think you could shoot me even if you tried. Your aim is horrible," he joked.

"Well, thanks. I'm glad you're taking this seriously. When I go berserk and start slicing up our neighbors or talking to animals, just remember me as I once was."

Riley laughed, wrapped his arm around my waist, and continued to remind me that I've always been a bit 'deranged' as he put it. It wasn't exactly comforting, but I realized how gingerly he was handling everything. I loosened up and came to the conclusion I wasn't going to win this discussion, as usual.

We sat by the water for a couple of hours, talking. We discussed everything from the weather to what super powers we wanted. In the back of my mind, I wondered if I really was slipping from sanity, but felt it best not to mention it again. If I wasn't crazy to start with and lost Riley over the whole mess, I definitely would be bonkers by the end of it all.

As much as I was enjoying my time with Riley, there were questions that I needed answers to. I over-dramatized a yawn and told him how drastically *tired* I was. We headed home for the evening, where I could take some melatonin and force myself into a dream world. Gabriel wasn't going to get off the hook so easily tonight.

CHAPTER EIGHT
HUNGER PANGS

I threw my clothes into a pile in the corner of the bedroom and ran to the bathroom. I popped a pill into my mouth and brushed my teeth in record time, in a hurry to get to sleep.

I normally avoided sleep or felt anxious, but not tonight. I wanted to know what was going on. I wanted to reassure myself that I hadn't lost my mind. I climbed under the blankets and yelled for Riley to come tuck me in.

"You do realize it's only eight o' clock, right?" Riley questioned.

"Yeah. I'm just really tired for some reason. Maybe it's just part of recovery." I yawned.

Riley's eyes narrowed. We both knew I was a horrible liar. "I don't know what you're up to, but I'd appreciate it if you didn't bring diseases back with you from your little field trip."

"I won't." I stuck my tongue out at him.

"Where are you off to tonight? Hopping on your magic carpet and sprinkling more plague seeds across the globe?" he gently kissed my forehead.

"I don't know. I was thinking about starting the Spanish influenza, or maybe crushing the Ming Dynasty with some dastardly disease." I grinned wickedly.

"Well, be careful on your time travel, don't get lost. I expect dinner ready when I get home from work tomorrow."

"Aw, I forgot you head back to work tomorrow." I pouted.

"Yeah, sucks."

"Anyway, enjoy your twisted fairytale land. I'm going to shoot up some undead for a few hours, I'll be in bed a little later. See you tomorrow after work." he kissed me gently on the lips.

"Good night," I smiled.

"Night." he closed the door behind him.

I rolled onto my right side and took a deep breath.

"Come on melatonin, kick in." I coached myself. I laid there, listening to the sounds around me. I could hear gunfire from Riley's game, Rufio scratching at the door, and the wind blowing swiftly through the trees outside. I listened to my breathing as it progressively deepened.

I was once again in a land I distantly recognized, although this time I knew going into it I was dreaming. I looked around the alley, my vision panned from the entrance of one corridor to the other end. I could hear people yelling, begging in Russian. Although I had never learned Russian, I could easily understand the terror in their voices.

Gathering my composure, I headed towards to street. I could see foot traffic as I approached. I felt a stabbing pain in my stomach and buckled to my knees. I felt a hand on my shoulder and turned my face upwards to see just the man I was looking for.

"Why are you doing this to yourself?" he asked, as he slid his arm under my own and helped me to my feet.

"I had questions. Where are we now? Why am I in so much pain?" I asked, cradling my stomach with my arms.

"You're in Ukraine. It's the Holodomor. You're starving to death, as we speak." Gabriel grabbed my arm and wrapped it around his shoulder.

"Let me guess, welcome to Famine?"

"Precisely," he answered, assisting me to the nearest wall.

"I'm not a fan of this ghost of Christmas past bullshit. Why can't you meet me in some normal dreams?" I asked as I curled myself into an awkwardly half-standing, half-ball.

"I've been trying to keep an eye on you. I'm attempting to keep you out of harm's way. These dreams aren't simply *dreams*. You're viewing the past," he confirmed, pulling back the hood of his lined coat.

"Well then, how about we head somewhere more cheerful, like the zoo? As for time, how about last week? The weather was really nice. Come on, give me a break." I slid to the ground and wrapped my arms around my knees.

"Why are you here, Eden? I'm sure you aren't here for sightseeing," he admonished.

"Like I said, I had questions. I'd like some answers, if you don't mind."

"I can't guarantee an answer, but go ahead," he was reaching into the pocket of his coat. When his hand emerged he handed me a small loaf of bread. I looked at the bread in my hand, and then passed it back to him as my stomach voiced its protest with an audible groan.

"There are kids starving here, I can't take this. I'm only dreaming," I said, curling myself tighter.

He shrugged and slid the bread back into his pocket.

"Where's your soul-sucking witch buddy? The one you were ogling in Ireland?" I asked coldly.

"Oh, Lilith? She's in Afghanistan," he answered without hesitation.

"*Lilith?* I thought her name was Nemain or something?" I contested.
He chuckled. "I see you did your research. And it's *Lilith*. She's been called many things throughout history, but *we* choose to use her *real* name. Lamia, Nemain, Helen of Troy, Cleopatra...they're aliases, pseudonyms so to speak," he continued.

"Wait, who is *we*? And whatever you want to call her, them... *it*, why is it helping you?" I asked.

"I can only be so many places at once. My hands are tied otherwise. Lilith is the General, the leader of a group of women in charge of taking innocent or valiant souls to their rightful place."

"So they are Valkyrie?" I questioned.

"In essence. Lilith is similar to the Valkyrie, but so much more. She actually commands the Valkyrie, but is not one, herself."

"Less riddles, more answers." my eyes narrowed.

"I can only say so much. Come, I have work to do." he offered me his hand.

I took his hand and pulled myself off the wall and fully erect. I closed my eyes and took a deep breath, and then followed behind Gabriel as he walked into the street. He pulled his hood over his head and continued walking through the foot traffic. We stopped in front of two children holding each other. Their faces looked deformed, with eyes sunken into the sockets and cheek bones jutting out.

Gabriel reached into his pocket and pulled out the small loaf of bread. The two children watched him anxiously. He tore the bread in half and handed each piece to one of the children. They took the bread eagerly, grateful, and consumed it almost instantly. We continued our trek through the streets, handing out pieces of bread as we found people in need.

"So, I don't understand. You came here to feed people?" I asked, confused.

"I came here to help. What don't you understand?"

"Well, last time I saw you, you were hanging out in a burning, disease ridden village and the surrounding fields. Just seems odd." I shrugged.

"I don't have to justify my actions. All you need to know is that I'm here to help," he said, defensively.

"Whoa, sorry. I wasn't trying to be rude." I backed up a step.

"I think you've seen enough. Now isn't the time. When the time *does* come, you'll be one of the first to know." he had grown cold.

"But when?" I asked, impatiently.

He leaned close to my ear and whispered, "It's time to wake up."

"Wait. Please. Can I stay a little longer? I want to help you. I won't get in the way or ask too many questions. I promise," I grinned.

He stared at me for a few seconds, and then nodded towards a group of people. I accepted his temporary invitation and followed behind him swiftly. My stomach ached and growled, but I ignored it. I wanted to help. I wanted to see more. I wanted to prove my worth, more than the flea ridden bird woman Gabriel seemed fixated on. I wanted him to *want* me around, instead of feeling like he was babysitting me.

I didn't understand where these feelings were coming from. I had never been a jealous person. I wasn't attracted to the odd being, but I felt an emotional bond with him, that I wasn't willing to sever. I wanted to find out more, about him, about this, about everything. I realized he wasn't going to give in. I knew if I continued to hound him, he'd push me away, waking me from our time together. I opted for silence and did exactly as he instructed.

We walked up and down the narrow city street, dispensing bread and prayers of healing as we passed. The women called us angels. I couldn't help but laugh at the thought. Doing a good thing for the starving people around me brought me comfort, even if I was only dreaming. I still felt as if I was helping.

I suddenly felt disoriented and sat down, "I don't feel so good."

"I knew I shouldn't have allowed you to stay. You must wake up now.

Goodbye, Eden." he gently kissed my forehead.

"Shit!" I shouted, pounding the bed with my fists as my eyes flew open.

I looked around my bedroom. He had forced me awake again. If he didn't want me around, why didn't he just do that right off the bat? I was glad that I knew a little more, but still felt as if I was being left in the dark needlessly. It was very frustrating.

I reached over to the nightstand and grabbed my cell phone. I slid it out of the cover and threw myself back onto my pillow. It was 5:40am. Riley must have left for work recently. It was Sunday morning. I had no reason to be up this early. I threw my phone onto the nightstand, startling Rufio, who had been sleeping next to me. I comforted him until he fell back to sleep. His purring soothed me more than I had expected.

I closed my eyes and pictured the country side I had seen ablaze. I visualized the children's faces as they wordlessly begged for food. I tried to force myself back to sleep, but realized it was impossible. I was wide awake. I walked into the living room and flopped onto the couch. I grabbed my laptop, waited for the screen to pop up and typed in *pestilence, famine* in to the search bar. I had a feeling that I already knew what was to follow.

Death.

War.

Also see: Four Horsemen of the Apocalypse.

"Impossible!" I snapped. I sneered and shook my head. I had an epiphany while I stared at my screen. It seemed that as of late, I had a few different encounters with people trying to feed me their religious sales pitches. I had questioned what I believed; I had questioned what was true.

I was sure that all this hype, the 'astral anomalies', the red tide combined with the pain meds, had caused me to delve too deeply into my psyche. I had pulled up things I didn't even realize I knew. I was putting faces and names together. There was a completely rational explanation for my irrational behavior. I felt very embarrassed. I realized that not only did I owe Riley an explanation, I owed him an apology. I was going to have to make some sort of effort to accept reality. I needed to accept the fact that all I had recently been through had all been in my head. I had spent so much time trying to disprove it, when in fact I had only proven to myself that I had lost my grasp on reality. I couldn't believe that I let it carry on this long. As skeptical of a person as I am, how did I fall for all of this bullshit?

I turned off my laptop and walked outside. I stared at the sky and snickered. How had I let it get this far? I was really starting to believe that I was wrapped up in some kind of supernatural phenomenon, that I was one of the wolves on the 'inside', instead of one of the billions of lambs left out to slaughter. I stood outside for a moment, smoking a cigarette and calming my nerves, then walked back inside and gathered the laundry together. I had left a trail of socks behind me, leading from the bedroom to the washer and dryer. I cleaned the kitchen and bathrooms, distracting myself as much as possible. I owed it to myself. I wasn't going to become lost.

I spent the morning and afternoon cleaning, arranging, and rearranging trying to lose myself in the rhythmic robotic repetition. Any time I thought about my dreams, I scrubbed harder; I turned the music up louder. I hid from reality. It was the safest thing I could think of. I was now one of the many people who hid from themselves. I was fake. But I felt safe. I felt sane.

…And it stayed that way much longer than I had anticipated.

CHAPTER NINE
THE LINES HAVE BEEN
DRAWN IN THE SAND

Much had changed in the past three months. I took the time to sit down with Riley and apologize for the way I had acted. He thought that it was a ploy at first, but accepted my plea in the long run and thankfully, dropped it altogether. It was fantastic to feel like everything was finally back to normal.

I called my doctor a few days after my cleaning spree and conned him into sending me back to work. The distraction helped. I spent a few weeks on light duty, cleaning and organizing, but eventually made it back out on the road. It was nice to be back to work with Mel, though they had changed our shift time and where we were based out of.

I also agreed to see a therapist, which I was never very pleased with. Our conversations always twisted, leaving me angry and leaving her more confused than when we initially started. In my opinion, if you don't want to hear about the gruesome truth, don't ask me what I do for a living or how I *feel* about it. It's just that simple. It seemed like she made shit up as we went along. Pulling terms and conditions out of her ass, like rabbits out of a magician's top hat.

Regardless of how I felt about that woman, she did do one thing that helped, slightly. She put me on some medications that were supposed to "help me sleep soundly, reduce anxiety and help me think clearer". It did, for the most part. What she didn't tell me was that the side effects included increased sarcasm, cynicism and one hell of an appetite. I haven't been letting things get to me. I've surrendered, but not without eating all of the chips and making fun of everyone in the process. Fair trade, in my opinion.

Here I was, again, in therapy. Today was no different than the other sessions I'd had with her. I dreaded going, but I still showed up, every month, to bullshit for an hour and get my prescriptions. Though I'd never been good at lying, I was getting a lot better at telling her what she wanted to hear... occasionally. She thought she was curing me. It was almost entertaining.

I'd been sitting in that damned waiting room for about forty minutes. I don't really understand why they give you an appointment time, if there's no chance in hell you're going to make it into the office within an hour of your scheduled harassment. Don't tell me to be punctual, if you can't extend the same courtesy. I hated being there, but I have to admit, getting some of this stupid stuff off of my chest made me feel quite a bit better. I didn't worry about her judgment. I just blabbed.

This was also my time to secretly stalk the entertainment industry without ridicule, by way of tabloids. If Riley ever saw me reading this crap, he'd make fun of me until death. Showbiz is like a really shitty mathematical equation. X sleeps with Y,

Y is currently married to Z. If X and Z wear the same dress to the award ceremony, then...

"Miss Eden? Are you ready?" the receptionist asked.

"Yeah. I have been, for about forty five minutes now," I stated as I stood and set down the outdated tabloid I was thumbing through.

"The doctor is ready to see you, just have a seat in her office. She'll be right back in a moment." the receptionist walked me back and opened the door. The walls were plasters with "hooray me" awards, diplomas and certificates saying she was more than qualified to handle my craziness. Even so, when I looked from frame to frame, nowhere did I see an award for *Outstanding Social Skills*.

I'm guessing that's because they aren't required. As long as you can blatantly tell someone what they're doing wrong in their life, without knowing a thing about them, you *too* could be a psychiatrist! Oh, and you can charge far too much money to go "mmhmm".

"Hello. How are you today?" the woman asked, as she walked in the door.

"You haven't started your timer yet, Doc. I can wait." I smirked.

"Cynical as always, I see. Such a pleasure," she commented. She pulled out a file and a legal tablet and began writing. I wasn't sure if she was writing the date, time, and my name or if she was writing about the "notable anger and nonconformist attitude" I displayed a moment ago.

I stared at her as she flipped through my file. I could tell she couldn't remember what all I had said, or what had bothered me. I'm pretty sure she couldn't have worked with me without reading up. Cheater. I could tell you all about her without having to read a file on her. She was in her mid-forties, wished she was still in her twenties. She obviously had had a boob job and some Botox. If vampires could survive UV light, I'd have assumed that she was one and had been trapped in a tanning bed for a few generations with the settings on high. Tanning torture. She reeked of fake and shame.

"So, where should we start today?" she asked, crossing her legs.

"I don't know, Cindy. I'm not the one who majored in psychology." I flouted.

"Has this been happening a lot lately? Have you been feeling more short-tempered again?" she asked, pushing her reading glasses up higher on the bridge of her modified nose.

"I didn't realize I *was* short tempered. Last I checked, that was called sarcasm," I continued, never changing my tone.

"Okay, so you've been feeling more *sarcastic*, lately?" she corrected her wording.

"Yeah, a bit," I dropped my attitude.

"Mmmhmm," she said, scribbling.

Lovely. I adore the "mmhmm" answers. There's the first one. Stay tuned for more.

"So how are things with you and your boyfriend?"

"You mean, Riley? My *husband* of almost six years? We're doing great," I said sarcastically. I couldn't believe she didn't even have her facts written down correctly.

"Mmhmm, mmhmm. Good," she replied, jotting down notes.

There's two and three.

I've spent more time with Riley, our friends and my family, lately. We've traveled to Houston to hang out with my brothers and their families. We've spent time with my parents. We've had drunken camping trips with Lamar and Fartleroy. We've had fun, and that's what really matters to me. We only have one life, one chance to be content, right?

"And how are you sleeping?" she asked.

"Better."

Things had really mellowed out in the past few months. I'd been able to think much clearer. I'd been able to focus. And lately, I'd been able to sleep. I saw Gabriel a few times in my dreams, but I cut it short. I figured it was for the best. I had decided that I needed to worry less about my dreams and focus on reality.

When my imagination began to stray too much, I'd wrangle it in. I spent the first few weeks sleeping only a few hours at a time. Then I retrained myself how to wake up, stopping the dreams short that I didn't want to witness. If at any time, it felt like it was going to be one of *those* chimeras, I'd force myself awake and find mindless busywork to clear my think tank.

"How is work going for you?" she continued, bringing me back from my reverie.

"Haven't we been over this? You don't like me to talk about work. You get that disgusted look on your face and turn an odd shade of green. I think it's best if we skip that question all together," I replied, honestly.

"You use your wit and tattoos as armor, Eden. Let down your wall," she countered.

"There you go again with the tattoo thing. What's your problem? Just because I choose to cover my skin with ink, with *art*, doesn't mean that I'm in denial, or that I can't accept myself. And I'm not hiding! I was *raised* in a culture that used tattoos as a way of telling your life story," I retorted, aggravated.

"But you aren't Samoan." she set her tablet down on her lap.

"And you weren't raised by plastic dolls, so why do you choose to convert yourself into one?"

"We aren't talking about me here."

"Oh, of course not. Excuse me. I'm the one with the issues," I scoffed.

"As I was saying, you aren't Samoan. That isn't *your* culture, *your* heritage."

"So? I love art. I respect the human body. I've chosen to combine the two." my annoyance was growing more evident in my tone.

"Why do you have the art that you have, then?" she asked, scribbling my last answer down hastily.

My entire right forearm is covered with a scarecrow in a pumpkin patch. Tombstones line the inside of my arm. A giant pumpkin, vampire, Frankenstein's monster and a day of the dead sugar skull fill in the rest. My left arm is a trick-or-treating scene, with candy and ghosts to fill in the empty spots. She hadn't even seen the rest of my tattoos. That was probably for the best.

"I love Halloween. It's the only time of year I feel like I can be myself. Three hundred and sixty four days out of the year, I feel like I'm wearing a mask. Have you ever sat back and seen the joy on a kid's face on Halloween?"

She looked up at me from her notepad to the top corner of the room, as if she was thinking; attempting to picture it in her own head.

"Mmhmm, continue," she replied.

Oh, look at that. There's four! This is starting to feel like one of those educational shows for kids, instead of inner dialogue.

"Have you ever noticed, how everyone lets go and just has fun? It's the only night that people can be whoever they want to be, without rules, fueled by creativity. I choose to carry a piece of that with me, every day. It helps me cope."

"How do your parents feel about them?"

"Well, seeing as how I don't live under my parents' roof anymore, I suppose it doesn't matter. But, for arguments sake, they accept me for who I am. They don't expect me to pretend to be someone that I'm not. My tattoos haven't changed their love for me, as they shouldn't. I don't have a contagious disease, I have multicolored skin."

"Let's move on, shall we?" Cindy said, obviously noticing the corner she had backed me into. "Have you been working on the exercises we talked about?" she flipped through her tablet to see what she had recommended.

I had started drawing and painting again. I used it as an exodus for my stress and creativity. It was never pretty, but at least it got some of the images out. I also had taught myself how to meditate. Granted, it was probably thanks to the medicine that turned me into a brainless zombie. But regardless, I had learned to clear my mind. I learned how to step outside of myself.

I used to attempt to meditate and only managed to think about what I was going to have for lunch, or question whether I had remembered to turn off the oven, or tried to remember what the main female Snork's name was. Through meditation, at peace and one with myself, I remembered: Casey Kelp. She was pink. I digress.

"Yeah, I have. I started working on my art again and I've finally started to meditate." I gave her the short version.

"That's great! Did you bring in some of your art?"

"Yeah, I brought a couple. Can you look at them without reading a lot into it or criticizing me?"

"I can't make you any promises." she mused.

I pulled my sketchbook out of my bag. I flipped the pages and walked over to her chair.

"It's... It's scary, but beautiful. What was your inspiration? What was your medium?"

She actually seemed interested, for once. I stared at the drawing I had done of Lilith, stealing souls in the field.

"I saw It in a dream. And I used colored pencils and pastels," I answered.

"How do you feel when you look at this art?" she asked, staring at it herself.

"Mixed emotions, really. I don't see the art; I see what I saw in my dream. I see a beautiful woman, harvesting human souls. I feel fascinated. I feel afraid. I feel helpless. I feel... jealousy." I sat down near her on the floor like a little kid.

"You can flip to the next page," I suggested.

"Oh, wow. What is this?" she turned her head sideways, trying to make sense of the art.

"That's what the sky looks like in my dreams. It's a view from the ground, up."

"Mmhmm, interesting. Why do you think it's always red?"

Five!

"I don't really know. It used to bother me, but then I just got used to it."

"But my dreams have been relatively normal lately." I shrugged.

She closed the book and handed it back to me. I carried my sketchbook back to the couch and placed it in my bag.

"How do you feel about the medication?" she asked.

"It's alright. I feel used to it by now," I replied with another shrug. I momentarily wondered if she counted my shrugs like I counted her "mmhmms", then decided I didn't care.

"So everything is going okay at home?" she asked.

"Yeah. So far, so good."

Things hadn't completely *changed*, but I'd learned how to pretend otherwise. I seemed to have adopted a new persona; that of the fifties style housewife. Riley didn't seem completely convinced of my new attitude, but he kept his opinions to himself. I think he just enjoyed the goofy apron and the piping hot muffins.

"Well, that's good to hear." she smiled.

So, that was life. Well, my new mockery of a life. It may not have been perfect and I may not have been happy all of the time, but at least I was making it by, without driving Riley insane. I was just thankful that he'd stuck by me as long as he had. I don't know if I could, if I was in his shoes. I don't think I'm worth the stress.

There was a knock on the door and the receptionist poked her head in.

"Miss Cindy, there's a gentleman on the phone for you. He says it's an emergency. I patched it through to your office." she winced, nervous to interrupt our session.

"Thanks, I'll be right there." she stood, setting her notepad upside down on her seat and took off her glasses, letting them hang down her chest on her little crystal and silver eyeglass chain.

"Why don't you take some time to relax and reflect; I'll be back in a few minutes and we can finish up for today. Try and think of something that makes you happy," she told me, before leaving the room.

She always said I'm never going to be happy in life, until I'm happy with myself. And I'll never be happy with myself, while I listen to loud "angry" music and watch horror movies. Apparently, I'm supposed to be a girly-girl and cry when I see puppies, or babies and watch chick flicks. Well, let me tell you lady... That shit's not going to happen. Ever. I *am* happy with who I am... I think. Kinda-sorta.

A few minutes passed, and the receptionist knocked on the door again. She popped in the doorway with an awkward smile.

"Miss Cindy had to handle a crisis. She isn't going to be able to finish your session for today. If you need to reschedule some time, let me know. We're very sorry."

That was the best news I had heard all day. I grabbed my bag and my purse and walked out into the hallway. The small woman was standing near the door, waiting to escort me to the front.

"I'm sure I'll be fine until next month. I have a lot going on in the next few weeks. I'd prefer to not have to come here, if I can avoid it at all," I told her as we walked.

"Okay. I'll make a note of it. I'll give you a call if Dr. Cindy wants you to come in before then."

"Oh, and here's your prescriptions. Have a great day. Remember to stay positive!" she smiled.

I walked out of the front door and was instantly blinded. The sun was so bright. The sky was crystal clear in all directions. The breeze was warm, comfortable. I was still having a hard time adjusting to the southern version of autumn. It was now the 2nd of October, and the only indication to that were the random Halloween decorations strewn about. I had gotten used to the forty degree weather of autumn in the North, I missed the colorful leaves. This was going to be my first fall and winter back in Louisiana. The high sixties to low seventies were genuinely throwing me off. But I wouldn't trade it, not for that shit hole in Michigan.

I got in my car and headed to the grocery store. I decided that I was going to be productive today. I was already out and about, might as well get some stuff done. As I drove across the interstate, I thought about my trip to see Cindy and felt a mixture of guilt and frustration, as usual. I knew I shouldn't be as hard on her as I was, but I can't help it. I know she was just doing her job, but she knows how to push my buttons.

I turned my music up louder and lit a cigarette. I tried my best to repress the feelings of guilt I was having. I pulled into the grocery store parking lot and snagged a parking spot close to the front. A little old lady gave me a dirty look and flipped me off when I pulled into the spot. I laughed maniacally. I was in a hurry.

The approach of Halloween meant many things to me. It meant I'd get to decorate the house with new decorations that would actually stay up until the next Halloween. It meant that I got to go pick out a pumpkin and carve it. It meant a shitload of candy that I'd never eat. Most importantly, it meant that I'd get to have some Count Chocula, Franken Berry and Boo Berry cereal!

I walked with an increased speed, grabbed my cart and made a bee line for the cereal aisle. I dodged cranky old biddies and college kids skipping class. I was anxious as I approached the section. If my cereal wasn't there, someone was going to feel my wrath. I held my breath as I rounded the corner. The sky opened up. A spot light of sun shone down on the boxes with a heavenly glow. A choir of angels sang praises. My cereal, my holy grail, was neatly organized in front of me. My mission in life was complete. I could now die a happy woman.

I threw four boxes of each into the cart, looked at the shelf, then looked again in my cart. I continued the epic battle in my head for a few moments, before deciding that one of each was probably going to be okay for now. I really didn't want Riley to question my motives for bringing home twelve boxes of cereal. He would assume that I was back on my "end of the world" conspiracy kick. I leaned against the shelf and read the back of the boxes. I was so excited. I took a moment to mourn the loss of my friend.

Rest in pieces, Fruity Yummy Mummy. You are forever missed.
Seriously, I don't know what they were thinking when they discontinued it.

I walked over to the holiday section and went through the Halloween stuff. I was pretty sure during the entire month of October I had a perpetual smile smeared across my face. I was like a kid again. It wasn't *just* Halloween that I loved. I loved the weather, the sense of anticipation on an autumn breeze, the preparation for winter, everything about the season really.

Everyone who knew me knew how important it was to me. I'd get a birthday card and something small from my parents for my birthday in May. But when Halloween rolled around, I received a *huge* box, loaded with candy, stickers, decorations, balloons… everything. It was the most exciting time of year. Just the smell of the aisles was enough to make me happy. I didn't need antidepressants.

When I was done shopping (I totally bought more glassware too), I took all of my things to the car, loaded up the trunk, hopped in and sped off towards home. My mind wandered beyond the car, beyond the roads, beyond the city. I was miles away in thought.

I slammed on my brakes when I noticed a man crossing the intersection I was fast approaching. He looked so familiar, although I was unable to pinpoint how or why. His eyes were a dull grey; his pale skin was almost translucent. He wore a tattered pea coat. In his right hand, he held a sign at his side:

"I WILL BLESS THOSE WHO BLESS YOU.
AND CURSE THOSE WHO CURSE YOU.
CHOOSE YOUR SIDE WISELY.
THE END IS NIGH."

I read his sign as he walked. He turned and looked at me as he passed in front of the car. His eyes pierced straight through me, making me nauseated. I gagged and turned my gaze to the light overhead which had turned red as I waited for the man to pass.

"Come on, light. Come on!" I shouted, drumming my fingers on the steering wheel.

The light changed to green and I glanced to the road, only to reassure myself that the man was no longer in my path. I didn't see him anywhere. I chose to put no more thought into it, put my lead foot on the gas and raced towards home, then pulled into the driveway and put the car in park. I sat in the driver's seat for a few minutes with my head rested on the steering wheel. I didn't want to think about why I had just gotten so sick, but I tried to remember why he looked so familiar. Where had I seen him? Had he been one of my patients before? And then it hit me. It had to have been the same man I had seen with Riley, that was crossing College Drive, months ago. He had a sign then, too.

I got out of the car and grabbed all of the groceries, unlocked the front door and was greeted by Rufio. He was always so cheerful and warm when one of us walked in. He was always so happy to see us. I set the bags on the floor and picked him up, scratching behind his ears and under his chin, while he purred and "made biscuits" on my arm. After our greeting for each other, I set him back on the floor and grabbed the groceries. He followed me into the kitchen and meowed loudly as I put the food and things away.

When I was finished in the kitchen, I walked into the living room and sat down on the couch. Rufio followed me and made himself at home on my lap as I channel surfed for something with entertainment value. Nothing seemed to be catching my attention. I flipped through channel after channel, disgusted by what I saw. People seem to thrive on one another's pain or drama. Talk shows stir up gossip or draw attention to someone's flaws, degrading people. Reality TV is as far from reality as the original movies made for the Sci-Fi channel. Infomercials make me want to put a brick through the screen. The cartoons people have made recently consist of bright flashing colors and no substance. What the hell has happened to entertainment? I watched the weather report long enough to tell you, from memory, what to expect across the nation for the next seven days. There was only one option left.

I stopped on the national news channel. I had spent the past three months avoiding the news, papers, radio stations or anything else that could report something extraordinary, provocative, or depressing. I figured it was in my best interest to become detached from the world outside of my life. I tried to focus on what mattered to me, what my life revolved around. I watched the news as they discussed topic after topic. All of which, made me sick to my stomach and made me wonder what the world had come to.

We're on our way to Hell in a hand basket and all we do is feed the flames. We scoff at the idea that we're destroying our world. Someday, we're going to blow ourselves up in the middle of a nuclear war. We'll spend the rest of eternity in a nuclear winter and die off quicker than the dinosaurs. At least they didn't do it to themselves.

Crime and violence had reached an all-time high, across the world. They talked about the possibility of World War III and the likelihood that if we didn't do something, our peace, or freedom could soon be lost. The country's debt was still on the rise, leaving families homeless, hungry and without medical help. The amount of reported suicides from June through the end of September was three times the amount reported for the entire previous year.

I felt sick as I watched. It didn't feel much differently than watching someone die, right in front of my eyes. It was disturbing. It was depressing. It was absolutely horrifying. But I couldn't look away. I felt helpless and hopeless, and then felt slight relief when the news broadcast went to commercials. I wanted to turn away, to turn my back on the world and continue living my life as a hermit, but I couldn't keep doing it. I'm not naive.

The news returned. They talked about the odd occurrences that had happened around the globe. The red tide had spread through the oceans of the world over the past few months, making all seafood inedible and endangering millions of creatures dwelling in the ocean, on the land, or in the sky. The light show over Rome had now been seen in hundreds of cities, in every country across the world. And of course, there's still no explanation for any of it.

Isn't that convenient?

I was blown away by all that had happened in the last few months. In the long run I didn't avoid anything, just hid from the truth and had it all blow up in my face at once. The lines had been drawn in the sand and the world, as we know it, had crossed the line. Like the man's sign said, choose your side wisely.

I turned off the TV and started to get the house cleaned up. Riley would be home soon. I turned on some music and played with Rufio. He chased his wind up mouse across the floor, until he finally keeled over and surrendered. I laughed as he instantly fell asleep on the rug, like a worn out child with ice cream and Kool-Aid stains on his face.

I heard Riley's truck engine turn off and the front gate swing open. I wanted to meet him at the door, but decided it was more important to keep the pizza from catching fire in the oven. Riley struggled with the door handle, talking to himself. At least, I had *thought* he was talking to himself. He walked in the door, with an awkward smile. I knew he was officially up to something.

"Hey," he grinned, sheepishly.

"Howdy, how was your day?" I played into it nonchalantly.

"Um, good. So. Uh, I decided to get you... something." he smiled, backing against the front door.

"Oh yeah?" I asked, as I tried to peek behind him.

"Um, can you go in the bedroom for a few minutes? I have to bring *it* inside." he fumbled over his words, with a large, awkward grin.

"Ooookay," I replied, as I turned to walk towards the bedroom.

"Bring Rufio with you? Please?" he handed me the cat.

I held Rufio and carried him into the bedroom, closed the door and placed my ear against it. I was trying to figure out what Riley was up to, to no avail.

"Ouch, shit. Stop! Sit!" he mumbled in the living room. I heard the sound of scuffling and something large banging against the kitchen counter.

"Okay, it's safe! You can come out, but leave Rufio in the room!" he yelled from the kitchen.

"Are you sure it's safe? Those sounds weren't very convincing!" I shouted back through the closed door.

I put the cat in the bathroom and ran to the bedroom door, spinning through, and closing the door behind me in one flowing move. I turned to face Riley, with his nervous smile. In his hands, he held a leash wound tightly. And on the other end of that leash was a behemoth.

"Holy Hell," I gasped, shocked. I knelt down on the floor and extended my hand to the gigantic beast sitting in front of me.

"I know you wanted a puppy, I'm sorry. But I also knew you wanted a big dog. He's great." he sounded almost guilty.

"He's beautiful. I love him!" I was petting my new companion.

"Good." he grinned, proudly.

"Where did you get him?" I asked, scratching behind his ears.

"Technically, I got him from work. He *was* going to be one of the K9s. He's apparently too young for the training." he rubbed the top of the dog's head.

"Dude, that's so *awesome!*" I was genuinely excited.

"I knew you wanted another Rottweiler, and he was just too amazing to leave living at the station." he smiled.

"How old is he? What's his name?" I asked.

"He's about nine months old and no one really named him. He was new to the force," he said, smiling at our new family member. The dog curled up on the floor and started chewing on a rawhide bone Riley had given him.

"Nine months? You mean this beast is still growing? Damn! He's already huge!" I laughed.

"I claimed him a few weeks ago and they put him through a light version of the obedience school, just to make sure he'd be safe to bring home." he was already very fond of the dog.

"So is that why you've been sneaky lately? Is that why you've been home late sometimes?" I asked, suspicious.

"Yeah, I kept going to visit him. I wanted him to get used to me, so I could introduce him to you."

"He's *huge*! He's like his own army," I said, staring at his giant paws.

"Yeah, that's what I thought. He's huge for his age. I don't know if you like it, but I've been calling him Azrael."

"Azrael? Yeah, I like that," I agreed.

"Well then, Azrael it is," he said, gently petting the new dog.

"Why does that sound so familiar though? What's it from?" I asked.

"It's the angel of death's name. I thought it was fitting." he grinned.

"That's really cool. I definitely like it." I smiled. "So, we should probably introduce the two kids to each other."

I walked into the bedroom and grabbed Rufio. I carried him to the door and set him down. Riley was kneeling down next to Azrael and had his leash wound tightly in his hand. He gently patted his head and whispered to him.

"*Nice. Be nice. You're okay, Az*," he talked into the dog's ear. Azrael let out a whine. Rufio was backed against the bedroom door, sniffing and hissing as Azrael tried to inch closer. Rufio ran off into the guest bathroom.

"It looks like our family is complete."

"Yeah, definitely," Riley said with his hands on his hips, looking down at his new dog proudly.

I grabbed Rufio and carried him over to his big little brother. They sniffed at each other suspiciously. Azrael continued to whine and try to break free of Riley's grip. Rufio growled and hissed. We both knew this was just part of adaptation and loosened our bonds on both animals, so they could adjust to each other at their own pace.

"Well, he's been stuck in the truck for the past couple of hours. I say we take him for a walk. I finally have the chance for revenge on the neighbors! I just hope Az can drop a bigger deuce than Samson." he grinned wickedly.

"That's disgusting! Hysterical, but disgusting!" I laughed.

"How horrible of me! Why would anyone choose to let their dog defecate on a neighbor's lawn? No one does that," Riley answered, sarcastically.

"Yeah, good point. Samson has booby trapped our yard more times than I'm sure I know of. They're going down! We're going to need a lot of fiber, STAT!"

"Atta'girl!" he winked.

We walked around the neighborhood for about an hour. Azrael seemed overwhelmed with excitement. He hadn't spent much time outside of a cage or kennel in his short life. We discussed our plans, or lack of plans, for the evening and decided that we would play it by ear. Now that we had a new buddy who needed attention and exercise, we figured we'd more than likely end up going to the park by the lake with him in tow.

The autumn days in Louisiana were mild, but the night cooled off much quicker than we had expected. We both were feeling the chill and decided to make our way back to the house. We returned to our street and walked slowly, to allow Azrael a few extra minutes of quality time, then stopped on the edge of our neighbor's lawn. He began to sniff the grass and walk in circles.

"Oh man! I think he's gonna do it!" Riley whispered, excitedly.

"You're *such* an asshole. This is ridiculous." I giggled to myself.

Azrael finished and returned to Riley's side wagging his nub tail. He had, in fact, left a steaming pile in the neighbor's yard. I gagged profusely. Riley had exacted revenge. The two of us laughed and praised the dog like two proud parents. Riley was entertained by this as if he was a teen leaving a flaming sack of crap on a neighbor's door step, after ringing the bell and running off to hide in the bushes.

"Good boy!" Riley chuckled, as we ran back to our house.

"They're going to be so pissed!" I laughed.

"We were just returning the favor," he rationalized. "Fertilizer."

"I *would* blame Samson, but Tom's trained him *not* to poop in *his* own yard."

We walked through the gate and latched it closed. Riley removed the leash from Azrael's collar and pulled a treat out of his pocket. He commanded the dog to sit, which he did, then gave him the treat and pet his head reassuringly. He romped around our small fenced-in yard while we sat on the patio and watched.

"I think he was a good choice. He acts like he's been with us forever," Riley stated as he threw a ball into the yard. Azrael ran after it, and then returned it to Riley.

"He's beautiful. I can't believe how big he is. Especially if he's supposedly that young. He's not even full grown." I was amazed.

Riley tossed the ball against the front gate. "Yeah, I was surprised by that myself. I couldn't believe that they didn't want to put him through the academy. He's so smart. He's still a little rambunctious, but I'm sure that will pass," he said, now holding a slobber covered ball. He threw the ball again.

"Well, I'm *glad* they didn't keep him." I smiled, watching him hauling ass across the narrow yard. The ground seemed to tremble under his tremendous paws. He looked ferocious.

"He's the Legion of Doom." Riley laughed.

Chapter Ten
Fecal Fury & Shit Fueled Shenanigans

I slept very restlessly that night. I tossed and turned for hours. I couldn't stop thinking, and the bed was much warmer than usual, with a new space heater lying between us. Az laid on top of the blankets snoring loudly and occasionally kicking my side as he dreamed. Rufio had slept on my pillow, as far from his new nemesis as he could be without giving up his throne. He, of course, kicked at my head all night as well. I'm guessing they were probably both dreaming of chasing each other.

Riley didn't even seem to have noticed the silent war raging between the two jealous animals hogging the bed. I was caught in the middle, like an intermediary, some kind of UN Peacekeeper caught in the age old war of cats and dogs. I was abused from both sides, yet no cease fire was made, no parley given. Stupid animals. I felt bad for Rufio. He was being forced to adjust to a nuisance canine.

Riley opened his eyes and yawned. He stretched and his hand landed on the heap of hot fur lying between us, which made him smile. Az woke and raised his head to see who was touching him, then wagged his stubby tail. This mild activity woke him from his slumber, and he eventually decided to get to his feet and stand on top of Riley, licking his face.

"Ugh, stop!" Riley tried to push Azrael off of him. The dog continued, ignoring his orders.

I laughed. "That's pretty sexy."

"I didn't miss dog slobber on my face. What was I thinking?" he sat up.

"You were thinking you wanted to one-up Tom and Samson and you knew Rufio's turds just weren't big enough to make an impressionable impact." I reminded him.

"True." he nodded. I threw my pillow at Rufio.

We both got out of bed and began our morning regimen. Riley sauntered to the kitchen like the Pied Piper, with both animals following him to their respective food dishes. I snickered and shook my head as I watched my boys. Gathering some clothes, I headed into the bathroom and jumped in the shower.

A few minutes later the shower curtain peeled back, revealing a black muzzle sniffing at the steam. I jumped when I noticed Azrael sticking his head into the shower like a peeping Tom. I covered myself with one hand with an unwarranted sense of modesty and splashed water on him with the other until he took off running into the other room. I could hear Riley laughing in the bedroom when he noticed his soaking wet dog running out of the bathroom.

"Did he get in with you?" Riley asked, poking his head into the shower.

"No." I laughed, splashing Riley just as I had with the dog. He left the bathroom, closing the door behind him.

"Thank you!" I yelled.

When I got out of the shower, I wrapped myself in a towel and began getting ready for the day. I plugged in the flat iron and put on some makeup, then changed into some clothes and walked out of the room. Riley and Azrael were running around in the backyard, while Rufio was sitting at the patio door, watching the scene unfold with what could have been a look of aloofness. The king, watching his peasants do peasant things. I knelt down and picked him up.

"Don't worry, you're still my favorite," I told him. He didn't seem comforted. He didn't seem amused. He didn't seem to give a shit about anything other than his felt mice, catnip and his tuna treats at bedtime. Oh, and those damned red straws...

I walked onto the patio and watched the two animals running around playing. Riley would growl and grab Azrael's backside. Azrael in turn would growl and bark, turning to chase Riley. I laughed as they ran back and forth. Riley eventually tired and sat on the patio. Az flopped onto his back and rolled around in the grass, kicking his feet in the air, his jowls flopping backwards, exposing a menacing smile.

"He's so happy." I removed my beer cap.

"You should have seen how happy he was a few minutes ago. Let's just say he created another peace offering for Samson." he grinned wickedly.

I laughed. "You're getting out of hand. Someone's gonna call animal control on the both of you."

Riley shrugged. He genuinely just didn't care. Revenge was the only thing on his mind.

We walked inside, trailed by the dog, which was covered in grass clippings. Riley grabbed his clothes and walked into the bathroom, followed by his furry companion. I sat down on the couch and turned on the TV. Rufio jumped onto the couch and began cleaning himself next to me. I flipped through the channels a few times before stopping on the Weather Channel. There was a small box with a rotating cloud formation in it at the bottom of the screen. That was never a good thing. I watched as they discussed the formation of a tropical storm, capable of becoming a hurricane. It was now off the coast of Haiti and headed towards the US.

I didn't have much fear of hurricanes, although, that did mean I was going to be stuck at work for far longer than I would want to be. Where the hell did this formation come from? Last I saw of the weather, there was no mention of a depression, or storm.

"What's going on?" Riley asked, walking into the living room.

"Tropical storm. Might turn into a hurricane," I replied. We both sat silently, watching the TV.

"Awesome."

"Yep," I agreed, sarcastically.

"Wait, what did they say? *Nestor*? You've gotta be kidding me. *That's* what they're going to name it? Who the fuck comes up with this shit?" Riley was dumbfounded. "Why do they always name something so destructive, something so homoerotic? I mean, seriously, *Nestor*? It sounds like an old dude living in his mother's basement playing Dungeons and Dragons, who spent his high school years as a leader of the Chess Club. I can't believe this shit!" Riley ranted.

I laughed. "Why don't they go for something slightly less creepy, like Bubbles or Tiny Dancer?"

"Actually, why don't they pick names that would be more accurate, more sinister. Something like Bubba or Butch, seeing as how they're just going to pound our asses," I offered.

"... Fucking Nestor, I can't believe it," Riley jabbed, shaking his head and leaving the living room.

"It's probably going to die off anyway. We've been really lucky this season," I said, walking behind Riley to the patio. He slid the patio door open and lit a cigarette.

"No. It isn't going to die off; it's going to commit suicide! It's going to leave a note, scribbled across the Atlantic Ocean, thanking the asses at whatever organization that named him. He's going to leave a big 'fuck you' and blow himself and half of the coast of Florida away with one shot. He's gonna kill himself on our front lawn and leave us holding the bag. Fucking Nestor," Riley continued his tirade.

I laughed again, caught up in his curse word laced rant.

We went back inside after Riley's smoke and I finished getting ready. I straightened my hair as Riley continued bitching in the other room. Every once in a while I'd hear him mumble something about "Nestor", which made me laugh every time.

When we were finished getting dressed and ready to go, Riley attached Azrael's leash to his collar. I made sure that Rufio had plenty of food and water before we left the house, then we walked out to Riley's truck and helped Azrael into the back seat. I handed him a treat, and he wagged his stubby tail in appreciation. As we were pulling away, we saw Tom standing in his front yard with Samson. Tom's eyes narrowed; like he was trying to blow up our gas tank with his laser vision.

"Must have found our gift," Riley stated. Azrael growled and barked when he saw Samson.

We pulled out of the neighborhood and headed towards the park. Az sat in the back, quietly watching his surroundings. He wagged his tail as he watched cars pass by, but never barked. He eventually nestled in the back seat and napped until we got to the park. Once we arrived, I grabbed the bag of food I had prepared for our picnic and Riley helped our big boy out of the back seat. He noticed a small dog running by with its owner and instantly tensed up, growling. The man noticed Azrael and tightened his grip on the leash, leading his dog away quickly. Riley laughed and gently pat our protector on his head.

I carried our stuff over to a large willow tree and spread the blanket down on the ground underneath it, taking the food and drinks out of the insulated bag and setting them out. Riley and Az had stopped on their way over and were now chasing a squirrel. Azrael barked and growled at the squirrel, which was now halfway up the tree. People turned to see where the menacing sound was coming from. Riley pulled on his leash and coaxed him towards our picnic. Sitting down on the blanket, he opened a container full of dog food, sliding it over in front of Az. Riley then grabbed himself a sandwich out of a bag and began eating. I sat against the tree and stared out at the beautiful park in front of me.

The sun was bright, when it managed to sneak out past the dark passing clouds. The birds were chirping. There was a light breeze that stirred the grass and flowers. It was hard to believe that there was a storm brewing out in the ocean.

"Do you think it's really going to hit us?" I asked, staring up at the fast moving clouds.

"What, Nestor? Probably. Just our luck. " He shook his head. "I have no clue, but it's going to suck if it does. You know I've never been around a hurricane like you have. We have to worry about Az and Rufio, and you know damned well that we'll both be stuck at work the entire time, or at least for the cleanup. I really hope it doesn't. I don't wanna think about it," Riley shoved his sandwich in his mouth.

"I guess we'll just have to wait and see." my brows furrowed.

We finished eating, packed all of our stuff back into the bags and brought it back to the truck then walked around the park, playing with Azrael and talking about life in general. I was startled when my cell phone rang in my pocket. I looked down at the screen.

"Who is it?" Riley asked.

"Mom," I said as I put the phone up to my ear, "Hey, Momma."

"Hey, honey. Did you hear about the hurricane?" she asked.

"Yeah, well kind of. I'm not that worried about it," I lied.

"Well, it's already been upgraded. I suggest you go get some food and things to prepare."

"What do you mean? It's only been like, three hours. How has it already been upgraded?" I asked, surprised.

"What's going on?" Riley asked, confused from only hearing my side of the conversation.

I covered the receiver as my mom continued to talk, turning to answer Riley. "She said it's already upgraded to a Category One, and it's headed towards Cuba," I told him, then returned to the conversation with my mother. "Don't get freaked out. Why don't you and Dad go get your stuff and get the windows covered. We'll figure out what's going on. Don't worry about us, we're fine," I tried to comfort her.

"Your dad's already outside talking to the neighbors. Why don't you kids head this way and come stay with us?"

"You know we can't do that. We're going to have to stay here. I'm sure we're both gonna have to work." My lip curled up instinctively.

"Well I think you should just come here, so we know you're safe. Can't you tell them you can't work?"

"Mom, really. We can't. There are hundreds of us that work here, what would they do if everyone said they couldn't work? There wouldn't be anyone showing up. I don't have a choice. Plus, we have Rufio and now a dog to worry about," I continued.

"A dog? I have a grand-puppy? Why didn't you tell me? What kind? What's its name?" she asked, now distracted.

"Riley just gave him to me last night. It's a Rottweiler. His name's Az for short," I answered.

"Ass?"

"No, Az. Azrael." I laughed.

"The angel of death!" Riley shouted to my mother.

"Oh, that's cute." she chuckled.

"I need to get going. But we'll be fine. You just worry about you and Dad. Don't worry about us. Please. We're adults."

"You'll always be my baby. I have to worry about you," she said.

"I know. But really, we'll take care of each other," I said.

"You always do."

"Exactly," I smiled.

"Well, what are you kids doing?" she inquired.

"We're at the park right now, but we're about to leave. I guess we should go find out what's going on and get some stuff taken care of. If the hurricane *is* going to hit us, I'm sure they'll be trying to call me in soon."

Riley noticed my irritation and smiled, then kissed my cheek.

"I need to go ahead and talk to Riley. We need to figure out what we're going to do. I kind of want to spend some time with him before the shit hits the fan."

"No problem, honey. I'll talk you later. I love you. Tell Riley I said hi," she said.

"Will do, and I love you, too."

"So what's going on now?" Riley asked, raising an eyebrow.

"Looks like we might get hit. I think we should head home and figure out what's going on." I frowned.

"Bah! That sucks," Riley growled. "Come on, Tubby!" Riley coaxed the dog to his feet.

The two of them ran to the truck. I followed behind at a slower pace, eyes locked on the sky. The clouds were pushing towards the west hastily. It was always uncomfortable to see the clouds zipping in the opposite direction. We loaded into the truck and drove towards home.

Traffic was thicker than usual. People looked anxious and irritated sitting on the interstate ramp. Honking horns and aggression thundered in the air. Riley's cell phone rang. I turned down the radio as he reached for it.

"Lamar," Riley said, looking at his phone. "Hey man, what's up?"

I stared out the window, attempting to ignore his conversation.

"Yeah, we heard about it. *Nestor...*" Riley laughed. "Three? What?"

My curiosity was now piqued.

"Nah, I didn't hear that. We're headed home to watch the weather and make plans. You coming over?" Riley asked. I slapped his arm and nodded. I wanted to know that Lamar was safe as well. "Yeah, we'll be there as soon as we're out of this traffic."

"See you in a little bit." he then hung up. "Lamar's headed to the house in a few minutes. He said he heard on the radio that there are now *three* storms brewing."

"What? Where the hell are they coming from? We've had no problem this season, and then 'poof'. Three of them?" I was so confused.

"Yeah, I don't know what's going on." he shook his head.

He turned the radio up, turning it to a local station. We listened as they spoke about the three storms festering in the sea. Nestor was now on its way to Cuba, Olga was further north, more than likely aimed at the Carolinas. There was also a tropical depression forming southwest of Mexico and California.

"Don't you think this seems kind of odd?" I asked him.

"What do you mean? It's hurricane season. You seem surprised."

"I don't mean just the storms. I mean everything," I explained.

"Everything, like what?"

"Look. We have three storms headed towards us, a possible third world war in the works, unexplained meteor showers, a red tide killing sea life, suicide on the rise... *something*'s going on. Something's wrong." I theorized.

"Did you take your medicine?" he asked suspiciously.

"Not funny. I'm serious!" I slapped his arm again.

"Come on, you don't seriously buy into that apocalypse bullshit, do you?"

"I don't know what I believe anymore," I said, distraught.

"Wow, emo kid. Need a razor?" he mused.

"Wow! You are *so* not funny." I couldn't help but laugh.

"Edie, there's a lot going on, I realize that. But I think it's all going to blow over and we'll be surprised how big of a deal everyone made over nothing. Like I said, it's hurricane season. This shit's bound to happen. There won't be another world war. It's just scare tactics. The meteor stuff is probably some kind of debris from an old satellite or something we blew up. We're destroying the Earth, the red tide is probably from some kind of pollution we've caused," he reassured me.

"You're right. I'm probably reading too much into all of it. But it's still scary," I said. A car swerved in front of us and slammed on its brakes.

"Douche bag! Do that again and I'll shove my truck up your Civic's ass!" Riley yelled out of the window.

The kid in the Civic flipped us off.

"Little bastard. I wish I could write him a ticket, just for being an asshole," he clenched his teeth, "Really though. Try not to get so freaked out. Everything will be fine."

"I know. You're probably right."

"As always." he smiled.

"Hardly," I laughed.

"Oh, yeah? That's news to me." he smirked.

After thirty minutes, we had moved about half a mile. We decided to exit off of the interstate at the first available exit and find another route. We inched down the ramp and waited to turn onto Perkins. There was a man standing at the intersection. I squinted trying to read the sign he was holding.

"Is that the same dude we saw a few months ago?" Riley asked.

"Yeah, I saw him the other day, too," I answered. "What does his sign say?"

"I can't tell, he's got it turned away," Riley replied, squinting and leaning forward over the steering wheel.

The man turned back towards us. We both read his sign.

How long, O Lord, holy and true, until you judge and avenge our blood on those who dwell on the Earth?

"What the fuck's wrong with that dude?" Riley asked.

"I don't know. But that's kind of creepy." I shuddered.

"Why can't he just ask for money like a normal bum?" he asked, staring at the strange man.

His sign was larger than the previous two, with bright red painted letters. He looked no different than the last time I had seen him. He had his hood up, his tattered pea coat buttoned, his face covered, with only his pale hands exposed.

We drove through our neighborhood and pulled into the driveway. Lamar was leaning against his car, on his phone. We pulled up next to him and parked the truck. Tom was standing out in his front yard. When he saw us pull in he turned quickly and walked back to his house. Lamar finished his conversation and hung up.

"Hey guys." Lamar grinned.

"Hey Llama!" I smiled.

"I called Mike and Lana. Looks like they might be coming over, as well. I hope you don't mind," he said.

"Hurricane party, eh? I think you guys are jumping the gun, a little." I let Azrael out of the back of the truck.

"Any excuse to drink works for me," Riley chirped.

"Ugh!" I walked to the gate and opened it.

Riley was standing by Lamar's car, talking to him.

"When did you get a dog? Rufio's gonna be pissed," Lamar said.

I walked to the front door and was instantly filled with anger. "Riley!"

"What's wrong?" he asked.

I handed him the stinking brown bag and the note that was taped to the door. "Look what you started," I said, frustrated.

Riley opened the note and laughed heartily. "Oooh, I can't believe he did that." Riley chuckled, handing the note to Lamar.

Mr. Nixon,
I believe your mutt left this on my front lawn.
I'd appreciate if you'd keep your crap in your own yard.
If there's a problem, I could call your supervisor and
get a _real_ cop over here to handle this.
Thanks,
Tom

"Holy shit. That's hysterical!" Lamar laughed. I had my hands on my hips.

"Yep. It's go time. This means war."

"Come on, Riley. The guy's an ass, but there's no need to retaliate. Just ignore him and be the better man," I suggested.

We heard the neighbor's door open and close and watched as Tom hurried to get his car door opened. He got inside and turned the car on then deftly pulled out of his driveway and stared at us as he passed. Lamar and I stared back, giving him dirty looks. Riley, however, smiled and waved. Tom was clueless. He really had no idea how much shit he had just stirred up, quite literally. We walked to the edge of the road, watching his car, as he pulled out of the neighborhood. As soon as he was gone, Riley began his strategizing.

"Okay guys, we're going to have to move quick," he said.

"What? Oh no. What are you up to, Riley?" I asked.

"I'm in." Lamar laughed, not even knowing the plan yet.

"Don't encourage him!" I shot a glance at Lamar. He shrugged and laughed.

"We have to hurry, we don't know when he's gonna be home," Riley said walking towards the shed.

"What do you have planned?" Lamar asked, curious.

"We need to split up. Here, take a bag." Riley handed each of us a plastic bag.

"Edie, do you have some gloves in your car?"

"Yeah, of course, why?"

"Oh no, no, no! Don't tell me you expect me to pick up dog shit!" I shook my head. "I can't believe we're actually going to do this."

"Come on! Let's go!" Riley shouted, heading out through the gate like he was charging off to battle.

After a few minutes of running around the neighborhood, we ran back to the house and Riley 'combined' our bags and wrote his own note to Tom. Lamar and I stood on lookout duty, watching for our victim while Riley walked over to Tom's doorstep and turned the bag upside down, dumping contents onto his mat. He had to outdo his foe. He stapled his note to the front door.

Tom,
It hurts me to know that you didn't appreciate my gift
to you. After all of your generosity, I felt it was only
fair to return the favor of a fertile lawn. Since you
didn't like my present, we decided to return your
goodies to you. I'm gonna go cry myself to sleep.

... I can play this game all day, sweetheart.

Riley returned to us with a very smug look on his face. I shook my head and watched him as he proudly laughed and bragged about his mischief. He was like a child, strutting around like a peacock. I wasn't surprised, either.

"The fecal fury is raging," I stated.

"Shit fueled shenanigans are fun and exciting!" Lamar laughed.

We went into the house and turned on the TV. Az and Rufio chased each other back and forth across the living room as we watched the weather. They talked about Hurricane Nestor, which was now a Category Two. If it continued on its current path and didn't lessen in strength, they expected it to reach Florida and Louisiana by Tuesday morning. Maybe earlier, if it strengthened further. Olga was still only a tropical storm, but was strengthening and turning more southerly. We didn't know what to expect. We weren't sure if we were going to get hit by one, let alone two hurricanes. The tropical depression in the Pacific wasn't a concern to us; it was just odd to have it come into creation while we had the other storms to worry about. It was as if the United States were being ambushed by natural disasters.

Mike and Lana knocked on the front door, and we yelled for them to come in. They carried in a case of beer and did their round of hugs and handshakes.

"Your neighbor is outside pissing and moaning about something," Lana said.

"Oh, yeah? Tom's having a conniption? Awesome!" Riley smiled widely.

"Yep. He's freaking out. What did you do?" Lana asked.

I scratched my head guiltily and smiled.

"Uh oh, I was joking. What did you guys do? Seriously," Lana asked.

"Let's just say, revenge. *Riley* covered his front porch with um, well, dog turds." I smiled awkwardly.

"Ew! Riley! Oh my goodness, that's disgusting!" Lana shrieked.

Riley didn't need to hear our conversation to know why Lana was squealing. He laughed maniacally. The rest of us snickered in response.

"He had it coming. Think about how many times your nice, expensive shoes have been covered in his dog's shit. Yeah, you're welcome." Riley returned to conversation with Mike.

"So what are y'all planning on doing about the hurricane?" Mike asked.

"Not sure. We don't even know if it's going to hit us," Riley replied.

"As shitty as our luck is, we'll probably get smacked with all three," Mike retorted. Lamar nodded in agreement.

We all watched the weather and formulated a plan. If we were, in fact, going to get bombarded with a hurricane, we'd be somewhat prepared and know we were all relatively safe. Although this was our first hurricane season in Louisiana, we knew that our home had made it through previous hurricanes with ease and without prolonged power outages. With our house located between two hospitals, we knew it shared a grid with at least one of them. The others in the group had lived in the area through multiple hurricanes and knew they weren't in great locations for a quick fix.

We all have our "children" to protect. Lamar is the proud father of Turkey Stamos, a monstrous cat. Mike and Lana have their puppy, and we have our two. Although it would be a handful, to say the least, we offered for our friends to use our home as a safe haven during the storm, in exchange for some babysitting if we were both forced to work. Everyone agreed that staying here, to at least ride out the hurricane, would be the best bet.

After we had finished discussing our plans, everyone went their own way. We decided that we'd get together tomorrow to stock up on food and other things we needed if it looked like we would be hit with the storm. Lamar said he'd keep an eye on the weather and give us all a call in the morning to determine what was necessary.

We all parted ways and went about our activities as planned. Riley and I opted for a quiet dinner alone at one of our local "go-to" restaurants. There really wasn't any 'romance' involved, but the solitude was nice, and the quiet ambiance helped calm my nerves. Once we were seated and had ordered our meal, we began to discuss the storm again.

"I'm sure we're both going to get called tomorrow. You guys start your evacuation soon after confirmation, right?" he asked.

"Yeah. If they suspect it to hit Tuesday, they're more than likely starting the evacuations tomorrow. We'll be transporting from hospitals and stuff nonstop." I pouted.

"I think we're going to have to start shutting roads down and setting up the routes." he sneered. "At least neither of us will be on the streets when it hits. *If it* hits. I'm sure we're preparing for the worst and nothing will come of it. Then again, I would never put it past a dude named Nestor to destroy everything. I would," he remarked sarcastically.

"You're pretty hung up on the name, aren't you?" I smiled.

"Come on, you don't think it's utterly ridiculous? *Nestor?* Oh man, I'd murder someone if I was named Nestor. Possibly myself."

"It could be worse. It could be Billy Bob." I mused.

"It's not headed for West Virginia." he laughed.

"Good point." We fell quiet for a few moments. "You think everything's going to be okay?" I asked nervously.

"With what, Nestor?" Riley asked.

"I don't know. With *everything.*"

Riley smiled and grabbed my hand. He paused, choosing his words carefully. "You know damned well, in all good conscience, that I can't tell you *everything* will be okay. I don't know what's going to happen, I didn't go to school for fortune telling. But, we've been through some rough shit and made it out with minimal damage." he smiled. I returned the smile with some effort. My phone rang in my purse. I pretended not to hear it.

"You gonna answer that?" Riley asked.

"Nope," I smiled.

Riley raised an eyebrow. After a moment my phone beeped, informing me of a missed call.

"Here we go," the waiter said, setting our plates down in front of us.

My phone rang again. People turned in their seats and looked at me, waiting for me to shut it up.

"Oh no, my cell phone's ringing. I can't believe I interrupted your conversation. How rude of me!" I remarked loudly, turning to the woman closest to our table that was glaring rudely. I locked eyes and stared silently as my phone continued to ring, unanswered, until she turned around. I returned my attention to

Riley, who was shaking his head with a barely concealed smirk on his face. My phone beeped again, indicating a voicemail. I searched through my purse and pulled it out. I listened to my messages.

"Awesome," I said sarcastically.

"What's wrong?" Riley asked, stuffing his mouth with a bite of steak.

"They're starting tonight and want me to come in."

"Do you have to?" he mumbled, with a mouth full of food.

"No, I'm not scheduled to work until Monday. They can't *make* me come in. But they'll keep me once I do." I frowned.

"Okay, so don't go in 'til Monday. That solves that problem."

"I better call them, they're not gonna stop calling until they talk to me. I'll be right back." I pushed my seat back and excused myself.

I walked outside, lit a cigarette and pulled up the number of the supervisor on duty, Dustin. We spoke for a few minutes about the hurricane and likely outcome. He wanted me to come in tonight. He had spoken to Mel, who agreed to return to work whenever I did. I felt torn, and highly annoyed.

"Are they saying it's going to hit us, for sure?" I asked.

"It's moving faster than normal. It's now a Category Four and it's destroyed most of Jamaica," Dustin replied.

"Ah, shit. I didn't know that." I rubbed my temple. "I'll see what I can do. I can't make any promises, but I'll try to get in before Monday."

"We'd really appreciate that. Just give us a call if and when you think you can make it in. I promise we'll take care of you," he said, then ended the call.

I put my phone in my purse, put out my cigarette and walked back inside. Riley was sitting there with an empty plate and talking on his phone, much to the annoyance of those around him. I pulled out my chair and sat down, then picked at my now cold dinner and pouted like a child. Riley forced a smile. I took a few bites, waiting for him to finish his conversation.

"Yeah, I know. Let me talk to Edie. We have to figure out what we're going to do before I can give you a straight answer," he said, spinning his knife on the table.

I stared at him, wondering who he was talking to.

"Okay. I'll call you back. Later," he said, then hung up. Riley looked up and saw my worried expression. "That was Jere. Looks like they've already started calling us in, too," his upper lip curled.

"Yeah, they want me to come in tonight or tomorrow. I told Dustin I wouldn't be in before tomorrow night or Monday morning. I told him we needed to get our place ready and stuff." I frowned.

"Jere and I will be rolling together. So, basically, it's all on you to decide when." he winced.

"Oh, thanks! As if work wasn't making me feel guilty enough, now I have to plan the demise of four people." I laid my head on the table.

"You aren't sending us off to our doom." he laughed. "I just didn't want to make any guarantees until I talked to you. I know how much you worry. I didn't want to run out on you, guns blazing."

"I know. I'm sorry."

"Let's get out of here. We still have the evening to ourselves. Let's make the most of it." he smiled.

The waiter walked by, asking if we needed anything else and suggested dessert. We declined and asked for our bill. Riley paid the bill and pulled my chair out, walked me to the car and opened my door for me. Before I sat down, he turned me around and gave me a hug.

"Don't worry," he said, then kissed my forehead.

"Easier said than done," I replied, smiling halfheartedly.

CHAPTER ELEVEN
BATTEN DOWN THE HATCHES!

The tide raged, battering the rocky cliffs. The water churned and bubbled like a witch's cauldron. The sky swirled and spun, a dark portal, an angry torrent, ready to consume everything in its path. The wind swept my hair into my face, temporarily blinding me from the mayhem that was approaching. A storm was on the horizon.

The cliffs moaned and shook, as the huge waves broke against them. I closed my eyes and took in a deep breath. The salt in the air stung the back of my throat. I coughed and gasped, clearing my burning airway. I listened as the wind howled and shrieked like a mournful banshee. There was more than just a storm on the move. The ground beneath my feet quivered. I knew I shouldn't be here, and the feeling was unnerving. I heard footsteps behind me and closed my eyes.

Ten, you're only dreaming.

Nine, you need to wake up.

Eight, you're at home.

"You've returned!" Gabriel exclaimed, surprised.

Seven, you're in bed with Riley.

Six, wake up.

"Eden, I've been trying to get your attention. We need to talk," he said.

I opened one eye and peeked at Gabriel, then let out a long sigh. "I'm not interested. I just want to get out of here," I replied, closing my eyes again.

"Eden, please. You have to listen," he pleaded, placing his hand on my shoulder.

"Fine. What do you want?" I asked coldly, opening my eyes and turning my attention to him.

"You still have two prophecies to witness. You have to hurry. Time is running short," he replied anxiously.

"What, now you want me around? Oh, please. I thought it was all just in my head, anyway?"

Gabriel shook his head.

"Wait, I mean, it *is* just in my head. None of this is real," I said, closing my eyes again.

Ten, wake up, Edie.

Nine, wake up!

"I can't allow you to keep running from the truth," he said, shaking my shoulders. "You're finally ready. And we don't have much time."

"What the hell are you talking about?" I asked, pulling away.

"The end is near. This storm is going to devastate far more than just your city. You must prepare yourself," he answered solemnly.

"Lovely." I winced at the implication.

"It isn't just a *storm*. It's an unstoppable force, capable of destroying most of the continent. It's Mother Nature, with a purpose, on a mission."

I snickered and folded my arms. "Seriously? This is ridiculous."

"Eden, this isn't a joke. I need you to accept the truth. I need you to work *with* me, not against me," he said sternly.

"Look, *Mom*. You can't expect me to take this shit seriously when you're telling me, *in my dreams*, that the United States is about to get swept off the map by a single hurricane. If you wanted someone to help you spread these glad tidings, you should have chosen a paranoid schizophrenic news reporter or a conspiracy theorist," I mused.

He shook his head slowly.

"I thought it was pretty amusing," I replied, grinning.

"As you would. Why would you be concerned? You've turned your back on the truth more times than anyone else in history." his eyes narrowed.

"Oh really? Isn't that something? You come to me for help, or whatever the hell you want, yet I'm unreliable, *at best*? Then why are you here talking to me? Come on. This is bullshit. And it *isn't* real!" I scolded him.

"Look, Gabriel, Mr. Figment of my imagination, you seem cool and all, but you aren't real! None of this is. This cliff, this conversation, this... *fear, I'm suddenly feeling... Oh, God*. What did you do to me?" I sat down heavily on the ground.

"You know more than you're aware of. I know you get the feeling that there's more going on than just...reality. You need to come to terms with your existence. You need to regain your strength," he said soothingly, attempting to calm me down.

"I'm fully aware of my existence. I realize that I'm just one of the numbers. I'm just another ant in this stupid farm. But you; *you* need to realize that I don't care! *You* need to realize that I care about three things. Me, my family, my friends. *My life!* Outside of that little box, I don't give a shit what happens to whoever. Or whom, or what-the-fuck-ever is grammatically correct!" I snapped.

"That just isn't true. Why would you do the job that you do? Why would you choose to put your life on the line to help others, if you didn't care?" he scrutinized.

"Because I'm realistic! Because I can handle blood and guts, while most people can't. Because I'm desensitized! Because I wanted job security! There will always be stupid people. There will always be accidents, jealousy, anger. People will always be off balanced, one way or another, and harm each other. Or trip over their walkers, for God's sake! It's the truth, whether you think that's sad and depraved, or not."

"That isn't true." he looked at the ground.

"Yeah, it is. Sorry, dude."

"That *isn't* true. There won't always be people who need your help."

"Oh really? I'm *pretty sure* stupidity is hereditary. I don't think I have anything to worry about." I smirked.

"There won't be people left, at all." he looked up at me somberly.

"Is this the hurricane thing again?"

"No, it's the end." he shifted his gaze to the sky.

"Man, you're a bit unbalanced yourself. They have medication to help you; I'd recommend finding yourself a good doctor," I replied, brow raised. "What time is it?"

"Your time?" he asked.

"No, in Japan. Yes! Central," I replied.

"9:32am," he answered, without breaking his gaze.

"Look, I've gotta go. I have to go get shit ready. We need to prepare for the hurricane and pack up for work. I need to make sure the animals are all set."

"Eden, you can't." he grabbed my arm.

"I can't what, leave?" I asked.

"You can't go to work. You just can't go in." He had a very serious look on his face.

"What are you saying? If I don't go in, I'll lose my job. We can't afford that," I justified.

"None of it is going to matter. You need to bunker down at home. You will be safer. You need to trust me."

"Trust you? I don't even know you. I can't trust my own baking, let alone an imaginary friend who can't decide whether he's made of shadow, light, or flesh." I stood. "Not to mention, I don't think Riley is going to go for that."

"If you care about him, which I know you do, you won't allow him to go either," he clarified.

The hair on the back of my neck stood on end. "I, I don't know what to say. How could you... why would you say that?" I tried to piece my thoughts together.

"Say you won't go," he replied.

"I don't know... this is stupid," I said, looking towards the water.

The sky rumbled and lightning lit up the sky. The scene was very ominous and frightening.

"Anyone left out in the elements tonight, isn't going to make it out alive."

"Tonight?! I thought it was coming in on Tuesday? Two days early? Come on, man. You must be crazy." I tried to make sense of everything.

"I'll find you today, before the storm," he said.

"I'm not going to be sleeping today. I have a lot of things to do."

"I never said you would be." he gently rubbed my shoulder and bolted into the sky with breathtaking speed.

I sat straight up with a sense of urgency and panic. Riley was startled by my movement. I grabbed my phone on the nightstand. Sure enough, it was now 9:36am. I set my phone back down, took my glasses out of their case and put them on. I gently nudged Azrael off of my legs, so I could get out of bed.

"Get up, we have to get dressed and get moving," I said, peeling off my soaked blanket cocoon.

"What? It's still early," he mumbled.

"No, we have to go. You have to get up," I ordered, climbing out of bed and running to the closet.

"We'll get it done. Just get in bed. We have all day." he yawned, patting the pillow on my side of the bed.

"We don't have *all* day. We have a few hours, at max," I replied, throwing clothes on the bed.

"We need sleep, there's no telling if we're going to get any at work. You need to rest up," he said, lying back down.

I paused at the closet doorway, looking at Riley. I was terrified. I worried more about his safety than my own. "Riley…" I paused, choosing my words carefully.

"What's wrong?" he asked.

"I don't think we're going in to work," I continued nervously.

He sat up, cocked on his elbow. "What? You know we have to. You know damned well we could both be fired if we don't make it in," he lectured.

"It doesn't matter."

"It *does* matter," he threw his legs off the side of the bed. "We can't lose our jobs. You know we don't want to end up in the same situation we were in. Neither of us wants to end up back in Michigan. There's nothing for us there. You know we don't want to have to go live with your parents," he reminded me.

"Damn! Mom and Dad!" I felt sheer panic rise in my chest. I grabbed my phone off the nightstand and ran outside. I dialed my mother's number and lit a cigarette. "Pick up!" I yelled, as the phone rang and rang. Her voicemail picked up instead.

"Mom! It's Edie. I need you to call me the second you get this message. I'm gonna try Dad's phone and the house phone. If you get my message before I get a hold of you, call me back! I love you, so much. I hope you know that," I said, then hung up the phone with a sigh.

I dialed my father's phone number, pacing.

"Hi, you've reached the voicemail of Kurt McDowell. Please leave your name, number and a message, and I'll get back to you as soon as I can. Thanks," the phone relayed.

"Dad! It's Edie… You have my number! Call me as soon as you get this. I really need to speak to you. Please, please, please call me. I love you!" I said, hanging up. I was absolutely petrified. I dialed my parent's home phone number.

"Hello?" my father answered with a yawn.

"Oh, thank God! Why didn't you answer your phones?" I asked.

"Edie?" he asked, sleepily.

"Yeah Dad, you're only daughter." I laughed lightly.

"Edie, I can barely understand you." he sounded so exhausted and confused.

"I've been trying to call you guys. It went to your voicemail." The fear was settling.

"I'm sorry, honey, the phones haven't been cooperating. I'm still having a hard time hearing you. Hold on," I could hear shuffling and sirens in the background.

"There, that's better. I had to come inside. Now, what's going on? You've been trying to call us both?"

"Yeah. I need you guys to do me a favor." I put out my cigarette, exhaling loudly.

"Kim! Edie's on the phone, she needs to talk to us!" he yelled. "So what are you kids up to? How are you doing?" he spoke nonchalantly, not seeming to hear the despair in my voice.

"I'm fine. But this is serious. I need you to really listen to me," I continued. I could hear my mother and father talking in the background. She was trying to explain to him how to put it on the speaker phone, which led to a full blown debate.

"Dad!" I tried to get his attention. "Hello? Dad?" and again, "DAD!" I yelled into the receiver.

"Oh, hello baby!" my mom said.

"Hey, Mom," I sighed, resigned to take this verbal ride that was common when speaking to my parents on the phone. They must've figured out how to work the speaker phone.

"How are you?" she asked.

"Now's not the time for small talk, but I'm fine. For now, at any rate," I replied. "I need you two to do me a *huge* favor."

"Need some money? Are you okay?" my father asked.

"No, no. Nothing like that. Thanks. I need you two to head this way."

"Oh, Edie. We can't do that,"she answered.

"Why not? You could get here in like, three hours," I argued.

"We just can't, baby. That hurricane is going to be here in a couple of days and we need to get everything around the house ready. We'll come to see you once it's all over with," Dad chimed in.

"We don't have a couple of days. It's going to hit tonight. Please, just trust me," I continued.

"Are you sure? We were watching the weather a little bit ago. They said it's picking up in strength and speed, but they never said it was that close," my mom responded. This was dizzying.

"No, I know for a fact, it's not going to wait very long. It's going to be tonight. Please, if you won't come here, I need you to at least hunker down now. Get ready and wait it out inside, safely," I pleaded.

"I trust the weathermen," my father stated.

"I know you do. But seriously. Just get everything ready today. If for some reason it doesn't hit tonight, you're just prepared early. It isn't a big deal. Please, please just get situated now," I begged.

"Okay, we will," my mother replied, trying to comfort me.

"Are you sure you guys can't head this way?" I asked.

"No, we can't leave this place," my father responded, somberly.

"I'm not going to argue with you. Can you at least call the boys in Houston and ask them to get ready for it?" I asked.

"They're fine! They don't even expect to be hit," he replied.

"I beg to differ. I think they will be. Please, just ask them to get ready for it. For me?"

"Baby, who is your source of information? Are you just panicking? Don't worry so much! You know we've lived through plenty of hurricanes. It was much worse on the islands. Back when we were in Guam, we had to rough it out," mom said.

"I know the stories. I'm just asking you guys to please take me seriously and get ready. Call the boys and get them to prepare," I said, exasperated.

The sliding glass door slid open. Riley was peeking his head out.

"Lamar's on the phone, we're trying to make our plans. We need you," he said. I nodded.

"I need to go. I'll call you guys back later. I expect you to tell me that the windows are boarded up and that you're fully stocked and ready," I ordered.

"Okay, honey. Call us back later. We love you," mom said.

"Bye, I love you, pork chop!" he said happily.

"I love you both, too. Bye." I said, hanging up the phone. "They're so difficult sometimes."

Riley had an awkward smile.

"Just tell Lamar to head over here, ask him to get a hold of Mike and Lana. We need to get Jere and Mel and start making things happen. We can all go together to get supplies," I said.

Riley relayed my message to Lamar. "He said Mike won't be free until after 2pm. He's at work," Riley shot back.

"Fine. We'll get shit without them. Just tell Lamar to come over soon."

"Okay. He's headed over." he hung up his phone.

"So how are your parents?" he asked.

"We didn't really small talk, well, I didn't. They tried to, as usual."

Riley laughed in response.

We walked back inside and began getting dressed. Rufio slept peacefully on the bed, oblivious to the events coming into play. A few minutes passed. We heard Azrael by the door barking and growling. Riley walked to the front door and after checking, let Lamar in. The two of them sat in the living room talking, while I finished getting ready in the bedroom.

I could hear them discussing the plans, deciding what would be the best approach to retrieve the supplies we needed for the coming onslaught. Riley told Lamar everything that I had said and it sounded as if they were taking me seriously. I finished up and walked out to the living room.

"Hey, Lamar," I greeted him.

"Hi, how are you?" he waved.

"I've been better, and worse."

"So, what's going on, exactly?" he asked.

"I'm pretty sure the hurricane is headed inland tonight," I said with a sigh.

"Last I heard, we were still safe until tomorrow sometime." he cocked his head to the side, with an inquisitive look on his face.

I made an attempt to change the subject. "So, did you guys get a hold of everyone else?"

"Mike's at work, Lana is over at her parent's place," Lamar stated.

"Jere and Mel are both at home, trying to get everything together before they head in for work tonight," Riley added.

"They're going in?" I asked.

"Well, yeah. They aren't freaking out quite like you are. They expect it to completely blow over." he finished the rest of his beer.

"And you do, too?"

"Well, no. I expect to get hit, but no time soon. It's hard for me to believe that the meteorologists would be completely caught off guard and have it swoop into town on its broom tonight. I'm not quite a damsel in distress, Dorothy." Riley grinned.

"And I am? We're not talking about the damned Wizard of Oz here, Riley." I frowned.

"Look, I haven't heard anything about it 'swooping' in tonight," Lamar chuckled. "But, I was watching the weather channel earlier, and they did say it had increased in strength and speed overnight. They aren't exactly sure where it's going to make impact or when, for that matter," Lamar continued very matter-of-factly.

"Thank you." I smiled triumphantly.

"I don't know. Someone has to be out there."

"Well that someone doesn't have to be you, or me," I stated, frustrated again. Lamar raised an eyebrow. He looked confused.

"I'll think about it. Anyway, we need to make a list of the shit we need to get, and head out," Riley said, changing the subject.

"Hey, Lamar, you still have your pillow and sleeping bag in your trunk?" I asked.

"As always." he laughed, "Dibs on the couch!"

We sat down at the dining room table and made an organized list of all the things we'd need. We were going to need some plywood for the windows, food, batteries, jugs of water, tarps, lanterns and a generator if we could find one. Lamar decided that we could split up to get things done quicker. He opted to head to a home improvement store to get us some essentials. Riley and I were headed to the grocery store and would be in charge of stocking up on the necessities.

We'd meet back up at the house as soon as we were able. We gave Lamar a spare key and told him to make himself at home, if he beat us back. Riley helped Azrael into the back seat of his truck as we got into our vehicles and headed off towards our destinations to fill up on supplies.

"Do you really think all of this is necessary?" Riley asked as we navigated the neighborhood streets.

"Yeah, I really do." I nodded. "I think this is going to be worse than expected."

Riley sighed, defeated, and turned the radio onto the local rock station. He expected them to report whatever was going on. They were obviously paying attention to the weather, as they had to give the reports every twenty minutes or so. We drove to the store without much more conversation. We were both thinking about the current events, although we saw things differently. I was concerned, thanks to my dream that we were in danger. He thought we were in danger of losing our jobs, thanks to my dream. I wasn't concerned about work. How could we work next week if we didn't live through the night?

I thought about it from every angle. What if I called my supervisor and told them I'd be in, in the morning. If the storm hits tonight, I could claim to be trapped at home. I could ride it out, safely, with Riley, rather than apart. But I knew I was a shitty liar, and I'd more than likely spill the truth and wind up jobless. I was at a loss.

"Are you mad at me?" he asked as he turned the radio down.

I looked at him, suspiciously.

Did I have a reason to be?

"No, why?"

"I don't know, you're just really quiet. I didn't mean to hurt your feelings about the dreaming thing. I just thought you were over that shit," he said.

"I'm not mad, I'm thinking. And I don't care about what you said. I understand where you're coming from. But I really just wish you'd trust me."

Trust me... I've heard that recently.

"It's not that I don't trust you, you know I do. I just don't want to think about losing our house or being unemployed, after all that we've been through." he grabbed my hand.

"What do you think we should do?" I asked.

"I don't know."

"Can we just stay home tonight? If the hurricane doesn't hit, then I was wrong. Then we can go to work in the morning, like nothing ever happened," I suggested.

"That works for me. I'll call'em in a little bit. I suggest you do the same," he responded.

I smiled and leaned over to kiss his cheek. I felt relieved. I hadn't won the war, but the first battle's victory was definitely mine. The least he could do for me was to give me the benefit of the doubt for tonight. From there, we'd just have to wait and see. I knew, deep down, we'd be caught in the storm tonight. He turned the radio off, complaining about the mainstream bullshit; that dudes wearing makeup were selling crap music to our youth. He popped in a CD and cranked it loudly. He smiled and began singing along to the punk that was blaring from the speakers. Azrael howled in the backseat. I chuckled and stared out of the window, watching people as we pulled into the grocery store parking lot.

People seemed to be going about their daily business, with no sense of urgency. Had I been wrong? Did we really still have until tomorrow night to prepare, instead of mere hours? I didn't think so. I watched the helpless lambs as they sauntered about before the slaughter.

As I watched, I thought about what Gabriel had said in my dream. What did he mean about me bailing out consistently? I had always been hardheaded and stuck things out. And when, where and how would I see him today? I didn't understand. Riley rolled down the windows a little bit to give the dog some fresh air while we were inside. We got out of the truck and began walking towards the store. Riley grabbed my hand and squeezed it tightly. I was glad we had reached an agreement.

We walked through the grocery store, tossing random things into the cart. I took the time to call other members of my family and ask them to prepare for the incoming storm. I called my brothers, cousins, and aunts. Most of the time I got their voicemail and left a message, probably more frantic than it needed to be, about hurricane Nestor and how quickly it was making its way to our doorsteps.

Riley stocked the cart with snack cakes and beer. They were his essentials and I knew better than to advise against it. We walked the aisles, tossing goodies into the basket, while people stared at us.

"We have the munchies." he smiled at an older woman. She shook her head in apparent disgust, and turned away.

"Nice. That's a great thing to say as a cop!" I snickered.

"Even better coming from a cop! Seeing as how I'm pretty sure I pulled her over last week." Riley grinned wickedly.

"You're horrible!" I laughed.

"And you love it." Riley's phone rang, "Hey, what's up?"

I turned and watched his reactions, trying to determine who it was on the other end.

"Really? Damn. Alright, grab all that you can and we'll meet back up at the house. We'll be done here in a little bit," he paused. "Okay, cool. Later." He hung up.

"Who was that, Lamar?" I asked.

"Yeah."

"What's wrong, no generators?" I questioned.

"No, he got a generator..." he said shortly, trying to end the interrogation.

"Then what's the problem?"

"No kegs." he frowned.

"You two are ridiculous!" I laughed as Riley smiled at me.

We wrapped up our shopping expedition and pushed our two packed carts to the front of the store. We waited in line behind the older woman that Riley had harassed. I turned away, embarrassed. I knew he was going to have to say something else to piss her off.

"Lovely weather isn't it?" he remarked casually with a smile.

"Yes." she returned the curt smile.

"Did you grab enough diapers and denture cream to make it through the hurricane?" he asked sarcastically. I slapped his arm.

"Excuse me?" she didn't look as irritated as I would've been.

"I asked if you'd stocked up on everything you need," he said loudly, smiling.

"Oh! Yes, we'll be fine," she laughed.

"Well good. Try not to break a hip during the storm. You know EMS will be hunkered down." he smiled charmingly. I turned beet red with embarrassment. I couldn't believe how far he had gone.

She finished checking out and turned to leave, "Try not to get alcohol poisoning during your hurricane party. You know, since EMS will be hunkered down and all." she smiled smugly over her shoulder.

"I'll be fine. Don't choke on your tapioca pudding!" he laughed.

"Bye, Riley." she laughed good naturedly and walked off.

"Tell Bill I said hi!" he yelled. She turned and waved.

"What the hell was that all about?" I asked, stunned.

"That was Ms. Becky. She's my boss' wife. She's funny as hell!" he laughed at my reaction.

"I thought you were serious. I thought you were just being an asshole."

"Have you ever known me to be mean to old ladies? Well, the ones that didn't deserve it?" he continued.

"I can't believe you!" I put my hands on my hips, giving him my best attempt at a scowl.

Riley chortled loudly. "We joke around constantly. She comes in and helps with paperwork sometimes. She's basically like Bill's secretary."

"I thought you had lost your mind." I smiled. "You didn't really write her a ticket, did you?" I asked sheepishly.

"You're so gullible." he laughed.

We finished checking out and almost lost consciousness when we saw the price tag on our little grocery shopping trip. We loaded the baskets back up and walked outside. The sky was starting to darken. The outer band must have been moving in already. I felt the anxiety surging in my body. We were too late!

Riley sensed my unrest. "Calm down, it's just a thunderstorm," he said, rubbing my back.

"How do you know? What if I was wrong? What if it's going to hit this afternoon? We have to get home!" I panicked.

"Lamar and I were watching the weather while you were getting ready. It's just some rain. We're fine. We still have time to get home, I'm sure." he reassured me.

We walked out and loaded the groceries into the bed of the truck. "We're gonna have to hurry so the food doesn't get ruined." Riley was looking up at the clouds.

I stopped, staring at the threatening sky. The color was an unsettling, unnatural looking, greenish-grey tinged hot mess. I felt my heartrate accelerate as I watched the quickly moving clouds zoom by. I imagined it morphing into the redness I had seen in my dreams. I held my chest, held my breath and silently prayed for a good outcome.

"Gonna get in?" he asked, holding my door open for me.

I slid into the passenger seat. Riley got in and turned to Azrael, handing him a treat he purchased in the store and reassuring him that he was a 'good boy' for not letting anyone steal his truck. Az sat peacefully in the back seat, munching on his biscuit and wagging his tail happily.

We drove home as quickly as we could, racing the thunderstorm that was nipping at our heels. We stopped at the red light on the corner of Perkins and Essen, waiting to turn.

"You've got to be kidding me!" Riley said, pointing out of his side window.

"What?" I asked, turning to see what he was pointing to. On the corner of the street was the man with his never-ending supply of ominous signs. This one was no different.

"STORMS ARE ON THE HORIZON.
BATTEN DOWN THE HATCHES!
THREE WILL BECOME ONE."

"Seriously? Is this dude the town crier? He needs to find himself a real job and stop with his sign crap," Riley shook his head and made the turn onto Essen Lane.

The man looked up as we were turning, removing his hood for the first time and allowing me a clear view of his face.

"*Gabriel!*" I gasped.

"What?"

"Nothing," I replied shortly.

We turned into our neighborhood and pulled into the driveway. Lamar was already there, his car parked in the driveway. I got out of the truck and walked around to the back, lowering the tailgate. Riley opened the back door and let Azrael out. Lamar popped out of the front gate with open arms. We all loaded ourselves up with grocery bags and walked them inside. Azrael stayed out by the truck as we filed in and out of the front gate, carrying arms full of bags.

"We'll need to run to the beer store on the corner and check for a keg." Riley nodded at Lamar.

"Cool, let's do it," Lamar said with a grin.

We finished unloading the groceries from the truck. I was in the kitchen sorting the bags and putting things away, as Lamar and Riley were devising a plan of some sort.

Riley and Lamar left the house. Riley's truck roared to life as they climbed in and headed out. I finished putting away the cold foods and toyed with the notion of hopping in my car and driving back down to the corner where I had seen Gabriel. At least, I thought that it was him. I weighed my options and opted not to go, more concerned with the idea of it *not* being him, and simply putting myself in danger. Instead, I finished putting away the groceries and walked out on the patio, letting Azrael outside with me.

I lit a cigarette and walked to the edge of the concrete pad, staring up at the clouds moving in overhead. They seemed ominous as they quickly moved in on the quickening breeze, whistling through the nearby tree limbs. Azrael sniffed at the air and began to growl. He ran to the front gate and growled again, deeper.

"What's wrong, Az?" I asked, walking towards him. There was a knock on the gate, startling me. I grabbed Azrael's collar, holding it tightly as I peeked through the cracks between the wood.

"Hello?" I opened the gate, slightly.

"Eden?" the familiar voice asked.

I pushed the gate open more. Azrael began to fight his bond.

"*Gabriel?* What're you doing *here*?" I asked. Azrael lunged at Gabriel, snarling and growling menacingly. "Az! Heel!" I pulled back on his collar. "Hold on," I said, pulling Azrael back towards the house.

I opened the front door and fought to get the dog inside. I returned to the shrouded man at the front gate.

"I told you I'd find you today." he smiled.

"Look, I don't know if you should be here. Riley will be home soon." I scratched my head nervously.

"I needed to speak to you in person, where you weren't able to wake up and run from me," he said.

I smiled awkwardly. "Well, come in."

He walked with me to the back patio and pulled out a chair. Azrael ran to the patio door, barking and snarling as he ran back and forth across the glass divide.

"The storm will be here in about seven hours." he removed his hood. His face was smooth, almost childlike. His golden hair blew in the wind. His skin was pale, almost translucent. His eyes were solid grey, with no pupils, no irises. I've never seen anyone wear contacts like that, and suspecting those were his natural eyes was unsettling. He was beautiful, in an eerie, terrifying way.

"When will Riley be home?" he asked.

"Soon." my brow furrowed.

"Good. I need to speak to him, too."

"I don't recommend that." I shook my head adamantly.

"It's too late, he needs to know the truth just as much as you do," he said. "He's impossible to reach in his sleep."

I chuckled in reply, uncomfortably. "Look, I don't think he's going to accept any of this as well as I did. Not to mention, we've seen you around with your signs, he's going to think you're insane. Then, when he realizes you've been talking to me in my sleep, he's going to think I'm insane. Which isn't that far off, I suppose."

"You worry a lot," Gabriel surmised, a slight smile playing across his lips.

"I hear that constantly," I said testily. My eyes narrowed as I looked him in the face. "What's going on with this storm?"

"I'd prefer to discuss it when Riley is here," he said loudly, over Azrael's barks and snarls. He was lunging at the glass doors now, trying to break through and get to the perceived threat.

"That's a great *guard* dog you have there." he smirked as he watched the increasingly hostile canine.

"I don't know what his deal is. He's normally really mellow."

"Dogs don't like us," he said.

"Us?" I asked confused.

Gabriel placed his hands in his lap, looking towards the sky. "Have you been paying attention to the weather?" he changed the subject.

"Relatively. I know we have a hurricane headed straight towards us."

"Have you been watching the *national* weather? Do you know about the other two?"

"I saw something about them the other day. I thought it was a little odd, but figured it wouldn't affect me." I shrugged.

"It's not only going to affect you, it's going to affect everyone."

"Okay, seriously. What the hell is going on?" I asked. My patience for this was thinning quickly.

"The three hurricanes are going to make their way inland. They're going to grow in strength until reaching Kansas and Nebraska. That is where they will clash and disperse, reforming into one giant super cell," he answered, somberly.

"Tornado Alley? And where will this *super cell* go from there?" I asked.

"In every direction. The hurricanes aren't the only threat. In fact, they may not even be the worst of it. The storms merging will be cataclysmic. The sky will explode with life when they meet, dispatching tornadoes and destructive storms in every direction," he continued.

"That's convenient. And how do you know this?" I asked.

"I just do."

"Are you psychic? Are you an alien? Are you fucking crazy? What? You have to give me some information here. How would a hurricane make it to Kansas, much less three? Why is my dog trying to rip through the glass doors to get to you?" I interrogated.

"It isn't easy to explain and it isn't the right time. All you need to know is that you can trust me; that I'm your guardian, in a sense," he answered calmly.

"My guardian schizophrenic? Nice," I mused. I turned to the patio door. Azrael was now whining as he continued his sentinel pace of the patio door. "If this was all you came to discuss, I suggest you head out. You need to find somewhere to squat until the hurricane passes. I'd offer you a spot here, but I don't think Riley or Azrael would appreciate it."

"*Azrael*? You named your dog after Death? Very interesting. Very fitting, to say the least." he nodded, "Though I do suppose you're right."

I rose to my feet and began walking to the front gate to see Gabriel out. I heard the truck engine turn off and the sound of two doors opening and closing. I could hear Riley and Lamar laughing about something. I felt a surge of panic in the pit of my stomach. How was I going to explain this?

Riley walked through the gate, with a keg on his shoulder. Lamar followed suit with bags of ice. Both of them watched the ground as they walked. Gabriel raised his hood when he noticed Lamar. Riley looked up, his eyes narrowed. Azrael was now at the front door, snarling.

"Who's this?" he asked me, lowering the keg to the ground.

"This is... Gabriel." I hesitated.

"Your brother?" Lamar asked me.

"No," Riley and I replied simultaneously.

Lamar stepped back slightly, startled by our reply.

"What are you doing here?" Riley asked Gabriel, walking forward.

"I'm here to warn you."

"Lamar, would you mind taking this inside and calming Az down?" Riley asked, never breaking his gaze from the stranger in his yard.

"No problem." Lamar readjusted the bags in his hands and grabbed the keg.

The three of us watched as Lamar walked inside the house. He turned to make sure we were safe, waiting until he received Riley's reassuring nod. He grabbed

Azrael's collar and pulled him back away from the door, closing it as he disappeared inside.

"Now, where were we?" Riley grinned menacingly as he took another step forward.

"Riley, calm down," I said, stepping between them.

"Calm down? I leave for ten minutes and come home to see a nutcase with apocalyptic forecasts in my backyard with my paranoid wife? How am I supposed to react, Eden? Am I supposed to be elated? He could have hurt you." Riley was fuming.

"I would never hurt her," Gabriel defended.

"Oh, okay. Never mind! I take it back. I didn't realize you were such a gentleman. What was I thinking?" Riley was getting more and more irate. I shook my head at him. This was what I was worried about.

"Riley, I'm not here to hurt either of you. I'm here to warn you."

"And how the fuck do you plan to do that, buddy? I think you should be concerned with protecting yourself at this point," Riley threatened.

"Would you just hear him out?"

Riley shot a glance at me and my stomach turned. I could see the anger in his eyes, "Make it quick," he said gruffly.

Gabriel paused for a moment, and then took a deep breath. He closed his eyes and pulled back his hood. When Gabriel opened his eyes, Riley gasped, staring at the strange man.

"I know it's a lot to take in. I know it's hard for you to trust me, but I'd appreciate if you'd listen and at least try to take me seriously. I've warned Eden for your benefit, not to make things more difficult," Gabriel said, calmly.

"Tell me what's going on," Riley said, staring suspiciously at Gabriel as he tried to recover from the initial shock.

"Not only is there a hurricane headed towards the southern tip of the nation, there is also a hurricane headed in from the east and the west. The three are all coming in at the same time, with the same trajectories." Gabriel paused again, waiting for Riley's reaction.

"So, they're all headed this way?" Riley asked, skeptically.

"No. The three are headed towards the middle of the United States. They're all going to merge near Nebraska and Kansas, forming one giant storm."

"But hurricanes typically lose strength when they reach land, how the hell is that even possible?" Riley questioned.

The front door flew open. Lamar was standing in the doorway. He stuck his head out of the door, attempting to keep Azrael behind him. He looked pale, uneasy, startled. The three of us standing outside turned as one to see what Lamar had to say, "You guys have to come see this shit."

"What is it?" Riley asked.

"We're boned," was all Lamar could muster as a response.

Riley and I looked at each other, and then turned to Gabriel. Riley and I walked. Riley walked in first and grabbed Azrael, taking him to our bedroom and closing him in the room. The dog protested, barking and jumping against the opposite side of the door.

"I'd prefer to stay out here," Gabriel said.

"It's okay. The dog is closed in the bedroom. You can come in." I smiled. Riley opened the door and we both followed him inside.

"It looks really bad," Lamar said, sitting on the edge of the couch petting Rufio, who was now comfortably sinking into the cushion beside him.

"What's going on?" I asked, taking a seat on the opposite side of the couch.

"All three have upgraded to category four and are making their way towards the States. They're still not sure when they're going to make landfall. They're moving much faster than normal. They've said this is going to be extremely destructive."

"Most people don't think it's going to be tonight, they're expecting morning by now. I tried to warn you, so you weren't stuck at work when it came inland," Gabriel said.

Riley turned to Gabriel, arms folded across his chest. "What's really going on here?"

"I don't know what you mean," Gabriel replied.

"You know *exactly* what I mean. How do you know this shit? How did you know about these three storms coming together and forming a super storm? The meteorologists didn't even know in advance. What are you?" Riley questioned.

Lamar and I stared at the TV, watching the radar imagery.

"Shall we step outside?" Gabriel asked.

"Yeah. We shall." Riley smirked.

Lamar and I sat on the couch for a few minutes, watching the reports on the weather channel. "Shouldn't we get the windows boarded up?" I asked finally.

"Oh shit, I need to get Turkey, like now," he replied.

I turned and just then noticed that both Riley and Gabriel were no longer standing there. I could hear Azrael sitting at the bedroom door, whining. I walked towards the bedroom, noticing Riley and Gabriel sitting on the patio, talking. I opened the door and let him out of the room. I went to the patio door and saw Riley shaking his head in disbelief. What had Gabriel told him? Was this still about the storms or something else? I walked out on the patio.

"Hi, guys," I said nonchalantly.

"Hey." Riley innocently smiled.

Thunder rumbled in the distance. The wind picked up, carrying the smell of rain on its back. The thunderstorm was finally moving in. Riley turned in his seat to stare at the approaching storm. Gabriel followed Riley's gaze, then closed his eyes, breathing deeply. I stared out at the fast moving clouds, wondering if we'd even have a break in between storms.

"We should probably start getting everything ready," I said.

Lamar stepped out on the patio, squeezing past Azrael and the sliding glass door.

"Yes, you should. And I should be going," Gabriel said, opening his eyes and rising to his feet.

"Well, I need to go grab my cat. Can I give you a ride anywhere?" Lamar asked.

"No, I'll be fine. I have my own mode of transportation. Thank you." he smiled. Gabriel began walking towards the front gate, pulling up the hood of his jacket as he moved. I turned to Riley and frowned, curious to know what was said.

"Wait."

Gabriel turned to face us.

"Why don't you ride out the storm here? We have plenty of space, food and I'm sure we could scrounge up a sleeping bag for you," Riley offered.

"I think you should." I nodded.

Gabriel glanced from my face to Riley's and back. "If you insist", he replied.

I smiled and pulled a chair at the patio table back out for him to have a seat. I lit a cigarette and opened a bottle of beer. I cleaned off my glasses, pulled my hair back into a ponytail and sat in one of the other chairs at the table. I was ready for business. We had preparations to make. "Okay, so. We need to get these windows secured, for starters," I began.

"I can help, if you don't mind giving me a few minutes to go pick up Turkey," Lamar said.

"We can get it," Riley said.

"I can assist in any way you need," Gabriel said, removing his hood again as he rejoined the group at the table.

Lamar stared at him, confused at the recent change of events. "Dude, you've gotta be hot as hell in that jacket. Do you need a t-shirt or something?" Lamar asked.

"I'm fine. Thank you," Gabriel replied.

"Holy shit, you're pale. Are you a vampire? Do you twinkle in the sunlight?" Lamar mused sarcastically.

Riley turned, covering his mouth with his knuckles. He chuckled then coughed.

"Alright, we should get started," Riley said, getting to his feet.

"Just let me know what you would like me to do," Gabriel said humbly.

"Just chill here for now. I need to let the dog out for a walk and talk to Edie." Riley grabbed my arm and led me to the patio door.

"I'll be back in a few," Lamar said, walking through the gate.

Riley and I walked inside the house and stopped in the living room. He called Azrael to his side and attached his leash. He walked to the closet and grabbed two hoodies. Slipping his arm into one, he threw the other at me then headed for the front door. I followed him out.

We stepped outside and pulled up our hoods. The wind was blustering heavily. The rain hadn't begun to fall yet, but we knew, as soon as we were far enough from home, it would kick in. We squeezed through the front gate, making sure that Azrael didn't catch sight of Gabriel.

We gave a wave to Lamar as he pulled out, and then began walking towards the end of our street. The thunder crashed in the distance, shaking the ground and startling all three of us. Azrael sniffed the air, whining. We both looked at him. He knew there was something very wrong and we couldn't help but agree.

"So what made you change your mind? What did he say to you?" I asked as we walked.

"He didn't *say* anything. It was what he showed me," he replied.

"And what did he *show* you?"

"I don't want to get into it." Riley mumbled as thunder cracked loudly, it was moving closer. "And besides, my opinion hasn't completely changed. I'm not sure I trust him, but right now, I feel he has more information and insight than we do. I'm going to let him stick around until I know what I need to know."

"So you're using him."

"No, it's a guy thing. It's mutual," he retorted.

"What could he possibly be using *you* for in return?" I asked cynically.

"Access to you." he sneered.

My brows furrowed. "I don't get it."

"Like I said, it's a guy thing. And I didn't want to get into it," Riley repeated.

"Fine," I crossed my arms and sulked. We walked quietly around the opposite side of the block.

"Edie, let's just say the hurricanes *do* come together and send out shockwaves of tornadoes and destructive hail. Let's just say that the world *is* coming to an end. What then?" Riley broke the silence.

"Who said anything about the world ending?" I asked.

Riley's face went flat. He nodded towards the house.

"Gabriel said that?"

"The long way around it, yes. He isn't very direct, is he?"

"I didn't hear anything about *that*." I played coy.

"You've *seen* it," he snapped back.

"I don't know. I'm not sure how I feel about any of this." I looked to the sky. "And to be honest, I don't know what I've seen."

The thunder rumbled.

"Why didn't you talk to me about all of this?" he asked.

"Jesus Christ, tell me you're joking? Because you thought I was bat shit crazy already! I didn't want you to have me committed," I said defensively.

"Nothing's changed; I still think you're crazy. Except now, I see a man sitting at our patio table who you've only met in your dreams, prophesying Armageddon and forecasting the weather better than the people who went to school for it. Not only are you insane, but now I'm feeling it, too," he said, cracking a smile.

"Thanks. That's comforting."

"You're quite welcome." Riley leaned over and kissed my cheek.

We got to the end of the road and turned around. The wind was beginning to blow harder, whipping leaves from the trees and sending birds tumbling from their flight path. Azrael continuously sniffed at the air and would occasionally growl. He was definitely uneasy.

"So now what?" he asked.

"I don't know. I guess we just take it day by day and see what happens."

"Well, now I really can't go to work tonight," he stated, which brought a forced laugh from both of us.

"I don't think it's a good idea." I shook my head vigorously.

"Nah, I don't wanna leave you and Mr. Creepy-fuckin' McPale-dude unattended. He may fill your tea with Rohypnol and kidnap you," he mused.

"You are so ridiculous. Where would he take me? Kansas?" I said sarcastically.

Riley laughed hysterically in response.

We continued our walk back towards the house. Azrael crouched down in front of the gate and let out a low, menacing growl. Riley bent down to comfort him and find out what was getting him so agitated. I opened the front gate and gasped. Riley looked up to see what had me shocked.

"Whoa. What the fuck?" he asked, staring intently.

"I don't know," I mumbled, taken aback.

We both stared at the strange glowing man standing in our backyard. Gabriel stood with his arms stretched and raised toward the sky. His face turned up, eyes closed. His skin shined brightly, like a supernova moments before the explosion. The light radiated from his skin in waves, burning our eyes. It was hard to focus. He stood, jacket at his feet, in beautiful golden armor. It shined and glimmered as the light from his skin bounced off of it in every direction.

"Oh God, he is a vampire? I thought that they just made that shit up?" Riley quietly mused, in awe.

Gabriel turned to face us; his eyes were black as coal, like two smoldering holes in the middle of the sun. We watched as his skin slowly faded back to the dull pale we had formerly seen with each growing second. He lowered his arms and sighed in resignation.

"It's time."

CHAPTER TWELVE
SUGAR & MOTHBALLS
IN MY THINK TANK

We stood in the doorway of the gate, awestruck and bewildered. Neither of us knew what to say, or how to explain what we had just seen. Azrael stared at Gabriel, snarling as he approached us.

He set his hand on top of Azrael's head. The dog pulled away and snapped at the armor-clad being. Gabriel didn't flinch, only stepped closer and knelt down, eye level with the angry dog. He placed his hands on the sides of Azrael's face. Riley and I turned to look at each other, then watched motionlessly as Gabriel stared into his eyes and whispered something to him we didn't catch.

Az whined and laid down at Gabriel's feet, staring up submissively. Gabriel patted him gently on the head and rose to his feet. Azrael followed suit and stood, wagging his stubby tail. Riley and I turned to each other again, dumbfounded.

"What the hell just happened?" Riley asked.

"Your guardian and I were just having a little discussion." Gabriel smiled.

"I didn't mean the dog thing. What was up with the light display there?" Riley asked, dumbfounded.

Gabriel smiled and walked back to the patio. Riley followed closely behind him with Azrael trotting alongside. I stood at the gate, still baffled and glued to the spot, unable to walk or speak. As Gabriel walked ahead, I stared at his back. Riley turned to me, shaking his head. He returned his gaze to Gabriel.

Riley followed him to the patio and sat down on one of the chairs. He stared at the ground and scratched Azrael's back, baffled. I slowly walked towards them, staring at the rumbling sky as it opened up. The rain fell with such force that it stung my face. I shielded my eyes and hurried to the porch.

I stepped up on the concrete and shook the rain from my hood, then took the rubber band out of my hair and ran my fingers through my soaked tangles. Riley glanced up at me, still shaking his head. He is such a practical man; I know he was having a hard time grasping what was real and what was fiction. Gabriel had put his jacket back on and was buttoning his coat.

"I'm so confused right now," Riley started, finally finding his words.

"What would you like to know?" Gabriel asked as he finished clasping the last button.

"Everything. But I have the feeling now isn't the time for a heart to heart. We need to get the house secured. Lamar will be back soon. We need to call everyone and find out when they'll be here," Riley said looking up at me.

"Let's do it." I nodded.

"How long do we have, Gabriel?" I asked.

"About five hours," he replied. "I don't know if this storm is going to let up before the hurricane heads in. This could actually be one of the outer bands. People aren't going to know what hit them until it's right on top of them."

"Is that why you had your sign out? Were you trying to warn people?" Riley asked.

"In a sense; I wanted people to look into it for themselves. I wanted people to be warned, but I can't interfere or say too much. It's not my place. When I do, people like *you* say I'm crazy and force me to spend three days in a hospital for psychiatric observation." he grinned.

"Maybe a commercial would have worked better than being yet another crazy guy with a board." I snickered under my breath.

"I'll be honest, I really don't know what to say or think about this. But we need to get moving. I expect some answers when the time comes," Riley finished. He got to his feet and pulled up his hood, then walked to the shed and started grabbing the plywood for the windows.

I turned to Gabriel, who was staring up at the sky again. I pulled my hair up into a damp ponytail and straightened my hoodie out, "Gabriel?"

"Yes?"

"What are the markings on your back?" I asked.

"They're like yours." he smiled.

"Those weren't *just* tattoos. I could see them through the slits in your back piece. " My eyes narrowed, skeptically.

He laughed awkwardly.

"Can I see them?" I asked.

He said nothing, turned his back to me and unbuttoned his coat. I helped him snap and unlatch the back piece from his golden armor and gasped. I shook my head as he uncovered an intricate design, covering his entire back. It took me a few moments to follow the lines as I traced them with my fingers. They were raised, like scars. They twisted and turned, forming the outline of enormous dark wings. Behind the lines my fingers traced, a trail of light followed for a moment, then slowly faded back to the color of his flesh.

"Wow. It's beautiful," I stated.

"Thank you," he replied humbly.

Riley walked back over to us and set down the stack of plywood. He smiled and let out a long exhaustive breath, "That shit's heavy," he said, wiping his brow with his sleeve.

"I'm sorry Riley. Let me help you," Gabriel said, setting the two large pieces of armor to the ground. He leaned down and picked up a full sheet of plywood with ease.

Riley shrugged and walked over to the three windows encompassing our porch. I grabbed the other side of the board Gabriel was holding, positioning it over one of the windows. Riley grabbed a few nails and held them in his pursed lips. He snatched his hammer from the table and placed it between his knees, while he shifted the board slightly.

"Can I ask you something?" Riley mumbled around the nails, glancing at Gabriel.

"Absolutely. What would you like to know?" he responded, confidently.

"How the hell were you glowing?" Riley asked, driving a nail into the board.

"Easily," Gabriel smiled.

"Funny." Riley hammered a nail in the second corner.

"It's just part of who I am. Eden has seen me in all three of my skin's forms."

"I have?" I asked.

"You have?" Riley responded simultaneously.

"Yes. You've seen my shadow skin, as well." he smiled.

"Ugh, I hated that shit. It was creepy." I shivered with the memory.

Gabriel chuckled loudly, apparently amused by my reaction.

"So, you change *form*?" Riley asked, pounding on a third nail.

"Somewhat, but... not exactly," he stopped to gather his thoughts. "My skin is very delicate, like human skin. When I need protection, I *summon* surrounding shadows to my skin, using it as armor, so to speak," he explained casually.

Riley and I stood, staring at Gabriel, bewildered.

"I'm sorry. I forgot that isn't anything normal to you," he said as way of apology.

"None of this shit's normal," Riley said, turning back to the board.

"So, what's the bright version?" I asked.

"That's just my skin." he shrugged.

"So what is it right now? Is that like a mask, so people don't freak out? Like camouflage?" I asked.

"Basically. It's not good to stand out in a world so full of judgment," he replied, dejected.

"You don't seem to have a problem telling *us*." I raised a brow.

"I'm also not concerned about *your* judgment."

"I'm sorry, this is just fucking bizarre," Riley said, nailing along the side of the board. "What exactly are you, Gabriel? Are you an alien?"

"Something like that." he smiled.

The gate flew open and Lamar ran through, yelling obscenities. Turkey was in his arms, bitching as usual, now soaking wet and angry. Lamar ran to the open front door and set Turkey on the living room floor. A few moments later, he came to the patio door. He looked drained, battered and overwhelmed. I couldn't help but laugh at his disheveled appearance. He also now had a new annoyance, as Azrael attempted to introduce himself properly.

"Turkey attempted to murder me on the way over. He wasn't very happy," Lamar said.

"Was he trying to whine you to death?" Riley asked, mimicking the fat cat's mouthy complaints.

We all laughed and went back to getting the boards in place. Lamar's phone rang and he stepped out of the way to answer it. He spoke for a few minutes and hung up. He looked frustrated.

"Mike and Lana are on their way, but they've been stuck in traffic on the Interstate for a bit. I'm not sure what's going on, but I guess it's really backed up," he said.

"They'll be fine," Gabriel replied to his concern.

Lamar's eyes narrowed and he shot a glance at me. I smiled and nodded reassuringly.

"What, is he some kind of meteorologist?" Lamar whispered to me.

"Not exactly, but I trust him."

"Doesn't mean I have to," Lamar replied, walking towards the table.

We continued working on the windows. Lamar grabbed a second hammer and I grabbed some nails. We split into two groups to get the windows covered quicker. Lamar and I walked to the side of the house with several boards, and then began getting a piece of plywood in place. I could hear Riley and Gabriel mumbling in the distance. I tried to listen, but wasn't able to make out what was being said. When we were finished getting all the side windows covered, I walked over to Riley and Gabriel.

"So, what're you two talking about?" I asked.

"Life in general," Riley answered shortly. "Are you guys done with that side?"

"Yeah, we are. And are you guys done talking behind my back?" I asked, dejected. I saw his swift change in conversation.

"For now," Gabriel smiled reassuringly. "You don't have to worry. I'm just trying to help Riley understand. I'm showing him pieces of the past, to rekindle his memories. Don't worry. I will fill you in fully."

"That's awesome. I'm so glad you guys have been able to bond! Too bad I don't have a clue what's going on myself." I felt my chest expand with that *attack* instinct. "Look Gabe, you've driven me crazy for months and I'm still left in the dark. When will you take the time to discuss this with me?"

"Be patient." Riley nailed into the plywood.

"I'm so tired of hearing that!"

"Whoa, someone needs a time out."

"You're such an asshole!" I stormed into the house, pushing Riley out of the way as I did so.

I walked into our bedroom and slammed the door. I threw myself on the bed and took a few deep breaths. I stared at the ceiling for several minutes and thought about my reaction. It was a bit overdramatic, I know. But it's frustrating to live your life through riddles. It was more than I could or wanted to deal with right now.

I could hear Lamar, Riley and Gabriel talking to each other on the patio. I could hear laughter and the banging of hammers. I felt extremely embarrassed by my actions and sat up on the edge of the bed. I cradled my head in my hands with my elbows on my knees, and decided I needed to apologize for my attitude.

The patio door slid open and there was a gentle knock on the door.

"Can I come in?" Lamar asked, quietly.

"Yeah."

"You okay?" he asked, opening the bedroom door.

"Yeah, I'm fine. I'm just tired. And overwhelmed. And tired… and overwhelmed," I replied.

"Ah, got it." he smiled.

"I was acting like a baby. Sorry about that." I frowned, disconsolately.

"Yeah, you totally suck," Lamar replied, straight faced. He sat down on the edge of the bed next to me and poked me in the arm with his bony elbow.

I snickered. "I take that as acceptance." I smiled. "Thanks."

Riley was standing in the doorway and raised an eyebrow. He ran in and power slid across the bed, tackling the two of us. I laughed and attempted to break free of Riley's hold. He pinned me down and smiled. Lamar chuckled and walked out of the bedroom.

"Are you done being an ass hat?" Riley asked.

"For now," I replied with a smile.

"Good. I don't want to spank you in front of your friends. I'm sure that would be embarrassing."

"You and who else?" I replied, struggling out from underneath Riley's weight. "Did you guys finish up outside?"

"Yeah, no thanks to you," he stated, "Come on. Let's go outside. We still have some shit to do." Riley stood, offering me his hand. We walked outside and began picking up the tools and securing loose objects.

"I'm sorry if I upset you," Gabriel said.

"It's not your fault. I was being a total baby. I don't know what's going on. I'm just really stressed out and a little nervous about all of this," I replied.

"Why are you stressed?" he asked.

"I'm not sure. I was doing really well for a while, before you came back." I ruffled my hair.

"Oh." he hung his head. "I'm sorry. I didn't realize I caused you so much grief," he continued crestfallen.

"No, that's not what I meant. I'm just really confused. I don't like feeling like I'm missing the big picture. And I know; you don't have to tell me again, be patient. I'm being as patient as I can." I smiled awkwardly. "That's just, not one of my skills."

Riley shook his head aggressively, eyes wide.

"It won't be much longer. Before long, you'll see the entire picture. At that point, you'll probably wish you were still in the dark. You'll pray to go back to being just Eden," he somberly remarked.

"I don't *pray* for anything. There's no point. Prayers go unanswered," I replied, walking off the porch.

"You're far more hardheaded this time around," Gabriel mumbled under his breath.

Lamar's phone rang and he answered it. He looked frustrated or worried, I couldn't tell which. He hung up after a moment and slid his phone back into his pocket as he said, "That was Mike. They're going over to Lana's parent's house instead. I guess she decided she didn't want to be away from them."

"Sucks," I replied.

"Yeah." he nodded agreement.

"Riley, did you call Jere?" I asked.

"Yeah, he's going into work. He didn't want to take the chance," Riley answered.

"So it's just going to be the four of us?"

"More beer for me," Riley smiled.

"No, more beer for *me*," Lamar chortled.

"Okay boys. Let's get this shit wrapped up," I said, ending the beer debate.

We spent the next hour putting things in safe places and making sure the windows were secured, while the rain had temporarily let up. Riley and Gabriel decided to take Azrael for a walk around the block, since none of us were sure when he'd be able to go back outside. Lamar helped me in the kitchen as I put dinner together.

"So, who is that guy?" Lamar nonchalantly asked.

"A friend of mine."

"Ah. And how does he *know* so much about what's going to happen?" he questioned.

"He doesn't."

"One of *those* guys, huh?"

"Yeah. He thinks he knows what's going on. But I'm sure he's wrong. Just like guys always are." I smiled.

"I'm pretty sure there's something going on that you aren't telling me." he raised a single eyebrow.

I turned towards Lamar and put my hands on my hips. "You know, you're right. There's plenty of shit I haven't told you. But the problem is I don't even know what's going on. I'm a ball of unanswered questions and half eaten thoughts. I couldn't begin to explain any of this to you, even though I want to." I frowned.

"Well, I'm here if you need to talk," Lamar offered.

"Thanks," I replied, content with his acceptance of the situation.

We finished getting dinner ready and sat on the couch, watching the weather channel.

"Damn. I've been so oblivious to the other two hurricanes," Lamar stated.

"Yeah, I haven't really thought much of them, since I didn't think they would affect us," I said.

We silently watched in awe as they discussed the three hurricanes in detail. They talked about how California hadn't been hit with a hurricane of this magnitude in about 200 years. Out of nowhere, I realized how significant the three storms now were.

I thought about how Gabriel had described them crashing into one massive cell. A surge of panic ran down my spine. I jumped to my feet and ran to the door. I ran down the street and caught up with Gabriel and Riley.

"Gabriel!" I called, out of breath.

"Yes?" he offered his hand to me.

I bent into the tripod position, trying to catch my breath and batting Gabriel's hand away. "What's going to happen with these hurricanes?" I asked.

"I told you what's going to happen. They come together, forming one."

"Why haven't people realized how monumental this is? Why are people acting like it's just another hurricane season?" I asked.

"What do you mean? It *is* just another hurricane season. We knew that moving into Louisiana," Riley responded.

"I'm not talking about just our storm. When have you ever heard of three hitting at once?" I asked.

"I don't know. Are we sure it isn't just a coincidence?" Riley asked, attempting to calm me down.

"Seriously? You think it's a coincidence? Showing up to a party wearing the same dress as someone else is a coincidence. *Three* destructive storms wiping out every U.S. coast isn't something I would just write off as a *coincidence*," I stated.

"Eden, there isn't anything we can do. The damage is already done. The events are already set to play out." Gabriel frowned.

"Is this like, something of biblical proportions? I don't know my prophecies. I haven't watched the Ten Commandments in a long time," I stated.

The wind began to blow heavily, almost as if it were responding to my questions. Azrael's ears tucked back and he began to growl. The three of us stared up at the sky. The clouds blackened like necrosis; plagued. Diseased. The wind stirred and whistled eerily through the bending branches. We ran back to the house as the rain began to fall.

"How long?" Riley asked as he opened the front gate.

"Less than three hours," Gabriel replied.

"Well, I hope everyone is okay. I need to call my mom and make sure they're ready," I said, closing the gate behind me.

We walked inside the house. I took Azrael's leash off of his collar and handed him a biscuit. Lamar was sitting on the edge of the couch, scratching Rufio behind his ears with one hand and Turkey's with the other. I walked to the kitchen and grabbed the bowl of salad, carrying it to the dining room table.

"Dinner's ready," I stated flatly.

We all formed a line in the kitchen with plates and forks, while Gabriel sat at the kitchen table. The mood was very somber. We all had our minds drifting off as we silently fixed our plates and found our spots. I sat down last and looked around at the faces at the table. Lamar looked deeply troubled. Riley played a drumbeat with his fingers as he chewed a mouth full of spaghetti. Gabriel stared at the TV screen, watching the scrolling message at the bottom, with an empty placemat in front of him. I set down my fork. I wanted to break the tension with something humorous, but I couldn't think of anything to say.

We wordlessly ate dinner, then cleaned up and returned to the living room to watch the weather. After a few minutes of unadulterated anxiety, I realized that I needed a minute to breathe. I slipped out of the front door and stood under the eaves. I lit a cigarette and closed my eyes, rubbing my temples. I heard the front door squeak open and turned to see Riley's soft smile.

"How's it going?" he asked as way of greeting.

"I'm fantastic. How are you?" I mused.

"Everything's going to be okay," he stated, rubbing my back.

"Oh, yeah? Did Gabriel tell you that?" I asked. We stared out at the roaring rain and overaggressive clouds pushing their way into the city.

"Gabriel's a little weird." Riley laughed.

"Hmm, I never noticed."

"Yeah. Sure you didn't. Paradigm of normal, that one," Riley lit a cigarette.

The awkward silence returned.

"Do you believe him?"

"About what?" Riley looked confused.

"I don't know; whatever you guys have talked about. All of it, I guess."

The thunder rumbled and cracked.

"It's a lot to take in. But I think there's more to all of this than I had originally thought. He's going to explain everything to you. I still don't know the entire story. But I know that *he knows*, if he didn't give me some info, he wasn't going to be near you," Riley clarified.

He grabbed me and pulled me against his chest, hugging me tightly. The wind began to blow towards us, showering us with cold, stinging rain. I squealed as we both flicked our cigarettes and ran to the door. He held it open as I ducked below his arm and ran in, shaking the rain from my hair like a wet dog. He stared out of the glass for a quick moment, then turned and closed the door behind him.

This entire situation was overwhelming. I was starting to feel trapped and knew that I needed to open up, but to whom? There were thoughts I needed to get out. I needed to vent. I decided to write. I grabbed my journal and wrapped myself up in a blanket in the papasan. This was the best form of therapy to me.

Life and the lines blur past me, like the button is stuck on warp-speed. And they say that we haven't mastered time travel? Apparently, scientists haven't witnessed my existence. Minutes turn into hours, hours morph into days. Wake-sleep-wake-wash-rinse-repeat. It's like a vicious current, pulling me under.
My mind is always numb from the speed, while my thoughts travel faster than my hand. Constant questions fill the void. Am I a badge of honor, or a burden?
I've been absent for the entire exchange. My hourglass is vacant, sand caught in the ebb and flow. Life's fueled by stolen time, borrowed and hand-me-downs.
Where has it all run off to?
I feel like Sleeping Beauty, sans the beautiful part. Somehow I've turned into a somnambulist. Sleepwalking through life, a zombie of a sort. Something is missing, but I can't reverse the clock. Everything ticks by, leaving me in awe. Leaving me on the sidelines of my own life.
What's the point if you never get to live it? What's the moral of the story that you never get to tell? The spiral encompasses, strangling and constricting.
Victory comes cheap when you forfeit your own game.
It's a good thing I've learned how to cheat...

I thought about the fact that I was *supposed* to see my therapist tomorrow, since she had rescheduled my appointment, against my will. The receptionist had left me a voicemail. Good news was that wasn't going to happen now. Even if her office hadn't been demolished, I was sure that the storm would have kept the office closed for a few days at least.

Riley walked over to his guitar and threw the strap over his head. He turned on his amp and pulled a chair out from the table. Lamar eventually got up from the couch and unlatched his case. He plugged his guitar into his amp and sat down at another chair. The two of them played random chords until eventually finding a harmonious sound that they continued to morph and twist into music. Rufio and Turkey curled up on the couch, content to take a nap. We nestled in for a while, listening to the music and wind intertwine.

"Where's Gabriel?" I asked.

"Stepped outside a little bit ago," Lamar answered over his guitar playing.

"Where's Azrael?" I asked.

"Out with vampire boy," Riley replied.

I threw off my blanket, got to my feet and walked to the front door. I could hear the wind howling loudly as I opened it. I couldn't see through the glass door, it was now covered with water droplets, leaves, grass clippings and dirt. I fought to get the door opened and stepped out into the wind and rain. I looked around for Gabriel and the dog and didn't see them.

"Gabriel?" I yelled out into the storm.

"Over here!" he replied.

I peeked around the corner of the house and saw Gabriel poking his head around the side of the patio. I pulled my hood up and ran over to him. Azrael was sitting next to his side, patiently staring out at the rain with him. He wagged his stubby tail when he saw me approach.

"What're you guys doing out here?" I asked, gently patting Azrael's head.

"Watching the storm roll in," Gabriel smiled softly.

"Mind if I join you?"

"That would be nice," Gabriel replied.

The wind tore through the air onerously. I folded my arms, holding my ribcage. I fought against the wind to keep my hood in place. The patio created a pocket against the worst of the weather, but even here the wind was fierce. My tangled tendrils whipped my face. I turned towards the house and tied my hair back into a messy ponytail.

"Less than an hour," Gabriel stated, very matter-of-fact.

"Fantastic," I replied, fighting with my flopping hood.

"This is it, Eden. This is the end of everything you knew. This is the beginning of the end."

"Is the world ending?" I asked.

"Something like that."

"It's time for the truth. I have to know what's going on." I held my hood in place, looking Gabriel in his solid grey eyes.

"And you will. There isn't much time left for secrecy," he replied.

"What do I do? What am I supposed to do with my life, knowing that it's ending?" I asked.

"Live. Live your life to the fullest in the little bit of time you have. Enjoy these last, fleeting moments." he smiled. "You need to look deep within yourself and figure out what it is that you believe. You will eventually fight to the death for those beliefs."

"I still have War and Death to see," I interjected.

"You've seen plenty of that."

"But, not like the others. I haven't had the dreams. Don't I still have to witness them, too?" I argued.

"You're a bit of a masochist, aren't you?" he questioned with a stern look.

"Not at all. I just want the whole story." I looked out to the sky.

"I'll show you while I'm here with you." he gently patted my back.

"So, what did you tell Riley?" I interrogated.

"The truth."

"Which is?"

"The 'Apocalypse' is on the horizon. There are very few who can make a difference, two of which are you and Riley. The two of you both play a very large part in the finale," he explained.

"So, when will I be told the whole story? When will I find out what part I play?" I questioned. I was glad that I was finally getting some answers from Gabriel, regardless of how miniscule they were.

Gabriel laughed. "Soon enough. Don't rush things. You need to realize who you are, what you will do. It is a burden. It's an affliction, an obligation you don't want to worry about right now. When the time comes, you will be spiritually, psychologically and emotionally prepared. I give you my word." he bowed his head.

"*Who I am?*" I repeated.

"You don't think we randomly chose an insane paramedic with a penchant for trouble to help us save the world, do you? If I were going to *choose* someone, I would've chosen someone a little more mentally sound and stable," he stated.

"Oh, hardy har, smart guy!" I guffawed.

"Eden, you are a wonderful being. You always have been. You really have no clue how much good you've done. You're very special, regardless of how you feel. You aren't one in a million. You aren't just another person. You are significant. You'll soon learn that the world is exactly what it is, partially due to you. And you'll probably wish you were still clueless."

My brow furrowed and my head cocked to the side subconsciously.

"I'll be here with you for a couple of days. It will give us time to truly talk. I'll show you Death and War, although I don't think you need to witness them to understand," he explained.

"I want to know what I'm up against," I clarified, crossing my arms stubbornly.

"As you wish."

"You aren't going to tell me now, are you?" I snorted, frustrated.

"No. Sorry," he replied.

The wind blew harder. I stumbled and began to fall backwards. Gabriel caught me and righted my stance. He held out his arm and I took it in mine. Burying my face in his coat sleeve. We ran towards the front door, leaving the protection of the patio and the boarded up glass door. Azrael kept pace at his side the entire time. As we walked inside, Riley stopped playing guitar and looked up at us. His eye brow rose curiously.

"Where have you guys been?" Riley asked.

"On the patio, watching the storm," I replied with a small smile.

"I guess it's on its way now?" he questioned.

"It's basically on your doorstep. About forty minutes. I assume everyone here is prepared?" Gabriel surmised.

"About as ready as we're going to be," Riley said, rising to his feet. He walked to the kitchen and dragged a large plastic trashcan from the pantry. It was full of ice and the keg that he and Lamar had retrieved. He walked over to Lamar, who was still playing his guitar, absent from conversation.

"Would you care to do the honors?" Riley said to Lamar, dropping to one knee and handing him the keg tap like a royal scepter.

Lamar smiled and set down his guitar. He rose from his seat and stretched, then grabbed the tap from Riley's outstretched hands and walked to the kitchen. The two of them tapped the keg and began pouring glasses of beer. I walked to the kitchen and grabbed a glass of beer from the counter, handing it to Gabriel.

"What's this?" he sniffed the foam.

"Beer!" I smiled.

"Alcohol?" he questioned.

"Yes, *beer*," Lamar stated, confused.

"I appreciate the offer, but I don't drink." he smiled politely and slid the glass across the counter.

"Who goes to a hurricane party and doesn't drink?" Lamar asked Riley. Riley laughed and shrugged. Lamar shook his head and held up his glass for a toast, "To the wind, the rain, the debris in the air and a few days off of work."

"Cheers!" Riley yelled, slamming his glass into the side of Lamar's.

I sipped from my 'douche bag' glass.

Gabriel had a very confused look on his face. "You *celebrate* disasters?"

"No. We celebrate days off of work," Lamar clarified.

I winked at Gabriel.

We refilled our glasses and went into the dining room. We sat around the table laughing and joking. The alcohol helped to loosen the tension in the three of us. Gabriel smiled and acted as if he were enjoying himself, regardless of the fact that he was sober. Silence fell when the wind began to pick up.

"This is pretty crazy," Lamar broke the silence.

We heard the house quake beneath the barrage of wind and rain. The howling sent shivers down my spine. I've been through hurricanes, when we lived out on the islands. Not only did I witness how devastating they could be, but I slept through the part where it ripped our roof off, sending my family running for their lives in the middle of the storm. I remember waking up, seeing the ground only during the lightning flashes. I had been thrown over one of my brothers' shoulder and carried, half asleep to the neighbor's house. I remember the wave of panic that coursed through my veins. I remember screaming for my mother and father. I remember crying and being absolutely terrified as we approached the neighbor's house, soaking wet and momentarily homeless.

I never realized how much the idea actually bothered me until I was back in that situation. My anxiety grasped my throat, making it hard to breathe. I clutched my chest and began to wheeze. I didn't realize how obvious my distress was, until I felt my inhaler resting in my hand and looked up to see Riley standing above me with a very concerned look on his face.

"Are you okay?" Riley asked, crouching in front of me.

I wheezed loudly and shook my head 'yes' instinctively.

"Use your inhaler, wheezy." he raised my hand up to my mouth.

I took a deep breath in and held the medication in my lungs. I counted to six and breathed out slowly. I sighed and repeated the process once more.

"How are you now?" he asked.

"I'm fine." I frowned.

"You don't look so good," Lamar stated bluntly.

"Really guys, I'm fine. I just got a little worked up," I said, embarrassed.

Riley grabbed my arm and helped me to my feet. I stumbled backwards, woozy from hyperventilating. The beer probably didn't help the matter, either.

"Come on." Riley escorted me to the bedroom. I walked clumsily next to him, my arms wrapped around his waist. He helped me through the door and gently guided me to the bed. He pulled off my shoes and smiled. I could see the worry on his face as he unzipped my hooded jacket.

"Why don't you relax in here for a little bit? I know it's been a long day, a long week for that matter," he suggested sympathetically.

"You're right." I nodded. "I'm exhausted. I still need to call my mom and make sure they're safe."

"Why don't you do that? I'll make sure everyone here stays safe," he offered, kissing me softly on the forehead. He got off of the bed and began to walk to the door.

"Riley?" I called.

"Yeah?"

"I love you." I smiled.

"I know." he grinned wickedly and pulled the door closed behind him.

I pulled my phone out of my pocket. I chose my mom's phone number and hit send. The phone rang for a few moments and ended abruptly.

"Hello? Edie?" my mother's voice sounded shaken.

"Mom! Yeah. How are you guys?" I asked.

"What, honey? I can't hear you. The wind is so damned loud," she stated, frustrated.

"I asked how you two were!" I shouted, annunciating every syllable.

"What, Edie? I can't hear you. Hold on a second," she said. "There we go. I had to get in the bathroom so I could hear you."

"Are you two okay?" I asked again.

"Yes, of course. We're fine! How are you guys doing?" she asked in return.

"We're doing good. I forgot how scary hurricanes actually are. I haven't been through one since Val." I fell back onto my pillow.

"I know they can be pretty scary. Just relax. I'm sure we'll all be fine," she said. I could hear the comforting smile in her tone. "If you don't mind, I need to let you go, though. I'm trying to keep your father under control. He's trying to sit in the living room and do paperwork in the middle of this storm." she laughed.

"Okay. Just give me a call and keep me updated every once in a while. Please?" I asked.

"No problem. I love you!"

"I love you, too. Tell Dad I said hi and I love him, as well."

"Will do!" she replied.

As she hung up the phone, I could hear her yelling something to my dad. I chuckled to myself. I felt slightly relieved after talking to her. I knew deep down that *they* would make it through the hurricane, unscathed. The two of them had lived in the Pacific much more than I had. They'd experienced the foul weather more often than I've even thought about it. The question was how would *we* fare?

I wordlessly listened to my surroundings. I listened to the howling, roaring winds as they tore through my neighborhood. I listened to the steady beat of a wrought iron gate, the entrance to the neighboring swimming pool, banging in the wind. I listened to the hum of the heavy raindrops as they tore into our roof like molten acid. The plywood covering the windows creaked and whistled as the wind found its weak spots, testing its durability.

There would be no peace tonight, no serenity. I knew deep in my soul that as weary as I was, I wouldn't be able to relax. I may pass out from pure exhaustion, but it wouldn't be peaceful. I anticipated a hellacious night. I knew my dreams would be frightening, even without Gabriel's help. Why did I volunteer myself for more torture? Why did I suggest for him to allow me to witness War and Death?
The last two. The worst two.

I couldn't help but think back on the crazy things that had taken place today. I woke up this morning, unsure of anything, nervous about what might, could, or would happen. I didn't feel like anything had been resolved, exactly, but I felt like I was at least a few steps closer to finding the truth.

What did Gabriel mean about the world as I knew it ending? The entirety of events that transpired today, from having Gabriel showing up at our home, to the new bond he and Riley shared, made my brain ache. It was like someone tossed sugar and mothballs into my think tank.

Chapter Thirteen
There Never Was a Good War or a Bad Peace.

The sound of bombs thundered in the distance. I flinched with every blast. The air was stifling, though a faint breeze washed through the land. It carried dust on its back, choking the breath out of my lungs. The booming continued and progressively became louder. It was getting closer. I could see flames in the distance, lapping at the small huts and anything else it touched. Dust wasn't the only thing in the air tonight.

No, there was also something else; something far more sinister. There was rage. There was hatred. There was merciless anger. I could sense the pain. I could smell the sickening odor of blood. My stomach turned as I tried to breathe. I felt ill. I covered my nose, trying to escape the pungent attack, but was too late. I dropped to my knees and wretched.

I looked down at my hands. They were covered in blood. Was it mine? Was it someone else's? I always hated this. It was a scary feeling to not know the difference. And then it hit me, like a ton of bricks. What difference did it make whose blood it was? I was going to be dead before sunrise. And I was surely going to hell. *Hell*? I'm in it. I sprung to my feet and ran with a sense of urgency. I had to escape this place. Call me a deserter if you must, but life is far more valuable than people care to claim. How did I let myself get wrapped up in this fiasco?

Why did I ever think it was a good idea to fight someone else's war? God only knows how many of my friends are lying in the foxholes, dead, near dead or otherwise wishing for it. I'm too young to have seen this much pain.

Let them catch me. Let them torture me. I deserve it for ever stepping foot on their land. I deserve whatever they throw at me. How could I have been so stupid? I don't belong here! I belong in college. I belong in my hometown. I belong with my family. I *don't* belong in the jungle, with a gun strapped to my back. I don't belong in this cruel place, watching women and children dying because of some bullshit excuse the government gave us. Career saving lives, *my ass*!

'If they aren't bad, then why are they fighting back?' they asked us. How about because we've invaded their homes! We've come into their yards and killed their children. We've desecrated their land, their women, their faith. All for what? Bragging rights. The ability to say we're top dogs, we're the cat's meow. We're the number one country on the planet. Well, how would *you* feel if someone came to your home front and destroyed everything you'd built for yourself and your family?

I can tell you what I'd feel. I'd feel rage. I'd feel hatred. I'd feel merciless anger. And I'd exact my revenge on every bastard I saw within one hundred yards, be he shooting back, sleeping or begging for forgiveness. War is not the place for repentance, which is why I know I'm done for.

I realize now, what I have done. I realize now how many I've hurt. It doesn't matter whether they were shot or detained, I've ruined countless lives. Lives that will never be repaired. I've ruined families who will never mend or sleep through the night without the nightmares of seeing our ghostly faces.

And it's for that reason that I run. I'm afraid. I'm scared to death of the pain they'll inflict on me if they find me. I have to run. I have to hide. What did I do? Uncle Sam is a rat-bastard! How could I have fallen for their cheap sales pitch?

"How could I have been so stupid!" I yelled into the night. I gasped and covered my mouth.

I could hear the snapping of twigs. Less than thirty yards, by the sounds of it. I dropped to the ground and closed my eyes. I squeezed my rifle like I wanted to hold my family. I pictured the life I'd never have. I pictured the beautiful rolling countryside I'd never get to see again. I saw the kids that I always wanted to have... and I froze. I tried to keep myself from sobbing. I tried to contain my anger, my hatred, but I no longer could. I wasn't mad at the enemy. I was mad at myself. *I was the enemy.*

I heard the sounds getting closer. I could hear voices. I couldn't understand what they were saying, I never learned the native tongue. I loosened my grip on my rifle and silently lowered my hand to my belt. I unlatched my gun holster and grabbed my pistol.

"Our Father, Who art in Heaven..." I whispered as I lifted my hand slowly up my chest.

"Hallowed be Thy name..." I released the safety and raised my pistol to my temple.

The sounds grew closer. I couldn't wait any longer.

"Thy kingdom come," I closed my eyes and pulled the trigger.

I shot up, gasping for air. My head was spinning and pounding at the same time. The room was pitch black. I cradled my head in my hands and began to cry hysterically. I couldn't control myself any longer.

I heard shuffling outside the bedroom. Riley barged in through the door, startled. Behind him, I could see Lamar and Gabriel, holding a battery powered lantern. Their faces were lit by the fluorescents, insinuating their furrowed brows. Riley ran to the side of the bed.

"Are you okay? What happened?" he asked, frantically.

"I'm fine." I sobbed, pulling the blankets up to cover myself.

"Edie, do you need anything?" Lamar asked, concerned.

"No." I sniffled.

Lamar turned from the doorway, placing his hand on Gabriel's arm, "Come on. Let Riley handle it." Lamar led Gabriel away.

I buried my face in Riley's chest and continued to sob.

"What's wrong?" he asked, painfully.

"I had a nightmare," I mumbled into his shirt.

"Was it one of the *prophecies*?"

"I don't know!" I sobbed louder.

"If you don't want to talk, I understand." he gently stroked my hair.

"I was in a war. I was in the jungle. But I wasn't me. I don't know who I was." I sniffled. "The thoughts. Oh my God, the thoughts were so fucking sad. How could anyone live with themselves after that." I cried heavily and tried to catch my breath.

"Just relax. You're safe. We're all safe." he rubbed my back.

"For *now*."

"Gabriel told me about your dreams. He tried to explain the entire thing. I asked him to show me, instead of letting you go through all of that."

"It's too late!" I sobbed. "He said he can't talk to you in your dreams."

"So he's been telling me. He said since I couldn't see it in my sleep, he'd have to tell me while I was awake."

"Riley, I don't *want* you to see what I see. It's horrible!" I said, grabbing his chest tighter.

"I'm so sorry," he said, squeezing me tightly.

"I couldn't stop him. I couldn't stop myself. I died. Well, *he* died. Whoever I was. He killed himself," I continued, rocking myself in Riley's arms. "I don't want to see it anymore. I don't want to go through this."

I pulled away from Riley, staring into his hurt eyes.

"I'm so sorry," he painfully repeated himself.

"I couldn't stop it. I just watched as it all happened. I watched from his eyes. My mouth moved as he said the Lord's Prayer and stuck his pistol to his temple." I rocked myself harder.

Riley gently brushed the hair off of my face and kissed my forehead.

"I woke up. My head hurt. Jesus! My head's killing me!" I pulled further away from Riley and cradled my head in my hands, rubbing my temples forcefully.

"Lamar!" Riley turned away and yelled towards the door.

"What's up?" Lamar asked as he peeked in the bedroom.

"Can you grab something for Edie? She has a headache," Riley asked as he rubbed my back.

"Yeah, no problem. Where is it?"

"Bathroom shelf," Riley answered.

Lamar returned a few minutes later with a couple of pills and a glass of water.

"Thanks," I took the pills in one hand and grabbing the glass of water in the other.

"No problem. Anything else you need?" Lamar asked, attentively.

"When did the power go out? I just realized it wasn't on," I asked.

"A few minutes before you screamed. Startled the shit out of us," Lamar clarified.

"Sorry. I didn't mean to," I said.

"It's cool. Don't worry about it." Lamar smiled and lit a candle, setting it on the nightstand.

He turned and walked out of the room, pulling Azrael by the collar, out with him.

"What time is it?" I asked.

"A little after midnight."

"How long have I been asleep?"

"About three hours." Riley shrugged.

"Felt like a lot longer."

He wiped the last remaining tear off my cheek and smiled softly. "Feel like joining us again?"

"Yeah, I definitely don't feel like being alone right now." I shook my head.

He offered me his hand and helped me to my feet. He handed me a pair of pajama pants and a t-shirt to wear over my tank top. I put my clothes on and slid my feet into my Bruins slippers. I pulled my hair back into a slightly less terrifying ponytail. I glanced up at Riley, who had a wide smile on his face. I smiled back and wrapped my arm around his. I rested my head on his shoulder and walked with him. He bent down next to the bed and grabbed a couple of pillows and a blanket, carrying them out into the living room.

"Hi, guys."

"Eden! How are you feeling?" Gabriel asked, concerned.

"I'm fine. War sucks," I replied.

"Excuse me?" he asked.

"*War*. It sucked," I repeated myself.

"Eden, I didn't show you War." he leaned down next to me and whispered.

"I don't get it. How did I just see the Vietnam War, if it wasn't because of you?"

"I don't know." he shook his head.

"Nevertheless, it was absolutely horrifying."

"I can only imagine that it was," he rubbed my arm, consolingly.

Riley carried an inflatable mattress into the living room and was inflating it with a pump. He stopped every so often to test its firmness. When he was done, he threw the pillows on and spread a sheet across it. He topped it off with a blanket and pulled it back, slightly. He walked over to me and grabbed my hand, then led me over to the mattress.

"Here. Now you can rest with us close by. I'm sorry for making you sleep in the bedroom."

"You didn't *make* me do anything. You were just trying to help. This isn't your fault," I said.

"Doesn't matter. You need to rest. But now you're with us."

I pulled the sheets back and kicked off my slippers. I slid under the blanket and pulled it up close to my chin. A few moments later, Azrael came to the edge of the mattress and began sniffing my face. He licked my cheek. His warm, moist breath smelled horrible. I pulled away, covering my nose and laughing.

He took that as a playful action and climbed onto the mattress. He flopped on his side, directly on top of my chest, forcing the air out of my lungs. I coughed loudly, took in a deep breath, and then snuggled next to my brawny companion. Rufio sauntered to the makeshift bed and found his place behind me, purring loudly.

I could hear the wind howling in the chimney. The eerie sound made my skin crawl. It sounded like the ghost of a freight train. The frightening memory of a damned locomotive. The windows buckled and whistled as the wind beat against them.

"I see the storm hasn't let up yet," I stated, scratching Rufio's neck.

"Nope," Lamar said, settling into his rightful place on the cozy couch. He pulled a blanket up to his chest and looked over at me.

"Looks like you're sleeping with me tonight, Riley. Your bed's full." he laughed, then covered his face with the blankets, to avoid seeing Riley's reaction.

"I have something for you to sleep with," Riley retorted. He walked over to Lamar, pressed his butt against the blankets and farted loudly.

"Jesus! That's fucking awful! What the hell did you eat?" Lamar laughed.

"Riley! Would you behave, please?" I asked, rolling my eyes.

I covered my face to keep from gagging. Riley laughed maniacally and walked over to the mattress. I looked around the room, noticing only the three of us were laughing.

"Where's Gabriel?" I asked.

"He's chilling in the spare room. He was watching the hurricane from the little window," Lamar replied.

"We didn't cover that one?" I asked.

"Nah, I didn't think it needed it. Besides, he asked for it to be left. I told him if the room floods, it's his ass," Riley chuckled.

"Nice. You're just bursting with hospitality," I mused.

"Yeah, I'm pretty awesome." Riley smiled.

I settled into the mattress and covered myself up, staring up at the ceiling. Within a few minutes, we could hear Lamar snoring from the couch. Riley rolled over towards me, with his arm tucked under his pillow. He stared at me. He began combing his fingers through my hair, calming me. He could see my noticeable anxiety.

"Everything will be fine," he whispered.

"But, what if it isn't? What if everything goes to shit?" I asked.

"You worry too much," he whispered with a soft smile.

I continued to stare at the high ceiling. I pictured the roof ripping off, exposing the ferocious sky. I saw the stormy-green clouds swirling overhead, dumping gallons of rain onto my screaming face. I gasped and covered my face, rolling over onto my side. Riley slid closer and wrapped his arms around me.

"Try to get some sleep. By the time we wake up, this will all be over," Riley whispered softly, playing with my hair.

I closed my eyes and listened as the thunder crashed and the winds howled and raged through the neighborhood. The hum of the wind rang in my ears, hypnotizing me into slumber. I slept through the storm without a dream, or at least, I didn't remember dreaming. My body was restless, tossing and turning throughout the night, startled with every creak and pop of the wood covering the windows. My mind seemed just as restless. Thoughts and memories filled the void that should've been dreams.

I awoke in the morning to the feel of cool air. Something was different. It wasn't hot or muggy in the house. It was bright. Sunshine? I opened my eyes and smiled when I saw the fan spinning overhead. I got up and walked to the kitchen. I saw Lamar and Riley sitting outside on the patio with beers in their hands and their feet propped up on the table.

"Um. It's over?" I asked as I opened the patio door.

"Yep," Lamar smiled, offering me a beer.

"No thanks, I'm good." I shook my head. "Where's Gabriel?"

"Out front. He's been kind of, *odd*, since the hurricane passed." Riley took a sip from his beer.

"So, when did the electricity come back on?"

"A couple of hours ago," Lamar nodded, happily.

"Awesome! I knew it was a good thing we live by hospitals." I grinned. "Any damage?"

"Nope! Nothing," Riley replied.

"I guess we really *didn't* have anything to worry about."

"Told you. It wasn't a big deal at all." Riley grinned.

Gabriel walked around the corner of the house. He had a very annoyed look on his face. His hands were on his hips. "It's no wonder you've all been given up on. Your cockiness and insubordination has led to this. You're forsaken and you have no one to blame but yourselves."

I could feel my eye brow raising, confused, bewildered.

"I thought you two were different. I thought you understood the value of life, the generosity provided to you. Instead, you smugly scoff at the heavens and turn your back to the One you shouldn't."

The three of us stared at Gabriel, confused.

"When the ugly truth rears up and bites you and you want help, I may not be there," he stated, turning back towards the gate.

"Gabriel, wait!" I ran towards him.

"I have nothing else to say. I should leave." he stepped out into our driveway.

I followed after him, trying to ease the sudden tension. "Please. I'm sorry. I don't know what we said that upset you so much. But if it makes you feel any better, we really do appreciate what you've done for us." I attempted to console him.

"It's sad for me to see that you've lost your faith. You, of all people. When you're ready, you know where to find me," he stopped in his tracks.

"Bye," I said discontented, staring down at my feet.

"Goodbye. I'll see you soon." he turned and began to walk away.

I turned and walked towards the gate.

"Oh, and be careful. It's the end, whether you're ready for it or not." he turned away.

I stepped through the gate and closed it behind me. I walked to the patio and grabbed the beer Lamar had offered me. I twisted off the top and chugged it quickly, then slammed it on the table. Riley and Lamar stared up at me wordlessly.

"So what's his deal?" Riley asked.

"I don't know. I guess he feels like we didn't take him seriously," I replied.

"I didn't believe him to begin with," Lamar stated, sipping his beer.

I looked at Riley and sighed. I walked into the house and sat on the couch. I turned it to the weather channel to see how the other states slammed with hurricanes fared. So far, so good. They reported minimal damage from all three hurricanes. The storm that hit the west coast fizzled out as soon as it made landfall. The storm that hit the east had lost momentum before even reaching land.

Watching the weather made me feel slightly more at ease. No one had been seriously hurt and the damage that was done could easily be fixed. The south had seen much worse. I continued to watch as they discussed the three cells which were moving towards the center of the United States.

They predicted thunderstorms throughout the Midwest due to the collision, but said it wasn't anything to worry about. Riley and Lamar came inside and sat down on the couch next to me. The three of us watched the report and the local weather update.

I got up from the couch and walked over to the coat hooks. I grabbed Azrael's leash and whistled for him. He ran to my side wagging his tail, then sat down and waited for me to attach the leash to his collar. I handed him a biscuit and gently patted him on the head, reassuring him that he was a 'good boy'.

"Taking Az for a walk. I'll be back in a little bit."

"Want some company?" Lamar offered.

"No thanks. I'd rather some time to reflect. Plus, Az will keep me safe." I smiled.

Lamar shrugged.

"Be careful," Riley said, as I pulled the front door closed.

"I will." I walked outside and raised my hood.

Azrael walked along side of me and never tried to get too far ahead. He was very protective and loyal. He was very gentle with me, even when he saw one of the neighborhood's stray cats. He knew better than to run after them. As we walked, I surveyed the damage in the neighborhood. There were some downed branches all along the road and leaves everywhere. The neighborhood had definitely taken a beating, but nothing too serious.

Had Gabriel been wrong? Was this really *that* simplistic? That's it? A couple of thunderstorms across the belt? They could probably use the rain. Or was Gabriel right? He said we 'scoffed' at the heavens. Had we really become so jaded that we mistook miracles for our ingenuity, or what we're owed?

The unknown sucks. It especially sucks when you don't know what side you're on, or who you believe. I wanted to truly trust Gabriel, but I was almost afraid to. If I trusted him and truly believed what he said, then the end of the world could be just around the corner. I was in the prime of my life! I didn't want to think about death.

It's not like I'm afraid of death, but I wanted to enjoy years to come. I wanted to have kids. I wanted to laugh when they cover themselves with demolished birthday cake that I spent hours preparing. I wanted to feel that pride, when they won the science fair, or feel that disappointment when they got suspended for shrink wrapping the principal's car. Okay, maybe I didn't want to feel disappointed in my kids, but I wanted the chance to have them. I wanted the chance to watch them grow, mature, and develop into wonderful adults. I wanted to be a mother.

The thought of never having that made me sad, which is a hard thing to accomplish, thanks to the antidepressants. I wanted the chance to live a full life, with a family. With *my* family. And with that being said, I hoped wholeheartedly that Gabriel was wrong. I hoped that he was just some crazy bum with off colored theories. But something told me he wasn't.

Oh, for the love of God! I saw the man glowing with my own two eyes! I'd seen him in my dreams for I don't even know how long. There was more to him than just crazy ideas. It's like he was a messenger. But a messenger for who?

When I asked him if he was some kind of alien, he said, 'sort of'. So, what exactly did that mean? Was he or wasn't he? Was he from an alternate reality? Was he from the future? I've watched far too much science fiction shit. I couldn't believe that I'd even consider some of this nonsense.

Azrael and I sauntered through the streets of our neighborhood, making small talk with the neighbors as they stepped outside to check things out themselves. Everyone seemed pleased to see everything intact for the most part. Some of the men of the neighborhood were outfitted with chainsaws and looked like Cajun lumberjacks. They laughed and chugged their beers from their LSU coozies while they cut the large limbs into smaller, moveable chunks. Their 'women' sat in lawn chairs like directors, yelling "cut!" when they were distracted.

When we made it back home, I stopped in front of our gate and stared up at the sky. It was relatively clear. There were a few renegade dark clouds striding by but over all, it was a beautiful day. It was hard to believe that we had just been through a hurricane until you looked at the ground and saw the mess the storm had left behind. It was like a child with his building blocks strewn all across the floor.

Although the storm was relatively short lived and had passed without major damage as far as we could tell, things still didn't seem normal. I noticed the lack of... well, nature. I didn't hear or see any birds. The stray cats that normally roamed the streets like a vicious gang of claw wielding hoodlums were nowhere to be seen. Something just didn't seem right. Even Azrael seemed to be slightly on edge, more attentive than usual. Was Gabriel right? Was this the beginning of the end?

I shivered when I thought about the possibility. I opened the gate and closed it behind the two of us. When I turned to face the house, I was startled. Gabriel was standing next to the house, leaning against the wall. I could feel my brow furrow.

"What are you doing here? I thought you left." I put my hands on my hips.

"I felt horrible for the way we parted," Gabriel replied, somberly.

"It's not your fault. I thought about what you said and it's true. We don't show our appreciation when something happens. We act as if it was owed to us, like we deserve for everything to work out. Then, we bitch when things don't go our way." I frowned.

"It's not that simple. I realize that's basic human instincts. But I expect more from you. Which I shouldn't; you don't know any better. You still don't know what you are."

"I know what I am. I know who I am. I'm me. I'm Eden. I'm a nerd. I'm a paramedic. I'm a person trying to live my life." I shrugged.

"Like I said, it's not that simple," he mumbled.

"Look, I'm not sure what you were trying to accomplish by coming back, but clearly, it isn't working. I apologized to you, but that just doesn't seem to be enough. What do you want from me? What do you expect me to do?" I was getting frustrated.

"I *want* you to be the creature that you are. I want you to be on our side. I expect you to fight and lead when we're called to arms. You aren't *just* a simple person. You aren't just a number. I thought we've gone over that."

"You know, if you'd kindly drop the riddles and metaphors, we'd probably get much further. You seem to forget that, *I still don't have a fucking clue what's going on!*" I shouted.

Riley and Lamar were at the front door within moments of raising my voice.

"Everything okay?" Riley asked, opening the screen door.

"Yeah, we're fine," I replied, shortly.

"I thought you left, Gabe?" Riley asked, eyes narrowed.

"He's not Gabe. Don't call him that," I snapped.

"I wanted to apologize to Eden, but if that's a problem, I can just leave," Gabriel said, walking towards the front gate.

"No, I want answers!" I reached for his arm.

"They'll come when the time is right," Gabriel said, walking towards the gate.

"I want you to stop avoiding the truth. I want to know everything now! The time is right. I'm ready. Some of us need a little time to process shit! Tell me!" I demanded.

"I couldn't tell you everything now, even if I wanted to. I'm sorry. I'll see you soon," he said as he stepped through the gate and closed it behind him.

"Gabriel! What the hell are you so afraid of?" I shouted.

I handed Azrael's leash to Riley and he took him inside. I walked around to the patio and sat down. I was so frustrated. Why couldn't he just tell me what's going on? Why was it so damned difficult for him to speak to me? I felt like our friendship or whatever you wanted to call it, was very one-sided. I tell him what he wanted to know, when he asked. But when I asked, I'm given the whole, "Be patient," bullshit. I was tired of it. I'm not a very patient person by nature, in case it hasn't been obvious.

"Are you alright?" Lamar asked me.

"Yeah, I'm just pissed off and not really in the mood to talk," I replied with a sigh.

I lit a cigarette and threw the pack onto the patio table.

"I know Gabriel made you mad, or whatever. But try not to take it out on us. *We* actually care about you. *We* tell you the truth." Riley rubbed my back, in an attempt to comfort me.

"Oh, yeah? Really? Then what were you and Gabriel talking about? What were you discussing that he couldn't seem to tell *me*?" I interrogated Riley, angrily.

He looked at the ground. He picked up the pack of cigarettes and took one out. He lit his cigarette and exhaled loudly. I could see the cogs spinning in his head, but nothing escaped from his lips. He wouldn't say a word.

"Yeah, that's exactly what I thought," I said, snidely.

I spent the rest of the afternoon in a relatively crappy mood. Lamar and Riley sat around in the living room playing games and guitar, while I sulked in the bedroom or on the porch. I didn't want to talk, or laugh. I didn't want to associate with anyone for that matter. And that is how I remained for the rest of the day.

Chapter Fourteen
In Nomine Patris, et Filii, et Spiritus Sancti.

The sounds of screaming and crying rang in my ears. It was damn near deafening. As soon as I was able to audibly recognize the sense, my stomach turned. This had to be it. This had to be the final apocalyptic prophecy. **Death.** But the question was, where was I?

I realized that I was in my own mind. I was myself. I didn't feel any foreign emotions; no symbiotic fears or recognition. I wasn't on the outside looking in, again. Once it dawned on me that I was in the fourth installment of the dream series, I realized that I was *supposed* to be here and that I more than likely would be meeting up with Gabriel. That gave me little comfort.

I rose to my feet, but was blinded. I was awestruck by the audible pain and anguish. There was a very morbid, somber feeling in the air, like a static charge. The smell of burning flesh and bone was unavoidable. The cries droned in the air, wails of mourning. The misery in the atmosphere was palpable. Sadness filled my heart, as I heard mothers' voices screaming for their babies. This was a place of agony that much was clear.

I felt my face, touching my eyes. There was a dense fabric covering my eyes, nose and mouth. I wondered what the point of the mask was. I untied the knot, choosing to witness Death with my own two eyes, rather than suffer only by sound.

As I looked around, I saw hundreds of cages and cells. But the cages didn't contain wild animals, they housed humans. The cells didn't contain criminals, they imprisoned the innocent. Innocent children, women, men, all with shaved heads and rags for clothing.

"Oh no, no, no, no," I gasped, as my eyes welled up with tears.
Death... The worst possible event in modern history.

"The Holocaust," I cried.

My chest tightened, it was so hard to breathe. I didn't know what to do. Why wasn't I in one of the cages? Why was I not seeing this from the victim's viewpoint? I was terrified to look down, afraid I would see a Nazi uniform on my body. I would've killed myself, instantly. Thankfully, I was in a black robe without any markings. I would never subject my hands, my mind, my *soul* to such heinous beliefs.

I heard two guards conversing in German as they checked each of the cells. I pulled my hood up and slowed my pace. I held my hands together as if I were praying and walked past the guards. I stared at the ground in front of me, stepping over pools of blood and broken toys.

How could anyone do this? How could anyone be so fucked up, that they truly felt massacring hundreds of thousands of innocent people would be beneficial? I felt guilty for witnessing this. I felt horrible that I couldn't just walk up to the doors and open them. These people deserved to be free. I watched the guards as they walked ahead of me. I checked my pockets, my belt, anywhere I could've possibly held a weapon.

I wanted to kill them.

I heard the slow trot of a horse as it approached me from behind. I glanced over my shoulder. The ground sunk where its massive hooves fell. I could feel the soft vibration in my body as it slowly stepped behind me.

"I told you I'd see you soon," a familiar voice said.

I turned my head up and over my right shoulder to see Gabriel. He was mounted on the horse, wearing a black robe. His hood was down, revealing his bright golden hair and piercing grey eyes. He offered me his hand and assisted me onto the back of his horse. I sat behind him and wrapped my arms around his torso.

"Why... why did you choose the Holocaust?" my voice quivered. I sniffled.

"Never has there been a more horrific deed done by man," he replied somberly as he patted the side of the horse's neck.

We strode slowly through the camp, my face buried in Gabriel's back.

"You need to witness this. I know it hurts you to see so much agony, but that's the entire point," he continued.

"I... I can't. I can't bear to see all of these people suffering." I shook my head.

"You must. There is a purpose for this visit. We will aid them."

"We're going to release them?" I looked up from his back and wiped my eyes.

"In a sense. We cannot free them from their cages. We can't change the course of history," he explained.

"There are kids here. There are mothers, separated from their babies. There are families, that have watched as their loved ones are mutilated, murdered. And for what? What good did any of this do? What purpose did any of this serve to history? What did any of this do for humanity? All this did was show hatred." my voice quivered as I spoke.

"Man is not perfect. They never have been, and never will be. This is merely an example of the power that one person can possess. The power of persuasion. The power of manipulation. What happened here was one of the most disturbing, horrifying moments in history. This is the reason God doesn't trust mankind," he explained, quietly.

"Then why did He create us in His image?" I threw my hands into the air, angrily.

"He didn't," he whispered. "That's the whole point! That's the problem! Open your eyes! Look at this pain! Look at the suffering," he ordered.

"No, I don't want to!" I cried into his back.

"Eden. Look," he said sternly.

"Why? Why do you want me to see this?" I asked, crying.

"Because if you don't begin to remember your past, if you don't return to who you are, this is going to happen again, on a global scale," he answered somberly. "This is what your family will endure, your loved ones. You must find yourself."

I turned my head to the side, resting my cheek on Gabriel's back.

A group of guards tossed body after body into a large pit. They acted as if they were merely taking out the trash. They showed no remorse, no respect... no feelings whatsoever. I take that back, they showed one emotion. They wore it on their sleeve like a badge of honor. Superiority. The fucking bastards. I wanted them dead, right then and there.

I looked down at Gabriel's side. He had a silver, glowing sword strapped to his belt. I contemplated unsheathing it, jumping down from the horse and running to the group of men. I wanted to massacre them as they had done with the thousands and thousands of Jews, Gypsies and more.

"You would be no better than they are. Killing out of vengeance is no different. Murder is murder." Gabriel attempted to reason with me.

I hadn't even noticed that I had slid my hand down to the latch on his sheath.

"It would be for a noble cause. How isn't that better?" I asked, bitterly.

"It just isn't. Don't you remember? *Thou shall not kill*," he replied with a sigh.

"Try telling that to Adolph and his piece of shit followers." my eyes narrowed. I could feel the hate welling inside of me.

"Accept this as your moment of clarity. Look past the cages. Look past the pain," he whispered.

"I can't. I can't see past any of it. What am I supposed to *see*?" I implored.

"Listen to your soul. It's trying to tell you something."

Heal.

"I don't feel anything, but anger." I shook my head, confused.

Heal them.

"There's something there. Listen." he grabbed my leg, squeezing tightly.

You must heal them.

We strode throughout the camp, slowly. I watched and wept as children were pulled from their mothers' arms, screaming and crying. I felt completely helpless. My tears drenched the back of Gabriel's cloak. He grabbed my hand and squeezed it, reminding me that he was there with me.

"I can't handle this anymore. I want to wake up." I sobbed.

"I'm sorry, but you can't." he shook his head.

"Why not? Please. Please, let me wake up. My heart is aching. It's hard to breathe. This pain is unbearable to watch." my voice trembled, muting half of my words.

"This isn't just a dream. This is a memory. We have a job to do. We must fulfill that before either of us are allowed to leave," he replied, somberly.

"What job?" I asked, sniffling.

"You must use your gift." he pulled on the reins. "We have souls to save. We have to reenact the past."

"We? This is my past?" I asked.

"It's your turn," he replied, patting the neck of his large steed.

"I don't understand. Why me?" I sobbed.

"You have to. It's *your* past and it's time," he ordered.

He jumped down from the side of the horse and offered me his hand. I folded my arms across my chest and closed my eyes. He sighed, aggravated and grabbed both sides of my waist, raising me off of the horse and easing me to my feet on the ground. I wiped my eyes and exhaled heavily, letting the last of my stubbornness out.

"I'm sorry. It's who you are."

We slowly walked to a cell and stopped at the barred door. I looked around nervously.

"They can't see us." he attempted to comfort me.

I watched as Gabriel held his arms out horizontally and walked straight through the bars. Once he was on the inside of the cell, he stuck his arm out, between two bars. I took his hand in mine, closing my eyes and stepping forward. I was now on the inside of the cell.

Gabriel frowned. I could see tears welling in his eyes. He knelt down and scooped a small child into his arms. He lowered his head until he was forehead to forehead with the child, "Reverto ut Deus, meus parvulus," he whispered, placing his hand on the child's chest.

I silently watched as the frail child smiled then went limp and lifeless in Gabriel's arms. He looked up at me, sadly. He wiped the tears from his own eyes and kissed the child's forehead.

"In nomine Patris, et Filii, et Spiritus Sancti," he whispered and laid the child down at his side.

I was so confused. He had, only moments ago, told me that murder was murder. Yet he took the life of a child?

"I thought you said murder was bad either way." I questioned him.

"I'm not murdering these children. I'm saving their souls. Would you rather them stay in this cage and starve to death? Would you rather their souls be trapped in this hell for all eternity? I'm not hurting them. We aren't hurting them," he explained to me.

I watched as he went around the room, grabbing child after child and cradling them in his arms. He performed the same ritual every time. "Reverto ut Deus, meus parvulus," he'd say, placing his hand on their chests.

They'd breathe their last breath with a smile. How could they be smiling? Was this truly a peaceful release for them? It hurt, so badly, to see these children living in such a horrific, hateful place.

"In nomine Patris, et Filii, et Spiritus Sancti," he whispered, kissed the child's forehead and laid the child down at his side, again.

I sat on the ground next to him, watching as he continuously euthanized the children. I felt helpless. I realized after watching a few of the children's passing that they *were* at peace. It finally made me realize why we were here.

"What are you saying to them? Is that Latin?" I asked.

"Yes. It means 'return to God, my child'. I'm basically giving them a free ticket home," he explained.

"Can anyone do that?" I asked.

"Not just anyone. But you can. And you need to." he nodded towards a group of children, huddled together in the corner.

I walked over to the group of children and offered my hand to one of them. He looked up at me and smiled. I helped him into my lap. I was sitting cross legged. He nestled into my chest and hugged me tightly. I hugged him back. My eyes filled with tears, as I said the Latin phrase I had heard Gabriel say, repeatedly. I kissed the child's forehead and held my hand on his chest.

I gasped loudly when I felt the surge from the child. It was like being electrocuted, except it wasn't painful in any way. I felt the child fall limp in my arms. I kissed his forehead again and set him down gently on the ground next to me.

"Was that his soul?" I asked.

"Yes."

"I stole his soul?" I was bewildered.

"No, you've protected it," he clarified. "You are helping them make their way to Heaven. Don't worry."

I turned back to the children, who were now sitting in a circle around me. One child stepped forward with his hands out. I grabbed his hands and helped him to my lap. He wrapped his arms around my neck and hugged me tightly. He pulled away and kissed me on the cheek.

"Vielen dank, engel." he sat in my lap and pulled my hand to his heart.

"Reverto ut Deus, meus parvulus. In nomine Patris, et Filii, et Spiritus Sancti," I wept as I spoke the words.

The tears flowed from my eyes. I cried as I kissed the little boy's forehead. He took one last breath and fell back in my arms. He had a grin stretched across his face. He was at peace for the first time, in God only knows how long. And I helped him achieve that. I realized then that I was in fact, doing a good thing. It *was* a noble deed.

We continued to save the children of the camp. Each one repeated the sentence the little boy had said to me. I had no clue what they were saying, but I was sure it wasn't anything insulting.

There were fifty three children in that single cell, ranging in age from toddler to teen. Each of them accepted our gift with a smile. They were happy to know they would have a peaceful release, instead of painful torture or being burned alive. When the last child was removed from my lap, I placed his body on the ground and stood up. Gabriel was standing behind me, with arms outstretched, ready to comfort me.

"Are you okay?" he asked, gently hugging me.

"Yeah. Yeah, I am," I replied, sniffling. I rested my head on his shoulder and closed my eyes.

"I know it was hard for you to do at first, but I know that you realized the importance of your job after a while," he stated.

"Do you know what they were saying to me? I couldn't understand," I asked.

"They were saying thank you. And called you an angel," he replied.

I felt the tears building up. I wasn't the angel. They were. It was so sweet, so moving to know that they appreciated our aid.

"It's time to go," he said, offering me his hand.

"What? No! There are still thousands of kids. And everyone else. We have to help them. We have to save their souls!" I felt panicked.

"It would take us days and it would alter history. As of now, it will seem to the guards that this cell had died from starvation. We can't save them all." he frowned.

"I don't care. Maybe history *should* be altered. This never should've happened to begin with," I argued.

"We've done all that we can. Others will come later. Others will save more. We can do no more here."

"We *can* do more! Just one more cell. One more group. Come on, Gabriel. We can do it," I pleaded.

"No, I'm sorry," he said stepping towards me.

"Well, if you won't help, I'll do it alone," I stated, tears welling in my eyes.

Gabriel put his hand on my forehead.

I pulled away quickly. I knew what he was trying to do. He grabbed my arms.

"Wake up," he whispered.

The next thing I knew, I was sitting up in bed. "God damn it!" I shouted.

I reached over to the nightstand and grabbed my glasses, put them on and grabbed my phone. Not only was it 3:45pm, I had nine missed calls. I growled and threw myself back into my pillows. I listened to my four voicemails and suddenly wished I hadn't woken up at all.

"Damn you, Gabriel," I mumbled to myself. To say I was upset was an understatement.

Riley had called twice and left a message that he was going over to Lamar's to make sure everything was okay there. Lamar called and left a message, wondering where Riley was, since he said he was going over there with him.

My mother called three times and left a voicemail, letting me know that everyone was safe, except for the gardenia bushes that apparently didn't fare too well. Two of my brothers had called, but didn't leave messages. And of course, one of my supervisors called and left a message for me to call them back.

I erased all of my messages and dialed Riley's phone number.

"Mornin' sunshine!" Riley said, as he answered the phone.

"Good afternoon," I corrected him.

"What's up, buttercup?" he asked, chirpily.

"That's what I was wondering. What're you guys doing?"

"*We* aren't doing anything. I've been trying to get to Lamar's for the past hour. I'm surprised you could even reach me. The network has been busy the entire time I've been stuck in this interstate parking lot," he explained.

"Why's there so much traffic? People returning home?" I asked.

"I'd assume so. But I can see a huge plume of smoke up ahead, as well. I'm not sure if that has anything to do with this traffic."

"Hmm. I'll put it on the local channel and see if they have any news. I'll call you back if I find anything out. Why don't you try to get off the interstate as soon as you can," I suggested.

"Yeah, I'll try. Call me back."

"I will. Bye." I hung up my phone.

I walked to the living room and turned on the TV and flipped through the channels. There appeared to be news or some kind of report on almost every channel. I flipped back to the local station and watched for a few minutes.

The smoke that Riley had seen had apparently come from a chemical plant that had exploded when something crash landed into it. The plant had tanks of different types of flammable, corrosive chemicals, some of which became toxic fumes when mixed with oxygen.

As soon as I heard the threatening news, I fumbled for my cell phone and redialed Riley. I listened to the report some more while I waited for him to answer. I didn't know how close he was to the plant, or if he was at a safe distance. His phone continuously rang, until finally going to his voicemail.

"Ah, c'mon Riley! Pick up!" I yelled, ending the call.

I redialed his number. This time, the line went to an odd tone.

"The number you are trying to reach is either disconnected or out of the coverage area. Please hang up and try your call again," the recording stated.

"Shit. Shit. Shit!" I yelled, hanging up my phone.

I dialed his number again, to no avail. I tried calling Lamar and got the same message. Was there something wrong with my phone instead? I tried calling Mike, but my phone beeped and said 'network busy' on the screen, ending the call. I began to feel panicked. I ran to my purse and grabbed my inhaler. I sat down on the couch and bent my head low to my knees.

"Breathe. Breathe. Slow. Breathe," I coached myself.

I closed my eyes and took in a deep breath. I let it out slowly and opened my eyes. I dialed Riley's number. It finally rang. After three rings he answered. I felt a huge weight lift off of my chest. I could breathe again.

"Hey," he said as he answered.

"You need to get out of there, you need to head home," I ordered.

"I know. I'm already off the interstate. I'm headed home, but the roads are just as packed. I'll be there when I can," he reassured me.

"There's news on every channel. Something's going on," I said.

"Did you find out what's going on with this traffic?" he asked.

"Yeah, apparently something crashed into one of those chemical plants. They said some of the chemicals are toxic when combined with oxygen. That's basically a cloud of poison, not just smoke."

"Oh, shit. That sucks. What happened?" he asked.

"They don't know. They just said some object crashed. They don't know if it was a plane or what. They're concerned about the surrounding plants," I explained.

"Damn. Any survivors? Or are they too afraid to get close to check?" he asked.

"No known survivors yet. Yeah, they don't want to get close."

"Well, hey look, uh," Riley cut himself short, pausing. He was obviously distracted. The line was silent for a few moments.

"What?" I asked.

"Yeah. What was I going to say? Oh. I'll be home in a few minutes. I'm gonna get off the phone so I can pay attention to this traffic. I'll be there in a little bit, don't worry," he said, hanging up before I could reply.

I flipped it to the national news and turned it up loudly. I walked to the bedroom and listened to the reports while I got dressed. Meteorologists were concerned about the three fronts coming together. As the bands drew nearer to each other, shockwaves of storms spun out. The storms produced by the huge storm cell, seemed to be more destructive than the three hurricanes had been, combined. Hundreds of tornadoes had sprung up, demolishing homes, neighborhoods, entire cities. As one would peter out, another would spring up behind it, devastating the same area and moving on.

It was as Gabriel had warned. It wasn't the hurricanes that were the threat, it was the super storm that developed from their meeting. Massive floods were drowning towns and cities. Lightning tore apart trees, roofs and towers, limiting communication. The winds ripped everything apart, sending unsecured objects through windows. Golf ball sized hail rained down, destroying everything that it touched.

No one was sure where and when the storms would end. It was as if the front itself was a giant kraken in the center of the country, reaching out with tentacle-like bands of destruction across the entire United States. Was there anywhere that was safe? I was afraid of the answer. I knew the truth, deep down.

I needed to find Gabriel. I needed to know what I could do to help. After the dream I had, I truly believed I did have a part to play in all of this. I had my doubts before, but no more. I returned to the living room and sat down next to Rufio. I gently stroked his back as I watched the news. He purred contentedly, his head bobbing as he fell asleep.

"Strange lights have continued to be seen all across the world, with no explanation as of yet. The military has declined to answer questions regarding the odd lights. And no two sightings have been the same. They've been seen in different formations, different colors and approaching the Earth at different speeds. Some speculate the military has something to do with this, stating 'why else would they choose not to speak on the matter?' Conspiracy theorists assume of course, that it's an alien invasion, leaving skeptics stumped and annoyed," the reporter said.

I thought about the conversation we had with Gabriel on the patio before the hurricane. I remembered asking him if he was an alien. Then I remembered his reply, "sort of." I knew without a doubt then, that he *did* know what was going on. Strange lights, the red tide, the huge storm, my dreams. Were all of these signs of the Apocalypse? I mean, *really* THE signs?

I always thought the Bible was just a good bedtime story. Fictitious. But what if this really was the end? I know Gabriel had been warning us, and my dreams seemed so real, so crucial. But I still had a part of me that was skeptical.

I figured I was reading too much into all of it and going along with the conspiracy theory. I hadn't sat back and really thought, "what if this is really happening?"

It is really happening. Right now, to be exact.

As I thought about the current events and how everything had been playing out, I felt nervous, very uneasy. What was my position in all of this? What will happen to me when this is all over?

What will become of my agnostic soul? I've spent so long confused about religion that I decided to take the easy way out and claim none. Was I going to pay for that? If there was in fact a Hell, was I headed there for not choosing a faith? The answers scared me. But the truth was, even faced with the threat of spending an eternity in hellfire and damnation I still chose not to claim something I didn't truly believe in.

What is the point of a baptism or communion if you really didn't mean it in your heart and soul? I'm sure God would know it was a mockery. He'd scream, "LIAR!", as I repeated the words. Empty of truth, void of love.

I paced through the living room, thinking about my options. I knew if this really was the end, if the Apocalypse was literally nipping at our heels, there was nowhere to hide. No caves or holes would shelter us from the truth. Judgment was coming. Death was coming.

"Gabriel's trumpet has sounded," I scoffed, stopping dead in my tracks.

The truth is, I don't really know how long I sat on the floor in the dining room. I knew that my ass felt numb, so it must have been a while. I remember realizing what was going on, well, that *something* was going on, and then I just kind of spaced out. The room spun, the sound from the TV warped and my breathing sped up to the point I thought my lungs were going to explode out of my chest like rocket-powered robotic organs.

Is he THE Gabriel?

I still didn't know what was going on, but I had started to piece things together. Riley still hadn't made it home. I looked at my phone and saw it was now 6:30pm. When was the last time I had talked to him? 4:00ish? Where the hell was he? My hands were shaking so badly while I tried to pull up his number in my phone. I felt like a total wreck. I was finally able to press send. The phone rang and rang.

"Edie," Riley said as soon as he picked up.

"Where are you? It's been almost three hours since we talked."

"Edie, get outside, look at the sky," Riley ordered.

"Why? What's going on?" I asked, confused.

"Just do it, please."

"Is something wrong?" I got to my feet and walked to the kitchen.

There was an odd lighting throughout the kitchen and the patio. Everything had a reddish tint. I had the phone pressed between my ear and shoulder as I slid the patio door open.

I could hear Riley breathing and people talking in the background. I heard what sounded like a woman screaming, then silence. I grabbed my phone and looked at the display. Did he hang up? I stepped out onto the patio and slid the door closed behind me, looking up. My phone dropped to the ground. I stood, staring at the sky, awestruck. Terrified. There were only three words I could muster.

"Oh… my… God," I gasped.

The sky was blood red. The clouds swirled and pointed as if they were going to birth a funnel cloud any given second. The hue shifted depending on what direction I looked. Some spots were a bright red, like candied apples. Some were blood red. Maroon. It was as ominous as it had been in my dreams. And the terror I felt was the exact same, without a single doubt.

This really must be it; the beginning of the end. The Apocalypse was upon us and all we could do was sit back helplessly like children as our world came to an end. My phone rang and vibrated on the ground beneath me. It took me a few rings to realize what was going on and pick it up.

"Hello," I spoke, very monotone.

"Are you outside?" Riley asked.

"Yeah," I replied in the same tone.

"Isn't that crazy?" he sounded amused.

"Yeah."

"They think it's just the chemicals and sunset," he continued.

"I don't think that's what it is at all."

I sat down and looked at my feet, "Where are you?" I asked, more alertly.

"I ran into Gabriel. Then we ran to the station. I just wanted to grab a few things," he replied. It seemed like he was leaving things out.

"Are you both coming here?" I asked.

"Yeah, we'll be there shortly," he said.

"Alright, hurry home and please be careful," I pleaded, and then hung up.

Why had Riley picked up Gabriel, I wondered. It seemed kind of fishy to me. Riley has been privy to some information I hadn't been. When they got home, I wanted the truth. I wanted it all laid out on the table.

I wanted to know what we were up against and how badly it really was going to be. Why had Gabriel made me witness pestilence, famine, war and death if it wasn't to prepare me for something to come? And if it was, in fact, to prepare me, what was I going to face?

The red clouds carried not only a cool breeze on their back; they also carried a static tension. It was like the calm before the storm, like a war was brewing, but neither side were in the know. It was as if everything was about to spontaneously combust and end. The clouds stopped flowing. They stood stagnant as if they were going to explode.

Tick. Tick. Tick. Boom!

The thought sent a shiver down my spine. William Shakespeare said it best, "Something wicked this way comes." I waited patiently for them to return home. Well, I suppose patiently isn't the correct adverb. I paced. I checked the time every forty seconds or so. I was nowhere near patient, in fact I was far from it. I sat on the couch and bounced my knee about forty-five miles per hour and chewed on my finger nails, counting the seconds. Finally, I heard the front gate open and heard Riley saying how someone was a good boy. I can only assume he was speaking to Azrael and not Gabriel.

The front door opened and in walked Riley, followed by Azrael, wagging his stubby tail and Gabriel holding up the rear. Riley smiled brightly, walked over to me and kissed my lips. Gabriel took Az off of his leash and handed him one of his biscuits. Gabriel smiled gently at me and sighed lightly. I knew that *he knew*; he had some explaining to do.

"How about we skip the crap and get straight to the point." I folded my arms across my chest.

"Hello to you, as well," Gabriel replied.

"I'm tired of being confused, but knowing there's *something* going on. I want to be included. Don't tell me that I have a major role to play, but refuse to tell me what it is."

I walked to the patio door and stepped out. I grabbed a cigarette out of my pack and lit it, tossing the pack and the lighter on the table. Riley and Gabriel stepped out, silently sat down and listened as I vented.

"I'm not stupid. Either both of you are hiding something or one of you is and the other is covering for him. I want to know the truth. Now."

"I don't even know where to start," Gabriel said, shaking his head.

"How about at the beginning?" I asked.

"Our beginnings would be two different things at this point," he stated.

"You two need to talk. I'm gonna run out to the truck and start unloading," Riley said, sneaking out of the ass-chewing.

I watched Riley hurry out of the front gate and returned my gaze to Gabriel. My eyes narrowed, "The truth. Now!"

He inhaled deeply and looked up at the sky. "Do you believe in reincarnation?"

"I don't know. What does that have to do with anything?"

"It has everything to do with everything," he smiled.

"I don't understand. Less riddles, please."

"It's hard for me to explain, because I don't know how much you'll believe. I don't know how much of the truth you'll scoff at," he stated.

"Try me." I smiled invitingly.

"You have always been a very hardheaded woman." he shook his head.

"I already knew that. Tell me something I don't know," I chuckled to myself.

"I don't simply mean in the past couple of decades. I'm speaking of thousands of years' worth of stubbornness," he replied. "There's only been one man who could tame you. Though many tried, one in particular, you always managed to blindside them all. Throughout history, you've managed to defy every force, every being, to be who you are. It's one of the more admirable and attractive of your traits, but also the most painstaking."

"You were always the favorite. Perhaps it was for those exact traits, the ones that bring the rest of us so much grief. But you were given gifts, offerings that the rest of them never had. I wouldn't say they were jealous, but they were slightly envious." he readjusted himself in his seat, settling in for story time.

"They? *We*, who?" I asked.

Gabriel held up his hand, gesturing for me to remain quiet. "After we were given the gift of companionship, you chose Thaddeus as your own. You refused to be courted by anyone else. You wanted to be with him and only him."

"Thaddeus? That's Riley's middle name." I cocked my head to the side, curious.

"Every lifetime, you chose him over everyone and everything else. You chose him over gifts of jewels, empires, farmlands. You chose him over the rich, the powerful. You crossed seas to find him. You fought wars to rescue him. And he, in turn, always did the exact same to be with you."

I didn't know exactly what he was saying, but it sounded very romantic. So I listened, quietly.

"You've been 'the muse' *so many times and to many men*. Sometimes they were driven mad by your defiance, sometimes inspired by your dedication and loyalty to Thaddeus. You've always been Juliet. You've always sacrificed your life and love, solely for him." he smiled awkwardly.

"What do you mean, exactly? Are you saying I'm reincarnated?" I asked.

"Yes. For thousands of years. You've always been the same challenging, problematic woman. You've yet to learn your lesson. Or, when you have, you've chosen Thaddeus over eternity." he shook his head.

"What have I been doing wrong? And why are you finally willing to talk?"

"It's not that you've done something *wrong*, it's just that you've never chosen to give up *this life* for the one you feel you're *meant* to have. You've always chosen earthly love over heavenly love. You've always chosen to relive your mistake, or have just made unforgivable decisions, that made it impossible to give you a choice," he explained, "And for the record, it's finally the time to discuss this. Hence my return."

"Well, good. I'm glad you're finally sharing. But... unforgivable, like what? What have I done that was unforgivable?" I asked, defensively.

"You need an example? Where to start? You've broken almost every law at some point or another. And I don't mean human laws, I mean God's laws," he clarified.

I guffawed loudly. That I could believe. "Was I ever a pirate? Or a ninja?" I asked.

"Yes, you've been a pirate. A horrible one, at that," he laughed.

I could feel a smile stretching from ear to ear. I pictured myself wielding a great sword and commanding men to swear I was the greatest or walk the plank. I giggled to myself.

"Was I, Edie The Meany?" I chuckled.

He laughed with no response to my awesome name, "But that wasn't the kind of act that led to your damnation. You've chosen to take your life, after losing Thaddeus, four times now." he frowned.

"And I'd probably do it again," I replied, straight faced.

"That's the problem. You've chosen Riley every lifetime. You've chosen him over every man on this Earth. You've chosen him over God, Himself. *That* is your eternal mistake. That is why you've been reborn so, so, so many times."

"Have you ever truly been in love?" I asked.

He looked at me and nodded somberly. "I have. And I face her constantly, knowing what we had in the past was magical. But we chose God, over our primal urges. We lost a part of ourselves in the process, that we pray to have back soon," he replied with sadness in his voice.

"There are thousands of soul mates, *thousands*. All of those 'fish in the sea', yeah. Those are people that you could be happy with. Whether that's momentary or not. But there is only one, *one* person who truly completes you. There's only one person out there that is your other half. Without them, you're nothing. Without them, there's no reason to exist. If Riley and I have always been together, then that's why. And the lifetime that I'm reborn and he isn't there? That will be the lifetime that I give up and do whatever it is that I'm *supposed* to be doing. Until then, I will *always* choose Riley over anyone and everything," I explained.

"You are so horrifically difficult."

"If that's true, if I've made a mistake by always choosing Riley, then I'm sorry. I really am. But I don't see it happening any other way."

"I do understand. Truly, I do." he nodded.

"So! What was the point of all of that?" I slapped my hands on my knees.

"I first wanted you to realize how long you've been stupid." he smiled.

I laughed loudly and shook my head, "Does Riley know about all of this?"

"Yes. And he said he felt that, all along." he snorted.

I smiled when I thought about the history Riley and I shared. Thousands of years? Has he always been this annoying? I apparently, truly was a glutton for punishment. Hundreds, and hundreds of times over.

Suddenly, there was a loud 'boom' in the distance. It sounded as if it were an explosion. Gabriel and I jumped from our seats and ran to the edge of the patio. Riley was standing just inside the front gate, staring up at the sky. We walked over and stood next to him. He wrapped his arm around my waist and pulled me close. The three of us stared up at the sky. I could feel the tension, the concern, the *questions*, radiating from us. I could almost see the vexation swirling in the breeze like the autumn leaves.

"What was that?" I asked moments later, afraid to hear the answer.

"I'm not sure. It sounded like thunder, but I haven't seen any lightning," Riley said.

"That was a landing. They're making their descent," Gabriel said.

"They who?" Riley and I asked, simultaneously.

"Riley, Eden, I think it's time you found out who and *what* you really are." Gabriel turned to the two of us.

We looked at each other, nervously. That was never a good thing to hear.

CHAPTER FIFTEEN
GARDEN OF EDEN & THE GREAT DIVIDE

We sat around the patio table and listened as Gabriel told us a story. The occasional booming continued for hours. Eventually the sky darkened into night, a canvas smeared with black and crimson wisps. The wind carried an uneasy chill. If you listened hard enough, you could hear a haunting melody in the wind. Like alluring sirens singing your name, beckoning you into the sea to your demise. I chose to stay on the deck. I wanted nothing to do with the bitches.

The story Gabriel told us was hard to believe, but the more I listened, the more I felt it to be true. It was hard to grasp, especially with the idea of being there myself to witness the entire thing. He shared so many details and sentiments, it was like having amnesia and being reminded of small aspects of your life that you had forgotten. Each new memory flooded back with a new emotion and excitement.

He began the story with simply telling us some of our adventures from previous lives. Riley smiled smugly when he was told how he had been a ruler of a great kingdom once or twice. How he had seduced a fair maiden, Eden, and made her his wife, the queen. Riley, a chivalrous romantic? Yeah, right.

We laughed when we were told about some of our less favorable lives. We weren't always noble it sounded like. We had a bit of a Bonnie and Clyde streak as well. Some lifetimes, we protected people, fought for justice, while other times we wreaked havoc and invoked fear in the hearts of humanity. That, of course, was our rebellious phase of eternity.

"So when did it all begin? What was our first life?" I asked, interested.

Whether Gabriel was telling the truth or manipulating us somehow, it was all very fascinating.

"For that, I suppose I'd have to start from the very beginning. I know you're going to laugh and probably saying I'm lying. But please, just let me finish. It's going to take a while."

Gabriel drew in a deep breath and closed his eyes. "In the beginning, we didn't live on Earth. We were in the heavens. We were nothing more than smaller, perfect versions of God, Himself. But as it seems, He grew weary of having only the company of Himself. So He granted us individuality. That may have been His biggest mistake." I could feel my eyebrows crumble. I wasn't fully prepared for a religious rant.

"By granting us individuality, we were all still a part of Him, but did not mimic His every move, like mirror images. We moved about freely. He decided that, that in itself, wasn't enough and gave us each our own personalities. He gave us voices. We then were more than just extensions of God, we were His companions."

"But the problem with individuality and personalities is that everyone becomes... different." he frowned. "At one point, God became very distracted, very... distant. None of us could figure out what was going on, but we knew He was up to something. Though He knew what was in our minds at all times, we didn't know what was in His. It seemed like forever before God called on all of us and said He had a surprise for us. It wasn't often that we were given gifts; just being in His presence was enough of one. We needn't much else," he smiled.

Gabriel stood up from his seat and began to pace. "When we arrived at God's side, He asked us to be seated and to listen carefully. He said He had made us something. He had put a lot of time, love and care into this special gift and He expected all of us to take great care of it. We all nodded excitedly. We were so curious, the suspense was overwhelming. He led us down to a new place, a strange surface we had never seen before. It was breathtaking. It was mesmerizing!" he closed his eyes and smiled brightly, as he reminisced.

"When we reach the land, we felt the ground beneath our toes for the first time. And when *you* arrived, Eden, God smiled and grabbed your hand. He pulled your hand down to the Earth with His, and you both knelt down." he knelt down mimicking the action.

"We watched in amazement as beautiful, vibrant colors sprung up in every direction. It was like you were God's paint brush and the Earth was your naked canvas. We watched as the land continued to change for miles and miles."

"...*me?*" I asked, confused.

Gabriel nodded. "He proclaimed then, that that very spot would be known forever, as the Garden of Eden. The beauty only a mind like yours could create. Dazzling flowers and plants sprung up, everywhere that you stepped. Trees grew and bowed before you as you passed. Your smile made the sun shine three times brighter, and has ever since." he sighed contently.

I was instantly reminded of my dream I had while at the hospital. Those steps I took, flowers springing to life. Was my mind trying to remind me of my gift? Riley stifled a laugh. Gabriel ignored his reaction and continued.

"As God created the landscape, He took you with Him, using you as His muse. Where you danced in circles, springs and creeks splashed with crystal clear water. The stones you kissed turned to mountains. Every image you saw in your mind, God laid down on the land. The dark and the desolate places arrived much later," he said, looking to the sky.

"God explained to us that it was our new home. He told us that we were to remain here and enjoy the beauty He had created, but that we were never out of reach. He gave us wings to return to Him when we wished."

"Is that what your tattoo is? Are those your wings?" I asked.

Gabriel nodded and unbuttoned his coat. He fumbled with his breast plate, removed it and set it aside. He turned his back to us. I rose, moving around the side of the table, to view his back once more. His tattoo glowed in the light of the moon. Beautiful, detailed wings. Wings that could only belong to an angel. *An angel!* Suddenly it all made sense. It was like I was blind to all the clues I had right in front of me.

"Some of us returned to God regularly, just to visit. While some returned to

Him with demands. He, the caring being that He is, granted their wishes. A group of angels approached God with a list of things they'd like to have. He sat down with the group and reviewed the list, stating that the demands were reasonable, while the rest of us thought it to be a mistake."

"What kind of demands?" I asked.

"They said they were lonely, so God created animals to have as companions. Like the Goldilocks story, some were too hot, or too cold. So God created the different environments, to suit everyone's tastes. As the environment changed, the animals changed with it." Gabriel stopped speaking and looked at me as I smiled and patted Azrael on the head.

"Then the real problems began." he frowned. "The demands continued. God was constantly being confronted about something. Some were bored, so God gave us a sense of humor, talents, the abilities to create art. Some felt under-stimulated, so He gave us alchemy, science, the ability to destroy and rebuild. The loneliness continued and God gave us the ability to love each other and things, other than just Him. That was the exact moment everything went wrong."

Riley and I looked at each other. We knew that we were included in the problem.

"With the newfound emotions, we saw each other in a different light. We used to only admire God, in His entirety. Now, we saw each other the same way. We felt that we couldn't live our lives or take another breath without that other being at our side. And with that feeling, many things sparked." he stood up, facing his back to us, he stared at the sky.

"Sounds like high school," Riley mused.

"With love, comes lust. With lust, comes sex. With sex, comes jealousy. With jealousy, comes madness and violence," he said, then turned back to us.

I listened to his words, taking them to heart. I nodded in agreement. His words made more sense than he probably realized. I thought about how many friendships, marriages, relationships in general, had been ruined because of sex. Because of lust and jealousy. People *killed* for these reasons.

"We became infatuated with ourselves, with each other. Craved things that we had never experienced before. Developing instincts that God, Himself, had not created. We were no longer the images of a perfect being, we were monsters." he sat back down.

"You mean we were human?" Riley asked.

Gabriel ignored Riley's words and continued. "Some of us watched as our race destroyed itself. They began to hunt the animals for the thrill of the chase, as a game. They knew God would create new ones in their place. They began to have sex for entertainment, for the pleasure, not for the physical and emotional bond it was supposed to imply. And before we knew it, these beings were returning to God, less and less. They'd create what they wanted, they didn't need His help."

"A few of us grew tired of the way the others had discredited our race and God. Three of us, to be exact. We returned to God and begged Him not to send us back to Earth. We pleaded that He let us remain at His side, even if that meant giving back all of the gifts that He had given us. He told us He would need some time to think it over and would give us an answer swiftly."

"A few days passed and God returned to us. He told us that He had reached a decision and that it would cause a lot of pain to Him, but that He was willing to do it to benefit us. He told us of His plans. He called it 'The Great Divide'. We were thrilled to know we would be able to stay, but some of us were saddened to know we'd be losing some of the others, that we cared deeply for." he hung his head.

I felt a wave of sadness rush through my core.

"God called our group His *Archangels*. We were now superior, given a special job and purpose. We followed Him down to Earth and knelt next to Him. He handed me a mighty horn. I sounded it, calling all angels to His presence. When everyone had arrived, He made His declaration." Gabriel turned, staring at the sky. He lowered his head and was silent for a few moments. I wondered if he had lost his train of thought, or if he was receiving some kind of message psychically. He turned back around, swiftly and continued the story.

"God said, whosoever desired to return to Him, must do so right then. They would be forgiven for their transgressions and would be rewarded for their sacrifice. Two angels sobbed and ran to His feet, bowing before Him, begging for forgiveness. He was quick to grant their pardon and allowed them back into His side."

"Wow, only two? That's one hell of an offer." I finished off my beer.

"Yes, only two. And it wasn't either of you," he stated, sadly.

"I figured as much."

"God was disappointed that only two had stepped forward. His lip quivered, and for the first time, we saw His anger. We felt His wrath. He rose and bellowed to the crowd of angels that those that *did not* return to His side, would be without His grace and would fend for themselves. He was no longer going to intervene if they chose the land and themselves over Him. He felt betrayed. Two more ran to His side begging for forgiveness. He granted their pardons as well, accepting them into the fold."

I held up my hand. Gabriel's head cocked to the side confused by my action.

"Hey, I hate to stop you, but I really need to use the bathroom. Pause the story." I ran to the patio door.

I could hear Riley and Gabriel murmuring as I sprinted to the bathroom. When I was finished using the restroom, I stopped in front of the mirror and looked at myself. I wondered if what Gabriel said was true. Was I really God's paintbrush? His *muse*? Did I break His heart by not returning? I suddenly felt a sharp pain in my chest. What have I done? Thousands of years…

I pulled myself together and walked out of the bathroom, through the bedroom and into the kitchen. I glanced out the patio door to see Gabriel and Riley talking and laughing. The mood seemed very light, considering the circumstances. I walked to the fridge and grabbed a six pack of beer. I opened a drawer and pulled out a bottle opener, sliding it between a bottle and the cardboard. I walked to the door and Gabriel slid it open for me. I smiled and nodded courteously.

"Want one?" I held out a beer to Gabriel.

"Oh, no." he chuckled. "We're not supposed to consume anything that clouds the mind," he explained politely.

"I'm sure you're also not *supposed* to be telling us all of this," I reminded him.

Gabriel looked up at the rolling, ominous clouds. "You know, you're right. The end is upon us, and I'm already going to be punished for restoring your memories, well, when God finds out. Why not?" He smiled awkwardly.

Riley chuckled loudly and opened his bottle for him. "Dude, that's fuckin' awesome."

Gabriel took a sip from his bottle and shook his head. He turned the bottle so that he could read the label. His lip and nose curled up into the typical 'eww that's gross' expression. Which made Riley and I laugh.

"Continue." I smiled, sipping from my beer.

"Where was I? I don't remember now," Gabriel asked as he slid his beer across the table to Riley.

"Two other sissies begged for forgiveness. God was all 'yeah, yeah, come on'." Riley mused, sliding the bottle back to Gabriel.

"Ah. Yes. So, God looked to His left, then to His right. There were now only seven of us. His eyes welled with tears as He looked upon the faces He had created. We were all at one point blank, claylike beings. Expressionless, featureless, asexual. He gave us all variations. He made each of us different, so that we'd *feel* different. But what He didn't expect, was that we'd all react differently as well." Gabriel stopped and sipped from his beer, turning his lip up, again.

"This is the best beer out there. Do you really not like it?" Riley shook his head, almost disapprovingly.

Gabriel shook his head and slid the bottle back across the table to Riley. "He looked from face to face, hurt. He asked if there was no one else that wished to be with Him? Was there no one else that longed for His company? He spoke of how He was so distraught to see the changes that had taken place. He was saddened to see the loss He had undergone. Three more approached Him, sobbing and somber. He accepted their apology, kissing their foreheads and allowed them to rejoin Him," he paused, looking at me. "He stared at you. *I* stared at you, Eden. We both expected you to be the first to run to Him. In fact, He was surprised to see you had ever left His side to begin with."

I hung my head, dejected. I felt guilty for something I did, so many lifetimes ago.

"He held His hand out to you, teary eyed, hoping that you would take it. Instead, you wrapped your arm around Thaddeus' arm and looked to the ground. You told Him you would go wherever Thaddeus chose to go, whether that was Earthbound or celestial. God felt betrayed! He felt humiliated. He turned to Thaddeus and asked him where he would take His beloved Eden." Gabriel stared at Riley.

"I chose to keep her in her garden. I had built her a shelter and did all that I could to keep her safe there," Riley said.

I turned to Riley. I was confused. Riley looked at me, sorrowfully.

"What? How'd you know that?" I asked, baffled.

"I've dreamt about it, all my life," he replied, somberly.

"That *is* what he told God. God was so upset. The skies turned black, clouds swirled overhead, and wind blew heavily and mercilessly through the crowd. God said then, that whoever chose to stay on the Earth would remain Earthbound for all eternity. Their spirits would remain, lost, hopeless until they realized what they had done. The only way they would ever return to Him would be if He agreed that they had earned it. They would live, life after life or wander as damned spirits for as long as He wished. And the pain would not end there. No. His wrath was as endless as His bounties." Gabriel cleared his throat.

"For the pain they had inflicted on Him, their pain would be tenfold. They no longer would be immortal. They would age, feel pain, become ill. They would love and lose, just as He had. They would turn their backs on each other and betray one another, just as they had to Him. He warned them of what was to come. Depression. Guilt. Living a life of sadness for one simple choice," he continued, shaking his head. I studied Gabriel's face. His expression reflected the sadness I felt in my soul.

"Two more ran to Him, dropping to His feet in fear. He agreed to allow them to join Him, but did not seem as enthused as He was before. His hands trembled with anger, sadness, despair. He was hurt beyond any words."

"That's twelve." Riley sipped from his beer.

Gabriel nodded. "Twelve? TWELVE?!" his voice thundered, mimicking God. I was startled by his theatrics.

"He was so angered by the fact that He had only twelve angels who chose Him over their earthly pleasures. He held out His hand for the last time, 'will no one else come home?' He asked. Everyone looked to the ground or their partners, refusing His offer. He let out a bloodcurdling roar that ripped through the land. Lightning lashed at the trees, the ground quaked with every boom of thunder. He cursed them all. He held out His arms and closed His eyes, dropping His head back. The air filled with screams of horror and pain as the wings were torn from everyone's backs, all but the twelve Archangels and one exception." he hung his head.

He looked so saddened. His mind was on that day, that moment.

"What or who was the exception?" Riley asked, curiously.

"One remained behind." he instantly moved on, avoiding the question. "When we left the land, God sobbed for nineteen days. And for those nineteen days, the Earth was beaten and lashed with storms from corner to corner. It wasn't punishment; it was merely reflecting His inner turmoil. There were a few angels who, after losing their ability to fly to God, felt the need to be with Him. They felt true remorse and genuinely missed His love. They prayed in small groups. Begging for forgiveness."

"Did He forgive them?" I asked.

"Yes, in time. And they were permitted to return to Him. As time progressed, more and more angels begged for forgiveness and pleaded for a chance to return to Him. He'd grant it, when He thought they deserved it."

"So how many angels were there that stayed initially?" Riley asked.

"Eighty three. There were ninety seven of us total."

"If there were only eighty three that stayed on Earth, where did all these other billions come from? And your math isn't adding up. If there were ninety seven, who are the other two, not included?" Riley asked.

"That is an entirely separate story altogether."

"Well, better get to explaining soon." Riley kicked his feet up on the table.

"Over the course of sixty years, seven more had returned to God. But the population on the Earth had begun to grow exponentially. Nineteen were with God, and three hundred were on the Earth. God had given us the ability to reproduce, as a gift. He gave each sex their own anatomy and internal homeostasis that made it possible. Any glitch in that balance, made it *impossible*. Conditions and timing had to be just right for an infant, which *would have* been a cherub, to be conceived. Those of us who were celestial beings conceived cherubs, where those that were Earthbound, had what God considered abominations," Gabriel said, somberly.

"Ouch." I frowned.

"Guess He forgot to take the ability to reproduce back from us when He took our wings. That was His own mistake." Riley shook his head.

"Well, humans weren't created out of His will and they were proving to be a nuisance. Over the course of a few centuries, He became slightly more accepting of them. He even allowed some of them to join us in the Heavens, when they proved to be honorable beings. They were given the rank of angel, but were still underlings. They didn't hold His love and affection like the twelve of us did. There were different classes, at that point; a hierarchy. The first twelve of us, were the Archangels, given preferential treatment. The Earthbound angels that returned were below us, but still very loved and accepted. Then the human were far, far below them."

"So it was like, royalty, nobles, peasants," Riley described.

"In a sense, yes."

"So if there's anyone to blame for all of this, it's God, Himself." Riley shrugged.

"How so?" Gabriel asked, intrigued.

"Like I said, had He taken away our ability to reproduce, we would've died off. There would be no humans and Earth would've remained sacred," Riley explained his point of view.

Gabriel was silent for a second, and then nodded in silent agreement.

"So how many of the original angels are left on Earth?" I asked.

"The final twelve."

"The exact opposite of The Great Divide," Riley mumbled to himself. "That's convenient."

"So, the other eighty five are already with God?" I clarified.

"Yes. Well, no. Not exactly. There is one in limbo and one we don't speak of."

"Wait, hold on. Who are these two? And when you said I had a role to play in this what did you mean?" I asked.

"You both have a role to play. You both have to face the truth and choose your side. But the problem is, your human life ends either way."

"So, if we decide to side with God, we'll be allowed to rejoin all of you?" Riley asked.

"Yes, but only if you truly mean it. And God also has stipulations. Because He was so fond of Eden, and she chose you over Him, you may both return, but your bond will be broken," Gabriel explained, his brow furrowed.

"Wait, I'm confused. Choose our side? Side of what?" I asked.

"Eden, the drums of war are echoing through the world. They've already started their descension. You have to choose between God and your world… again." he frowned.

"So, I'm supposed to choose between the love of my life, wait, the love of my *lives* or go to a place where I will have to live without him? That doesn't sound like Heaven to me. That sounds like hell. That sounds like a life I don't want to live," I argued.

"You know nothing of hell," Gabriel replied, somberly.

I looked at Riley. It was a pretty hefty burden to bear. I couldn't imagine my existence without him. The thought made my heart ache. I felt nauseated. I stood up and ran to the edge of the patio, I knelt down and began to dry heave. I was breathing rapidly. Riley ran to my side and started rubbing my back.

"Don't worry. We'll figure this out," he said, attempting to comfort me.

"And if we side with the *humans*? If we decide to go against God?" I asked, staring at the ground below me.

"You will finally end your life, no reincarnation, no reliving," Gabriel stated, sadly.

"I think I'd rather die, than live an eternity without my family." I stood up.

Riley smiled wide and wrapped his arms around me, hugging me tightly. "Is there any way we can stop this?"

"I don't know. If there was a way you could convince God to stop, then maybe." he paused. "There is one who might be able to help, but he's impossible to control. But even with his help, I doubt it. They're geared for war and armed to the teeth. God wants His world back," Gabriel confirmed.

"Who could help? And why now?" I asked.

"Edie, do you really have to ask that? Look at what we've done to this planet. The violence, the crime… We've smeared this world with blood. We've killed our own. People have killed over shoes. *Shoes*, for fuck's sake… there's people out there that rape and murder children. And the systems that we're supposed to trust to do justice, give those exact assholes a warm place to live with free college education and cable TV. We deserve to lose." Riley slammed his beer.

"I understand that, but could we change? What if we united, promised to make a difference?" I asked.

"Humans will never learn. It's impossible. God feels that the people of the world have ruined His utopia, vandalized His masterpiece, defiled His throne. It isn't that He wants vengeance, He just feels like it has done more harm than good to let this go on for this long," Gabriel stately bluntly.

"So how long do we have? When does this *war* begin?" I asked.

"Technically, it already has," Gabriel replied.

CHAPTER SIXTEEN
INTERJECTIONS OF MY INNER MONOLOGUE

Tick. Tick. Tick. Tick. Tick.

I listened as my mechanical heart attempted to confirm the truth with breakneck speed. What does my soul tell me? If I could tell you, then I wouldn't be in this situation. I would know where I truly stood. I've stepped out of my own mind and turned the investigation inward. If what Gabriel says is true, then my life, the life I was living was just a faded copy. A plagiarized lie with the true author scribbled out. How could all that I knew be false?

But I had lived this.

I could still remember my fifth birthday. I still remembered my first kiss. My memories aren't false... they just aren't my "firsts". I remember my first love, and those beautiful blue eyes. I remember the pain, the anguish of my teen years. This hasn't been a farce!

If I *have* lived before, why do I have no memory of it? Where is the proof? Did I leave myself a time capsule somewhere? Did I leave myself hidden messages written in invisible ink, an S.O.S in the sand? The rains of time would have more than likely washed them out anyway. This felt like a sickening prank played on me, even God was in on it, possibly the mastermind. That made it even more frustrating. I didn't know what to think. I didn't know who to trust. It bothered me that I was unusually comfortable around Gabriel. It bothered me even more that Riley accepted him and listened, without threatening to break his face.

There was something about Gabriel that confused me. I felt like we had some sort of bond that I was unaware of. How did I recognize him as *Gabriel* when I met him in my dreams? I know at first I was scared shitless of him, but I also didn't know it was him. It's like he was a part of me, not just a figment of my imagination. He was a part of my mind, my heart, *my soul*.

I didn't get it. If I really was an angel, did my parents know? Were they even my parents? They gave birth to a child who's soul isn't even her own. A symbiotic relationship. In reality, I took over the body of an infant, their child, to relive this joke of a life, to correct my missteps, my mishaps. That little girl could have grown up to be a hero, a martyr in her own time. But no, she's taken over by a selfish immortal soul, who steals bodies to relive her sadistic mistakes.

Guess what, kid, I'd do it again.

But what if that wasn't the case? What if I was me, just a continuation? What if I didn't take over someone's body and this was my own. My body, my soul, just reinvented? Then I guess I had nothing to be sorry for. Well, at least not to a soulless child that I kidnapped. That sounded far too familiar, soulless child. And to think, that's what I always thought I was. I saw the world in a different view. I always saw

God as a puppeteer, pulling the strings and changing outcomes like a child who was having a meltdown for not getting the lead part in the school play. I thought that when I was well on my way down the assembly line, it short circuited and forgot to implant my soul. I figured I continued down the line, vacant. Missing that mysterious weight. But somehow I slipped through the cracks. Somehow the inspectors didn't notice the flaw. They didn't notice the one thing that I needed the most. But they stamped me as O.K. anyway. Call it a quality control issue, call it what you will.

Apparently I was wrong. Not only did I have a soul, I was in fact, an *old soul,* as my mother had always said. Did she know more than she realized? I felt like I needed to tell her all of this. But I knew the outcome. I knew what she would say. She'd ask me if I was doing the old drugs again, or not taking the new ones. She'd assume that the doctor's diagnosis was correct. That I was manically depressed. But what can happen to severely manically depressed, bi-polar people when it isn't controlled? *Paranoia.*
Also see: Schizophrenia.

None of this was the case. I was not paranoid, I was too realistic. Seriously, how could I be thousands of years old, but still make so many fucking mistakes? For posterity? I know I'm hardheaded, but I'm not stupid. Then I saw Riley's face in my mind and I realized *exactly* why I'd make the same mistake, life after life. Let me explain this in simple English. Let me explain myself in layman's terms.

Love. Love made me make the same mistake every time. If that's a crime, then I will accept my punishment with a smile on my face. I will always choose my soul mate. I will always choose my other half over anyone, anything else.
I am nothing without him.

This was all illogical. I'm not sure I even believe in reincarnation. I'm not saying that it's not possible, but how could someone be reborn, like a phoenix in flesh, without an imprint from their past? Then I thought about some of my dreams. Spirits I'd never met before; maybe I had met them in a past life? Places I've never seen before, so familiar, so sentimental that my senses instantly recognized them. Maybe it was true? I can't believe I never knew my own soul until this point. Thirty years. Wait, no. *Thousands of years. Impossible. Impossible. Impossible.* Improbable.
Tick. Tick. Tick. Tick. Tick. Tick. Tick. Tick. Tick. Tick. Tick. Tick. Tick. Tick. Tick. Tick. Tick.

I took in a deep breath and listened to the clock on the wall, as I attempted to keep the rhythm synced with my heartbeat, but it was out of tempo, out of cadence. Far too slow, but I couldn't match them up. How could everything I'd believed for so long be so very wrong? I thought I didn't believe in Heaven or Hell. I thought I didn't believe in angels and demons. I threw out the idea of mysticism. I believed in science. Chemistry. Biology. Math. Probability. The fundamentals of proof. You can't prove any of this shit that Gabriel has said.

How do I know that he isn't feeding us bullshit? Silver spoon-fed angelic bullshit. But how do I rationalize what I'd seen? How do I debunk the dreams I'd had with him? How did I justify seeing him glowing like millions of LED bulbs in my back yard? How did I explain the wings on his back?
Saturday mornings. I was four, maybe five. I ran to the TV, first thing in the morning

with my cereal sloshing over the edges of the bowl. I planted myself a foot and a half away from the screen and stared blankly into the pixels of the screen; the tricolor formation that make up every color of the rainbow. I watched as that Great Dane and his overly optimistic teen friends solved every mystery they encountered.

That's it! This had all been a trick. This was all an elaborate scheme to try and get me to sell him my hotel on the hill. There's gold buried in the caves below. Wait, no. The family treasure, that's what he wanted. Ugh, that couldn't be it. It's the oil fields. The circus. The racetrack. The... It's a projector! A smoke machine? A dummy on a line and pulley?

Why couldn't I justify any of this? I'm a skeptic. I'm a skeptic with conspiracy theories. I'm reaching. I'm grabbing onto anything I can, to put the blame on him. There's no way this is my fault. There's no possible way that this is true. How could I not have known? I'm smart. I figure things out before I'm supposed to. How did I not know my own soul?
Tick. Tick. Tick. Tick.

The clock was driving me insane. I felt like a robot that was short circuiting. Steam and smoke billowing out of my ears as my brain has finally blown its fuse. *Quick! Someone grab an extinguisher! Save me before I'm completely lost!* It's too late. By the time someone would find me, I'd be a crumpled ball of charred, rusted gears, rocking in the corner, humming the theme song to that damned cartoon. This is all your fault, Gabriel. No, this is all my fault for trusting him. I truly trusted him. How?

I was doing so well for so long. I managed to keep all of my thoughts inside my head. I managed to hide my true self from everyone. And there I was, venting. Letting it air itself. The truth stinks. Literally. It made my stomach turn and flip. I imagined the smell of dust and mothballs filling the room, as the door I left locked in the back of my mind creaked open.

Millions of memories flooded to the floor. I scrambled to catch them as they flowed out of my eyes. And then it hit me like a blow to the head. My lungs burned and screamed for carbon dioxide. Instead of trying to time my heart rate, I should've tried to slow my breathing. Too little, too late.
All was black. Black as pitch. Black as Gabriel in his creepy fucking shadow armor.

I woke up with a headache. I felt like I was hung over, but I hadn't drank enough for that. My lungs ached. I must've hyperventilated. I must've freaked.
Also see: Panic attack.

How long had I been locked in this room? How long had they been yelling and banging for me to 'just open the door'? How long had I been pulling this heist? Holding myself hostage, with that knife in my hand. I'm too selfish to hurt myself. It must have all been an elaborate hoax. That blade was meant for someone else. Someone who threatened my life. Someone who threatened to make me live a lie.
Gabriel.

What the hell was going on? I couldn't even remember when I came in here. I walked to the door and held my ear up to the hollow wood. I could hear mumbling. I heard Riley blaming all of this on Gabriel. *You tell him, Riley!* My phone vibrated, startling me. I pulled it out of my pocket.

Riley Calling...

I sighed and hit the cancel button, sending him to my voicemail. I held my ear to the door to hear how close they were. I listened. When I felt like it was all clear, I opened the door slightly and threw my phone out. I heard the crash as it made contact with whatever it hit. I hurried to close the door again, locking it. I threw myself onto my bed and sobbed into the pillow. How could this be true? I felt robbed. I felt betrayed. I wished that I had never met Gabriel. I wished that I had never been born. I felt like my heart, *my soul*, had been taken advantage of.

"Eden? Can I come in please?" Gabriel asked.

Gabriel. *Gabe.* I have a brother named Gabe. Why couldn't it have been him here? He wouldn't put me through this much pain. This wasn't sibling rivalry. Or was it, in a sense?

Gabe, I miss you. Come home. I'll never call you a douche bag again, I promise.

As I lay sobbing, I thought about my brother. I thought about how he rescued me from our dog trying to kill me when I was little. He held me over his head, as the dog clawed at his body, trying to get to me. Trying to tear me apart. I thought about how many times I cried when he left home to go about his life. I never let him see my tears. I thought about how I cried when I was packing to leave Michigan, after he had left our house. I never let him see me break down. We fought for years. We argued and bitched when we were together. But always, in the background, I cried for my brother. He was my best friend growing up.

Gabe, please come save me. I'm sorry for getting you grounded. I'm sorry. I love you.

"Edie, open the door," Riley ordered sternly.

I walked to the door; held the lock between my fingers as every thought rushed through my brain. *Don't open it! Open it! It's a trap! Just cut and end it...* I twisted the lock and stood back as Riley burst through the doorway. He walked in and grabbed my hands, then squeezed the pressure point in my wrist. The knife dropped to the ground with a clatter. I stood, blank. Empty. He hugged me tightly and ran his fingers through my hair as he told me repeatedly that he loved me. Would he sacrifice eternity for me? Would he choose me over God? And then I realized the truth. He had. If he hadn't, he wouldn't be here. I buried my face into his chest and cried. I told him I was sorry. But the truth was I wasn't sorry. It was instinctual. I didn't know what to be sorry for. I guess I was sorry for doubting his devotion. I guess I was sorry that I didn't realize he had given up just as much as I had over the past centuries.

He said he forgave me, but did he know what he forgave me for? Did he forgive me for locking myself in our bedroom and scaring the shit out of him? Or did he forgive me for damning his soul to this Earth for all eternity, just for loving me?

I don't think either of us knew what to say. We both stood, vulnerable, holding each other. It was like we were both reading from a script, or cue cards. We said what we felt the other needed or wanted to hear, but it wasn't what we wanted to say.

I didn't know what was in his mind, but his heart raced. His heart was trying to tell me something his brain wouldn't. I pressed my ear against his chest and fought the urge to ask him to help me. I fought the urge to ask him to save me. There was only so much he could do. There was only so much either of us could do. And I knew he felt uneasy, just as I did with this whole new revelation. Although Gabriel told us where we were from, who we were, he never told us what was to come. He couldn't. The decision was ours to make.

As I held my ear to Riley's chest, I thought about Gabriel's signs. Were they warnings to the people, or warnings to the angels? To us. Were they truly warnings at all? Maybe he was trying to reawaken something inside of us. Maybe he was rubbing it in our faces.

I pulled away from Riley and sat down on the edge of the bed, staring at the floor in front of me. I made patterns out of the treads in the carpet fibers with my toes. Riley sat down next to me and grabbed my chin, turning my face towards him. He looked me in the eyes. I could see a sadness I had never noticed before. It was new. It was current. It was me.

"You're not alone." he smiled sadly.

"I know."

"We'll get through this. We'll figure it out," he reassured me.

"How? How will we do that? We don't even know if we'll live through this." my voice trembled as I spoke the words.

"I don't know, but we've made it this long. You really think something could tear us apart?" he bowed his chest out smugly.

"So you *do* believe this?" I asked, skeptically.

He looked away, looking out into the living room were Gabriel sat patiently, "Yes."

"How? Why?" I asked, shaking my head.

"I don't know how to explain it. You know I can see through people's bullshit. He's telling the truth. I really believe that."

"You said you dreamt of God and the garden. You really remember that happening?" I asked.

"I always just thought it was a crazy dream. When I first met you, I thought it was amazing that you looked just like the girl from my dreams. It made me love you more. Like, I had been dreaming of *you*, my entire life." he smiled.

I returned the smile, feeling my cheeks flush with heat. I looked at the floor, bashfully. He brushed my hair back out of my face, tucking it behind my ear. He chuckled heartily. He kissed my cheek and I couldn't help but grin more. I grabbed his hand.

"It always surprises me when you're sweet." I laughed.

"Don't get used to it," he said seriously, brows raised.

I winked. "I never am."

"Edie, I love you. I always have. I always will. If we have to give ourselves up, then we will. Not even God could deny our love. It would return. The memories would come back. We'll figure this out," Riley reassured me, kissing me gently.

He grabbed my hand and led me into the living room. Gabriel was sitting on the couch watching TV. He looked completely enthralled. We sat down next to him and watched the news broadcast. The screen flashed with coverage of the war raging in the Middle East, images of the dead and dying. They spoke of suicide bombers and the mass multitude of casualties associated with the war.

"They'll never learn," Riley said somberly.

"People are violent creatures. It seems they always have been. And you're right, they won't learn. By the time they might have had a chance to, it'll be too late. These bombers, they think they're doing a noble deed for *their* God. If they only knew how much He detested them for their actions, they'd be ashamed. They'd blow themselves up in a private place, taking out only themselves," Gabriel spoke angrily, eyes never leaving the images on the television.

I thought about what Gabriel had said. I thought about what Riley had said. I thought about everything that had run through my head, and realized that I wasn't as confused as I thought I was. What I was confused about wasn't whether or not I believed Gabriel, it was whose side I chose. Who I felt was in the right. I couldn't help but see God as an Indian giver. *Give us the world, and then take it back.* But could I really blame Him?

It was hard to take the side of people, when I knew how horrible they could truly be. I've seen pictures, heard horror stories of what people had done to each other. I'd even witnessed it myself first hand, working in EMS. How could I choose to defend them after knowing what they were capable of? But at the same time, I also knew the *good* things they were capable of; unconditional love, sacrifice, generosity, humility.

God saw them as abominations because He, Himself, didn't choose for them to exist. But when they *were* created, they showed all the same qualities as the beings that He loved so much. They were like the stepchildren He didn't want, but that He grew slightly fond of. As time progressed with these creatures, they began to become needier, more demanding, just as the angels had. But the difference is, *people* didn't ask God to step in and give them these gifts. They created them for themselves. They used science and education in place of asking Daddy for presents.

It's obvious. As people became more independent, God became less attached to them. Once again, just as He had with the angels on Earth. I didn't need memories of the past to figure this out, it was self-evident. Although I did have some questions about my soul.

"Does my soul have amnesia?" I turned and asked Gabriel.

Gabriel chuckled lightly.

"I mean, if it's the same soul I've always had, why doesn't it remember? That has to be part of the reincarnation, right?" I asked, curious.

"Yes, it's the same soul. In fact, you look the exact same every life as well. Minus the tattoos, of course." he smiled and nodded towards my bare arms.

"You're not answering my question. Why don't I remember any of it?"

"If you knew the answers to your test, you'd cheat."

"I'm not much of a cheater." my eyes narrowed.

"You've had glimpses. Your dreams have shown you some of your past," he explained.

"But I don't always remember them," I stated.

"That doesn't mean that you haven't experienced it. You lock so much away in your mind. You are capable of so much, but you hide things in that hard head of yours. Now that you know the truth, the memories will begin to flood back to you. Probably sooner and quicker than you'd prefer. It will be hard for you to sort them. Both of you will remember things you didn't before," Gabriel elaborated.

"If I truly have seen my past in my dreams, then I actually remember a lot from my past. Some of them have been reoccurring, some haven't. But I remember the garden. I remember so much, but only as dreams. Distant memories; twisted in my mind and sprinkled with the present," Riley explained his feelings.

Gabriel was right. I did hide things. I hid things from others. I hid things from myself. I've managed to convince myself that it never happened, if it's something I wanted to forget. I have many flaws, many skeletons. But I pile those skeletons in the back closet of my mind like a mass grave. They're nameless, unidentifiable bodies, tossed into a black hole and buried shallow, in hopes that someone will find them and bring me to justice. Give me the help I truly need! I'm like a mass murderer! But the only things I've killed, has been pieces of myself. Tiny bits of my sanity, torn off and tossed into the wind. Some pieces have gotten caught in drains, some in trees. Some have gotten stuck in women's hair and they scream "get it off me!" as I laugh and watch my mind terrorize humanity.

"What's so funny?" Riley asked me, breaking me out of my trance.

"Nothing," I smiled awkwardly. I must've let the laughter slip out.

I walked out to the patio and lit a cigarette. I sat down in one of the chairs and stared out at the sky. It seemed less oppressing knowing that I held the bargaining chips in my back pocket. Too bad my pants have so many holes; the chips could slip out and leave my plan foiled.

My right leg bounced to the rhythm my heart produced, like an eighty mile an hour bass line. *Boom. Boom. Boom. Boom. Boom. Boom. Boom.* I could hear a constant pounding in my ears, in my head. My blood pressure must have been through the roof. My head ached with the blood flow. It was hard to think. It was hard to focus.

I blew out the last of the smoke and coughed to clear my lungs. I stepped out into the tall, wet grass and sat down. I folded my legs and drew in a deep breath. I closed my eyes and listened as the wind whipped past me. The storm was over, but we still had some lingering effects. The winds hadn't completely passed and the clouds still loomed. Was this from the actual hurricane? Or were these new storms rolling in, offshoots of the big bad wolf in the center of the nation? I drew in another deep breath.

In through my nose. Out through my mouth. In through my nose. Out through my mouth.

I repeated the lines in my head until they were no longer thoughts, they were merely actions. My mind was blank. I was tranquil. The wailing wind sounded sad. The lament reminded me that something was amiss. I listened as the mournful element told me a story. It led me back in time, back to days I had forgotten. I followed the footsteps I had made, retraced my steps as I approached the giant tree in the center of my mind. Everywhere I had placed my feet, small wildflowers sparked to life. I danced in circles, humming and laughing as I created a masterpiece of endless life and color. The wind was my cape. It moved through my hair and followed my feet, a silent dance partner, never missing a step.

I bounced from side to side and kissed the leaves folding low enough to reach. A drop of dew slid down the fold, like a single tear. I smiled and laughed, continuously spinning in my safe haven. There was nothing to fear. Nothing to worry about. I picked up the sides of my long flowing skirt to keep from getting the pristine white fabric dirty. My toes were cold in the damp grass. I spun and spun until becoming so dizzy, that I had to sit down. I fell backwards and let out a single, ear piercing cackle. My mind spun in circles, continuing the dance I had to stop. I closed my eyes to regain my balance.

When I opened them again, I was staring at the most brilliant smile I had ever seen. I pulled myself up, onto my elbows and stared at the angelic face. I had to remind myself to breathe. I felt my cheeks flush with heat and I looked away, bashfully. The handsome angel brushed the hair away from my face and tucked it behind my ear.

I looked back up at my unexpected company and smiled. He offered me his hand. I took it in mine and rose to my feet, and then brushed off the backside of my glowing white clothing. I was instantly smitten. I remembered his face from his creation. But that was centuries ago. I remembered nothing else, but his face.

He bowed his head and held out his hand once again. I curtsied and accepted. We danced in circles, spinning and laughing, but never spoke a word. The Earth struggled to keep up with our steps, spitting out baby's breath and clovers, as it no longer had the energy to form full blossoms. I stared intently into some of the most beautiful eyes in all of existence. As we danced, our wings lifted us off of the ground.

I felt my heart flutter, skipping beats and forgetting its rhythm altogether. I felt the cocoons burst open in the pit of my stomach, moths and butterflies vying for their chance to erupt from my body. This was a feeling I didn't recognize. I felt woozy when he smiled. I melted in his arms. What was this feeling? I struggled to place it, but tried to keep it in the back of my mind, as I enjoyed this amazing moment.

A horn sounded in the distance and our dance was cut short. He bowed before me again and grabbed my hand, gently kissing the top. I felt every hair on my arm stand at attention, sending a shockwave through my body. My breath quivered and I giggled lightly. I then covered my mouth, embarrassed, which made him smile that much wider.

I watched as he sped off through the sky towards the direction of the trumpet blast. I stared into the distance for a long moment, then dropped back to the ground and fell to my knees, sighing heavily. It dawned on me like an epiphany strapped to a bolt of lightning. That was *love.* Love at first sight. I had never felt that before, other than for God, and the flowers, and the trees, and the animals, and the wind. I had never felt that for another being, such as myself. I had never felt it *that* strong, *that* heavily. I wanted more.

I sat there, my knees gently resting in a patch of clovers. I stared out in the direction that my new friend had flown off to. I waited, patiently, hoping he would return to dance. I wondered why he had come into my garden. Not that I wasn't ecstatic to have him here, I just rarely had company. I was a recluse, not by choice, but by the will of God.

Recently, I had been venturing out, alone, without God at my side. I wanted to see the world I had helped create. I wanted to meet the other smiling faces. I wanted to spend time with the others. It was my right, after all. I did help create them.

There was one face that stood out in the crowd, stood slightly *away* from the crowd. One that I didn't recognize or know the name attached to. I was not involved with his creation. His face was not the one I had just seen, but the temptation I felt was the same. His glowing blue eyes tempted me to approach him. But our acquaintance was always cut short, as I was herded away by Gabriel or the others. And he would be gone, as quickly as I had found him. He was like a wolf, hidden in the darkness.

Darkness...

The air became cold; the land grew darker as night approached. I crossed my legs behind me. My elbows were firmly planted in the soft grass. I rested my chin on my knuckles, staring through the trees. I wanted so badly for my dance partner to return. I silently prayed that he would come back. *Please, come back.* The fireflies eventually dimmed and my eyes became far too heavy to stare any longer.

I awoke the next morning, warmer than I typically was. I sat up and began picking the tiny heart shaped leaves out of my tangled locks. I giggled to myself when I realized how silly I must've looked, sleeping in a bed of clovers, pining for a soul I didn't even remember the name of. I rose to my feet and yawned, stretching widely.

Turning to the giant tree in the center of my home, I tripped and stumbled to the ground. I reached for my knee, which had struck a hard object in my tumble. I turned around to see what had threatened my balance and saw motion under a blanket of fur and cloth.

An angel.

My eyes narrowed, confused and curious. He shook his head, dazed and turned to face me. Our embarrassed smiles greeted each other warmly like old, long lost friends. I bit my lip anxiously and sat down next to him.

"You never told me your name," I said, folding my arms in petition.

"You never *asked* it of me," he smiled smugly.

I laughed heartily. I instantly knew he was a complex creature. I loved it.

"Thaddeus." he continued to smile, sitting up.

"Well, Thaddeus. I'm Eden." I blushed.

"I know who you are."

I felt my cheeks heat up with embarrassment, or was it flattery?

"You're the handmaiden, the muse, the life giver. I am but a face amongst the nameless crowd," he continued.

"That is not true," I offered. How could he consider himself just a nameless face? I remembered staring down from my cloud, asking God what his name was. It was my fault for forgetting it over the years. I was instantly drawn to him then, and I was instantly drawn to him now.

"You are far more than simply a face. You are a beautiful face, radiating from the nameless crowd," I said nervously.

"Then apparently, I have a challenger for that title. For you are far more stunning than anything that you create. Haven't you wondered why the flora bow as you pass?" he smiled charmingly.

My cheeks ached from smiling so widely for so long.

We sat together for hours. We talked about the Earth, the heavens, God and ourselves. I asked him about his abilities, his passions. He was a peacekeeper. He brought swift justice. He was the commander of the Earthbound Army.

He was given a special assignment. He received the duty from God, Himself, charged with watching over me. When I asked him why I would need protection, why I was to be watched over, he said God was trying to avoid me becoming 'overwhelmed by temptation'. He was protecting me from *someone*. He didn't want to see me become lost, the way some of the others had. He knew I had been venturing out of my garden, alone. So he provided me with my very own guardian.

What He didn't expect, was for Thaddeus and I to become so drawn to each other. Thaddeus was a warrior, a protector. I was merely an artist, a muse. Our kinds rarely met, let alone grew fond of each other's company. No one saw it coming. It took even *us* by surprise. But it was a bond that was unmistakable. It was absolutely undeniable. We complimented each other, even from the first second.

Weeks came and went, but each day was the same. I'd wake to see Thaddeus' smile. I'd spend the day bringing life to the Earth as he watched from a distance. He'd fly off, leaving me every time Gabriel sounded his horn, bringing orders from God. He'd return to me in the evening, bearing gifts either from himself or from God. He'd build a fire to keep me warm through the night and settle in for rest, across the flame from me. Every night, the distance between us grew shorter.

Months passed and we had grown accustomed to our routine. He rose one morning before I had awakened and returned with gifts. I awoke to find a tray of fresh flowers and stones that shone brilliantly in the sunlight. I was blinded by the prisms they created, mesmerized by their sparkle. They were the color of his eyes, beautiful shades of green, gold, blue, and crystal clear. I was awestruck. I had never seen anything like them, and did not remember them being something of my creation.

I didn't know how to thank him or what to say. I ran to him and hugged him tightly. I stood on my toes, wrapped my arms around his neck and kissed his lips for the first time. It was like a chemical reaction; a new creation discovered that was both breathtaking and Earth quaking. I knew, at that very moment, that he wasn't just my protector. He wasn't just my companion. He wasn't just the warrior, doing his duties. He was my love. Every second that he was away from me, I mourned. Every night that he slept across from me, I wished that he'd join me, at my side. I realized that of all the beautiful things I had created, nothing even came close to the ravishing emotions that he created in me, just with his presence.

God had given me the very best gift any creature could ask for. Though, that was not His intentions. Had He known He had given me the exact thing He was trying to avoid, He would've taken Thaddeus away from me. I couldn't allow that to happen. I would have to hide my infatuation from my Father, my Creator.

One morning, Thaddeus smiled wide and stared into my eyes, and I knew that he felt the same connection to me as I did to him. We spent the whole day together, ignoring our duties. When Gabriel sounded his horn, Thaddeus chose to stay with me instead of responding. We shared moments of love and laughter. Though I was worried Gabriel would note his absence, I ignored the nagging thought.

When night fell, he made the fire, as he always did. But something was different. The bed of furs and blankets that he normally laid out for me was much larger and there were none across the fire. I looked at him, perplexed. He had a wild look in his eyes and a wicked smile, as he hovered above me. I lied down on my pallet and felt my heart race as he joined me. A single wolf's howl erupted from encroaching darkness.

The next morning, I awoke feeling different. I felt complete. I was ecstatic. I felt changed. But, I also had a twinge of guilt, of sorrow, that sprung in the back of my mind. It wasn't that I regretted a moment with Thaddeus; it was that I felt we would be punished for our actions. But if anything we had done was wrong, why did it feel so right? So perfect.

I spent the rest of the day with my mind elsewhere. I was concerned and the concern was growing. It spread through my mind like a vicious disease. Was I going to be punished? Was *he* going to be punished? Would he be taken away from me? I couldn't bear to be without him. It tore me apart. Thaddeus could see my obvious distress and showed concern, himself. Although he felt he had done something wrong, he had in fact done *nothing* wrong. What he had done was everything *right*.

Gabriel's horn sounded and Thaddeus battled with himself, whether he should go or stay with me. I told him to go, that it would be less conspicuous if he attended the gatherings. He reluctantly agreed and left my side.

I paced the garden while he was gone, twirling my long locks between my fingers. I felt a great unease. Something was amiss and I knew it. Something happened last night, something changed. I could feel it deep within my soul. The balance had been disturbed. Thaddeus returned to me shortly thereafter and said that this was a meeting that even I must attend. God, Himself, had come down and wished to speak with all of us. My heart raced as I heard the words that he spoke. I had known there was something wrong, and this only further proved my theory.

I was panic-stricken as we flew to the meeting grounds. My arm in his, he escorted me through the ring of trees, into the brightly lit meadow. I looked overhead as we approached and saw the swirling dark clouds. I looked to God, met His gaze, and instantly looked to the ground. It hurt me to see the anguish in His eyes. He was bothered by something. Gabriel blew his horn every few minutes, until the last of us had reached the meadow. We stood in silence as God glanced from face to face. Gabriel, Lilith, and Michael were standing at His side. What was this? Some form of interrogation? My guilt and nervousness swiftly shifted to confusion and betrayal.

I looked around the crowd, recognizing familiar faces. But the one face I searched for, *the lone wolf*, was nowhere to be found. I didn't know what was happening, but I suddenly longed for my garden. I wanted to be away from this gathering.

"It has come to my attention, that some of you have chosen to live a life other than how I had intended," God announced.

The crowd gasped and mumbled.

He continued, "I do not wish to hear excuses, so provide none. I have witnessed this myself, firsthand."

I squeezed Thaddeus' hand tightly. The nervousness grew in my heart.

"You have changed. You've gained independence. You've gained strength and talents. Yet you've also become selfish and greedy. I've seen lust, envy, and gluttony. Sins that I told you I shall not accept. Yet you continue to defy me!" He bellowed, the anger rising. The clouds continued to swirl overhead. The lands shook, as thunder rumbled across the sky.

"Because of these changes that have come to light, I will give you a chance to make your choice. Choose wisely, for you will rue this day otherwise."

He continued with his speech, telling us to choose between the heavens or the Earth. As He spoke, my mind was elsewhere. My mind was dancing in the garden with Thaddeus. I realized then that there was only one place I was truly content and that place was in the arms of my beloved. I squeezed his arm tightly and stepped out of my trance with a gasp and mental clarity.

As God spoke, looking from face to face, I stood my ground. I spoke no words, offered no remorse. I did not regret a second with my love, nor would I falsely apologize for my actions. I would not beg for forgiveness like those yellow-bellied snakes at His feet. God looked me in the eyes and held His hand out to me. His eyes welled with tears and His expression grew weary. He motioned for me to approach Him. I wrapped my arm around Thaddeus' and turned my gaze to his face. Thaddeus looked down at me and smiled warmly.

"And to which side do you choose, Eden? Do you not wish to share my company any longer?" God asked me directly.

My heart stopped. Having to choose between the two beings that meant the most to me was almost more than I could bear. I had to choose to forever sleep in solitude again, cold, mournful, or to be at rest in the warm embrace. I had to choose between the Creator and the created. Between my soul mate and my Father. The fact that He was forcing me to choose filled me with anger. And this was an emotion I had never once felt.

"I go where Thaddeus goes, my Lord," I said, squeezing his arm tightly and turning my gaze away.

"And where shall that be, Thaddeus?" God asked him, arms folded across His chest.

"If it is her wish to be at your side, I cannot deny her that," Thaddeus said, staring at me as I continued to look away. "Yet if she chooses to stay at my side and it is my decision of where our haven will be, I wish to remain here, on Earth. She has only ever been truly happy in her garden. I have built her a suitable home, well kempt and perfectly safe. I will not leave her side or allow any harm to come to her." Thaddeus stepped in front of me, spreading his wings widely. He was shielding me from our Creator.

"Is this what you want?" God asked me.

I stood on my toes, peaking over Thaddeus' shoulder. I nodded, bereft.

Our decision seemed to have incensed God's rage. Of all the others who had chosen the Earth over the Heavens, it was *our* decision that tipped the scales of His wrath. He roared loudly and raised His arms out in front of Him. His massive hands curled like sharp talons as He flexed His arms towards the sky. The lightning cracked and thunder rumbled as the screams filled the air. No words could describe the multitude of pain we all felt, as our wings were ripped from our flesh. We dropped to our knees, all of us screaming in agony, writhing in pain. It was as if thousands of razor sharp whips lashed at my back in the same moment. It was physical pain, a new and horrific sensation to the children of God.

Tears filled my eyes. My hand shook as I reached out to Thaddeus. His face twisted in pain, but never once did he voice his torment. He crawled to my side on his hands and knees and lifted me to his lap. He cradled me, sheltering me from the stinging rain and blustering wind that fell now from the swirling clouds above.

"The pain you feel on your flesh is nothing compared to the pain I feel in my heart!" God shouted, his voice quivering.

We watched as He turned His back to us and disappeared in the sky, followed by his *loyal* subjects. We betrayed Him, they betrayed us. I looked down around us. The ground was covered with mud and bloody feathers. I tore my gaze from the Earth and looked into the dark portals, the pools of green and gold that were Thaddeus' eyes. They weren't as vivid as they once were. A spark was gone. He slumped his shoulders and leaned in closer to me, then gently kissed my forehead as I felt myself lose consciousness to the sound of crying coming from the fallen around us.

Fragments of memories, thoughts and emotions filled my mind. But it was impossible to focus. The pain was too great. The loss was unbearable. My return to reality struck me. I fell forward onto my hands and knees with a gasp. Tears were flowing from my eyes as I stared at the grass in front of me. I looked up towards the darkening sky and closed my eyes.

I sighed, opening my eyes again. I blew a kiss into the wind, as a humble "thank you" for the gift it had just given me. I knew it wasn't simply a memory stored away in my mass grave of wretched thoughts. The wind itself had blown the memory into me. My cape had been restored. I was reunited with an old friend. I rose to my feet, which were quivering and shaking like a newborn fawn's legs, fighting to keep my balance as I righted myself. I thought about my initial choice. *I'd do it again. I will do it again.* I laughed to myself and began spinning in circles as the rain gently fell to the Earth.

The sky rumbled as the storm rolled in and blanketed the city. I danced in the rain, laughing to myself and humming the same tune I had in my memory. What was once a blissful melody was now a war torn lament, thousands of years in the making.

I ran to the patio, drenched and laughing. A breath of life had been blown into my lungs, filling me with a lighthearted feeling. I was beaming. I felt light. I felt as if my wings had been restored. I slid the sliding glass door of the patio open and stepped into the kitchen. Riley and Gabriel turned to face me as I sloshed across the room. I knelt down in front of Riley, who was sitting on the couch. I looked up, into his eyes and smiled.

"You are far more than simply a face. You are a beautiful face, radiating from the nameless crowd," I said. I watched as his expression changed from confusion to understanding and sentiment.

My eyes filled with tears. Something had awoken with that memory. Something had changed in those moments of meditation and enlightenment. As I looked into the eyes of my husband, it was like a reunion. I wasn't just his wife, Edie anymore. I was *Eden*, his soul mate, the handmaiden he had sworn to protect. I was the being he had traded his immortality for. As he leaned forward and kissed my lips, I felt the same flutter, the same jolt of emotions I felt the very first time our lips met. This was my heaven and I wouldn't trade it for anything.

Chapter Seventeen
Oh, What a Tangled Web We Weave.

Riley and I shared our moment of remembrance with pure unadulterated happiness. My memory seemed to have sparked something in both of us. He remembered far more than I knew, but he had seen it as being just strange dreams. He had blamed the videogames and movies for his visions. I knew exactly where mine had been triggered from. The love I felt for Riley was eternal. It had always been there, since the second he was created. I couldn't imagine that love being threatened. But it was; there was someone trying to tear us apart. The pain and anger I felt was deep.

I turned to Gabriel and rose to my feet. I felt different. I felt reluctant to trust him. My eyes narrowed as I stared at my "friend". He looked at me confused, thrown off by my new demeanor.

"*You...*" I said, brows furrowed.

He looked baffled.

"You betrayed us, now you come to us with guidance? Whose side are you really on?" I questioned, as the water began to pool around my feet.

"What do you mean?" he asked, confused. "You know exactly whose side I'm on."

"I remember everything. I remember the garden. I remember the evening of The Great Divide. You *sided* with God. You chose *Him* over us, over your brothers in arms." I shook my head.

"What's your point?" he crossed his arms, trying to read my intent.

"I'm asking *you* the questions. It's your turn on the docket. If you chose God, if you returned with Him, giving up your life with Lilith, why are you here? Why are you choosing to warn us?" I asked, incredulously.

"Because I love you. I've loved you more than you'll ever understand, since the moment I was created." he hung his head, seeing I didn't mirror his emotions.

I folded my arms silently. Why didn't Riley fight him for that comment? Was this all over jealousy? Riley turned, arm cocked on the edge of the couch. He had a wild smirk. I knew he was thinking something he more than likely shouldn't be.

"Despite your feelings, your love for Eden; despite your motives, you *did* betray us. Give me one good reason not to send your ass back to Heaven in a body bag?" Riley was pissed after all.

"The truth is simple. Well, it's a number of reasons. I felt responsible, *partially* responsible, for the entire event. It's not like it was *my* idea! But I did go along with it," he mumbled the last few words.

I shook my head. I couldn't believe the way things had changed so suddenly.

"I felt that maybe, if you two knew your past, you'd realize that the best thing you could do would be to surrender. I hoped that you'd realize your mistakes and choose to return to God's side. I wanted you to return to my side, Eden," he continued.

"Clearly you don't know how damned hardheaded either of us are," Riley mused.

"Why did you show me all the dreams then? Why did you walk me through the prophecies?" I asked cynically.

"I thought, maybe, if you had seen what humans truly were capable of, that it would help you make the right decision. If you only knew the pain and anguish they've caused God over the years, you'd feel remorseful for ever leaving the fold," he explained.

I shook my head violently. "You used me. YOU *used* me!" I yelled.

"Oooh, what a tangled web we weave, eh, ol' chap? I think you're in trouble. And guess what, *pal*? I'm not saving your ass. You think God delivers wrath? Ha ha! Lemme tell you, Heaven and Hell hath no fury like a woman scorned. And Edie can be pretty wicked when she wants to be. You of all *angels* should know that," Riley guffawed loudly and nodded.

"I didn't use you. My intentions were only to help you," he attempted to justify.

I sat down at the table, staring at the wood grain floor beneath me. I felt my hands shake, my lips quiver as I attempted to speak. I wasn't sure if it was my soaking body or my blinding fury that caused me to tremble, and I didn't care. Gabriel's face was so somber, so pained as I continued to berate him.

"You think God's felt pain? Anguish? Do you have any idea the amount of pain we felt as our wings were ripped from our backs? It wasn't a quick, surgical incision with anesthesia and sedatives. No, it was vengeful. It was out of spite. It wasn't just the physical pain either. When He removed our wings, He removed our bond to Heaven. He made us helpless. The words He spoke in our minds were just as painful. We were disowned."

I looked up at Gabriel with tears in my eyes. He looked down at me, with tears in his. He wiped his cheeks, silently listening to my tirade. Why wasn't he fighting back? Why was he allowing me to put so much blame on him? His lack of defense only managed to make me more furious.

"I've spent the past, God only knows how many years, reliving a life because I chose love, true love, as my driving force. I didn't murder someone in the garden. I fell in love. You should understand that. You gave up Lilith. I've seen death. I've seen murder. I've seen abuse. I've seen all of the horrible things that humans do, but they have nothing, *nothing*, on the betrayal that you, the Archangels, created."

"I'm sorry. I never intended to hurt any of the angels. And I especially never meant to hurt you. You're my heart. I didn't want to remind you of that pain. I was only trying to make things right," Gabriel replied, dejected.

"Oh, don't give us that load of shit. If you cared so much for her, why'd you let any of that happen? Why didn't you fight the other Archangels? You're just the humble messenger, right? Well, you know what we do to messengers in the real world? We shoot them, but only after beating the shit out them and carving our own message into their flesh." Riley advanced towards Gabriel.

Azrael stepped out of the bedroom and walked into the living room. Our raised voices must have gotten his attention. He walked to my feet and sat beneath me. He looked up at me, and then turned his gaze to Gabriel, instinctively. Gabriel turned to me with pleading eyes.

"I thought you were a friend. I thought you were my guardian. I thought you were trying to protect me, not throw me to the wolves," my voice cracked as the tears flowed down my cheeks.

Riley walked over to me and rubbed my shoulders lovingly. *Protectively.* "I think it'd be best if you left. You've caused enough grief and damage. Give her time to think for herself. Give her time to *remember* the past. *I will not do your dirty work. I will not tell her anymore,*" Riley spoke his words very carefully.

Gabriel rose from the couch and walked towards the patio door. Azrael's eyes followed his every move, a low growl echoed in his throat. As Gabriel stepped through the door, Riley, Azrael and I followed him. We stepped out onto the patio, tense and expectant. I watched as Gabriel shed his coat. Riley and Azrael stood in front of me. *My loyal protectors.* Gabriel stepped out into the grass and turned around to face us. Azrael's growl grew louder, more menacing. He began to bare his teeth as his head lowered and the hair along his spine rose, a very clear and poignant message.

"I'm sorry for everything. I love you, Eden. I hope you'll see that. I hope that you'll remember what we share. Call on me, when you're ready. I'll be waiting." Gabriel smiled faintly, wiping the tears from his eyes.

He turned his back to us and gazed towards the sky. He raised his arms towards the heavens. We watched wordlessly as the tattoos on his back first began to glow, peeking through the slits in his armor. Sparks of light danced off of his skin and with a burst of light and feathery down, his wings emerged. They were huge, just as I had remembered in my mind. They flapped and stretched, as if they had just woken up from a long slumber.

I felt the tears welling in my eyes again as the mixture of emotions swelled in my soul. I felt betrayed. I felt scared. I thought he was my friend. How were we going to face the war ill prepared and alone besides each other? I felt longing. I suddenly missed my wings. My beautiful wings.

As Gabriel prepared himself to depart, he turned to us for the last time. He pulled a piece of folded paper out of his pants pocket and plucked one of his feathers from his wing. He tucked the feather in between the folds of the paper. He walked towards us and handed the two items to Riley. He smiled awkwardly, full of regret. He bowed his head, then turned and flew off into the night sky. The speed was uncanny. He flew like a golden bolt of lightning, away from the Earth. The draft off his wings gusted heavily, throwing debris and leaves in every direction. We stood motionless and silent for a few moments.

I ran my fingers down Azrael's back. "Thank you, my loyal little friend." I kissed the top of his head as his growling subsided and turned instead to a slight whimper of reassurance. He wagged his stubby tail and panted, content with my appreciation.

"So, now what?" Riley asked.

"I don't know. But we have to figure something out. And quick, by the looks of it," I replied. Riley stared out into the night sky. He looked troubled.

"Is there something you need to tell me?" I asked.

"It's not my place," he replied.

I stared as his expression changed from somber to amused, "Why are you smiling?" I asked.

"If we've been together since the dawn of time, since the angels roamed the Earth... never mind." he cut the thought short.

"What were you going to say?"

"Does this mean we have more anniversaries? Do I have to buy you more shit?" he asked, nervously.

I laughed hysterically and wrapped my arms around his waist. He leaned his face down, with a pout and kissed my lips.

"Yes. And I expect them to be retroactive." I smiled.

"Oh, come on!" he yelled. I smiled wickedly then shook my head no. "Oh, thank God." He relaxed his shoulders, slumping a little.

"I don't think we should be thanking Him for anything," I muttered under my breath, my mind back to the issues at hand.

"Technically, we should. Had He not asked me to guard you, we may never have met."

"Ugh!" I walked back inside the house.

"Well, it's true!" he yelled, muted by the closed glass door.

I walked to the couch and sat down, turned on the TV, and felt my stomach turn as I watched the report on the news. Thousands were dead or homeless, thanks to tornadoes and massive storm cells sweeping the nation. I leaned forward, elbows on my knees with my hands cupped over my mouth. It had in fact begun. People were dying, *murdered* by Mother Nature, the wrathful hand of God.

I thought about my dream, my vision of Pestilence and wondered if Lilith and the Valkyrie were at least reaping the worthy souls. The banshees were probably enjoying the carnage and harvest.
Bitches.

Riley walked in through the patio door with Azrael at his side. "He won't quit sniffing and growling at this shit Gabriel handed me. I don't know what his deal is."

I turned to face him, inquisitively. "Did you look at it yet?"

"Nah. I didn't know if it was too soon. He *did* just leave. It could be a trick, or a booby trap or something." he laughed. Azrael jumped, snapping at the paper in Riley's hand. "No! Get down! *Bad boy!*" Riley scolded.

"I wouldn't put it past him. A wolf in sheep's clothing," I muttered.

"He wouldn't really do that. Not to you, anyway."

Azrael jumped again, trying to retrieve the items in Riley's hand. "Knock it off!" Riley fussed at the dog.

"Anyway, I'm curious. What's the love note have to say?"

"If he'd stop trying to steal it from me, I could open it and tell you," he replied. Riley unfolded the paper. The feather floated to the floor. Azrael lunged for the feather, grabbed it in his mouth and took off running towards the spare bedroom. We both jumped to our feet and chased after him. Riley yelled, ordering him to drop the feather. Azrael ignored his master. He backed into the far corner of the room, his hackles raised. He growled and crouched, baring his teeth.

"Whoa! What's wrong with him?" I asked.

"He really wants that damn feather, I guess," Riley replied, surprised. Riley walked slowly towards the crazed beast, arms out in front of him, like a well-trained lion tamer. "Azrael! Drop it, now!" he ordered, pointing to the floor. Azrael backed further into the corner, growling louder and more terrifying.

"Something's wrong, Riley. Just let him have it," I pleaded, backing towards the door, startled.

"No!" Riley snapped. "There's a reason he left it for us." he stepped closer to our angry dog. Azrael growled louder, baring his teeth in warning. His hackles were raised like a mohawk, from the back of his neck to his stubby tail.

"Azrael, DROP IT!" he ordered, advancing toward the dog. Azrael lunged forward, snapping at Riley's hand.

"Oh my God!" I shouted. I didn't know whether to run from them or run to them.

Riley and I both noticed as Azrael had lunged for Riley, he dropped the feather. Riley sprinted forward and grabbed the slobbery plume in his hand. I watched, horrified as Riley dropped to his knees. His back arched backwards, his face turned towards the ceiling. His blood curdling scream sent chills down my spine. I ran forward, my eyes full of fear. Azrael howled, as if he was in pain as well. He crawled towards Riley. He grabbed the feather with his teeth, pulling it from Riley's hand, and began to whine uncontrollably.

Riley fell forward, catching himself in my arms. He was breathing rapidly and mumbling under his breath. Azrael laid down in front of him and whined. Riley leaned back on his knees, held his quivering hand out, and pet Azrael's head gently. He whined in reply, licking Riley's hand. I stood up, with my hands over my mouth, shaking. I was afraid to move, I didn't understand.

"Fucking dog," Riley finally said.

"What? What did he do to you?" I asked through my fingers.

"*He* didn't do anything. He was trying to protect us," he replied weakly.

"From what?" I asked, slowly walking forward. I placed my hands on Riley's back and he pulled away with a quick howl. He winced, cringing in pain.

"I'm sorry! I'm so sorry!" I said horrified.

"It's okay, it's not your fault," he replied through clenched teeth. I knelt down and helped him to his feet.

"Do not touch that feather," Riley said, very sternly.

"I won't. I won't." I shook my head violently.

I helped Riley hobble back to the living room. Every step he took he gasped loudly. I tried not to touch his back, but noticed his shirt felt damp. Once we were in the living room he lifted his shirt over his head.

"Whoa! Oh my. Wow. What? No." I couldn't piece together a thought.

"How bad is it?" Riley asked me.

"What. What happened to you?" I asked painfully.

I stared at his back. There were two large gashes. They were deep and flowing with blood. I felt panicked. I was used to treating trauma patients, but I wasn't used to the victim being someone I loved. I tried to think of what to do. I ran to the bathroom and began searching the shelves for equipment. I knocked everything over, bottles crashed to the ground, shattering. I ran out of the bathroom and grabbed the car keys off of the table. I sprinted through the rain to the trunk of my car. I unlocked the trunk and grabbed my jump bag from work, then ran back to the house and closed the door behind me.

Riley was leaning forward on the floor, on his hands and knees. I could tell from his rapid breathing that he was in severe pain, but trying to fight it. I opened my bag and pulled out a bottle of sterile water. I grabbed a hand full of 4x4 inch bandages, trauma dressings, gauze and cling. I searched through the pockets for my shears and tape, then remembered I wasn't in work clothes and pulled the necessary items from the outside pockets of my bag. When I had gathered what I needed I ran to his side.

"I'm so sorry. I know this is going to hurt, but I need to get it bandaged," I tried to reassure him.

"Nothing you could do could possibly come close to the pain I just went through," he answered.

I leaned forward and grabbed the bottle of sterile water. He grabbed my wrist and turned his face up towards me. "Please. Before you start. Get me a beer?"

I paused for a second, and then ran to the fridge. I handed him his beer. He leaned back; his legs were folded under him. He rocked back on his shins and swallowed the beer in four gulps. I helped him to a chair at the dining room table. He grabbed the edge of the table and squeezed as I poured the sterile water into his wounds. He gasped and groaned in pain as I flushed the gashes. He leaned forward, resting his head on his forearms as I applied the dressing and bandages to hold it in place. I wrapped the bandages around his ribcage continuously to apply pressure. Once I was done, he leaned back and sighed deeply.

"I told you. That shit was a booby trap." he chuckled lightly, then winced.

"What happened when you grabbed the feather?" I asked nervously.

"I saw everything at once. I remembered what God said and our reply. I saw Him raise His hands as He ripped our wings off. I felt the lash of pain course down my spine and saw your face. It was horrible." he shook his head. "I just relived The Great Divide."

"I'm so sorry. This is all my fault."

"You didn't do this. I chose this life, just as much as you did. If anything, this is my fault. I could've chosen for us both to return to Heaven. If I would've only done my job," he attempted to justify the pain.

"If you had only done your job? Then neither of us would've ever gotten to enjoy the life, no, the *lives* that we've shared." I smiled and kissed his forehead.

"But it seems that my actions have brought us just as much grief as it has pleasure," he replied with a frown.

"What marriage hasn't?" I mused.

He laughed. "Hey, don't steal my thunder. Only I can make a mockery of our union," he grinned wickedly, color finally beginning to creep back into his face.

"We *both* chose this. We *both* have to persevere. If it's a war He wants, it's a war He's going to get. I'm not going down without a fight and I'm not giving you up. I didn't when I was staring into His eyes, and I won't again when He steps down off of His high horse," I replied self-righteously.

"Seems as if we've had a little role reversal here. Normally I make fun of the Creator and you pussyfoot around situations. What's gotten into you, Eden Quinn?" he asked, hands on his hips from his seated position.

"Life," I replied. "I saw what I had. What we had. I watched as it was all taken away from us, leaving us writhing in pain and incomplete. That isn't something that I will let go of, ever again."

"Then I guess we suit up. I'm gonna have to get some shit together." he attempted to stand, but buckled in pain and fell to the floor.

"No, it looks like I'm gonna have to pull some strings. You need to rest." I helped him back to his seat.

"What are you saying? It's 3am. What can you do this late at night?" he asked.

"I can get you out of pain."

I kissed him on the lips and grabbed my car keys. I bolted out of the front door and ran through the rain to my car. I stared out of the front windshield, gathering my courage. I was about to do something against what I believed. I was about to break an oath, break a code. But it was something I had to do. I didn't want to think about it. I knew it was wrong, but I knew my intentions were pure.

I turned the engine on, put the car into reverse, backed out of the driveway and sped down the street of our neighborhood. I turned the corner sharply and drove towards the interstate. I entered on the ramp and sped down the road, weaving through the traffic at breakneck speed to get to my destination. I knew I had precious little time; I had to get my mission done before it was too late. I exited the interstate and reached the base in record time. A drive to work that normally took me thirty minutes of dragging my feet and whining, was done in seventeen minutes flat. I looked around the empty parking lot and sighed with relief. No one was here. I grabbed the backpack out of backseat and emptied out its contents.

"I'm sorry, Hippocrates." I frowned.

I ran inside to the safe and began to dial the combination. I stopped myself midway, realizing they'd know it was an inside job if I did it that way. I paced the lounge for a few minutes, peeking out of the window every so often. I didn't want to get caught. It wasn't because I didn't want to have to face the punishment or explain myself; I didn't want to have to hurt anyone. I didn't want them to see my sad expression, knowing damned well that I had broken an oath I swore I never would.

That was it; I didn't have time to fight my conscience.

I put on a pair of gloves, dialed the combination and winced as the safe clicked open. I grabbed every vial, every pouch of narcotics that I could and loaded the front pockets of my backpack. I walked to the cabinet and loaded the large pouch of my bag with IV supplies. I grabbed needles, tubing, saline bags, alcohol pads, tourniquets, IV covers and tape.

Heal them.

I fumbled through the cabinets, grabbing anything and everything I could. I realized that if we were going to war, there would be casualties. There would be injuries. I was sorry I had to steal from the company I loved, but I needed to prepare myself for battle. I was to be a battle medic, armed to the teeth with pain killers and proper bandages.

I zipped up my loaded backpack and headed for the door. I toyed with the notion of leaving a note. I wanted to apologize for my actions, but figured they'd send the cops to get me before we could figure out our game plan. I ran to the car and threw my bag in the back seat. I bit my lip anxiously, trying to concoct a plan.

"Ah, ha!" I whispered to myself. *It was a break in.* I ran back to the bay and grabbed the wrench used to open the large oxygen cylinders, sprinted back inside the base and bashed the key pad on the safe until the numbers flew off in random directions. I wasn't sure if that would have made the safe open *beforehand*, but I thought it at least looked good. Maybe they'd think it was a junky that broke in, taking the heat off of me, just long enough for me to devise a plan with Riley.

I threw things around, knocking over the table and chairs. I closed the front door behind me and once again realized my mistake. I took an oxygen bottle and smashed the front door in, breaking it free from the frame. I marveled at my handy work, then ran to the car. I got in and peeled out of the driveway as quickly as I had arrived.

As I drove down the interstate, I slowed my pace and thought about everything that was going on. I couldn't believe what I had just done. Under normal circumstances, that would've never happened. But, alas, desperate times call for desperate measures. I felt as if anyone in my situation would've done the same thing. I saw it as a preemptive strike to the riots and looting that were going to occur once the battle begun. Marshal Law is going to happen, I might as well stock up on what I need while the getting is good.

By the time I made it home, it was 4:24am. I stared at the clock on the dashboard and let out a sigh of relief. I made it, free and clear. I reached into the backseat and grabbed my backpack. I got out of the car, locked it and hurried to the front door.

When I walked in, Riley was still sitting at the table. He was staring at the piece of paper in his hand. He didn't look up when I walked in. His undivided attention was drawn to the page. He shook his head and ran his finger down the sheet, tracing lines and mumbling to himself.

I set my bag down on the table and stared curiously at him. What was he looking at? I watched as he continuously traced lines and mumbled incoherently. He tried to stand up and slumped over in pain.

"Sit still a few minutes," I ordered.

"I can't. I have to get started," he replied.

"So do I. I need to start an IV on you."

"Like hell you do! You're not poking me," he replied, defiantly.

"Thad... *Riley*, I need to. You need fluids. Plus I got some pain medicine for you," I tried to reason with him.

"Did you just call me Thad?" he asked with a chuckle followed by a wince.

"All this Eden, Thaddeus, stuff! It's throwing me off. Stop trying to change the subject!" I rebuked him.

"You're *not* stabbing me with a needle." he folded his arms in petition.

"But you need it."

"No. I don't. You're just trying to play doctor. I'm not playing with you!"

"You need the fluids; you've lost a lot of blood," I attempted to negotiate with him.

"So, I'll make more blood. The body is an amazing machine, you've said so yourself." he smiled faintly.

"You're so goddamned hardheaded! Would you please, please just trust me? You really do need the fluid replacement. Let me do my job." I was beginning to lose my patience.

"I've seen how you do your job. You're into bloodletting! You're going to kill me!" He held his index fingers out in front of him like a cross.

"I'm not a vampire, ass hat. I'm a paramedic." my eyes narrowed.

"So crosses don't work on you? Hmm. What will ward you off? An attorney?" he laughed to himself.

I shook my head and started to zip my backpack up. I set my bag on the floor. "Fine. I brought Morphine home so that I could get rid of the pain. But, since you're going to be such an asshole about it, you can just suffer. Imagine how you'll feel in the morning. That's gonna burn like fire, not to mention ache like hell. Sucks to be you!" I shouted with a large, smug, shit-eating grin.

"Morphine, you say?" he asked, brow raised.

"Yep, but you don't want it. I guess I'll just save it for the other people I find in pain during the war." I shrugged. He was caving and I knew it.

"Can't you just give it to me as a shot?" he asked, like a child.

"Can? Yes. Will I? No," I replied.

"Why not?" he asked, with a tinge of a whine in his tone.

"It doesn't matter how I can give it. You don't want it. I'm just gonna let you sit around weak from the blood loss and hurting. Too bad you're so stubborn. You could've already been feeling better."

"Fine. But you only get one shot to get it," he caved.

"That's all I need." I smiled arrogantly. "They call me the One-Hit Wonder for a reason."

"Ha! Tell that to your voodoo doll, pin cushion patients!"

"You're pretty brave to taunt someone with needles," I mused.

"I trust you," he lied.

I pulled out a tourniquet, pierced the bag of saline with the tubing and ran it a few moments to drain the air from the line. I closed off the tubing and grabbed a vial of morphine. I popped off the top and cleaned it with an alcohol swab. I grabbed Riley's arm, twisting and turning it looking for a good spot to start his IV. His arms were full of what we called "pipelines". His veins were huge, which was a good thing and a bad thing all in one. The good news was, if I could get an IV in without blowing the vein, they could hold a larger gauge needle, giving him more fluids in a shorter amount of time. The bad news was, as soon as I poke him, I risk the chance of blowing the vein because of the amount of pressure in his *pipes*.

I found a spot that I trusted. I grabbed a needle and pulled it out of the packaging. I grabbed the vial of morphine and a syringe. I filled the syringe with air, equal to the amount of medication I was going to withdraw. I squeezed the plunger, forcing the air into the vial, causing a vacuum. I drew out the entire ten milligrams, and recapped the needle.

"Ready?" I asked, nervously. I had never given Riley an IV, he'd never let me.

"Yeah," he replied, wincing already.

"Oh you're such a puss," I mocked. I applied the tourniquet to his arm and cleaned the area with an alcohol swab. I waited a second for it to dry.

"On the count of three," I removed the cap from the IV catheter and turned it.

"Okay." he turned his face away.

"One... two..." I stabbed him. "Three!" I slid the needle back into the chamber and laughed.

He laughed as he yelled, "You cheater!"

"That wasn't so bad, now was it?"

"You're about as 'light handed' as your brother when he gives tattoos!"

I laughed. I knew that was a jab at both my brother and I, but couldn't help myself.

"Nah, really it wasn't bad," he said more seriously.

I smiled and connected the catheter to the tubing, then ran the fluids for a moment to make sure the IV was patent. Once I knew it was safe and that there wasn't a leak anywhere, I slowed the fluids down some and cleaned off the medication port.

"Is it going to hurt?" he asked.

"What? The morphine?" I asked in return. "Nope. You shouldn't even notice it in your arm. You'll feel kind of light headed after a minute or so, then get kind of numb. Then you'll babble a lot and annoy the hell out of me." I smiled.

"That's your professional opinion, of course."

"Yes sir," I replied, twisting the syringe into the port. "Let me know if you get nauseous."

I slowly pushed the plunger of the syringe and watched his face for changes or reactions. I gave the medication very slowly to make sure he didn't get nauseated. I watched as he went from an anxious expression to blank, getting the all too familiar glassy eyed expression associated with morphine.

"Whoooooooooa," he said.

"What? Are you okay?" I asked, stopping the meds.

"I'm fuckin' fantastic! How are you?" He chuckled.

"Wow, you're a total lightweight. That was only 4 milligrams." I snickered. I continued to push the plunger, slowly. He began to drum on the table and make motor boat noises with his lips. I pushed the last of the morphine and threw all of the trash away. He sat at the table drumming with his fingers and laughing.

"How are you feeling now?" I asked when I returned.

"I need a cigarette."

I walked to the table and helped him to his feet. He staggered a bit, and then wrapped his arm around my shoulder to stabilize himself. I grabbed his IV bag and carried it in my other hand as I helped him to the patio door and slid it open. He stepped out, laughing, and stumbled to a chair. He sat down heavily, nearly tipping the chair on its side.

"Whoa there, junky!" I jumped to his side to catch him.

"I'm fine! I'm fine." his speech was slightly slurred.

I hung his IV from a plant hook then handed him a cigarette and lit it for him. He pulled his head back as I lit it, dazed. He moved his hand in front of his face over and over again, laughing. He looked like a high school stoner, amused by tracers.

"Shiiiiiit," he mumbled around the cigarette in his mouth.

"What?"

"I hope they don't give me a drug test at work," he replied seriously.

"I don't think you'll be working much more anyway," I said with a sarcastic giggle.

"How will we pay rent?" he asked, like a child, still not making the connection.

"I don't think we'll have to worry about rent either."

"Then where will we live?"

"I'm pretty sure we're gonna be moving, a lot." I blew smoke out of my nose. He was silent for a few seconds. "Like nomads?"

"Like people, trying to survive the Apocalypse," I answered, annoyed.

"Like in that movie with Australian What's-his-face?" he asked again.

"Yes, Riley. Like in Mad Max or *whatever*." I rolled my eyes.

"I'm gonna have a mohawk like that crazy broad!" He laughed. "Wait, wait. No, YOU should grow a mohawk again." he smiled and nudged me with his elbow.

I cradled my face in my hands. "What was I thinking?" I mumbled into my palms.

"My back feels much better." he smiled.

"Good," I replied groggily. It had been such a long day.

"Thanks."

"You're very welcome," I replied, pulling the rubber band from my hair and scratching my head.

"You're really hot with your hair down." he grinned in his best attempt at a seductive stare.

"Thanks," I laughed and yawned at the same time.

"You're like a MILF, but you don't have kids. Well, you have Rufio and Azrael, and those damned cactuses you always seem to kill..." he trailed off. I couldn't help but laugh at him.

"Cactuses? Cacti. What-the-fuck-ever." he giggled.

I stared at my drugged up husband, amused.

"Dude, your mohawk would be like, ten feet tall." he squinted as he looked up, trying to imagine it.

"My hair's only to the small of my back. It'd be like, three feet tall, except it wouldn't be tall at all. It would fall over," I corrected him.

"Not if we got the same person to do yours that did hers," he shot back. I laughed loudly at his insane thought processes.

"That would be awesome." he nodded to himself.

"I'm not gonna shave my head again. No mohawk. I'm sorry," I replied.

"That's okay. Just keep your hair down then."

We sat for a moment in silence. Well, relative silence. He drummed his fingers on the edge of the patio table and made guitar sounds with his mouth. I wished for a second that I hadn't given him so much medication. I was glad he was out of pain, but I really needed him to be able to focus. I really needed him to help me devise a plan. Then he broke the silence, *the relative silence*, with something somewhat useful.

"Man, Gabe wasn't that bad of a guy," he said, staring up at the sky.

"Gabe, my brother? Or Gabriel, the traitor?" I asked, confused.

"Gabriel, your brother," he replied.

"What are you talking about? What did you mean '*not that bad of a guy*'? Of course he isn't a bad guy. He's my brother," I asked, mimicking Riley.

"He really helped us out." he nodded.

"How so? I'm confused." I shook my head. I couldn't follow his thoughts.

"Giving us the feather and shit. Warning us about the storm."

"Oh, you did mean Gabriel, the traitor. How the hell did he help us out? Reminding us of the pain we've lived? Causing you to writhe in agony, with blood running from your back? Yeah, that's really helpful," I scoffed.

"You didn't see what I saw," he shook his finger at me.

"I saw it, I just didn't have my back lashed up," I replied dryly.

"No, no. The list. He gave us the list."

"What list?" I asked.

"*The* list." he nodded with a grin.

"He left us a list and a feather? What, a grocery list? A 'to do' list?"

"Your bro left us the answers to all of our problems." he smiled, wide.

"Stop confusing my brother with that sellout!" I shouted. "And I still don't get it." I shook my head, confused and annoyed.

"Oh, but you will. You definitely will."

Chapter Eighteen
The Pen is Mightier Than the Sword.

Riley mumbled incoherently and eventually began to fall asleep. I helped him to bed and laid down next to him. I tossed and turned for about thirty minutes and then decided to just get back up. I had too many thoughts running through my mind for sleep.

I got out of bed and put my glasses on. I slid my legs into my favorite Washington Capitals pajama pants and walked out to the kitchen, closing our bedroom door so that Riley could get some much needed rest. I filled a coffee filter with grounds, poured a pot full of water into the back of the coffee maker and turned the beast on. I needed fuel for my think-tank. I was running on fumes. I stood at the kitchen counter for a few minutes, dazed, staring blindly at the coffee pot as it began to fill. I could hear a repetitive sound, like laughter or the high pitched whine of a foreign car's engine revving, somewhere outside the house. As I stood staring at the coffee pot the noise intruded on my reverie, beginning to grate on my nerves as I tried desperately to focus on my next move. Eventually, I couldn't take it anymore and decided to go outside and investigate.

I walked out to the patio and lit a cigarette. The sound was louder, closer. From outside the house I could decipher the noise better and recognized it as a bird's squawk, though I still could not see the source. I peeked around the corner of the house and saw a large crow, seated on the tall dog-eared picket fence. I tried to quietly shoo it away. I waved my hands and jumped towards it. It refused to budge. It only cawed louder in defiance.

"Stupid bird," I mumbled around my cigarette. I searched the patio for something to startle it. I moved plants and slid chairs, but couldn't find a single thing to get the crow to leave. I finally found a small rock on the ground just below the patio deck and picked it up. I chucked the pebble at the bird, but being the girl that I am, I meet the stereotype and threw the stone like a pansy. The rock hit the fence, ricocheted off and hit the side of the house.

"Damn it!" I yelled, louder than I intended. I could hear Azrael barking in the house, startled by the sudden sound of the pebble pinging off the house and my loud reaction.

The crow held its position, cawing repeatedly. It sounded like a laugh. The little bastard was taunting me! I walked towards the bird, waving my arms in the air. It bobbed and weaved like a well-trained boxer, then lunged towards me from its picket as if it was going to peck me. I let out a shrill squeal and decided to retreat to the deck, running hunched over with my arms protecting my head, cigarette still in hand.

The crow grew louder, louder, louder. I tried to think of a way to get rid of the bird. It was wasting my time! But I knew damned well if I didn't shut the thing up, I wouldn't be able to think. It would wake Riley up. I sat at the table for a few minutes, my leg bouncing a hundred miles an hour, my nails chewed to the quick. I turned to my left and saw Azrael standing at the patio door, his muzzle pressed against the glass; condensation advancing and retreating across the surface of the door with every breath. His jowls were pulled back, baring his sharp teeth. My eyes narrowed and my head cocked to the side. I chuckled. I looked back at the cackling crow, and then returned my gaze to Azrael, who was scratching at the bottom of the sliding door. He stopped and looked back up at me. I looked closer. His hackles were raised. He was pissed!

"Oh you're gonna get it now, you *stupid* bird." I laughed to myself.

I slid the door open and caught myself as he bolted past me, almost knocking me over. He ran straight to the fence and lunged at the bird, jaws snapping loudly. I watched as the crow rose off of the fence and hovered for a moment. Azrael returned all four paws to the ground and stood, growling, louder and louder as he snarled at the menacing nuisance. The crow dove at Azrael, as if to taunt him. He jumped slightly to the side and caught the bird in his vice-like jaws. I turned away, disgusted. I heard Azrael growling and the crow cawing, panicked, pain stricken; its wings flapping helplessly. My stomach turned and my heart stopped as I listened to the dying bird. It sounded as if it was screaming "repent" as it died, though that had to be my imagination.

"Azrael! Drop it!" I yelled.

Azrael unlocked the hinges of his jaw and dropped the bloodied bird to the ground. I threw my cigarette into the yard, walked over and stood above it. I knelt down and poked at its breast. It was dead, and I felt guilty. I felt as if I had personally murdered the creature. I looked at its battered face and saw its glowing white eyes.

"What the hell?!" I fell backwards onto my butt. Azrael sniffed at the carcass and growled.

"Morrigan? Mórrígna? Oh shit." I stumbled to my feet. I gently pat Azrael's head, "Good boy. Good boy," I said, breathless.

I brushed the grass and dew off the back of my pajama pants and coaxed Azrael back to the deck. He was still distracted by the bird. It was as if he wasn't done tearing it apart. He wouldn't follow me, so I grabbed his collar and pulled him up to the patio with me. He struggled in his bonds and tried to turn away. Once I had successfully gotten him to the deck, I commanded him to sit. He obeyed, but whined, staring at the dead crow.

I scratched my head. Was that a bad thing that I had done? Was I going to be, I don't know, punished? I thought it was just a bird! It still *might* just be a bird. But I was also upset when I felt like I had personally damned the bird to die. I paced the porch, trying to figure out what I should do with the carcass. Azrael began to growl and whine, nearing the edge of the deck.

"Stay," I commanded. He howled a long, high pitched whine in response. "No, Az. Stay."

And then I heard flapping. I turned to the spot in the grass that had been speckled with bird blood and ripped feathers, and saw the crow twitching, flapping its wings. I watched, stunned as it twisted and contorted, snapping its joints back into place. I tried to hold Azrael's collar tightly, but I was overwhelmed. He broke loose of my hold and dove off of the patio. He darted towards the crow, but missed as the bird shot into the air.

"Repent! Repent!" it cawed as it flew off.

I stood on the edge of the patio, traumatized. I thought about the Edger Alan Poe story and instantly thought, *that bastard wasn't crazy; he just had to deal with the damned Mórrígna!* Azrael relaxed and sauntered back up to the patio, satisfied the threat was gone. He sat next to me and raised his head, looking up at me expectantly. I gently pet him and smiled.

"You're still a good boy."

He wagged his stubby tail, unsure.

I turned to walk back inside, Azrael poised perfectly at my side. As I slid the door open, I heard a woman's chuckle. The chuckling continued until it was full-fledged cackling. *She* was laughing at me. I felt my jaw clench and my shoulders tighten.

"Oh, *screw you*, Lilith!" I yelled, as I slammed the door shut.

Azrael walked back into the living room and took his place on the couch, near Rufio. I returned to the coffee pot and poured myself a mug full, looking at the clock on the stove. 6:47am.

"God, I *hate* her," I muttered under my breath. I didn't realize how true that statement was. How true it had always been.

Another sleepless night. Another day of yawning and sandpaper eyelids was ahead of me. Just what I always wanted! What day was it anyway? Tuesday? Wednesday? They were all starting to run together. I grabbed my cell phone off the counter and looked at its display. It was now Thursday, October 9th. What? Did I lose a day or two? I thought back over the past week.

I mumbled to myself. "Friday, saw Doctor Boob-job. Saturday we hung out. Sunday, boarded up the house for Nestor. Monday it had passed. Tuesday, everyone left. Wednesday... What did I do yesterday? Oh... yesterday I found out the truth."

I sighed heavily when I thought about the memory I had, the pain I had felt, the betrayal. I thought about the pain Riley had endured. I wanted to take it all back, but I couldn't. And now I had to worry about Lilith. What was she up to? Gabriel must have sent her. But if he was still trying to "talk sense into me", he wouldn't have sent one of the women I despised, and she sure as hell wasn't going to make me beg for forgiveness, not as a squawking pest.

"*Bitch*," I spit out the word.

I grabbed my cup of coffee and walked to the dining room, turned the light on and sat at the table. I could still hear the laughter outside, muted by the insulation and closed windows. She was *really* proud of herself, or a glutton for punishment. I wasn't sure which.

The room began to glow with a faint red and pink, as the sun broke free of the horizon. I battled the ominous bird in the dim light, but it wasn't going to happen again. She wouldn't get away with that racket during the day. People would be up; kids with pellet guns would be awake. Well, kids would be at school, but the *parents* of kids with pellet guns would be awake and pissed! I laughed to myself.

I saw the folded up piece of paper on the table and toyed with the notion of opening it. Riley had said it was a list, of some sort. I wasn't completely clear on the details, seeing as how he babbled in a morphine-induced haze. I bit my lip and reached for the paper, then stopped. He had wedged the feather back in its fold and I was extremely nervous about touching it. I saw the wounds it had inflicted on Riley, I didn't want that for myself.

The cackling outside continued. *Caw. Laugh. Caw. Caw. Laugh.* I felt like I was going to lose my mind. I walked over to Azrael and woke him up. I acted excited and said "outside" in a happy voice. I could see the gears in his mind turning slowly as his tail began to wag. He thought he was going out to play!

"Oh no, no, silly dog. You're going out to take care of business again," I said as I pat Azrael's back.

I slid the glass door open slightly. He stuck his muzzle through the crack and sniffed at the air. His breathing became more rapid and I heard a growl erupt in his chest. *Yes!* He noticed she was back. I giggled to myself as I slid the glass door open further and stepped out onto the patio. Azrael ran off the edge and into the grass on a mission.

I threw my arms up into the air, "I unleash the hounds of hell on you, witch!" I yelled, then did my best impression of a maniacal, diabolical laugh. I smugly watched her take flight. Azrael barked and snapped at the air as she hovered and eventually flew off. Satisfied my job was done for now, I walked back toward the patio door and left it partially cracked so I could hear Azrael and know when he wanted back inside.

I returned to the table and my now cold coffee and took my place in a chair across from the alluring folded paper. I reached for it and stopped. I reached for it again, but stopped. I stood up and walked over to the opposite side of the table. I reached for the corner, furthest away from the feather and lifted the edge. I shook the pain-filled trap until the feather released and fell to the table. *Victory!*

I unfolded the sheet carefully. The paper was thick, like handmade parchment. The edges were worn. As I inspected the dense, yet seemingly delicate paper, I completely overlooked what was written. My eyes wandered from the edge, my hands shifted from the texture to the print. The script was obviously handwritten. It was beautiful and elegant. It was feathery, yet heavy, like Old English. The words, *themselves* , meant nothing until three, together, caught my eye.

Roy Anthony Bergeron

Roy Anthony Bergeron? Of all the names to catch my attention, it wasn't even my own. My curiosity was piqued. I traced my finger down the list of names on the left hand side of the parchment. Some names seemed so familiar, so relevant, but I didn't catch the connection. Only three of them were directly known to me. Most of the names had a very faint red line through them, as if they had been crossed off.

"What the fuck?" I gasped, as my eyes ran down the page.

It dawned on me, about halfway down the list of names that *this* was the list of angels left on Earth. Nine out of the twelve listed had names that ran along the opposing side of the page. The only one that was crossed out and didn't have a name on the opposite side was Matthew Jefferson. The man from the bridge? The suicidal man that had murdered his family? It was hard to believe that anyone who could kill the love of his life and children was an angel.

The red lines were only on the left hand side, which led me to believe that the names on the left side were the angels previous or current earthly names, if they had not yet died and reincarnated. That was the only way to explain the two that were left intact, without an alias. I read the list as a story. Jonah Smith, died at *some point*, and became Jonah Alexander. Victoria Nichols also died, then was born again as Victoria Stewart. Paul Andrews was now deceased, but Paul Lee was born with his soul. Mary Elwood was apparently still alive and guessing by the order of the names, was very old. Thomas Adams died and was reborn as Tom Hatcher. Roy Anthony Bergeron had passed away and was reborn as Anthony Hedderman. Thaddeus Boyd had passed on, becoming my Riley. Riley Thaddeus Nixon. Eden Haley had croaked and had spawned again as, well, yours truly! Eden Quinn McDowell. Eden Nixon, now. Jeremiah Primo died and was now Jeremiah Connell. *The* Jeremiah Connell? Riley's best friend? No way. As weird as all of this had been up to this point, that would just push things over the edge. Four names were now connected.

Next on the list was Matthew Jefferson, who was crossed off, with no name to follow up. If in fact, that was the same Matthew from the bridge, it had only been a few months since his death. It was probable that he had been conceived, but there was no way that he had been born again. Then, there was Elijah Ryan, who was *also* still alive. The final name on the list baffled me. Brandon Sullivan. His name wasn't the issue. What boggled my mind was the fact that Brandon Sullivan, who died, became Brandon Sullivan, Jr. How could he have died and been reborn so quickly? How could he be his own father?

As much as I was pissed off at Gabriel, I now knew that he was in fact, trying to help us, in a sense. He could've taken the list with him, which, he probably was *supposed* to. But he chose to give it to us. We now knew who else was out there. We didn't have phone numbers or addresses, but we had a means to work with. I grabbed my laptop and popped my knuckles. I knew this was going to take some research. It was time to get to work.

I had become a Guru of the search engines over the years. There wasn't much out there in the world that could hide from me. Well, at least not if it was on the internet. I didn't know how to hack, or how to encrypt or anything like that. But I could Google like nobody's business. The internet is both a blessing and a curse. It can either help you, giving you answers and easy step-by-step instructions, or it can bend you over a dirty site and violate you. It can leave you without an identity, penniless, and flush your credit down the can. But much like a loaded gun, the "inter-web" is harmless without the douche bag hiding behind the keys.

My laptop screen looked like a mosaic, a collage of half opened internet pages and their accompanying tabs. I was on a mission and nothing was going to sway my need for answers. I was crazed. Dedicated. Irrationally obsessed. Call me what you will. I guess it all depends on your views or educational background. I was going to find these people, by any means necessary. The only thing that would *possibly* keep me away would be a restraining order... and chances are I'd probably just kidnap them anyway. Who was going to worry about sending me to jail or court once the world was in absolute chaos?

The coming days, the future, was going to scare a lot of people. All of those people who survived by their money and "bling"? Lemme tell you something, honey, it wasn't gonna do a damned thing for them. And to all of those kids who walk around with their thick black eyeliner and giant anarchy patches sewn onto their jackets? Those kiddies, they were up for a rude, rude awakening. Anarchy was on its way in, and it will be frightening, while it lasts. Right before the end. But I digress.

My dining room had been turned into a giant flow chart. Names and notes slathered the wall. Thumbtacks strewn around the floor like landmines. I was unable to think of anything but finding these people. It was proving to be slightly harder than expected.

I worked as if I was in a trance. I scribbled down information as I found it and tacked it on the wall adjacent to the corresponding name. I went through archives and obituaries from across the globe. I flipped through countless social media profiles. I guess I never realized how many people shared the same name, until now. I was completely unaware of my surroundings. I lost track of the time. I was *in the zone* as I researched. I didn't even notice when Riley had woken up and lumbered into the living room until I heard a groan.

"Ugh. I feel like death warmed over."

I jumped out of my skin, startled by his approach. He looked awful. His skin was pale, paler than usual, which was hard to believe. His eyes looked sunken, the dark circles under gave the appearance of a bandit mask. His short brown hair was slightly more disheveled than usual. It poked up and twisted in odd spots. He looked like a zombie. He shambled towards me to give me a hug. I was reluctant to return the affection. What if he was after my flesh? What if he wanted my brains? I needed sleep. I was losing my mind.

"I feel like poop." he frowned.

"I'm sorry. How's your back?" I asked.

"Hurts. Not as bad as it did last night, but it's still pretty painful," he replied, tugging at the bandages wrapped around his ribs.

I smiled awkwardly. I didn't know what to say or do to make it better.

"So I see you opened the list," he said, staring at my messy mural.

"Yeah. It's crazy," I replied, following his gaze.

"I don't remember much. I just remember seeing us and Jere. You think it's the same Jere?" he asked.

"I wouldn't be surprised. It seems we're all connected to each other, one way or another," I replied, staring at my progress.

"What do you mean?"

"Well, obviously the two of us are connected. And then there's Jere. But some of the others are too. Like this, look." I pointed to Roy Anthony Bergeron's name, "Do you know who he is?"

"Nope. Doesn't ring a bell."

"He was one of the most amazing men to ever grace this Earth. He worked so hard to take care of his family. He was funny, loving, generous. He was wonderful." my voice shook as I described him.

He looked at the notes corresponding with the name. "Asbestosis?" he asked, baffled.

"Yep. He died in 2000 of Asbestosis. It really sucked," I replied.

"So how do you know all of that about him? Where'd you find it?"

"That's my grandfather." I smiled up at him. I smiled for the right reasons, the sadness of his loss as well as the celebration of his life, the memories I had. As wonderful of a man as he was, it was only fitting that he was an angel. It was horrible to lose him, especially to something so painful, but I knew that he was more than simply a *man*.

"Really?" he asked, surprised.

"Yeah. I really wish you would've gotten to meet him."

He wrapped his arms around me and kissed my forehead. "You'll see him soon."

I frowned. "I don't know. I wonder if I should leave him alone."

"Why would you do that?"

"Because. He died in 2000; he'd be in his teens now, if we're lucky. I don't think I should pull him into this mess. And for all I know, he isn't the same person I knew and loved. What if he's one of those bad kids that I hate to be around?" I questioned.

Riley chortled loudly. "I doubt it. As much as the two of us connect every lifetime, I'm sure the second you make eye contact with him, the love returns. Do you remember him from any other life?" he asked, trying to comfort me.

"No. I wish I could remember everything else. All I remember is this life. Well, other than the flashback or whatever that was," I responded. I stared at the lists on the wall, honing in on my grandfather's name. "I hope you're right. I hope we would have an instant connection. I wonder if he'd look the same, or have the same traits." He rubbed my back as we stared up at the mess strewn about the dining room wall.

"Watch out for the tacks. I keep losing them," I changed the subject. Riley raised one foot, looking beneath it. "Yeah, I noticed that you had booby trapped the dining room."

I laughed.

"So. Do you think I should call Jere? Think I should tell him to come over?"

I bit my lip anxiously. "I don't know. I'm not sure how you should tell him. You know he's like a damned zealot."

"Mmhmm. True story." he nodded. "So how many of these guys have you found information on? What all have you found out?"

"Fragments. I've found bits and pieces of seven," I replied, staring at my tangled web of information.

"I wonder when we should start trying to communicate with them?"

"When we know what to say and how to explain it without sounding crazy," I stated.

"I think that's what the feather is for," he suggested.

"Hi, my name's Eden. I'm an angel. You are, too! Here, hold this feather. It's going to hurt like hell," I jeered.

"That sounded pretty good for a trial run." he laughed.

I shook my head. "Yeah, that sounded great. I'd be sold!"

We stared at the list of names on the wall. I knew, if anyone else saw our spread, they'd wonder what we were up to. Was this a hit list? Were we stalking people? No, it was a help list. These were the people that could help us save the world. Maybe. Doubtful. But we could try, right? I really hoped that they'd be willing to join forces. I was afraid of the hunt, the journey to band together, the team building montage that was to come. But staring at the list that Gabriel had given us, I realized, the pen is mightier than the sword. Maybe if we came together it would make a difference. Then again, maybe it wouldn't.

Chapter Nineteen
My Armor, Torn Asunder

We spent hours scouring over my notes and staring at the screen of my laptop. Riley noticed how on edge and distracted I was. I couldn't remember the last time I had slept. With everything going on, I didn't know when the shit was going to hit the fan. The last thing in the world I wanted was to be caught off guard when the world ended, or worse, to somehow sleep through the End of Days.

It was early evening when Riley made me a grilled cheese sandwich and convinced me to take my "night time" medicine. I reluctantly agreed and was soon losing consciousness on the couch. Despite Riley's wounds, he picked me up and carried me to the bedroom. I drifted in and out of reality as I felt my body weightlessly moving. I watched the ceiling, confused, tired and drugged. He laid me down on the bed and pulled back the sheets around me. He slid my glasses off and smiled. He sat down on the edge of the bed and laughed at me as I tried to hold a conversation under sedation.

"You really need to sleep," he suggested.

"We have too much to do," I replied, attempting to sit up.

"It can wait until tomorrow." he stood and turned off the light.

I felt my eyes grow heavy. I fought to keep them open, but eventually surrendered to slumber.

I awoke under a soft canopy of green and orange leaves. I could hear the thunder rumbling, lightning cracking in the distance. How long has this storm continued? I sat up and pulled my knees to my chest, staring out at the land; a reflection of myself. The flora was battered and bruised, the beautiful leaves and petals torn from the onslaught of wind and rain. Heavy tears fell to the Earth for weeks, drowning life and our spirits. I stared out, helplessly. *Hopeless.* I sobbed for days, my tears kept company by the falling rain. If I hadn't truly known where this weather had come from, I'd have thought it was only reflecting my emotions. I felt battered. I felt bruised. I was drowning in sadness.

Thaddeus had been gone for days. I yearned for my love to return. This was the longest we had been separated since the day we met. I thought about that moment, dancing in the garden. I buried my face in my knees. Everything I loved and longed for was gone. After The Great Divide, many of the men began to form hunting parties. Thaddeus left with the last group, to retrieve food and supplies. It seemed that when God retreated, taking our wings and all of the traits that made us heavenly beings, he also left us with many burdens.

We no longer hunted for sport, no longer ate for enjoyment. The two were crucial for sustainment. We felt hunger. The cold no longer gently tickled our skin, it burned like fire, numbing and aching. We no longer felt joy and happiness as a part of our being. The land reminded us of what we were. We were fragile. We were breakable. I looked down at my quivering hands. Everything had fallen apart, slipping between my fingers. I felt a horrible pain in my chest. My heart ached. My heart was broken. God had in fact found the perfect punishment for me. I was tormented. I was miserable in my own skin.

I looked at the weeping clouds, the waterlogged land, and felt a sadness rush through my body. The Great Divide was a detachment. I had been detached from my Father, my Creator, my inspiration and the joy that made me who I was. I hadn't created life since the day they left us. I wasn't sure if I was even capable of it any longer, whether He had taken my ability or if my agony was to blame.

I laid down, curling my legs into my chest and stared out into the storm. My heart raced with every rumble of thunder. When would this end? I closed my eyes and drifted to sleep as the wind attempted to comfort me, cradling my cold body.

I awoke to birds chirping. The sound startled me after only hearing the sounds of the storm for the past nineteen days. I sat up, stretched and yawned. I rubbed the sleep from my eyes and looked around my neglected garden. The land hadn't fared well through the storm. Branches were broken and strewn about the ground. Flowers had been too downtrodden to raise their faces to the sun. It was a very sad sight. My beautiful home, my garden, my safe haven had been attacked. I rose to my feet and stepped out of my shelter. My toes sunk into the Earth as the ground had soaked up the water. My meadow resembled a marshland. I looked around, distraught.

I walked around my garden and tried to heal the injured. I tipped the flowers' heads to drain the water. I held their faces towards the sun's warm rays. I picked up the broken branches and set them below their respective trees. I wasn't able to reattach the appendages, but I returned them to their rightful owner.

"I'm so sorry," I said, kissing the side of the battered tree.

I hopped from large stone to large stone, avoiding the muddy ground until I reached the edge of trees that divided my garden from the surrounding land. Stepping between the trees, I stared out in horror.

The land had been demolished. Trees lie broken, toppled. Animals scurried above and below the fallen giants. Were they searching for food or were they searching for their families? I stepped out into the torn land and dropped to my knees.

"You're going to soil your dress," a familiar voice said.

I felt my heart skip a beat and a smile returned to my face. "Thaddeus! You've returned!" I said happily, as I sprung to my feet and turned to him.

He reached down and lifted me at my waist. I wrapped my arms around his neck and kissed his lips, "Of course." he smiled.

I smiled widely in return.

"Come," he said, setting me down on my feet and grabbing my hand. He led me back through the tree line into the garden. As we stepped into the garden, I saw the many gifts and provisions he had retrieved while away. There were bags strapped to a horse, a beautiful white creature. Furs lined on top of the animal. I smiled when I saw the hard work he had done while away from me. I suddenly felt very selfish. The entire time he was away, I cried and stayed under the shelter. I remained cold as I never learned how to properly build a fire. He had built one for me before he had left, but with all of the rain, the wood was far too wet for me to keep the fire ablaze. I had sulked and flooded the garden with more self-pity than rain.

"Why do you look so sad?" he raised my chin. I stared into his beautiful eyes.

"As you were away, struggling to provide for me, I wept and stayed put. I feel unworthy of your gifts."

"I'd give my life for you. Some food and furs are no comparison. You deserve the best, and I will do anything in my power to assure your comfort." he smiled then gently kissed my forehead.

I wrapped my arms around his waist and buried my face in his chest. "I missed you so very much," my voice quivered and broke.

"I missed you more," he replied, running his fingers through my hair. He reached down, pulling my arms away from his body. He knelt down and grabbed my hands. "You are far too marvelous of a creature to be so saddened."

I chuckled slightly, thinking about how silly I must appear. I wiped the tears from my eyes and sat down in front of him, resting my head on his chest. I looked out into the garden as he continued gently running his fingers through my hair.

"The garden was destroyed," I whispered, sadly.

"Then we will rebuild it," he replied.

"Many of the flowers have died."

"Then we will bring them back to life," he kissed the top of my head.

"I don't believe I can." I frowned, leaning forward.

"You have just as much of an ability as you did before The Great Divide. When you smile, the land smiles with you. You must find that happiness again." he began to rub my back again.

I flinched slightly, wincing. My back wasn't fully healed. "I found that happiness in your return." I smiled, turning to face my beloved.

"Then they will return to life, just as I said."

"You truly think so?" I asked, leaning back into his arms.

He cradled me as we stared out into the humbled garden. The white horse trotted around our outdoor home, feeding on the wet grass. We watched in amazement as the sun began to set in the distance, lighting the sky with dazzling shades of pink and purple. Although I was still saddened by the loss of God and the Archangels, I was able to overlook my sadness with Thaddeus at my side. I watched him as he rose from the shelter and built a fire, laid down our bedding and prepared a small feast.

We sat together, discussing his adventures while away. It sounded as if the land had become much more feral in the short amount of time since The Great Divide. The animals became less tamable, more timid and reluctant to settle. He told me of the struggles to catch the beautiful mare. We shared laughs as he described the process. He was fairly certain that she was carrying a foal. Judging by her size and hunger, I agreed. She seemed fairly comfortable in the garden, and didn't require any bonds to stay within the confines of the trees. I slowly approached the mare. She looked at me, slightly nervous. She neighed and stepped away apprehensively. I knelt down, grabbing a handful of tall grass and held it out in front of me. She stepped forward timidly and ate the grass from my hand. I stood slowly and gently stroked between her eyes, brushing her mane aside and staring into her beautiful black eyes.

I stepped to the side of the breathtaking animal and gently stroked her coarse coat. I paused and left my hands on her side. I closed my eyes and silently held my hands over the side of her stomach. I felt a small nudge. I smiled widely and returned to the front of the mare. I kissed her nose and knelt down for more grass. When I had finished my time with the mare I skipped across the stones back to Thaddeus. He sat, smiling, watching as the simple joys began to return to my life. He and I both knew it would merely take time. All wounds take time to heal. Though the injuries I had to my heart and soul were far deeper and would take much longer.

"She's carrying a colt!" I smiled as I skipped.

"Wonderful!"

"Yes, it's a blessing." I chuckled softly.

"There will be many blessings ahead, you needn't worry about that." he smiled.

"I'm sure there will be," I replied, reluctant to share my true feelings.

Thaddeus held out his hand and I accepted. He pulled me down to the fur bedding. I laid next to him, staring at his chiseled profile. When God created Thaddeus, He gave him the most masculine, yet breathtakingly beautiful body. His humbling hazel eyes could calm the angriest of seas. His smile could brighten the cloudiest of days. His rugged features resembled calm, snow covered mountains, rocky, yet still elegant. His hair was a mixture of beautiful, bronze and claylike Earth tones.

He stared out into the garden, scanning the tree line. He looked restless, something was on his mind. Something was bothering him. I didn't want to disturb him as he was watchful. I didn't want to break his concentration or make him aware of my anxiety. I'd much rather he stay at my side than walk through the garden patrolling. I fell asleep lying next to him; my face rested on his chest. I drifted into slumber listening to his heartbeat as it synced with my own.

I woke up to the sound of Thaddeus' laughter. I sat up and stretched, twisted my hair into a knot and stood. I walked around the side of the tree and saw him playing with a young wolf.
The wolf...

I wondered what had become of the mysterious angel. The piercing blue eyes, standing out in the sea of beings. I hadn't seen him in so long I couldn't remember what he looked like. I could only recall his eyes, blue as forget-me-nots glowing in the brilliant sunshine.

I shook the thought from my mind and returned to the present. I watched as Riley and the wolf ran back and forth. It seemed as if they were enjoying themselves. I leaned against the tree and laughed. Thaddeus stopped running, looked over towards me and smiled. The wolf barreled into him, knocking him on his back and licking his face before jumping off and bounding away again. Thaddeus laid there. I realized after a few moments, that he wasn't moving. I ran to his side. He had his eyes closed, as he drew in deep breaths. He sat up, placing his hands on his back.

"Are you alright?" I asked.

"I'm fine. My wounds are still as tender as your own," he replied.

My brows furrowed. I raised the back of his tunic and ran my fingers gently over his wounds. I could feel him shiver and wince. I placed my hands on each of his shoulder blades and closed my eyes. I saw the beautiful canvas of skin that once covered his spine in my mind. I opened my eyes and saw the horrible gashes' failing attempt to heal. On impulse, I leaned forward, kissing his injuries. He turned his face to me, concerned. I smiled warmly and placed my hands on his back again. I closed my eyes. I pictured dancing in the garden, rising off of the ground, spinning in the air. I imagined the beautiful flowers born from my footsteps, the life that rose from my kiss.

I opened my eyes again and looked at his back. There were scarred markings, but the wounds themselves had healed. I smiled brightly and wrapped my arms around his neck kissing his cheek. He reached his hand behind him and smiled, baffled.

"Thank you. You are an amazing creature. Yet, how will you heal your own?" he asked.

I took in a deep breath and shifted my position onto my hands and knees. I pressed my hands to the still damp ground. I closed my eyes and pictured my wings. I pictured the pain I felt. I wasn't able to see my own skin in my mind. I heard Thaddeus gasp.

A bloodcurdling scream pierced the air. I sat up in my bed. I was back from my dream, my memories. I wasn't sure if the scream was in my dream or in reality. My head felt like it was filled with cotton. My vision, my thoughts were clouded. I could hear raised voices outside of my bedroom. I realized then where the sound must've come from.

I struggled in the blankets, stumbling to my feet. I put my glasses on and stepped out into the kitchen. I walked out to see Riley standing over Jeremiah with his arms folded across his chest. Jeremiah was on his hands and knees, staring at the floor as he gasped for breath.

"Told you, dude." Riley shook his head.

"What did you do to me?" Jeremiah asked.

I leaned against the kitchen counter and rubbed my eyes, lifting my glasses to the top of my head. Riley looked proud of himself. He turned to me and nodded smugly. Jeremiah glanced up at me in obvious pain.

"Is this true? Is this real?" he asked me, fighting the pain. "How is this possible?"

Riley and I both looked at each other, recognizing the feeling Jeremiah had, the questions, the disbelief.

"You are who you are," I replied.

"It goes against everything I've ever believed. You know I go to church every

Sunday. You know I have my faith. How could I not have known this about myself?" He shook his head.

"It caught me off guard, as well. I thought I was agnostic!" I reminded him.

"Yeah, but I'm not surprised that *you're* a hypocrite," he jabbed.

"Dude, we're still trying to figure everything out. Sorry I used you as a guinea pig with the feather thing," Riley apologized.

"What? I thought you had touched it, too?" Jeremiah asked.

"I did. I was just trying to find out if you were the Jeremiah Connell on the list," Riley explained.

"Wish we could've found out another way." he cringed.

I stared at Riley, "Me, too. I was sleeping, asshole!" I shouted, though a smile played across my lips.

Riley helped him to his feet and assisted him to a chair. Jeremiah was leaning forward, cradling his head in his hands. He mumbled incoherently through his fingers. Riley sat down next to him at the table and showed him the list as I bandaged his wounds. He refused pain medication. I stepped out onto the patio. I felt that Riley could handle explaining the strange news to his best friend. I didn't need to get any more involved. When he was ready to discuss things with me, he'd let me know.

I stepped off the deck into the dew covered grass. The night sky was crystal clear. The moon was in its first quarter, slumping towards the western horizon. I shivered as the wind blew. A noticeable chill was in the air. I crossed my arms, stared up at the star filled sky, and thought about my dream. I stepped out further into the yard and knelt down on my knees. I folded my legs underneath me and gazed up at the heavens, then closed my eyes and pictured myself back in the garden. I imagined Thaddeus' beautiful face, the same face as my Riley. I smiled. I envisioned the flowers, the soft sea of grass waving in the wind. The sweet smell of the last remaining wildflowers filled my nose, overwhelming my senses. I took a deep breath in and leaned forward on my hands. I felt my body flush with heat, remembering the warm rays of the golden sun.

The grass was cold beneath my fingers. I smiled fondly as I remembered my connection to the Earth. I slowly breathed in through my nose and out through my mouth, concentrating my energy. I focused on my soul, my body. As I focused my energy on my past, I connected with it, spiritually. I felt heat emerge from my back, like giant white wings of light. I imagined them flapping and stretching, yearning to take flight. A shockwave of energy shot through my body, like an electrical current. It moved from my feet, up my legs, through my torso and my arms into the ground. I gasped and opened my eyes.

Looking down at my hands, under the dim moon, they looked darker than usual, though my arms glowed with a pale white in the fading light. Something was different. I rubbed at my skin, baffled. How could this have happened?

I jumped to my feet and ran to the deck. I flipped on the light and stared at my naked arms. My skin! So pale, so blank. I ran into the house, slamming the glass door behind me. I ran straight into our bedroom, into the bathroom and turned on the light. I stared at myself in the large mirror, then looked down at my ink covered hands and stumbled towards the sink. I turned on the water and let it run over hands and arms, scrubbing myself compulsively with soap, washing the ink off my hands as an artist would upon completion of a masterpiece.

Riley knocked on the door, "Edie? Are you okay?"

"I'm fine," I said instinctively.

"You don't *sound* fine. Can I come in?" he asked.

"I don't know," I replied, scrubbing my arms.

Riley twisted the knob and stepped into the bathroom. "What the hell?" he asked, looking at my reflection in the mirror.

"I don't know."

"What happened?" he asked, grabbing my arms and turned me to face him.

"I don't know!" I shouted, voice trembling.

He turned and twisted my naked arms in his hands, inspecting them in the light of the bathroom.

"I had a dream that I had healed you. You asked me how I would heal my own wounds," I explained.

"So you went outside and somehow healed yourself? Your tattoos…" he shook his head.

"I know. I mean, I don't know. They weren't wounds, they weren't an illness, a disease. I don't understand." I stared down at my white skin.

"How did you do it?" he asked, amazed.

"I was meditating. I pictured the garden. I pictured you. I felt a current, a charge, through my body and then they were gone." I shook my head.

"It's like you're reverting," he suggested.

"To what?"

"To Eden, the handmaiden, not the smart ass. Not *you*. It's amazing." he grinned.

My brow raised. What did he mean by that? "But that would mean I wasn't the girl you fell in love with," I replied, cynically.

"You've always been the girl I fell in love with. Did you forget that? Every lifetime. Every chance I could." he smiled, and then pulled me close. I nestled into his chest and slid my hands under his shirt, placing them on his back. He flinched, but didn't pull away. I closed my eyes and pictured Riley's perfect back. I imagined his skin as it once was, soft, intact. I rose up on my toes and kissed the side of his neck.

A pulsating heat began to emanate under my palms, and I lost focus for a second, thrown off by the odd sensation. I shook my head, trying to refocus. I closed my eyes, took in a deep breath, and pushed my hands firmly against his back. The pulsing raced faster, thumping against the palms of my hands like a tribal drum beat. The heat intensified. We were both breathing faster, in sync, in tune with one another. With my head rested against his chest, I listened to his heartbeat. It was like hypnosis. I was suddenly inside his body, like a mechanic in a large, damaged machine. I could see his heart, his mind, his soul. Two lines ran vertically, emitting bright red, pulsing light. It was his wounds. I could see them in my mind. I felt the pain from his injuries radiating to me. As his wounds sealed shut, the light burned white.

"Thank you," he said, softly.

I blushed bashfully.

He lifted his shirt from his back and turned looking over his shoulder into the mirror.

"Are they gone?" he asked.

I pulled the bandages aside gently. "Yes," I said, just as taken aback as he was.

"We need to show Jere! He totally needs to see this," he exclaimed excitedly.

"You can show him."

"Imagine what you could do. You don't need medicine, you don't need needles. You can heal with your hands," he said, amazed. He grabbed my hands and gently kissed their palms, then pressed them against his cheeks, cradling his face in my hands.

I stared into his hazel eyes.

"Come," he said, grabbing my hand and leading me out of the bathroom.

"I'll be there in a few." I smiled and pulled my hands from his.

After he had left I stared into the mirror. My reflection sent so many thoughts through my mind. Memories came in fragments. I felt like a jigsaw puzzle, slowly piecing myself together. I wondered how many of my pieces had gone missing over the years. I wondered if I would ever be complete again. I couldn't help but question what I truly was.

How was it that I of all people had the ability to bring life, to heal? I found it hard to believe, hard to accept. I've spent my life confused about religion, why would someone so disbelieving be trusted with such an amazing gift? I realize I've always been the same person, but still. I felt as if I wasn't worthy of such a talent. How was it that Riley seemed completely comfortable with all of it?

My life has completely changed since moving down to Louisiana. I don't even know who I am anymore. I've been disarmed and given a new weapon, my armor, torn asunder. All that I have is trapped in my mind, stored in my soul. If I only knew the combination. If I only knew the trigger to open it all. I wanted to know who I was, who I've been, who I am.

I stared blankly into the mirror. Pieces of me wished I could undo this entire event, walk through life, naive, ignorant to the epic battle ahead. Parts of me understood why Matthew took it upon himself to "save" his family from the horrors ahead. He knew the truth. He probably was able to see it clearer than I could. I seemed to see the past in fragments, but was terrified to see the future. I was horrified.

Now I understood why Gabriel wanted me to wait. He truly was saving me from *this* pain. Before I knew the truth, I was carefree. Now, I'm lost. I'm confused. I'm scared. He was right. And I felt like an idiot.

The truth was, I didn't know what was going to happen and that was a terrifying thought. But when you factor in everything else that I did know, it was suddenly too much to bear. If I wished to return to Heaven, if I chose to leave this world behind and escape the pain and anguish, I could. But in doing so, I was leaving the people I loved, the *humans* I loved, to perish. Alone. Unprotected. And that in itself was a reason I couldn't give in.

At the exact same moment, I knew that by choosing to fight this, choosing to side with the *abominations* I loved so deeply, I would perish eternally, as would they. The eternal love I've shared with Riley, *Thaddeus*, would be no more. I didn't want to make the choice. I hated that I had to choose a side. I felt the pain of The Great Divide all over again. My chest ached. I stared into the mirror. I stared at my pale skin, growing paler on a daily basis.

Gabriel, I need you. I'm sorry.

I pulled off my tank top and stared at my reflection. My body, the colorful canvas, was now blank. Ivory. Alabaster, becoming more and more angelic as my memories returned. Was that a trick? Was this a way of God attempting to remind me what I once was? What I would be, when I returned? *If I returned,* without my connection to Riley.

I couldn't bear to think about choosing anyone over my love, over my family, over my friends. I would rather die than choose. What difference does any of this make? I'm riding into battle armorless, weaponless and fragile. I don't need to question my existence; I'm not going to exist much longer.

I stared into the mirror, into my eyes, my ever-changing eyes. They were cold tonight, despite the magic at my fingertips. I felt vacant. I felt hollow. I felt like a porcelain doll. I felt as I did under my leafy canopy, helplessly hopeless. I was crumbling under the pressure. I was caving.

Repent. Repent.

The easy way out.

Repent!

I thought about the words. I thought about Lilith.

Repent...

I'd rather die with honor, alongside my friends and family.

CHAPTER TWENTY
SOLE AWAKENING

The night went much better than I had expected, once I realized my rightful place in this battle. Riley and I discussed the situation with Jeremiah. We told him about Gabriel. We told him about my dreams, Riley's dreams and the imminent death we were sure to face, if we marched ahead as planned.

Riley had shown him his back, which was now fully healed. He had also grabbed my arms and forced my sleeves up, revealing to Jeremiah my lack of tattoos. He was rather surprised to see both of our revelations. When Riley explained my *ability*, he allowed me to heal his wounds as well. I didn't realize until after healing Jeremiah, how tiring it was to do so.

Jeremiah had the same concerns in mind that Riley and I had discussed, and an added fear, as well. As he reminded us, Riley and I have spent lifetime after lifetime together. But what about Melanie? Lamar? Our families? They were human. They were just numbers in the eyes of God. We knew better. They were wonderful people who had brightened our lives. They were good souls and deserved to live their lives to the fullest. Thinking about their fragile existence reminded me of all the memories. Mom, my absolute best friend. Daddy, my hero. My brothers. My nieces and nephews. My aunts and uncles. Lamar, my partner in crime. Our crime? Optional stupidity. We shared a ridiculous sense of humor.

"We have to do something. And we're probably going to have to move quick. Gabriel never gave us a timetable of what's to come. All we know is that this giant storm that's terrorizing the nation is the start," Riley explained.

"How can we prepare? How are we even going to fight?" I asked.
Riley and Jeremiah looked at each other and both grinned. I was instantaneously nervous.

"Oh ye of little faith. If we can survive Flint, Michigan, we can survive an invasion," Riley mused.

"We can head to the station and load up on guns and ammo. They won't really notice it. Well, it might go unnoticed if we take the confiscated shit anyway," Jeremiah suggested.

"That's probably because we're the ones that usually do the inventory and logging," Riley shot back with a chuckle.

"Yeah. We could definitely do that. We could just remove them from the log, entirely," Jeremiah nodded to himself, satisfied.

"It's totally how I envisioned the Apocalypse, except it's not zombies. I never expected to be killed off by angels instead," Riley stated.

"Do we have any other options? Is there another choice?"

"Yeah. We choose to repent. We choose God," I replied honestly.

Riley stared at his best friend. He studied his expression. He knew that that wasn't something farfetched. Jeremiah had his moments of sin, but had always been a religious man, whether it was out of fear or love. I wasn't exactly sure. We didn't debate religious views. That's a slippery slope.

"You know this puts me in a really tough spot," Jeremiah replied.

Riley's expression was unreadable. "I know. I'm not asking you to choose me over your religious beliefs," Riley said somberly.

"It's not just that. I'm pretty steadfast in my convictions. I'm pretty sure I've gotten it right this time around. I'm more concerned about Lamar, Mike and Lana, Mel," he reminded us. "I'd fight for them, for my family. But what if it isn't the right thing to do?"

"We'll figure this all out," Riley attempted to reassure us both.

I got up from the table and walked to the kitchen. I made myself a glass of iced tea and sat down on the couch, turning on the TV. The death toll associated with the giant storm cells was now somewhere around nine thousand. The homeless were innumerable. The missing? They couldn't even guess.

Riley walked over to the couch and sat next to me, Azrael followed.

"How are you?"

"I'm doing okay. Kind of tired. How are you holding up?" I inquired.

"I'm doing much better, thanks." he nodded.

Jeremiah's phone rang. He stepped outside and began a quiet conversation with the caller. Riley and I flipped from channel to channel. Almost every station had some sort of news coverage ranging from the storms, to the war ever-brewing, to the rising conflicts in the East, to the strange lights in the sky. Ah, yes. The "strange lights" in the sky. Conspiracy theorists claimed it was aliens. Ha. Evangelicals claimed it was God's gift. Ha ha. The truth was the exact opposite. God's curse was more like it.

The red tide had spread, plaguing all connecting waterways. It was now even affecting the Mississippi River. I wanted to go check it out. I needed to see the red waters. I needed to see the bridge. *Jump.* The connection was now even more noticeable. Matthew swan diving into the Mississippi and the red tide is now in the river. *Jump!* Thinking about that dream sent shivers down my spine. *JUMP!* My skin crawled.

How was everyone so oblivious to the obvious? Even without the knowledge that I had, even before I knew the truth, I knew something was wrong. I knew something was amiss. Were people choosing to play ignorant? I wondered, since the suicide rate had increased, were people leaving notes? I wondered if anyone else out there had these sugarplum visions in their minds. I wondered how many others had taken their life, the life of their loved ones to save them from the hellfire and damnation.

Jeremiah emerged from the patio and sighed, "Looks like they need me to come in. They're finally investigating that plant. I guess there's some rather interesting shit they've found."

"Want me to come with you?" Riley asked.

"I'm not sure that's such a good idea. They're pretty pissed at you for not showing up for hurricane duty. I'm not sure how long your suspension is." he curled his lip, reluctant to bear the bad news.

"Shit, I needed to go get some things, too." Riley's brow furrowed.

Jeremiah began stepping towards the door. "I'll get a hold of you tomorrow. We'll get something lined up."

"Be careful," I said, as he unlocked the deadbolt.

"I'm a heavenly being. I'm not worried," he replied with a wink.

"*Were!* You *were* a heavenly being!" I shouted to him as he stepped outside.

I got up and walked to the kitchen, glancing at the clock on the stove. It was 12:17am. I had only been asleep a few hours, yet it felt like days. I wasn't well rested, just well-traveled in my slumber. Riley walked up behind me and wrapped his arms around my waist, resting his chin on my shoulder.

"I think we should call it a night and get back to this in the morning," he suggested.

"We need to walk Azrael."

"I did, before you got up," he replied.

I continued to resist, "I need to find out more information."

"You need to sleep. You need to be well rested. You aren't much use to me delirious," he reasoned.

"Fine," I caved.

I walked to the pantry and filled the animals' food dishes. Rufio chirped and stalked me, circling my feet like a shark out for blood, Azrael slinked behind. I walked into the bedroom and pulled off my pajama pants. I put my glasses in their case and retreated to the bathroom for my nightly bedtime ritual.

When I had finished, I climbed into bed and settled in my spot. Riley turned on the TV and put it on cartoons, turned off the light and curled up in bed with me. He gave Rufio his bed time allowance of snacks and handed Azrael a couple of biscuits that he so generously crumbled into the sheets.

Once our *kids* were done munching on their treats, they climbed into their respective positions and settled in for the night. I wrapped my arms around Riley and kissed his back. The last thought I remember having before falling asleep, was that I needed to see Gabriel. I needed to apologize for how I acted. I needed to thank him for the list and find out if there was anything else that could help us with the search. I needed to see him, even if it was for the last time.

I awoke in a field. The grain around me rolled in the wind like waves. I stood up and stepped out into the sea of gold. Turning towards the *sun*, I swept my hair from my face, and then began walking against the wind. I held my hands out, brushing the tops of the grain as I walked. My flowing white skirt billowed in the breeze; my hair blew behind me like a fiery mane.

The ground was firm. Broken stalks stabbed at my bare feet. I ignored the pain and pressed on, recognizing the rocky cliffs ahead of me. I continued forward and stepped out onto the jagged ledge, staring out into the angry sea beneath me. It crashed into the side of the cliff, splashing on the rocks below. It was a strange juxtaposition, seeing the waves of the land and the waves of the sea, divided only by the base of this solid crag of rock.

"Gabriel!" I yelled out into the wind, where my voice was swiftly carried away.

I closed my eyes and breathed in the warm salty air. The smell of the sea was unmistakable. It brought back so many memories. I sat down on the precipice, pulling my knees to my chest, staring out into the choppy ocean as it churned. I thought about the wonders of the world, the natural beauty I had once helped God create. *And what color would you choose for the tumultuous seas?*

I looked to the sky. The heavy clouds sagged and twisted. A single opening in the billows appeared, sending down a bright spotlight on the rocky cliffs I had made my vantage. I watched as a bright figure emerged from the opening.

"Hello, Eden," Gabriel said as he hovered over the ridge.

I smiled a greeting, "Hey there."

He gently landed by my side and offered me his hand. I took it in mine and rose to my feet. He held out his arms and I stepped towards him, hugging him. I rested my head on his chest for a moment. He held me tightly, neither of us speaking until I pulled away.

"You called for me?" he asked.

"Yes. I wanted to apologize," I began, staring into his dull grey eyes.

"You owe me no apologies. I am the one who wanted your forgiveness." he smiled.

"You didn't do anything. You tried to convince us to do the right thing. I appreciate your concern," I said, hanging my head dejected.

He laughed loudly. The sound carried on the wind. "I only ever wanted what was best for you. Thaddeus is a wonderful man. Although I do miss having time to spend with you myself, I do understand. As your memories return, hopefully your cognizance of our bond returns, as well."

"What?" I asked, confused.

"When God created all of us, he created *us* together. We share a piece of each other. We weren't lovers. We were siblings, twins. Conjoined by spirit, linked by soul," he stated, holding my hands in his.

"I don't understand. Why didn't you tell me? Why didn't I know? Riley knows, doesn't he?" I asked. "That explains why he called you my brother." I felt sheepish. I thought about my dreams. I thought about the three prophecies we shared, the instant connection, the safety I felt with Gabriel, now that I realized who he was.

"You know just as well as I do that as your memory returns, it's fragmented. There's only so much interfering that I can do. Once God realizes that our link has been rekindled, I will be forbidden to speak to you, unless it is to carry out a message." his brows furrowed.

"How have you been able to come to me?" I asked.

"Every so often, throughout history, God has sent me down to the Earth. He sends me down with a message, a proclamation, a declaration. When I've been able, I've found you. I've spent time with you, which you've seen in your dreams. I'm unable to come to you on my own, outside of your mind, otherwise," he explained.

"But, Gabe… My Gabe. What about my *older* brother?" I asked.

"Anthony was a wonderful being. He shared much of his past experiences with your mother. Though she doesn't *know* of our past, directly, she has had spiritual dreams, envisioning her children walking hand in hand, in the cloudy fields of Heaven. When she gave birth to her son, there was only one name befitting." he sat down on the rocky ledge, dangling his legs over the side.

"So my grandpa told her about the *two of us*?" I asked.

"He told her stories of the beautiful angel twins, Eden and Gabriel. From there, he imprinted us into her dreams. She named you both, after you and me. As a dedication to her father."

"That's wonderful. So, my grandpa remembered us, he remembered everything before The Great Divide?" I asked.

"It's almost as if we all have gifts, abilities different from one angel to another. They're pieces of our soul, pieces of our personality. You of course, know your gifts. You're a healer, a creator of life. Anthony, I mean Roy, your grandfather, had the gift of eternal memory; infinite recollection. Most of it will return to him as he ages, and by the end of his time, he will have full memory of the past," Gabriel explained.

"Wow, that's amazing. So he shared that with my mother. She's so spiritually receptive." I smiled fondly.

"When you were born, Gabriel, your *earthly* brother, was given glimpses of our past, as a gift from me. Though he was far too young to understand them, he felt the same protectiveness for you that I have. I engrained in him the importance of your bond."

"Well, thanks. But it didn't seem to keep us from acting like assholes to each other growing up." I chuckled.

"Although the two of you have fought far more than the two of us ever did, he shares the same love for you that I do. Perhaps you should go easy on him." he smiled, staring out into the violent sea.

"Go easy on him, or go easy on *you*?" I mused.

"Yes." he winked as the corner of his mouth raised in a smirk.

"Yes, you, or yes, both?" I laughed.

"Both."

"So, what you're saying is that my mom had visions of *us*. You and I. Which is why she chose the names that she did, for my brother and I? Then you filled his mind with your memories of our life?" I asked, attempting to clarify the tale.

"In essence. Your brother was named after me, your *soul* twin. You have always been Eden. Your name goes with your soul. Your mother was simply more perceptive than most. Your grandfather definitely helped with that."

"Was it a coincidence that Anthony was born, then became my grandpa?" I asked.

"No, it was no coincidence. As you'll find out, following the list, we're all connected. Our lives are intertwined. One way or another, we are joined. That of course, includes all of you," he explained.

"That makes sense." I nodded as I pictured the list. "So, I have to ask, when you showed me the previous dreams attempting to convince me to return to Heaven, it wasn't just for God, was it?" I asked, speculatively.

"No, absolutely not," he answered, instantly. "I wished for your return, just as much." he stared at the intemperate waters.

"I'm so sorry," I whispered softly. The wind carried my words, stirring up a chilling breeze. "I never intended to hurt you. I never wanted to hurt God." my voice weakened.

"Love is a very unpredictable beast." he leaned back on his hands.

We sat quietly for a few minutes. Staring at the raging sea, the stormy sky reflected the turmoil churning in the waters. He reached over and grabbed my hand. He held it in his own, squeezing gently.

"You miss being able to fully connect yourself with Lilith, don't you?" I asked, finally able to understand.

"More than anything. We've both made such a huge sacrifice for the greater good, even for humanity." he frowned, reminded of his loss.

"How will I tell Riley?" I asked.

"You needn't say a thing. He knows we share a spiritual connection. He knows we're soul siblings. You don't seem to realize his power of perception. He can see through any guise. He knows the truth, whether he chooses to inform you of that fact or not."

I chuckled, "Yeah, he kind of blew that tonight."

"I'm not surprised. He's very honest with you," he replied with a snicker.

"Will I see you again?" I asked, teary eyed.

"If you choose to remain Earthbound, I'm afraid not. I don't know if I'll be able to return to your dreams either. Time is running short. God must be aware."

"When will this end?" I asked.

"Samhain," he replied. "The first of November, if you make it until then unscathed."

"If I choose the Earth, if I choose Thaddeus again, what will happen to my soul when this is all over with?" I asked, afraid of the truth.

"You will be lost. A waste of a beautiful soul. A wonderful heart, a precious mind, simply discarded," his voice quivered as he spoke. "I wish that you would reconsider," he muttered softly.

"My mind isn't made up." I turned to him, with sincerity in my eyes. The wind blustered heavily. Thunder rumbled in the distance.

"We don't have long. I have to return soon," he said, squeezing my hand.

"What are our odds?" I asked hastily.

"You know the answer to that. Well, as of this moment."

None.

"How will I know which are the other angels? There are multiple people with the same names," I asked while I still had time.

"You'll *know*. I can't do this for you," he replied, rising to his feet.

"Please don't go." my eyes welled with tears. I reached up for my soul twin.

"Come with me," he said, gently pulling my fingers.

"You know I can't do that," my voice fell flat as I pulled my fingers from his hand.

"Goodbye," he said softly, tears in his eyes.

"Goodbye," I mouthed, unable to utter the words.

I sat up with a gasp, tears flowing from my eyes. *Goodbye, my brother.* I cradled my knees, burying my face in the sheets. I sobbed as I felt the pain radiating from my chest. Riley propped himself up on his elbow, rubbing my back. "Bad dream?"

"Gabriel's gone," I replied, between sniffles.

"He'll be back. You know he won't leave you helpless," he said, wiping the tears from my cheek.

"I don't know," I replied, stifling my tears.

"Any news?"

"November 1st. It'll all be over then," I said, wiping my cheeks.

"*Day of the Dead?* All Saint's Day, very fitting," Riley flouted.

I reached over to the side table, turned on the small lamp and grabbed my glasses, then slid them on and pulled my hair back into a lazy ponytail. I grabbed my phone and looked at the display. *Friday, October 10th 7:49am.* We only had a few weeks left to prepare, a few weeks to spend with each other… a few weeks to *live.*

"We have to get to work," I said, staring at my phone.

"Yup," he stretched while yawning, and then fell back onto his pillow with a grin.

I looked at my long list of missed calls. They weren't missed, they were *ignored.* I hadn't gone into work on Monday. I hadn't called them. I hadn't answered their calls to me. As far as I knew, I was probably fired. And for all they knew, I could've been dead. I flipped through the list of contact phone numbers in my phone, and stopped on **Gabe**. I wanted to call him. I wanted to tell him I was sorry for always being such a bitch to him. I wanted to tell him I loved him, and that he'd always be my brother, my protector. I set my phone down. Now wasn't the time.

I got out of bed and walked to the dresser, grabbed some clean clothes and went into the bathroom. I closed the door behind me and slipped off my tank top and underwear. I stared at my figure in the mirror. My naked flesh reminded me of the truth; *my armor is gone.* My wings had been ripped from my flesh. My tattoos had flowed off my skin, like toxins shed through sweat. My heavenly protection had been taken, and now my soul twin. Everything I had ever been able to hide behind had been stripped from me. At least I still had Riley.

I turned on the shower and stepped inside, standing motionless under the warm water as it caressed my skin, attempting to comfort me. I breathed in the steam, filling my lungs with the humid reality. *Jump… drown with me.* My thoughts were racing. I closed my eyes under the warm running water as flashes of images flickered in my mind like a stop motion movie. I saw bits and pieces of my past, my life in fast forward. I opened my eyes under the free flowing waters. My eyes burned momentarily, adjusting to the spray as the tiles came into focus. I wiped the water from my eyes and smiled.

I was complete.

I was a phoenix, born again in the flesh.

I was the strong woman, the muse, the creator of beauty and giver of life.

My soul had woken like an angry sleeping dragon, *my sole awakening.* I finally knew *exactly* what I had to do. And I was no longer afraid.

Chapter Twenty One
Altered Ulterior Motives

My family has always been religious. We were brought up in a household that was very devout, very spiritual. I was raised going to children's classes and attending religious functions on a regular basis. It was a principle of the faith to investigate other religions, to ensure that we understood the inner working of all of man's religions. I researched all of them and had a very good understanding of each.

Every religion has its key factors, encouraging closeness with God. They may all have a different name for Him, but the premise is the same. This idea was the only one I truly believed in. Some religions have this philosophy that they are the *right* choice, while everyone outside of their organization will be damned for all of eternity. Ha. That's funny. If they only knew, we were *all* damned.

It is for these reasons, these atrocities that I decided long ago that I was better off without a religious tag. It's not that I think I was taught wrong, I feel like my parents did a wonderful job. It just seems like religion drives too large of a wedge between humans. I wonder what people would think of themselves, if they knew the truth? Would they still be religious if they knew their life was a mockery? A satire.

I thought about my parents. I thought about how hard they tried to make sure that I had a very stable upbringing. They gave everything they could to make sure I was never hungry, that I always felt loved, that I had a good education. They were always so supportive of me. They were so amazing. I knew deep in my soul, that they were the type of people that would be allowed into Heaven. That gave me more comfort than I could even describe. They have always believed in me. They were always my number one fans, my own personal pep squad. They always backed me, no matter what my decisions were. They were the first people to praise me for a good job, and the first to give me a shoulder to cry on when things crumbled. They were the parents that every kid wanted to have.

They knew I would never intentionally lie to them. They knew that I was a very truthful person. Yet I couldn't help but wonder what they would have to say when I told them the truth. How did you tell the two people that raised you, that changed your diapers, that helped you with your homework, that grounded you, and attended your wedding that you aren't the person they think you are?

How did you tell the people who know you better than you know yourself, that you aren't *human*? How could you tell the people that you love that you're a renegade angel, damned for all eternity to walk the Earth with a mortal life, reincarnating repeatedly? How could you convince people with different religious beliefs, that what they believe is wrong?

I paced the patio with my cell phone in hand. I knew that I needed to make the call. I needed to tell my parents, whether they chose to believe me or not. I needed to get this off my chest. I hoped that they would hear me out, but I also knew how farfetched it sounded. I stared at my phone, pulled up my mother's number and hit send.

"Hello?" she answered.

"Hey, Momma."

"Hey, baby! How are you?" I could hear that smile in her voice.

"I'm…" I paused. I really didn't know how to answer that.

"Are you there?" she asked.

"Yeah, I'm here. And I'm okay. How are you and Daddy?" I dodged the question.

"We're doing good. Your father's off running some errands. Are you sure everything's okay?" she asked.

"Yeah, basically."

"*Basically*? Baby, what's wrong?" there was obvious concern in her voice.

"Mom, I really need to talk to you. I need you to listen to me very carefully," I began.

"Oh God, what's wrong? Are you pregnant?" she panicked.

"No! No. It's nothing like that. I wish it was that simple."

"Damn." She wanted me to have her grandbabies.

"It's really hard for me to explain. I don't really know where to start," I said.

"Are you gay? Are you and Riley splitting up?" she continued guessing.

"No! Everything's fine with me and Riley." I chuckled.

"Did you kill someone?" she asked.

"No, but I might have to." I cringed and dodged the question again. "Why are you asking me silly questions?"

"Well, honey, it sounds like something big has happened. Just talk to me. Tell me what's on your mind," she pleaded.

"Promise me you won't laugh," I ordered.

"What's going on?" she asked, avoiding my last statement.

"Okay. Um, did Pawpaw ever tell you stories about angels?" I asked.

"Maybe, when I was little. I don't really remember anything specific. It's possible though, he was Catholic. Why?" She sounded confused.

"Okay, how did you pick out our names?"

"Please stop with the riddles. What's going on with you?" she sounded more worried than confused now.

"Please, just answer me," I begged.

"I had a dream when I was younger. I saw the two of you holding hands and playing in a field. It was a beautiful dream. When I asked the two of you what your names were, you said, 'I'm Eden and this is my brother Gabriel'. I instantly fell in love with the names."

"What if I told you, that was real? What you saw was in fact me and my brother Gabriel." I knew this wasn't going well. It didn't even make sense in my own mind.

"It was a dream. I loved it, but that's what it was. What are you getting at?"

"If I told you I was a zombie, would you believe me?" I asked. "If I told you I was a vampire, would you believe me?"

"No," she stated simply. "Did you stop taking your medication?"

"If I told you I was a fairy, would you believe me?" I continued to question her.

"Unfortunately, no. That wouldn't surprise me with you, though."

"If I told you I was an angel, would you believe me?" I asked and winced. The phone line went silent. I continued, "If I told you that Pawpaw, Riley and I were angels, would you believe it?"

"I... I don't know," she said. "I do believe Pawpaw *is* an angel, and you're a close second, but not Riley." she chuckled.

"Look, I know it sounds crazy. It's hard for me to even explain. But I need you to stay open minded."

"I'm listening," she said, then went silent.

I didn't even know how to start the explanation. "There was a time when we all were in Heaven. We were God's creations, His companions. He decided that He wanted us to be individuals. He gave us our own traits, our own minds. Some of us were given a piece of another's soul, linking us as twins. Gabriel and I are an example of that link."

"So Gabe is an angel?" she asked, confused.

"What you saw in your dream, *was in fact*, me and my brother Gabriel, but not *your* son Gabriel," I continued. "My brother is God's personal messenger, his errand boy. And my soul twin."

I continued with the story. I explained about meeting Thaddeus in my garden, how I was a muse and created life. I told her about how we became so independent and selfish that God told us to choose Him or the Earth. I explained what happened at The Great Divide. I told her about reincarnation and the fact that the only way we would return to Heaven was if we corrected our mistakes, if we repented.

"So you're telling me that my dad isn't with God?" she asked, sadly.

"No, he isn't. Not yet," I replied.

"I don't like that. The only thing that gave me relief when he died, was that I knew he was in the Abha Kingdom and that he wasn't in pain anymore." her voice shook as she spoke.

"Mom, you don't understand. It isn't a bad thing. It isn't like he's being punished. He made the choice to remain earthbound," I clarified.

"So if what you're saying is true, then he's out there somewhere. My dad is still alive?" she asked.

"Not exactly. Yes, he's alive, but he isn't the same man. He'd be a boy. He's a teenager. I doubt he has any recollection of his past," I tried to simplify.

"Oh," she replied, morose.

"It isn't bad. Don't look at it that way."

"Wouldn't that mean that you aren't really my daughter?" she asked.

"No, no. I'm still your daughter. You gave birth to me. I'm a part of you, but I'm much more than *just your* daughter, at the same time."

"Edie, this is a lot to take in. Honestly, this sounds like an amazing story, but it sounds like something you'd see in a movie, or read in a fiction novel," she replied. "And a more obvious explanation is that you are simply off your medication, and I should truly be worried about you."

"I know, Momma. But there's more." I sighed.

"What do you mean?" she asked.

"God never intended for humans to be born. Reproduction was a gift God gave us. When we had a perfect union, we'd conceive and deliver a cherub. When God and the Archangels left the Earth, we were still able to reproduce. Which is where humans came from."

There was an awkward silence. "What are you getting at?" she asked.

"God is sick of the wars. He's disgusted by the murdering, the raping, the way we've destroyed His perfect planet. He's sending down His army to reclaim the Earth." I rubbed my right temple methodically. I was trying to calm the screaming voices, urging me to stop telling my mom everything.

She sat silently.

"There's going to be a war. The human race, as we know it, is going to be exterminated."

"Well, doesn't that just suck," she replied.

"Yeah, it does. And I'm not kidding. I'm not on drugs; well, other than the ones I'm supposed to be on. This isn't some conspiracy theory. I know this for a fact."

"I want you to really think about what you're saying. I know you've been under a lot of stress and I know that you have nightmares. But are you really trying to tell me that the end of the world is coming?" she tried to negotiate with me like I had explosives strapped to my brain.

Red wire? Green wire?

"I'm not joking. I'm not fibbing. I'm not messing around. It doesn't matter how you word it, I'm telling you the truth." I was getting frustrated.

"I really think you need to go lay down. Try and relax. You sound exhausted." *Beep, beep, beep... BOOM!*

"Alright, well. I can see we aren't getting anywhere in this conversation. Maybe we can discuss this later, once you start noticing all of the crazy shit on the news," I jabbed.

"*Eden Quinn! Don't be mean,*" she ordered.

"I'm sorry, you're right. I need to relax. I'll talk to you later." I didn't need to rest. I needed someone to hear me out and believe me.

"Don't just blow me off because I don't know how to take this. You know how I feel religiously. It just goes against my beliefs. I'm sorry. Give me some time to take in what you said," she reasoned with me.

"That's fine. I'm not going to argue with you. Regardless of how you feel now, or what you believe spiritually, that's all going to change, and soon. I've got stuff to do. You sit back and think about what I told you."

"I will. Call me back later. I love you."

"Love you, too," I replied and hung up.

I lit a cigarette and tossed my phone onto the patio table. I knew it was a hopeless cause, why did I even waste my breath? I sat at the table for a few minutes, trying to calm myself down. I wasn't mad at her; I was frustrated that I have to deal with something so bizarre. I was mad that I had to live a stupid lie. I was mad that I only had a few weeks to spend with the people I love.

I put out my cigarette and stared at the sky. I shook my head and went inside. Riley had already gotten to work, trying to find the others. He still had the ability to log into the police data base and cross reference our research. He clicked through files, typed in names, addresses, everything that we had available.

"So, find anything?" I asked, leaning over his shoulder.

"Well, we know where we live. We know where Jere is. And we now know where to find two others." he turned to me and smiled.

"Oh yeah? Which two?" I asked.

"Mary Elwood is in a nursing home in Florida. While you were on the phone with your mother, I took it upon myself to do some snooping. So, I found the nursing home's name, I called and told them I was a police officer from Baton Rouge, and had reasons to believe Ms. Elwood had been involved in a hit and run."

"And they said?" I prompted.

"They said it was impossible. That she's bedridden and has Alzheimer's. Apparently she hasn't gotten out of bed in over a year. I asked if she had any family, any relatives that might share her name. They said no, that she's alone. She never married or had children. She was a nun. All of her immediate family is dead. She's 96 years old," Riley said incredulously. "I told them it must've just been a mix up. So now we know. She's not going to be of much use to us."

"So what do we do? Do we find her?" I asked.

"I don't know. She may be safe. What difference does it make, anyway? If she doesn't die in the next two weeks, she will when everything goes tits up," he said.

"I just don't know if we should try to tell her, or if it would be a wasted effort. I'd hate to waste a day driving to Florida just to try and talk to a crazy old bird who doesn't even know who she is. Maybe she became a nun to plead her case."

"For all we know, she may have all the facts already. She may have already learned her lesson. She obviously led a religious life," he suggested.

"Yeah, you're right. I guess we shouldn't waste the time." I stared at my personal investigator. "So who was the other one that you found?"

"Heh. Funny story. I didn't even have to do much searching for this dude. He had a pretty lengthy rap sheet. Which is great! I'm thankful that there's one of us still around." Riley laughed and pulled up the screen.

"Paul Lee, eh?" I read though the reports. "Ugh. Michigan, of course. My least favorite place in the world." I cringed.

"I'm sure he'll be really useful. He's a bit of a hotheaded scrapper, but then again, he always was argumentative. All of his charges are for bar fights. Looks like he's taken out quite a few people at a place called, Booze & Caboose," he snickered.

My eyebrow raised. "Booze & Caboose? Is it a bar dedicated to trains? Or, ooooh... It isn't a 'bar' is it?" I laughed.

"Not from the looks of it, no." he laughed.

"Lovely. Sounds like a real winner," I remarked.

"Never know. He *was* a great guy. He may be a real asset." he shrugged.

"Or a real ass hat."

"Only one way to find out."

"You remember him or something?" I asked.

"I've had dreams about my *army*. He was in it. Well, Paul was. Hopefully he's the same," Riley replied.

I nodded. I understood what he meant a lot better now. I had no memory of the guy.

"So what do we know so far? There are you and I, Jere is still undecided, Mary's old and out of her mind so she's out, then Paul? What if he doesn't even want to get involved?" I asked.

"Something tells me if we offer him some whiskey, tell him there will be chicks and promise a good fight, he'll be in. At least, if he's anything like he used to be." he smirked.

"Sounds like a good offer, I suppose. How are we gonna get him?" I asked.

"At Booze & Caboose, of course. I have his address now. Maybe we should fly up there and talk to him. And if I remember correctly, he had a *brother*. I don't remember his name."

"I guess we don't need our savings anymore. We might as well make the trip quicker," I agreed.

"Yeah, if you want to start looking into tickets, I'll try to find some of the others." he turned his attention back to his computer.

I grabbed my laptop and carried it to the dining room table, grabbed a drink and settled in for a day of research and frustration. Riley cracked his knuckles and adjusted himself in his seat. He started typing and scanning pages of names and numbers. After about thirty minutes, we were a little further ahead. After researching flights, I realized that most of the airlines were grounded due to the weather. It would be nigh impossible to find one without paying with a vital organ and risking our lives in the process. It was a price we were willing to pay if it was necessary. We decided that we'd buy tickets once we knew where everyone lived.

"Ah. Found another," he said with a grin.

"Who is it?"

"Your grandpa. He was a little harder to find than I expected. He's so young and hasn't gotten into shit, so he doesn't have a record. I found the high school he goes to though, and his school picture. He goes to the same school as Rendon and Kadence. Weird, huh?" he smiled.

"My grandpa... *Anthony's* in Houston? That's insane!" I was surprised by that.

"Yeah," he nodded.

"Wow, it is a small world." I couldn't believe that not only did he live in the same city as two of my brothers, but he just so happened to go to school with two of my nephews.

"We'll have to go to Houston at some point. I need to see them anyway," I said. "Or maybe, we should have everyone gather at my parents."

The mood became very somber. Both of us thought about the fact that we were going to have to say goodbye to our families. I wanted to just show up on their doorsteps with a smile and hugs, but I'm sure they'd suspect something. They'd assume I had ulterior motives. They all knew I was normally really busy with work, so I was sure there'd be a ton of questions. Couldn't a girl just show up and visit her family without having *end of the world* type news? Hmm. Guess not.

"Yeah. I'll have to talk to my mom at some point soon. Maybe she should go to Texas, too."

"Sounds like a plan," I agreed.

There were a few moments of silence before Riley broke it with a loud slap on his computer desk. "And another!" he shouted, looking at me over his shoulder.

"Who now?" I asked.

"Jonah. He's in Boston." he stood up and tacked some more notes on the wall, corresponding with the names. We stared at our masterpiece, marveled by our discoveries. As the day progressed we managed to find the information for all but one of the angels. We found that Victoria Stewart was living in Chicago. Tom Hatcher was in Memphis. Brandon Sullivan was in Seattle. Yet so far, we weren't able to locate Elijah Ryan.

We found it kind of odd that there were groups of us that stuck together throughout history, but the others apparently spread out, despite Gabriel's comment. Anthony and I were linked in this lifetime; Riley and I were linked together in every lifetime. Jeremiah and Riley have been close throughout history. They both served as protectors before and after The Great Divide, which was when their friendship kindled.

So were any of the others in contact with each other? I supposed there was only one way to find out. We were going to have to travel. We opted against plane tickets, since we were headed to multiple locations. We decided we were going to ask Lamar to come feed Rufio and we'd take Azrael with us. I grabbed my phone and dialed Lamar's phone number.

"Hey," he answered.

"Howdy!" I shot back.

"What's up?"

"I have a *huge* favor to ask of you." I bit my lip.

"Oh, yeah? What's that?" he asked nervously.

"Do you think you could keep an eye on Rufio for a few days? You don't need to take him home, just stop by to make sure he has food and water," I asked nonchalantly.

"Wait, what? Why?" he replied.

"Riley and I need to head out of town for a few days. It's kind of a road trip," I answered.

"Little last minute, huh?"

"A little." I cleared my throat.

"You guys gonna be home in a little bit?"

"Yep. Coming over?" I winced and punched myself in the leg.

"Yeah, I'll be there in a few," he replied, and then hung up.

I suddenly had the feeling that Lamar wasn't the right person to ask to watch the cat. He was going to ask questions, then get himself involved. Although I see him as one of my closest friends and I love to have him around, the last thing I could have possibly asked of him or wanted for him, is for him to get wrapped up in this war.

Riley turned and saw my irritated expression.

"Didn't go well, I take it?" he asked. "Did he say no?"

"Lamar knows we're up to something. He stopped asking questions and said he was coming over." my brow furrowed in frustration.

"You could've told him no or lied."

"Why would I do that?"

"Good point. You suck at lying," he replied, turning back to the wall.

"Do you think we should take this stuff down?" I asked. "You know, maybe it would be best that we don't look crazy."

"No. I think it'll validate our point more, if he wants the truth," Riley answered.

"Do you really think we should tell him?" I frowned and slid my arms into my hoodie.

"He has the right to know," he replied simply.

We printed out a map of the U.S. and marked the spots that were home to the angels. We discussed a route that would encompass all of the locations, and began to strategically plan the next couple of days. We were going to be on the road a lot and weren't going to have much time to stop and relax. But we needed to gather everyone that was willing to stand at our side.

A short time later, Lamar knocked on the front door and I opened it with a smile. He walked in and folded his arms across his chest. His eyes narrowed as he looked from Riley's face to mine, and then cracked a grin.

"What are you two doing?" he asked suspiciously.

"Oh, nothing," I replied with the same awkward smile.

He laughed. "You suck at lying, Edie. Why do you even try?"

"I seem to hear that a lot lately." I smirked.

"If you really want to know what's going on, we'll tell you," Riley said, coming up behind me.

"Riley!" I uttered through my clenched teeth.

"Well, if it's none of my business, then no, I don't want to know. Edie just made it sound so, *sneaky*, so fun!"

"Way to go," Riley said to me, with raised brow.

"Yeah, this is my fault." I walked to the fridge and grabbed three beers. I popped the tops of the bottles and walked back over to Riley and Lamar.

"So what's all of this shit? Who are these people?" Lamar pointed to the wall.

"It's kind of hard to explain. It's complicated," I said, handing him a beer.

"Try me."

"Edie and I decided that we needed some extra money, so we found these people on the FBI wanted list. We're gonna be bounty hunters," Riley said, straight-faced.

Lamar shot me a glance and waited for my reaction. I could see him counting down in his mind.

Three. Two. One.

And I cracked. "The Apocalypse is coming. We're going to gather up the last remaining angels on Earth so that we can build a suitable army to try to save all of humanity from extinction," I said in one breath, then winced.

Lamar laughed. "I think I believe the bounty hunter story more. I told you, you *suck* at lying!"

I stared at him without the slightest hint of sarcasm. He studied my expression.

"Holy shit! You aren't lying?" Lamar stumbled over his words as his grin fell flat.

"I figured you wouldn't believe me if I told you the truth." Riley shrugged.

"Well, yeah. I wouldn't believe *you*. You bullshit all the time," Lamar said excitedly.

"I know it sounds absolutely insane. I really didn't want you to even know, but I don't think we have much of a choice anymore. It's going to happen whether you know about it or not." I frowned.

"I guess that explains a lot. I mean, these storms have gotten out of control, we're on the brink of a third world war, the oceans are toxic, people are killing themselves left and right. How long have you guys known?" Lamar sat down on the arm of the couch, steadying himself with his free hand.

"A couple of days," Riley said somberly.

"Does this have something to do with that creepy vampire bum that was here?" Lamar asked, staring at the floor.

"You mean Gabriel?" I asked, confused.

"Yeah," Lamar replied. "Creepy vampire bum guy, Gabriel."

"Kind of. He's one of us," I muttered.

"*Us?*" Lamar shot a glance at me and Riley.

"What do you mean, us? How are you involved?" he asked, shaking his head in disbelief.

"I need another beer," Riley chimed in, walking to the fridge. I hadn't even noticed how quickly he had drained the one he was holding only a moment before.

Lamar slammed his beer in response. "I need another one, too."

Azrael sauntered out of the bedroom and approached Lamar as he stood by the kitchen.

"Tell me the truth, guys. Don't leave me clueless," Lamar urged, gently patting Azrael.

"I still think you should stay out of this." I pleaded with my eyes.

Riley, Lamar and I grabbed replacement beers and headed to the table, beginning a discussion about the past. We explained to Lamar everything that we could. Riley told him about having dreams about our past and how Gabriel also "showed him visions", which I didn't know about. Lamar was very interested and peppered us with questions through the whole exchange.

We spent a few hours and killed off a few six packs before we were done telling him the back story and filling him in on the current situation. I was very surprised by how quickly he accepted the truth without skepticism. He realized we weren't lying to him. Whether it was actually happening, or we just believed it was.

"Ask Mike and Lana to watch Rufio," he suggested.

"So you won't do it for us?" I asked.

"Not unless Rufio is going, too."

Riley was shaking his head, "Whoa, whoa, whoa. Nope. Not happening."

"I'm not staying behind. I'm going with y'all," Lamar said, sternly.

"Dude, you really shouldn't get involved with this. It isn't like we don't want you around. It's just not going to be safe," Riley argued.

"So, it'll be safe for me to sit here and watch my life end? Yeah, that sounds fun," Lamar jeered.

Riley and I knew exactly how he felt. *That* was why we were getting our asses in gear.

"I'd rather die with friends than die alone."

"I'm not going to tell you to stay or go. You're a big boy," I interjected.

"I'm going."

"No, you aren't." Riley shook his head emphatically.

Lamar folded his arms across his chest, "Yeah, I am."

"Riley, can I talk to you a second?" my artificial smile didn't mask my concern.

"Whatever," Riley said, following me to the sliding glass door. We stepped out onto the patio and lit cigarettes. "I don't want him going."

"I don't think we have the right to tell him he can't. You heard what he said. He'd rather be with us than alone. I respect that," I tried to negotiate with him.

"It's putting him in danger. I can't do that. He's like a brother to us both!"

"He's in danger no matter where he is," I continued. "Probably more so without us. The world is *ending*, Riley! He has a right to choose where he is when it happens."

Riley's brows furrowed. A plume of smoke blew out of his nose like he was a massive cartoon bull. The glass door slid open and Lamar stepped out. He stared up at the sky.

"You have two choices; either you *let* me go, and allow me to help you, or you continue to tell me no, and I just follow you. Either way, I'm not staying here." Lamar lowered his gaze, locking eyes with each of us in turn.

"Wanna go on a road trip?" I smiled.

"When are we leaving?" he asked.

"Tomorrow morning. Have your shit packed and ready first thing. Or we're leaving your ass behind," Riley said defeated, then walked inside with a huff.

"Sweet... Road trip!" Lamar gave me a high five.

Chapter Twenty Two
The Besmirching of Honor

I called Mike and Lana and asked them if they'd be able to stop by and check on Rufio for a few days. They asked far fewer questions than Lamar, and Lana was more than willing to take on the task. She was excited to play mother to our little hellion. She agreed to also check on Turkey, Lamar's behemoth feline when Lamar followed our phone call with one of his own seeking kitty care. We called a company and requested a rental van, which they said we could pick up in the morning. We spent the night packing and strategizing. Lamar went to his apartment to gather his belongings and returned to us a short time later. The three of us snuck in a short nap between preparing and planning.

Morning arrived far quicker than any of us had expected. We awoke and shrugged off the slumber. I brewed a pot of coffee while Riley printed off all of the angel's addresses and directions to their homes, in case our phones stopped cooperating. Lamar took Azrael for a brief walk. We all got dressed and ready, then sat around the dining room table as we ate breakfast. I savored every bite of my scrambled eggs and bacon, the whole time wondering if this was the last time I'd get to have a good meal. The thought seemed to be in everyone's mind, though no one said it. We all ate silently, chewing each bite obsessively.

Riley called Jeremiah and let him know we were going to be headed out of town. It seemed that he was still undecided as to what he was going to do. He told Riley about the plant, telling him that something had crashed into it and apparently *walked* away. He was still confused with the whole ordeal, but wanted to help Riley get some guns and ammo from the station. Riley kissed me goodbye and loaded Azrael into his truck. Lamar and I jumped into my car. We were headed to the rental company to pick up the van while Riley met up with Jeremiah. We didn't know how long all of this would take, but we planned to leave as soon as possible. Saturdays always sucked for traveling, and that's without apocalyptic weather across the country.

"So, have y'all talked to any of these guys yet?" Lamar asked me.

"Nope. We figured if they didn't remember anything from their past, they probably would just laugh and hang up on us," I replied truthfully.

"So how do you know whether they'll agree to join us or not?"

"We don't know. But it'll be easier to convince them in person."

"How's that gonna work? What if they won't listen?" he continued his interrogation.

"We have a little *help*, you could say."

"Oh, yeah?" he asked, eye brows raised.

"Yep. You'll see." I smiled.

We arrived at the rental company in short order, then filled out all of the paperwork and waited as they ran my credit card. They handed me a set of keys and showed me to the conversion van. We decided bigger was better in case recruitment went well. I climbed into the driver's seat of the large van and followed Lamar as he drove my car back to our house. Riley was already back and carrying things out to the driveway. There were piles of pillows, blankets, bags of food and clothing. Lamar and I got out of the vehicles and began to load everything into the back of the van.

"How'd it go?" I asked Riley.

"Fine. At least until they find out how much is missing." he walked over to the side door of his truck. I followed behind him.

"Holy shit!" I shouted then covered my mouth when he opened the door.

Riley smiled widely and grabbed one of the guns. The back seat of Riley's truck was loaded with more weapons and ammunition than I knew the names for. I was completely blown away by the large arsenal we now had in our possession. If we got pulled over at any point, we would be so screwed.

Riley inspected a pistol in his hand. "So, whatcha think?" he smiled smugly.

"Good God!" Lamar said, as he stepped around the side of the truck and saw the massive amount of weaponry.

I was at a loss for words. "We may not be able to kill'em, but we'll at least piss them off," I mused.

"If this shit doesn't kill them, nothing will. I'd rather send them back to God in pieces than roll over and take it," Riley said.

"Agreed," Lamar smirked.

We loaded the van with all of our supplies and weaponry. I ran inside the house and gathered my things. I kissed Rufio on his head and filled his dishes. He was my baby. I was going to miss him more than anything. I grabbed Azrael's leash and headed back outside to the van. Riley was grabbing the last of his things and helped Azrael into the van, then asked Lamar to go into the house with him. When they returned, Lamar was waving the snow white feather in the air like a winning lottery ticket, which got me to laughing.

"So what's the big deal with this feather?" Lamar asked as he climbed into the van.

"That's our little help I was talking about," I replied, still chuckling to myself.

"What? Your bargaining chip is a feather? Gonna tickle them into submission? This shit is getting weirder and weirder," he mumbled to himself.

"That's one of Gabriel's feathers. When we touch it, we relive The Great Divide. It's very painful, physically and mentally. If they don't want to listen, we'll just force them to see the truth."

Riley sneered as he put the van in reverse. "You mean Lamar will force them. I'm not touching that damned feather again."

"I knew you guys needed me. I'm gonna bring the wrath of God onto their asses!" Lamar shouted.

I burst into laughter at the unexpected declaration.

"Wait, no. That's what we're trying to avoid. You know what I mean." Lamar laughed.

We pulled out of our neighborhood and down Essen Lane. We jumped onto the interstate and headed towards Hammond. From there, we would begin heading north towards Mississippi. Riley listened to a mixture of heavy metal and hip hop as he drove. Lamar and I talked, pouring over the map and arguing which highways would be quicker to take. After a while we both became bored and tired. Lamar fell asleep in the back seat with Azrael drooling all over him, while I settled in up front. I plugged my headphones into my phone and set my music to loop. I was in a never ending play list of mellow rock, metal and instrumental, and enjoying every moment of it. I closed my eyes for a minute and let the music wash over me until I had cleared my mind of all thoughts. Then I opened my eyes and watched the trees zip by. I was going to miss this place.

No matter what happened with this war, it was evident that I wouldn't be around to see my home anymore. My empty mind was filled with all the things I would miss, all of the adventures I'd regret not having. I'd never see the moss covered oak trees again. I'd never get to bitch about the humidity again.

I concentrated on the rhythm flowing into my ears. I pictured the words as stories. I saw images of my past, connecting to the songs in a way I never had before. Each song gave me a different feeling, a different memory. I felt a smile stretch across my face as the music faded from reality and my eyes once again closed.

I opened my eyes to see a room full of people I didn't recognize. The music was still present in the background, though slightly muffled. I got up from the couch and wandered through the crowd. I was at a costume party. I looked at people's masks as they stepped aside, opening a pathway for me to walk through. Ahead of me I saw the soft glow of snow white wings. The gentle light bounced and ricocheted off of his golden armor, lighting the ceiling like a disco ball. I walked up behind him and wrapped my arms around his shoulders, placing my hands over his eyes and smiling.

"Guess who?" I whispered in his ear. He pulled my hands off of his eyes and turned quickly.

Gabriel's smile seemed to glow and illuminate the room more than his wings and golden armor did. I was always much happier to see his eyes grey, not the lifeless dull glow of his shielding shadow armor. He hugged me tightly, "I've missed you."

"I missed you, too," I replied, as I returned the hug of my heavenly brother.

He grabbed my hand and pulled me towards a doorway. We stepped outside onto a balcony. His long golden hair blew in the wind, whipping and curling then settling on his shoulders as the breeze calmed. I pulled off my mask and set it on the railing.

"Have you found them yet?" he asked.

"All but one. We've found their addresses. We're actually on our way to talk to them now," I replied.

"I think you'll be surprised when you reunite with them. Paul, especially."

I laughed. "He sounds like he's a little wild."

"He's the same as he always has been. He's rough, tough and always ready to rumble," he replied with a grin.

"We weren't able to locate Elijah. But we're guessing he's too old to get involved as it is." I shrugged.

"I'm guessing you don't remember Elijah yet? I'm sure you will soon, or at least when you see him. He's with one of the others. He's safe and well protected."

"Well, that's good to know, I guess," I replied.

"He's... 'different' from everyone else." a fond smile crept across his face.

Now I was curious. "What do you mean?"

"You'll see when you find him." his expression and mood changed suddenly.

"Will we find them all in time?" I asked, guessing the cause of his shift in mood.

"That, I can't answer. I don't know the future. All I know of is the plans." he frowned.

"So you don't know how it's going to end, exactly."

"No, not exactly," he replied as he shook his head.

"Don't worry. I have a plan." I grabbed my brother's hands.

"That makes me nervous," he responded, looking me in the eyes.

"I've made up my mind. I just have to play through the moves correctly." I smiled at him. He held my gaze, head tilted to the side. It was like he was *reading my soul*. "You'll see me again, I promise," I stated matter-of-factly.

Gabriel's face slowly lit up like an over decorated Christmas tree. He sighed with relief then hugged me tightly. "I knew you were brilliant."

"I just play the hand I was dealt."

"Does Riley know of your plan?" he asked.

"No. No one does, yet."

"Will he agree?"

"I'm positive he will. I know for a fact that he feels the same," I replied.

I felt a gentle tap on my shoulder.

"It's Riley. Goodbye for now," he bid me farewell.

"No! Not yet!"

I felt my shoulder shake, more urgently this time. I opened my eyes. "God damn it." I gritted my teeth.

"Sorry, we're almost out of Tennessee. I stopped at a rest stop so we could get out for a minute. I'm gonna go walk Azrael, let him stretch his legs. I figured you'd like to use the restroom," Riley said as he opened his door.

Lamar and I got out and stretched widely. I lumbered towards the restroom and walked in, looking at myself in the mirror. I looked ill. The circles under my eyes were darker than usual. My hair was a mess. My makeup was smeared like an old woman with shaky hands and cataracts had applied it. I laughed at my reflection and grabbed a paper towel.

I finished up in the rest room and walked back outside. A sudden wave of nausea hit me like a crash test dummy hitting a wall, buckling my resolve and my knees. I crumbled into a heap and held myself up with one hand.

"Whatcha doing?" Lamar asked.

"I just feel sick. I don't know if it was something we ate, or all this… shit. It's probably just nerves," I replied.

"Ah. That sucks."

Riley and Azrael walked up to the two of us. "What's going on? We ready to roll out again?" Azrael wagged his stubby tail and panted.

"Yeah, I'm fine. Just felt kind of sick," I replied, using Lamar's arm as a crutch to climb to my feet.

"Let's get going," Riley ordered, throwing the keys to Lamar, "Your turn."

I was in and out of consciousness as we drove. It was difficult to stay awake. My dreams were scattered, broken and incomprehensible. Every time I awoke, we were in another part of the country. The further we headed north, the more colors we were beginning to see. I had missed autumn living in the South.

The sun was setting over the terrain, scattering light as it bounced off of the trees and rock outcrops. The colors flooded my mind. Beautiful hues of red and orange cascaded to the ground. I thought of the dreams I'd had recently. I thought about all that was going on with me, with the world, with everything. It was hard to filter my thoughts, to separate them. I felt like I was caught in a wind tunnel. Images and thoughts swarmed in my head, blinding me. It wasn't long before I was out again. We made a few pit stops, but most of the time, I chose to stay in the van and rest.

Before I knew it, we were back in Michigan. It was the last place on Earth that I wanted to be, but one of the most crucial. With all of the stops, it took us almost eighteen hours to get from Baton Rouge to Detroit. It was almost 2am. We decided to head straight for Booze & Caboose, in hopes that Paul would be crawling out of there soon. I used the GPS system in my phone, and found exactly where it was. We pulled into the parking lot, and waited outside.

Lamar broke the silence of the van, "How will we know it's him?"

"I saw his picture in his file. Not to mention, he should still look like he did when we knew him," Riley explained.

"When *you* knew him," I corrected.

"Whatever. You, me, we, them. Who gives a shit?" Riley replied dryly.

We waited impatiently for him to emerge from the sin bin. Lamar began losing his patience. "We've been here for like, two hours. Should one of us go in and look for him?"

"We've been here for ten minutes and I'm not going in," I said, folding my arms in petition.

"Well, I could." Lamar smiled.

I looked up at the neon sign. It was one of those motion signs of a naked woman shaking her *caboose*.

"Yeah, why don't you head in and look for him. Just tell him that there are people out front that need to speak to him." Riley pulled his printed mug shot out of a manila envelope and handed it to Lamar.

"Something tells me I don't want to piss this guy off," Lamar replied, looking at the pictures of Paul Lee.

He hopped out of the van and ran to the door, quickly disappearing into the neon lit doorway. Riley and I sat in the van, hoping that he would return with Paul. *Like, now.* We didn't know what to expect. Unlike Riley, I couldn't remember anything about the man. As far as I knew, I had never met the guy. Or should I say the angel.

My right leg tapped the floor board as I chewed my fingernails and stared out of the window. I watched the door like I was a getaway driver waiting on my friends to return with the heisted jewels. In this case, I just hoped my friend returned with his jewels intact and nothing broken. Paul sounded like a beast.

"I think something's wrong. Should we go check on him?" I asked, never breaking my gaze from the doorway.

Riley chuckled softly. "I thought you refused to go into a nudie bar?"

"Well, that was before I thought about Lamar's face being bashed in with a stiletto." I frowned.

"I'm sure he's fine." Riley continued to snicker at the scenario we now found ourselves in.

"I hope you're right."

"I bet you could do a lot of damage with a stiletto, though," Riley trailed off into thought.

"That's not funny," I scolded as I shot him a glance.

I looked at the time on my phone. It had only been seven minutes since Lamar left the van. Riley leaned over and placed his hand on my knee. I didn't realize how heavily I was rocking the van with my nervous leg shaking. I smiled awkwardly and stopped, until he moved his hand. He made some snide remark under his breath. I looked at the time again. It had only been a minute since the last time I checked. *Eight minutes. Someone could easily be killed in eight minutes.*

"I think I'm gonna puke." I reached for the door handle and poured myself onto the sidewalk below.

"Try not to get it on the van. I don't want to wash this bitch!" Riley shouted to me. A few minutes passed and I returned to my seat, feeling refreshed.

"Why are you so fidgety? And.. sickly?"

"Not sure. Might be the gallons of caffeine I've had since we crossed the border. Or the fact that I'm worried about Llama. Or just the fact that the world's ending. Pick your poison," I pouted as Riley simply shrugged his shoulders and turned his attention back to his own thoughts.

I stared at the door, hoping they would emerge soon. I saw the door fly open and out walked Lamar with a behemoth of a man next to him. Riley laughed and got out of the van. I recognized Paul from the pictures, but had no memories of him. He had his arm around Lamar's neck, like they had been the best of friends for years. I stepped out of the van timidly.

"What's up!" Paul shouted into the night air, like a bedlamite. I looked at Riley, nervous and confused. Paul stepped away from Lamar and hugged Riley, lifting him off the ground.

Paul was beaming. "Dude, it's been how many years since we've seen each other? Few hundred at least?"

"How do you remember all of that shit?" Riley asked.

"Because I'm awesome… Plus I'm still pissed about the whole *exile* thing. I lost a pretty sweet piece of ass in the process. I'm not gonna get over that shit anytime soon. As far as I'm concerned, they can all tongue-wash my balloon knot!"

Paul guffawed. Riley and Lamar laughed with him.

"You remember The Divide?" I asked, incredulous.

"Fuck yeah I remember! I'm a bitch when it comes to grudges," he paused and wagged his finger at me. "No offense to you. You're a woman, I'm sure you can hold a grudge like a bitch, too."

Riley looked at me and nodded his head vigorously.
Charming, both of them.

"So what's going on? What brings you guys up here?" Paul asked.

"Paul, we really need to talk. I don't think in front of a strip club is the proper place." I eyed the catty sign, feeling uncomfortable.

"It's Paulie. Not Paul. Not *Paul Lee*. Paulie," he clarified, "And this place is top-fuckin'-notch. I can get y'all in for free. They love me here."

I snickered. "Okay, well, no thanks, *Paulie*. We need to talk. Mind going for a ride with us?" I asked.

"Are you going to give me candy if I get in your van?" he asked.

Lamar dug in his pockets and pulled out lint and half a bag of skittles. "Sure. Want some?" Lamar offered them to Paul, picking the lint off the bag.

"Sweet ass!" Paul laughed maniacally and climbed into the van, snatching the bag of skittles from Lamar's hand. "Let's go to my place. It's cold. I'm ready to get out of this shit. And I really have to piss."

We all got into the van and drove to his apartment. He shouted obscenities and blurted out memories as we drove to our destination. He seemed to have quite the memory. He apparently didn't remember me, as I didn't recall anything of him. Though he was very fond of Riley, and remembered him from the days of leading the guardians and their hunting pack. He kept calling him Thad.

We pulled into his apartment complex and waited as he punched in the code for the security gate. We drove around the complex and parked in the spot he indicated. The group piled out of the van and followed him to his door. Azrael was very reluctant. He seemed on edge as he sauntered towards the door, glancing from side to side.

Paul headed for the kitchen as soon as we walked in. Lamar and I sat down on the couch, while Azrael laid down at my feet. Riley followed Paul to the kitchen and stood in the doorway, within earshot of Lamar and me.

"So, who's the chick and dude in there?" Paul asked Riley, as he popped the top off of a bottle of beer.

"That's Eden. I'm not sure if you two have really formally met."

"*The* Eden? As in, Garden of?" Paul asked, handing Riley an opened beer.

Riley locked eyes with the bigger man, "Yeah. We've been together ever since."

"Damn, Thad! Nice. I miss Gwendolyn." Paul smiled and made humping motions. "So, is he *damned,* too?" Paul asked, gesturing towards Lamar. Lamar shot a glance at me, raising a brow.

"Nah, Lamar's just a really good friend of ours. He refused to stay put."

The two of them walked into the living room and sat down to join us.

"So, what's up with the hell hound? He doesn't seem too comfortable around me," Paul asked, pointing at Azrael.

"He's able to sense us. He just doesn't know what to think of you," I replied.

"Like mother, like pup, eh?"

"I guess you could say that." I smiled awkwardly.

He looked at Riley quizzically, "So how the hell did you guys find me? Is there records of us somewhere?"

"Something like that." Riley paused, and then slowly nodded.

"Well, you sir, seem to have quite the record and reputation," I remarked, brow raised.

"Oh... *that* record. Well," he looked me dead in the eyes. "You see, I have a bit of a temper. It takes a lot to set it off, but when it happens, it's catastrophic. Let's just say, when you besmirch a lady's honor, I'll besmirch your fucking face." Paul smiled and bowed his head to me.

We all laughed.

"So your fights were chivalrous, you're saying?" I asked.

"Always. Or at least the ones involving cops," he reassured me.

I grinned. "Note taken."

Riley gave me his little 'I told you so' smirk and chugged his beer.

"Alright, now that the formalities are out of the way, wanna explain what the hell y'all are doing here?"

"We need your help," I stated simply.

"With?"

"God and the Archangels are returning to reclaim Earth. They're going to wipe out humanity," Riley explained abruptly.

Lamar kept his mouth shut and pet Azrael. I could tell by his expression, that he didn't like this conversation piece.

"So, you're planning on going up against them?" Paul surmised.

"Exactly. We may not be able to stop it, but we can at least put up a fight and not give in easily," I replied.

"Who all is involved so far?" he asked, looking at Riley.

"Well, so far it's just me and Eden," Riley responded.

"And me," Lamar interjected.

Riley jumped back in with the slightest twinge of annoyance in his voice. "Okay, so far it's just the three of us. But we know where basically everyone else is. We have a few more that can join in if they want. We'd appreciate it if you'd help."

"Fuck, yeah! I'm not going down without a fight. Those assholes won't know what hit'em." Paul smiled wickedly.

"Alright then. That settles it." Riley smiled widely and offered Paul his hand.

Paul slapped his hand out of the way and hugged Riley firmly.

I was in awe. I stared wordlessly as the giant, sitting next to the statuesque man that held my heart bantered back and forth. It was so bizarre to see two men, who had never met in *this* lifetime, recall so many stories and adventures that they had once shared. I was starting to realize we each had a special talent just as Gabriel had mentioned. As we know I'm able to spark life, or heal. Riley is a natural leader; a guardian. He has the power to read people's persona. He is justice incarnate. Although I was unsure of what Paul had to offer, I wouldn't be surprised if his gift was his sheer size and his bear-like strength. Or the fact that he could hold one hell of a grudge for thousands of years, if such a thing could be considered a gift.

Conversation continued. We explained to him how we had found out about all of the current events and the future. We told him about the list and he explained how he was still in contact with Jonah in Boston. He was very curious about the others, and whether or not we had made contact with anyone else yet.

"I hope you realize that there isn't much time for anything. We really need to be leaving tomorrow, whether you leave with us or just meet up with us later," I said.

"That's cool. I don't have shit to do here. If the world's going to hell in a hand basket, I might as well skip town while I can. Detroit's completely falling apart as it is," he replied.

"So where do we go from here?" Lamar asked.

Riley and I looked at each other. We hadn't *exactly* planned past this point. We thought about going to Chicago next, but we didn't know if that was definite. I think we were expecting to run into a snag, or have some kind of divine intervention to assist us. Nope, we were left high and dry.

"You say you've been in contact with Jonah? That was your brother, correct?" Riley asked, cocking his head to the side.

"*Is. He is* my brother. We've stayed close throughout the years. Back in the 20's we were low on cash, so we joined the circus. I was the 'strong man' and he was a fortune teller, 'Jubilant Jonah, *Mystic! Oracle!*' It was stupid as shit, but we did what we could." Paul laughed.

"So, does he know about our history?" I asked.

"Yeah, he's the one who always finds me and has reminded me of a lot. It seems that we all have our memories of the past, they're just kind of locked away. Repressed. It doesn't take much to restore them."

Riley looked at him curiously. "How does he remember all of it?"

"I don't know. He always has. Probably helps that he's like a warlock, or some shit. Probably leaves himself clues. But he always knows where I am and how to remind me. I guess it's that brotherly bond, you know?" Paul continued.

"Must be like me and Gabriel," I pondered.

Paul scoffed, "Ugh, I don't even want to think about that dill-hole."

"Hey, he may be one of the archangels, but we wouldn't have a clue what was going on if he hadn't told us," I shot back defensively.

"They're all the enemies to me." Paul's eyes narrowed.

"If Jonah knows about all of this already, can you get a hold of him and see if he's in?" Riley asked Paul, attempting to change the subject.

"Yeah, I'll give him a call," Paul replied and pulled his cell phone out of his pocket. He walked down the hallway and into another room, shutting the door behind him.

"You sure we can trust him?" Lamar asked.

I shrugged. "I don't know. What choice do we have?"

"Paul is a good guy. He's gonna help a lot," Riley reassured us. "He's just a bit of a loose cannon. Give him time to settle down."

I stood up from the couch and walked to the front door.

"Where are you going?" Riley asked.

"Out. I need some fresh air."

"Let me go with you." Lamar began to stand.

"No, thanks. I want to be alone."

"At least take Az," Riley suggested.

I grabbed Azrael's leash and led him to the door. We stepped outside and walked out into the parking lot. I stared up at the moon. The Michigan night was just as I remembered it; clear, cold and able to make you feel completely insignificant. I held my arms close to my chest and shivered as I watched my breath disappear into the bitter air.

I pulled my phone from my pocket and looked at the display. It was almost 4am. I knew it was a bad idea, but I couldn't hold out any longer. There was a phone call I had to make. I scrolled through my phone's address book and stopped on _Gabe_. I took in a deep breath and exhaled it out slowly in a puff of blue glowing condensation as I pressed send. I didn't know exactly what to say or how to even converse. A million thoughts rushed through my head as I listened to the phone ring.

"Hello?" he finally answered, half asleep.

"Hey Gabe, it's Edie." I winced, waiting for the yelling to begin.

"Edie? It's 4 in the morning. Is everything alright?" he asked, sounding slightly more awake.

"Um, yes and no."

He yawned into the phone. "Are you okay?"

"Look. I don't really want to drag you into the mess I'm in, but I just wanted you to know how much I love you," I replied.

"I love you, too, kiddo. Even if you are a turd that calls at 4am," he laughed with his husky, sleepy voice. "What are you doing up so late, anyway? It's what, 3am there?"

"No... No, it's 4am." I cringed, waiting for the perfect moment to explain myself. "Gabe, I'm in Michigan," I blurted out.

"Wait, what? What's going on?" he asked, fully awake and attentive now.

"It's kind of hard to explain. If I drove to Flint, would you leave with me?" I asked, crossing my fingers.

"What about Sara? What about the kids?" he asked.

"They can come, too. They can stay with Mom and Dad."

"Hold on a minute."

I heard the muffled sound of Sara's voice in the background. I couldn't make out the conversation over the sound of his heart beating as he pressed the phone against his chest.

"Are you in some sort of trouble?" he asked when he returned to the line.

"We all are," I replied cryptically.

"What do you mean?"

"The world's going to end. I'm not joking. I'm not on drugs. I'm not drunk. I'm serious as a heart attack."

"Oh, come on. Don't tell me you believe this alien bullshit?" he sounded baffled.

"*Alien* bullshit?" I asked.

"People are freaking out. They say there's been sightings all across the globe. Weird *light up* people and laser guns or some shit. I don't fucking know. It's so ridiculous."

Oh God... We're too late.

I couldn't say anything. I was literally stunned silent.

"Edie, you there? It's a hoax! Don't buy into the bullshit." he tried to comfort me.

I managed to choke out, "Oh, shit."

"Hello?" he sounded worried.

"Oh, my God. It's already started." I didn't even notice my phone leaving my hands until it clattered on the pavement.

CHAPTER TWENTY THREE
WE'RE COMING TO GET YOU, BARBARA!

Our phone conversation ended on an awkward note. I picked my phone up off of the cold ground, told Gabe I would call him later, then hung up without another word and ran inside with Azrael. I searched for Paul's TV remote and turned it on, found the news, and sat on the edge of the couch.

"What's going on?" Riley asked, confused by my sudden actions.

"I just got off the phone with Gabe. He said there's shit on the news about aliens. People are seeing them, like this is some sort of invasion," I said while staring at the screen.

Paul walked into the living room and slid his phone in his pocket. "I've got good news and bad news."

"What's up, Paulie?"

"Jonah is definitely in. He said he saw this coming. He's excited to reunite. That's the good news. Bad news, he said the shit has already started hitting the fan and if we don't move extremely fast, we're fucked," Paul replied with a serious expression.

"We already knew that," I said, pointing to the TV screen.

"Well, that is definitely good, and bad to hear." Riley nodded.

We all sat silently as we watched the news unfold before us. Amateur home videos depicted large glowing beings, morphing into shadow form, walking the streets. The shaky screen flashed from the Archangels, to the ground as the person filming the coverage ran for their life. I cradled my head in my hands.

"We'll figure something out, right?" Lamar asked, wrapping his arm around my shoulder to comfort me.

"I hope so," I mumbled between my fingers.

"So, what's happening with Jonah? Do we need to go get him?" Riley asked.

"No, he's gonna try to get a ticket for the next flight out. So maybe he'll be in Detroit in the morning," Paul replied.

"Hopefully the weather doesn't ground them and planes are still flying," I added. I couldn't believe my eyes. I couldn't believe my mind. How could this be happening? I've seen so many horror movies, so many sci-fi movies, but never in my life did I expect to be living one. The heroes always succeeded. Granted, there were always casualties. Was that going to be true in our case? I had to get my brother. I had to be sure that he was safe. I grabbed my phone and redialed his number.

"Hey, shit head. Why'd you hang up?" Gabe asked as he answered.

"Sorry. I was a little freaked out." I rubbed my temples. "I need you to get up and get dressed. Gather some clothes and supplies."

Riley walked towards me and grabbed the phone from my hand. I could hear

Gabe talking as the phone was pulled away.

"We're coming to get you, Barbara!" Riley shouted into the receiver and laughed. He handed the phone back to me.

I chuckled as I stepped out of the room and held the phone back up to my ear.

"What the hell's going on?" Gabe asked, snickering about the zombie movie reference.

"I'll explain everything once we have you, but Riley's right. We're coming to get you. If you want to fight us, we'll just have to kidnap you. Your choices are go willingly, or be hogtied in the back of a big black van," I said only half joking.

"I'll go, preferably without the hogties. But Sara wants to stay with her family."

"She'd be with family. Us. Tell her to get the kids. We'll take them all to a safe place."

"I don't know. She doesn't want to leave her parents," he replied.

"That's between the two of you. I just think it would be better if we could get her and the kids to Texas. They can stay with Mom and Dad. I'm gonna get a hold of Ross, Lucas and Eli and ask them to do the same. I want to know that everyone is together. It's easier to keep them safe that way."

"This is fucking crazy. I hope you realize that," he mumbled.

"We'll take care of it. Just get everyone ready. We're wasting time," I said frustrated.

"Let me go talk to her. I'll call your punk ass back."

"Okay, please do. Either way, we'll be there to get you in a couple hours," I said.

"Alright. I'll see you soon. I love you, Kiddo."

"I love you, too." I smiled.

I walked back into the living room. Riley, Lamar and Paul were staring at the TV screen with disturbed looks on their faces. I sat down between Lamar and Riley and turned my attention to the TV. They kept replaying a video clip. One of the pitch black "aliens" picked a man up by his chest and held him in the air. A blinding burst of light flashed, then the being dropped the man to the ground and sauntered off.

"Oh my God," I clasped my mouth shut.

"What are they doing?" Lamar asked.

"They're reaping. They're *harvesting* souls," I explained.

"Is that a bad thing?" he asked.

"In this case, no. It sucks that they're killing people. But they're saving the souls of the worthy. The others will just be killed," I continued.

We watched as they cut to live feed. The reporter shot around the front of the camera and began narrating the story as it was unfolding. Suddenly, a large, burly man shot at one of the angels. The glowing skin morphed into a shadowy mass instantaneously and sped towards him, with blinding speed. He grabbed him by his throat, made one quick jerking motion and snapped the man's neck, then dropped him to the ground. The person behind the camera screamed an obscenity and took off running, the camera pointing at the ground and picking up sounds of chaos. The feed was cut and the screen returned to the newsroom, where the anchor had a look of fear and disgust smeared across his face.

I shook my head. "We don't stand a chance."

"You don't know that for sure," Paul replied.

"We're boned." I whined.

"There you go, getting all emo. Give us a chance," Riley said, rubbing my back.

I looked over at Lamar. My brow furrowed even though he was smiling at me, "I'm so sorry," I whispered to him. He didn't say a word. He didn't have to. I knew why he was here.

"We need to head to Flint. I'll go alone if you guys want to stay here and rest," I said to the room.

"No. You aren't going alone. All we need is for you to run into one of them by yourself and have them reap *your* soul," Riley said determinedly.

"Somehow I doubt they'd save my soul. I'm one of the traitors, remember?" I replied somberly.

"I'll go," Lamar said.

"We can all go," Paul interjected.

"No, you need to get ready. You also need to be here so you can pick up Jonah if he makes it here before we do," I shot back.

"Riley, why don't you stay with Paulie; Lamar and I can run to Flint. We'll be fine. You know that I know my way around. I'll be sneaky if I have to. I know all the back roads," I tried to comfort him.

"Fine, you two go. But take Az. He may prove to be one of our most valued members," Riley suggested.

"Okay," I smiled. "Come on, Scoob!" I hooked Azrael's leash to his collar and walked over to Riley. I kissed him and gave him a long hug.

"Please be careful," he whispered in my ear.

I nodded, "I will."

"I love you." he frowned anxiously.

"I love you, too," I said, then kissed him again.

Riley walked us out to the van. Lamar and I opened the side door for Azrael, and then jumped in the front seats. I gave one final wave to Riley as we backed out, then we were away. We sped through the city as sirens blared from every direction. We got onto the expressway and made our way towards Flint. Gabe hadn't called me back yet, but I didn't care at this point. He was coming with us, whether he was ready or not.

"So we're going to pick up Gabriel? Why did he come to Michigan?" Lamar asked.

"No, we're going to get my brother," I replied, never breaking my gaze from the road.

"Wait, your real brother, like *blood* brother?" Lamar asked, trying to keep up.

"Exactly," I clarified.

"So you have two brothers named Gabe?"

I summed up the story, explaining how my mom had dreamt of the two of us.

"Ah. Crazy," he said quietly when I was finished.

"Yeah, a little bit. Not any crazier than any of this shit though," I mocked.

"I couldn't imagine anything else being this insane." He stared out the window.

After some time in silence, Azrael got off of the back seat and stuck his head between us. Lamar gently patted his head and scratched behind his ears as he continued to stare into the night. "I'm worried about my family. I'm really worried about Chuck," he finally broke the silence.

"Yeah. I'm worried about Chuck, too," I replied, worry creasing my face.

"Think it'd be okay if I call him and get him to come along?" he asked.

"I'm scared enough to have you involved. I don't want to have to worry about your brother."

"I don't like being away from him. If something happens, he wouldn't even know." he began chewing his fingernails and paused. "I think he should be with us."

"Honestly, that's your call. I'm not going to say he isn't welcome," I replied. "I know exactly how you feel. Shit, we're going to get my brother. Do what you feel is best."

I wish people would stop volunteering themselves or others to die for a 'noble' cause.

I popped in a CD and drove as fast as the van would allow. I sped down the expressway, weaving around the sporadic traffic. Lamar continued staring out the window and sighed occasionally. I didn't know what was on his mind, but I knew what was on mine. If I was able to heal us, heal the angels, was I able to heal humans? Could I really keep Lamar safe? Could I protect Gabe? The tables may have turned. My phone rang, startling me and breaking my concentration. I pulled it out of my pocket and read the display.

"What's up?" I answered.

"Good news," Riley said as way of a greeting.

"Oh yeah? What's that? Did they retreat? Are they leaving us alone?" I mused.

"No, not that good. Lower your standards of 'good'," he replied with a laugh.

"Wishful thinking."

"Jonah's on the next flight out. He'll be in Detroit at 9:45am. And he's bringing friends," Riley said with a smile in his voice.

"No shit? Awesome."

"Where are you guys?" Riley asked.

"Just outside of Auburn Hills. We're making good time."

"Be careful," he pleaded again.

"I will," I reassured him as I hung up.

"Can I ask you something?" Lamar said, looking from his phone to me.

"Yeah, of course."

"Why is it that Riley remembers these people, but you don't?"

"Well, a lot of it has to do with who we are, who we *were*," I explained as I changed lanes. "I stayed in the garden, for the most part. I wasn't really *allowed* to venture out much," I continued, swerving around a small car.

"Thaddeus... *Riley*, was a guardian. He was ordered to keep me safe. But he also led the group of guards that were on Earth. Gabriel brought them orders and he was in charge of making sure those orders happened."

"So he led God's army?"

"No, Michael has always led God's crusade. Riley was just in charge of the 'Earthbound'. Michael never wanted to set foot on the planet. In fact, he only did twice; when we were introduced to the planet, and The Great Divide." I realized I was trailing off on a tangent. "Riley took orders only from God, Himself, but he led the guardians that we had."

"So he had more time with everyone, unlike you," Lamar surmised.

"Basically. He spent a lot of time with Paulie and the others. Whereas I wasn't able to. When I wasn't in the garden, I was walking the fields with God. I was creating things, with my Creator." I peeked into the rearview, checked my side mirror, then returned my gaze forward instinctively. "I did, occasionally, sneak off. But it wasn't as often as I wanted to. I had a few friends... and this one angel in particular fascinated me, but I was never really allowed to make contact."

"Who did you spend time with? Are there others that you remember now? It seems like your memories are returning slowly."

"Yeah, they are. Definitely not as quickly as I'd like, but maybe that would be too overwhelming or something. There were a few I remember though. Lilith and Gabriel spent a lot of time with us. I was never fond of her, but I kept my mouth shut. Victoria also spent time with me. I wouldn't be surprised if we feel that bond that Riley and Paul feel when we meet."

"That's cool." he nodded, trying to make sense of it all.

We were silent for a few minutes. I could tell he was thinking.

"So, are you happy that you're more than just a regular person? Or were you happier when you thought this life was all you had?" he asked nervously.

"I have mixed emotions, I guess. It's a bit of a catch-22. I wouldn't take it back, if I could. But at the same time, everything was much easier before I remembered."

"That makes sense." he returned to typing on his phone. His phone beeped occasionally and he chuckled to himself. I thought about his questions as I drove towards Flint.

We crossed over into Genesee County and I cringed. I didn't miss this place. I didn't miss the pain that it had inflicted on me. I didn't miss the stress and pressure of wondering how we were going to pay bills and eat with the little money that we had. I didn't miss this... ghost town, one bit.

My phone rang and I answered it, "Hello."

"Hey, where are you?" Gabe asked.

"Just crossed into the county. We'll be there in about 20 minutes. I hope you're packed."

"I am. And Sara agreed to go to Texas with Lily, Ian and Aiden. Do Mom and Dad know they're coming?" he asked.

"Um, not yet. I'll let them know." my forehead crumpled.

Shit. I knew I was forgetting something. I just volunteered my parents to baby sit during the Apocalypse.

"Just get yourself ready. I'll explain what I can to Sara when we get there."

"Alright, see you soon," he said, then hung up.

We drove into the city and headed for downtown. We exited the expressway and pulled onto Saginaw Street. Lamar looked around, taking in the sights of the dead city. I slowed as we approached a red light. The homeless shambled across the street like aimless zombies.

We pulled onto the street my brother lived on and parked in the lot. We stepped out of the van, leaving Azrael inside, and made our way to the front door where we pressed the call button, and Gabe buzzed us in. We got into the old elevator and rode up to the fourth floor, stepped out, and began to walk towards my brother's apartment. He met us outside the door and picked me up with a huge bear hug and a smile.

"Hey, kiddo!" he said, as he squeezed me tightly.

I wrapped my arms around his neck and kissed his cheek. Lamar just smiled as he watched our reunion. We stepped into his apartment. Sara was sitting on the couch watching the news. She glanced up from the TV and folded her arms across her chest. She had a faint smile. She was normally very affectionate and friendly with me. I knew she was worried.

I smiled at her, "Hey, Sara."

She yawned as way of greeting and responded with a "Hi."

"Oh, you guys, this is Lamar. He's a good friend of ours," I introduced him. He politely grinned and waved sheepishly.

"What's up, man?" Gabe smiled and shook Lamar's hand.

"Edie, what's going on?" Sara asked.

"I, um. It's kinda hard to explain. If I even attempted to, you guys would just think I'm nuts." I scratched my head awkwardly.

"Too late for that. Y'all want something to drink?" Gabe stepped into the kitchen.

"Sure, water please," I replied, looking at Lamar and nodding towards the kitchen. He followed my brother out of the room.

I walked over to Sara, gave her a big hug and kissed her cheek, then sat down beside her. "You know I would never lie to you. You know I'm almost honest to a fault. I would never say anything to you that I didn't know for sure," I said, grabbing her hand. "I want to tell you the truth and I want you to keep an open mind. I want you to listen to what I say and not pass any judgment or make any assumptions until I'm finished."

Gabe and Lamar walked back into the living room and sat down, beers in hand. Sara muted the TV and turned to me.

"I wish I could tell you guys that this was all an elaborate prank; a hoax. But unfortunately, it isn't. Gabe, I know you're one of the most skeptical people I know. Sara, I know you're one of the most logical people that I know. Together, you may be the toughest people to convince, but I would never lie to either of you."

Gabe opened his mouth to talk. I held my hand out in front of me and closed my eyes. "Just give me a few minutes to explain, please," I said before he could start.

He leaned back in his chair and crossed his arms.

I gave them a brief rundown of the entire story. I explained everything I could, as easily as possible. They sat silently as I spilled crazy babble all over their living room floor.

"I know it's totally sci-fi, but I'm not kidding. If you want proof, I can show you proof," I finished.

I unzipped my hoodie and threw it onto Lamar's lap. I held my arms out for my brother and Sara to see. I knew, he, of all people would realize something was bizarre, something had drastically changed my body and not just with the missing tattoos.

"Edie..." Gabe stared at me.

"What happened to your tattoos? What happened to your skin?" Sara finished Gabe's question.

"She's one of them. But she's a good one," Lamar interjected.

My pale skin almost glowed under the light. "It's not a matter of good or bad. They aren't *bad*. They believe they're justified. They just don't care for humans. They see them as bastard children. Completely unwanted."

"Fuck *them*!" Gabe shot back.

Sara began to have a panic attack, hitting her inhaler hard and trying to calm her shaking nerves as the reality sunk in. I assured her that I had a plan. Not only was I trying to preserve the planet, but I was trying to do so with minimal sacrifices. I told her there was no way around it; we were going to have to go against the Archangels and the others. But, it was possible that we could avoid the entire annihilation of the human race. I never told them exactly what I had in mind, but I tried to make sure that they understood. I knew what I was up against.

"I know it's hard on both of you, but I'm asking you to trust me. I need Gabe to come with me. I need you and the kids to go stay with my parents. I know you don't want to leave your family, but we can only keep tabs on so many people," I continued.

"Edie, we're running out of time. It's already 7:45," Lamar cut in, looking at his phone. "Jonah will be here in two hours."

"We have to leave. Get one way tickets to Beaumont, Texas for you and the kids. My parents will pick you up there. Call me and them, when you know what time you'll be departing and arriving. I need you to act fast," I explained, pulling a mangled wad of cash from my pocket and placing it in her lap. She nodded numbly.

Lily walked around the corner and stared at us. Her bright blue eyes blinked and squinted in the bright light. Her golden curls spiraled out in every direction. She held a decrepit stuffed duck, worn out from years of her love and affection. She smiled brightly at me. Her adorable gapped smile made my heart melt. I missed my niece. I walked to her and picked her up, hugging her.

"Aunt Edie!" she exclaimed and squeezed my neck tightly.

"Hey, Lily bug! I missed you." I sighed into her hair. She giggled and kept squeezing.

I closed my eyes and rocked from side to side as I held my niece. I could feel the tears rolling down my cheek as I thought about the beautiful girl in my arms. I worried I would never see her again. I set her down on the ground and knelt down to be eye level with her angelic face.

"Lily bug, I need you to do me a favor, okay?"

"Okay!" she replied. Her enthusiasm mixed with her high pitched little voice made me smile.

"I need you to go with your mom and your brothers. I'm taking your daddy with me for a little while. You'll see him soon," I promised.

"Oh... Okay!" she replied with a frown, then a smile.

"You're gonna be a big girl, you're gonna be strong for me, right?" I asked.

"Yes." she nodded with a smile.

She was almost 8 years old. She's so smart for her age. I wish I could watch her grow and develop into a beautiful woman. My heart was breaking, looking into her crystal blue eyes. She looked so much like my brother, gapped smile and all. The only difference was that she wasn't over six feet tall with tattoos everywhere. That, and she was innocent.

Gabe walked over and picked up his daughter. He gave her a hug and kissed her. He blew raspberries on her belly, as she squealed and laughed loudly. He stared into her eyes and whispered something to her. She whispered back and hugged his ink covered neck with a vice-like grip. He acted like he was choking and she squealed louder. She kissed him one last time, then kissed her hand and stuck it in his pocket. *A kiss for later.*

"I love you, Lily," he said as he set her next to Sara.

"Love you, too, Daddy," she replied with a pout.

"Bye, Sara. Bye, Lily bug! Kiss the boys for me." I stepped out of his apartment and wiped the tears from my eyes.

Gabe followed me out of the apartment with a heavy sigh. He looked me in the eyes. Nervous. Concerned. I had never really seen this side of my brother. He grabbed the straps of his backpack and started walking with us. We got in the elevator and went down to the first floor. No one said a word.

Once we were downstairs, we ran across the street to the parking lot. I opened the side door and Azrael burst out, bolting out into the concrete jungle. I chased after him, yelling for him, but he didn't react.

"Az! Stop!" I shouted, chasing after him. I couldn't see what he was after, but he appeared to be on the hunt. "Azrael! Sit! Damn it!" I shouted again. He was beyond me catching up.

I watched from where I was as he lunged into the air and heard the loud 'snap' of his jaws locking. He turned towards me and began jerking his head back and forth. I ran towards him and stopped within a few feet. He had a crow in his mouth.

"Oh, Az," I said, short of breath.

Gabe and Lamar caught up with me, Azrael's leash in tow. "What the fuck? He was chasing down a bird?" Gabe asked bewildered.

"It's not just a bird." I shook my head. "It's Lilith, also known as the Morrigan... The war goddess."

"What?" Lamar asked, confused by my statement.

I sneered, "It seems as though she's spying on us. This is the second time Azrael has caught and killed her."

"Apparently he didn't kill her right the first time," Lamar said, raising a brow.

"Azrael, come on." I attached the leash to his collar.

I made sure he didn't drop the bird from his clenched jaws, as we walked back to the van and opened the back doors. I grabbed a large water thermos, unscrewed the top and dumped out all of the water. Lamar and Gabe stared at me, confused.

"Drop it!" I commanded. He dropped the bird and walked off to relieve himself in the lot.

I quickly picked up the dead crow by the wing and slung it into the thermos, secured the lid hastily and grabbed the roll of duct tape from one of the bags. I wrapped the tape around the thermos several times then tossed it into the back of the van. Azrael returned to my side. I brushed my hands off on my jeans and patted Azrael's head, "Good boy."

Lamar and Gabe stared at me, speechless, jaws agape. Gabe's cigarette hung from the corner of his lip. I pulled a cigarette from my pack and lit it, opened the side door of the van and let a stunned Gabe and excited Azrael in. Lamar took the keys from my hand and made his way to the driver's side, now too used to weird happenings to be slowed for long. I hopped in the passenger seat and turned around to talk to my brother. We hadn't seen each other in over a year.

"So, how did you find out about all of this?" Gabe asked before I could say anything.

"I guess it all started with dreams," I replied, flicking my cigarette butt out the window as Lamar navigated the roads.

"So you're an angel? I'm calling shenanigans on that load of shit. I helped raise your ass. There's no way that you're *heavenly*." he laughed.

"Yep," I replied nonchalantly, as I unzipped my backpack and pulled out a granola bar. "Believe it or not, the Garden of Eden was all mine."

"You know, when I was little, I used to have dreams of us grown up. It was really weird. You were my sister, but I wasn't me. It was really bright and colorful." he paused. "It was pretty fruity."

I had to laugh at his assessment.

I turned forward and watched the road as Lamar pulled onto the expressway and sped towards Detroit. The sun had risen in the east, blinding me as it settled just above the tree line. I rolled down my window to get some fresh air as we drove southeast towards our destination. I thought about what I had just put my brother and his family through. I felt horrible. I felt selfish. But I truly felt it was for the best.

I wasn't acclimated to the northern weather anymore. The breeze rushing in through the window was bone chillingly cold. I watched as my breath momentarily clouded in front of me, only quick enough to fog up my glasses before it was sucked out the window. I bundled myself up in a blanket and pulled my knees to my chest as I stared out of the window.

There was one thing I truly did miss about the north. There was nothing more beautiful than fall leaves. I had a special place in my heart for autumn. I knew it was another one of those things that I had helped influence, in an earlier period of time. But, as a woman that abided by and appreciated science, I felt that I owed my friends carotenoids and anthocyanins a special tip of the hat. The chemical changes of autumn were by far, one of the most breathtaking.

I turned around and saw Azrael fast asleep, head on Gabe's lap, while Gabe himself was snoring softly. It was so funny to me how innocent my brother looked when he was asleep. His short shaved hair glowed golden in the passing light. His tattoos, from neck to toe reminded me of a child's body artwork, created with markers. He still had the same gap in his top central teeth as he did when he was little. His bright blue eyes had never lost their sparkle. He's five years older than me, and had always been the ultimate protector. It was odd to feel the other way around.

As we raced into Detroit, I went into copilot mode to help Lamar navigate through the city traffic. I looked at the clock on my phone; it was 9:30am as we were entering the outskirts. For the slightest of moments, I was surprised by the heavy traffic on a Sunday morning. Maybe everyone was racing to church to suck up to their "Holy Father". *Ha.* And then I instantly remembered. Some people aren't as dumb as others and are actually evacuating, as opposed to blindly believing the military will take them out. Not that the angels won't catch you eventually. But, people don't *know* that yet. It's all still just assumptions and grainy smart phone videos.

I gave him turn by turn directions as we approached the airport. I woke Gabe up and let him know we had arrived. He opted to stay in the van with Azrael while Lamar and I ventured through the airport to meet up with the rest of the party.

Riley sent me a text message informing me that they were at the luggage area and that the plane was delayed by twenty minutes. That was good news to me. That gave me and Lamar time to get to them before the crowds rushed to get their luggage. I replied to let him know we were on our way in.

We got out of the van and began walking through the parking garage towards the moving walkway. We hopped on and rode towards the sliding glass doors, entered the airport and found the nearest escalators down to the luggage area. I saw Riley and Paul sitting on a bench near the turnabout.

"I guess I should warn you about Jonah." Paul winced and scratched at his beard. "He's a bit, um, how should I say it? Eccentric."

"He's not bringing friends, he's bringing followers," Riley interjected.

Paul nodded. "He brought his coven."

"His coven? I thought he was an *angel*, not a *vampire*. Jesus. How many of y'all are creatures of the night?" Lamar gibed, only half kidding.

"He's a Neo-Pagan. Big difference," Paul replied defensively.

Lamar looked at me, we both shrugged at the same time.

We sat around for a while waiting for Jonah and his *coven* to arrive for their knapsacks of herbs, sticks and stones. I pictured men and woman that looked like they had just left a renaissance festival, prancing down the escalators playing ocarinas and pan flutes.

My mind trailed off as we sat in the luggage area. Riley and Lamar attempted to ride the turnabout like surfboarders, avoiding security guards and the overhang. They eventually had a wipeout, which led to bursts of excessive laughter. We tried to muffle our racket to avoid confrontation. Paul, being the behemoth that he was, pretended to scold them for their actions as a security guard walked by. The laughter soon resumed.

My eyes darted to each entry point. I wondered what direction they would be coming from. I also wondered if I would recognize Jonah once I saw him, maybe sparking some dormant memory we shared. I waited, impatiently, as always. My right leg bounced, shaking the bench.

And then they descended. There was no doubt about who they were. They had a very mystical aura about them, drawing your attention to the group immediately. As they rode down the escalator, I was awestruck.

In the front of the group were two stunningly beautiful women in solid white, long, flowing dresses. Their hair draped over their shoulders like waterfalls of gold and bronze. Their stance was very eloquent, very mysterious. Behind them were two men in snow white tunics and black pants. They looked like regal bodyguards, strong, confident and dedicated to their coven. They were obviously very devout in their beliefs. Behind the four people, I saw Jonah, and the air was sucked from my lungs.

CHAPTER TWENTY FOUR
ARE YOU A GOOD WITCH,
OR A BAD WITCH?

As the coven descended and exited the escalator, Paul stood up and walked in measured steps towards his *soul brother*. Jonah stepped forward, gently pushing his friends aside and approached Paul. They nodded at each other in unison, then hugged each other and did the manly pat on the back thing. Paul escorted him towards us, and we stood up as they approached.

"Jonah, I'd like you to re-meet Thaddeus, Eden and their friend, Lamar."

"It's Riley now. Thaddeus is my middle name. Pleasure to see you again, Jonah," Riley said, shaking his hand.

"The pleasure's all mine, I assure you," Jonah said and bowed his head slightly.

The four others stood behind Jonah. One of them cleared his throat loudly, attempting to use the subtle '*what about us*' trick. It really wasn't subtle...

"Oh, how rude of me. Eden, Riley, Lamar, Paulie, these are the members of my circle. This is Erick, Corey, Paige and Brooke." he smiled as he pointed to each of the members.

"It's nice to meet all of you." I smiled.

We all exchanged pleasantries, then the new additions, along with Riley and Paul walked over to the luggage carousel and waited for their possessions to spin around to them. Lamar and I sat back on the bench, exhausted. I scoped out each of our new companions.

Erick seemed very shy. He had a friendly face, but didn't seem to say much at all. His shoulder length hair was black and fell in his face as he looked to the ground, rather than looking any of us in the eyes. He looked like he was in his late twenties. He had soft brown eyes and a beautiful smile. His olive skin tone shouted that he had an interesting heritage. He had an aura of warmth and comfort about him. He appeared to be very down to Earth, very centered.

Corey seemed to be quite more outgoing. He appeared to be the polar opposite of Erick. He had a relatively dark complexion. I'd imagine he's half African American and half Caucasian. He looked as if he was in his late teens, possibly in his early twenties. He wore glasses and had his lip pierced. He joked around with Jonah and danced to music blaring from a single earphone dangling from his ear. His dreads looked like he was statically charged. That made sense. It felt like he emitted an electric energy. He was like bottled sunshine, if it was possible.

Paige was the quiet blonde. She had that new-age hippy vibe. She seemed like one of those women who were vegan and would protest animal cruelty. Hipster, if you will. Granted, I didn't know if it was true, it was just what I expected. I tend to stereotype. Her blue eyes reminded me of the large clouds that roll in with a heavy thunderstorm.

Brooke had long, wavy reddish-bronze hair that stretched to the small of her back. She was very bubbly and friendly. She hung on Jonah's arm, smiling and sighing like a love struck puppy. She looked like she was in her mid-twenties. She also had a brilliant smile and golden eyes. Her freckles speckled her cheeks like a blotch painting or a game of connect the dots. She was breathtakingly beautiful and seemed serene.

Lastly, but not least in my observation… Jonah. He was much shorter than Paul, much smaller in stature. He had a very welcoming air about him. He had a smile that could light up the darkest room. He had almost glowing green eyes that pierced as he gazed. He had a neatly trimmed goatee and very well groomed, long black dreads. He looked to be in his later twenties. He wore a loose fitting white tunic and cotton gauze pants.

Paul looked very happy to be near Jonah and as I studied Jonah's demeanor, I realized why. He was a very charming man. I understood why he had *followers*. Though, as a coven, each member was an equal. Each had an important role to play. I wondered if they knew the truth about Jonah. I could only imagine the truth would only further fuel their love and devotion for him. He had the look and image of a messiah. A shepherd; and his sheep looked very obedient.

They gathered their belongings and returned to us. We rose to our feet and led them out to the parking garage, where Gabe and Azrael napped in the van. I thought about how odd we all must look together and laughed to myself quietly.

Paul, Jonah and the two women left us and began walking to Paul's SUV. Corey and Erick followed Riley, Lamar and I to the van. I warned them before they approached the van that we had two beasts snoozing in the back seats. I opened the side door and Azrael began barking and wagging his stubby tail. He hopped out and ran to Riley's side.

I don't remember much of the drive back to Paul's, as I was in and out of consciousness catching up on much needed sleep. When we pulled in and parked, everyone exited the van and stretched. I stumbled out of the side door and lumbered towards the apartment, tripping over my own feet. Riley walked over to me and grabbed my arm, wrapping it around his neck as support.

Paul unlocked the door and let us all in. He showed me to his room and offered me a pillow and blanket to relax on his bed, while they planned our next move and decided how to extend our convoy. Through the walls, I could hear mumbling and the occasional laughter erupting from the living room where everyone was gathered. I closed my eyes and buried my face in the pillow. It wasn't long before I no longer noticed the voices and drifted off to sleep.

I stepped out of reality and back into my dream world. I was actually beginning to enjoy sleeping, now that I wasn't frightened by my dreams. I had managed to lucid dream, controlling my actions and manipulating the situations I encountered.

I was back in the golden field of grain. I turned towards the cliff and held my hand over my eyes, shielding them from the bright beams of sunlight. I began walking towards the cliff and saw the figure of a man standing on the ledge. My steps quickened until I found myself sprinting towards the precipice.

As I approached, the figure turned around. It wasn't Gabriel. I stopped suddenly and started to back away. The man was staring right at me. He cocked his head to the side. I could see his eyes, glowing bright white as his body suddenly morphed to a pitch black figure. He dropped to all fours and began to run towards me, like an animal.

Wake up! Wake up! Wake up!

I panicked as I watched the being barrel towards me. I turned away, and began to run through the grain field as fast as I could. I could hear the heavy footsteps, almost at a full gallop as it approached me from behind. I closed my eyes and ran with all of my strength. I ignored the burning in my chest as I overexerted my lungs. My diaphragm screamed as it attempted to keep pace with my racing heart. The adrenaline coursed through my body. I let out a sharp cry as I pushed my body to its absolute limit. It wasn't enough. Tripping, my body was hurled through the air and I hit the ground violently. I raised my head and looked back in fear as the shadowy figure raced after me. His glowing eyes looked bloodthirsty. I held my arm out in front of my face, shielding my head from the coming attack and closed my eyes.

At the very second that I expected an impact with the creature, I felt my body lifting off the ground and heard the sound of gently flapping wings. I slowly opened my eyes and looked up to see Gabriel, cradling me like a child. I envisioned him with a bright cape and a horrible color ensemble of spandex and latex. He was my hero. He didn't say a word as he carried me off. The expression on his face told me that something was deeply troubling him. Somehow, I knew I was at the root of his anxiety. I tried to focus as we flew, but the cold wind dried my eyes, forcing them to close. I fell asleep in his arms; exhausted from my travels and the close call I just had with whoever that was. I awoke as he lay me down in a bed of delicate clovers. I opened my eyes to see his worried expression.

"Who was that?"

"That was Michael. He's infuriated," Gabriel stated.

I looked away, averting my gaze from Gabriel.

"Lilith has yet to return and he feels you have something to do with that. Tell me you have nothing to do with this, please?"

I said nothing.

"He found out that we meet in your dreams and he invited himself in," Gabriel continued with a concerned look on his face.

"Bastard."

"You know where she is, don't you?" he asked.

"Maybe," I replied, falling back into the bed of clovers and yawning.

"It would be best if you let her return. Don't let this become a personal vendetta," he suggested, attempting to reason with me like a hostage negotiator.

"I'll let her return when I know we won't be spied on. Consider her a prisoner of war until then." I smirked at my soul twin. "And for the record, this is all *very* personal to me."

"You *have to* let her go. The only thing this is going to do is stir up more trouble for you. God will send them directly *for you*, first and foremost. Not to mention, you're hurting *me*, by proxy."

"*If* I let her go, I expect you to tell her to get off my ass. *Anytime* I see her, or her little feathered friends, I'm gonna let Azrael rip them apart. Next time I won't tell him to drop her. Next time I'll let him finish her off for breakfast. I can't imagine she'd return to Heaven smelling very fresh," I mused.

I felt my shoulder shake gently.

"Let her go," Gabriel said sternly.

I awoke startled. I sat up and rubbed my eyes. Riley, Gabe and Lamar were standing in the room staring at me. Riley sat down on the edge of the bed next to me and smiled. I looked from face to face, confused. The others began to walk through the doorway. Eventually, all of our party was standing in Paulie's room, watching me.

"What the hell is going on?" I asked.

Lamar smiled, "We just came to check on you."

"*All of you?* Bullshit. What's up?" I asked.

"Jonah, care to speak up?" Paul presented him to me, like a door prize.

"Eden, we know you have a plan. We know you also have leverage in the back of the van. We want to know what you're thinking," Jonah said, sitting on the edge of the bed.

"If you're so mystical, 'Mr. Jubilant', then you wouldn't need to ask me what my plan is," I mocked.

He crossed his arms. "Is she always this cynical?" he asked Riley.

Riley nodded, "Yup. Especially when you back her into a corner."

"What I have in the back of the van isn't leverage at all. It's a homing beacon, and I have to get rid of her, before the wrath of God is brought down directly onto us. I thought it was a good idea, initially," I said, swinging my legs off the bed and standing up.

I stepped around the crowd of people and walked out of Paul's room into the hallway. I didn't realize at first that I had a trail of people walking behind me. *What the hell is their deal?* It felt like one of those games you play in kindergarten or like, a conga line of old people on a cruise ship.

I opened the front door of Paul's apartment and stepped out to the van. I opened the back door and heard muffled squawking coming from underneath some blankets and pillows. Pushing everything aside, I pulled the thermos from the van. I popped the tiny top nozzle used for pouring fluid from the jug. I took a deep breath in and pressed my lips to the nozzle.

"Hey!" I yelled into the thermos. The crowd of people that followed me was now staring at me like I was insane.

"Lilith! I know you can hear me!" I yelled into the thermos.

Lamar and Riley laughed. I had told them about her harassing me.

"Listen to me. I'm going to let you out of this thermos. If I see you, hear you, or *even think* that I saw or heard you *ever again*, I'll let Azrael rip you to shreds. I'll let him mangle your body to the point that you aren't able to reform. I'll scatter your stupid little bones in every corner of this planet. You understand me?" I said, mouth pursed to the nozzle.

I heard flapping in the thermos and the sound of her banging into the sides.

"Bring Azrael over here. If she tries *anything*, let him have her," I demanded.

Riley walked towards me with Azrael on his leash. He sat down at my side, staring up at the jug in my hands, attentively. I began tearing the tape off, layer by layer. I didn't realize until I tried removing it, just how much I had used. Once I had removed all of the tape, I unscrewed the lid slowly, and set it down. I stepped back, waiting for her to spring from her cell, but she didn't. I shook the thermos, holding it above my head. She didn't budge. I thought about dumping her on the ground, but I knew Azrael would automatically assume she was a snack.

"What the hell?" I asked, turning the thermos to look inside.

I saw the bright glow of her white eyes as she sprung from the bottom. I tried to block myself as she flew out. She ripped at my arms and face. Riley let go of Azrael's leash, and he clawed my flesh trying to reach her. I could hear his vice-like jaws snapping near my ear. She took off, flying away from us, cackling loudly.

"Repent! Repent!" she cawed as she flew off to safety.

I dropped to my hands and knees. The gashes she had inflicted burned. My skin felt like it had been slashed with razors then had salt poured into the wounds. Riley ran to my side and helped me to my feet. Blood dripped slowly from my arms and pooled at my side, soaking my shirt.

"Holy shit. What the fuck just happened?" Gabe asked, staring at us.

"It's okay dude, you start to get used to the craziness after a while," Lamar reassured my brother. He then came to my side, opposite Riley and the two of them helped me back into Paul's apartment. I felt very weak, very drained.

They assisted me to the couch and I sat down with a cringe and a groan. I looked at my arms and shook my head. I had large, deep gashes all along my forearms from attempting to protect my face. I felt my cheek. It was painful and sticky. I knew that she had gotten me pretty good. Riley left my side and went to the kitchen with Paul. They returned with wet wash clothes and helped me clean my wounds. Paul ran out of the room and disappeared down the hallway. He returned a few moments later with some hydrogen peroxide and handed it to me.

"Are you okay?" Riley asked, concerned.

"I'll be fine," I replied. I was livid.

I lifted my shirt slightly and looked at the claw marks on my flank from Azrael. I knew he didn't mean to hurt me; he was merely using me as a stepladder to reach the wretched bird. Every scratch, every cut, burned immensely.

"So what did you guys figure out while I was napping?" I asked, trying to take my mind off my wounds and pain.

"We found another rental company. We have to head back to the airport to pick up a van, or two. We assumed that Chicago was our next best move," Riley suggested.

"Sounds good. When are we going to get it?" I asked.

"We can go now, if you'd like to stay here and relax for a while," Jonah stepped into the conversation.

"Paulie, can I borrow your shower? I need to go clean up and hopefully heal these wounds," I said.

"Yeah, definitely. Riley, why don't you stay here with her? We can take care of the van pick up."

"I planned on it," Riley confirmed.

"I'd like to stick around as well. I'm so sick of riding in vehicles," Lamar chimed in.

"I'm pretty hungry. I'll go with you guys and snag some food while we're out, if you don't mind," Gabe added.

"Hell yeah! No problem, Bro. We'll get you some food," Paul replied smiling.

Jonah and the two women walked outside, followed by Gabe. Paul led Riley to the cabinet where all of the towels and wash clothes were. Lamar kicked off his shoes and threw himself back onto the couch. He smiled at me then rolled over onto his side, facing the back of the couch. Azrael sniffed at his hair and the back of his neck. Lamar rolled over with a laugh and faced us. He gently pet Azrael, as he sat and wagged his tail. Corey and Erick were seated near me. I looked at both of them. Corey looked as if he had something he wanted to say. My eyes narrowed as I looked at the young Pagan.

"Yes?" I asked, smirking.

Corey smiled bashfully, "Nothing."

"What did you want to know?" I asked him.

"Jonah told us about your ability. Can you still *create* life?" he asked skeptically.

Erick turned to him and shook his head. He backhanded his arm. "Ignore him. That really isn't any of our business."

"It's fine. The truth is, I don't really know. I just recently realized I can heal things. I'm not completely positive I'm capable of that."

"What about resurrection? Have you ever tried it?" Corey asked, amused.

Erick turned to him again and punched his arm.

"Ouch!" Corey laughed, holding his bicep.

"No, I've never tried it," I replied, baffled.

"Would you?" he asked again curiously.

"No. It's not my place. It isn't my right to choose when people live or die," I explained.

"Yet, you're in the medical field?" he interrogated.

"I'm a paramedic, yes," I answered.

He grinned, "So, you interfere with death on a regular basis."

"I used the ability I was given, to assist humanity. Science, technology," I justified my reasoning.

"Yet you could've avoided their death altogether by healing them," Corey suggested.

"Dude, stop!" Erick cradled his face in his hands, shaking his head.

"I didn't know I was capable of it," I replied, saddened by the reality of his statement.

"I'm sorry. Corey's still young. He's full of questions and hasn't figured out when to use *tact*," Erick excused his fellow coven member.

"It's okay. I never really thought about it that way," I replied.

Erick looked at Corey and shook his head with the *'I'm so ashamed of you'* look.

"If only I had known what I possessed," I added, pressing down on a bandage on my forearm.

Paul stepped into the room and nodded to Erick and Corey. They rose from the couch and headed towards the door with Paul.

"Thanks for talking with me. You're very enlightening." Corey smiled gently.

Erick smiled and bowed his head. "See you soon."

Riley was standing at the entrance of the hallway, leaning against the corner. He was staring at me, looking confused. "What was that all about?"

"Corey was harassing your woman," Lamar mumbled through his pillow.

I chuckled and walked towards Riley. He offered me his hand, and I took it. He led me to the bathroom and turned on the water. He helped me take my shirt off so I didn't touch any of my wounds then left me alone in the room. I got into the warm shower, flinching as soon as the water touched my tender skin.

I curled my arms up to my chest and leaned against the wall and tried to slow my breathing. I knew in the state that I was in I wouldn't be able to heal myself. I couldn't concentrate, I was in pain, I was sleep deprived and worried. I rocked back and forth under the warm water.

I pictured the garden. I imagined the shower as a soft rainstorm passing through as I danced under a canopy of drenched leaves. I was at peace. I was tranquil. I had stepped into a trance, leaving reality far behind. After a while, I looked down at my bare arms, relieved. I turned around to face the water and let the blood and pain wash off my skin like dirt and debris. I pulled my hair into a twist around the side of my neck.

I must have spent an hour in my trance, letting the water of the shower work its therapeutic magic. When I was ready to face the world I exited the shower, got dressed, and left the bathroom for the living room. There wasn't a soul to be found inside, so I walked outside and found everyone standing around conversing while Lamar and Azrael ran back and forth, playing.

"It's 4:15. We should head out soon. If we hurry we can hopefully find Victoria tonight, instead of having to wait until tomorrow morning," Riley was saying.

"Let's get ready to roll out then," Paul replied.

"I'll gather the circle. We need to do a quick blessing ritual before we depart. You guys go get yourselves ready," Jonah said with a faint smile.

Riley and I walked back into Paul's apartment to grab our belongings. Corey stared at me as I passed, stopping me. Riley continued without me.

"You... You really can heal," Corey said, grazing my arm with his hand.

"You knew that, why do you seem surprised?"

"Sometimes you can't help but wonder how much wool someone's pulling over your eyes. I wasn't sure if it was just bullshit or if Jonah was serious," he replied.

I smiled. "You're a smart kid. I'm glad you truly think for yourself and not buy into everyone's ploys."

"So, are you a good witch, or a bad witch?" he asked with a grin.

I snickered and shrugged, unsure of a response.

"She's bad," Gabe answered, as he walked by with a large box in his arms.

"I'm serious! Watch out for her voodoo hexes, she's coon-ass!" Gabe yelled to Corey, as he walked to the back of the van.

"He means Cajun, if you haven't heard that expression before," I explained.

Corey chuckled lightly. He looked concerned for a second, like maybe what my brother said was true. I winked at Corey and walked into Paul's apartment. I found Riley and gave him a peck on the cheek. He turned to me and smiled suspiciously. I grinned, my most innocent grin. He chuckled and wrapped his arm around my shoulder.

Corey followed us into the apartment and sat on the floor near Jonah and Paige. Jonah held out his hands. Corey and Brooke took each of his hands in one of their own and linked their free hand with Erick and Paige. They sat on a white silk cloth embellished with an ornate pentagram. The design was formed with multiple colors, woven together. The pentagram had a medley of natural items spread across it. There were crystals of several colors, twigs bundled together with silver twine, herbs, feathers and flower petals. Jonah reached into a small pouch and poured a small amount of dirt in the center.

The five of them closed their eyes, bowed their heads and began to chant. It sounded like Latin, but I wasn't sure. I felt the hair on the back of my neck stand on end. I had goose bumps on my arms as I watched and listened to their ritual. I could feel my heart racing, as I breathed in the aromatic herbs. I walked towards Jonah, and sat close by, closing my eyes. I listened to their chanting as I delved into my subconscious. I saw myself dancing around a fire, white dress blowing in the cool night breeze. I spun over and over again, throwing herbs and flowers into the blaze.

When they finished their ritual, I opened my eyes. I felt very relaxed. I felt safe. I felt protected. I smiled widely and thanked the coven for their blessing. We all rose to our feet as Jonah gathered up the crystals and twigs, gently placing them in a small silken bag. He pulled the strings tightly and tied it into a bow. He carried the ritual items out with him to the van. We all followed behind him.

"Well friends, I suggest we leave now while we're protected," Jonah said. We all piled into the two vans and departed for Chicago.

CHAPTER TWENTY FIVE
THE WINDY CITY BLOWS

By the time we left Detroit, it was almost 5:00pm. We knew that we were going to have to pick up the pace if we wanted to get to Chicago at a reasonable hour. We didn't want to have to wait until morning to find Victoria. Time was of the essence, anything wasted could mean more lives lost.

Our group was split up evenly. Paul, Jonah, Corey, Paige and Brooke were in one van, while Riley, Lamar, Gabe, Erick and I were in the original rental with Azrael. We had exchanged cell phone numbers in the event that we got separated, though it wasn't needed. People were continuously texting each other with updates and jokes.

The trip felt much longer than it should have. We were only traveling about two hundred and eighty miles, yet it felt like we had been driving for days. I guess I was still feeling the travel lag from the trip north. Our troop held conversation for a while, but I was too exhausted to get involved. I laid my head on the door of the van and began to doze off. I realized after a little while that conversation had also nodded off. I turned around and saw Gabe, Lamar and Erick asleep in the back.

"Are you sure you're okay to drive for a while?" I asked Riley.

"Yeah, I'm fine. Go ahead and rest," he replied with a soft smile.

He didn't have to tell me twice. I grabbed a pillow and drifted off to sleep.

I awoke in a place I had never seen before. I knew it was a dream. I was becoming much more aware of my subconscious as of late. I was standing in a field full of thorny weeds and sun burnt wildflowers. The unkempt plants ripped at my bare feet as I walked. The sky was darkening; a storm was brewing on the horizon. I could see the lightning's quick, continuous flashes. I needed to find shelter.

I turned around and saw a line of trees. There was an opening in the tree line, a dark break, in the tightly woven foliage. I grabbed the burlap bag next to me, and started walking towards the opening. I pushed aside the branches and leaves as I stepped through the untamed woods to the interior. I could hear water dripping, a trickle somewhere nearby. I crouched low, attempting to look around a shrub and saw what appeared to be a massive bayou in the distance. I stood up, stepping through the bushes and brush, then stepped into the open swamp.

The feeling immediately changed. I became uneasy and nauseous as I breathed in the stagnant air. There was something foul penetrating my nostrils, and it wasn't the swamp water. I jumped over a tree limb and landed on a mossy bed that sank under my feet and continued towards the water.

The air was humming. I knelt down and stuck my hand into the water, cupping some of the fluid in my palm. I pulled my hand back and saw the red wine coloring. I stood up and wiped my hand off on my skirt, staring out into the distance. The hum was getting louder. There was no sky in this place. In its place was a mixture of large oak, willow and cypress trees. Spanish moss hung from every branch, like musty cobwebs in the forgotten attic of a long abandoned home. There was definitely an eerie feeling. I needed to get out of here as quick as possible.

I grabbed my bag and jumped from stone to stone across the flowing, boggy water onto a small island of mossy logs and large rocks. I swayed to catch my balance, giving my equilibrium a second to readjust. Once I felt centered, I hopped across to the other side of the embankment, again from stone to stone, the rhythmic humming sound continuing to grow louder.

I traced along the flowing water, stepping over branches and avoiding holes. I pushed the low hanging Spanish moss aside and continued my trek. I had a nagging voice in the back of my mind, telling me to move forward.

Press forward. Don't look back. Don't turn around.

As the voice continued, I increasingly fought the urge to do the exact opposite. I noticed my pace had increased. My breath and heart rate raced as my feet moved quicker.

Keep going! Keep moving!
Don't look back!

I heard rustling, twigs snapping under a heavy foot. I heard splashes in the water and a moan in the distance behind me. My heartbeat doubled. I knew I wasn't alone. My pace increased again. The noises sounded closer. I wanted to stop and close my eyes. I wanted to wake myself up.

Don't stop.
Move faster. Move!
Run! Run! Run!

My quick pace transitioned into a run. I was tripping over my own feet, over branches and roots. I was becoming so afraid that I wasn't able to react properly. My chest ached as my lungs attempted to pump the putrid air faster through my lungs. I reached for my inhaler. I'm dreaming. It isn't there.

Oh God.

The humming sounded like a chant.

You're dreaming. This is just a dream. Nothing can hurt you. Nothing can...

I stopped in place and closed my eyes. I took in slow, deep breaths. I could feel my feet sinking into the soft, wet ground. I could still hear the snapping of twigs and branches behind me. The sounds were getting much closer as something was closing in on me.

Ten, It's just a dream.
Nine, Just wake up.
Eight, Breathe slowly.
Seven, Just wake up.
Six...
snap!

I stood motionless. The sound of wood breaking was right behind me. I couldn't concentrate enough to wake myself up. I opened my eyes for a second then closed them tightly.

Ten... Oh, God. I can't do this.

I was panting, sweat dripped from my forehead. I opened one eye and peered ahead of me. The marshy land was dark, malicious and intimidating. I closed my eyes again and tried to slow my breathing. I felt a warm rush of air on the back of my neck. It was timed with my own expirations. *It was breathing on me.*
Don't turn around.

I ignored my mental warnings and turned around quickly. There was nothing there. I sat down on a broken and battered log and stared out into the water, incredulous. I was embarrassed, even in my own mind. As I stared into the flowing water, I saw a small doll float by, face down. I cocked my head to the side and watched as it drifted by. My eyes stayed trained on the doll as it glided downstream. Once I couldn't see it any longer, I returned my gaze forward. There were bodies everywhere. *Human* bodies, animals. Women, men, *children*. The bodies bumped into each other, buoyantly drifting ever downstream.

Oh my God... I dropped to the wet ground, my eyes welled with tears. I was afraid. I clasped my hands over my mouth and pulled my knees to my chest. I watched, mortified, as hundreds of bodies floated by like a macabre parade. A black parade. I buried my face in my knees and tried to think of anything else. Anything other than their water logged, bloated, twisted faces. I tried to count backwards; the numbers weren't even registering as a thought. I tried to think of a silly song, but the only thought that flashed through my terrified mind was the corpses.

I heard cries of children, moans of women, screams of men. I couldn't look up. I wouldn't. How did I get myself into this mess? Why was I so compelled to delve into this swamp? The humming continued, meshed with cries.

I felt something drop onto my back, then my knee. I felt the wet splatter of something slimy land and slide off my hand. I raised my head slightly, to see over my forearms and knees. There were frogs, everywhere. *Dead* frogs, falling from the tops of the trees. I felt another one hit my neck. I reached back and grabbed it, throwing it into the water with a girly squeal. I clasped my hands over my mouth to muffle my loud shrieking.

I stood, flinching every time an amphibian touched my skin. I grabbed my bag and started to run forward, following the trail of the dead. I tried to watch where I stepped, avoiding the frogs' slimy dead bodies. I tried not to look in the water. I just wanted to get out. I wanted to wake up.

The air felt statically charged and there was a hissing sound all around me now. It started out low and progressively became louder and louder, almost deafening. I turned around to see a cloud of small objects moving rapidly towards me. As the cloud moved closer, the noise continued to grow. I dropped to my knees and covered my ears, clenching my eyes shut. I hummed to myself, rocking back and forth. I tried to drown the sound as it approached. I hummed the same rhythm I heard throughout the swamp.

I opened my eyes and saw the swarm dissipating, breaking formation and dropping to the ground. A few of them landed on me. I squealed and jumped, throwing what I now saw were bugs, off me. I knelt down and grabbed one by the leg.

Locusts? You've got to be kidding me.

I stared at my surroundings. I was encircled by death. I dropped my bag to the mossy ground and slumped over, defeated. At this point, I knew I couldn't wake myself up and that was the scariest part out of all of this. How long would I have to endure this hell? I decided to just let *whatever* was intended to happen, happen.

I looked at the curious bag. I didn't even know what was in it. I grabbed the burlap sack and set it between my folded knees, then slowly untied the top and began opening it. In the distance, I could hear a faint cry. I stopped opening the bag and turned my attention to the noise.

The crying was getting louder as it approached. It sounded like a child's cry. I could hear it, tracing along the last bend in the water. The crying became quicker, louder. As the rhythm sped up, the crying sounded more like laughter. It started as a light chuckle and ended with loud maniacal cackling.

The sound was above me. I looked above my head, to the mossy eave. Bodies floated by, pushing aside the branches and low hanging moss. It was exactly like the bodies in the swampy waters, only now they floated in the air, dripping blood as they drifted by, snapping twigs and branches as they snagged their flesh and clothing. Some were face up, while others were face down. The laughing continued.

I couldn't tell where it was coming from, only that it was close. I glanced from face to face, trying to locate the sound. It was so loud. I squeezed my temples. What the hell was going on? I glanced back up and watched a young girl float by, alone, without the company of the other corpses that had come before. Her skin was a pale blue, her lips were a darker blue, lifeless. Her eyes were open and had the milky white hue of death glazed over.

I watched, horrified, as the girl floated above me. Her black hair hung like the Spanish moss, blowing in the light, putrid breeze. The laughter had stopped. I stared at her face waiting to see her expression change. I was startled when I felt the bag in my hands move slightly. I broke my gaze from the dead girl and looked down at the bag.

I pulled back the top of the sack and tried to peer inside. It was so dark, I couldn't see a thing. I peeled the sides back and saw a black mass. I reached in and picked up the cold, clammy object, retrieving it from the burlap sack. As I raised it up to inspect it, that nagging part of my subconscious returned

Don't pick it up!

Throw it! Drop it!

I raised the object in front of me and gasped. I dropped it and watched as it rolled down the embankment into the swamp. It was the head of the girl. It laughed loudly as it hit the water. I looked at my shaking hands. They were covered with blood and strands of black hair. I felt something grab my shoulder and I screamed loudly.

"Are you okay?" Riley asked, staring at me.

"Oh, shit! Whoa," I said, trying to catch my breath. "Whoa, fuck." I turned around to glance in the back seat. Everyone was staring at me, with concerned looks on their faces.

"What were you saying?" Riley asked me.

"What are you talking about?" I asked him, confused.

"I don't know. You were babbling incoherently," Riley replied.

"That wasn't babble. She was speaking Latin. I don't know exactly what it was, but I scribbled down some of it." Erick held up a napkin covered in nonsense and stains.

"But I don't know any Latin." I shook my head, confused.

"I'll have to ask Jonah to translate it. He's good with it," Erick continued, ignoring me.

I looked at my brother. He looked bothered. Was he worried about me? "Where are we?" I asked, trying to change the subject.

Riley was focused on the road. "We're right outside Chicago. We'll be there in a few minutes. Traffic was pretty shitty on the way over."

"Want something to drink, Edie?" Lamar asked me, holding out a bottle of water.

"Sure, thanks," I said as I took the bottle from him. I unscrewed the lid and thought about my dream.

"Latin? It doesn't make any sense. Man, that was so creepy," I mumbled.

"What did you dream about?" Lamar asked.

"I don't know exactly. It was a pretty bad nightmare," I replied. I didn't want to talk about it. I chugged the bottle of water and tossed it in the back seat.

"Did it have anything to do with what's going on? Did it give you any new information?" he continued interrogating me.

"I don't think so. I don't really know."

"I guess we'll find out once this is translated," Erick interjected. "Hopefully it makes sense. Sometimes Latin is hard to translate."

Riley asked, "Did you see Gabriel?"

"No. I wish he'd been there. I might not have freaked out so bad."

"I heard you counting," Riley said. "That was the only thing that made sense."

"That's how I wake myself up, it wasn't working." I frowned.

"If I'd have known you were having a nightmare, I would've woken you up sooner." Riley grabbed my hand. "Sorry."

I sat quietly, watching out of the front windshield as Riley weaved through traffic. I looked at the sky from the side window. I couldn't see a single star, thanks to the low ceiling of clouds and the overabundance of street lights in the city.

Riley exited the interstate and stopped at a gas station. He turned off the van and watched in the mirror, waiting for the second van to pull in. I saw the headlights draw closer and sighed with relief. We had all made it to Chicago unscathed.

"We need to fuel up," Riley said, opening his door. "You guys need some snacks or drinks? Might want to stock up now. We don't know how long we'll be on the road once we pick Victoria up."

"I'm gonna take this to Jonah," Erick said, waving the napkin in the air.

I watched Gabe and Lamar walk into the convenience store, followed shortly thereafter by Corey and Paige. I lit a cigarette, standing off in the grass. Riley and Paul were getting gas for our vans at adjacent pumps. Jonah was stretching outside the van when Erick approached him. Brooke stepped out of the van and clasped Jonah's hand.

I couldn't hear what they were saying, but I watched Erick hand the napkin to Jonah, who stared at it for a minute, then looked back at Erick with a very odd expression. Erick pointed at me and nodded. Jonah let go of Brooke's hand and stepped away from her and Erick. He walked towards me at a quick pace.

"Tell me what you saw," he said loudly from a distance as he approached.

"What does it say?" I asked.

"What did you see, Eden?" he asked again, more urgently.

"What does it matter? Whatever I was saying, I didn't hear in my dream. At least I don't remember hearing it," I continued evasively.

"What you said, I've seen before. What did you dream?" he asked again, lowering his voice and slowing his speech.

I gave him a brief synopsis of the dream, told him about the bag, the trees, the water, the bodies, the frogs and locusts. I told him about the creepy little girl and the head in the bag. I told him everything I could remember. Nowhere in that dream did I recall hearing whatever I supposedly said in my sleep.

"You were basically saying an incantation; a foreshadowing. Erick did not catch all of it, but he did get four lines written correctly," he said.

"What did I say?" I asked nervously.

"Vestri cruor mos spill, amo flumen, rutilus. Vestri viscus mos occulto terra, iam mortuus. Vestri bones mos congeries, constructum quod tumbus. Vestri placitum mos vado incuratus in tempestas rugio."

I studied his expression. *What the hell did I say?* As much as I wanted to, I never learned Latin.

"So what does all of that jargon mean, exactly?" I asked confused.

"The exact translation is debatable. Latin words have multiple meanings; it's hard to say word for word, what the translation is. But the English version of the incantation, I know. It's been around for centuries, based on the old Latin version," he said, then grabbed my hand. "Your blood will spill, like the rivers, red. Your flesh will cover the land, now dead. Your bones will pile, build and tumble. Your pleas go unheard in the storm's rumble," he translated then crumpled up the napkin.

"Where did that come from? I don't understand," I asked, shaking my head.

"I wish I could tell you. It isn't a good sign though."

Gabe and Lamar were walking out of the store when they noticed us talking. They made a beeline towards us, curious about what Jonah had figured out. They stood by my side, arms loaded with snack cakes, bags of chips, beef jerky and drinks.

"It was a sort of war chant. A tactic used to scare the enemy. Witches, warlocks, whatever you choose to call them, would chant it and spit blood to intimidate the opponents. It was very dark, and a lot of the time, it was associated with demonic summoning, Satanism and dark magic."

Paul joined us when he was done pumping gas.

"Ew, that doesn't sound good." Lamar frowned.

"So is it something to worry about? Was it some sort of repressed memory resurfacing?" I asked.

Riley walked to the side door of the van, attached Azrael's leash and lit a cigarette as he walked over to join us.

"I hope not. For all of our sake, I hope that wasn't a memory." Jonah shook his head.

"So what did she say? She's always talking in her sleep. It's just typically in English," Riley said, exhaling smoke.

"It seems as though Eden was *channeling*."

"Channeling what?" Gabe asked, chewing a mouthful of beef jerky.

"I don't know exactly, but it typically isn't something positive. It's seems as if there's other forces at work as well," Jonah replied.

"As well as?" I asked, confused.

"As well as us. As well as God and the Archangels," he replied.

"Who the hell else *could* be involved?" Riley asked.

Jonah looked at him, "I don't know, but I don't think I want to find out."

Riley looked at me. He could tell I was worried.

"Do you mean something else as in, something demonic?" I asked.

"Let's get going. Victoria's place is only 10 to 15 minutes away from here and it's getting late," Riley interjected, attempting to distract us from the uncomfortable news.

He wrapped his arm around my waist and kissed my cheek.

"Fuck. What if there's something dark *in* me?" I whispered to Riley.

"Don't worry. You know he's into all that bogus hocus pocus," Riley whispered back.

Jonah decided to ride with us for the final leg of our trip into Chicago. He hopped in the back seat and sat silently. I got that eerie feeling like someone was boring a hole into the back of my head. I knew he was staring at me. I turned around and met his gaze. He attempted to look away quickly and avoid my eyes.

"So, why me?" I blurted out randomly.

"What do you mean?" Jonah replied.

"Why was I the one to say that shit?" I clarified.

"You've always had strange dreams and visions, right?" he answered my question with another question.

"Yeah, but they're typically in a language I understand," I replied.

"Or so you think. I believe there's a part of your past that we aren't aware of. I'm guessing you have a darker side." Jonah sneered. "Have you ever had any encounters with the dark arts? Or with 'The Devil'?"

I shook my head, "I don't even believe in the devil."

"He's there, always has been. I'm sure the others remember him. We don't want to have any darkness wrapped into this mess," Jonah replied.

"Says the guy who practices witchcraft… with followers," Riley jabbed.

"Neopaganism isn't 'witchcraft'. It's white magic. We don't have anything to do with the dark arts. Some stray, yes, that's true. But *we* don't," Jonah shot back defensively.

"So what you're saying is Edie was spouting off something bad? Like, really bad?" Riley asked skeptically.

"Well, it *wasn't good*, by any means. Some would outright say she was speaking in a demonic language," Jonah answered.

"Riley didn't get to hear what I had said," I reminded Jonah. I turned to Riley, "I said something about blood and bones and flesh and stuff. Like a crazy version of a Mother Goose nursery rhyme."

"I blame the horror movies. You probably just picked it up from all the shit you watch," Lamar jested.

Gabe interjected, "Hey, don't blame the arts. You sound like one of those crazy parents that blame video game developers for their fat, spoiled, asshole child failing in school. It's bad parenting, not bad games. Just like its Eden's twisted head, not the movies."

We all chuckled lightly at Lamar and Gabe's debate.

Jonah continued when the laughter abated, "It doesn't matter much where it came from. My only concern would be if there were others involved in this upcoming war."

"You think it's something that may arise soon? Can you *see* anything?" I asked.

"The only thing that worries me would be the arrival of a much darker force also fighting to claim the Earth. And no. No, I do not see anything, as of now. Things are still so cloudy, since we haven't had the chance to communicate with the others. But I do see some of the war."

"Like what?" Gabe asked, curious, or skeptical. I couldn't tell which.

"Can we change the subject? Please?" I asked and turned around, facing forward.

"We're almost to Victoria's. Everyone chill out. We don't know how much convincing we're gonna have to do. And I doubt we'll be able to convince her to join us if we're bickering back and forth like a bunch of hormonal old biddies," Riley ordered.

The van became quiet other than the occasional sigh, yawn or cough. We turned the corner onto Victoria's street and stared at the beautiful houses. Her neighborhood was very well kempt. Large, extravagant homes lined the streets, with perfect landscaping and expensive cars in the circular driveways. I felt out of place.

"Damn. Looks like she's done pretty well for herself," Riley said, staring at the giant white house at the end of the cul-de-sac. He turned off the engine. We all sat quietly, wondering if we should approach the house.

"What if she's like, all snooty and tells us to leave? We don't look like we should be here," Lamar whispered.

"Well, we won't know that until we get up there, will we? What if she's just the maid or something? You never really know," Riley replied with a grin.

"Are you sure we've got the right girl?" Gabe asked.

"Yes, I'm sure," Riley confirmed.

Riley, Lamar, Paul and I began to shamble towards the huge house. It had four large pillars in the entryway, with ivy spiraling upwards. The landscaping looked professionally done, with rounded, pruned hedges and mosaic walkways. There was a fountain in the center of the lawn, ornamented with a beautiful angelic girl pouring water from a pitcher above her head. Paul and I studied the fountain.

"We're definitely at the right place," we said simultaneously.

"What if someone sees the vans and thinks we're coming to kidnap her? I don't wanna go to jail." I swallowed nervously, only half joking.

"Would you guys stop being little bitches? *Jesus*," Riley scoffed.

"Lamar, you have the feather?" I asked.

"Yes ma'am."

We stepped onto the well-lit front porch and collectively held our breath. Riley leaned forward and pressed the doorbell. I winced and waited for the killer Doberman to attack us, or the trap door to open under our feet, sending us to a watery grave of piranhas and sharks below. Or maybe we'd get sucked into a deadly game of Parcheesi or chess. Either way, I was afraid to see what the outcome was going to be. Something didn't feel right.

Riley leaned forward and rang the doorbell again. He cleared his throat and held his hands behind his back.

"Just a minute!" a female voice answered from inside the house.

I realized there were only three of us standing on the porch. I turned around to see where the rest of our party was. Gabe stayed in the van with plans to nap. The pagans stayed behind, discussing whatever it is that pagans discuss. Cool rocks and flowers or something, I don't know. But I digress; Paul was still in front of the fountain, jaw dropped, staring at the perfectly carved, naked breasts of the marble angel. I chuckled and turned back around to face the house.

The door opened slightly, "Can I help you?" the woman asked through the crack of the chained door.

She appeared to be in her mid-fifties. She was well dressed, wore too much makeup and smelled of wine and perfume. She reminded me of my therapist. Well, my ex-therapist.

Riley smiled politely. "Yes, ma'am. We're looking for Victoria Stewart."

"Are you friends of Tori's?" she asked skeptically.

"Yes, ma'am. We've been trying to reach her, but haven't been able to get ahold of her. We had plans for tonight. I suppose she must've forgotten," Riley continued charmingly. He sounded so proper, it was throwing me off. I was expecting him to cuss out the lady and have us arrested for something.

"It's *abhorrently* chilly tonight. Come on in and have some warm apple cider," she said with a smile, as she opened the door widely.

We took that as an invitation for all of us to enter. She looked cross. I suppose the invite was only for Riley. We didn't care, she was right. It was cold. And we hadn't had a chance to sit down and warm up with anything, let alone apple cider by a fire place in a swank pad. She excused herself and stepped out of the room.

We all stood around, gawking at the paintings and fine art décor coating the embellished walls. Paul and Lamar walked over towards a golden colored statue and were quietly arguing whether it was real and whether they should try to sneak it out.

"I'm sorry, honey, I didn't catch your name. What was it?" she asked Riley, as she returned to the parlor with a pitcher of cider and a tray of glasses.

"My name's Riley. Riley *Thaddeus* Nixon," he said, emphasizing the Thaddeus, in case she was trying to trick us.

"Hmm. Your name doesn't ring a bell. I don't believe I've ever heard her mention you. Are you sure you're a friend of hers? You could be a friend of *mine* if you'd like." she winked and placed her hand on Riley's arm.

Lamar, Paul and Gabe snickered behind them, then began to fake cough and clear their throats with a failed attempt to cover their laughter.

My hands clenched tightly. I wanted to punch the cougar in her Botox-injected face.

"Uhh… " Riley nervously pulled his arm away and smiled politely, "Not to be rude ma'am, but we're kind of in a hurry."

"Claudia."

"Excuse me?" he asked.

"I'm not *ma'am*, I'm Claudia." she winked slyly at Riley and slid closer to him.

Paul let out a sharp hyena laugh and clasped his mouth shut quickly. He saw my eyes narrow and mouthed "sorry" to me.

"Do you happen to know where Vic… Where Tori is?" Riley continued.

"Oh, you know Tori, always off on some harebrained scheme to save the world through art and protest. I thought I taught her well. I thought she was aware that the sycophant, activist cliché is *such a* faux pas," she sipped from her wine glass. Riley and I looked at each other and mouthed "what the fuck?" at the same time. How could *an angel* have been born from *this woman*?

"Oh, how rude of me. Riley, would you prefer some wine instead of cider?" she asked with a flirty flitter of her lashes.

"No, thank you, Mrs. Claudia," he replied.

"Oh, you're *so* proper! I bet your mother is so proud of the strapping young man you've become." she smiled and ran her hand down Riley's arm, seductively.
Don't bash her face in with the fake gold statue.
Stop staring at the telephone cord, strangling takes too long.

"Miss Claudia. It's very important that we speak to Tori. Do you know where she is or not?" Paul interjected with a twinkle in his eye. He was excited to play.

"Oooh, and who might you be, fine sir?" she asked, staggering towards Paul, tripping over her own feet and giggling like a high school lush.

"I'm Paul," he replied with a smile. "I'm not really a friend of Tori's, just an acquaintance. I'd rather be *your* friend." He laughed.

I ran to Riley's side. "Holy shit, what's going on? She's gonna molest all of you guys. The cougar's on the prowl. I repeat, the cougar's on the prowl!" I whispered to Riley.

He chuckled and turned to see Paul's reaction.

"And who are *you*? I didn't catch your name either, honey," she said, running her finger across Lamar's chest.

"I'm... Llama." Lamar smiled awkwardly.

Paul was standing behind her, pretending to 'hump' and spank her. Laughter erupted across the room.

"What's so funny?" she wiped her mouth. "You boys wanna go swimming?" she asked, speech slurring.

I crossed my arms. I'd had enough.

"Look, lady. I realize you probably haven't gotten any action lately. I can tell by the huge house and giant rock on your wedding finger that your husband obviously is too obsessed with work or golf to play 'widow and the cabana boy' with you. But we aren't here to sate your sexual hunger." I sneered, arms crossed and eyes narrowed.

"Shit, I will," Paul mused with his hand in the air.

"You aren't helping," I said through my clenched teeth.

"We just want to know where we can find Tori," Riley said with a sigh.

"Well, why didn't you just say so? I thought you were a group of swingers that saw my ad," she guffawed.

"Well, for the tenth time, we're friends of Tori's. That's who we're here to see." I rolled my eyes. "Okay, so now that you know we aren't swingers for you to play with, where the hell is she?" I asked, getting very annoyed with the lousy lush.

"I don't know exactly. I haven't spoken to her in weeks. Last I heard she was gallivanting off to California, or was it Oregon? Oh, I don't know. Somewhere on the West coast. She said something about eloping with her little boyfriend Brandon. I think it was all just to spite me. She knows I don't approve of the kid," she pouted and sipped from her wine glass.

"Her boyfriend, *Brandon*?" Jonah asked.

"I think that's his name. Short for... Brandon or what have you." she rolled her hand in the air, snob style.

"What?" I laughed. "Was she going to Seattle?"

"Oh, yes! I'm sorry. Seattle, San Francisco... both teeming with people living *alternative* lifestyles. Ugh, so distasteful." she shook her hands as if just saying the words gave her some transmittable disease.

"Well, clearly you pay attention to your daughter very well. I'm so surprised to see her leave you. I don't understand why anyone would want to do that," I mused, shaking my head patronizingly.

"Aren't you just *darling*!" she smiled at me with those same 'kiss me, you fool' eyes. I shivered.

"Well, thanks for all the information and cider ma'am. We're going to head out. It was nice to meet you," Riley said, making a break for the door.

"Oh, no. Don't leave yet, I really enjoy your company." she pouted and squeezed his arm again.

"I'm pretty sure his wife wouldn't want that," Lamar said nodding to me.

She followed his gaze and met my eyes.

"Oh, I'm sorry," she giggled. "This must happen a lot, with such a handsome husband."

"Not really. Most people know how to show tact and keep their fantasies in their head," I replied, jaw clenched.

"Well, thanks lady," Paul said as he opened the front door and began ushering us all outside.

"Do come back and visit, *any* time!" she winked at Riley.

I grabbed his arm and pulled him out of the house.

"Ouch. What're you doing? I wouldn't let her do anything. Relax," Riley tried to calm me down.

"I wasn't worried about you." I sneered. "I was worried if I didn't get out sooner I was going to bludgeon her to death with a table lamp or half naked statue."

Riley laughed loudly and kissed my cheek.

We all gathered near the vans and tried to figure out our next move. We still needed to head to Washington, Tennessee and Texas. It was too difficult to make a spur of the moment decision, especially standing out in front of the sex crazed cougar's den. We decided to head back towards the interstate and hit up one of the diners, if we could find one. We all hopped into the vans and sped off towards our food-filled destination.

We got lucky. After countless failed attempts, we actually managed to find a diner open and serving food. When we arrived, Gabe offered to stay outside for a few minutes and give Azrael a chance to relieve himself and do a little munching. The rest of us piled out of the vans and walked inside. We got a little corner booth and pulled another table up to it so we were all able to sit together. We ordered a round of coffee for everyone and slid the salt and pepper shakers off to the side. I pulled out the map and laid it down on the sticky table.

"Okay, let's see," I said, tracing interstates and highways from Illinois to Washington.

"Why's that say I-l-l-i-n-o-i-s-?" Paige asked.

"Um, because that's what state we're in. Illinois?" Paul replied confused.

"But I thought the 's' was silent?" she continued.

Everyone at the table glanced from face to face.

"The 's' *is* silent. That doesn't mean it isn't in the name," Lamar interjected.

"Oooh. I thought it was Chicago, I-l-l-a-n-o-y!" she blushed.

She's going to be really helpful.

Everyone at the table chuckled to themselves. We poured over the map, scouring for our easiest route. We thought about splitting up and meeting back in Louisiana or Texas, but realized if anything happened our defense would be weakened by being separated. We decided to head straight for Seattle.

But before doing so, we were going to have to make sure that Brandon, at the very least, was still there. Riley pulled out his little notepad filled with information. He flipped through multiple pages and then stopped. He pulled his cell phone out of his pocket and began dialing numbers. As the phone rang, he put it on speaker phone. We listened as it rang and then stopped.

"Hello?" a male voice answered.

"Hello, Mr. Sullivan?" Riley asked.

"Yeah. Who's this?" Brandon asked suspiciously.

"Yes, hello. I'm calling in regards to the drawing for the cruise you've won. I was wondering if I could speak with you for a minute, to clarify some information."

"What cruise? I didn't enter any drawing for a cruise?" he replied, sounding alarmed.

"I believe your name was put in by a Ms. Victoria Stewart? Does that name ring a bell?" Riley asked and cringed.

"Yeah, that's my girlfriend. I didn't realize she entered us for a cruise," he replied, sounding slightly more relaxed.

"Well, she did and you've won! Now I just have a few questions for you. It'll only take a moment of your time then we'll send the confirmation letter to your email address with instruction on how to pick a date and such." Riley straightened his imaginary tie and pushed his invisible glasses up on the bridge of his nose.

"What do you need to know?" he asked.

"Are you still living at the same address your girlfriend recently used, in Seattle?" Riley asked, being very vague.

"Yeah," he replied.

"And is the number I called you on the best number to contact you?" Riley smirked.

"Yeah," he sounded annoyed by Riley's barrage of questions.

"Lastly, in order to determine what style of suite and cruise line to send you aboard, how old are you and your girlfriend? You'll receive two tickets. I'm assuming you'd want to bring her." Riley smiled, holding his finger up to his mouth to hush our giggling.

"Yeah, it would be the two of us. I'm 27 and she's 23," he replied. We could hear a woman's voice in the background. Brandon tried to muffle the receiver, "Apparently we won that cruise you put in for."

I looked at Riley.

"Oh, shit," Riley whispered.

We could hear her clearer as she was now closer to the phone. "I didn't enter any contest for a cruise. What're you talking about? And it's midnight. Why would anyone be doing business out of business hours?" she asked.

"Motherfuckers!" he said as he returned to the phone call in question. "Listen here, you asshole..."

"Hang up!" I whispered. All of us were doing the 'end call' mime hand signals.

"What the fuck... Who are you? We didn't enter for a cruise. Tell me the truth!" Brandon said, obviously angry.

"Oh, Maybe I have the wrong Brandon Sullivan and Victoria Stewart. I'm sorry for bothering you," Riley said and quickly hung up.

We all started laughing.

"That was great!" Lamar said.

Corey nodded, "Dude, you're great at making shit up on the spot."

"If they don't want to take their cruise, I'll go!" Paige added with a smile.

The laughing died off and smiles fell flat as everyone realized she was serious.

"It was a trick, Paige. We were just trying to make sure the two of them were actually in Seattle," I attempted to explain.

"Oh. Ha!" she laughed. She really didn't get it... still.

"Where did you get this one?" I asked Jonah quietly.

"Long story." he hung his head, ashamed.

Gabe walked into the diner and sat at the table, "Damn, why's everyone laughing, what did I miss?"

"Riley called Brandon in Seattle pretending to give him a cruise vacation, just trying to see if they're there," Erick explained.

"It was awesome," Corey confirmed with a chuckle.

"Damn it! I always miss the good stuff."

We ordered our food and continued to make our plans. We decided that we would go ahead and make a run for Seattle, while we knew the couple was there. It would've been quicker for us to all fly, but we didn't have *that* much funding. So we opted to spend the night in Chicago and leave first thing in the morning.

"You know, it seems like everything has started to go downhill since we hit Chicago," Lamar speculated.

"I noticed that, too. I just didn't want to complain," Riley said.

"I hope it isn't our fault," Corey added.

"No, it isn't," Riley and I said simultaneously.

"It's just bad timing, or our shitty luck," I explained.

"I hope it gets a little easier on us," Brooke spoke up, finally.

"Me, too," Lamar agreed.

"I'm sure it will. Don't lose hope, guys." Paige smiled.

I chuckled lightly, seeing how happy-go-lucky and easy going she was. She took everything with a grain of salt. Despite her attempt to cheer us up, I just wasn't feeling it. It was starting to dawn on me that this entire trip sucked. It wasn't that I was worried about not getting everyone together, or concerned about our safety any more. I was more or less just sick of it. Literally. My stomach turned constantly.

I wanted to be at home, in bed with Riley. I wanted it to be just us, and our animals. I wanted everything to go back to the way it was. The more and more I thought about it, the more I realized that even if we managed to save the day, even if we managed to save all of humanity, nothing would ever be the same. Nothing would ever just 'go back to normal'. Not after all of the death.

"Ugh!" I threw my head back onto the seat. They all turned to face me. "The windy city blows!"

Chapter Twenty Six
Filling in the Blanks

I awoke the next morning feeling well rested. If I had dreamt, I didn't remember any of it. It was fantastic to sleep in an actual bed, rather than the seat of a car. We all rented rooms at one of the last remaining open hotels. We struggled to find one after we left the diner and decided that we'd head out once everyone had gotten enough sleep, had time to shower and eat a full breakfast.

Riley and I took Azrael for a short walk, then went into the lobby and enjoyed a *complimentary* breakfast. It seemed that everyone was downstairs eating and eager for an early start. We all conversed about our *game plan* for convincing Brandon and Tori to join up with us.

"It may be a little harder to do now, since the whole *cruise* thing," Gabe suggested.

"I didn't plan on walking up to the dude and being like, 'oh hey, I'm the ass hat who called you and tricked you into giving me information by lying about a nonexistent cruise'. Don't think that would be very smart. He sounds big," Riley mused, shaking his head.

"Still, he may be a little more reluctant to listen," Gabe stated.

I grinned, "You haven't seen our leverage. We haven't had to use it yet."

"Oh, no. What do you have? Rohypnol?" Gabe asked nervously.

"No, much better," I nodded to Lamar. "Show him."

Lamar pulled a single, white feather out of his coat pocket.

Gabe laughed loudly. "Nice... tickle torture? It's very cartoon-esque. You'd make one helluva' villain, Edie."

Lamar nodded emphatically. "I said the exact same thing. Yup."

"Wow, thanks for the vote of confidence, you guys!" I slapped Gabe's arm. "It isn't *just* a feather. This is one of Gabriel's. When we touch it, we see The Great Divide."

"Like visions or flashbacks?" Corey asked, getting curious by our conversation.

"Not exactly," I responded.

"Like astral projection?" Erick chimed in.

"No. It's more similar to time travel. Riley, why don't you explain?" I asked, trying to dodge the trouble of describing it.

"Ugh, I hate that shitty feather." Riley rolled his head back, aggravated.

Gabe and Erick looked at each other confused.

Riley stabbed his muffin with a plastic fork, leaving his food impaled. "Basically, when we touch that cursed plume, we *relive* The Great Divide. And by relive, I mean, we feel the horrible agony of having our wings ripped from our backs. We feel the pain in our chest as God takes away every bit of us that makes us heavenly. Our souls feel like they're drowning in sorrow and ineffable pain."

The group fell silent as they imagined Riley's words.

"So, if they don't want to listen, we make them *see and feel* the truth," Riley continued, sipping from his paper coffee cup.

"It's just in your mind though, right?" Erick asked.

Riley slid his chair backwards and turned his back to our companions. He raised his t-shirt up, revealing two long, disfiguring scars. "No, it's not 'just in our minds'. We literally relive the feeling. The wounds are inflicted again. And I can't even begin to describe the pain I felt. Thankfully, Edie was there."

"That's horrible," Brooke said with a frown.

"Yeah, it wasn't very fun. I was the first to find out what the feather did," Riley said.

"Has anyone else taken some convincing?" Corey asked.

Riley turned to look at him. "So far, only one other person has touched it."

"Wait, people see it, too? Or did you mean angels?" Erick asked.

"Oh, yeah, how did Jere handle it?" Lamar added.

"Jeremiah didn't believe me. He thought I was drunk or trying to pull some ridiculous prank. I tried to warn him, but he just wouldn't listen. He called me a liar, so I changed the subject completely." Riley smiled. "I told him I had seen a huge white bird that looked like an eagle. I knew he knows birds pretty well, so I asked him if there was such a thing as an albino eagle." Riley laughed at his own ingenious methods of madness.

"I motioned towards the feather on the table, asking him what he thought. As soon as he touched the damned thing, he dropped to the floor and started screaming in pain. I laughed for a second then used a pair of tongs to grab it from his hands." Riley snickered.

Paul laughed and shook his finger at Riley. "Dude, that's wicked as hell. There's something wrong with you."

Riley shrugged. "I needed him to see the truth, he wouldn't listen."

"So you let your best friend writhe in pain?" Gabe asked. "That's a dick move."

"No, he didn't hold it as long as I did. And God didn't mutilate his body quite like he did with me. My pain was a vendetta. He had it pretty easy," Riley replied defensively.

"I thought you guys just found out about this recently? Your scars look like they're old, fully healed. Did Eden heal you?" Jonah asked, speculating.

"Yeah, the night I told Jere, which was the night after I had touched the feather, Edie found that she could heal. It was the same night that her tattoos exuded from her skin," Riley said, then bit into his rock hard muffin, using the impaling fork as a handle. He chewed for a minute then sneered at his bran nemesis.

I took a bite of my soggy, room temperature bacon and spit it out, changing my mind on how hungry I was.

"So, you never told us how you coaxed Paulie out of the sin bin." Riley smiled widely, looking at Lamar.

Paul and Lamar laughed loudly. "He's a lying bastard!" Paul shouted with a chuckle, punching Lamar's arm.

"Ouch!" Lamar laughed and caressed his abused extremity.

"He walked up to me and was all like, 'dude, you look like you like to party. There's some totally hot, drunk chicks outside looking for guys to party with'. I was like, whoa, awesome. Who is this amazing man? He must've been a gift from the heavens!" Paul said. "So yeah, then I walk out and see Riley's ugly mug," Paul continued, laughing heavily.

"Oh thanks, douche. Like you have much room to talk," Riley joined in the laughter.

There was a gasp and we all turned to see a little old lady sitting at a small table behind us with a young child. We all snickered lightly when we realized she had heard Riley's remark. How long had she been there? How much had she heard of our story?

"Excuse us, ma'am," Jonah smiled politely.

"She knows too much. Maybe we should, you know, *take care of her*," Riley said sarcastically, doing the throat slit motion with his finger.

She looked at us as if we were a table full of lunatics. She grabbed her purse and walked to the other side of the table. "Come on, honey, we'll just eat something once we get back on the road," she said as she grabbed the child's arm and walked out of the dining room, staring at us.

We all laughed until we couldn't breathe.

"Oh, man, that was awful," Lamar said between breaths.

"*Awfully awesome!*" Paul added. "So, anyway, back to the story; your little pet monkey, Lamar, is one helluva' good con artist. He had me fully convinced there was a limo full of hot, half naked chicks looking for a shmuck like me to get shit faced with," Paul began as the laughter died down.

"Yeah, I thought you were gonna kill me when we got outside. I stuck my hand in my pocket and was all kinds of prepared to shove that feather down your throat if I had to, to get you off of me." Lamar chuckled with a nervous glance in Paul's direction.

"Ha ha! That was funny as hell, dude. I'm impressed, seriously," Paul said to Lamar, patting him on the back.

"So what's your part in all of this mess, Lamar?" Corey asked.

"I didn't want to be alone. Not that I'm afraid of being alone... it's just that I'd rather be with friends when the world ends," Lamar replied with a shrug.

Paige looked at him curiously. "What about your family?"

Lamar sighed and took a bite of his scrambled eggs.

"We'll get Chuck, I promise," I said to Lamar, leaning in towards him.

"What about your family? What are all of you doing here?" Lamar replied.

Erick nodded. "Good point."

"We all have to keep in mind that we're in the middle of a horrible event. Sometimes it's best to lighten the mood. It's always easier to deal with traumatic ordeals with laughter," I interrupted. The room became silent as everyone looked to the floor, or their bowls, or at me. "We need to help each other. We need to keep the smiles up. If we give in and let the dark side of this get the best of us, we'll wind up killing ourselves before we ever get a chance to change this."

"Just like Matthew..." Riley mumbled.

"Exactly," I agreed.

"What did happen with Matthew? Did you guys find him?" Paul asked.

"Matthew was technically the first angel we met. He, um. He..." I struggled to speak.

"He saw what was coming. He saw the future. He killed his family then jumped off of a bridge over the Mississippi," Riley filled in where I left off.

"We tried to save his family. We all rushed to Houma, to his address. But it was too late by the time we made it," I finished, voice shaking.

"That's fucked up," Gabe said somberly.

I shrugged. "I kind of understand why he did it. He didn't want them to see what happens. It's going to be terrifying."

"What was terrifying was seeing a dead woman cradling her dead children in a corner of the room with 'I'm sorry' scribbled on the walls in blood," Riley said coldly.

"That must've been terrible for you both," Brooke said teary eyed.

"Well, what can you do? It's part of the job," I replied as I stared at the table, sweeping the memory under the rug, piling the skeletons back into the closet.

"Wow, okay. Now that we've thoroughly ruined the atmosphere, I suppose we should get the hell out of this jip joint," Riley suggested with a sudden loud voice, sliding his chair back.

"Yep," Lamar agreed, taking his tray over to the trashcan.

Jonah walked over to me and placed his hand on my shoulder. "I'm sorry you had to see that. I know how badly you wish for a family of your own," he said remorsefully.

"You don't know anything about me," I replied snidely, watching everyone leave.

"I wasn't trying to hurt you, I meant it. I know you want your own children. I'm very sorry that you witnessed that," he said again and gently hugged me.

I laid my head on his shoulder and let down my armored wall.

He gently placed his hand on my back. "You've led a remarkable life, full of amazing experiences. Hopefully, someday you'll see that for yourself and realize that you aren't missing anything," he paused for a second. " Though... curious. Eden... I *do* see children in your future," he pulled away and smiled widely.

"Bullshit. I call shenanigans on you Mr. Jubilant Jonah, mystic, oracle." I chuckled at his lame attempt to cheer me up.
False hope.

"I assume Paulie mentioned our circus tour." he smiled. "We used the gifts we had to get into that gig. I do have glimpses of the past, present and future. It's not complete, but it *does* happen."

"Then what's going to happen with this battle?" I asked skeptically.

"Well, that I truly can't answer. There's too many different influences on the outcome. Too many variables. Namely, your little stunt you plan on pulling." he raised an eyebrow.

"Oh, no, no, no. You..." I shook my head, nervously.

"I know what you have in mind, but I swear to you, I give you my word, I will not tell a soul what you house in your little noggin of schemes." he looked me in the eyes as he swore. I believed him. "If it'll work, I'll be at your side, as well. If He'll accept your compromise, I'll follow you to the end," he smiled softly, squeezing my hands gently.

"Come on, we need to catch up to the others before they start to worry or wonder what we're up to." he grabbed my hand and walked me out of the dining room.

Could it be true? Children?

We walked to the elevator and pressed the up arrow. I stared at the numbers as they ticked down, stopping on the floors above. I thought about everything that Jonah had said to me. I realized how bewitching his personality was. I could see the allure of his aura and fully understood why his coven would follow him to their doom, just to be at his side.

"Did you really see kids in my future?" I asked, staring at the floor numbers as they ticked by.

"Yes."

"But, if I die, it'll never happen. How is it possible?"

"I told you, I can't see the outcome of this war because of all the influences. Who's to say the world is going to end? Who's to say that it doesn't blow over, or change with your idea?" he responded simply.

"How far into the future can you clearly see?"

"Clearly, I can only see the immediate future. It's almost like Déjà Vu," he attempted to explain.

"Like what?" I asked, trying to understand.

"Like for instance, when the elevator doors open, Riley and Lamar will be standing there in a very awkward position." Jonah winked at me.

I cocked my head to the side, eyebrow raised, smirking as I watched the elevator indicator flash for the lobby. This was going to be a good test of his gift. As the elevator dinged and the doors began to open, my jaw dropped.

Lamar was on his hands and knees and Riley was sitting on his back like a cowboy. He was holding on to the collar of Lamar's shirt with his left hand, like reins. Riley had his right arm in the air, frozen. They stared up at us with awkward, embarrassed expressions.

"It's totally not what it looks like!" Lamar shouted, sitting up, forcing Riley off of his back. His face was beet red.

"It's totally what it looked like. I was riding Lamar like a well-trained trick pony," Riley said with a straight face. The two of them began laughing hysterically. I stood with my arms folded across my chest, staring at my mentally disturbed companions.

"Going up?" Lamar asked us with a smile.

"I don't know, I wouldn't wanna interrupt you guys going down," I mused.

"Ugh! Come on. He's not my type," Lamar replied.

Jonah and I laughed as they entered the elevator. I leaned forward and pressed the button for the sixth floor, where our room was. "So, do I even want to know what you guys were up to?"

Riley smiled. "It was actually for *two* reasons."

"We thought it would be funny if they checked the security tape." Lamar laughed. "And it freaked people out when the door opened. So we didn't have to share the elevator with anyone. They all offered to take the next one down."

"You guys are ridiculous." I shook my head.

"Thanks," they answered simultaneously.

When we reached the sixth floor Riley went to help Lamar with something, while Jonah followed me into the room and sat on the bed as I gathered my belongings.

"You're wondering why I'm Pagan, when I know the truth. You're wondering why I've chosen a 'primitive' spiritual high road, rather than giving my faith to the Creator."

"Yeah, basically."

"There's more to the world than simply what God or even *you*, created. There are elements to this planet that weren't created by either of you. They're there, you may just not be able to see them or believe them for yourself." he smiled.

"So, you're saying that the mystical aspect of the world is real?" I asked, dubious.

"Yes, very much so. If you could remember what it was like living in the 15th or 16th century, you'd know exactly what I mean. There was a time when gravity, fusion, the things we consider common sense thanks to science were seen as dark arts or miracles," he explained. He looked at me with a roguish smile that made me want to believe him.

"With that in mind, does it not make you realize how primitive we are to doubt the natural ways of faith? I don't say prayers, I say incantations. I don't ask God to watch over me, I use protective blessings. People call it magic, but it isn't. What we do is use the Earth as our power source," he concluded.

I thought about every word he said and realized how much sense it made.

"Are you and I any different?" he asked.

"Of course we are," I replied confused.

"How so?" he interrogated.

"Well, first off, I have boobs, which you don't," I mused with a grin.

"No, no. I mean, in the fact that the two of us use the Earth as our power source," he suggested.

I stopped what I was doing and looked at my hands. I closed my eyes and pictured how I healed myself, how I formed life. *He was right.*

He smiled knowingly, "Eden, you were one of the original druidic goddesses, so to speak. At least that's how we see you."

I sat on the bed next to him and didn't say a word. I was speechless.

"And to answer your question, I found Paige living on the streets in Salem. I was nineteen when I met her and took her in. She was 10 years old. I basically raised her. It was difficult, being a child myself," he paused momentarily, "I home schooled her, giving her any knowledge that I could, including spiritually. I know she sometimes seems to be a bit, how do you word it properly, ditsy? But she's a sweet girl. I see her as my daughter."

I realized then how wonderful of a man he was. He was a modern day messiah. He was a prophet of the digital age. Even I was taken aback by him. Even I was willing to follow him to the ends of the Earth, and I had only known him for roughly twenty four hours.

CHAPTER TWENTY SEVEN
THE DELUSIONAL PIED PIPER

"Baby, let me just say this, and I mean it politely... *you* appear to have shitty luck. Pardon my French, sweetie," the cashier said as she rung up our new and improved tire.

"Yeah, trust me, I know. You don't know the half of it."

"You want it mounted here, Baby? Or are you taking it elsewhere?" she asked.

"Here would be good." I shoved the receipt in my pocket. "Thank you, Beatrice!" I looked at her name tag.

She smiled. "You're welcome, baby. I hope your vacation turns out better for you."

Why was I buying a tire and having it mounted? Hmm. Let's rewind a bit, shall we? We left Chicago and got back on the road, headed for Washington. Everything seemed to be going well. Our van full of dorks had high spirits, singing ridiculous songs and telling crude jokes. I wished I had volunteered to ride with Paul. I'd rather have to explain why lemons aren't called yellows like oranges are to Paige, than listen to the *boys*. At the same time, it was nice to know that even though the Apocalypse was nipping at our heels, we still had that nagging gusto to push on.

We made it out of Illinois alive and well, before everything began to go haywire. Paul was pulled over for going 90 miles per hour in a 50 mile an hour road work zone. Okay, first off, I thought that only counted when there was construction *actually taking place*. There weren't any workers present! Not to mention, we were just following traffic. And why are there still cops on the road with this craziness afoot? We stopped ahead of them and waited for the officer to write his ticket. Little did he know, we wouldn't be making it to the court date, the world would be barren by then.

Once they caught up to us, we were back on the road and hoping that would be the last of our problems. Oh, trust me, it wasn't. You know that saying about all hell breaking lose? Yeah well, it happened.

As we were headed towards Madison, Wisconsin, we could see a giant storm cell in front of us. The sky was pitch black, other than when it was glowing green as the lightning struck. I thought about the fact that we were lucky we had avoided all the aftermath storms and then wondered if this could, in fact, be one of them. I knew that those storms in particular were very deadly, very dangerous.

I had *politely* asked my darling husband to slow down and ease up going into the storm, which he so kindly ignored as he barreled towards Madison, guns blazing and tires squealing. Needless to say, when we reached the storm the winds were blowing ridiculously hard and the hail wasn't as small as I was used to seeing.

Riley kept his speed, stating that slowing down would probably pose more of a threat for an accident than keeping to a normal pace. Seeing as how he's a cop and trained to do all the crazy maneuvering, I assumed he was right. Heaven forbid my ideas make any sense. So, I cringed and held onto my seat belt for dear life, repeating *"please don't let us die, please, please, please don't let us die."* Riley took that as an insult to his driving and threatened to pull over and let me drive. In the middle of his speech he glanced over at me and had to deal with the ear piercing shouts and realization that a piece of scrap metal was flying through the air. He swerved to avoid hitting it head on, thankfully. It could've easily gone through the windshield. Instead, we hit it from the side, sending it spinning like an out of control saw blade that bounced and turned like a boomerang as it sliced into our rear, driver's side tire.

Riley pulled the van over and turned on the caution lights, not that it did much good in this weather. You couldn't see two feet in front of you. I was sad to confirm the death of our beloved rear tire. No amount of rescue efforts or duct tape was going to work. I decided that it wasn't the time to write an obituary for the tire, much like the Douche Bag glass.

At this point, I was wet. I was cold. I was hungry and getting rather cranky. We unlocked the back doors of the van and slid all of our possessions aside to lift the flap covering the spare tire. Lo and behold, the spare tire wasn't in there, nor was the tire iron. Fantastic! For future reference, when you arrive to rent something and you ask if that said item is ready to leave the lot, you typically mean, does it have all of its essential accoutrements? For instance… a spare tire or the tire iron. Next time those lazy bastards tell you yes, do yourself a favor and check for yourself.

Four hours later, we were back on the road. I learned quite a few things from Wisconsin. Never stop for vehicle maintenance at a store with a bar across the street. And *never* trust a drunk man who swears he isn't, who asks to hold on to plumage that will send him on a painful, tyrannical tangent.

Lamar had been driving for a while. I was sitting up front, keeping him company. We made an executive decision to stop for fuel and snacks. I was ready for a break.

"Where are we?" Riley asked as he sat up in the back seat and stretched.

"Don't know," I replied with a shrug and opened my door.

I stepped out of the van and opened the side door, then attached Azrael's leash to his collar and let him out. He seemed very reluctant to leave the side of the van, which was understandable in this weather. I had to coax him away, tugging on the leash lightly. I pulled up my hood and lit a cigarette. We stepped out into the rain, headed for the nearest patch of grass. Suddenly, Azrael stood stiff and emitted a low growl.

"What's wrong, Az?" I asked, tugging at his leash. "Come on, do your business so we can get back to the van." I attempted to pull him to the grass.

He stepped into the grass, sniffed a few spots then stared out into the darkness. The gas station was in the middle of nowhere. There was one streetlight overhead, and two between the exit and the gas station. Otherwise all was darkness. I didn't even understand why there was a stop light. It seemed like the only people that lived in this tiny town, were the people that owned the gas station. Azrael finally got to the business of relieving himself then began sniffing at the air.

"What's wrong?" I asked again, leaning down to him, rubbing his back.

I could feel the tension between his shoulders. I felt his hackles rise under my hand. He stared out into the darkness and again began growling. It started as a low rumble, progressively getting louder. I stared out into the black night, trying to see what he saw, but was blinded by the overhead street light. I covered my eyes and squinted.

Azrael began walking forward slowly, his growl taking a loud menacing tone. I saw a quick motion, like a shadow darting in the dark background and felt the hair on the back of my neck stand on end. I suddenly had the horrible realization that we were not alone.

"Come on," I said, slowly backing up.

I heard a loud rumble and backfire behind me. A little white truck with loud exhaust pulled into the gas station and sputtered before idling off. I turned for a split second to see who else was here. I returned my gaze to the darkness and saw another quick movement in the distance. I tugged on Azrael's leash urgently.

"Let's go," I ordered the dog. "Riley!" I shouted over my shoulder as I continued to back up. He was still in the van, more than likely still asleep. Lamar peered around the side of the van as I turned and started walking hastily towards them. He put the gas cap on and walked around the side towards me.

"We need to go," I said simply.

He looked at me confused. "What's wrong?" then looking over my shoulder his face suddenly changed. "Whoa. What the hell was that?"

"Jonah, get in the van," I ordered as he placed the gas cap back on the second van.

"What's..." Jonah turned to me. "Oh shit! Eden, run!" he shouted, hopping into the driver's seat.

I sprinted towards the van and jumped between the two pumps. There was now gas pumps and the little white truck between me and whatever it was that was running after me.

"What the fuck is that?" I heard a country-twanged voice ask as I jumped into the passenger seat and slammed the door closed.

Lamar started the van up and sped around the pumps, headed for the exit. I watched horrified as the solid black being lifted the man off of the ground and snapped his spine like a twig. He threw him to the ground and moved towards the vans.

"Oh, my God!" Gabe shouted in the back seat.

"Go! Go! Go!" I screamed.

Lamar slammed down the gas and fishtailed as we pulled out onto the road and headed for the interstate. I bent down, placed my head between my knees and tried to slow my breathing.

"Oh, shit. Where's her purse?" Riley asked.

"What the fuck is going on?! What was that thing?" Gabe asked as we made it onto the interstate ramp.

"That was one of *them*. Now, where is her purse?" Riley insisted, turning on the dome light and digging through bags.

"The other van's behind us. Do we have everyone?" Gabe asked excitedly, staring out the back window.

"I don't know, call them!" Riley said, tossing Gabe his cell phone.

I couldn't slow my breathing down. I started to feel dizzy as my wheezing began. I sat upright and grabbed the arm rest tightly.

"Holy shit," Lamar said, shaking his head and speeding into the storm.

The commotion in the van was sending my head spinning. Or maybe it was the lack of carbon dioxide. My ears rang as all I could hear was my wheezing and my rapid heartbeat.

"Oh, God," I whispered as I blacked out.

I awoke a short time later with a horrible headache and my heart racing. I looked around the van, trying to familiarize myself to my surroundings. What the hell happened? Was that a dream?

"How're you feeling?" Riley asked, leaning forward between the seats.

"I feel like shit. What happened?" I responded, massaging my temples. "My head is killing me."

"Here," Lamar said, fishing in the side compartment of the door. He handed me a bottle of acetaminophen. I unscrewed the lid and shook two tablets into my hand, then recapped the bottle. I reached for the nearest bottle of liquid around and unscrewed the top. I took a sip of the lukewarm water and swallowed the pills.

"Where's Azrael?" I asked.

"He's fine. He's in the other van," Lamar replied reassuringly.

"What happened? I don't remember everything."

"What's the last thing you remember?" Riley asked me.

"It's all fuzzy. Just give me a recap."

"You were walking Azrael at the gas station. One of those bastards ran after you. Az tried to stand his ground, to protect you, but you dragged him back," Lamar summarized. "As you were running back, Paul saw the *thing* chasing you and jumped out of the van. He scooped up Azrael and jumped into the other van with him."

Gabe picked up the story from there. "As you made it in this van, that asshole killed that dude at the gas pump. We pulled out of there as fast as we could and jumped on the interstate."

Riley shook his head. I knew that he was happier with me *not* remembering the events.

"We're all fine, that's all you *really needed* to know," Riley stated flatly, looking at Gabe, irritated.

"So everyone made it out safely?" I asked.

"Yeah, I called the other van. We're all present and accounted for. Though I can't say spirits are very high right now," Gabe answered.

"That happens after watching someone get murdered," I scoffed.

The van fell silent for a few moments, other than the sounds of the road and the rumbling of thunder overhead.

"I think we all need a breather. What's the next big town?" Riley asked, turning to Gabe.

"Um, let me look." Gabe turned on the dome light and unfolded the map. He sat in the back, turning and twisting the map, tracing lines and looking up every once in a while to see the mile markers.

"Looks like the next big city would be Sioux Falls, South Dakota," Gabe answered, looking up from the map.

Riley nodded. "We don't want to take a chance again in one of those Podunk towns. So let's try and make it to Sioux Falls."

"Aye, aye Cap'n," Lamar said sarcastically.

Riley called Paul and made sure they could all hold out. The general consensus was that it wasn't worth the risk to stop in the middle of nowhere. I pulled my phone out of my pocket and looked at the time. It was 11:10pm. Scrolling down the list of names, it appeared that I had gotten a text message from just about everyone I knew.

Mel had texted me, asking what was going on. I didn't know what to tell her. I didn't want to tell her anything that would scare her. It was a tough spot to be in. Mike had texted me to let me know that Rufio was not only doing well, but was fantastic… ever since he had managed to eat an entire container of lunchmeat while Mike was using the bathroom, then apologized for raiding our fridge while we were gone.

Lana had texted me to apologize for our cat that was now passed out from his turkey feast. She then reminded me that she meant the lunchmeat, not Lamar's fat cat. They weren't eating each other, of course. I laughed at that. I have some ridiculous friends.
I miss them.

Sara texted me to let me know that not only did Ian think it was the coolest thing EVER to fly, but Lily decided that she wanted to be a flight attendant, or something that would allow her to fly 'like maybe superwoman'. ***OMG! LOL…*** was the only thing I could think. Sara had also texted me, apologizing for spilling the beans to my mother and father, about my grand entrance to Flint and their apartment. So yeah, now they know why Gabe is with me and all of that.

I threw my phone on the floorboard.

"What's wrong?" Lamar asked.

"Nothing. I just have a lot of messages that I don't feel like dealing with," I replied. "That and Sara told our parents what was going on. Well, what she knew of it."

"Aw, seriously? Damn it," Gabe responded from the backseat.

"Yeah, I'm gonna call Mom," I replied over my shoulder. I dialed my mother's number and waited for her to answer.

"Hey, honey!" she answered.

"Hey, Momma. How are you guys?" I asked cautiously.

"We're fine, just relaxing. The kids and your dad already went to bed. Sara and I have just been sitting here, talking."

"Oh, yeah? That's nice." I swallowed hard, nervously.

"Yeah. So, how's everyone?" she probed.

"Good, I guess," I replied. I wasn't sure who all she was referring to. I didn't know what all Sara had told her. Then again, I didn't know what all Sara knew.

"Excuse me for a minute, Sara," she said, turning away from the phone.

I could hear her patio door squeak as she had obviously walked either inside, or outside, to have a private conversation with me. "... Edie," she began, very calmly.

"Yeah?" I responded with a wince. I bit my lip and rubbed my forehead with my free hand.

"Tell me the truth," she ordered.

"Okay?" I responded.

"You were serious when you were telling me about the angel business, weren't you?" she asked.

"Yep," my jaw clenched as I answered her.

"Sara said she saw all of your tattoos gone and that you just... looked different. She said it was hard to explain, but that as soon as Gabe saw you, he refused to go against anything you said."

"Yeah, I thought it was kind of weird how easily he went along with the whole thing. He normally blows me off," I replied, thinking back on the entire event.

"Honey, please. Tell me what's going on," she pleaded. "Why is everyone supposed to gather at our house?"

I could tell by her tone that she knew something was in fact happening and that she was worried about her kids.

"I'm sorry. I just can't talk about it all right now. I promise you, as soon as we're done with... what we're doing, we'll be headed your way. I'll explain everything. I promise." I said with a sigh.

"So, I'll see you soon?" she asked.

"Of course," I felt the tears forming in my eyes as my heart thumped nervously. I swallowed what I really wanted to say, "I love you, Mom."

"I love you, too, baby," she replied.

"I need to go. I'll call you tomorrow. Tell everyone I said hello. And tell Dad I said I love him, please," I concluded then hung up.

"Everything okay?" Lamar asked.

"Peachy," I replied flatly, choking back the tears.

I turned back around and watched the rain as it spattered on the glass and slid down the side of my window. The stripes of water merged and twisted as we sped down the road. I wanted to cry, to scream. I wanted to open the door of the van and jump out. I wanted this to be over with. I wanted it to have never started. I hated who I'd become, but wouldn't change it if I could. The truth is unavoidable. *The truth.* The truth is, I didn't want to see the people I love die, but I didn't want to be away from them. So I lead them to their deaths, like a delusional pied piper.

I continued staring at the rain drops and the merging trails as they illuminated in the glow of the random street lights. Looking at the little lines, it reminded me of our group. We were those rain drops, coming together to form one solid, staggering being, nervously pressing forward. Just like the water on the windows, we had no clue where we were going in the long run, or what we were going to run into at the end.

I wondered if we would hit the ground and splatter. I wondered if we would evaporate, if we'd return to the sky just to fall to the Earth once again in the future. What future? The future was about as dismal and dreary as this dark, gloomy night.

These were the last memories, the last days I'd get to enjoy. And by enjoy, I mean, drudge through with deep regret and unbridled sadness.

So many things I've meant to say. So many things I've wanted to do...

It was a little after midnight when we arrived in Sioux Falls. The place still seemed to be alive and kicking. That was definitely a good sign to me. Even if the angel had followed us here, he'd have a hell of a time dispatching us with so many people around.

They don't care who sees. It isn't like some secret mission or anything.

I shivered at the thought.

"How's this look?" Lamar asked.

Riley looked up from his book of notes and squinted at the neon sign. "Pancakes at midnight? Hell, yes!" He smiled wide and jumped for the side door.

I couldn't help but laugh.

We all piled out of the vans. Once outside, I stretched and waited for the other van to park, then ran over to it and pulled the side door open. Azrael was standing there, wagging his stubby tail and panting. He jumped down from the van and started jumping on me and barking. I laughed and knelt down to give him some love.

"He wouldn't stop whining. He was driving me insane," Paul said.

I looked up at Paul gratefully. "Thanks for grabbing him. I never realized how much he meant to me until I was worried that he was gone."

"No prob' Edie. He's a pretty cool mutt." he smiled.

I pulled a biscuit out of my pocket and attached his leash. I started walking towards a patch of grass near the side of the diner.

"Hey, where are you going?" Riley called after me.

"Letting Az use the bathroom before I go in."

"Did you forget what happened last time? I'll take him," he said catching up to me.

"No, but you can come with us."

He wrapped his arm around my shoulder and walked with us to the grass. I turned around for a second and noticed everyone standing outside, watching us. "They aren't gonna let that happen again. We're all sticking together now," he said, guessing my thoughts.

I leaned in closely to his ear, "What if I have to pee?"

He laughed. "Hope you like an audience."

"No way. Not a chance."

"I'm not saying the dudes will follow you in, but I think we need to use the buddy system," he suggested.

"And what good would Paige or Brooke do me? Come on. Are you even remotely serious?" I asked in a whisper.

"Fine, one of us will go in with you." he shrugged.

"No!" I shrieked.

I could hear an eruption of laughter, followed by coughs and throats clearing, coming from my group of miscreants. I turned to face them. They instantly turned away and pretended to be discussing… whatever it is that they discuss when they aren't near me, video games, porn, God only knows.

We walked back towards everyone and grabbed Azrael's food and water dish, setting it on the ground next to the van. I sat down next to him while he munched on his food and sloshed water everywhere but in his mouth. When he was finished we helped him back into the van and all entered the diner together as a pack of hungry beasts.

We all followed the hostess 'Britani' to the table and sat down. We flipped open the menus and drooled over the perfectly arranged plastic pictures depicting delicious dishes. We were all starving, scared, anxious and exhausted. This trip was proving to be more than any of us could have expected. It was more than we were prepared to handle. All we could do to make things easier was try to stay positive and supportive. Easier said than done with limited food and rest.

I looked around the diner, studying the faces and characteristics of the people of Sioux Falls. I picked up on pieces of people's conversations. I wanted to scream at them to go home, to spend time with their families and friends. I wanted to shout, at the top of my lungs, that they'd be lucky if they survive a couple more days.

There were so many different types of people here. The artsy beatniks sat in the dimly lit corner, talking about art shows and whatever the hell they're into. There was a table of little Goth teens whining about something. There were older couples discussing boring adult stuff. Wasn't it past their bedtime?

I was pulled from my trance long enough to order. My stomach was doing flips. I felt sick again. But I decided to ignore it long enough to refuel with gallons of coffee and bacon. Everyone at our table was looking at me when I was done ordering.

"Edie, are you okay?" Riley leaned over and asked me.

"I'm fine. I'm just thinking."

Gabe pushed the maple syrup bottle, salt and pepper aside and pulled the map from his pocket, spreading it across the table. He pulled out his cell phone and used the wireless internet to access a map website.

"Looks like we still have almost 1500 miles to go."

"We're never gonna get there," Corey said, resting his head on the table with a thud.

Paige frowned, "I'm so tired."

"We all are," I said.

"Should we spend the night here?" Jonah asked.

"I don't think we should stop longer than necessary. We can start switching on and off for driving," Riley suggested.

"I don't think we should take any more chances," Paul added.

I nodded. "I agree."

"There's a lot of people here, I'm sure we're fine," Erick stated.

"You really think they care who sees? They're *killing* people. People aren't a threat to them and they know it. They'll do what they want, where they want," I replied.

The table grew somber. Maybe I should've left that thought to myself.

"At any rate, I'm good to drive now," Gabe said, breaking the tension.

"Me, too. I'm tired of sitting in the back," Brooke said with a sigh.

"We're all tired of sitting. But we have to get to Seattle," Riley replied.

"So when are we leaving here?" Corey asked.

"As soon as we're done eating," Riley confirmed.

"Are we going to get a chance to stop for more than an hour?" Paige asked.

Paul leaned back in his seat, "When we're in Seattle, sure."

"You guys don't have to stay with us. You can go home whenever you want." Riley shrugged.

"I'm not going anywhere that you guys aren't," Erick shot back.

"Thank you," Jonah smiled.

Corey shook his head. "Shit, me either. I'm not missing the action."

I turned away from the group, focusing my attention to Lamar, "What time is Chuck flying in?" I asked him quietly.

"I guess he'll be in Seattle around midnight tomorrow, well, today. Wait, is that tomorrow?" He stared at the ceiling. "Either way, you know what I mean. Not tonight, well, now," he shook his head, confusing the both of us.

"I hope we get there in time," I replied, turning to the glass next to me.

I stared out the window, watching people as they walked to their vehicles and went about their life, as if death was not imminent. I wished I was in their ignorant positions. I wish I was so naïve, that I could flaunt my mortal body, and twirl my hair under a bright light in the parking lot like the girls outside. They made me sick. *Do something good with your life! You only have weeks left, for fuck's sake!*

Knowing the truth was a burden I was sick of bearing. I ignored the conversation at our connected tables. I wanted to step away from all of this and just be. Be alone. Be anyone but me right now.

I guess what I really wanted, was to be sleeping in my own bed at home. I wanted to curl up with my cat, eat ice cream and watch a movie, without these thoughts storming in my mind. I wanted to be back in my childhood, with my family, with my parents. I wanted to forget this entire atrocity. I wanted to crawl into a hole and stay there until this all blew over. But I knew better.

It won't just blow over.

CHAPTER TWENTY EIGHT
A LULLABY FOR THE WAYWARD & WEARY

I'm pleased to announce that we made it through our meal without any major disruptions or scares. There were no screaming patrons, or shadowy beings lunging at us through the glass. It was just good old fashioned pancakes and Belgian waffles.

Conversation lightened up quite a bit after we started to notice we were safe. It seemed as if the fuller our bellies got, the looser our nerves became. We began to laugh and joke around again, recalling some of the more ridiculous of moments as now fond memories. Such as, when Paul decided he was tough enough to handle the feather and dropped to the ground like a whiny baby.

Okay, he never actually whined and he handled it like a man, but still. It was much funnier with our spin on it. Riley and Gabe decided to convince him that while he was 'reliving' it, he was sucking his thumb and calling for his mommy. He of course laughed and threatened to shove random condiments up their exit holes.

All was light and entertaining, until someone recalled the gas station. The mood changed quickly. Smiles fell flat, sighs hummed in the air. I choked on my spit as I tried to swallow the thought.

I closed my eyes and cradled my head in my hands. I opened my mental closet and shuffled some items around. I moved a couple of oddly positioned skeletons towards the back to make room for the new members of my macabre collection. I slammed the door shut and opened my eyes with a smile.

"Alright, let's get out of here. Shall we?" I asked, holding my hand out to Riley.

He grabbed my hand and threw a handful of bills on the table as a tip.

Chairs squeaked and creaked as they slid across the floor. Everyone rose from the table and shuffled towards the front counter. We stood in line and paid our tabs, then turned and walked out. It was almost two in the morning. We spent quite a bit of time in the diner. We filled our tanks with caffeine and protein and were ready to get back on the road. We all nervously looked around, scanning all of the shadows and dark spots.

"Think we're good?" I asked, turning to Jonah.

"As far as I know."

I glanced around and made a mad dash for the van. I stopped at the front of the van and peeked around the corner. I walked to the side and pulled the door open. I attached Azrael's leash and let him have a little bit more walk around time, before he was confined to the back of the van. He's been trapped in this piece of shit for almost three days. Then again, so had I.

"Maybe sometime today we can find a nice quiet place to sit and relax for a bit. Hopefully we can give Az some time to run around and really stretch his legs," Riley said, walking towards me from behind.

"That would be nice. I feel horrible for him," I replied.

"I know you do."

"I feel like maybe he should've stayed home with Rufio." I frowned. I hated to think about poor Rufio at home alone.

"Edie, if Azrael hadn't been there," he paused, choking on his words.

He wrapped his arm around me and squeezed me tightly.

"Stop," I looked into his sad eyes.

"I don't even want to think about it."

"I wouldn't have known it was out there," I completed his statement. "What happens if they do kill us, though? I mean, do we face God? Do we disappear forever? What happens?"

"That's what we're trying to avoid. I don't want to find out," he replied.

We loaded up our living cargo and hit the road. We headed back towards the interstate and continued westbound. Gabe was driving our van. Lamar was reclined in the front seat. I leaned forward and pulled my pillow out from underneath our snoring dog that was sleeping between the front and our seat.

Gabe turned down the volume of his music. I opened my eyes and stared, upside down, out of the side window as we sped towards our destination. The rain had finally stopped.

The random streetlights flashed in the van as we passed, like a stop animation film, like snapshots in a scrapbook. Photos of memories I wasn't sure I wanted to keep. Riley wrapped his arm around my waist and squeezed an awkward perpendicular hug. I smiled and pressed my ear to his chest, listening to his heartbeat. This was a memory I'd love to preserve. We passed another streetlight. I closed my eyes like a camera shutter.

Click. I'll keep this one.

I closed my eyes and felt my body relax. I felt the tension release in my shoulders, my jaw, my temples. I kicked off my shoes. They hit the floorboard with a loud *thud.*

"Did we pass a swamp?" Gabe asked sarcastically.

"No, Edie took her shoes off," Riley replied with a laugh.

Lamar pretended to gag.

"Shut up! You guys are such assholes!" I laughed.

We all chuckled as Paul snored in the backseat, unaware.

I turned over, burying my face in Riley's warm chest. He wrapped his arm around me, caressing my back. I felt the shaking of him quietly chuckling. He was obviously thinking of something funny he should've said or some sort of prank he was planning. I was too tired to ask what was on his mind.

My eyelids felt as if they were weighed down with sandbags. I felt my breathing slow. I felt my body completely relax. I felt his fingers passing through my hair, slowly becoming less frequent as his breathing became heavier, deeper. I glanced up with blurry vision and saw him falling asleep, as well.

Click. Definitely saving that one.

I felt myself drifting in and out of consciousness as I listened to Riley's melodic heartbeat and rhythmic breathing. His body silently sang me to sleep, a lullaby no one else could even remotely attempt to perform with such grace.

The hum in the air was as sweet honey. It was buoyant and blithe. I opened my eyes for the first time. I gasped and felt the warm, sweet air fill my lungs like sugar caught in the wind. I was blinded. Blinking and squinting, I tried to adjust my vision to the magnificent light.

I felt my body rise, felt the gentle breeze as my body rose to eye level. I stared forward, awestruck and dazzled. I was overwhelmed with joy and admiration as I gazed at the face of my Creator. No words can even begin to describe His beauty. No sounds could ever mimic His wondrous laughter as He marveled at His magnum opus.

"I shall call you, Eden," He smiled.

I felt warm liquid run down my cheek as I heard my name for the first time.

"Do you like that? I thought it befit your beauty." He grinned, proud of Himself.

"I love it," I choked, as I spoke for the first time.

"Then Eden it shall be!" He kissed my forehead and set me on a soft shoal of celestial mist next to Him.

"I have given you much, little one; as you are very much, a piece of me." He smiled.

I bowed graciously.

I watched as He molded another being in His hands. He carefully bent and moved its appendages, shaping it into a tall, statuesque figure. He set it down in front of His crossed legs and held His hand to His chin as He pondered the style this one would take.

"Eden, would you like to help create your brother?" He asked me.

I smiled and nodded.

"Much like the piece of me given to you, to create your brother you will have to also give a piece of yourself."

I looked down at my hands. I didn't understand how to remove a part of myself.

"What color shall his eyes be?" He asked me, with a grin.

"Grey! Calm and serene," I smiled and clapped my hands excitedly.

"And his tendrils?" He asked.

"Golden, as sunshine," I grinned.

"And his hide?" He asked.

"Alabaster!" I jumped in place.

"Close your eyes, little one. And do not peek." He chuckled.

I closed my eyes, squeezing them tightly. I wouldn't go against His words, as much as I wanted to see our creation. *Together*, we had created my brother. I waited anxiously. I was so excited, I squealed with glee.

"You may open your eyes," He whispered.

I slowly opened my eyes and gazed at the beautiful man held out in front of me.

"Now, you must give your contribution to make him complete."

I looked nervously from the motionless face of my brother, to the magnanimous face of my Creator.

"What shall I do?" I asked.

"Come," He said, holding out His hand.

He picked me up in one hand, holding my brother in the other. He closed His eyes. I watched a smile stretch across His divine face. He moved His hands closer together. I watched as my brother slowly moved closer towards me. I held out my hand, grabbing my brother's. I kissed his cheek.

My head fell back and I gasped as the air was pulled from my lungs. My eyes rolled to the back of my head. I felt part of my essence escape from my chest. He held His mighty finger against my core. I watched as the bright, glowing mist moved from my chest to my brother's.

His eyes sprung open. He gasped and staggered backwards, catching himself. He turned his eyes upwards and blinked rapidly. He smiled wide and turned his gaze from our Creator's face to my own.

"And you will be Gabriel," God said with a content sigh.

"Wonderful!" I clapped.

Gabriel smiled and bowed, pleased.

"Gabriel, your sister has given a piece of herself to create you. She is no longer complete. Do you wish to share a piece of yourself to make your bond unitary?" God asked my brother.

"As you wish," Gabriel bowed his head.

God held His finger to Gabriel's chest. Gabriel gasped as his head dropped back. I watched, both startled and in awe as a glowing, pulsating haze rose from his chest and settled in our Creator's hand. He carried me closer and gently blew the essence into my being.

"Perfect!" God smiled, proudly.

He returned me to the cloud shelf above His shoulder. He gently carried Gabriel over to me, set him down, and returned to His work. We turned to each other and smiled. Gabriel grabbed my hand and held it tightly. We were very similar, very much a part of each other. Our eyes reflected the same emotions, our hearts beat to the same rhythm. We were one and the same, yet immaculately sole.

We quietly laid on the shoal, resting our chins on our palms, our elbows buried in the silk like cosmos. Our feet swayed in the air behind us, gently tapping into each other. We looked down from our nirvana as we watched our Creator mold more delicate beings.

He now had a pile of mannequins lying next to His side, incomplete and without individuality. He continued to mold more beings, setting them down. I couldn't help but wonder when he would complete each of them.

"Eden!" He called to me from below.

"Yes, Father?" I responded.

He stood, holding the new being in front of me. I stared at the flawless face and felt my heart flutter as my eyes traced his perfect lips and sharp, strong features. He was more breathtaking than Gabriel. Our Creator had made his true masterpiece.

"What color shall his iris' hold?" He asked.

"Blue. The purest shade of azure." I smiled.

God smiled at me, "That is all."

I cocked my head to the side, curiously. I tried to watch as God finished creating the being and set him lifelessly on a cloud out of view. Why had he not brought him to life? What was his name? Why wasn't he with us? God drew my attention away from the cloud and asked me to help Him create the next being.

"Green! No, gold!" I shook my head.

Gabriel laughed at my indecision.

"Grey, very warm," I whispered, staring at the being's handsome face.

"I must've given you my creativity when I made you." He laughed heartily.

I blushed and hid my face in my brother's shoulder.

"They will contain all three shades!" God smiled.

I bit my lip with anticipation.

He will be stunning.

Gabriel laughed at my thought.

"And his tresses?" He asked, again.

"Bronze," I suggested.

"Crimson!" Gabriel shouted.

"Crimson is far too bold for such a humble creature. Though I do believe you're on to something." God nodded.

He turned away from us and held the being in front of Him. I tried to look around His shoulders to see the flawless entity in His hands. Curiosity raced through my mind. He finished with the breathtaking marvel and set him at His side. I looked over the cosmic shelf, trying to see the last work of genius our Father had made. His face eluded me. I sighed with a slight frown then rose to my feet.

"Father!" I called down to Him.

"Yes, little one?" He responded.

"What is that one's name?" I asked with a smile.

"Thaddeus," God gazed at me with a smug grin.

"Thaddeus, how lovely!" I replied and laid back down next to my brother.

We watched as He created more beings. He began to create so quickly, leaving them incomplete. They began to collect in even larger piles next to His folded legs. Gabriel and I stared down, curiously. Why was He not completing each as He had with us?

"Eden," He called to me once more.

"Yes, Lord?" I responded.

He held up another statuesque male specimen. "Help me, with your *magnificent* imagination. Choose hues fit only for a leader."

"Copper hair! Golden eyes."

"And what is his name?" Gabriel asked.

He stared at the lifeless being in His hand, "Michael."

God held His finger to Michael's bosom and marveled as he sparked to life. He set him down by Thaddeus and picked up another lifeless shell.

"Gabriel, this one is your choice. What color shall her hair be?" God asked my brother.

Gabriel stared at the breathtaking female body in awe.

"Ebony. With eyes that are jade, as mysterious as the heavens themselves."

"As you wish," God smirked.

"What is her name?" Gabriel asked, peeking over the edge to see his sleeping beauty once more.

"Lilith," God replied, returning to work. "Eden. These two will be brothers. Though they do not look the same, they will also share a piece of each other, as you and Gabriel have. Grace me with your ideas."

"Hair as onyx as the cosmos. With bright gold eyes and golden skin," I said.

"Very interesting," God nodded.

He knelt down and set the larger one at his feet. He held the shorter one in his right hand and blew life into his body. He gasped and opened his eyes. Gabriel and I smiled at each other as we thought about how amazing it was to witness such a miraculous event.

"Jonah, son," God whispered.

"Thank you, Lord." Jonah bowed.

"Let us bring your brother to life, together."

"Yes, please!" Jonah smiled excitedly.

God knelt down and picked up the large body. "Jonah, help me summon your brother's essence."

The two of them closed their eyes and laid their hands on the burley male. He sat up with a gasp, shaking his head.

"Welcome, brother."

"And his name?" God asked, turning to Jonah.

"Paul," Jonah suggested.

"Hello, Paul, my son."

Paul nodded and smirked. He had a much different air about him. *Bizarre*, Gabriel and I thought with a grin.

The handiwork continued. Consistently, God came to us with questions, asking for suggestions. I excitedly shouted my opinions and clapped as I saw His concoctions.

"And this one?" He'd ask. He'd ornament the beings with my suggestions, "You will be, Daniel."

Gabriel and I were soon distracted by the stars above us.

"What about these sisters?" He asked.

"Hmm, red, with brown eyes," I replied, without looking, lying on my back.

He'd grab another and complete the figure.

"Welcome to life, David."

We had been through dozens of combinations. Black hair, blue eyes. Brown hair, grey eyes. Dark skin, light skin and every warm tone, imaginable. He named each creation and introduced Himself, needlessly. There were so many of us now. How had He not grown tired?

At His feet, rested Kenneth and Michael, now brothers. Anthony and Thomas wandered through the heavens, admiring the marvels. Gwendolyn and Theresa were holding hands and laughing as they also watched our Creator bring life to the masses. I looked down at the amazing arrangement of angelic faces, with perfect features and names. There was now Callin, a fiery redheaded beauty. Emily, her dark haired sister. There were twins, Jacob and Tobias. Seth was running around with his new acquaintances, Marcus, Bethany, Mary and Paul.

Meridith and Jeremiah were resting on the banks of the cosmic river, watching the stars float by. I looked from face to face, but couldn't find the one I wished to see the most. God kept Gabriel and I on the cloud shelf above Him at all times. Though we wanted to retreat to the ground below, and socialize with the others, we knew God had a reason to keep us separated.

At least we had each other, we both thought.

God paused, glancing up at us wearily and shook His head. He looked exhausted. He had created numerous beings, without resting. I called for Him to join us. He nodded in agreement, and rested with us on our celestial shelf.

"They are wonderful!" I smiled, staring down at the perfect creations.

"Yes. Each will become their own being, feeling *their* own emotions apart from mine," God explained.

"Why have you created us?" Gabriel asked.

"As perfect as this Utopia is, I'm sad to say I had grown lonely. I decided it was time to create beings capable of companionship. As I breathed life into each of you, I gave you all the attributes and emotions I have," He replied with a fond smile. "You each have a gift. You will discover these presents as time progresses. I can't reveal all of my tricks." God chuckled to Himself.

"What is mine?" I asked with a smile.

"You will see soon enough, little one. Your talent will help me create my greatest masterpiece. A gift, to all of you," He explained with a whisper.

"And mine?" Gabriel asked nervously.

"You, son, are my voice. You will grow to spread my word. That is no secret."

Gabriel and I looked at each other.

"I will not be able to be everywhere at once, as much as you may wish for it to be true. I will need you to speak on my behalf. Your words will be as respected as my own."

"That sounds like quite the task."

I heard his thoughts. His chest bowed out with pride.

"You are the only one worthy of such a gift. It will be a burden at times, but never more than you can bear," God explained, gently resting His hand on Gabriel's shoulder.

The three of us stared down at the angels, as they ran about and socialized with one another. Gabriel and I questioned God for hours about each of the angel's special gifts. Some of which, we were more curious about, than others.

"And what ability does Lilith possess?" Gabriel asked, with a nonchalant grin.

"She is able to shape shift. She is also a Commander, in a sense. Lilith will not only be able to change her form, she'll be able to change the minds of others with her talents and beauty. She is three spirits, in one." God explained.

"And what of Meridith?" I asked.

"She is a fine specimen, indeed. She has the power to soothe, like a warm embrace. She is the essence of love, comfort and compassion."

"That's amazing. And what about Thaddeus?" I asked.

"He is a warrior; a leader. Anyone is capable of leading a group, but not with such a clear mind. His abilities to strategize and detect the truth are uncanny. Not even Michael compares to his ability to lead. The angels will follow Thaddeus to the ends of the Earth," God explained.

"Earth?" I asked, confused.

"Well, I seem to have ruined the surprise!" God chuckled.

"I suspect that's the masterpiece you were referring to?" Gabriel asked.

God smirked and shook his head.

"When do we start creating Your masterpiece, Lord?" I asked.

"Tomorrow," He winked.

I grinned wickedly and turned to my prideful brother. His smile radiated like the sun itself.

"But for now, we rest, my angels."

I laid my head back on a pillow of clouds and thought about the blue eyed angel and the warrior, Thaddeus.

I was startled back into reality by the violent shaking and terrifying sound of the van horn as Gabe pulled the van onto the side of the road. He tread across the rumble strip and laid his forearm on the horn. I shot straight up, looking out the front windshield.

"Shit!" Gabe yelled.

"What? No! No! No! No!" I shouted as I threw my head back into the seat.

"Sorry, guys. I don't know where all this traffic has come from."

"What's wrong?" Riley whispered in my ear, rubbing my arm.

"Nothing," I was heartbroken.

I wanna go back.

Lamar was leaning against the dashboard, trying to see around the mass of vehicles in our path. "I can't tell why they're stopped."

Paul yawned loudly and growled like a bear in the backseat as he sat up. "Morning, ladies." he scratched at his days' growth of a beard.

Lamar rolled down his window and climbed onto the door. He held onto the handle on the inside, as he hung out of the side.

"What can you see?" Riley asked.

"Not much. I can't see beyond the semi up ahead," Lamar replied, poking his head back inside the van.

Paul's cell phone rang. "What's up, bro?" he answered it. He was silent for a second. I turned to look at him, to watch his reaction.

"Oh, no shit? That's not good. We'll go check it out." he turned around to look at the van behind us.

I glanced through the back window. Jonah was seated in the front passenger seat, waving at us.

"Okay, I'll let you know as soon as we get back," Paul said, then hung up his phone. He growled loudly as he scratched at his beard.

"What's wrong?" I asked.

"Fuck!" he shouted, punching the back of the seat.

"Dude, what's going on?" Riley asked, turning to Paul.

"Come on, you and I need to get out," Paul said, sliding between the side of the seat to the door.

"Wait, no! What's going on?" I asked.

"Edie, please. Just let us check this out. We'll be right back, I promise you. I'll keep him safe, don't worry," Paul said, trying to comfort me.

"I just want to know what's going on," I replied, folding my arms.

"We don't have *time*."

Riley and Paul jumped out of the side doors.

"Well, I'm coming with you," I said, unbuckling my seatbelt.

"No. You're not. No one is," Paul insisted.

I looked to Riley and frowned.

"Sorry. You're staying here." he shrugged.

"At least take Azrael?" I pleaded.

"Nope. You need him more than we do," Paul replied, closing the side door.

Paul and Riley walked to the driver's side window and tapped on the glass. Gabe rolled down his window and stuck his head out. Riley whispered something to him and then pat him on the shoulder. When Gabe pulled his head back in he sighed heavily and rolled his window up. He locked all of the doors with the push of a button.

"What's going on?" I asked.

"I don't know," he replied. "I was just doing what I was told. Don't ride my ass."

I watched as Riley and Paul walked around a large truck and disappeared from sight. I cradled my head in my hands and peeked through my fingers. I stared through the windshield, waiting to see them return. A few minutes after they disappeared, there was a loud boom, the ground shook and a blindingly bright light flashed.

"Riley!" I shouted, reaching for the door handle, "Oh my God! Riley!" I ripped at the handle. It wouldn't open. "Gabe unlock the door!" I yelled with tears in my eyes.

"No," he replied somberly.

"Unlock the fucking door!" I shouted at the top of my lungs.

"They told me not to. I'm sorry."

I felt my heart stop beating, altogether.

Chapter Twenty Nine
We Call That 'Karma' Down Here.

I sobbed heavily into my pillow. I gasped for air and wept uncontrollably. Azrael licked my cheek, trying to console me. The louder I cried, the more he began to whine.

"Edie…" Lamar placed his hand on my shoulder.

I slinked away, burying my face deeper into my pillow.

I should've gone. I should've fought them. I should've gone!

"Edie, please," Lamar said.

I knew he was only trying to help. He was trying to comfort me. Nothing was going to comfort me. For all I knew, Riley and Paul were now dead. Nothing was going to change my emotions, no amount of apologies or false hope. I shouldn't be here. I should be at his side, no matter what condition that put me in. How could I have let this happen?

Gabe's phone rang. He was quiet for a second. "Holy shit! Okay. Be right there," he said then hung up his phone. He unlocked his door and stepped out. "Edie, stay in the van. Lamar, keep her in here. Please," he said as he slammed the door shut.

I sat up, sniffling.

Not only did I have to worry about Riley being dead, now I had to worry about Gabe running out into danger. I didn't sit up quick enough to see which way he had run. I looked at the van behind us. The doors were opened. Jonah, Corey and Erick were all standing outside.

"Lamar, I'm sorry. I didn't mean to push you away."

"It's okay. I understand," he replied.

"Where'd Gabe go?"

"He ran ahead," Lamar pointed towards the hazy scene in front of our van.

"Who called him?" I asked, sniffling and wiping my eyes.

"No shit!" Lamar said with a chuckle as he threw his door open.

"What?" I shouted as he stepped out.

My attention was drawn ahead. I watched as Lamar ran towards the semi and stopped. Riley popped around the back end of the semi-truck. He waved to me and bowed as if the production was over and the curtain was dropping behind him. Lamar hugged him and pointed to him, presenting him to me like a new car I had just won on a game show.

I climbed over Azrael and into the driver's seat. I hit the button to unlock all of the doors and began to open the driver's side door when my phone rang. I looked down at the display, it was Riley. I looked back up at him. He was shaking his head and pointing to his phone.

"Riley! I was so scared!" I said as I answered.

"Stay in the van."

"No, I want to…" I began to speak, but was cut off.

"No, I need you to stay in the van. We're all fine. We're totally safe," he reassured me, very calmly.

I stared out of the front windshield. "Is that blood?"

"Nah, it's ketchup," he replied. "Of course it's blood! What the fuck else would it be?" he laughed.

"Ketchup," I mumbled.

"Edie, it's not my blood. It's not Paul's or Gabe's either. That's all that matters. Okay?" he paused. "Now, listen to me. I need you to stay in the van, with Azrael. Lock all of the doors and do NOT open the doors until we come to you. I'm sending Lamar back to you. Let him in, and only him," Riley gave his orders very clearly, very concise.

"Okay," I repeated. "But…"

"No buts," he sounded annoyed. "I need to get off the phone with you. I have some *business* to attend to."

A couple of minutes later, Riley disappeared from view and Lamar sprinted back to the van. I unlocked the passenger door for him. He ran to the driver's side and shook his head. I shrugged and shook my head back, confused. He motioned for me to scoot over. I slid into the passenger seat.

"They're fine." he smiled as he jumped into the driver's seat and closed the door.

"What're they doing?"

"Hmm, I'm not really sure." he shrugged.

"You're lying," I replied, brow raised.

"You'll see," he replied, with a conservative grin.

"I thought you didn't know what they're doing?" I said skeptically.

"I don't."

"You're lying again." I chuckled.

"Just wait." he smiled, staring out of the windshield.

Gabe stepped around the backside of the truck and flagged Lamar to pull forward. Lamar threw the van into drive and slowly inched forward. Gabe held out his hands for Lamar to stop after a few yards. He put the van back in park and sat still.

I grabbed my phone and dialed Riley's number.

"Yes, Edie?" he instinctively answered his phone.

"Um, you have a second?" I asked anxiously.

"Not really. I'm kind of busy at the moment," he replied, distracted.

"If I can't get out of the van, can Lamar, at least?" I asked.

"Why are you asking that?" he inquired.

"Well, I just realized it was almost 9am. Az hasn't been able to pee or anything in like, 7 hours. I'd really like him to have some time to stretch his legs and stuff." I winced and bit my lip, nervously. I didn't want to make him mad.

"You need to stay in the van. So yeah, ask Lamar to take him out. Tell him to stay *right* by the van. But I need to go. We'll be back in a few minutes."

He hopped out of the driver's door and walked around to the side. He pulled the door open and attached Azrael's leash. He helped him out and walked towards the grassy shoulder next to the road. I watched as Azrael stared forward, hackles raised and growling.

"Is everything okay?" I asked, rolling down my window slightly.

"Yeah, he's just a little, observant, I think," Lamar replied turning to face me. Azrael stared forward, ignoring nature's call.

"What's he looking at?" I asked Lamar, rolling my window down further.

"Uh, I'm not sure I want to look." Lamar squinted and turned to me.

"Is one of the angels out there?" I asked.

"Uh, yeah, kinda," Lamar said. He sounded nervous.

"Turn Az the other way. Make him walk towards the other van," I suggested.

"Okay," he replied then gently tugged on his leash.

Azrael followed suit and turned away from the action.

I stared through the windshield, trying to see through the fog and collection of vehicles. Gabe ran around the corner of the truck, grinning. He ran straight to the back of the van and knocked on the back door. I pressed the unlock button and waited for him to pull the doors open. I turned to face the back of the van.

"Hey, what's going on?" I asked him.

"Hunting season has officially begun!" he grabbed something from the back then slammed the doors shut.

"What?" I yelled.

He, of course, didn't answer me. I pressed the lock button and stared at my brother as he ran by the van. He was carrying a machete and an armful of rope. I felt very anxious, not knowing exactly what was going on. Time seemed to be passing like molasses. I continuously stared at the clock, wondering when they'd be back from whatever they were doing.

I looked at the clock on the dashboard, again. It was now 9:45am and I hadn't seen Gabe, Riley or Paul in at least forty five minutes. I was beginning to worry that something had happened. I contemplated calling Riley or Gabe, but decided it was probably better if I didn't. I rested my head against the window with a loud 'thud'.

"They're fine, Edie. Don't worry," Lamar responded.

"I wish they'd hurry back."

"I just saw them moving around. I'm sure they're headed back in a minute."

He cleaned up Azrael's dishes and let him walk around some more. I saw movement in the hazy foreground. Lamar and Azrael stepped out in front of the van, protectively. I watched as Lamar's stance changed from cautious to lighthearted. He turned to me with a smile.

"Told you!" he shouted and ran towards the approaching shadows.

I watched as Riley walked out around the back of the semi-truck with a ring of light spinning on his finger. He danced and showboated like a Las Vegas showgirl, sans the sequin pasties.

Paul ran around the back of the truck with giant pure white wings flapping on his back. He jumped and frolicked like a little girl, giggling and prancing as he approached the van. "Look! Look at me! Edie! I'm an aaaangel! I'm a pretty little aaaangel!" Paul laughed and spun around on his imaginary catwalk.

"Oh my God," I clasped my hands over my mouth.

Gabe lumbered around the corner with a hogtied body, tossed over his shoulder. He looked exhausted and out of breath, as Paul and Riley danced and laughed on their way to the van.

My phone rang. "Hello?" I asked, staring at the dancing imbeciles.

"Pull the van forward. This bastard is heavy," Gabe said.

"Wait, what?" I asked, confused.

"Pull the van for-ward," Gabe annunciated each syllable slowly.

"Okay, fine." I jumped back into the driver's seat.

I crept forward and stopped when Riley held his hands up.

Gabe lugged the body towards the van and dropped it down on the hood. I stared out of the windshield at the bloodied, disfigured corpse that was rested on the hood of our van. My heart raced and I felt a surge of panic.

I stepped out of the van and walked around to the front of the van. I stared at the lifeless face and gasped. *And I will call you David, my son.* I recognized the face instantly.

Oh shit. What have we done?

"How?" I asked, baffled.

I watched Riley climb onto the top on the van as Paul continued to prance around like a damned fairy.

"The bastard was so cocky, he didn't even put up his shadow armor," Riley explained as he hoisted the corpse to the top of the van. "Gabe, hand me some rope."

Riley motioned to 'hurry up'. Gabe tossed the coil of rope to Riley on the roof of the van.

"I don't get it. How were you even able to?" I was at a loss for words.

"Edie, he was slaughtering people. He was wiping out cars full of women and children. He didn't spare anyone," Riley said, looking me in the eyes. "He wasn't cloaked in shadow. We did what Jonah told us to do. We killed him to protect ourselves."

"And he was all like, we call that karma down here, mother fucker!" Paul laughed maniacally.

"Paul, not now," Riley shook his head and tied the body down.

"He was gonna kill us, Edie. Don't get upset. Eye for an eye, *remember?*" Paul continued, flapping his wings.

"Dude, seriously, I got it. Thanks," Riley said.

Gabe wrapped his arm around my shoulder.

"You know, just as well as I do, why they're here. They aren't here to murder, pillage and plunder. They're not fucking pirates, Riley. They're *reaping.* They're *harvesting!*" I shouted.

"Who's side are you on?" Paul asked me with a sarcastic tone.

"Paul, enough! Please!" Riley threw his hands in the air. He finished tying down the angel's body to the top of the van and jumped down. He wiped his brow on his shirt sleeve, and slumped his shoulders. "It's okay. I know this is a lot for you to take in, still." Riley rubbed my arms, comfortingly.

"I was just worried about you guys." I gazed up to the familiar angelic face.

"You know I was just fucking with you. I know whose side you're on," Paul said with a sheepish smile.

"Yeah, Paulie. I know you do," I replied, staring at Paul. I shook my head and chuckled. I couldn't help but laugh at him. He stood in front of me, covered in blood, sulking with puppy-dog eyes and donning floppy stolen wings tied on to his back.

"You look ridiculous." I laughed.

"What?!" he spun around like a ballerina. "I look damned sexy. I look classy."

"You look like an idiot," Riley confirmed, pulling his shirt off.

"Says the guy who frolicked with a halo balancing on his head like a crown? Yeah. Uh huh," Paul mused.

Paul grabbed the tips of the wings and ran around flapping them like a vulture circling his dying prey.

"Take'em off. We need to mount'em," Riley scolded.

"What are you doing with them?" I asked, confused. I put my hands on my hips and waited for this to start making sense.

"We're gonna mount them on the front of the van. As a bit of a warning," Gabe said wiping off his hands.

"I want them to realize we took him down. I want them to know that we can and will kill them, if they threaten us," Riley explained with a very monotone, gruff voice. "I'll do anything and everything to keep you safe. Even if I have to kill God, Himself."

"You know that's impossible. Don't be so fucking arrogant," I replied.

"Edie, come here," Lamar called from inside the van.

"What?" I responded peeking in.

"I understand you're really torn. I know you're pretty shaken up about all of this," Lamar explained. "You're the only one here that sees it from both sides. You're the only one who isn't doing all of this out of vengeance. Just sit in here with me and try to relax."

I didn't say anything. I stared out at the woods. I noticed the black silhouette of a large bird on one of the branches.

"Oh, shit…" I stepped back, staring into the woods. "Lilith! Everyone get in the vans!"

I jumped into the passenger seat and closed the door. I watched in my mirror as the van behind us closed up. Gabe jumped into the back of our van with Paul. Riley ran around and slid across the high hood of the van, hopped into the driver's seat and put the van in drive.

"Edie, consider the body on top of the van a scarecrow and nothing more," Riley said as he began to drive forward, slowly. "Now, as we drive around all of this *traffic*, I want you to close your eyes. I want you to think of cartoons, or a concert, or your garden. I don't care what you think about, just *don't look up.*"

I took in a deep breath and closed my eyes. I heard a gasp in the backseat and instinctively opened my eyes. "Oh, God."

The road was covered with stranded cars, for miles. There were bodies everywhere. Some of them rested in their vehicles, some outside. Men, women, children, scattered across the road in pools of blood. I didn't understand. I thought they were claiming the souls of the innocent? This was genocide.

"What…" I choked on my words.

Riley looked over at me and frowned. "I… I'm sorry." he grabbed my hand.

"I don't understand," I replied, staring out the window at the mass murder.

There were cars on fire, trucks overturned. There were bodies huddled together. They died, trying to protect each other, trying to shelter each other from this atrocity. They were helpless. How could God let this happen? How could the Creator that I loved so much, let His *children* do this sort of act?

"It's pure cruelty," I mumbled. "If God doesn't see humans as His own children, I understand, but this is still inhumane. That's not like Him."

"I think God has turned away," Gabe said, as he stared out of the window.

"I think God smote us. This is damnation. This is hell," Paul replied.

I undid my seatbelt and crawled between the two front seats. I got into the middle of Gabe and Lamar in the next seat back and buried my face in my brother's chest. I was horrified. I couldn't imagine *him*, being one of those bodies lying on the ground, disfigured and discarded like trash. *My brother. My blood.*

I sobbed into my brother's shirt as he rubbed my back and attempted to tell me it was alright. *It wasn't alright*, it was so fucking far from it, it was ridiculous. When I had stared at David's face, I felt remorse. I felt like *we* had done the injustice. No, they were justified. I owed Riley and Paul an apology. They *were* just trying to protect us.

Those feathers that were flapping on the grill were merely part of a trophy. It was no different than mounting a tiger's head on your mantle, after that said tiger, mauled and murdered an entire village. It wasn't revenge, it was as Paul had said; it was an eye for an eye, or a life for the hundreds of lives that were now scattered across the road.

"Where are we?" Paul asked.

The van was silent. A few minutes later, the silence was broken.

"We're passing through what used to be known as Alzada, Montana," Riley replied as we drove by a small welcome sign.

"Holy shit," Lamar whispered and covered his mouth with a gasp.

"There's no one left," Paul said somberly.

"They must've been trying to leave. I wonder if they had some kind of warning? Or were these just people passing through?" Gabe asked.

"Who knows what's been on the news lately. We haven't stopped and caught up with what the media's saying in… I can't remember how long," Riley replied, speeding around the abandoned vehicles.

Gabe wrapped his arm around me and held me there tightly. He wasn't allowing me to see the town.

"We need to stop soon. I can't help but wonder if anywhere is safe anymore," Riley said.

"How are we on gas?" I asked, mumbling into Gabe's chest.

"Low, almost on E. Gabe, you stopped while we were sleeping, didn't you?" Riley asked.

"Yeah, about five hours ago. I don't remember where we were, it was crowded though. I figured we were good," Gabe replied.

"Who's got the map?" Lamar asked.

"It's in the back seat," Gabe said.

Paul dug around and pulled up the map. Riley slowed down and I sat up.

"Does it look like we'll hit a big city any time soon?" Riley asked, looking in the rearview mirror.

"Um," Paul scratched at his beard. "Next name I even see is Hammond. It's the same situation as here. There's like, two roads," Paul responded, tossing the half-assed folded map into our seat.

"Call Jonah, ask him if he *sees* anything," Riley suggested.

Paul called Jonah. I tried to focus on the one sided conversation, but was unable to piece together the situation. Paul ended the conversation with an irritated expression.

"Jonah said we need to stop and turn around. He said we better just suck it up and get fuel in Alzada. He doesn't see much ahead, but more possible scares." he rubbed his forehead.

"What? We can't go back there. You saw that place!" Gabe threw up his hands in petition.

"I trust Jonah's word," Riley said.

"So do I. He also said that since we took out what's his face, that we're safe in Alzada for a little bit. So we might as well get some supplies," Paul continued.

"And how are we going to do that?" I asked, naively.

"Well, I can tell you they won't notice," Paul mused.

"Edie, you've seen all those zombie movies. This really isn't any different," Riley said, looking at me in the rearview mirror. "Don't go getting a conscience on me now."

"Well, looking at it that way, I guess it's not a bad idea. At least they aren't gonna get back up and try to eat us," Lamar interjected with a smile.

"Jonah wants the halo," Paul said suddenly.

"What?" Riley asked.

"Jonah requested the halo," Paul repeated. "He said he thinks he can use them."

"How?" I asked, skeptically.

"How the hell am I supposed to know? He's fuckin' nuts. He sees shit!" Paul scoffed.

"He can have it when we stop," Riley said, pulling to the far right and doing a wide U turn.

We drove back towards the gruesome site. I didn't want to return. I didn't want to have to see any of that again. I knew I didn't have a choice and that it was only going to get worse as we went. I climbed over the middle console and back into the passenger seat. Riley looked over at me and smiled faintly. The look in his eyes said 'I'm sorry'. He grabbed my hand and held it as we pulled off the highway.

We turned onto the feeder road and stopped at the only convenience store we could see. Paul and Riley jumped out of the van and looked around. There was no one to be seen. This place was a complete ghost town. Lamar and Gabe exited the van and ran off towards Riley and his gang of thieves.

Riley, Paul and the others congregated in front of the van and discussed their strategy. Jonah explained to them that we had roughly an hour to get ourselves together and back on the road, before trouble found us. He seemed anxious, distracted.

It wasn't long before Jonah walked around the side door and opened it. He climbed into the back seats and looked around for the glowing halo. I watched in the rearview mirror as he leaned over the back seats and picked up the ring of light. It surged and pulsated as he held it. He sat down, stared at the ring, and closed his eyes.

I watched as everyone ran off to get things done. Lamar and Riley ran inside and disappeared. I hoped that we'd get everything we could use and be out of here quickly. I looked at the clock on the dashboard. We had already been here fifteen minutes. Time was running short. We may be safe here, for an hour, but we don't want to be leaving, just as *whatever*, is coming in.

"Jonah?" I turned to look at him.

He didn't respond. He looked as though he was in a trance. I stared at him, both confused and amazed. He was sitting on the seat directly behind me, with his legs folded and his head bent down. His eyes were closed as he held onto the bright ring of light. Azrael sat on the floor board next to him, staring at him with his head cocked to the side.

I watched Azrael as he concentrated on Jonah's face. We've only had him for a few weeks, yet he's proven to be such a loyal, wonderful asset. I love my little guardian. Well, he isn't very *little*, at all. I hadn't noticed how much it looked like he's grown over the past couple of weeks. He's such a regal, majestic animal. His umlauts over his eyes shifted and bounced as he looked from Jonah's face, to the halo. I could tell he wanted to take it, whether to snack on it or to play catch, I wasn't sure.

"Eden," Jonah finally spoke.

"Yes?" I asked.

"Your instincts were correct," he said as he opened his eyes.

"What instincts?" I asked, confused.

"The massacre, it wasn't God's wishes."

"Michael's orders?" I asked.

"Yes. It seems that he has quite the distaste for humans. He ordered David to just 'get rid of them', rather than to reap them, as God had intended."

"So, God does want them to filter out the good from the bad." I nodded.

"Yes. Judging by what I saw, the Valkyrie and the Morrigan are out collecting souls as they were told. Lilith, however, doesn't seem to be cooperating as she was ordered." Jonah sighed and turned to the window. He stared up.

"She seems to have some kind of personal vendetta with me. I'd assume she's following us, rather than commanding her troops," I suggested.

"It would appear so," he stated.

"So, what do we do?" I asked.

"We continue as we were. We head for Washington. We need to get there before any of the angels do," Jonah replied.

"And what of the corpse on the top of the van?" I asked.

"We leave it, for now. It's going to work in our favor for the time being."

"What did you tell them, when you called and warned them?" I asked, finally able to fill in the gaps.

"I informed Paul that there was an angel ahead of us. If we proceeded as we were, he was going to catch us off guard and would've been able to wipe us all out," he said. "He was arrogant. He chose to fight and kill without his shadow armor. I knew we had a chance to take him down. I told Paulie to flank him from the north. As I saw it, Riley would be able to incapacitate him with bullets."

"Do we stand a chance if there's multiple angels? If they have their armor up?"

"Not as far as I know. But, that doesn't mean it's impossible. I just can't see it."

"How do we completely 'dispatch' them?" I choked on the words.

"We have to remove their wings. It makes them unable to return to the fold. In essence, it makes them human. From there, they're just as fragile and delicate as our friends." he smirked awkwardly.

"So it's a matter of getting them, without their armor, caught off guard, and getting their wings off. That doesn't sound as easy as this last one was." I shook my head.

"It won't be. Like I said, he was arrogant. He thought he was untouchable as he murdered this entire town." Jonah looked down at the ring of light in his hand.

"How did you see all of that? Was it stored in his halo?" I asked.

"Basically. Do you ever remember wearing a halo?" he asked me.

"Nope," I shook my head.

"That's because we, they, don't wear them. I know you've seen Gabriel glow. These halos are the remnants of their souls, once their bodies are deceased. If they belong to anyone at all, they belong to you." he sat forward, leaning between the two front seats and held out his hands. The pulsating, brightly glowing ring of light balanced perfectly on his palms. He held it out, waiting for me to grab it. I was nervous. He was able to see information from David's soul, what would I do with it?

"Take it," he ordered.

I nervously looked down at the clock. We only had twenty minutes to get out of here.

"I don't have time to deal with it. We need to get those guys together."

"You helped create all of us. You helped create the world. Each one of us, each piece of our existence is part of you. Take it back." he said, nudging my arm.

I leaned out of the driver's side window, "Corey!" I shouted.

"Yes m'lady?" he grinned.

"Make sure everyone is wrapping up. We're almost out of time."

"No problem," he replied and ran into the store.

"Don't ignore the truth. You can't." Jonah held the halo out to me.

"What will happen?" I asked.

"If I could tell you that, I'd be a mighty oracle, indeed."

"So, you don't even know what will happen if I take it? What if nothing happens? What if the van blows up?" I asked.

"Eden, just take the damned thing!" he laughed.

I reached for the glowing ring of light and gasped as I did. I could feel my head snap back as the air was ripped from my lungs. *Much like the piece of me given to you, you will have to also give a piece of yourself.* The memories rang in my head like loud, chapel bells. I was deaf to the world around me. I saw the face of my Creator. I saw the creation of David, the proud smile God wore once He introduced Himself to His new son.

"Eden?" Jonah called to me. His voice was muffled. "Eden, can you hear me?"

I couldn't respond. The ringing in my ears became louder. My chest burned and ached. It felt like an elephant was sitting directly on my heart. I stared at the ceiling of the van as my vision blurred and tunneled. I couldn't sit up, I couldn't move a muscle.

"Edie?" a familiar voice called, muffled and distorted.

Oh shit.

CHAPTER THIRTY
THE SLEEPING DOG LIES.

When all else fails, trust new friends. They may prove to be far more valuable than you once thought. At least, it was that way for me. Though I was not the least bit surprised. Obviously, I didn't know all the details, as I wasn't conscious when the little turn of events happened. But I, of course, trust my companions.

Apparently, when I touched the *halo*, I basically slipped into a coma of a sort. I can't recall anything that happened, both in reality and in my subconscious. It's completely blank, void, empty, kaput. When I awoke, I was told everything that happened with me and the rest of my traveling circus of misfits.

From what I was told and what I gathered by interrogating everyone in our group, all hell had broken loose and I snoozed straight through it. Jonah wasn't able to see the future clear enough; quick enough. There was very little time for them to make an escape without sacrificing one of our own. That news was very troubling. I was relieved to know that everyone was safe and that they all watched over me. However, I felt as if the stress and anxiety they felt was my fault.

We were now in a little town, God only knows how far from Alzada. It was 8:48pm and my mind was troubled. I had missed the entire day so far and didn't know exactly where we were. We pulled into the dirt lot of a diner called The Sleeping Dog and parked right out front. The old lit up sign with changeable letters claimed it was the best food in the world. Somehow I doubted it, but we were starving and needed a few minutes of peace.

We got out of the vans. I attached Azrael's leash and let him do his business. Everyone stretched their legs and yawned loudly, but never spoke a word. We all stuck together, waiting for Azrael to finish up. Once he was done, we all walked to the front door of the little diner and stepped in.

The atmosphere was overwhelming. The smell of burning flesh and charred wood filled the little country chop shop. Animal heads ornamented the walls with pride like PhDs from the finest university. The dim lighting was dimmed even further by the thick smoke. The country music blaring from the mono speaker reverberated and distorted into even worse noise. I didn't know you *could* make country music any worse.

"Y'all can have a seat wherever you want to," the waitress told us.

"Um, thanks," Riley replied and looked around the desolate room.

There were numerous tables, booths and barstools strewn about. There was only one occupied spot in the joint and that was in the far corner, under a red light. There were three men seated in the corner booth, eyeing us suspiciously. I stared at them nervously.

"Edie, you want to sit on the end?" Riley asked me.

"Sure. Thanks," I said, turning to my friends with a muted smile.

I hated sitting next to a right handed person. Being the lefty that I am, we always ended up bumping elbows. And seeing as how I'm clumsy, I wind up with food everywhere but in my mouth and stomach. Riley was very observant of that and frequently catered to my anal retentive pet peeves.

"What can I get y'all to drink?" the waitress asked.

"What do you have?" Gabe asked, searching his menu for the answer.

"Coffee, tea, milk, soda pop and orange juice," she replied, removing her pen from her bun and preparing to write down our order.

... *Soda pop? Ha ha!*

We ordered our drinks and she disappeared into the haze, walking behind the counter.

"This place is creepy," I mumbled lowly to Riley.

"No shit. I'm pretty sure I've seen this place in horror movies." Riley smiled.

Gabe nodded adamantly in agreement. "You sure do got a perdy' mouth, mmhmm," he mused with a horrible, fake southern accent.

We all laughed nervously. It was far too realistic for this place.

"So where are we, exactly?" I asked.

"Not too far outside of Spokane," Riley replied.

"So, we're in Washington now?"

"Yep. We didn't want to wake you up or anything, so we decided to just keep going until you were ready," Riley explained.

"Ah. You guys didn't have to do that." I frowned.

I knew they were hungry and tired.

"Here y'all go." She sat our drinks down in front of each of us. I was surprised by her accuracy.

I looked up at her name tag, embroidered on her red and white striped frock. Her name was Peggy. She appeared to be in her late forties, maybe early fifty. Her bright red hair screamed 'unnatural', but in a subtly pleasant way. She had a very comforting smile, despite her surroundings.

"Y'all know what you wanna order, or do y'all want to hear the specials?" Peggy asked, propping her tray on her cocked hip like a toddler.

"What are your specials?" I asked politely.

For some reason, I was amused by her country accent. I always found it fascinating how common that drawl had become, in every state, in every corner of the continent. I guess I just wanted to hear her speak. Maybe it was silly. I liked the distraction.

"Let's see. We have some ribs, pork chops, fried chicken, baked beans and hot links," Peggy rattled off.

"And that's the special? All of it?" Gabe asked, confused.

"No, it's special because we actually have it all here!" she smacked her mouth and rolled her eyes at me.

I snickered at her reaction. She was sassy and it entertained me. She sneered at me. I thought she was being sarcastic. *Guess not.*

"So what'll it be?" she asked.

"I'd just like a house salad." Paige smiled.

"Me, too," Lamar said.

"Sorry, out of salad."

"Um, I'd like your quarter pound cheese burger, please." Corey smiled, excitedly, pulling the ear buds from his ears.

"Did y'all not hear what I said we had? We don't have *cheeseburgers* or *salads*. If you haven't noticed, the country is in chaos. Deliveries just ain't happening right now," she responded with her hands on her hips.

"Can you repeat what you have then, please?" Jonah asked nervously.

Peggy sighed heavily and rolled her eyes again.

I realized her smile had been false advertisement. She wasn't comforting at all!

"Listen up. We have ribs, hot links, fried chicken, pork chops, some baked beans and corn on the cob. Maybe some potato salad."

We all anxiously ordered from our few choices and tried to summon a healthy, balanced meal out of their artery clogging selection. She scribbled down our orders and disappeared into the back, like a stealthy, hog wrestling, hick ninja.

"She's practically begging us not to tip her," Paul said.

"I really don't think she gives a shit. I think she'd rather us leave," Lamar replied.

I stared out the window. The street was dark. There was a streetlight a few hundred yards away and no traffic. How did we keep finding these little tiny shit-hole towns? I stared out into the darkness, afraid that *something* could be watching us from the shadows. Of course, we all know what that *something* is. I was afraid to take any more chances. We should've just eaten some of the food we picked up at the convenience store and skipped the stop. I hated the idea of something coming after us *again*.

"It's safe, Eden. Don't worry." Jonah walked over and whispered to me.

"My gut says otherwise."

"Well, I would never tell you to ignore your instincts, but I don't foresee us having any more problems. We'll be out of here soon. Try not to let it bother you," he said.

"I don't trust this place or these people," I responded, turning my gaze back outside.

"Those guys in that corner keep fucking staring over here. It's giving me the creeps," Lamar whispered across the table.

"Me, too," I agreed, intentionally not looking at them.

"You two sissies need to settle down. They're just hillbillies. They're not used to people with so many teeth. They probably think we're celebrities," Riley mused quietly, then laughed loudly.

"Ha! Nice. Yeah, you're probably right." Lamar nodded with a smile.

The table of friends continued to chat amongst themselves while we waited for our food. I stared out the window, waiting to see something dart in the darkness or crash through the glass. I didn't want there to be a replay of Alzada. I was glad that I missed the entire thing; I didn't want to witness it here.

I thought about what everyone had said, how everything went wrong and how we barely made it out alive and without prosecution.

Jonah told me, when I wasn't responding, he called for Riley. Riley came to my side and noticed the time. He rallied the troops and ordered that everyone get in the vans and get ready to go. Apparently, as the side door of our van was opening, Azrael shot out and ran off barking and growling.

Riley told me that he couldn't leave my side, regardless of how much he cared about the dog. He knew Az was after something, *something dangerous*. If Riley ran after him, he wouldn't have been able to protect me. So Gabe and Lamar ran after him and found him cornering a shadowy form.

Lamar told me that Azrael snapped and snarled at the angel. And that as Azrael lunged for him, the angel shot into the air like a rocket, and flew towards the van. They were terrified, but Gabe told me he didn't even seem remotely interested in killing them. There was something, *someone else*, that he was after.

He flew towards our van, faster than anything they had ever seen, they both said. Azrael ran with them back towards the group. Paul was apparently standing outside the van and had grabbed a shotgun, when he saw the angel barreling towards them. Lamar said as they were running back, a crow dove towards them, attempting to peck Azrael. So, of course, he recognized the feathered nuisance and snapped at her, instead.

Jonah said that Riley shouted for everyone to get in the van and told me that everything kind of went to hell in a hand basket all at once. As Paul shot at the angel, the angel dodged the round entirely. Paul said it looked like he basically teleported, lightning fast.

As they were trying to fight off the descending angel, a sheriff drove up and flipped on his lights. The angel apparently landed on top of our van and stood there, waiting for the sheriff to make a move. Gabe said he was about ready to shit his pants when the cop got out of his car and pulled his gun out, aimed at them.

Paul apparently set down the shotgun and tried to explain what was going on. The sheriff wasn't buying any of it and was ordering the "guy" on the roof of the van to "get his black ass down". Paul said that the angel didn't budge. The sheriff walked forward and kept his gun trained on everyone as he interrogated them.

He asked why there was a body strapped to the roof of the van. He was yelling at them and asking about all the dead bodies, all of the townsfolk. He believed, after seeing the corpse on the roof of the van that *we* had basically gone on a killing spree. He apparently wouldn't listen to a word that was said. He became aggressive.

They were trying to explain, but he cocked his gun and told everyone to get down on the ground. Jonah said they all listened, other than Riley who he hadn't seen in the van with me. The angel refused to move. The sheriff warned him again and said he had three seconds before he "shot his ass down".

Needless to say, those weren't words that bode well with the heavenly beings. The 'crow' left Azrael alone and flew towards the sheriff. Paul said it was the *hottest* thing he had ever seen. Once Lilith was directly above the sheriff in crow form, in a liquid movement, she shifted from flight into human form. She dropped down behind him, silently, and snapped his neck. The sheriff dropped to the ground without ever even knowing what touched him. Jonah said they all rose instantly, switching to defensive mode. She apparently approached the group, Azrael stood between her and Lamar. She said nothing, but smiled coyly. She was up to something, as usual.

Paul said that he blew her a kiss and she cackled as she morphed back into crow form and flew off. Paul picked up the shotgun and turned around to make a mess of the angel on the roof of the van. They all said that when they turned around, they were startled to see *both* of the angels were gone. The angel had apparently come to claim the *deceased*.

The questions raised in my mind were would he have killed them all if he wasn't more concerned with retrieving the body? Would we have run into him either way? Or had he specifically hunted us down, with the sole intention of removing the corpse?

"Holy shit. I just thought about something," I said, suddenly less frightened.

"What's up?" Riley asked me.

Everyone turned, waiting for my reply. I turned and looked at the three men in the corner. They were staring directly at me. I leaned in, close to the table and began whispering. Everyone huddled together to hear what I had to say.

"I think I see what happened in Alzada," I stated with a smug smile.

"Oh, yeah? We all know we got bent over and almost screwed," Gabe replied.

"No, it's not as bad as you guys are thinking. It's not as bad as I was thinking. I'm pretty sure of it, anyway."

"What did you surmise, Eden?" Jonah asked.

"Look, why was there no traffic on the roads? Why weren't there any vehicles around us, other than the ones that were filled with dead people?" I asked, trying to get them to think along the same lines that I was.

"Shitty day for travel? Not a commonly used road?" Riley responded.

"No, I don't think so. I think David was working with others. I think they were wiping out everyone as they approached, like a trap," I suggested.

"So? That doesn't really change anything." Paul narrowed his eyes, confused.

"Who would David be with?" I asked, trying to spark a memory or two.

"I give up," Riley said, shaking his head.

"How about his brother, Daniel," I smiled and nodded.

"You think that was *Daniel* at Alzada? You think he was the attacking angel?" Paul inquired.

"Technically, if what you're telling me is the truth, he never *attacked* anyone. I think he was only there to claim his brother's body. I think *that* was his only concern," I explained.

"That does sound like him. He was always the more gentle of the two. But I didn't really see Daniel in David's memories of the event. But that definitely sounds like something he would do." Jonah nodded in agreement.

"Maybe David and Daniel weren't 'working' together, so to speak. But they could've been down there together. David could've been working with others. For all we know, Pestilence is on the loose, already," I suggested.

"Fuck, I don't even want to think about that," Paul said, throwing his head onto the table.

"It's always a possibility," Riley added.

"I'm sure he's up to something, by now," Jonah agreed.

"Wait, so how do you explain the deal with Lilith, then?" Paul asked.

"I don't know," I responded.

"She could have snapped all of our necks, just as quick if she wanted to," Riley said solemnly.

"She chose not to, obviously. Maybe she was doing all of that as a favor." I shrugged.

"A favor to whom? To you? You guys have always had bad blood," Riley jeered.

"And why is that?" Paul asked, curiously.

"That's not something I want to talk about, Paul, even if I could remember all of it. As for my thoughts on her *favors*, it could've been a combined effort. Maybe she was trying to make sure that Daniel could reclaim his brother's body. And maybe, just maybe, she's watching our backs for Gabriel," I explained my views.

"That could be true, as much as Gabriel cares for you," Jonah agreed.

"Now, how could you not see them coming?" Gabe asked Jonah.

"See what? Daniel, or whoever that was, with Lilith? I was more worried about Eden. Not to mention, I did say we only had an hour, safely," he defended himself.

"We all were worried about Edie." Gabe looked at me. I could see the big brother look in his eyes. "That isn't a valid excuse."

"Lay off of him, will you?" Brooke became defensive of Jonah.

Jonah raised his hand in the air slightly, trying to defuse the situation. "I knew something was headed our way, I just couldn't focus on *what*. I told you guys we only had an hour or so to clear out. We shouldn't have waited around as long as we did. I'm not perfect, neither is my vision of the future."

"I know. I'm sorry," Gabe replied.

"It's fine. I know you weren't blaming me. I just wish it would've worked out better." Jonah rubbed his forehead.

"As much as you don't want to hear it, I think that worked out perfectly," I said.

"How so? We don't have the dead angel anymore," Paul reminded me.

"I'm pretty sure, driving into busy cities, with a dead body strapped to the roof of our van, wasn't a very good idea. I don't know what I was thinking. I was just feeling that bloodlust and revenge, I guess," Riley stated.

"We did what needed to be done. And I think having him on the roof was going to keep us safe," Paul argued.

"No, I don't think it would've. Don't forget, the entire world doesn't know what's going on yet. Who knows if they ever will," Lamar interjected.

"Exactly," Gabe agreed.

I heard the swinging doors of the kitchen and watched as Peggy emerged from the back with a tray full of steaming food. She sat the tray down on the front counter and returned to the kitchen. She exited the kitchen a minute later with a second tray of food and walk around the counter towards us.

I stared at the mess on my plate. She continued to call out the orders as I stared at my dish, trying to determine whether it was edible or dangerous. The 'ribs' were charred and uncut. It was a slab of black and red crunchy, smelly *something*. The potato salad was yellow. And I don't mean like mustard potato salad, it was intimidating. I was concerned to ingest it.

"I'm scared." I stuck my tongue out, curling my lip, as I poked at my potato salad.

"Don't be a wuss. You've eaten island food! Your stomach can handle it," Gabe joked between bites.

"Bleh," I frowned.

Everyone was quietly eating for a few moments. No one looked impressed. The sighs and groans spoke for themselves. I think we were all secretly wishing we hadn't stopped at this jip joint. The food was gross, the air reeked of dead, ill prepared animals and burnt flesh. I thought about the stupid sign out front. I was now annoyed.

"Best food in the world, my ass. The Sleeping Dog *lies!*" I said, much louder than I should've.

"I'm sorry, is there a problem?" Peggy asked, from behind the counter. She sounded offended.

"Yes, ma'am. There is, in fact, a bit of a problem," Paul said, standing up.

"Oh, yeah, sonny? What's that?" she asked, folding her arms across her chest.

"This food tastes horrible and I found hair in my beans," he said with a slight gag.

"If y'all are just going to bitch and try to start a ruckus, I'm gonna have to ask you to leave," she said loudly, pointing to the front door.

"With pleasure," I jabbed, cradling my tumultuous stomach in my hands.

"Yeah, this shit is disgusting. I think I'm gonna throw up," Erick said, covering his mouth.

"Get the hell out of here!" she shouted, pointing towards the door.

We all got up and walked towards the front door. I personally, would much rather have starved than eaten that crap. There's no telling what was in any of it. I bet a health inspector would have had a field day in there.

"Thanks for the food poisoning, Peggy." Paul laughed, as he stepped out of the screen door.

"No shit." Riley chuckled.

"Get the hell out of here, before I call the sheriff," she threatened.

"Damn, Lady. Chill out!" Gabe shook his head and stepped out onto the front porch of the chop shop.

We all walked down the stairs and headed towards the vans, laughing.

"God damn. That was horrible." Paul laughed awkwardly.

"I'm just glad we didn't get murdered. That was totally like one of those chainsaw movies." Gabe laughed loudly.

"Guys, we have plenty of food in our van, if you want to grab something edible," Brooke offered with a smile.

"Thanks. I could use something," Riley replied.

"I'm really not hungry now. That killed my appetite," I said, shaking my head. "In fact, I just feel sick again." I ran to the nearest bushes and vomited.

"We need to get out of here, before she pops out on the porch with a shotgun and hunting dogs," Gabe mused.

Everyone else found snacks and piled into the vans. I started the van and pulled behind Paul, who was driving the other. He knew I didn't know where I was. I followed him back to the interstate and then sped around him. There wasn't much traffic on the road, but what there was, seemed to be heading away from the direction we were headed.

"You know what I just thought about?" Riley leaned forward between Gabe and me.

"Boobs; you wish you had a pair. It's okay, dude. I was thinking the same thing," Gabe mused.

"Me, too," Lamar yelled from the seat behind Riley.

"No, you jackasses!" Riley laughed and smacked Gabe with a pillow.

"Liar. You're just saying that, because Edie's right here. I know the truth," Gabe continued.

"Were you dropped on your head repeatedly when you were a baby?" Riley asked Gabe, shaking his head, baffled.

"It's possible. Our mom was 17 when she had me. If she was anything like I was at 17, I wouldn't doubt it," Gabe retorted.

"Enough, guys. What did you just realize, Riley?" I asked, changing lanes.

"Well, I don't know. Do you guys think it's weird that all of the angels that are left are here in the U.S? I mean, that doesn't seem odd to you? Why haven't we had to travel outside of the States?" Riley asked.

"Hmm. That is kind of weird, now that you mention it," I replied.

"Well, I thought you guys don't know where one of them is. Maybe he's elsewhere," Lamar said, from the back.

"No, we don't know where he is, exactly. But Gabriel told me he was with one of them. That would also put him stateside," I explained.

"Well, maybe it has something to do with the fact that we're all kind of linked together. Maybe we just all migrated towards the States," Riley suggested.

"Where was your garden, Edie?" Gabe asked, hinting at his idea.

"I'm not really sure where it is." I shook my head.

"There's really no telling. And honestly, I'm glad we weren't all spread out across the globe. I couldn't imagine this being any more of a pain in the ass, than it already is. We wouldn't have had time to scour the world for everyone," Riley said.

"Yeah, that's a good point. Couldn't have afforded it, either." I agreed.

"I bet I know exactly why," Lamar said, sitting up.

"Oh, yeah? What's your opinion?" I asked, curiously.

"Well, look at it realistically. The United States leads the world in so many things. Unemployment, violence, obesity, just to name a few. All of which are negative things. We claim to live in a democracy, freedom for everyone, right?" he said.

"Supposedly," Gabe scoffed.

"That's the thing. The rest of the world is far more enlightened, far more advanced. Maybe all of the angels everywhere else saw the truth and returned. It's just you guys left, because you choose to live in this bullshit. You've chosen to thrive in this misled, mistaken society," Lamar continued.

"It's not like it's our fault. We didn't choose to be born to people in U.S., or even on this continent, for that matter," I defended.

"That's also true. We don't control where or what we're born into," Riley agreed.

"So maybe it was God's doing. Maybe he wanted all of us, that were left, born in the exact spot that the bomb would drop," I said.

"You don't think they're attacking the entire planet?" Gabe asked, turning to me.

"No, I know that they are. But, the United States has been taking the brunt of the blow. Like the storms. Technically, that's one of the prophecies of the impending apocalypse. That could've been anywhere, but he chose the good old U.S. of A," I explained.

"That's kind of fucked up," Gabe said.

"Yeah, it is. But it's to be expected. Just like Lamar said, look what we lead the world in. Violence, depravity. We let rapists and pedophiles back onto the streets, with a slap on the wrist and a little black mark in their record," Riley said.

"I really don't know what to think about all of this. The more and more I *do* think about what's going on, the more I feel that this world *does* deserve to be wiped clean. But the thing is, the *good* people, don't deserve to suffer for the fuck ups," I said.

"But, we're not supposed to, right?" Lamar asked. "Well, you said yourself, Edie. God told them to 'reap' the good souls, right? Aren't they supposed to save those of us that deserve to go to Heaven and just 'take care' of those who don't?"

"In a sense. I'm not sure what His plan is. I'm not sure if He's telling them to take in everyone who has been a good person, or just the exceptional. Either way, they aren't even doing that."

"But they're supposed to. Won't God punish them for not listening?" Gabe asked.

"I don't know. They may get away with it. If God is really that angry about what's happened to the world, He may not care how it's done, just as long as the humans are gone," I replied with a sigh.

"All merciful... fucking lies." Gabe put his earbuds back into his ears.

"I think that only applies to the beings *He* created," I responded.

"Ha! Yeah right. Ripping our wings off and lettings us live, life after life, full of pain and anguish is *very* merciful. Just *bursting* with love and mercy. He doesn't give a shit about us either. Don't be naïve," Riley said, very snidely.

"This conversation has become counterproductive," I said.

"You're just being defensive. You seem to forgive Him, regardless of everything He's put you through," Riley argued.

"Everything He's put *me* through? I'm sorry, Riley, but don't forget what *we* did. We chose each other and the Earth over Him. I'm sure that was a total kick in the balls." I folded my arms across my chest.

"You're right, this conversation *is* counterproductive." Riley sneered.

"So, how about them Yankees?" Gabe asked with an awkward smile.

The van became very quiet. I'm sure we were all thinking about what was going to happen. The truth is we didn't know what was going to happen. That's a scary enough thought to begin with, but now we had to think about whether we were going to be murdered, with our souls left to rot. At least I have to worry about that. I have to think about my family, my friends, everyone that means anything to me, lying dead, *somewhere*, without eternal rest.

After about an hour of driving without conversation, I realized that the van full of some of my favorite people, were all sound asleep. Azrael was lying on the seat with Riley, snoring and kicking his legs. He whimpered a couple of times and lightly barked. He was obviously dreaming.

"You still okay to drive?" Lamar asked me.

"Yeah, I'm good. You need to rest up. You have a lot to explain to Chuck," I said.

"Ah, shit. I forgot about that."

I laughed and he flopped back down in the back. I could hear him sighing occasionally. I knew he wasn't sleeping; he was trying to figure how he was going to explain all of this to his brother, without him thinking we're insane. I knew how he felt. So far, I had been really lucky with people understanding. I know my mom had a hard time accepting it, at first. It wasn't because she thought it was a lie, or because it was so farfetched. It was because she religiously, believed differently. Those aren't feelings or beliefs easily changed. In the long run, she handled it well and had become an asset to me.

I know she would do anything I asked of her, whether that was to help keep my family safe or say goodbye to me for the last time. It wouldn't be easy for either of us, but I'd do anything in the world that I could, to attempt to save the ones I love and those I've never even met. I just wish I could tell someone what I was thinking... Even God will be caught off guard. You can't say that, every day.

I tried to ward off the highway hypnosis by slamming cans of sugary, carbonated goodness, to no avail. I couldn't stop yawning. Riley sat up in the backseat and leaned forward between the seats, gently resting his chin on my shoulder.

"Pull over, let's switch," he offered.

"Okay," I yawned.

I put on my hazards and pulled over along the side of the road. I put the van in park and watched in my mirror. There were no headlights behind us, other than those of our companions. They pulled over behind us and stopped with their flashers on, as well.

I jumped out of the driver's side and ran around to the side doors. Riley was standing towards the front of the van, peeing in the grass, facing away from everyone. I laughed and climbed into the backseat. He closed the doors behind me then ran around the front to the driver's seat.

Gabe sat up and yawned looking at Riley confused.

"Hey, baby. I just wanted to be closer to you," Riley said to Gabe, with a wink.

"Edie, you married a moron." Gabe laughed and curled back up to sleep.

Chapter Thirty One
This Isn't Poker,
It's Russian Roulette!

It wasn't long after I rolled over that I woke up in an out of body realm. I knew something was different. This wasn't a *normal* dream, there was no way I had been asleep long enough. This was more of a meditative state. Either way, I felt an odd sense of comfort.

Surrounding my cold, bare feet, were swirls of multicolored, misty clouds. I saw my breath as I exhaled. It was unnaturally cold here. I stepped forward, cautiously. I wasn't sure where I was or why I felt so at peace, but I didn't want to fight it and cause myself to slip into a nightmare.

"There you are," the heavenly voice echoed behind me.

A smile stretched across my face and my shoulders dropped instantly, relaxed. I turned around quickly and faced my soul twin. I ran towards him and hugged him. He smiled and laid his head on my shoulder, squeezing me tightly. I looked up into his beautiful eyes.

"I've missed you so much," Gabriel said.

"I've missed you, too." I smiled and hugged him tighter.

"You look exhausted." he frowned, tracing the dark circles under my eyes.

"I am. I've been running on fumes for days," I replied with a yawn.

"Who's driving?" Gabriel asked.

"What do you mean? I am… Oh God!" I smiled. "Haha, just kidding. Riley just took over. He made me stop."

I realized then, how lucidly I was dreaming.

"I really wish the two of you could just enjoy your time together and didn't have to deal with all of this." he wrapped his arm around my shoulder.

"All of this is really beginning to take its toll on me." I frowned and slumped my shoulders.

"I know. I wish there was more that I could do to assist you. How is everything?" he grabbed my hand and led me through the cloudy haze.

"I'm not sure. It seems as if we're making progress, then something gets in our way." I followed my angelic brother's steps.

"I heard about David and Daniel. Lilith told me everything." he shook his head.

"So it was Daniel? Fuck. I'm so sorry."

"Don't be. I would've killed him myself if I were there and worried about your safety. But Daniel is truly in mourning."

"Why? Won't David just be reincarnated or healed or something?" I asked, confused.

"No. He went against God's will, mercilessly killing all of those humans. God has refused to allow him to be reborn. Daniel has taken it very hard," Gabriel explained.

"That's horrible." I thought about the pain I would feel if I lost any of my brothers. Gabriel was connected to me deeper than my earthly brothers, but I didn't feel any more love in my heart for him than any of them. He was a part of me. But, I had spent my life, this life, with my four brothers and would do anything for them. I couldn't imagine what Daniel was going through right now. They've never been apart.

"Eden, it wasn't your actions that brought about his death. God wouldn't have allowed him back into His fold, had He found out. Daniel is ashamed of what his brother has done. He told God, himself." he stopped in place.

I stopped abruptly to avoid a collision with my soul twin. "Why did God react so harshly, if He doesn't approve of humans?"

"Would you condone someone killing dogs or cats in your home? He may not have created humans Himself, but they are still alive. They're still creatures that think and feel. They're still created in His image, regardless of who created them. He wanted this to be executed with mercy." he continued walking.

"Well, then I guess David got what he deserved." I was emotionally torn.

"In a sense. Although, Daniel is the one who is truly suffering." he frowned.

He sat down on a misty bank. He gently tugged on my hand, forcing me to sit beside him. I curled up close to my brother's side and laid my head on his armored shoulder as I stared out at the stream of stars and cosmic dust that floated by our feet like a heavenly creek.

"Do you remember this place?" he asked me.

"No. I wish I did," I replied and turned to my brother.

"We used to sit here and mix up the galaxies."

"What? You're lying!" I replied with a smile.

"No."

I looked at my brother, skeptically. My eyes narrowed. He had to have been pulling my leg. "We'd spend hours here, discussing life as we knew it. I'd watch as you'd create little works of magic and set them loose in the stream of cosmos. Then I'd add my personal touch by chaotically swirling them." he laughed and squeezed my shoulder.

"I can't believe that. There's no way I had a part of that. I make flowers, not planets!"

"You're right, you didn't make them." he laughed loudly.

"You're such an ass! I was like, 'holy crap! I'm pretty freaking impressive!'" I laughed and slapped his arm.

"But we did sit here and watch them pass by." his smile fell flat and he turned his gaze to my hand, in his.

"What's wrong?" I asked him.

"I'm just worried about you," his voice cracked as he choked on his words.

"You worry far too much." I smiled.

"I saw what happened to Daniel. He's been devastated. Yes, they've spent their entire lives together, but *we* are joined at the soul. I'd feel that same pain, tenfold. I can't imagine the pain I'll feel if something happens." he frowned and rubbed his temples.

"You don't trust me? My plan is infallible."

"If you make it."

"Have a little faith in me, geez!" I grabbed Gabriel's face in my hands.

"Eden, if anything happens to you, I've lost you forever. Riley loses you forever. Even God loses you forever. That's a risk that shouldn't have ever been taken. The odds are starting to stack against you." Gabriel shook his head concerned, pulling away from my hold.

"I think you're worrying for nothing. I think the odds are more in my favor than you realize. Don't forget what bargaining chips I hold." I smirked.

"Eden, this isn't poker, it's Russian Roulette! You're playing with your *life*, not plastic chips!" he scolded me.

I stared out at the swirling stars and sparkling twilight below my feet.

"Give me a little credit. I have this well thought out. I'm not deliberately taking any chances. We're all being as cautious as we can be," I responded, calmly.

"Promise me you won't do anything stupid." he squeezed my hand.

"Define *stupid*?" I grinned.

"Eden Quinn! Don't even joke around." he looked at me sternly.

"Damn, Gabriel, did you just channel my mother? What the hell?" I laughed.

"You're not funny, you're being reckless," he reminded me.

"I'm being as careful as I possibly can be. I'm doing my best. I'm trying to avoid as much death as humanly, *and heavenly* possible," I reassured him.

He hugged me tight to his chest.

"I know. Lilith has been keeping an eye on you for me." Gabriel smiled fondly.

"Why? You know she hates me." I tossed a small stone.

"You're wrong about her," he paused and watched me throw a second stone. "Way to go, Eden. They're all going to die. You just hurled a meteor towards a planet of living creatures." he shook his head.

"Oh, shit!" I said, leaning forward.

He laughed loudly and pulled me back.

"I was just joking!" he chuckled, proudly.

"When did you become so smart ass?" I laughed.

"You say *I* worry too much." he smirked. "And Lilith doesn't hate you. She's hoping you stop hating her for something that she did, with the best intentions. When you remember everything, you'll remember I'm half to blame, as well. We never wanted to do what we did, but the choices were limited. She knew what was to come."

His smile faded quickly, "It's time to go."

"What's wrong? No, finish explaining this, please," I asked, suddenly worried by his reaction.

"You're at the airport. Go get Lamar's brother." he stood and leaned down, kissing my forehead.

"No, not yet. They can wait. I don't have to get up. They don't need me!" I pouted.

"Goodbye, Eden. I hope to see you soon." he waved and disappeared into the Technicolor clouds.

"I want to stay here with you!" I folded my knees to my chest, waiting to awaken.

I felt my body shake awake. I sat up, squinting and yawned loudly. I fell back on my pillow and covered my eyes. The lights under the overhang were blindingly bright as we stopped in front of the doors of the airport. Lamar opened the side door and stepped out. He stretched widely and sat on the edge of the doorway.

"He should be landing any minute now," he said then yawned.

I sat up, straightened my glasses. I pulled the rubber band from my hair, and twisted my hair into a loose bun, barely balancing on the overstretched elastic. I yawned again and climbed out of the van, squeezing between Lamar and the frame of the van. I reached into my purse and pulled out a granola bar.

"Breakfast of champions," Lamar mused, looking at my tiny snack.

"Brain fuel," I replied, shoving the last bite into my mouth.

"You didn't have to get up." he told me.

"It's cool, don't worry about me. I got a power nap in." I shrugged.

"You were only out for like 45 minutes."

"I'm fine, don't worry about me." I smiled.

Azrael walked to the edge of the doorway and sniffed at the cool night air.

"Smells different around here, doesn't it, Az?" I smiled and scratched behind his ears.

He wagged his stubby tail and panted with approval.

I attached his leash and gently tugged on it. He jumped to the ground and stretched with a yawn and a whine. I walked him across the road, towards the nearest patch of grass I could find, under the closest overhead light. I didn't want to trail off too far or wind up in the dark. I didn't want to make Gabriel worry, but of course I was concerned. I know my plan would be a complete waste, an utter failure, if I manage to get myself killed.

"Wait up!" Gabe shouted, as he ran towards me. He zipped up his hoodie and pulled his hood over his beanie.

"What's up?" I asked, as Gabe approached me.

"Ah, nothing. Just wanted to keep you company." he smiled.

"Oh. Thanks." I wrapped my arm around my brother's waist.

"So this is it, huh?"

"What do you mean?" I asked.

"We're in Seattle. We're getting the last two that will join us, right?" he clarified his question.

"Oh, no. We still need to go to Tennessee," I smiled sheepishly.

"Ah, there's another?" he asked.

"Yeah. Tom."

I heard Riley's phone ring. He stepped out of the van, and spoke to whoever it was. He pulled up his hood and pulled his cigarettes out of his pocket. We were pretty far from the van, near the parking. I wasn't able to hear what Riley was saying, but I could tell by his body language, that something troubled him.

"Come on, Muttley. You lay around enough. Let's walk." I gently tugged on Azrael's leash.

We walked through the grass and let him stretch his legs for a while before taking him back to the van. I felt guilty for how long he's been trapped in the van without proper exercise. He's such a well-mannered, well behaved animal.

"Talked to Sara recently?" I asked, as Gabe and I walked back towards the van.

"Yeah, she sent me a text a bit ago. They're all doing good. She's freaked out a bit by the news, though," Gabe said.

"What news?" I lit a cigarette.

"I don't know exactly. I guess everything is starting to really go to shit. The internet is buzzing with so much conspiracy theory stuff, it's hard to tell what's really going on. We need to get a paper or something."

I inhaled and gathered my thoughts, then exhaled forcefully. "Yeah, we will. I think we're gonna hit up a hotel tonight. We'll go after those two in the morning."

"Good. I could really use a shower." he sniffed at his armpits, through his hoodie.

"Yeah, we all could." my lip curled up instinctively.

When we returned, Chuck was now with our group. It was great to see Lamar and his brother together. They stood side by side, with wide smiles and instantly began their friendly bantering.

Though Chuck was younger than Lamar, he was much larger than his brother. Chuck had a good, three inches in height on Lamar and had a larger frame. He stood next to the van, head clean shaven and goatee neatly trimmed, making fun of Lamar's gruff appearance due to our travels and lack of time to devote to personal hygiene.

"It's good to see you, Chuck," I said as I approached them, flicking my cigarette butt into the air.

"Hey, Edie. Good to see you, too." he smiled.

"How was the trip?" I asked with a grin.

"Not too bad. We pretty much stayed out of the storms. It was kind of rough there for a little bit, but we got here relatively unscathed." he shrugged. "It's cold as shit here, though. Why didn't you warn me?" he asked, bundling up in his coat.

"We just got here, too. Stop your bitching." Lamar laughed.

"Whatever." Chuck rolled his eyes at his brother.

"Settle down, ladies," Riley said to Chuck and Lamar as he rounded the corner of the van.

"Hey, Nix! What's up!" Chuck smiled and walked towards Riley with his hand extended.

They shook hands like gentlemen then Riley pulled Chuck in for a man hug, with the traditional pat on the back.

I laughed and grinned at Lamar.

"You two wanna stop making out so we can get the fuck out of here?" Paul asked as he walked towards the van.

"Ah, Chuck, this is Paulie. Paulie, this is Chuck, Lamar's little brother." I smiled as I introduced the two.

"Nice to meet you." Chuck said, as he shook Paul's hand.

"You too, man." Paul smiled. "Little my ass," he mumbled to me.

The rest of the group filed out of the van and walked towards us.

"Oh, geez! It's freezing out here!" Paige shouted as she stepped out.

"You guys are all pussies," Paul jabbed.

"I'm fine." Riley smiled.

"You two were raised in Michigan, you dorks!" I laughed.

"Okay. Let's get the hell out of here," Riley said with a grin.

Riley had gotten into the driver's seat and I had jumped into the front passenger seat. Lamar and Chuck were in the seat in the far back, discussing whatever it was that they were discussing, quietly. Gabe and Azrael were seated directly behind us, staring out of the windows as we drove through the busy city. I was very surprised to see so many people out and about this late at night. Everyone moved in a hurry, almost suspiciously. "So, who was that on the phone?" I asked, quietly leaning towards Riley, attempting to change my focus.

"Jere," he replied, short.

"Everything okay?" I asked, staring at a running woman as we passed to her left.

"No."

"What's wrong?" I continued my interrogation, returning my gaze ahead again.

"We'll talk about it once we stop." he slammed on the brakes, avoiding an abandoned car.

"Okay," I turned to look out the side window again, people watching.

The streets were covered with a soft glow of the reflecting neon lights, bouncing off of the wet pavement. It was impossible to see the lines on the road past the water and refracting light. We pulled into a nice looking hotel and parked in the turnabout. Riley opened the door of the van and stepped out without saying a word. I didn't bother to ask him what was troubling him; I knew it had something to do with Jeremiah.

I knew his body language. I knew how he acted when he needed space or time to think for himself. Thanks to the close quarters we're all stuck in, he didn't have the luxury of solitude. I figured he was going inside to check the availability of rooms and that he'd return with an answer. I didn't need to follow him or bother him while he was obviously bothered by something. This was something between him and his lifelong best friend. He stepped out of the front door and smiled.

I rolled down my window, "All good?" I asked.

"Yup. Let's go park and unload," he said, running towards the driver's side.

After parking, we all headed towards the front door with our backpacks strapped to our backs and bags in our hands. Azrael walked with me on his leash, acting very casual and relaxed. I sighed with relief to see him so calm. I felt like we may be able to sleep through the night, without any kind of surprises.

We all stepped inside the well decorated foyer and were greeted warmly by the clerk.

"Hello, everyone." he smiled fondly.

"Hey, again." Riley set his bag down. "Thanks, man. We really appreciate your help."

I looked at his name tag. His name was Aaron.

"Here are your keys, Mr. Nixon." Aaron handed Riley a stack of key cards.

"Thanks," Riley replied as he grabbed the keys.

"Your rooms are all consecutive. You're all on the seventh floor. Once you get off the elevator, turn right. All of your rooms are down that hallway," Aaron explained.

"Thank you, so much," I responded.

"No problem, ma'am." Adam smiled cheerfully. "Well, you all have a wonderful night. Sleep well. The breakfast bar opens at 5am and is free, of course."

As we began to walk away, Paul stopped dead in his tracks and turned towards Aaron. "Why are you still here? Why are you still working? Why aren't you home with your family, or hiding, or running?"

I grabbed his arm to pull him away.

"I have nowhere to go. My family is gone. All I have left is this place. I don't even have a car." Aaron laughed uncomfortably.

"May God have mercy on your soul," Paul shook his head and left the poor boy alone.

We all walked towards the elevator and pressed the up button. Everyone waited patiently for the elevator to arrive. Azrael sat next to me, well behaved as always. Once the doors opened, we all piled into the elevator and hit the button for the seventh floor.

Everyone discussed the room arrangements and split up accordingly. I followed Riley into our room and threw my bag on the bed. Azrael pranced in behind me, nosedived onto the bed and began wallowing all over the clean, white bedspread. I followed Riley out onto the patio and lit a cigarette.

"So, wanna talk now?" I slid the glass door shut.

"I guess," he stopped and lit a cigarette, then pulled a chair out.

"What's going on with Jere?" I asked, turning to see his face.

His beautiful features shown in the moonlight like a soft white, marble statue. "He said that everything is going to shit. Apparently, they called him in and put him on patrol in the city. They've declared Martial Law," he explained, rubbing his temples.

"What happened?" I asked, shaking my head.

"There was an attack in the city. There were a lot of witnesses, a lot of people that managed to get away. But they're seeing it as some kind of terrorist attack. They're still saying it's aliens. How fucking stupid can people really be?"

"Riley, this isn't anything someone would ever expect to happen," I reminded him.

"I know, but I don't understand how they think they stand a chance." he buried his head into my side.

"But people got away, that's a good thing," I said with a faint smile.

"Edie, Mel was there." he frowned.

"Oh, shit. Please tell me…" I started to panic.

"She's fine. But she saw everything," he responded.

"You scared me. I thought, oh God. I thought she was *killed* or something." I leaned forward catching my face in my hands.

"No. I'm sorry. I wasn't trying to scare you. But it's still bad." he wrapped his arms around my waist.

"If she's safe, then its fine," I tried to reason with him.

"No, the problem is, Jere's been trying to shelter her from all of this. He didn't even know what he thought about it and now he's got one of our best friends freaking out."

"Well, he should've told her about it beforehand. She's a big girl, she can handle the truth."

"How so? He didn't know what to believe. He didn't want her to think he was nuts. Then we took off on him. Here we are, gallivanting off like some fucking pack of vigilantes, prancing around, trying to save the world from pissed off angels. He's stuck in the city, face to face with the heartless bastards. He has no clue what he's doing." Riley cradled his head in his hands, speaking through his fingers. "*You* haven't exactly taken this with a grain of salt, either."

"Shut up!" I retorted and paused. "So what are you going to do?"

"I told him he needs to join us." he pulled me close. "He's going to."

"Well, that's good news! What's the problem? Why are you so upset?"

"Mel wants to be with us, as well."

"What's wrong with that?" I asked.

"Edie, it's hard enough to keep a few of us safe. We're stockpiling people that we're trying to protect. I think we're getting too sidetracked. Maybe we should send everyone to your parents' place," he suggested.

"No, no chance. You know Gabe and Lamar aren't leaving our side." I shook my head.

"And Chuck? We basically just threw him to the wolves. He doesn't even know what's going on," he reminded me.

"Riley, I know this is stressful. It's stressful to me, too. But I know it's especially hard on you. They look to you for guidance. Everyone expects you to play commander. You have to keep your chin up," I said, kissing his forehead.

"That's easier said than done, when you're putting your friend's lives in jeopardy. And what about my family? I haven't even told them what's going on."

"That's a choice you've made. That's something you have to do. I'm not doing it for you. You know what's best." I rubbed his back.

"I know. I'm just worried. We're dragging so many people into battle with us.

These are lives we have to protect. These people should be spending the next couple weeks with those they love. They shouldn't be risking their lives. Not for us; not with us," he said, lighting a second cigarette.

"Riley, you need to remember something very important. *Free will*. It's what got us into all this trouble to begin with. It's what we're fighting *for*. You can't take that away from any of us," I reminded him.

He nodded and exhaled his smoke with a sigh. "You're right. I can't stop these ass hats. They won't leave!" he laughed awkwardly.

"What if this was the other way around? What if we found out the truth, but Chuck, Lamar and Gabe were the angels? Would you still want to be involved?" I asked.

"Yeah, but I'm a fighter. I'm a warrior. I'm a leader. And I've always been so. They haven't. That's what I was created to do. That's who I am."

"And this is who *they* are. They're just as faithful. They're just as loyal. If the roles were switched, if they told you to run along home and hide, you'd tell them to kiss your ass and you'd be here with them." I smiled.

He nodded and chuckled lightly at the thought.

"Let them be where they want to be. We aren't their parents. We aren't their guardians. Whoever chooses to be at our side needs to be welcomed with open arms. We all know the risks and implications. Relax," I offered.

"You're right," he agreed, finally. "You always are."

"Now, call Jere. Tell him what's going on. Tell him that he and Mel are welcome to join us. Let him know, that we'll do everything in our power to keep her safe. Let him know, that being with us, may be the safest place for her. Don't forget, we have some heavenly protection, ourselves." I lifted his chin and looked him in the eyes.

Chapter Thirty Two
Blitzed and Blindsided

10am arrived much quicker than I had hoped for. We decided it would be best if we awoke early, ate breakfast and attempted to find Tori and Brandon soon. The alarm clock was extremely annoying and made it nigh impossible to sleep through, which I supposed was a good thing. Riley and I were big fans of the snooze button, but neither of us wanted to have to experience that racket again.

I rolled over and smiled at Riley. He smiled back and softly kissed my lips. He rolled over and handed me my glasses. I slid them on with a loud, overdramatic yawn and stretched, kicking the sheets and heavy comforter to the floor, at the foot of the bed.

"I'm hungry," he said, yawning, as he lumbered to the bathroom.

"I'm nauseous," I responded, struggling to get out of bed.

"Well, let's go get everyone up and get some food. Maybe that'll make you feel better," he said loudly then flushed the toilet.

"Okay," I agreed then yawned again and flopped back down on my pillow.

He walked back into the room and pulled his pillow from the bed.

"Get up!" he shouted, as he continuously pelted me in the butt with his cotton filled weapon.

"No!" I grunted and buried my face in the pillow.

He grabbed my ankles and began to pull me off of the bed. I squealed like a little girl and tried kicking free of his grasp. I grabbed onto the edge of the headboard, attempting to hold my position as he pulled at my legs. I continued to scream and laugh.

I could hear Azrael barking across the hall, responding to my noise. He sounded anxious, worried. I smiled and covered my mouth. Riley stopped tugging on my legs and slid into a pair of jeans, lying on the top of his bag. There was a knock on the door, followed by whines and growls.

"Who is it?" Riley asked, laughing.

"Open up," Gabe said.

Riley opened the door slightly, leaving the chain linked in place.

"Yes? We don't need room service, thank you," Riley mused.

"I think the mutt was worried you were killing her."

"Oh, he's gonna get you!" I laughed, pointing at Riley.

Azrael stuck his muzzle in the crack of the door, sniffing and snorting loudly. He whined and clawed at the crack aggressively. I jumped out of bed and slid on some pants, then ran to the door to greet my furry guardian.

"Hey, Az!" I said, excitedly. "Open the door." I looked up, smiling at Riley.

He closed the door slightly and undid the chain lock. Azrael pushed the door in, nearly sending Riley and I toppling over.

"Hey, boy!" I said as he climbed on my lap, knocked me over and attempted to get to the balcony in one fell swoop.

"Jesus. It hasn't been that long," Gabe stated.

"I know. He's obsessed with her. Fucking momma's boy." Riley shook his head.

"Come on, momma's boy. Let's go outside," Riley said, reaching for Azrael's leash, and pulling the reluctant behemoth towards the door. "I'll go walk him if you want a few minutes to get ready," he said, pulling a t-shirt over his head.

"Thanks." I smiled, excited about the solitude.

I leaned down and kissed the top of Azrael's head and watched them leave the room, as the dog whined and attempted to pull away from Riley's grasp.

Shortly after they left, I could hear a vibrating noise coming from the room. I peeked around the bathroom door frame, trying to locate the origin of the vibration. I noticed my phone, moving across the small end table and walked over to it. I had two missed calls, a voicemail and a few text messages.

I had a voicemail from my mom, letting me know that my three other brothers and their families had made it to my parents' home. Everyone was now safely together, besides me and Gabe. It was a huge relief. I opened my inbox and looked at all of my text messages.

Hey! We're headed your way.
I'll see you soon. You have a
LOT of explaining to do!

I didn't want to have to be the one to explain everything to Mel. She hadn't seen me in a while. Which means, she hadn't seen me since my tattoos disappeared. She was going to freak out and I knew it.

I returned to the bathroom and took off my glasses. I started putting on my makeup when my phone rang again. I looked down at the display and argued with my conscience, whether I should answer it or not. *Damn it.*

"Hello?" I said as I answered my phone.

"Hey, Edie. What the hell's going on? I've been trying to get through to you for hours," Mike sounded concerned.

"Hey, Mikie. Uh, not much, how are you?" I replied.

"Huh? I'm fine, kind of. But uh, what's going on?" he asked again.

"I can't hear you, there's some kind of static or feedback or something."

"Bullshit. You're such a bad liar." he laughed.

"Why does everyone say that? And I don't know what to tell you."

"The truth would be a good start," he mused.

"I don't think you'll like that as much as my horrible lies. Those are much better." I laughed awkwardly.

"Okay, how about I ask you questions and you just answer them," he suggested.

"We can try that game," I said, pinning the phone between my ear and shoulder as I applied eyeliner to my eyelids.

"Alright, first question. Where the hell are you?"

"In my hotel room. In the bathroom, if you want me to be really specific."

"Okay, let's try that again. What city and state are you in?" he asked, more direct.

"Oooh. We're in Seattle. That's in Washington," I replied sarcastically, puckering my lips to apply lip gloss.

"Good. You did great that time. Now, are you ready for the next question?" he asked, patronizing me like a child.

"Was that your question?" I laughed. "No, give me a minute. I'm running out of retorts."

"Oh, come on! Would you give me a little bit of a break, please?"

"Was that your next question?" I asked with a chuckle.

"God, you're so difficult!" he laughed, angrily.

"Thanks, I've been practicing." I grinned and rubbed my lips together.

"Edie, are we in danger?"

I sighed and grabbed the phone, moving it to my other ear as I held my mascara brush in my hand. I didn't want to lie to him, "Yes."

"That isn't sarcasm, is it?" he asked with a very low tone.

"No."

"What should we do?" he continued to inquire.

"Spend as much time with your family and loved ones as you can," I replied, lost for words.

"Now, will you tell me what's going on? And don't give me some bullshit, fragmented answers or false hopes. I know something's up."

"I'm telling you, you'd prefer my lies," I responded.

"No, I really wouldn't. Why do you think I called you? I know you can't lie to save your life. Tell me the whole story."

I set down my makeup and stepped out of the bathroom. I walked out to the patio, lit a cigarette, pulled up a chair and sat down. If he wanted the truth, I wasn't going to deny him. How he chose to tell Lana and what he chose to do with the information I gave him, was up to him. I wasn't going to keep sheltering my friends and family from something that was inevitable.

"Have you been watching the news?" I asked him.

"Of course. What the fuck are those guys? What's with their armor, or skin, or whatever that is?"

I explained everything to the best of my ability. I explained that the creepy pitch black dudes, or brightly glowing guys, were one and the same. I explained their origin and their reason for being here. I even took the time to explain that God had commanded that they save souls, but that they all weren't doing so. I explained that it was all Michael's fault.

"Uh, okay, wait. Isn't that a lie? I thought you said you were going to tell me the truth," he jeered.

"See? I told you you'd rather one of my lies. The truth is weird, scary and total bullshit."

"Okay, so you're telling me the truth?" he asked nervously.

"Yes."

Mike let out a long sigh, "Great, so I'm named after a vengeful asshole, not a heroic angel who saves humanity... that's awesome."

"I don't know what his deal is. But, his army listens to him. They take orders directly from him."

"Isn't that how it's always been? I mean, that's what it says in the Bible, right?" he asked.

"Not exactly, but I'm not entirely sure. I never read the Bible. The only story I know, is the true story, not one created by man. Riley led the Earthbound," I explained.

"Wait, what? Riley? I think I'm missing something here." he chuckled lightly. "So, you're telling me, that *you* and *Riley*, are *angels*?"

"Yeah, that's what I said, like, 15 minutes ago," I replied, aggravated.

He laughed maniacally, "I've seen how much you guys drink. I've seen your tattoos, your crazy decorations. Come on, Edie, you guys don't even believe in God, do you?"

"Of course, I do. I just don't choose a manmade religion."

"So you guys are like, heavenly beings?"

"No, not anymore. We're screwed," I responded.

"Let me get this straight. You guys are angels. We are bastard mutts. God wants the Earth back. He wants us all killed. So Michael has taken it upon himself to massacre humanity, but somehow that's against God's will?" he surmised.

"Yes, that's the gist of it," I agreed.

"I don't know what the hell to think."

"You're not the only one." I rubbed my temple.

I heard a light knock on the door.

"Just a second," I called out. "Mikie, I need to go. Can I talk to you about this later?"

"What's there to talk about? I might as well just go sit outside and wait for the end."

"It's not like that. We're trying to stop this. We're trying to save people."

The second knock on the door was louder. "Hold on!" I shouted, pressing the phone to my chest.

"Mikie, just please, take care of yourself. Just try to be careful for the next few days. We'll be home soon," I said, worried about my friends.

"Well, we're staying here at your place until you come back. We saw some of those, *whatever they are*, by our apartment."

"No! Don't stay there. I don't think it's safe. They know we live there. If they come looking for us, they may take you out," I said, attempting to look under the door. I couldn't see a pair of feet.

The third knock on the door was booming.

"Hold the fuck on!" I shouted. I was livid.

I walked towards the door and tried to look out the peephole. I couldn't see out. Whoever was outside the door was covering the glass. I felt my heart race and my breathing increased. I quietly slid the chain across the lock and made sure all three deadbolts were fastened. I slowly backed away from the door and raised my phone back to my ear.

"Mike. I need to go. I think something's wrong. Please, be careful. Get Lana and go to Lamar's. I think you'll be safer there. Just please do this for me. We'll be back soon. I need to go. I have to get Riley," I whispered into the phone then hung up.

I took a deep breath in and exhaled slowly. The knocking continued; a rumble of rapid succession.

"Who is it?" I asked, as I dialed Riley's cell phone number.

There was no answer from behind the door.

I dropped to my hands and knees and crawled towards the door, holding the phone to my ear as his phone rang. I looked under the door, looking for shoes or anything I could identify. I still couldn't see anything, only a silhouette. *Blackness.*

"Hey, where are you?" Riley asked as he answered his phone.

"Um, good question. I'm trapped in our room, where are you? Where is everyone?" I whispered.

"I'm downstairs, eating. We're all down here. What do you mean you're *trapped*?" he asked.

I heard the door handle jiggle.

"Oh, shit. Get up here, please. *Someone*'s trying to get in here," I whispered then covered my mouth, terrified.

"I'll be right there. Paul! Let's go!" he said as he hung up the phone.

I crawled around the side of the bed, furthest from the door and folded in my knees, holding them tightly against my chest. I tried to keep my breathing controlled. My brain swirled as I thought about what could be waiting for me right outside the door. But they're unstoppable. Why hasn't it just broken in?

I heard the sound of loud flapping and quickly backed into the corner of the room. I peeked through the curtains and saw a brightly glowing being hovering just outside the patio. He swept from side to side, attempting to peer into the room. I covered my mouth to choke back my tears.
Oh God, it's over.

There was a loud bang and snarls as I heard Riley and Paul approach the door, obviously with Azrael in tow. "Paul! Don't let him out!" Riley shouted.

I was far too terrified to move.

"Edie, open the door! I can't get past the chains and deadbolts!" Riley shouted through the door crack.

I was frozen solid. I didn't know what to do. I dialed Riley's number and listened to it ring from the hallway.

"Why won't you open the door?" he asked as he answered.

"There's one of them, right outside the glass door. I'm scared to move. He doesn't see me," I whispered, my voice cracked.

"Oh, fuck."

I could hear heavy traffic in the halls and the loud crash of glass breaking, outside of the room. I decided then to make a run for the door. As I rose to my feet and jumped over the edge of the bed, the flapping became louder. There was a deafening burst as the angel dove through the glass patio door, barreling towards me. I lunged for the chain, sliding it aside. I fumbled with the deadbolts and dropped to the floor in a tight ball as the angel came down on top of me.

Riley crashed through the door. His fist connected with the angel's jaw, in an instant, slow motion combo. I buried my face in my knees and felt large arms grab underneath mine, slinging me from the floor in the room, onto the floor in the hallway. I let out a sharp, ear piercing shriek, kicking and fighting as much as I could. I looked up to see Paul crouched over me, like an over aggressive, protective bear.

"Get her out of here!" Paul said.

I turned to see Gabe, Jonah and Corey standing directly behind me. Gabe grabbed my arm and ran me towards the elevator.

"No, we can't leave Riley and Paul!" I shouted, voice quivering with fear.

"Edie, get downstairs!" Riley ordered, poking his head around the corner of the door.

Gabe helped me to the elevator and hit the button for the first floor. "What the fuck happened?"

"I was getting ready, and on the phone with our friend Mike, from Baton Rouge. I don't know what was going on exactly. I just know someone kept knocking on the door and there was an angel outside the patio," I tried to slow my breathing.

"There were two of them? All we saw was the one in the hallway. Damn, you could've been killed and we wouldn't have even known it," Corey stated bluntly.

Gabe shot him a 'shut up' glare and smiled at me gently. He wrapped his arm around me, "It's okay, Kiddo. We're all good." He squeezed me tightly.

"For now. But how long will that last?" I asked, looking at Jonah.

"I didn't see them. I was distracted. I'm so sorry," Jonah apologized.

I stared at the numbers overhead as they ticked down to the first floor. When the doors opened, everyone was standing there, with concerned looks on their faces. I followed them to the foyer.

"Is everything okay? Where's Paulie?" Paige asked, concerned.

"They're upstairs, don't worry about it. They'll be down in a few minutes," Jonah said, wrapping his arm around Paige's shoulder.

"I hope you're right." she frowned.

We sat on the couches and waited for them to come downstairs. I chewed my fingernails to the quick and stared at the numbers on the elevator, indicating what floor it was on. It stopped on the seventh floor. I waited patiently, watching as the floor numbers very slowly ticked down.

"You should've seen Riley throw that dude out the window." Corey smirked. "It was awesome. Home-dude lunged at Riley. Azrael snapped at his neck, taking him down to the ground. Riley totally grabbed his legs and did one of those spinning tosses like a fucking Frisbee, and threw his ass out the seventh story window."

The elevator dinged loudly. I looked up to see my two heroes.

"We need to get out of here. Everyone upstairs, together. Gather your shit, we're splitting," Riley ordered as he held the door open for everyone to walk through.

"Yes, sir!" Corey answered, jumping to attention and running towards the elevator.

"Where's Azrael?" I asked.

"Um, he's a bit busy." Paul smirked.

"By *busy* you don't mean, *dead*, do you?" I asked.

"Oh, hell no! He's uh, cleaning up. The um, room?" Paul replied, obviously making the shit up as he went along.

"Please tell me he's okay," I said, turning to Riley.

"He's fine, Edie. He's upstairs," he replied, grabbing my arm and shuffling me into the elevator.

Everyone looked startled, confused, tired and completely ill prepared to begin our day. We all stepped into the elevator and hit the button for the seventh floor. Chuck seemed unusually quiet. I wasn't sure what Lamar had told him, but I knew something was troubling him. Something was troubling all of us.

The elevator opened and we all stepped out together and surveyed the damage in the hallway. We were sure to hear something from what was left of staff. The small tables and vases with fake flowers that lined the walls between the rooms were almost all destroyed. The paintings hung in disarray. There was glass all over the floor towards the far right end of the hall. We all stood, staring at the damage, silently.

"Okay guys, get in your rooms, get your shit and get out. I don't want to find out anyone was *anywhere* alone. Understood? You need to use the bathroom? Keep someone close," Riley ordered. "Alright, Edie. Let's get our stuff and go. Az is in there. Don't be freaked out by what you see," he explained to me and grabbed my hand.

We stepped into the doorway and I instantly gasped. Azrael was lying on the floor, munching on *something*. I could hear the cracking and tearing as I entered the room. I peeked around the corner and saw him ripping apart, what appeared to be a body.

"Oh God," I gasped, covering my mouth.

"Listen, before you panic, this was the bastard that was after you. Paul took his wings, they're in a bag. His halo is yours. I'll give it to you later. The one out in the hall was injured, but took off. I kind of *helped* him out of the window. "

"I can't believe this. It's like they *knew* we were here." I shook my head, staring down at the disfigured corpse.

"They did know we were here. They were specifically after you."

"How do you know?"

"Let's just say, he told me, before he died." Riley pulled off his hat and scratched his head, with an awkward, saddened expression.

"I'm sure I don't even want to know." I closed my eyes and breathed in slowly.

"Hmm, not really, no." he smiled the fakest of smiles, trying to lighten the mood.

I shook my head and started grabbing my things. I threw everything into my bags as Riley stood by me, arms folded across his chest, scouring the room and the sky outside. I stepped into the bathroom and gathered my makeup and accoutrements, tossing them into my backpack. I walked back out into the room and grabbed my clothes off of the floor. Shaking the fragments of glass from them, I shoved them into my bag and stepped over Azrael and his, now deceased, chew toy.

"About ready to go?" Riley asked me.

"Yeah, I'm ready. What about you? And what about the body?"

"Don't worry about that," Riley replied, pulling his cell phone from his pocket. I watched as he pressed a few buttons and held the receiver to his ear. "Hey. I need a cleanup on aisle 2. You ready?" he asked.

There was a short pause, he nodded, said good bye and hung up his phone. A few minutes later, Paul entered the room, followed by Gabe.

"Alright, let's get the hell out of here," Gabe said.

We met up with everyone else in the hallway; everyone but Riley, Jonah and Paul. The elevator dinged and the doors opened. We stepped into the elevator and silently rode it downstairs. There were occasional sighs and coughs.

The elevator stopped on the third floor, the door opened and an old couple stepped in. They stared from person to person, suspiciously. I felt uncomfortable and claustrophobic enough, before the elderly couple joined us, staring.

The doors opened and we stepped out into the lobby. We all walked to the front counter to return our keycards. We tried to be as nonchalant as possible. The less obvious we made it, the less likely they were to run straight upstairs and see the damage. We wanted to be out of the area before that happened.
Oh God, I'm so nervous.

I heard rustling behind the partition connected to the back wall.

"Excuse me," I paused for a reaction. No one emerged. "My husband will be downstairs momentarily. He'll get us all checked out. He has the cards."

A short brunette popped her head out from behind the partition.
Stop panicking! She looks clueless.

"Oh, okay. Thanks!" she smiled. "Oh, wait… one second."
She knows! She's calling your bluff! She's going to run upstairs, see them manhandling a corpse and call the police.

"Is there a problem?"
Shut up! Stop giving her ideas!

"Oh, no ma'am. I just forgot to give your husband a message that had come in for you guys."
Dodged a bullet…

"Would you mind taking it? I'm not sure whether it was meant for you or your husband. It just said Nixon," she said, holding a folded piece of paper.

"My pleasure," I grinned politely.

"Well, safe travels. I wish you the best of luck. God bless." she ran behind the partition.

"Strange ass girl," I mumbled, shaking my head.

I was quickly shuffled out of the lobby by Lamar. We walked out to the vans and stood around talking while we waited for the guys. Gabe and Erick seemed especially watchful of the skies. I pulled a cigarette from my pack and lit it. I bundled up tightly in my hoodie, and pulled my hood over my curly ponytail.

"How long are they going to be?" Paige asked, staring at the front doors.

"Not sure," I replied.

"What're they doing?" Corey asked.

"Cleaning up," Brooke answered.

"Did Jonah decide to join them?" I asked, exhaling slowly.

"Yeah, he wanted to check out the halo before it was given to you," she explained.

"What time is it?" Chuck asked, turning to me and Lamar.

"11:16am," I replied, looking at the display on my phone.

"Did you even get a chance to eat, Edie?" Gabe asked me.

"Nope. I was going to head downstairs, then I was so rudely interrupted by an asshole dive bombing me through the glass door."

"Here, come with me," Brooke said.

I followed her to their van. She opened the back doors and started digging around in the some bags. She pulled out a couple individually packaged blueberry muffins and handed them to me. I couldn't believe how good they looked. I was sure that it was more than likely because it felt like I was starving to death. It seemed that the adrenaline had knocked the nausea out of me.

"Thank you so much," I said as I ripped open one of the muffin's packaging.

"No problem. You need to eat."

"We haven't gotten much time to bond, have we?" I asked.

"No, but I understand. I don't take it personally. I know you're very busy and under a lot of stress. Under normal circumstances, I'm sure we'd be very close." she grinned, reassuring me.

"So, you're Erick's sister? That's awesome," I said, biting into my muffin.

"Yeah, he's a pretty cool guy. I was so thankful that he introduced me to Jonah." she smiled fondly.

"That's great. How long have you two been together?"

"Almost 2 years," she replied with a wide smile.

"That's so awesome! I'm very happy for you."

Her smile fell flat, "Not that it matters much longer."

"Try to stay positive. We're doing our best to save this," I replied, clutching my muffin like a treasured object.

"I know... But I know either way, I'm going to lose him," she responded, her sad eyes welled with tears.

I didn't know what to tell her. I just stood, speechless, next to the beauty. She rubbed her arms, to warm herself. I wanted to tell her it was going to be okay. I wanted to tell her that everything would work out just fine. I wanted to tell her that she'd live a long, fruitful life with Jonah. But I couldn't force myself to lie. I couldn't pretend to know what was ahead of us on our journey.

The two of us watched the front doors of the hotel, waiting for our significant others to emerge from the building. The quiet was awkward. She was silently begging me to tell her not to worry, that everything was going to work out. I was battling my conscience.

"There they are," Brooke said with a smile in her voice.

"About damned time!" I replied.

We watched as Azrael drug Riley hastily to us. Paul and Jonah were walking behind them joking and laughing about something.

"It's all taken care of." Riley smiled as he approached us.

"Really? How'd you explain the broken window, the patio door and the halls?"

"I told the truth," Riley replied, smugly.

"You told her that a vindictive angel blitzed and blindsided me, and his comrade with no interior design experience, attempted to redecorate the halls to make them more Feng Shui?" I asked sarcastically.

"Basically."

"Bullshit. What did you tell her?" I asked.

"I asked her if she's been watching the news. She told me yes, so I told her one of those *'aliens'* were upstairs. I said that he crashed through the patio door, the dog chased him down the hallway and he exited the end window." he laughed, proud of himself.

"And you honestly think she bought it?" I asked, shaking my head.

"Oh, she bought it." Paul nodded.

"How do you know?" I asked.

"She gave us a refund," Riley chortled loudly.

"What?" I asked, eyes narrowed, confused.

"Exactly. Crazy shit," Paul agreed.

"So, not only did she not charge us for the damage, but she paid you back for *five* rooms?" I shook my head.

"Yep," Riley replied.

Stupid girl. Well, I guess not a total loss.

"Alright, everyone in the vans. We need to go meet the next two." Riley clapped his hands loudly and ordered us to move.

We all piled into the vans. Paul decided to drive, so that Riley could be co-pilot with the directions. Gabe and Azrael sat in the back, barking and growling at each other. I was sitting with Lamar and Chuck, getting Chuck caught up to speed. I was surprised by how much Lamar had told him and now he wasn't being argumentative. That wasn't like Chuck, at all.

Gabe growled at Azrael, who barked loudly at Gabe.

"Edie, show him your arms," Lamar said, nodding towards my sleeves.

I reluctantly rolled up the sleeves of my hoodie.

"Whoa, what happened?" Chuck asked.

"She can heal. It's like her body treated the tattoos as an injury," Lamar explained, quicker and more accurate than even I could have.

Chuck looked at me, waiting for my reaction. I simply nodded in agreement.

"That's crazy. Are you pissed?" Chuck asked with a slight grin.

Azrael barked loudly, pawing at Gabe's chest and swatting him in the face.

"Kind of. If I wanted to waste thousands of dollars for nothing, I would've at least blown it on something I'd get to keep," I replied with a light chuckle.

Chuck laughed loudly, which Azrael accepted as a challenge and barked even louder.

Chapter Thirty Three
I've Heard Better Lines From Politicians and Vacuum Salesmen.

It was almost 1pm, by the time we found the apartments that Brandon and Tori were in. It was a very interesting Victorian style high rise, more than likely an old hotel converted into apartments. Its architecture was beautiful.

We parked across the street and stared at the front doors. The tension in the air was so thick you could've cut through it. Well, we would've needed one of those fancy knifes that can cut through a brick then slice your tomato with ease, not like a plastic butter knife or something. We were all nervous. Very nervous.

"Alright, who all is going?" I asked.

"I think it would be best if the four of us go," Riley replied.

"There's six of us in here," I responded, confused.

"I mean the four of us, angels."

"What about the feather?" Lamar asked.

"Yeah, we may need it for him. He sounded a bit rowdy," Paul said.

"Says the guy who could knock out a grizzly bear? You really think we need a feather to take him down?" Riley guffawed.

"I don't think y'all should take any chances," Lamar said.

"You're just saying that so you can go," Riley laughed.

"So? You know I'm the feather keeper," Lamar jested.

"Well, you girls decide. I'm getting out to smoke," I said, pushing the side door open.

I stepped out and lit a cigarette. A few moments later, Gabe and Riley joined me. We stood around, smoking, thinking; strategizing. It wasn't long before everyone was congregated outside our van. We all stood around, trying to figure out the best course of action.

"Wait. Do we still have that last halo or did Edie suck it up yet?" Gabe asked.

"We still have it in the bag with his wings," Paul replied.

"Could you show that to him?" Gabe asked.

"That might help, it's not like it's manmade." Riley nodded.

"I have a question," Chuck said, raising his hand like a child in school. "Why is it you can't touch Gabriel's feather or whatever, but you can hold on to a full set of wings?"

"Fuck if I know." Paul shrugged.

"Maybe because they're already dead?" Lamar suggested.

"Maybe because Gabriel is a messenger. *He's not just an angel.* He's very special," I said.

"It's something to do with Gabriel. He was able to *show* me part of my past to remind me," Riley said.

"How'd he do that?" Jonah asked.

"By touching me," Riley replied instantly.

"Where on the doll did he touch you? Was it in your no-no spot?" Gabe talked to Riley like a child, patronizing him.

"Shut up, asshole! I'll kick you in your no-no spot!" Riley threatened Gabe, while laughing.

"Okay, on a serious note. It sucks that we don't have Gabriel here to help. If he was able to show and convince Riley of his past, he could convince *anyone*," Lamar said.

"What the fuck is that supposed to mean?" Riley asked, defensive.

"He's just saying you're a hardheaded, skeptical, cynical twat," I explained.

"Oh, that's fine, then." Riley nodded in agreement.

"Alright. The fewer, the better," Paul suggested.

"I'm not touching that damned feather, so Lamar goes," Riley said.

"I can sit it out," Jonah said.

"I'm going. I'll dance with the punk, if he wants to get physical," Paul said.

"Well, we need Edie, for sure. So I guess that'll work. Me, Edie, Paulie and Lamar," Riley said. "Okay, if we're not back or haven't called in about thirty minutes, get up there with guns."

The four of us walked towards the front of the building. We stopped on the sidewalk and waited for a second.

We opened the door and stopped at the mailboxes. We scoured all of the boxes until we found the one that said "Sullivan, B." on it. He was in apartment 437. We all looked at each other and headed for the elevator. The doors opened as soon as we pressed the up button. We stepped in and pressed the button for the fourth floor.

"I really hope this goes well."

"Me too," Lamar agreed.

"They're coming, either way. We don't have a choice in the matter anymore. We need them just as much as they need us," Riley said.

The elevator dinged and the doors opened. We looked at the wall directly ahead of us. It had a sign on it with two arrows, pointing left and right. Towards the left, were apartments 401 through 420. To the right, were apartments 421 through 440. We all started walking towards the right end of the hallway.

"I really hope they don't freak out on us," I said.

"Shit, were you guys this nervous about getting me?" Paul asked.

"Hell, no. I knew I could lure you into battle with the promise of some beer and tits." Riley laughed quietly.

"I'm offended. There's more to me than just alcohol and bitches." Paul frowned.

"I'm sorry, did we leave out the fact that you'd get to do face bashing?" Riley smirked.

"I'm a very complex creature. Give me a little bit of credit," Paul said, smugly.

"Shut up." I laughed.

We walked down the dimly lit corridor and stopped right before Brandon's apartment. We looked from face to face, making sure we were all ready for whatever we were about to encounter. Riley stepped forward, breathed deeply and knocked on the door.

"I'm still waiting for my brew and honeys, by the way," Paul mused.

"Who is it?" a female voice asked from inside the apartment.

"Victoria? May we speak to you a moment?" Riley asked.

"We don't want to buy anything, thank you," she answered.

"Tori, we just need to talk to you and Brandon, please," I said.

"He's not here," she replied, through the door.

"Even better," Riley mumbled to us.

"Tori, could we please speak to you? It'll only take a few minutes," I asked politely.

We heard the deadbolt unlock and the doorknob turned. She left the chain in place.

"What do you want?" she asked, peeking through the crack in the door.

"We need your help," Riley said.

"With what?" she asked suspiciously.

"It's very hard to explain, is there any way we can come in and speak to you?" Riley asked.

"I don't think so. I'm not comfortable with that," she responded, beginning to shut the door.

"It's very important. Like, life or death. What about just me? Will you at least talk to me?" I asked, forcing the door open as far as the chain would allow.

She looked from face to face and returned her gaze to me. She closed the door and slid the chain. "Alright, *you* can come in. Only you. Everyone else stays out in the hall," she ordered. "I have pepper spray if anyone tries anything."

"Thanks for the warning, but we're not here to hurt you." I smiled and stepped into the apartment.

She closed the door behind us and locked it. I stood in the entry way, waiting for her to relax. She walked into the living room and sat down on the couch. I followed her and sat down across from her.

"It's a beautiful apartment." I smiled.

Her eyes narrowed and she cocked her head to the side, staring at me. "Do I know you from somewhere?"

"Yes, actually you do. I'm sure you don't remember, but we used to be pretty close."

"Like, when we were kids or something?" she asked.

"Something like that. It was a really long time ago."

"Would you like something to drink?" she asked me, letting down her guard, ever so slightly.

"Sure, if you don't mind."

"Well, come with me to the kitchen. You can start explaining," she said, standing still momentarily.

"Okay, sounds good." I rose to my feet and followed her into the kitchen.

"So, what is it that you need my help with? Some kind of protest?" she asked as she opened the fridge door.

"Kind of. Can I ask you something?" I inquired as she handed me a glass.

"I suppose," she replied.

"How much of your life can you remember?"

"A lot of it; I still remember my fourth birthday and stuff," she said, grabbing a pitcher of tea out of the fridge.

"What about *before* this life?"

"Excuse me?" she tilted her head, as if she didn't hear me correctly.

"Do you remember any of your past lives?" I questioned.

"I don't really know how to answer that." she shook her head with a slight grin, pausing on random syllables.

"What are your religious views?"

"I'm Buddhist," she replied, proudly.

"So you believe in reincarnation, correct?"

"Of course. But, I don't remember any of my past lives." she paused, and then pour herself a glass of iced tea.

"What if I told you, I had a way to make you remember? If I offered you the chance to see your past, would you accept that?"

"I don't know. I don't really understand what you're getting at." she grabbed my glass, filled it with ice and poured my tea.

"Can I bring one more person in? I want to show you something. It'll explain a lot."

"I want to trust you, really, I do. But it's really hard to, with everything that's going on."

"Please, it'll only take a few minutes. Once you see the truth, you can make the decision, on your own, whether you want to know more or if you just want us to leave," I tried to reason with her.

"I guess. But it better be quick. Brandon will be home soon and he'll be pissed if there's people he doesn't know in his home. Especially with all of this craziness going on. We plan to leave," she replied with her hands fixed on her hips.

"Okay, cool. That's perfect. We'll make it quick."

She walked with me to the front door and opened it. "Lamar, come in," I said.

Lamar looked from Riley's face, to mine, then to Tori's.

"Well?" she asked, leaning against the door jamb.

"Yeah, okay." Lamar nodded and walked towards the door. He stepped in and followed the two of us to the living room.

"I want to show you something. Lamar, get out the feather."

"Here you go," he said as he pulled the feather from his inside coat pocket.

"What, are you guys some kind of bird activists?" she mused.

"No. Lamar, hold it out."

Lamar held the feather out in front of him.

"Do you recognize it, at all? Does it remind you of anything?" I asked her.

"Uh, nope. Just looks like a white feather to me," she said, shaking her head.

I looked at Lamar, "I want to try something, okay?"

"What're you planning on doing?" he asked me nervously.

"Hold on," I said, unzipping my hoodie.

I stepped over to Tori and knelt down in front of her, facing away.

"Will you lift my shirt and look at my back?" I asked.

"What?" she asked; baffled.

"No, don't do it, Edie. Riley didn't want you touching it. Remember?"

"*Riley?* Are you the same assholes that showed up at my mother's place looking for me?" she asked.

"Yes, and please, just do it," I pleaded.

"Fine, whatever." she lifted my shirt. "Now what? I don't understand this."

"Lamar, give me the feather," I ordered. "Just watch."

He knelt in front of me and looked at the floor. He held the feather out to me.

I grabbed it and felt a shockwave of pain course through my body. I felt myself drop onto my hands and felt the tears stream from my eyes. My sob grew louder and louder as I fought to hold onto the feather.

Images of my past flashed in my mind. I saw the garden, Heaven, God's immaculate face. I saw everything wonderful and everything hurtful in the exact same moment. I felt my wings, ripped from my back. I heard the lightning crack as the screams of everyone around me filled the air.

"Eden!" Lamar yelled as he finally ripped the feather from my hand.

"What the fuck is going on in here?" I heard a voice say.

I stared at the floor, trying to regain my composure. I could hear the voices around me murmuring, arguing. They grew louder, but still incomprehensible. My heart raced, my chest ached from hyperventilating. I couldn't think of anything except how horribly bad my back hurt. I looked around me, there was blood, everywhere.

"Who the fuck are all of you? And what the fuck are you doing in my apartment?" Brandon said, setting plastic bags full of groceries down on the table.

"Calm down, we're here to talk to you both. We need your help," Riley said, holding out his hands in a peace treaty sort of way.

"Need my help with what? Murdering this chick? Why the hell is she bleeding all over my living room floor?" He was pissed.

"I'm sorry. I didn't mean to ruin your carpet," I said, my voice trembled.

"Get up," he replied, offering me his hand.

I grabbed his hand and used all of my strength to raise myself off of the floor. He helped me to a chair at the kitchen table. I sat down and laid my head on my forearms. I tried to catch my breath.

"Now, what's going on? Start talking before I start smashing your faces." Brandon stood, arms folded across his chest.

"Watch it, Bub." Paul stepped forward, chest bowed and fists clenched.

"Tori..." I winced.

"Yeah?" she responded.

"Come, look at my back."

She stepped over to the table and raised my shirt, "Oh shit!"

"What the hell did you guys do to her?" Brandon asked.

"No one did anything to her, Brandon, calm down!" Tori ordered.

"How about you tell me what the hell is going on. Now!" Brandon demanded, fists balled.

"Just watch, please, and keep quiet," I replied.

I pulled my shirt over my head, revealing only my back. I couldn't tell how bad it was, but I assumed it wasn't pretty. I could feel the blood trickling and heard everyone's reactions once they saw the gouges, running down my spine. "Now, watch closely and please, keep quiet."

I thought about my garden, the beautiful flowers swaying in the wind. The tall tree in the center, covered with blossoms, singing softly as the wind blew through its massive branches. I thought about dancing, spinning, singing in my garden. I envisioned all the animals that gathered to see me perform my art, like quiet spectators. I laid my hands on the ground, pressing my fingers firmly into the Earth. I inhaled slowly, exhaled even slower, concentrating on the sky, the land, the water, the fire that burned deep in my spine. I imagined extinguishing that flame. Using the pulsing power of the Earth, I felt the pain subside, I felt my flesh stretching and fusing, molecule by molecule.

"Holy shit," a voice said, pulling me out of my trance.

"How the hell did you do that?" Brandon asked.

"If you'd like the truth, I suggest we all sit down and have a little chit chat," Riley said.

"Edie, are you okay?" Lamar whispered to me, leaning down by me.

"I'm fine."

"If you guys are pulling some kind of bullshit with me, you're gonna pay. You have 10 minutes to explain what the fuck is going on, before I beat your asses and call the cops," Brandon said.

"We need a little bit longer than 10 minutes," Riley said.

"Well, then you better start talking," Brandon said, walking over to the couch and sitting down.

Lamar and Paul lifted me to my feet and helped me to the couch, across from Brandon and Tori. Riley sat down on the floor in between the two couches, facing the two nonbelievers. I was drained. I felt completely exhausted. I was hurt, not physically, anymore, but emotionally.

"Now, what are you doing here? What the hell just happened?" Brandon asked.

"There's a war on the horizon and the two of you, joined with us, may be the only hope humanity has. I know you're probably thinking we're full of shit, and to be honest, I don't blame you, but I'm telling you the truth," Riley said.

"Are you talking about those *aliens*? Bullshit," Brandon jeered.

"They aren't *aliens*, they're *angels*. And so are you. *Both* of you," I added.

Brandon laughed loudly.

"Seriously? Come on. I've heard better lines from politicians and vacuum salesmen. I'm not an idiot." Brandon laughed.

"We're being very serious," Riley said.

"Yeah, right," Brandon replied.

"We can show you," I said.

"Oh, yeah? How so?" Brandon asked.

"Well, there's two ways about this," Riley responded.

"Which one is less painful?" Tori winced and looked at me.

"We have two pairs of wings downstairs and a halo. If you'd like to check them out for yourself, we can either take you downstairs, or call the rest of our group up here," Riley explained.

"I'm willing to try holding the feather. I want to *see* what you're talking about," Tori said.

"What the fuck, Tori? Are you really buying into this bullshit?" Brandon shook his head.

"You didn't see what just happened. Something strange is going on and I want to know the truth," she snapped back.

"It's just like you to get pulled into something stupid. You trust people far too easily," Brandon said with a snarl.

"Well, just because I'm not an asshole, doesn't mean that I'm not skeptical. I want to see what she saw. *I want to know the truth,*" Tori said, folding her arms in petition.

Tori insisted that she hold the feather. I explained to her that I wanted to try something. Before she was handed the plumage, I placed my hands on her back and focused all of my mind on her. I thought of Victoria, the angel, and Tori, the woman sitting in front of me.

Our memories entwined. We discussed the current situation, while viewing the past, present and possible future. It felt like an eternity as we walked through our minds, side by side.

We returned to reality, and I was pleased to see no harm had come to her. She was able to witness part of The Great Divide, without feeling the physical pain associated with it. It was as if we were both viewing it from the outside, rather than living through it once more.

She told Brandon exactly what she had experienced. He, of course, opted to call it "voodoo, witchcraft or some kind of fucked up hypnosis." We both tried to defend the truth. I offered him the same experience, void of pain and suffering. He denied my offer.

"Give it here." he motioned with his hands.

Brandon grabbed the feather and let out a sharp yelp. His head snapped back, his back arched. He held his arms up towards the sky, grasping the feather tightly. He dropped to his hands and knees and began to sob, lightly.

"Lamar, take the feather. He's had enough," I said.

"No, let him see everything." Riley held out his hand to stop Lamar as he leaned forward.

"He's hurting! Take the feather!" Tori said.

"No, let him see," Riley repeated himself.

Brandon struggled to his feet and let out a loud roar. His rage reverberated in my chest, filling me with more anger and fire to fight than I had expected. He dropped the feather to the floor and opened his eyes, widely.

"What the fuck…" he said, with a low growl.

"I told you we weren't lying to you," Riley retorted.

"How is that possible?"

"What all did you see?" I asked.

"Everything. Flashes of everything. God, the others, Gabriel and his trumpet. I saw my past, The Great Divide, life afterwards. I saw pieces of all the lives I've lived. I felt the pain as God ripped my wings from my back. I felt the lash as I tried to shield Victoria in the meadow."

"Let me heal your back, you're bleeding a lot," I offered him my hand.

"No, I'm fine." he swatted my hand away. "I don't understand. How is it that I could've lived this long, without remembering, without knowing?" he sat down on the edge of the couch.

"We all felt that way," Riley confirmed.

"How many of us are there?" Brandon asked.

We showed him the list and explained what we knew. We told him about the rest of our group and our game plan. He seemed more enraged and ready to battle than even Paul had been. The revenge burned brightly in his eyes. He was out for blood.

"So, what do you need from us?" Tori asked.

"We need to all come together. Those of us that are able bodied," I replied.

"We need to band together. We need to prepare for battle. God has sent everyone down to reclaim the Earth. If we don't make a stand, we're all going to die. We'll die, your families will die, everyone. We have to stand up. We have to fight for the rights of humanity to keep the Earth," Riley said.

"Who's leading this *battle*?" Brandon asked.

"Riley, *Thaddeus* as you might remember him, is leading *our* side. Michael is leading the attacks," Paul clarified.

"So how long do we have?" Tori asked.

"Well, what's today?" I asked.

"Wednesday, the 15th," Tori replied.

"Um, 17 days, or so. The *end* will be November 1st. If everyone lasts that long, anyway," I replied.

"Wow, doesn't give us much time to do anything," she said.

"Not really." I shook my head, dejected.

"Where do you stand, Brandon? You have to choose, and you have to choose fast," Riley asked.

"Do you really have to ask? They're dead. All of them." Brandon slammed his fist on the table.

"I'm totally with you guys," Tori said, without hesitation.

"Great," I smiled, relieved.

Riley looked at his phone. "We have to run to the airport. We have another angel flying in, with one of our human friends."

"Go to the airport and come back. That'll give us time to pack," Brandon said.

"Eden, why don't you two stay and fill in some of the blanks?" Tori asked me, pointing to Lamar.

"See you guys in a little bit. Call me if you have any problems," Riley said as they stepped out of the front door and closed it behind them.

Lamar and I sat across from Brandon, explaining all of the current events. I described how I found out about all of this. I tried to explain as much as I possibly could. Where my memory was fuzzy, Lamar chimed in, filling in the rest.

We told him about the gas station, Alzada, all of our experiences as we traveled from Baton Rouge to Michigan, then from Michigan to Chicago. We laughed as we told him about the tire blowout and drunken Paul with the feather. He laughed lightly, but never completely loosened up.

Brandon filled us in on what was happening outside of our little convoy. War was now full force in the Middle East. The tension was continuing to rise, spreading fear and anxiety across the globe. Countries, rising against each other, have readied their weapons, readied their missiles. It was going to be a global war, the likes of which had never been seen in history. Of course, there have been horrible wars, in the past. But never did humanity have such strong, deadly hatred. And even stronger, deadlier weapons.

The storms had now not only left millions homeless, but had also *killed* tens of thousands. They, of course, had no idea when it was going to stop and blamed all of the killer tornadoes and lightning storms on high and low troughs. They claimed it was the combination of hot and cold air. We knew better.

There had also been storms raging across the rest of the world. Killer tsunamis, typhoons, earthquakes and other natural disasters swept across the globe. All in all, millions were dead, millions were injured, and even more were homeless, scared and losing hope. Everyone felt we needed a miracle. I knew there was only one chance for that. There was only one hope, and it brought little comfort to me.

There had also been more *meteor showers*, where people had claimed to have seen the *aliens* land. I wondered, for a moment, whether the truth should be brought forward to the media. Then I realized how little good that would do, they would think we were insane.

The death toll was rising, thousands by the day, all across the world, not just the country. Cities, large and small, were being found to have all of its occupants deceased or gone. There was panic in the streets, looting, rioting, murders, bombings, pure pandemonium.

On top of all of the death and destruction, there was a flu strand that was apparently worsening, killing off the weak and elderly. It was becoming more and more evident that we were on the brink of the apocalypse. People were becoming more fearful, more superstitious, more religious. At the same time, they were becoming more paranoid, and self-sufficient in a *kill or be killed* type of manner.

There were multiple disease processes, illnesses and viruses that were attacking the human immune system crawling across every inch of the Earth. People were starting to mockingly call it "the time of Pestilence". *Ha! So true.* There had also been many signs of Famine; with all of the fresh produce being destroyed by Mother Nature, people looting all that they could get their hands on, and everywhere being battered by destruction, there was little left to salvage.

It was everything I had ever expected to see on the news, but I expected it to be about zombies, not angels. The news was devastating. It was sad. It left me with so little hope. The worst of the situation wasn't even inflicted by the angels. The worst parts were caused by people, against each other.

This world has become a lost cause.

Chapter Thirty Four
And the Claws are Out!

I wasn't happy when I opened my eyes and saw the dead field again. I knew exactly where I was. I looked down and saw the burlap sack next to my foot. I wasn't going to go through that again. This time, I knew what was in the bayou. I *knew* what was beyond that eerie tree line. I wasn't going back.

I turned away from the trees and left the bag exactly where it was. I instead began to walk in the opposite direction when I heard a faint cry. I stopped and cocked my head to the side, trying to pinpoint the direction of the sound. The cry was muffled, but distinct. I turned around and walked towards the sound, back to where I was previously standing. The cry was coming from the burlap bag. I stared at the bag apprehensively, fighting the urge to turn and run. It was obviously the source. I leaned down closer, studying the size and shape of the object inside. As I leaned, contemplating what I should do next or how I should react to the noise, I realized that the cry was that of an infant.

"You've got to be kidding me!" I shouted. I figured it was a trap. I thought I'd open the bag and find the head of the dead girl; the girl that was floating in the trees. I assumed as soon as I'd open the bag, she'd begin laughing, taunting me. Terrorizing me. I debated whether to open it or not. I was terrified as I had been in the dream before.

It's only a dream.

There's no child in there.

It's only a dream.

"Just wake up," I coached myself.

The cry grew louder, more urgent. I fought my intuition; battled with my conscience. I was afraid to open the sack. I turned to walk away, but stopped short. The cry was very distraught, panicked. I returned to the bag and knelt down, my mind made up.

"Why are you doing this to yourself?" I stopped, holding the bag in front of me, listening. I felt a strange pulsing in my hand and held the burlap sack close to my ear. I could hear a heartbeat. And at that moment, it felt as if my own stopped. My instincts kicked into high gear and I pulled the top aside, peering into the dark, dirty bag.

There was an infant, lying naked in the sack. He cried loudly. I picked him up out of the bag and held him to my chest, rocking back and forth as I gently pat him on the back and cooed to him to calm him down, which in short order he did.

"I was wondering if you were ever going to take him," a female voice spoke behind me.

I turned to see Lilith, sauntering slowly in my direction.

"What're you doing here?" I rocked back and forth on my pained shins.

She grinned, "I might ask you the same thing?"

"I'm dreaming, why the hell are you here? You weren't invited," I hissed, eyes narrowed.

"Oh, but you're wrong. I was very much invited." she giggled.

I felt a sharp pain in my chest and looked down. I wasn't holding a naked child anymore; I now had my arms wrapped around a large and angry crow. I gasped loudly and dropped the bird to the ground. Lilith threw her head back and chuckled loudly, proud of the deception.

"Oh, come now. You didn't think I'd let a baby lie in a prickly field all day, in a burlap sack, did you?" Lilith asked smugly.

"I wouldn't put it past you. Wouldn't be your first time to abandon a child," I replied, kicking at the filthy bird as it clawed at me from the ground below. Lilith lunged forward quick as lightning, picking up the wicked pest and cradling it in the crook of her arm as she took a defensive stance.

"Stop it, now!" Gabriel ordered.

We both turned to see him walking towards us, the displaced mist forming tendrils in his wake.

"Hello, lover," Lilith said with a sly grin, tossing the giant crow into the air. "Hey, Gabriel."

"Why can't you just be civil?" Gabriel asked, looking from Lilith to me.

"Because she's a total bitch," I said, folding my arms across my chest.

She let out a haughty chuckle. "Ah, so eloquent. It's no wonder God wants you dead." she returned her eyes from Gabriel to me and smiled menacingly.

"Lilith, watch your mouth. I will not warn you again," Gabriel said sternly.

"Why the fuck did you invite her here? If I have to deal with *her* to see you, I'd prefer to be on my own," I said coldly, and then turned to walk towards the woods.

"Aw, such a tough little girl, isn't she? She's willing to face her nightmares to get away from little old me," Lilith patronized me from behind with a pout.

I balled my fists and turned to face my brother and his conniving companion. "Shut your fucking beak, Lilith! No one cares about you! You've always been a manipulative harpy! Can't you see that?" I snapped.

"Oh, hardly; I'm quite the opposite. *You're* the only one who brings this side out of me. I'm *still* an angel, remember? God *loves* me, Gabriel loves me, too." she smiled smugly as she slowly ran a finger down my brother's arm.

"You're so full of shit!" I shouted, pointing angrily at the stupid bird woman.

"Ah, she *can* be made jealous! Luke *was* right. You're not such a tough cookie after all, are you?" she spoke to me like a child, using the most condescending tone she could muster.

"Gabriel, shut her up before I snap her neck," I threatened.

"You both need to *calm down*," Gabriel admonished.

"*Calm down?* You bring her into *my* dreams and *I* need to calm down? You need to put a muzzle on your stupid bird before she gets bitten," I said, middle finger raised in Lilith's direction.

"This is most amusing." Lilith grinned, placing her hands on her hips.

"What the hell is your problem, anyway? What did I ever do to you?"

"You really want to know? Come on, it's common sense. Or are you really *that* dense? There you were, God's favorite little pet. You were given everything you desired, *everything*! You threw it all away. You threw *God* away, for this disgusting planet and a *boy*." she shook her head.

"I didn't throw anything away. Like you have any room to talk, as it is," I retorted.

"I can't believe how naïve you are. How many lives have you lived? Hundreds? Thousands? And you still haven't learned a single thing. You're nothing. You're worthless."

"I don't have to take this shit. I'm waking up," I said, turning away from them.

"Like hell you are!" Lilith replied.

I closed my eyes and took in a deep breath.

Ten, please wake up.

Nine, get out of this horrible place.

Eight, get away from Lilith!

"You're not going anywhere," Lilith said, shaking my shoulders.

"Don't you *dare* touch me!" I growled.

"Would you both please *stop*!" Gabriel shouted in a voice that boomed. Lilith and I both stood still for a second as he composed himself. "This is not what I wanted. This isn't what we need."

I stared to the sky, watching the crow make its rounds above us, circling like it was on the hunt. "What did you want, *Gabriel*? Did you want us to be the best of friends? Did you want me to tell you that I'm happy that you're with her? How could her presence here be beneficial in any way?" I asked, sitting down on the thorny ground and picking at the undergrowth with my fingers.

"You share a common goal. You share a common love. You are so much alike, *that* is your main flaw. If you could, for once, set your differences aside. Embrace the fact that you're trying for the same thing. You might realize the value of an alliance," he explained.

"What could we possibly have in common?" I asked skeptically.

"Well, for starters, you both care for me. In different ways, of course, but you do. You both want humanity to keep the Earth, though you have differing reasons. You both want this to be over with. Together, we could make that happen."

"What do you want us to do?" Lilith asked calmly.

"I want the two of you to be civil. I want you to be able to be in the same place, at the same time, without trying to murder or belittle each other. I just want there to be peace!"

"I'll be civil, as soon as she stops fucking around with me, my friends and my damned dog!" I responded.

Lilith smirked, "I'll be civil, when she stops being a drama queen. Tell her she isn't God's little muse anymore."

I focused my gaze directly on her. "*I don't care*, Lilith! I've been paying for my mistakes. When this is all said and done, I'll have made things right again."

"You really think you can make a difference? You really think you have a strategy to fix this?" she asked.

I nodded, "I do."

"And what is that?" she asked cynically, brows raised in mock disbelief.

"I don't trust you enough to tell you."

"But I do," Gabriel assured me.

I shook my head. "I'm sorry, I'm not saying anything. She can watch quietly as it unfolds, but I will not tell her my plans, just to have her sneak ahead of me and foil them."

"I guess you're smarter than I gave you credit for," she said with a sideways grin.

My anger was far from being abated. "Look, I'm not trying to screw you over. I've never once told Gabriel to stay away from you. I'd appreciate if you'd show me the same courtesy. If you aren't going to help, just stay away."

"I haven't helped?" her eyes narrowed. "I'm sorry. I'm pretty sure that if I hadn't stopped that 'donut-eating redneck' in Montana, you and all of your little miscreants would be dead or incarcerated. I thought that *was* help!"

"Yeah, well, I think you had ulterior motives. I think you were just trying to help Daniel retrieve David's body," I replied.

She shrugged. "Well, two birds… one dead officer of the law."

"We don't *need* your help. We need you to stay out of the way," I repeated.

"Oh, you will need me before you know it. Besides, what if I want to help?" she asked innocently, watching her feathered friend circling over us.

"You don't. You want to ruin all of our chances to succeed," I jabbed. *Why does she think I'm so stupid?*

"I've been following you and the rest to make sure you didn't run into trouble. On top of that, I'm keeping an eye on the Valkyrie, to assure that they're doing their job. I went to Alzada to *warn* David; to stop him from murdering everyone. I've *been* helping," she said, lowering herself to the spiky Earth opposite me and leaning back on one elbow languidly.

"I guess your version of help and my version are two different things. When I think of the word 'help', I think of something positive. Someone trying to make things easier on you. Not trying to kill your dog, or laughing and yelling 'repent' every second for hours on end." I looked to Gabriel for support.

"Fine. I'll leave you be, if that's what you and Gabriel want. But I can assure you, I haven't been trying to harm you or anyone with you," she said calmly. "If I wanted you dead, you would be."

The crow began cawing loudly, incessantly.

"Where were you when I was almost attacked in Seattle?" I asked.

"In Chicago, cleaning up a mess. There are angels on your tail. They leave people dead in their wake. I tried to catch up, to save some of the souls before it was too late. A lot of innocent people have died because of your little charade." she paused, whistling sharply for the crow circling overhead.

"Because *of* my trip? Come on. We're on the road, gathering together in the hopes to *save* them," I argued.

"Kill one to save a thousand, right?" she asked snidely, gently petting the large crow now rested on her shoulder. She paused for a second, turning her cheek to the bird, as if she were listening to a report from the battlefield.

"No. I don't want a single person to die for me, or because of me," I replied.

"It's a little late for that. Not to mention, those aren't all angels in your vans. Sure seems like you're herding your little flock of sheep to slaughter," she said as she casually tossed a pebble at me and shot me a wink.

"They chose to go. I didn't force anyone. That's the difference between you and me. People choose to follow Riley and me because we care. Because we're honest and trustworthy. Because we're doing a noble deed. The Valkyrie follow you out of fear," I retorted, aggressively throwing a small rock back at her.

Lilith sneered and moved out of the way instinctively, as her companion shot into the air, defensively. "You really are a foolish little girl. Fear is in fact a strong talent of mine. Alas, they don't *fear* me. They respect me," she replied, bowing her chest. "As do most who have come to know me. Present company excluded."

"Ladies, I don't think this debate is getting us anywhere." Gabriel sat down next to us, legs crossed.

"You're right. I need to be going anyway. The cries from the bloody battlefield in the Middle East are deafening me." Lilith rose, turning her attention to Gabriel.

"Be careful," Gabriel said softly.

"I will, my love." she leaned down and kissed him on the lips. "Oh, and by the way, Eden, I didn't come here to fight with you. I came to give you some information on Yeled Ad," she said, brushing off her backside.

"Who?" I asked, confused.

"My little *Pele*. You'll find him in Memphis with Thomas. He's very valuable. Be cautious," she continued.

"Who is Pele?" I asked.

"Must I do *all* of your work for you? Isn't your oldest *blood* brother a Hebrew scholar? Ask him!" she leapt into the air. In a bright flash and a cloud of black mist, she transformed into a crow and hovered over us, "Repent! Repent!" she cawed, then laughed as she flew off, her companion bird in tow.

I pulled my knees close to my core.

"She isn't all bad, you know," Gabriel said with a faint smile.

"If you say so. I just want to see her dead."

"That isn't a very nice thing to say," Gabriel scolded me.

"Well, the truth isn't always nice," I replied testily, turning my attention to a small root I was trying to pull from the ground.

"And the claws are out!" Gabriel mused.

"Oh, come on! Seriously? She totally started it this time."

"I realize her 'trick' wasn't very nice. But, you can always be the bigger person and not let her get to you," Gabriel continued to rake me over the coals.

"Easier said than done," I pouted.

"Hopefully soon, you'll realize how useful she is, and can be to you."

"If she helps me in any way, you know damned well it's for you," I reminded him.

"That isn't necessarily true. She is a very complex, complicated creature, but I think she genuinely wants to see you succeed. She's just, I don't know." Gabriel shook his head, at a loss for words.

"Just a bitch, is what she is," I said under my breath, the root finally giving in to my tugging with a gentle snap.

"I wish you both would get over yourselves. Thousands of years' worth of bad blood, that's just ridiculous. Why can't you behave? Why can't you try to act like an adult?" he cradled his head in his hands, obviously distressed.

"I'm sorry. Really, I am. I'll try, I promise," I told him. I felt horrible to see him so upset over something I had helped influence.

He smiled lightly, "Thank you. You know I love her deeply."

"I'm not sure why, but I know you do."

"Now. Let's discuss your trip!" Gabriel clapped his hands, changing the subject.

"What about it?"

"Let me know your progress! I've had to be cautious watching you. It's getting harder to tell the wolves from the sheep these days."

"Well, we made it out of Seattle unscathed. I'm not really sure where we are now exactly, but we're on our way to Memphis. Brandon and Victoria weren't as difficult to coerce as I thought they'd be," I filled him in.

"So, who all is with you now?" he asked.

"Um. Me, Riley, Lamar, his brother Chuck, Gabe, Paul, Jonah, the members of his Wiccan circle; Erick, Corey, Paige, Brooke, Jeremiah, my partner from work Melanie, Brandon and Victoria," I counted on my fingers.

"You have more humans in your party than angels? That's a bit dangerous for them, don't you think?" he asked.

"These are people that have openly stated that they'd rather fight at our side than die alone, helpless." I wasn't sure who I was trying to convince.

He shrugged his shoulders. "That's very noble. I only hope their deaths are met with respect and dignity. I would hate for them to die needlessly."

"Me, too. I don't want them to die, at all. You know I'm trying to avoid that altogether, if possible."

"Yes, of course." he nodded. "I'll be coming down soon. I'll try to find you as swiftly as I'm able."

"You're coming down? To Earth? Uh oh," I tried to make sense of what I had just been told.

He frowned, "Unfortunately, yes. Well, I'm thankful that I'll be able to see you and hopefully assist you in some way, but I'm not happy with the reason I'm going to Earth."

"Are you coming to announce the end?"

"Basically. My horn and I have a date with destiny." As he spoke he stared at the ground in front of me, where I had now amassed drawings in the soil and a pile of small roots and debris.

"Well, I'd rather hear it from you than someone else, if that helps," I replied.

He chuckled lightly, "No it doesn't help, much. How do you tell billions of people that the end has arrived? 'Go home, kiss your children, your husbands, your wives, your mothers, fathers, your brothers and sisters, for the last time.' This is the first time in history that my proclamation won't be a warning, it's a promise. It isn't a threat or an omen. It's impending. It's imminent." he rubbed his temples with the thumb and middle finger of one of his hands.

"Hopefully I can beat you to the punch and get this taken care of, before your message has to be declared."

"I can't count on that. I have to prepare," he replied as he continued to stroke his temples, eyes closed.

"I understand. But don't take my hope away from me," my brows furrowed.

He stopped what he was doing as he heard the disappointment in my voice and looked up at me. "I'm sorry, Eden. I love you. And I'm sure your plan is fantastic. I'm just worried you won't see the day to put your plan into action."

"Oh, ye of little faith!" I guffawed.

He smiled, "I have immeasurable faith in you. It's not you that I'm afraid of. It's the others, following out their orders. Michael has personally requested your death to be dealt swiftly. He feels that you're causing a stir, a cog in the gears of the End of Days. I believe he's threatened by you and Thaddeus."

"Riley," I corrected him.

"You and *Riley*, sorry."

"Why does he think that?"

"Because you're not only getting the angels on Earth involved, you're getting humans ready to fight. Some of the angels are noticing what's going on. They're hearing stories of your determination and have considered aiding you. Michael is worried that your actions will cause a revolution, so to speak."

"Wow. Really? He's threatened by us?" I smiled smugly.

"So it appears."

"Ha! Riley's gonna love that shit!" I laughed.

"I don't know about that."

"Well, he'll love the fact that Michael feels threatened for his hold on the angels. He won't be happy to hear that they're being sent, specifically, to kill me, or us," I corrected myself.

He paused, holding up his index finger for a second. "Edie, I need to go. I'm needed elsewhere, unfortunately." Gabriel stood swiftly, turning his face to the east with a concerned expression painted across his face.

"Everything okay?" I asked, concerned by his sudden change in demeanor.

"No, it isn't. Something is very, very wrong. You need to wake up. Stay alert. Stay safe," he ordered urgently.

"Is there anything I can do to help?"

"Keep your eyes open. Watch the skies! Keep an eye trained behind you.

Something dangerous, *something deadly*, is on the horizon," he replied frantically.

"What is it?" I asked, rising to my feet.

"The Horsemen." he leapt into the sky and hovered over me, looking as impressive in his glory as he had the day he was made. "I have to go, now! It's Lilith. Something's wrong!"

"Be careful!" I shouted as he soared out of sight with a speed that expressed the crisis at hand.

Without Gabriel at my side, I suddenly felt very alone in this place. I pulled my knees to my chest and spent a few moments thinking. I could feel my blood boiling in my veins. I was fueled for battle. I was ready to coat my skin in paint and beat the drums of war. This was far from over. In fact, it was just beginning.

I closed my eyes and breathed in deeply.

Ten, Get up.

Nine, Wake up.

Eight, Up! Up! Up!

Seven...

I awoke with a gasp and sat up, looking around. We were stopped at a gas station. I looked out of the window and noticed a lot of people out and about, including those traveling with us. I must've slept through the stop entirely. I yawned and stretched. I looked around the van for Azrael then saw him outside, rolling on his back in the grass, with Gabe and Lamar standing nearby. I laughed and opened the side doors.

"Where the hell are we?" I asked as I approached them.

"Potatoland!" Lamar clapped his hands excitedly.

I smiled, "Oh! Nice!" I pulled a cigarette from my pack and lit it.

"We're in some place called Coeur D'Alene. In Idaho," Gabe elaborated.

"Damn, already? How long was I asleep?" I asked.

"I dunno. I was crashed out, too. Maybe 4 hours?" Lamar replied.

"Yeah, it was about 4 hours. Don't worry, you didn't miss anything." Gabe laughed, gesturing with his arms at the flat Middle America surroundings.

"Hey!" Riley yelled from the doorway of the convenience store, "You guys want anything to eat or drink?"

"Yeah. I'll take some coffee," I replied.

"Me, too," Lamar agreed.

"Okay, then get your asses in here and get it. What do you think I am? Your barista?" Riley laughed and turned around, walking back inside.

"He's such an *ass*! How do you put up with it?" Gabe laughed.

"Well you see, when you've been with someone for thousands of years, you kind of become immune to the bullshit. I basically have like, a permanent reflective coat on my skin to deflect his sarcasm and snide remarks. Occasionally, they bounce back and splatter in his face," I mused, to which Lamar and Gabe both laughed.

I left the two, and snuck inside to stock up on drinks and snacks. What was left in that tiny shithole was sparse and in general disarray. There was a pot of relatively burnt coffee, sitting alone on the counter, for God only knows how long. I carried my cup of coffee and knock-off snack cakes to the counter, and followed the directions left for patrons by the shop owner. I sifted through my pockets, attempting to obtain exact change as requested of me, by the crudely, handwritten note taped to the bulletproof glass, at the register. I was two dollar bills short, forcing me to leave more money than necessary. I shuffled off, returning to the van. Riley was seated in the driver's seat, scouring over maps. I stood next to the open passenger door, cracked the plastic lid on my coffee, took a sip and let out a loud 'ah'. It was gross, but it was caffeinated. Riley raised a brow and looked at me as I made the noise again.

"Are you still cool to drive or would you like me to?" I asked.

"Nah, I'm good. You can continue resting," he replied, turning his attention back to the maps.

"Nope, I'm staying awake. I talked to Gabriel. He told me that I needed to be *ever vigilant and watchful.*"

"Anything we need to be worried about?"

"I'm not exactly sure."

"Well, get in the van. We'll talk about it once we get out of here," he suggested.

"Sounds good!" I hopped in.

"Idaho sucks," Corey said irritably, climbing into the backseat of our van in an exaggerated manner, knocking things off seats and making the van rock.

"Agreed," I said as I looked back at him.

"I don't know. They're like, potato capital of the world," Riley argued with a shrug of his shoulders.

"Wouldn't that be Ireland? Besides, we only eat red potatoes," I reminded him.

"Potato's a potato. I'll eat any of 'em," he said with a sideways grin.

We pulled out of the gas station and waited for the light to turn green. There were quite a few cars on the road, which surprised me. The light turned and we sped towards the interstate ramp, continuing our journey eastward.

"So, what did Gabriel say about being watchful or whatever?" Riley asked.

"He said something dangerous and deadly was coming. He told me to keep my eyes on the skies and to watch behind us," I replied. "The Horsemen are out there."

"Are we leaving breadcrumbs or something? Are they following us?" Gabe asked.

"I don't know, exactly. I just know we need to pay attention. We probably need to keep a couple of people awake at all times, to be on watch," I responded with a nervous glance in his direction.

"I'll help keep an eye out," Gabe replied with a nod.

"At any rate, he wants us to be watchful of our surroundings. I don't know if he's expecting an ambush, or maybe the war is starting soon."

Riley shook his head with a confused look on his face. "I'm really curious what we need to watch for. I mean, if its war, wouldn't it be widespread?"

"War between humans is escalating. I can't imagine what it's going to be like once the angels get involved," Brandon interjected leaning forward to join the conversation.

I shook my head, throwing my hands in the air in frustration. "To be honest, I don't really know why it's even called a war. It's more of an annihilation. Another holocaust."

The Holocaust. God, I didn't want to ever think of that again. It was one of the most difficult experiences, yet so crucially important. I've seen so much death, so much sadness in my life. But never have I seen pure, unadulterated hatred. It was sickening to see human beings, treated like vermin, like diseased animals. It was by far the most horrific event in human history, in my eyes.

It was for that reason alone that I realized why God would think humans were nothing but primitive, evil, sadistic parasites. Humans, as a whole, have fed off of each other for centuries. The poor are fed upon by the wealthy, using them as slaves. The villainous have preyed on the weak, the desolate.

Maybe I'm wasting my time. Maybe I should just keep my mouth shut.
Maybe I am on the wrong side. This planet truly deserves a clean slate.

"Edie?" Riley snapped me out of my thoughts.

"What? Did you say something?" I asked.

"Yeah. Yeah, I did. Why don't you call Jonah and ask him if he sees anything?"

I grabbed my cell phone and tapped in his number. He answered after a couple of rings, sounding very distracted, very pensive. He asked how I was, which I, of course, turned against him, reminding him that he's supposed to be psychic and know.

"I was curious. I saw Gabriel in a dream, between Seattle and Coeur D'Alene. He told me to be very mindful of our surroundings, to keep a tight watch. Do you know what we're supposed to be watching for? He said to keep my eyes on the sky, and behind us."

"Well, I was trying to rest once we left Seattle, but I wasn't able to. I felt very ill at ease. Something is definitely dark on the horizon. I saw fire, blood and black feathers falling like raindrops from the sky. There were embers and ashes swirling like tornadoes, destroying everything in sight," he spoke in a soft, somber voice.

"You didn't think to mention this? Where? When?" I asked.

"I don't know. I couldn't tell you where it was, or if it's something we'll experience soon, or two weeks from now. All that I know is that it was terrifying and it's left me restless and weary."

"Well, that's not good," I replied, stating the obvious.

"What's not good?" Riley asked, studying my expression with concern. I held up my hand for him to 'hold on'.

"I have a very bad feeling, like we're going to *lose* something, or someone," Jonah concluded.

"What should we do?"

"We should do exactly as Gabriel advised. We should keep watch at all times. We should pay attention to the sky, pay attention to the roads and the tree lines."

"Do you think they're following us?" I inquired.

He sighed into the phone. "It's probable. I'm sure someone has eyes trained on us. The question is, who and where? I'm afraid to find out."

"You know, when you were talking about what you saw, it sounded an awful lot like the dream I had about Pestilence, the Horseman," I said nervously, seeing the connection. "And Gabriel did say the Horsemen are loose."

"I wouldn't be surprised if that was exactly what we're facing. It may in fact, *be* Pestilence on the horizon. The feathers could have been from the Valkyrie, falling as they take flight, collecting souls," he hypothesized out loud.

"So, does this mean we may run into the actual Horseman, or just witness his destruction?"

"I don't know. I don't see *him* specifically." Jonah sounded frustrated.

"I'm sorry if I'm bothering you."

"Oh, you aren't. I'm bothered by how fragmented the future is appearing. It's very difficult for me to focus. It's so chaotic and spastic. The more people that get involved, the harder it is for me to see our paths. There's so many that are crossing. And I see a massive amount of people coming together soon." he sounded exhausted, and I realized the toll trying to keep so many of us safe was taking on him.

"Is there anything we can do to help you focus? To help you see clearer?"

"Not as of yet. I think once we get to Memphis, *if we reach* Memphis, more will unfold and the answers will be much more apparent. Especially once I see who all of these people are," he replied.

"Can you see anything concerning Memphis?"

"I see a child. And protectors. That's all," he answered wearily.

"What kind of child?" I pressed.

"I don't know. He's beaming with charisma, he attracts everyone that lays eyes on him. I'm not sure who, or what he is. But his protectors make it impossible to pry," Jonah explained.

"Does he have a name?"

"I could hear multiple people calling him *something*, but it wasn't something I recognized. It was almost a chant. It was hypnotically rhythmic," he replied.

"Was it *Pele?*"

"Bingo! How'd you know?" he asked, suddenly alert and attentive to the conversation.

"Lilith had also appeared in my dream. After arguing and bickering, she told me that we would find *her* Pele in Memphis, with Thomas," I explained.

There was a long pause on the phone. "Hmm. Now I'm curious."

"I asked her who he was, but she wouldn't answer me. She told me to talk to my oldest brother, Ross. He's a Hebrew scholar. I have a feeling I have some connection to him, but for the life of me, I can't recall what it is," I explained.

He chuckled lightly, "Interesting! Very interesting, indeed."

"I guess we'll find out in the morning, when I'm able to call my brother. Maybe his expertise will help remind me."

"Well, Mrs. Nixon. You've proven to have more information about the future than I. Perhaps you're the one with the psychic ability."

"No, I cheat. I'm given the answers or clues. I guess Gabriel and Lilith think I'm too dumb to do my own detective work." I laughed.

"Well, cheating or not, you and your sources are indispensable," he replied. I could hear the smile in his voice.

"We'll see," I responded with a sigh.

"That we will. That, we most certainly will," Jonah agreed.

I ended my conversation with Jonah and found my ear phones. I plugged them into my phone and leaned back in the seat, attempting to get comfortable. I set my play list to loop and delved into an endless wave of instrumental music. I felt my body relaxing as my brain began to warp the music blaring from the tiny speakers. My thoughts shattered like glass as they drifted through my mind. My chest felt feather light as my heart gently fluttered like delicate butterfly wings. I could hear my breathing, slowly echoing in my ears, blending like an infrequent drum beat with the whimsical rhythm. I tried to think. I tried to focus. But the thoughts slipped through my fingers like grains of sand. I was lost in my own head, falling deeper and deeper in the rabbit hole. Darkness consumed my mind. *Quiet, infinite darkness.*

I awoke, sitting in a beautiful field. The wind blew lightly, interlacing wildflowers and grass together like lovely braids. The sun felt warm on my face. I fell backwards and closed my eyes with a sigh and a smile. Even in the worst of times, I could find peace and solitude. I was thankful for the gift my subconscious had given me.

I propped myself up on my elbows and crossed my legs in front of me. The soft grass tickled my feet as the breeze blew by with a swift gentleness that tousled my hair. I took in a deep breath. The smell of honeysuckles and gardenias was carried on the air.

Something wasn't right. In a world stricken with fear and panic, how was I able to escape so easily? I stared up at the sky, waiting for it to morph into an eerie crimson omen, as it usually did. I looked to the trees, waiting for them to twist, deformed and bereaved. I waited to see the shadowy form of an angel, stealthy, cloaked, and waiting to attack.

But it never came. The darkness kept its distance, far beyond sight. I leaned back once more. Folding my arms behind my head, I rested my gently curled hair in the palms of my hands. I closed my eyes and enjoyed the sweet smell of the flowers, savoring every second in my nirvana. The breeze carried only a slight chill, mitigated by the warm rays of the golden sun. I listened to the birds chirping and singing in the distant trees. The wind itself sang a melodic hymn.

"Eden! It's wonderful to see you!" someone shouted in the distance. I opened my eyes and propped myself up on my elbows. "Hello," I smiled widely, sitting up. There were three brightly glowing men walking towards me, from the far side of the meadow. The light they emitted was warm and welcoming. I knew them from my past.

The one called Flemming bowed as they drew near. "Sorry to interrupt your rest. I'm sure you're exhausted."

"No problem. How can I help you?" I asked, grinning at the chiseled faced angel.

Kenneth stepped forward and smiled. "Eden, we're not here for your help. We're here to offer you *our* assistance."

"What? Why would you want to risk yourselves for us?" I asked, pulling my knees to my chest apprehensively.

"Because what *you're* doing is the right thing," the third, Seth answered. He came closer and sat down on the ground in front of me.

Kenneth again spoke, "Gabriel told us of your struggles in secrecy."

"Oh, yeah?" I replied nervously.

"Eden, you have nothing to worry about. We know what we face by assisting you," Flemming stated.

"I really don't think you should get involved. I'm sorry," I replied with a frown.

"It's too late. We're involved regardless, by being here," Seth reminded me.

"Well, you don't need to risk your souls for us. We've chosen to fight. You've been given orders. I suggest you follow them," I responded, rising to my feet with determination.

"What is happening on Earth right now is completely uncalled for. If the end is here and history will be written, we want to be on the proper side," Kenneth replied resolutely.

I shook my head. "I don't know."

"We know of your plan. We wish to help fend them off until you are able to accomplish it," Flemming stated, palms laid out to me in placation.

"This isn't your choice. We've made up our minds. You have two options," Seth explained, rising to his feet, looking down into my eyes with a stern expression. "You can either accept our help and have us at your side, or we'll have to speak to Thaddeus and have your opinion overruled."

"Have we not made it clear to you? We have *chosen* this. We were not asked. We were not ordered. We *want* to be at your side. Thaddeus was our commander, we wish to be under his command once more," Flemming added.

"I'm sure he'd be honored to hear that," I replied, bowing my head slightly in gratitude.

"Do you accept our help?" Seth asked.

"What about Michael?" I asked, turning to Kenneth.

"What of him?"

"You're brothers. How could you choose to fight against him?" I asked, baffled.

"That is one of the saddest endeavors of war, when brothers turn on one another. However, he's chosen to abuse his powers. He's becoming that which he's sworn to destroy. He's become a tyrant of evil," Kenneth explained.

"Then why doesn't God step in and stop him? Does He not see what's happening?" I asked.

"God has turned a blind eye towards Earth. He has left the war and spoils in the hands of Michael. What He doesn't know will not hurt Him, so to speak,"

Flemming joined.

Seth picked up, "Currently, God is ignoring this entire event. He's completely turned away from the Earth. We meet in secrecy, even He knows not of our plans. Michael is also unaware."

"So, why doesn't someone talk to God about it? Why doesn't someone stand against Michael and what he's doing?" I asked, confused.

Seth grinned. "There are such people that are. You, Thaddeus, the others. This is why we want to join you. You're standing against Michael."

"I meant in Heaven," I mumbled, casting my eyes downward.

"There are those of us who wish to fight against Michael; though we don't wish to fight him in God's kingdom. We will take it to the earth, as he's chosen to do," Kenneth said.

"So it's just the three of you?" I asked.

Flemming and Kenneth looked at each other and laughed loudly as Seth smiled broadly, white teeth glistening in the sun.

"What's so funny?" I asked.

"No," Flemming continued to chuckle lightly.

"We were merely the voice of the masses. Much like The Great Divide, there has been another separation, another faction. There are many who wish to fight. Many, who wish to be led by Thaddeus again," Kenneth explained. "As we speak, his army is regrouping, gearing for battle and waiting for the command to descend. We act in concealment, working in the shadows and away from Michael's prying eyes. We will be ready, whenever Thaddeus gives the orders."

"How many of you are there?" I asked.

"Between the original angels and some of the humans that have ascended, we're now roughly 60 strong. Granted, Michael's forces are much larger and geared far better, we will still be able to stand tall in due time," Kenneth said proudly.

"Wow. Thaddeus hasn't led that many people since The Great Divide." I smiled and shook my head.

Seth nodded, "I'm sure his strategies will return to him when the time comes."

"You do realize we may not be successful," I reminded them.

"We will never know unless we try," Kenneth said with determination.

"We also bring word from the others," Flemming stated, suddenly remembering his *other* mission.

Seth laughed, "Oh yes, that's right!"

"Meridith, Callin, Emily, Bethany, Haley and Gwendolyn have decided that they refuse to allow you to go to battle without them. As they are all part of the Valkyrie, they demanded to fight alongside of you. Lilith has given them her blessing. The Valkyrie will also be with us, namely to save the fallen. Your precious families will not be lost to the underworld," Kenneth proclaimed.

"Oh, wow. That's amazing. I have to admit, I'm slightly surprised by Lilith, but none of the others. Callin and Emily have always been the sense and sensibility among the group. I can't believe how blessed we are." I sighed contentedly. "I'm so thankful to have you all."

Kenneth nodded with finality. "Well then. I suppose this meeting is adjourned. Please pass on the message to Thaddeus and make sure he understands, we're fully at his disposal."

"We'll return to see you within the next day or so. By then, hopefully there is a plan set. Just speak to Thaddeus and tell him we're ready," Flemming reaffirmed.

"Thank you for your time, Eden. And blessed be your travels."

"Rest well. We shall see you very soon," Kenneth concluded as he turned and walked towards the trees.

The other two bowed and followed behind Kenneth. I stood in the beautiful meadow as I watched the three angels ascend and hover for a moment before flying off. The breeze had picked up; the sun was no longer overhead. I felt the chill, drilling down to my bones. I shivered and folded my arms across my chest, rubbing them to generate body heat.

I followed the direction the angels had taken. The wind blew harder, stinging my face. I looked to the sky. It was growing dark. I was concerned. If I didn't get out of here soon, I was likely to run into someone I didn't necessarily want to see. As peaceful as this locale had been, I didn't want to overstay my welcome. I chose to leave immediately. Besides, I had very important news to share.

I awoke in the van, staring up at the pale grey upholstery. I sat up and rubbed my eyes. The day light was blindingly bright. I yawned loudly and looked around. We were speeding through barren farmlands, laden by fire and ash. What had happened here? I watched the smoke and embers spinning and twirling in the breeze like burlesque dancers.

Pestilence.

"Oh, shit."

"Good morning, Edie," Lamar said sarcastically.

"Where are we?"

"Well, we're about 30 miles outside of Rapid City. We're hoping this shit doesn't stretch all the way there, seeing as how we haven't stopped since Bozeman," Riley replied.

"We need to talk," I said, turning to Riley.

"What's up?"

"A lot. A whole helluva lot," I replied, shaking my head and trying to determine where to begin.

"Did you see Gabriel again?" Riley asked.

"No."

"He wasn't there? You seemed at peace," he asked, confused.

Everyone in the van turned to listen in on our conversation. I thought about lowering my voice, to keep them unaware, but what would be the point? They're in this just as deep as we are. They deserve to know what's going on, just as much as we do.

"Nope. But I was given a message to relay to you," I began.

"Oh, yeah? I'm pretty sure I didn't owe anyone any money." Riley laughed then cleared his throat nervously.

I grinned with excitement at what I was about to tell him. "Kenneth, Flemming and Seth paid me a little visit."

"And?" Riley asked, head tilted curiously.

"And they wanted me to let you know that your army is ready and awaiting your summons," I said with a wide smile.

"What? You've got to be fucking kidding me!" Riley shouted in excited disbelief.

"Nope. I'm dead serious. They said that they've been preparing in secret, that Michael doesn't know what they're doing. Even the Valkyrie are coming to our aid," I replied, my mouth relaying the information as fast as it was entering my brain.

"Why are they doing this?" he asked, shaking his head in bafflement.

"Because you were their leader. They'd rather go down with their captain and the ship, even after all of these years. Apparently there's even some ascended humans that have chosen to join us, after hearing about your leadership and our fight. It seems we've caused quite a stir." I chuckled.

"That's crazy shit!" Corey grinned from behind us.

"That's awesome is what that is!" Brandon chimed in.

"So, we're not going to be fighting alone?" Gabe asked.

"Doesn't sound like it," I replied turning to them.

"What if I don't call on them?" Riley asked.

"Don't think you have a choice. They made it abundantly clear, that they *want* to be at our side. They know what they're facing. I fought them about it, at first. They wouldn't back down."

"How many are we talking about?" Gabe asked, glancing in my direction.

"They said there were 'roughly' 60 of them. Not including the Valkyrie," I responded.

"Holy shit!" Brandon shouted, elated.

"That's not many," Gabe replied.

"But they're *angels*," Lamar added.

"Don't get your hopes too high, we still have to make it to Memphis," Riley reminded us all. "But, it's a good start."

"How bad was the trip from Bozeman?" I asked, coming back to the current situation.

"It looked the same as this. There hasn't been anything left standing. Just flames, ash, smoke and destruction," Lamar cut in.

"Has it been like this all along?" I asked.

"For the most part. Traffic has practically disappeared. There's been a few cars, but mainly helicopters flying overhead. They've been dropping that powder shit, trying to put out the flames," Chuck answered.

"It seems whatever is causing these fires is just ahead of us," Riley said with a nod ahead.

"I hope we don't catch up to it," I replied nervously, settling back in my seat in preparation for what lie ahead.

"What could it be? Is this one of the prophecies?" Corey asked.

"Well I don't know for certain, but when I had my dream about Pestilence, there was a lot of fire. The Horseman had burned the town to the ground once the people were stricken with the plague," I replied. "Not just the people, the crops as well."

"That's fucked up. So not only were these people suffering with an illness that was killing them, they also had been burned alive?" Chuck shook his head, appalled.

"We don't know for sure that's what's going on," I stated, trying to dismiss the thought from my mind.

"But didn't you say yourself talking to Jonah that was a possibility?" Lamar asked.

"Yes, but it isn't a guarantee. Anything and everything is a possibility," I replied.

"Looks like we're about to find out," Riley said loudly, leaning forward on the seat in front of us.

He was staring out of the front windshield, which drew all of our attention forward. Lamar eased up on the gas and turned to look at us, his mouth hung open. He slowly returned his gaze to the front and stopped the van.

We all leaned forward, staring ahead of us. In the middle of the road, no more than 200 yards away, was a pillar of smoke spinning around a large stallion with flaming hooves and a rider as black as the darkest depths. He was enormous. We watched as the horse neighed and stood on its hind legs. The rider stared back at us with bright glowing eyes.

"Oh, fuck," Gabe said, leaning against the dashboard.

"What do we do?" Lamar asked, eyes never leaving the Horseman.

"Well, we could politely ask him to move," Riley mused in a barely audible whisper.

Brandon scoffed, "Yeah, you go do that."

"Uh, guys. He's headed this way," Lamar said nervously.

Riley took off his hat and scratched at his head. "And now for the moment we've all been waiting for."

CHAPTER THIRTY FIVE
PESTILENCE, THE ONE TRICK PONY

We stared out of the front windshield, terrified and frozen in place. Paul inched the other van forward and parked parallel to our own. Jonah and Lamar rolled down their windows so we could communicate between the vans. None of us knew what we should do, what the implications were, or how we got out of this alive. I was torn. Part of me felt that I could get out of the van and reason with the Horseman. The other half of me felt it was a death wish to even breathe too loudly.

"Edie, you've worked with the Horsemen before, haven't you?" Jonah asked me.

I leaned over Lamar to speak with Jonah in a hushed tone, "Um, not exactly. More like I helped clean up their messes."

"Why's he just staring at us?" Corey asked, staring back at the colossal mounted being.

"He's probably trying to figure out what the hell we're doing," Riley replied.

"You talking to him may be our only way to get out of here alive," Paul stated excitedly.

"You don't know that!" Lamar snapped.

"Ah, but I do," Jonah retorted.

"Oh, yeah? Half the time you say that you can't see shit." Gabe jabbed.

"Boys, calm down. This isn't helping anything," I whispered urgently.

I looked forward, drowning out the sound of everyone arguing. I stared at the behemoth eqqus caballus, and his ominous rider. The horse piaffed, waiting for orders from his master. The Horseman gently pat the side of his neck, pulling upwards on the reins. The two spun in a wide circle, taunting us, daring us to come forward.

"So, it would be better for us to send her out and fucking die here? Fuck you, buddy!" Gabe gave Jonah the finger.

"Calm down! All of you!" I shouted through my clenched jaw.

Gabe shook his head, throwing his hands in the air, "I'm sorry, this is just total bullshit."

"Gabe, we know you're being protective of Edie, but she may be the only one who can approach him and get us the fuck out of here. You need to trust us. Trust Jonah," Riley said, attempting to placate my brother.

"I missed most of that conversation; I was kind of spaced out. What do you see, Jonah?" I asked.

"Not much. I told you I saw fire, ash, embers. This must've been what I was seeing," Jonah replied.

"Yeah, well, you also said something about blood and feathers. So? Do we get out of here alive or not?" I shot back with a glance.

"I've had visions of Thomas, the child, and the protectors. So I would assume so. How we get through, I'm uncertain of," he replied with a shake of his head.

"I don't know what else to do. I think our only option is for me to approach him," I responded as I began to steel my resolve.

"No, I don't think that's a good idea." Gabe was shaking his head again.

"Do you have a better idea?" Paul asked.

"Well, sending my sister to her doom isn't exactly a brilliant strategy. Why can't we just run him the fuck over?" Gabe suggested.

"It wouldn't do any good. They're indestructible," I replied.

"How do you know?" Lamar asked, skeptically. He seemed to approve of the idea to mow the mounted rider down.

I explained, "All we'll do is wreck the vans *then* be killed. The Four Horsemen are the incarnation of God's wrath. They're basically an extension of His being. They're His dark side, so to speak."

"Do they have His thoughts and memories?" Brandon asked.

"I'm not sure." I shook my head.

"If they do, then you would be our only chance for survival. He wouldn't want to watch you suffer from disease or burn alive," Riley interjected.

"Yeah, but Pestilence is a bit of a one trick pony. That's basically all he's good for. I don't think he makes decisions on his own. From what I've seen, he breathes death into the air then trots around on his flaming steed, devouring the land with fire," I continued.

"We need to think fast, he's walking this way," Lamar said nervously.

"Shit, I'm going," I replied decidedly as I reached for the side door.

"No! Edie, don't! Take me with you, at least!" Gabe shouted, reaching for my arm.

"I can't let him see you. I love you." I smiled sadly, then vacated the van.

"Let her go," Riley said flatly. He placed his hand on Gabe's shoulder, refraining him from chasing me.

"Dude, that's your fucking wife! She's your soulmate. Stop her!" Gabe's eyes narrowed with tears streaming out. He was livid.

"I have to do this. Please, trust me," I said as I walked along the side of the van.

"Be careful," Riley said after me.

"I'll try."

He frowned, "I love you."

"I love you, too." I grinned and turned my back to the van, focusing on the task at hand.

I watched the horse rear up on his hind legs as the Horseman again pulled on the reins. I exhaled heavily as I slowly stepped towards the deadly being and his destructive beast, watching the flames and smoke billow from the horse's flaring nostrils as he breathed.

"Okay, Edie. You can do this," I spoke to myself out loud.

A female voice spoke behind me, "But you probably shouldn't."

I turned around and watched as Lilith morphed from her wiry crow form into a beautiful angelic being.

"What the hell are you doing here?" I asked nervously.

Which of these two monsters would be worse to face, alone?

Lilith grinned. "Oh, come on. I'm here to save you."

"How so?" I asked skeptically.

"Follow me," she smirked and sauntered forward towards the Horseman.

I turned to face our vans. I could see everyone staring at me, scared. They knew Lilith and I weren't two women that should be spending time together.

The two of us walked side by side towards the incarnation of Pestilence. Standing tall and keeping my chin up, I pretended to stride with unfailing confidence and power. I thought about what Kenneth, Seth and Flemming had said. She had given us her blessing, but that didn't guarantee it was in earnest. I didn't know whether Lilith was truly here to help me, or if this was her final trick to get rid of me. At this point, I had no choice but to trust her. I never thought I'd put the name *Lilith* and the word *trust* in the same sentence, other than by saying 'I don't trust that stupid bitch, Lilith'. That thought alone made me chuckle to myself.

"What's so amusing?" she asked, cocking her head to the side.

I grinned, "Oh, nothing."

She shot me a menacing glance. "Bullshit, Eden. You've never been able to lie."

"You sure do have a dirty mouth for being so heavenly." I grinned wickedly.

"Ah, yes. And you are the *prime* example of *eloquence*." she laughed sarcastically.

"I have an excuse. What's yours?" I jabbed.

We were no more than twenty yards away for the Horseman.

"Breathe, Eden," Lilith commanded. "Don't allow him to smell your fear."

"I'm trying," I mumbled as my voice trembled. "It's easier said than done."

"Explain to me why I shouldn't kill you where you stand, mortals?" he bellowed before us.

"Clearly, you do not remember who I am, Great King. For I am no more of a mortal than you are," Lilith curtsied as she spoke.

I bowed my head to the enormous being, averting my eyes.

"And who might you be, little shape shifter? My memory eludes me as of late," the Horseman inquired. His voice was so terrifying, so deep, that it rumbled in my chest like thunder. He resembled the modern, historically inaccurate rendition of a Viking. His shining black armor appeared to have runes etched into the surface, shimmering and shattering in the light from the flames. His long red hair and beard blew in the breeze underneath his massive, horned helmet. He was a force to be reckoned with, a warrior, a murderer.

"Do you not remember the Black Death? We worked together," Lilith stated with a slight smile as she looked up at the being.

"Mórrígna?" he questioned, eyes narrowed.

"In the flesh," her smile grew and she bowed again.

He bowed his head slightly in response, "Pleasure to see you once more, my Goddess."

"The pleasure is all mine," she replied.

"Why is it that you've come?" he asked.

"I ask you to pardon these strangers and allow them safe passage beyond your flaming barriers."

"Why should I allow anyone, save you, to escape my scorn?"

"Because they, too, are on a mission and have orders from the Heavens to proceed. Much like your lack of memories of me, you seem to have lost your memory of Eden, muse of God," she said, presenting me like a game show door prize with an extravagant wave of the arms.

"If this is some form of trickery, there will be far more destruction than called for, I can assure you of that," he threatened. His eyes narrowed and he leaned his hulking form forward above the head of his steed, trying to recollect my features.

"This is no trick, Great King. Eden and Thaddeus are traveling to collect their army, as ordered. They need safe passage to Tennessee. If you would allow this, we would be forever in your debt," she explained, bowing low.

"Why aren't they traveling by wing? And why haven't you spoken for yourself, little *muse*?" he asked, turning his unwavering gaze towards me.

I felt the heat on my face as his flaming beast exhaled embers and smoke in my direction. "I didn't feel worthy, my Lord," I spoke, voice trembling much like my hands. "And we've been instructed to not make ourselves noticeable to the humans. We've been ordered to blend in."

He laughed loudly. "I will step aside. As I said, if I confirm this was chicanery, justice will be dealt swiftly and without mercy," he roared, pulling sideways on the reins. The giant steed trotted to the right side of the road. "*Mórrígna*, if you have deceived me you will find yourself in far more pieces than the three beings you can manifest."

Lilith smiled, "Thank you for your generosity. Please return to your duties."

The two of us bowed and turned; beginning the return trek towards the vans. I could see everyone moving around inside the vehicles anxiously. As we walked Lilith turned to me and grinned with true pleasure, revealing a beautiful smile. She wrapped her arm around my shoulder and pat my arm. I knew I was going to pay for this.

"So, next time you want to say I'm not helpful, I'll find Pestilence himself, and let him know you're actually going *against* God's will," she threatened with a whisper.

"Those words will never slip from my mouth again."

"Good," she grinned.

"What were you doing here?" I asked.

"Like I said, coming to save you."

"Were you following us again?" I interrogated her.

"Yes and no. I was trying to reap some of the remaining souls, before it was too late. He's making a horrible mess. To be honest, I hate his work. So detached. So impersonal. So ugly."

"So it was just good luck and perfect timing that you found us?" I asked.

She nodded, "Basically."

"Thank you. Really," I grinned sheepishly, lowering my eyes to the road in front of me.

"Yeah, don't mention it." She pretended to brush off her shoulders.

I stared from the corner of my eyes at the beautiful woman standing beside me. I tried to look past the grudge I felt for her. She was still just as stunning as the day she was created, with her pitch black hair and neon green eyes. I could see the attraction that Gabriel had.

"So, I heard you gave us your blessings, and will post the Valkyrie with us," I said as we approached the vans.

"Yes, I heard you promised Gabriel to behave. I made the same promise once he arrived and sprung me loose. I seemed to have gotten myself a bit *snared*, so to speak, while trying to stop the birth of this *human* war." I could tell she detested humans, but still, she aided them.

"So now what?"

"Now, you get out of here and drive as fast as those things can carry you. I suggest you get as far away from him as possible, quickly. If he notices those vans are full of humans, he's going to go berserk," she replied with a look of concern.

"Wait, so we're still in danger?" I asked as we reached the side of the van Riley was in.

"If you don't get away from here, yes."

I opened the side door and began to climb in, turning towards Lilith, "Do you want a ride past him?"

She snickered as she looked past me at the travel weary companions in the van. "No, I'll be fine."

"Well, I'm still in disbelief, but thank you again." I shook my head as I spoke the words, a look of confusion and shock painted across my face.

"You're welcome, Eden. I'll let Gabriel know that you made it safely past Pestilence. I suggest you all cover your mouths and noses as you drive past him. I can't guarantee your safety from the plague," she replied. "Now, go!"

I nodded once more to Lilith, then climbed into the van and closed the side door behind me.

"Now what?" Lamar asked, turning around to speak to me.

I leaned forward to speak so that everyone in our van and Jonah in the opposite van could hear what I had to say. "Cover your mouth and nose. Turn off the AC. Let's haul ass past him and *do not stop* for *any* reason until he's completely out of sight. Got it?"

"Yep," Lamar replied. "Ready?" he asked, rolling up his window and pulling his shirt over his mouth and nose. I looked over and saw that the other van had likewise closed all the windows.

"Ready," I mumbled through my shirt and hands.

Lamar put the van in drive and firmly pressed down on the gas pedal and we flew forward. I watched the Horseman as he and the horse piaffed on the side of the road. He looked at us, gazing suspiciously as we passed. I could see Lilith hovering near him. He turned towards her and plucked her from the sky with one of his giant hands. He yelled something incoherent and tossed her delicate body to the ground below.

"Lilith!" I shouted.

"What happened?" Riley asked urgently.

"Should I stop?" Lamar shouted.

"No! Keep going! Get out of here!" I yelled back.

Oh my God, what have I done? I shouldn't have let her get involved.

"Don't worry Edie," Riley said, rubbing my arm.

The Horseman turned towards us and began riding after our vans. I was filled with sheer terror. If he caught up to us, we were all dead. I was worried about Lilith. It was all my fault. Someone was going to pay the price for my mistakes and I was afraid it wasn't going to be me. Or at least, not *only* me.

"She's back up!" Riley exclaimed, staring out the back window.

"Are you sure?" I asked.

"Yeah, she just staggered a bit then flew off," Riley shouted up to me.

"Oh, good. I felt horrible."

"I can't see the Horseman," he stated nervously.

"I can't either," Gabe said, looking around the vehicle.

"Oh shit! There he is!" Corey shouted, pointing to the forest next to us.

Pestilence was riding on his horse, head down. A plume of smoke trailed behind him as he weaved through the trees, occasionally glancing in our direction with a look of pure hatred. We watched, horrified, as each step of his steed's hooves set the forest floor alight, consuming the trees behind him.

"We're not gonna make it!" I screamed and buried my face in Riley's shirt.

"Oh yes we are," Lamar said with a slight chuckle. The look in his eyes was almost crazed as he buried his foot in the floorboard, bringing a roar from the engine as he tried to get the last bit of speed out of our ride.

Gabe laughed, "Nice!"

"What?" I asked, looking up from Riley's body.

We had reached a long bridge. The two lane expanse spanned a slowly moving river, too wide to traverse without crossing the bridge. The Horseman stopped at the bank of the water, pulling on the reins. He stared after us as his horse scratched at the ground expectantly. I watched, pleased, as the Horseman pulled on the reins, forcing the steed to turn slowly around. With one final hate-filled glance over his shoulder he put his boots into the animals' sides and sped off in the opposite direction.

"We're so fucking lucky," Gabe muttered as he watched the departing rider.

I nodded emphatically, "Yeah. Definitely."

"How did you and Lilith convince him to let us go to begin with?" Riley asked.

I summed up the events and explained his conditions.

"And why did he come after us after letting us pass?" Riley pressed.

"He must've noticed that we have humans with us."

Riley slowly pulled his hands through his hair, "Ah, shit."

"Yeah, I have a feeling that isn't the last we'll be seeing him. Lilith asked for our safe passage *to Tennessee*. So now he knows what direction we're headed," I continued.

"You think he knows the layout of the United States?" Chuck asked skeptically.

"He's an extension of God. You think he needs a map and compass to get around? I highly doubt it," I replied sarcastically.

"Tennessee is a pretty big area," Brandon interjected.

"True," Tori nodded in agreement.

"Yeah, that is true. But that doesn't mean he won't catch up to us before we get there," Gabe said.

Lamar looked to Riley. "So what do we do?"

"Just keep speeding. We'll still stop in Rapid City, if the coast looks clear. But we'll have to hurry. In and out, back on the road," Riley ordered.

"Got it," Lamar agreed, once more picking up speed.

"20 more miles," Gabe said, pointing out the mileage sign as we flew past.

I pulled my phone from my pocket and stared at the display. It was now 4:30pm. It was definitely late enough for me to call Ross and find out if he knew about what Lilith had said to me. I opened the contacts in my phone and scrolled down the list of names and numbers until I found my brother's cell phone number. I pressed send and waited while it rang.

"Hello?" Ross answered with a southern twang in his voice.

"Hey, Ross. It's Edie."

"Hey, Edie!" he responded excitedly.

"Hey, how are you?"

"Good, all things considered. What's up? How have you been?" he asked.

"Uh, little good, little bad. You know. Everything's been pretty weird."

He began to chuckle. "I've noticed. Have you seen that crap on the news? Aliens... right. This is the end, my dear."

"Yeah, I'm in agreement with you there. I know it isn't aliens."

"Oh, yeah? What do you know? Give me the dirt! Give me the scoop!" he mused.

"Well, that's kind of what I was calling you about. I need to ask you something. If you can give me the answers, it might help explain what's going on a little better."

"Alright, shoot. What'cha got for me?" he asked excitedly. The man loved a challenge.

"Okay, here goes. I need some translations, and I probably need help figuring out what the words are. As far as I'm aware, it's Hebrew. Seeing as how the person that told me said that I should ask you what it meant, being a Hebrew scholar and all."

"Alright, what were you told?" he asked.

"Well, Riley and I are on our way to Memphis to pick up a *friend*. But it appears that our *friend*, is the guardian of someone called *Pele*? And she said that he is a *yellow odd*? I don't know what any of that means. Does any of that ring a bell to you?" I chuckled awkwardly. I felt ridiculous telling him this.

"Very interesting that you'd mention that. There is an old Hebrew prophecy, that a child will lead us. He was even spoken about in the Old Testament, but his name was never mentioned, though in one story a family sees him in the shadows and asks him what his name is. He tells them his name is Pele, which means 'Wonder' or 'Miracle'. It was the name given to him by the Israelites," he explained.

"Wow, okay. Weird. So Pele is a kid?"

"Supposedly. It never said how young he was. He could be a few years old, or in his teens. There was no description to completely identify him" he continued.

"Now what about the yellow odd, thing?" I asked.

"I don't know. Is he jaundiced? Maybe he has liver failure?" Ross mused.

I laughed, "No, no. It's supposedly Hebrew as well."

"Hmm. *Yellow odd. Yellow odd,*" he mumbled to himself. "Wait, do you mean *Yeled Ad?*"

"Yes! That's what she said!"

Thank God for smart brothers.

"Well, Yeled Ad would basically mean everlasting child. A boy. Eternal boy. Like immortal," he explained.

"So, like Peter Pan?"

"Not exactly. That's a fairy tale. Pele was a prophecy," he corrected me.

"Prophecy... fairytale, same thing," I joked.

"You know better than that, and I'm assuming by the questions you're asking, something is going on. Something that I should be aware of?"

"Well, there's definitely something going on," I replied nonchalantly.

"Why did Dad ask me to bring the family to their house?"

"Well, for safety mainly," I replied cryptically.

"Safety from?"

"I was going to explain everything to everyone when I made it back, but you aren't going to let this drop, are you?" I asked.

"Not a chance."

"Safety from the Apocalypse. The end is coming. I'm gathering the last of the angels in an attempt to save the world from God's wrath. The Four Horsemen have started to descend, as well as the Archangels. The prophecies are unfolding and we're all going to die unless my plan works," I explained in one breath, then waited for his reaction.

"Whoa, whoa, whoa. What?" he asked sounding confused.

I wished I knew how to explain this situation without everyone thinking I'm insane. "Exactly. I'm not good at explaining this shit. Just trust me, please. I think the safest place for everyone is together. I'm trying to do everything I can to keep you all alive."

"Eden Quinn. Are you on drugs?" he asked me.

I laughed, "No! God, no."

"I've gotta get home to the family. I don't have time to talk about this right now. But I'm gonna call you back later and I want you to explain everything to me, piece by piece. Okay?" he demanded.

"Sure, gotcha," I lied. "Be careful, I love you."

"I will, and I love you, too," he replied and hung up.

I slid my phone back into my pocket and thought about everything my brother had just told me. Something seemed odd, not *Ad*. I was thoroughly confused. I tried to tie everything together, hoping to have some kind of idea of what we were walking into, but I was stumped and at a loss for words.

"What did Ross have to say?" Gabe asked.

"He said that Pele was the name of an immortal child. He was talked about in the Old Testament, but they never said his name. I guess in some Hebrew story, he told someone that he goes by Pele."

"Okay? Weird," Gabe replied with a look of confusion.

"What else did he say?" Riley asked.

"And it's *Yeled Ad*, not yellow odd. Not that I can tell the difference anyway. I don't remember ever speaking Hebrew."

"What does that mean, did he know?" Riley continued to question me.

"Apparently it means something like 'eternal child' or 'eternal boy'."

"Whoa, so what're we getting wrapped up in now?" Brandon chimed in.

"I don't know," I shrugged.

"Is this immortal boy like a vampire or something?" Corey asked.

Chuck started to laugh, "I wouldn't be surprised. Look at all this angel bullshit. Maybe we'll team up with some zombies and werewolves to defeat God's army."

I shook my head. "No, of course that's not it. I think that it's Elijah. I don't know for certain. I have an odd feeling that I'm supposed to remember more about this than I do. "

"Wait, then who is Pele?" Lamar asked.

"Maybe another angel no one knows about?" Tori suggested.

"Maybe Elijah *is* Pele. That's what I was trying to say," I surmised.

"There is no Elijah. There's only Pele," Corey said, jokingly.

"No, *Elijah* was on the list. There wasn't a Pele on there."

"We're here, guys," Lamar said, turning on his blinker and exiting the interstate.

Gabe leaned forward to look out the front of the van. "Thank God. I was about to piss on myself."

"I already did. Fucking Pestilence was scary as hell," Chuck joked.

"Yeah, I agree. My bladder's empty now. So is my colon." Riley chuckled.

"How do you think I feel, I had to stand below the huge ass guy!" I mocked.

"We know you wet yourself, it's okay. We won't tell anyone." Chuck grinned at me.

We pulled into the first gas station we came across. The pumps were all filled with vehicles lined up, front to back. Looking across the street to the other two gas stations, we noticed *they also* had long lines of cars.

"What the hell's going on?" Lamar threw his hands into the air, frustrated.

I began moving for the door, "No clue. But I'm getting out to use the restroom. I'll ask around. I'd imagine this is part of a mass evacuation."

Tori followed suit. "I'm coming with you," she called after me, squeezing past Brandon to get out of the side door.

Tori and I stepped out of the van and walked towards the convenience store. There was a long line of people waiting at the register. The entire interior and exterior of the service station was a sea of humanity. Men, women, and children hurried about in various states of panic and disarray. We hastily walked to the back of the store and opened the restroom door, where we were confronted by five women waiting outside of occupied stalls. We all simultaneously began doing the *pee pee dance.*

"What's going on around here?" I asked, dancing in place.

An older woman turned to me, puzzlement written across her face, "What do you mean?"

"Why are the gas stations and stuff so crowded?"

A third woman joined the conversation, "You aren't from around here, are you?"

"No, we're not. We're just passing through. What's going on?" I asked again.

"Everyone is evacuating," the old woman answered.

"With that wildfire spreading, everyone getting sick, the tornadoes and everything else going on, we're all getting the hell out of here," a young woman holding a child at the front of the line explained.

"Damn. Where's everyone headed?" Tori asked.

"Anywhere but here. My family and I are headed north. It seems to be relatively safe up there," the young woman with the child replied.

The older woman began shaking her head emphatically, "Not from what I've heard and seen on the television."

"Excuse me?" the young woman asked, switching the child to the other hip.

"From what I've seen and heard, they're getting it just as bad up north. There's been thousands of deaths. They say it's like a killer strand of flu, an epidemic, or pandemic. Whichever the hell means more deaths," the old woman replied with a shrug.

The young woman rolled her eyes, then looked dubiously at the other, "Oh, bullshit."

"Suit yourself, honey. Take that little baby of yours up north. You'll be holding her in your arms when she dies from this *plague.*" the old woman made the sign of the cross and shook her head.

"You need to learn some manners. And you know what, you superstitious old hag? I'm going to enjoy laughing when this all blows over and leaves close minded, crotchety old bitches like yourself clueless, as usual. It's like the Y2K scare all over again," the young woman shouted, then turned on her heels and walked out of the restroom.

"Kids these days." One of the women turned to the old lady and shook her head.

I'm so tired of these pushy old biddies that think they know everything there is to know about the universe, just because they made it to seventy.

We waited our turn to use the restroom and squeezed between people to use the sinks when we were finished. We walked out into the loud, crowded store and weaved our way through the mass of people towards the front door. I wasn't going to even attempt to pay for a snack or drinks. I'd be in line for hours. I knew we still had plenty of food in the vans.

"How bad is the line in there?" Riley asked, approaching us.

"Which one?" I answered with a question.

He raised a brow, "Huh?"

"There's lines to check out. There's lines to use the restroom. There's lines to make a cup of coffee. There's lines to grab a fountain drink. Take your pick; they're all long and ridiculous," I replied with a flurry of hand waving, wildly gesticulating.

"Sucks. I'll just go whiz on the side of the building. Bet there isn't a line there!" Riley grinned.

"No, there isn't. That's what I just did!" Paul laughed loudly.

"Same," Brandon grinned.

"You boys and your little caveman instincts to pee on things…" I mused.

"You're just jealous of our superior intellect and ability to pee standing up. You get all bent out of shape from having to use the toilet seat covers, or get your ass wet from someone else's mess," Gabe chuckled at himself smugly.

"Shut up, jerk!" I scoffed, punching my brother in the arm as hard as I could.

"Told you!" Gabe smirked and elbowed Paul's arm.

"Superior intellect? Don't make me tell them about some of your stories growing up," I reminded him, folding my arms across my chest.

"Oh, yeah? Like what?" Gabe asked, eyes narrowed with challenge.

I noticed the crowd of our companions gathering to hear the juicy gossip.

"Oh, I don't know," I replied.

"See, you have nothing. Nothing!" he shook his head.

"*As I was going to say*, hmm. Like how you drew on the walls with your own poop as a toddler, or how you hid your cookies in your toy box, then Mom found'em like, months later all moldy!" I laughed at the look of horror on his face at the retelling and group laughter that ensued.

"Ha ha! Oh, yeah! That's funny shit though. That's nothing to be ashamed of. I was like, two. That doesn't count!" Gabe yelled with a smile, trying to recover.

I threw my hands up, "Meh, you're right. I got nothin'."

"Knew it!" he grinned.

"I'll think of something."

"So, you ladies ready to go?" Riley interrupted.

Gabe looked at him, "Yeah, we're all gassed up and ready to roll. Traffic will probably start getting shitty. I heard everyone is under mandatory evacuation in the area."

Lamar nodded; a look of concern on his face. "I heard the same thing."

"Alright, let's go ahead and do a head count, find out who wants to ride in what and get ready to go. Has the mutt gotten to do his business and stuff his muzzle?" Riley asked, turning to me.

"I'm not sure. I haven't checked," I replied with a frown. I suddenly felt like a neglectful parent.

"He's good. I took him for a walk and Chuck gave him some food and water," Corey chimed in.

I smiled, "Aw, thanks guys!"

"No problem, Ms. Edie," Corey shot back with a wink.

"Okay. Who's driving now? We have roughly five hours to go," Riley continued.

"I'm ready to drive!" Brandon yelled, hopping up and down.

"Me too," Jonah replied, far less enthusiastically.

"Alright, everyone hop in. Let's get the hell out of here before Pestilence catches up," Riley said, walking to the side door of our van.

I hopped into the front seat so I could keep a good look out for trouble. And by trouble, I meant the lumbering pandemic and his flaming horse. We merged into traffic and were stuck at a light. I looked towards the western woods and could see smoke. I knew that we needed to hurry; Pestilence had made it to the city. I stared out at the tree line, waiting to see the behemoth beast and heartless rider emerge from the forest, setting the dry field ablaze.

"He's coming," I said, turning to Brandon.

"Not before we get the hell out of here." he smirked and gunned the engine when the light turned green. As we accelerated he swerved around slower vehicles, riding the shoulder as he got onto the interstate ramp. Flying onto the interstate, he weaved in and out of traffic, until we were finally at the front of the line of cars. We sped eastbound, the trailing van close behind.

I kept an eye out for any approaching dangers, but was pleasantly surprised to say it was relatively quiet. Everyone looked around us, watching the sky and sides of the road carefully, until the inactivity slowly calmed everyone's frayed nerves. It wasn't long before I began hearing snoring from the back. When I turned around, everyone, including Azrael was asleep and either curled up, propped against a window or propped against the person they shared a seat with. I checked my side mirror often, half expecting to see the Horseman nipping at our heels, but never did. All I saw was the other van, matching our speed. It was a momentary reprieve.

CHAPTER THIRTY SIX
HAND-ME-DOWN HEARTS AND HALF-ASSED SINCERITY

I was surprised by how quiet the rest of the trip to Memphis really was. We ran into a few snags here and there, but overall it was fairly gentle. There were a few accidents on the roads, bad traffic, more fires and sheer panic, but we were becoming accustomed to this new way of life on the road. I now knew how the Gypsies felt. Granted, I didn't have everything I owned strapped to the roof of my caravan, but I could see what it was like to be on the move, day in and day out. It sucked. I always referred to my family as nomads, but we at least stayed in one spot longer than two hours. And we never had to watch our backs.

We traveled back through Sioux Falls, stopping for a brief rest. We ate dinner and had the chance to stretch our legs with ease and comfort. The area was quiet, unscathed so far. Because of this the people didn't move with as much panic in their step.

We hadn't seen Mr. Pesti-pants since we left Rapid City, luckily. Of course, that didn't mean that we wouldn't be seeing him again in the future. We were just able to reach Tennessee without him gracing us with his presence. *Good riddance.*

As lucky as we *were*, I'm not sure I can comfortably tell you that luck lasted, seeing as how I'm a horrible liar. The truth is, everything became even more confusing, even more unnerving once we found what we were looking for. After being wrapped up in all of this drama and fearing the worst, it was hard for me to wear a smile. It was hard for me to be optimistic, when I truly felt the worst was just ahead of us. I felt like I was peddling stolen, hand-me-down hearts and half-assed sincerity. I was pretending to be calm, pretending to feel confident, when in truth, it was all failing.

It was 8:45am when we reached Memphis. Traffic had been horrific. Then again, any time I had been through Memphis, the traffic was shitty. We spent an hour driving in circles, trying to find the correct address we had for Tom. After circling the same block or two for the twentieth time, we stopped where the numeric should've been. Okay, obviously I was exaggerating about the twenty circles, but still.

We piled out of the vans and stared up at the beautiful, pristine, white synagogue. We couldn't see any numbers on the building, but the street numeric skipped straight over the numbers we were looking for. Perhaps there was a small house behind the iconic temple.

Lamar walked to my side, "Should we knock on the door and just ask?"

"I don't know," I replied with a sideways glance.

"Should we just walk around the building and look?" Gabe asked, craning his neck and standing on one leg to see what was on the side of the structure.

"I don't know," Riley responded.

"Do you guys have any clue what we're going to do?" Gabe asked with a laugh.

Riley shook his head, "Nope. Don't know."

"Wow, we're really organized, aren't we?" Chuck laughed.

"Nah, we'll be fine. I just hope he's around here somewhere," I said, trying to exude more confidence than I felt.

"Did we maybe get the wrong address?" Tori asked.

"It's possible. But I doubt it. I got his address the same way I found all of yours," Riley responded.

Corey was scratching his head, "Hmm, seems weird. Is there maybe multiple roads with the same name?"

Chuck shook his head, "Don't think so. That would be too confusing for people. Especially if they used the same numbers."

I thought the conversation I had with Ross and suddenly it hit me like a ton of bricks, right between the eyes. "Guys, this *has* to be the right place."

"Oh, yeah? How do you know?" Gabe asked skeptically.

"Well, what is a synagogue?"

"A Jewish temple, right?" Lamar replied.

"Exactly. And what is Hebrew?" I continued the lesson.

"A language?" Chuck answered, confused.

"Never mind. I'm going up." I laughed and turned towards the synagogue. I heard the van doors open and slam shut as the other van arrived and the occupants filed out. I walked up the perfectly landscaped pathway, admiring the love and attention each flower had been shown as it had been immaculately placed in its desired location. Someone had shown great care and obviously spent much time outside, preserving the natural beauty of the grounds.

I approached the front steps and felt as if I should be nervous, anxious to knock on the door. But all I felt was warmth. I felt welcomed. I felt as if I was supposed to be here. And suddenly, my heart filled with pure joy. I was happy. I was excited. I soaked in the unfamiliar feeling and smiled widely. It was so bizarre. I giggled to myself and knocked on the enormous, heavy wooden door.

"Hello. May I help you?" a young man said as he opened the door.

"Hi, yes. I'm looking for Mr. Thomas Hatcher," I replied with a smile.

He looked from my face to the two vans below me on the street, "May I ask who you are, ma'am?" he asked nervously.

"My name is Eden Nixon. It's very important that I speak to him, if he's in fact here and available," I responded politely.

"And may I ask the nature of your visit?"

I shook my head. "No, I'm sorry. It's a private matter."

"Well, then I'm sorry to tell you that I cannot allow you to meet with Mr. Hatcher. Good day," the man said as he gently closed the front door in my face.

"Excuse me?" I shouted, banging on the front door urgently. There was no answer. I could hear talking coming from around the side of the building. It didn't sound like English, but from a distance I couldn't make out anything anyway. I ran down the stairs and followed the sound around the corner. There was a man that appeared to be in his mid-thirties, walking with a young child.

"Excuse me!" I called out loudly as I walked towards the two. The man stopped, turning to face me and stepped defensively between me and the child.

"Yes ma'am, can I help you?" The gentleman asked.

"Hopefully. I'm looking for Thomas Hatcher. It's very important that I see him."

"I am Thomas," he responded with a slight nod.

"Oh, thank God. The guy that answered the door wouldn't allow me to speak to you unless I told him what it concerned. And frankly, it didn't concern him at all," I let out with a sigh.

"How can I help you?" he asked again.

"We desperately need to speak. Is there somewhere we can go? In private, preferably."

He turned and looked at the child behind him. The young boy smiled and nodded his head. "Come," Thomas ordered.

The child stepped forward and smiled widely up at me, then ran back to take his place beside the retreating Thomas.

I followed the two as they walked hand in hand to a small house behind the synagogue. The dwelling was very simple and humble, though the pathway to the home was elaborately adorned with beautiful flowers and green life. Thomas opened the front door and the child ran in, jumping onto a small couch with fanfare and giggles. He adjusted himself on the couch cushion and motioned for me to come in.

"What is it that you wish to speak to us about?" Thomas asked, taking a position in the doorway to the small living room.

"Well, it's *you* that I wanted to speak to," I clarified.

"This does not concern Pele?" Thomas asked, turning his head to the side suspiciously.

"So *this is Pele*?" I asked, pointing to the smiling child that was now waving in my direction.

"Yes, Eden," he chimed in from the couch.

"How did you know my name?" I asked, surprised.

At the look of confusion on my face he began laughing hysterically, kicking his feet in the air as he did so, "I remember you," he managed through fits of giggling.

"This is the group you foresaw?" Thomas asked, turning to the child.

"Yes," the child regained his composure, but the smile never left his eyes.

"You knew we were coming?" I asked with a grin.

"Of course. I know everything that is occurring," Pele smiled widely again, amused and proud of himself.

"Well, don't leave me in the dark, little one." Thomas shook his finger at Pele.

"Ain Sof," Pele replied simply.

"What of Him?" Thomas asked.

"The army is descending to reclaim the Earth. Ain Sof has sent the angels down," Pele replied in a more somber tone.

"This is what you've spoken of in your lectures. It's happening soon, I assume?" Thomas asked, sitting next to the child.

"I informed the members of the synagogue in some of my teachings that the end was upon us. Most of them have sworn their allegiance to us. I told them there would come a day, a day when a group of angels would come to aid us in our endeavors. This is that great day," Pele explained with a smile and a wink in my direction.

The boy was confusing me. "This isn't a great day, Pele. This is nothing to be happy about."

"Eden, you being here is a wonderful omen," Pele shot back, not to be dissuaded.

"The end of time is hardly a good thing." I shook my head.

"I will be able to assist you, much like I need your assistance," Pele explained cryptically.

"I don't understand."

Thomas interjected, "I'm sure you have many questions, most of which he can answer for you. There are a few that I may be able to answer as well."

I turned my attention from Thomas to the boy, "Pele, do you know what we're doing?"

"Yes. You've been traveling, uniting the remaining angels and gearing for battle. You intend to save the Earth for the humans."

"Are you going to join us?" I asked.

I can't believe I just asked a boy to join our fight.

Pele's smile was radiant in the light of the room. "Of course we are, Eden." Thomas looked at Pele, obviously not as confident in this course of action. "Don't worry, they're doing the right thing." Pele smiled and grabbed Thomas' hand reassuringly.

I was still confused about something. "You seem to know a lot of what's going on. Can I ask you something?"

He turned from Thomas to face me once more, "Of course."

I figured it was a silly question, but I needed to be sure of the truth. "Where can we find Elijah? Are you him?"

The boy chuckled heartily, "Yes, I *am* Elijah. Pele, was a name given to me by the people. Though I don't agree with them, I appreciated the moniker. The Israelites felt I was a miracle because of my 'immortality'. They didn't comprehend the truth the way *you* do."

"So, do you go by Pele, or Elijah?" I asked.

He smiled gently then let it fade with a sigh, "I would prefer to be called Elijah, as that was the name given to me by my parents."

"How old are you, Elijah?" I asked.

"That's a bit of a trick question." he laughed. "I was born in Heaven. I was a cherub. My parents brought me down to Earth once it was given to us. I grew over time, until The Great Divide."

"Who are your parents?"

"Lilith and Gabriel," Thomas replied as his attention returned to the conversation.

I gasped and covered my mouth, too much in shock to immediately formulate words. "What? How could I have forgotten that? I knew we were connected somehow."

"When God called everyone to the meeting grounds, my mother kissed my cheek and left me at our shelter. I told her about the coming events. She knew I must remain on Earth, but remain heavenly intact. She told me that she'd watch over me, but she knew there was a great task for me in the future," Elijah explained, his beautiful face now serious.

Thomas took over the story, "She told me what was to happen. I, of course, chose to stay on Earth and protect my nephew, rather than return to Heaven with Lilith and the others. It broke her heart to leave him behind. But as she told me, he would be a savior one day. We all had to sacrifice to fulfill his destiny." As he spoke, Thomas ran his hand down the back of Elijah's head lovingly.

"So you're my nephew, as well." I grinned, staring at the radiant child.

The beaming smile returned to his face. "Yes. Uncle Thomas is Lilith's brother."

"So you haven't aged since The Great Divide?"

"No, I've been 10 years old since that day forward," he replied.

I shook my head, amazed. Then a realization hit me that changed everything. "If you weren't at the meeting grounds, then…" I covered my mouth, amazed at the thought.

"Yes, I still have my wings," he replied quietly.

"How has God not found you and demanded your return to Heaven?" I asked in disbelief.

Thomas raised his hand slightly as he began to speak, "I've been very careful to keep him hidden, throughout time. Well, *we* have."

"But you were at The Great Divide. You've aged and died just like the rest of us," I surmised, head cocked as I tried to place the pieces.

"Yes. We've had this synagogue for generations. For hundreds of years, our faithful followers have aided me in protecting Pele. Though we've moved around the globe, numerous times, they've always taken him to my location. He's always reminded me of my promise, my duty," Thomas elaborated.

Elijah picked up when Thomas paused, "There have also been times that I spent with you, but because of your connection with my father, it's always been feared that God would see me. So, I've primarily stayed with Uncle Thomas."

"So, you both remember the past completely?"

"Of course," Elijah nodded, a smile edging up one side of his mouth.

"Are you sure you want to join us?" I asked.

"Unfortunately," Thomas replied with a reluctant shake of his head.

"What's wrong?" I asked.

Elijah looked from Thomas to me, brows creased in concern now. "He's worried. This is the part of my life that he's dreaded since The Great Divide. This is the time that I fulfill my destiny. This is what the prophecies foretold. I will lead my people into battle and then walk them to the gates of Shamayim."

It was hard to believe that this young boy was as old as he was based on appearance. But hearing him speak, he was far more intelligent and enlightened than any children of his apparent age, and most adults, for that matter. He had curly brown hair, bright, piercing green eyes and a smile that sparkled only slightly dimmer than the radiant twinkle in his eyes. He was a dazzling kid and I was proud to know that he was my nephew, spiritually.

"Where are the others?" Elijah asked me with inquisitive eyes.

"They're out by the vans."

Elijah shook his head with a small laugh at my misunderstanding. "I was referring to the angels that are going to descend for Thaddeus."

"Oh. Well, he hasn't called on them yet. We aren't exactly sure when, or how to do that."

"It must be done soon," Elijah stated with a serious look.

I nodded, "We'll be sure to let him know that, then."

There was a knock on the front door. We all turned to face the sound. Thomas rose from his seat and walked to the entryway, opening the door slightly. The young man that answered the synagogue door was standing out front. Through small pleasantries between the two, I learned his name was Justin. After a brief exchange Thomas excused himself and stepped outside, closing the door behind him. I turned to face Elijah. He smiled brightly and shrugged.

"Do you ever get to see your parents?" I asked, afraid of the answer.

His smile never left, "Of course, I do. They come and see me whenever they can come down to Earth. But mainly I see them the same way you do. They visit me in my dreams."

"How do you know so much?" I grinned and shook my head.

"I'm still 'heavenly' as you call them. I'm still an angel. I still possess all of the gifts and traits that were bestowed upon me at birth," he replied.

"So you see the past, present, future. What else?"

"I see everything that has ever been and ever will be," he replied with a mischievous grin.

I frowned, "That must be a lot of pressure."

"It is. Well, it can be. Luckily, everyone that surrounds me, loves me and has never tried to exploit me," he replied with a meek shrug of his shoulders.

"Yeah, that is a good thing."

He looked at me seriously. "I know you want to know what's going to happen. I know that you're worried, you're concerned about everyone. I cannot tell you the outcome, as it could change the course of the future. But what I can tell you, is your plan will come into play and I will be the one who helps you."

"What about my family?"

"They're safe, though I can't promise their safety for any specific length of time," he replied.

"That's what I was afraid of."

"You should go get your friends and the others. We can provide you with warm showers, food and lodging for the night. We need to pray and meditate on our strategy. We can leave tomorrow morning," he suggested with a soft smile.

"Do you think that's best?"

He laughed, the smile returning to his small face as quickly as it left, "I wouldn't have suggested it if I knew there were any threats."

I nodded, having to laugh at his logic. "That's a good point."

"I'm sure you know, the future is always changing and can be manipulated by outside forces. As of now, we're safe here. I know my mother is keeping an eye out for us and will give one of us a warning if we need to move quickly," he explained.

I was still curious about something, "Why didn't she tell me who you were? All she did was tell me that we'd find 'Pele' here with Thomas. Why didn't she tell me it was you and how the two of you were connected?"

"I'm not sure why she's chosen to omit the truth. I'm sure she has the best of intentions. Perhaps it was to keep one of us safe."

I shrugged. "That's possible, I suppose."

"I know that Michael has managed to sneak into your dreams before. Maybe she was trying to make sure someone with the ability to read you, wouldn't find out where I was," he surmised.

"You're very clever for a child," I said jokingly.

To this he again erupted into a fit of laughter, "I'm fairly certain that *you're* more of a child than *I am*."

"I guess you're right," I said, joining in his laughter.

"Well then, I suppose you should go get your friends and have them join us." he sighed contentedly.

"Yeah. I'll go get everyone. Are you sure it's okay if we stay through the night?" I asked once more.

He closed his eyes and nodded. "Yes, Uncle Thomas will respect my decision."

At that moment the front door opened and Thomas stepped in. He smiled nervously at me and sat down on the couch next to Elijah. They conversed about Elijah's plan and Thomas agreed to allow us to stay and rest for the day. He seemed very reluctant to trust us, but it was obvious how much he trusted Elijah and his decisions.

When they had finished their discussion Thomas looked to me. "We can set up some pallets in the back of the synagogue. There are three bathrooms, total, between the temple and our home. I'll ask Justin to assist me in preparing a meal for all of you."

"I truly appreciate the hospitality. Thank you, so much," I smiled at Thomas.

"You're quite welcome. A friend of Elijah is a friend to us all," Thomas replied with a slight bow.

"I will join you in a little while. I'd very much enjoy meeting everyone," Elijah called as I departed.

"Okay, cool." I opened the door and stepped out. I walked down the pathway from their humble home, looking at the beautiful landscape surrounding this sacred spot once more. As I approached the vans I noticed everyone staring at me expectantly. Jeremiah and Melanie came to my sides then followed me to the van. Azrael was running in the street, chasing Gabe, who was carrying his rope toy. Lamar and Riley were sitting on the curb, singing. Chuck was sitting on the hood of the van, doing something on his cell phone. Corey was flipping through a magazine, pointing things out to Erick, Jonah and Brandon. Paul was pacing back and forth on his phone, while the girls sat in the grass, obviously having a *girl talk*.

"I hope you have good news, you've been gone awhile." Riley looked at his watch.

"It hasn't been *that* long," I replied.

"Felt like it."

"But yes, I do have good news. Let's gather some of our stuff and head up to the synagogue," I pointed. "We're staying here until tomorrow morning."

"Really? Are you sure that's a good idea?" Riley raised his brow.

I grinned at his ignorance of the situation. "Once you see why, you'll agree wholeheartedly."

"Hmm. There must be something rather impressive going on to have gotten you comfortable," Riley replied skeptically.

I raised my voice to be heard, "Alright, listen up! Grab some clean clothes and such. We've got a chance to get cleaned up and rest for the day. We'll be leaving again in the morning."

"A whole *day* to relax? This place *must* be Heaven!" Paul exclaimed sarcastically.

"If you're going to be smart ass, then you can stay in the van," I replied, placing my hands on my hips.

"No, no! I'm glad, really." he grinned sheepishly.

Brooke smiled and hugged me. "I think it's awesome. Thank you."

"You're welcome, though I had nothing to do with it." I chuckled, pulling away from her grasp.

Everyone walked towards the front of the synagogue. Justin and Thomas were standing at the front door, waving everyone to go inside. I strayed behind a bit, allowing everyone a chance to get inside and relax. Jonah walked beside me, smiling. He grabbed my arm and escorted me towards the pristine white temple.

"Elijah is here?" Jonah asked in a whisper.

"Yes." I grinned.

He smiled at me, "Wonderful. Then our search is complete."

"Yup," I returned his smile.

"I assume Elijah and Thomas will be joining us?" he continued.

"Uh huh."

"Fantastic," he nodded. "Yes, I'm starting to believe we may have a very good chance to put your plan into action."

"I hope so."

As Jonah and I approached the front doors Thomas spoke up, "Come in.

Please, make yourselves at home and relax"

Jonah smiled at Thomas kindly, "Thank you, very much."

"It's my pleasure. I serve Elijah any way that I can. If this is what he wishes, then this is what I must allow." Thomas bowed his head slightly.

"Sounds like a spoiled little turd to me," Paul mused.

"Far from it, friend," Thomas shook his head.

Paul looked at me and made the 'oops' expression, then grinned and ran off towards Riley and Gabe.

"When will I get to meet Elijah?" Jonah asked, excitedly.

"Soon. He's meditating at the moment," Thomas replied.

Thomas left Justin, Jonah and me near the door and walked towards the back of the synagogue where everyone else was gathered. He was a very gracious host. He seemed to be tending to everyone's needs, pointing towards the restrooms and opening a closet, revealing pillows and blankets.

"Is there anything I can get for you, Ms. Eden?" Justin asked.

"No, thank you. I'm fine."

"I'm very sorry for interrogating you earlier. I'm sure you now know why I was so concerned. You know who I've sworn to protect," he said awkwardly, embarrassed.

I nodded, "I completely understand. There's no need to apologize."

"Thanks. Well, my wife is in the kitchen trying to figure out what she could whip up for dinner for so many people. We have some other members coming over, as well. There are a few of us that have dedicated our lives to Elijah, and will not allow him to leave the temple without us," Justin explained.

"So you plan to leave with us tomorrow?" I asked.

"Yes, some of us will be."

"How many of you, if I may ask?" I questioned.

"Well, my wife and I, for sure. I'm not sure if anyone else will be going. And I should warn you, we have children that will need to travel with us," Justin explained.

I looked at him skeptically, "Yeah, I don't know if that's a good idea. We'll need to discuss it with Elijah and Riley."

"I guess we'll just have to wait and see." he shrugged. "Now, why don't you go make yourself at home? There's snacks in the kitchen and clean towels in the bathrooms."

"Where can we keep our dog?" I asked.

"There's a fenced section in the back of the grounds. We can put him in there so he can get some exercise. Unfortunately, he won't be allowed in the temple." he frowned apologetically.

I shook my head. "Oh, no. That's totally understandable."

"Would you like me to show you where to put him?"

"Yes, please." I smiled.

"Okay, follow me." Justin opened the front door, and I followed him as he led the way back to the van.

When we got there I opened the side door and attached Azrael's leash to his collar. He jumped to the ground and stood at my side, waiting for his next command. I gently tugged on the leash, leading him to the fenced portion of the grounds. We followed behind Justin as he led us up the pathway and around the backside of the synagogue. He unlatched the gate and stood aside as Azrael and I stepped into the well-kempt, fenced yard.

"He'll be safe here. No one will mess with him," he reassured me.

"Cool, thanks." I smiled and looked down at my faithful companion.

"There's a shed in the corner that he can use as shelter if it rains. I'll gather some towels for bedding and some bowls for his food and water," Justin continued.

"This is great. Thank you." I gently rubbed Azrael's back. He looked up at me, tongue hanging out of the corner of his mouth and wagged his stubby tail, panting excitedly. I was so glad that he was going to have time to run around and be a dog, instead of being crammed in the van. I removed his leash and walked to the gate, closing it behind me. Justin escorted me back around the side of the synagogue, and then disappeared into the temple through one of the side doors. I walked down the colorful pathway towards the van to retrieve Azrael's supplies.

The wind was beginning to stir, carrying a cool autumn breeze. The multicolored leaves danced in the wind as they broke free from the overhead branches and spiraled to the ground below. I paused for a moment where I stood, and closed my eyes. I inhaled deeply, breathing in the sweet smell of the flowers and crisp air. This place was phenomenal. Everything about it exuded tranquility. Pure calmness. I hated to take our collective away from this little slice of Heaven on Earth. I returned from my momentary reverie and opened the side door to the van.

"I see you've met my son," a female voice said behind me.

I turned to see Lilith standing on the curb, arms folded across her chest. "Yeah. Great kid you've got there," I replied, once more turning my back to gather Azrael's belongings.

She smiled coyly. "I know. He takes after his father."

"I was thinking the same thing." I chuckled, shooting her a backward glance.

"Why am I not surprised?" She raised an eyebrow and grinned.

"Did you come to visit him?" I asked, changing the subject and turning my attention to her.

Her demeanor grew more serious, "No, I don't have time to spend with him. I came to ask a favor of you."

"I guess I do owe you, technically. What do you need?"

"Please, do everything in your power to keep him safe. I'm sure you haven't spent enough time with him to love him yet, but you have before and you will again. He's a part of you, just as he's a part of Thomas. Family is family, whether you're expecting it or not," she paused, then smiled suddenly, then squinted her eyes at me. "Whether you *like* it or not."

I shook my head, "Lilith, I wouldn't let any harm come to him, whether he was my nephew or not. Even if he was your bastard child, I would do everything possible to keep him out of harm's way."

"Well, I do appreciate that. And so will your brother." she curtsied slightly.

I couldn't tell if she was being sincere or sarcastic. "You're welcome, I guess." She turned and began to walk away.

"So, where are you off to now?" I called after her.

Lilith stopped and half turned to me. "Famine has now descended. I have souls to harvest. Not to mention I need to keep an eye on Pestilence. If he goes unchecked he could catch up to all of you, unseen."

"Gotcha," I nodded.

"I'll see you soon," she said, as she shifted forms and flew off, gaining altitude until she was above the roofline, then headed to the west.

"Can't wait," I whispered to myself, rolling my eyes. I grabbed the materials I had collected from the interior of the van and closed the door. Turning around, I was startled at the sight of Elijah balancing on the curb. His arms were behind his back and a smile was stretched across his angelic face from ear to ear as he rocked back and forth, trying to tip toe as close to the edge of the curb as possible without falling off.

"What're you doing out here?" I asked with a smile.

"I came to see you," he replied, not looking up from his game.

"Is there something I can do for you?"

He shook his head with a grin, "Nope."

"Is there something you wanted to ask me?"

"Nope," he shook his head again, smiling wider.

I stared at my newly introduced nephew and cocked my head to the side. My eyes narrowed suspiciously.

"Are you done guessing?" he stopped his balancing act and now met my eyes with the familiar smile still dancing across his face.

I couldn't help but return the smile affectionately. "I didn't realize we were playing a guessing game."

"Hold out your hand and close your eyes."

I did what I was told. He stepped forward with a giggle and grabbed my hand. I could feel his small, warm hand encompass my fingers. He set a cold piece of *something* in my palm and curled my fingers around it gently, then wrapped his arms around my waist and hugged me. I opened my eyes, still smiling and returned the hug, then opened my hand.

"Oh, Elijah!" I gasped, staring down at the familiar trinket.

"You asked me to hold on to this, a very, very, very, very long time ago," he spoke barely above a whisper, looking up at me with his gleaming green eyes.

"I'd forgotten all about this," my voice trembled as I turned the silver and crystal talisman in my hand.

"I knew you'd want it back one day. I promised you I wouldn't lose it," he sighed. He looked saddened.

I looked at the beautiful, silver, filigree locket that was once the most important material possession I owned, and then looked at his beautiful face, his furrowed brows. He was sad to give it back to me. Maybe keeping it safe was an important task to him, one he wasn't ready to quit. Or maybe, by returning it to me, he realized that this was it. This was the end.

"On second thought, maybe you should hold on to it a while longer. I may need it a few years from now," I said with a grin.

His face lit up like a Christmas tree. "I'll keep it safe, I promise!"

I wrapped my arms around his shoulders as he rested his head against my sternum. I felt his head turn as he pulled back slightly, staring at my core. I looked at him curiously. He looked concerned, or as if he was concentrating.

"What's wrong?" I asked.

"Shh…" he replied and pressed his ear to my stomach.

I felt my stomach rumble, and we both laughed. He placed his hands on the sides of my stomach, "You need to eat."

"I'm not that hungry."

"Nonsense, you have no choice in the matter, Aunt Eden," he said, shaking his head.

I placed my hands on my hips and stared at the hardheaded child standing in front of me. He was very much like his mother, just as he was his father. "I will. Let me get these things to the dog, and I'll go grab a snack."

"No, please. Allow me to go visit him. I'll make sure he's set up nicely. You should go in and eat, right away," he argued.

"Okay, just be careful. He doesn't know you."

"He'll be fine with me!" Elijah shouted, shoving the talisman back into his pocket and running towards the fenced in section of the grounds, with Azrael's food under one arm.

I chuckled lightly and shook my head as I watched him scamper off. I felt my stomach rumble again and suddenly felt very ill. My breathing increased and I was suddenly nauseated. I ran to the edge of the street and leaned down, vomiting into the drainage ditch.

"Oh, shit," I caught my breath and wiped my mouth.

CHAPTER THIRTY SEVEN
THE DINGLEBERRY FAIRY AND OTHER MYTHICAL BEASTS

We spent the night in Memphis, holed up in the synagogue. There were others that joined us, as Justin had predicted. We had a large, hearty meal and sat around discussing the predicament we were in. Everyone listened with open minds and kept their fears to themselves. All of our new comrades seemed reluctant to fight, other than Justin. He was easy to rile, easy to bait. I knew he was going to be a wonderful addition to our group. As for the others, they seemed more on the laid back, 'let's talk this out' wave. Unfortunately, that wave crashed against the cliffs thousands of years ago and left us without a Heavenly Father or a true home.

We all went to sleep relatively early and awoke the next morning, fully rested and chocked full of hope and energy. There was something magical about the tranquil temple. It filled my spirit with peace. It made me feel almost as close to God as I was before The Great Divide. The temple was a divine place, simplistic, yet very ornate and breathtakingly beautiful.

For the first time in I don't even know how long, I slept completely restfully. Well, for the most part. There were no shadows, no heckling from corpses. There were no ominous messages or warnings. There was silence, other than the cool autumn breeze's whistles from beyond the walls of our sanctuary. There were beautiful colors as the leaves spun and spiraled in the current of the air outside the windows.

As happy as I was to have such a good night's sleep, I had woken up quite a few times ill. I was also slightly troubled that I didn't get a chance to see Gabriel. I had questions. I wanted to speak to him about Elijah. I wondered why he hadn't mentioned the eternal boy to me before. He knew I didn't have *all* of my memories back. He *told* me that Elijah was *different*. Why didn't he just explain everything to me up front? It annoyed me greatly the more and more I thought about it.

After we had eaten a light breakfast we bade farewell to those of the congregation other than Thomas and Elijah, loaded up, and rolled out. We felt it was safer and more convenient to not add any more stragglers to our hectic wolf pack. More bodies, meant more people to have to watch out for and protect. It was more trouble than any of us were willing to undertake. Though it was rather difficult to tell them they weren't allowed to follow the sweet being they had dedicated their lives to protect, it was for the best. Justin took it exceptionally hard. We damn near had to have him restrained until we were far enough away to not worry about him jumping onto the back of a van, spy style.

It was now Saturday, October 18th and we were on our way back to Louisiana. We had 'borrowed' the van belonging to the synagogue to expand our convoy, rather than spend the money to rent a third van. We were trying to limit our expenses, since none of us were working at the moment and our resources were dwindling. It was getting just a little too confining to all be squished into two vans and two extra bodies just pushed us over the limit.

We felt it was best to keep Elijah in the van with me, Riley, Jonah and Paul. And of course, since Thomas has sworn to protect him at all costs, he was adamant about riding with us as well. As a group, we needed to discuss the future and our plans with the boy. Although everyone was curious about what we were up against, we were the ones that faced the burden of executing decisions and putting said plans into action.

About thirty minutes away from the synagogue, I turned around in my seat and smiled. I watched Elijah softly snoring and bobbing his head as he napped, rested against Thomas' chest. He was such a beautiful boy. Those green eyes were breathtaking. They were as vivid as Irish fields, lit by the midday sun. The dimples in his cheeks showed themselves as he grinned in his sleep. I was glad to see he was having a good dream. It was hard to find anything positive to think about in the last month or so. I'd imagine it was worse for him, as he was able to see the outcome before we even began to know our strategy. What a horrible burden to bear, for a child especially.

Thomas stared down at Elijah's soft face and gently ran his fingers though the angel's curly brown locks. He smiled as he watched the boy sleep. I could tell by his expressions, that he was a wonderful father figure for Elijah, even if the boy knew everything there was to know about life itself. Every child, even ancient, immortal ones need discipline, structure and stability in their life.

We were just outside of Hammond, about half an hour away from Baton Rouge. I spent the entire trip staring out of the window at the horrific scenes, checking on my companions in our van as well as the other two, and spent a lot of time on the phone with my family and friends. It seemed that in the week we had been gone, everything had gone to shit. There were fires speckling the roadsides randomly, bodies lying dead near the roads or hanging from signs. It was truly the Apocalypse and people were in a sheer state of panic. There was no need to hide our intentions any longer; the world was beginning to see the awful truth for themselves.

I was at least comforted to know that my family was smart enough to take my advice and unite in a single location. All of my brothers and their families were now gathered at our parents' home. This wasn't a permanent fix, but it gave me and Riley enough time to finish up our duties and head to Texas to meet them. I didn't find out until we had stopped in Mississippi that Riley had contacted his family and they had also gathered, and were safely tucked away in Michigan.

As we approached Hammond, my senses heightened. I was on full alert, aware of anything and everything happening around us. The sound of sirens filled the air, as well as the boom and hum of gun shots as we drove through the city. It seemed that the entire nation was now under Martial Law and the streets were flooded with panic and chaos. We still had a little less than two weeks to endure. At this rate, people will end up killing each other and themselves off before we even get the chance to try and save them. They were jumping off of buildings, off of bridges, ending their lives before they were murdered by the merciless *aliens* or killed by the unstoppable strand of flu that was sweeping the globe.

Between Hammond and Baton Rouge, the tree lines were thinning. Fire danced between the limbs, lacing the brush and shrubbery with flame licked leaves resembling thousands of candles on a cake. But this wasn't a celebration; this was a disaster, a catastrophe, a funeral pyre.

As we sped towards our home, I felt guilty pangs in my stomach as I viewed all the misery on the sides of the road. The stranded, the homeless, the despondent masses begging for us to stop. But we dared not, we had neither the time nor the room in the vans to stop and help them. The guilt ate at my core, making me nauseated and heartsick. It wasn't a choice that was easy to make, but it was one that had to be made. With the events unfolding as they were, we couldn't take the chance of someone commandeering our vehicles at gunpoint, despite our generosity. And we couldn't get involved with other people's struggles. We all had our own families, our own friends in our mind and in our hearts. These were the people that we had to help. These were the people that needed us most.

We were just outside of Denham Springs when traffic suddenly came to a complete standstill. People were honking and throwing their arms up in the air. Obscenities and rage electrified the stagnant air, as plumes of thick black smoke blew towards us from multiple directions. I tried to see around the large semi-truck that was in front of us, but was unable to peer around the large trailer.

"What the fuck is this?" Riley asked, smacking the steering wheel with his palms. There was no movement; the interstate had become a parking lot. "Someone needs to get out and look."

"Want me to go?" I asked.

"No. You don't need to move around and get all sick again. Last thing we need is you puking everywhere." he put the van in park and unbuckled his seatbelt.

"Whoa, no, no, no. You need to stay in and drive if traffic starts to move. I'll get out and check," Jonah said, unbuckling his seatbelt and climbing to the side door.

Paul grinned from the back and followed suit, "Yeah, I'll walk with him. Keep'em safe."

"Should we wake up Elijah and ask him what's up?" I asked, turning to Riley.

Riley shook his head, "I don't want to wake him."

"It's too late," a gentle voice said from the back seat.

I grinned at the angelic face. "Morning, sleepyhead!"

"Good afternoon, Aunt Eden," he replied with a yawn.

"So, Kiddo. Do you see anything? We're kind of in a pickle here," Riley asked, turning in his seat to see Elijah's expression.

"Hold on. I'll let you know." Elijah unbuckled his seatbelt and leaned between the two front seats. He held his hand out in front of him and closed his eyes. His head cocked to the right as he moved his hands side to side, concentrating. Suddenly he opened his eyes with a loud gasp, looking panicked, "Get them back in the van, quickly!" Elijah ordered, putting his hand on Riley's shoulder.

"What's wrong?" I asked.

"We don't have time, just get them!" he replied frantically.

Riley opened his door and stepped to the front of the van, searching for Jonah and Paul. He ran to the passenger side of the van and looked around the large truck ahead of us, then sprinted forward and began shouting for them to come back. I rolled down my window and opened my door, hiding behind it like a barrier. I watched nervously over the open window ledge as Riley, Jonah and Paul ran full pace back to the van. I was beginning to feel queasy again.

"Move, move, move!" Riley shouted, as he pushed me back in and closed my door.

Paul dove into the side door repeatedly shouting, "Oh, fuck!"

"Watch your fucking mouth around the kid!" Riley yelled at Paul as he threw himself into the driver's seat and yanked the large vehicle into gear.

"Uncle Riley, please get on the shoulder and get off the interstate as quickly as you're able. It's headed this way," Elijah ordered frantically pointing to the side of the road from his perch between the two front seats.

"I'll try," Riley replied as he cranked the wheel to the right.

"You have to, we don't have a choice!" Elijah responded.

I looked over at Riley, deep in concentration as he began to navigate us out of harm's way. "There's back roads that run from Denham Springs to Baton Rouge."

Elijah nodded adamantly, "Yes, take them. We have to get out of here, quickly."

"I'll call Brooke and tell her what's going on. She can tell the others," Jonah called from the back seat.

Riley continued to ride the shoulder, trying his best to avoid the many obstacles on the narrow stretch of road. There was a loud, grating sound as he ran the side of the van against the metal railing. We all covered our ears as we squeezed through the narrow pass until the shoulder widened again. Then Riley found a break in the guard rail away from the sloping interstate and drove off, through the grass, towards the empty feeder road. I looked behind us; the two other vans followed the same way. I looked ahead to the cause of all of the traffic.

In the distance, huge, towering flames rose as a column from the middle of the road. I couldn't see the cars or the passengers of the vehicles to know whether or not they had gotten out safely or if they had been casualties. I instantly wondered if this was the work of the pyromaniac, Pestilence.

"Oh, goddess..." Jonah choked out and covered his mouth.

"What?" I asked.

"So much death. So much pain." he shook his head as he rubbed his temples. I looked at Elijah's face, studying his expression. He looked sorrowful. He looked so sad. It made my heart ache to see such a beautiful face, so distraught.

"It'll be okay, sweetie," I told Elijah, reaching for him.

He climbed onto my lap, curled his legs in and buried his face in my chest. I unbuckled my seatbelt and wrapped it around us. He was weeping heavily into my shirt as I rubbed his back and rocked from side to side, attempting to comfort him.

"Was it Pestilence?" I asked, afraid to pain him more by my question.

"No," Elijah replied, his quivering voice was muffled and distorted by my chest.

"Was it another Horseman?"

"No," he answered, looking up into my eyes.

I stared into his teary green pools. He was so saddened, it was painful to see.

"The angels. They've done this," he sniffled.

We silently watched the events from the feeder road as we passed the trap set by the angels. It appeared that they had blown up a tanker truck, blocking all traffic from getting past that point. They moved forward, murdering everyone in their vehicles as they walked through the trapped prey. People didn't see them coming due to the smoke and flames.

I held Elijah's head firmly against my chest. I knew he could see the images in his mind, but I didn't want him to see it all with his eyes, as well. I rocked him as he cried and attempted to comfort him as we passed the murder and mayhem. Bodies lined the interstate, as people made a fruitless attempt to run from the flames and the murderous angels. We sped forward, ignoring all traffic lights and sliding around the little traffic that was still moving. Large signs were posted on streetlights and buildings, ordering an immediate evacuation of all residents.

As we approached the typically busy intersection, we saw the barricades and large military vehicles parked under the overpass. It was clear to me that they either had not heard of what was happening a few miles back on the interstate, or that they had chosen to not get involved, preferring the relative safety of their barricade.

"What the hell's happened?" Paul asked, staring out the window at the abandoned ghost town and the massive military outpost.

"I guess the Army is getting involved," I replied flatly.

Thomas finally spoke up, "They probably think its aliens, too. They're trying to neutralize the invasion."

"It seems so. I wonder when they're going to learn that their efforts are wasted," Riley stated as he swerved to avoid a car in the road.

"They always run in, guns blazing. They won't learn," I jeered.

Elijah peeked up from my chest and looked around. "Take this road to 190."

Riley quickly turned right, turning onto Range Avenue. A military Humvee roared to life from behind the barricade and quickly began gaining ground on our convoy. It went around the side of the two trailing vans and began inching up to Riley's window. He looked in his side mirror and laid his foot down on the gas pedal. "Hold on guys!" Riley shouted as he sped forward, ignoring a red light.

We sped through the intersection, barely avoiding hitting a camouflage transport truck filled with soldiers holding rifles in the back.

"Pull over!" someone shouted into a speaker from the Humvee.

"Not a fucking chance," Riley mumbled under his breath, speeding towards 190.

"Stop your vehicle now and pull over!" the soldier repeated.

I looked in Riley's direction nervously, "Should we just stop?"

"No," Elijah stated flatly.

"I'm not going to warn you again," the voice called over the speaker. "Use of deadly force in this area has been authorized!"

Riley flipped the Humvee the finger and rolled up his window as he turned sharply onto 190 westbound towards Baton Rouge. The Humvee slowed, then stopped as we accelerated away, as if it wasn't allowed to leave the vicinity. Riley sped down 190, swerving around abandoned cars and crossing into the oncoming lane where intersections were blocked by overturned vehicles or barricades.

I frowned out my window at the devastation. "This is insane. We've only been gone a week."

"Everything has been destroyed," Riley whispered, a tremble in his voice.

We hastily drove towards Baton Rouge, paying close attention to the road ahead of us and the sky above us. Riley hit 90 as we fled towards the city we once called home. Entering Baton Rouge city limits, the roads were much more cluttered. As Riley adjusted his speed to the increased obstacles we could see, there were still cars on the road, obviously evacuating or headed somewhere to find supplies before leaving. The streets were strewn with flaming, overturned vehicles, the occasional dead body, paper and trash flying in the light breeze like tumbleweeds.

"We're almost there!" Riley yelled, attempting to ease everyone's minds.

I stared out of the window at the demolished city. We turned onto Airline Highway and headed towards Bluebonnet Boulevard. It seemed that we were no longer being tailed by either the military or the angels. We were lucky to have made it into the city without being stopped and turned away, or even killed if that Humvee was serious. We needed to get to Mike and Lana. We wanted them to be safe, with us, but we also wanted our damned cats.

"Damn it!" Riley shouted, pounding the steering wheel with his fists.

"What's wrong?" I asked, turning to him.

He pointed ahead through the windshield, "Just look."

I followed his gesture. The part of Airline that we were approaching looked like it had a bomb dropped on it. Chunks of the road were missing, areas of the asphalt were peeled up like a layer of tape, twisted and mangled. The entire road was pocked and cratered, completely impassable.

Riley threw his hands up in fury. "You've got to be kidding me!"

"Well, I guess we're doing a little bit of off-roading." I sighed.

Riley turned the wheel sharply and revved the engine. We hit the curb hard, jolting us all forward as the van climbed onto the grass alongside the road. Riley straddled the curb as he drove on the grass and the small shoulder of the right hand lane. The ditches were deep along the highway. If we went too far over, we would roll the van or end up stuck. As he carefully traversed the destroyed road, I turned around, watching the rest of our caravan. They mimicked Riley's idea, straddling the curb for safety. We slowly made our way through the heaps of rubble as my stomach did summersaults with every jolt and bump, and were able to return the van to the road after a few hundred yards.

"Good job," Thomas said with a massive exhale of breath as we returned all four wheels to the road.

"I've had to do that to get the hell around cars when I had a call," Riley explained with a determined smile on his face.

"Bullshit. You only did that when the 'hot fresh donut' light was on," Paul mused in an attempt to break the tension.

Riley laughed, "Yeah, you're right."

I turned to look out the back window. All three of our vans had now safely made it back onto the road.

Riley glanced in my direction and quietly asked, "You sure you're feeling okay?"

"I'm fine, why?"

"You look a little 'under the weather'," he whispered, pointing to my pale skin.

"Yeah, I don't know. My stomach's just pissed off. It's probably all that jerky I ate," I replied with a light laugh.

"I hope you didn't catch the plague, talking to that asshole," he stated derisively.

"Bah, I highly doubt it."

We turned onto Bluebonnet Boulevard and sped towards our home. I was surprised to see as few vehicles and people as I had since we got into Baton Rouge. Granted, there were a ton of neon orange evacuation orders posted and the occasional military vehicle. But for the most part, we were left alone.

We were approaching I10 when we heard an extremely loud boom. The ground trembled, forcing Riley to slam on the brakes instinctively.

"What the hell was that?" Riley asked, looking from window to window.

"It was one of the chemical plants," Elijah replied, opening his eyes and putting his hands back down in his lap.

I shook my head in confusion, "There aren't any plants very close to us."

"It wasn't close by," Elijah clarified.

I gasped and covered my mouth at the implication. "Oh, shit. That had to be huge."

Elijah shook his head, sadly, "There no longer is a 'downtown' Baton Rouge."

"How far are we from your place?" Paul asked, leaning forward in the seat.

"Just a few more minutes," I replied.

Riley accelerated again and sped towards Summa Avenue, then turned the corner sharply. We passed by the hospital, flames billowed from the roof and windows. There weren't even sanctuaries left. There was nowhere to go and find help or shelter. As we pulled into our driveway, I was smacked in the face with reality and my stomach fell through my ass.

"Damn," I sighed quietly as I stepped out of the van.

"God damn it!" Riley screamed, pulling off his hat and scratching at his head.

We all stood, staring at the destruction. Our front gate was shattered into thousands of wooden splinters, blanketing the sidewalk. Just past the gate, our cement birdfeeder was tipped over on its side. The glass panel of the storm door was shattered and the front door had been kicked in.

We approached our home tentatively, Riley taking point. His handgun was loaded and cocked in front of him, with trigger happy bullets ready to find a new home in an intruder's cranium. Riley gave us hand signals, flagging some of us to go around the side of the house. Jeremiah pulled his own gun from his belt and released the safety with an imperceptible 'click'. He walked forward around the side of the house followed by Gabe, with a baseball bat and brass knuckles at the ready. I held onto Riley's belt, forming a human train. Melanie and Tori held onto my arms, nervously as we advanced. Paul and Thomas stood directly in front of Elijah, protecting him from anything coming from the front, while Corey and Erick guarded him from the back.

We all cautiously approached the house. Riley indicated silently for us to stay outside, while he went in and investigated. Jonah grabbed a backup gun from Paul and walked in with Riley. I watched through the broken windows as they passed from the living room into the spare room methodically, Riley's training impressive to watch.

"I'm scared," Paige whispered, wrapping her arm around Paul's.

Elijah smiled softly up to her. "We'll be okay."

Paul wrapped his arm around Paige's shoulder and pulled her close.

"Who the hell would've done this?" Melanie asked, surveying the damage.

"I'm guessing it was probably the angels. I'm sure they came here, looking for us," I replied as I glanced over my shoulder.

"Yes, it was. They were here looking for Eden," Elijah explained.

"This is such *bullshit!*" Lamar replied through his clenched teeth, stepping over the mangled front gate as he joined us in front of the house with Azrael in tow. Chuck was walking on Lamar's left side as they joined me, taking up defensive positions to protect me. I always felt safe around Lamar and Chuck. They were like brothers to me. I was thankful to know them and have them in my life, even if it wasn't going to be for much longer.

"It's all clear. You guys can come inside," Riley called, flagging us in.

We stepped through the rubble and tried to balance on the destroyed door as we entered what used to be our beautiful home.

"I'm so sorry, Edie." Brooke said, hugging me tightly from behind.

"It's okay. It's just material possessions. At least we're all safe," I replied with a sniffle. I lifted my glasses to the top of my head, resting them on my curly hair and wiped the heavy tears from my cheeks with another sniffle.

"Are you okay?" Chuck asked with a frown.

I was still taking it all in. "I'm fine, guys, really. It's just hard to see my home demolished."

"If there's anything I can do for you, let me know." Tori smiled sympathetically.

"Thanks. There's a few things I want to gather from here before we leave again," I said, looking around.

"If you need help, just let us know," Paul added.

"Thanks. I really appreciate your understanding," I sniffled, trying to regain composure.

"You guys need to see this!" Jeremiah shouted from our bedroom.

We all walked towards the bedroom, congregating at the door. My eyes were instantly drawn to the large wall across from the door. Written in what appeared to be blood was an eerie, spine tingling message, scrawled across the wall. There were random splatters and symbols surrounding the message.

Atone for your sins or suffer the same wrath as the human scum you travel with. We will find you. You will face us. Repent, traitors!

"Who the fuck are *they* calling *scum*?" Gabe sneered.

"Who the hell do they think they are, calling *us* traitors? We're not the ones that are murdering everyone we can get our hands on. We're not the ones threatening to kill our own!" Riley shouted, punching the doorjamb repeatedly.

Paul started laughing and threw his hands in the air, "This is bullshit."

"We have to get out of here. They knew you weren't here, so they must've known we'd come back here," Jonah interjected urgently.

"We must leave quickly!" Elijah agreed quietly.

"Let's get your stuff," Tori said, wrapping her arm around mine with a frown and gently nudging me into action.

"We need to go. Edie, grab what you need and we can get out of here. We'll find a quiet spot and hang low until we're able to get ahold of Mikie and Lana," Riley ordered.

"Okay. I'll try to make it fast," I replied, returning from my momentary distraction to the task at hand.

"Everyone use the bathrooms if you need to, raid the fridge and pantry for any food that might be useful. Grab towels, blankets, pillows, flashlights, batteries, knives or anything else that might come in handy. There should be some stuff still lying around from the prep work we did for the hurricane. We need to be out of here in 10. Understood?" Riley barked. Everyone nodded and split up.

I climbed across my bed and pushed the mattress aside. Wrinkles, the stuffed dog my dad had given me as a Valentine's Day present when I was seven years old, had been wedged between the mattress and the wall. I pulled it out and held it to my chest, squeezing it firmly. This stuffed animal was my most treasured material possession.

I walked to our ransacked closet, flipped on the light and searched for a backpack. I quickly found the green one I often used for overnight trips, unceremoniously dumped its contents onto the already messy floor and returned to the bed. I gently shoved Wrinkles into my bag and began flipping through drawers, searching for old pictures and mementos that were important parts of my life I would want to keep close. When I was finished with that, I went into our bathroom and gathered up my jewelry. I shoved everything into a small silk bag with a pull string and zipped it into the front pouch of the backpack. I next ran to the living room and gathered some of my journals, sketchbooks, and framed pictures of my family, to which I added small trinkets from my parents.

None of these were things I planned on keeping. These were things that I wanted my parents to have, when this was all said and done. I knew they were things they would cherish and remember me by, when my time on Earth had finally ended. I wasn't going to be here to give them grandchildren or share any more birthdays or holidays. But hopefully, if my plan was a success, they would be around to enjoy those events with the rest of my family, and these physical possessions would give them something to hold and treasure.

"Are you ready to go?" Riley asked from the sliding glass door.

"Yeah, I guess so."

He frowned, studying my expression. He wiped the fresh tears from my cheek and gave me a hug, squeezing me tightly. I laid my head on his chest and breathed in the smell of him. I was going to miss that. I was going to miss everything about him.

"We need to move. I know this is hard on you, but we don't want them to come back and find us here. There's no telling how big their hunting pack is," he reminded me gently. "I'm sorry."

"Don't be. I know you're right," I agreed with a single nod.

Riley clapped his hands loudly, "Let's go! Everyone outside! Back to the vans, we leave now!"

I laid my head on his shoulder as we stood by what *used* to be the front door and watched everyone file out of the remnants of our home. They all walked by us with armloads of useful things. Everyone had contributed to the search and provided us with more materials for our travels, wherever that may lead us.

"I got ahold of Mikie," Lamar said as he approached us.

"Awesome. Where are they?" Riley asked over my head.

"They went back to my place. I guess Lana's parents took off to hide with some other family members. Mikie said that he wanted to stay in Baton Rouge, since he knew we would come for them. She isn't comfortable here. He doesn't know if she's going to go with us or not. But, he said Turkey and Rufio are safe."

"That's great," I grinned, looking up from Riley's chest.

"I bet those boys miss their mommas," Riley mused jokingly.

Lamar punched Riley in the arm with his free hand.

"Ouch! Ha! Ha!" Riley chuckled and grabbed his arm.

"You're such an ass," Lamar shot with a smile.

"Alright, let's head to your place and get those guys. From there, we'll head out to Texas. It's only going to be about a two and a half hour trip, as long as there isn't any complications," Riley said.

"Okay, sounds good," I said as I disengaged our embrace.

Lamar, Riley and I walked towards the vans together. Riley and I turned around, looking at our destroyed home for the last time. We walked out of the yard and through the spot where our gate used to stand. My eyes began to well with tears again, but stopped short when Riley gently kissed my cheek and rubbed my back. I knew we shared the same sadness, the same pain. But we also shared the same hope. *We are going to save the Earth, no matter what the stakes are.*

We made it over to Lamar's apartment complex with relative ease, hurried through the gate and sped to his building. Riley, Lamar and I bolted up the stairs, then Lamar unlocked the door and we slipped inside. Time seemed to speed past us as we attempted to discuss the current events with Mike and Lana. She had decided that she wanted to be with her family. Mike, torn between his love and the friends he saw as family, opted to stay with her. It was a hard decision for him to make and the emotion penetrated the air. *Goodbye* was never fun to say, but even harder when you know it's your last. We were all going to miss them, but the decision was theirs to make.

With tear-filled eyes, we hurried downstairs towards the ground level. Rufio clung to me calmly as we descended the stairs and walked towards the van. I looked up at the sky and noticed why Riley had been so anxious to leave. There were green tinged clouds swirling in front of what appeared to be a red background. I swallowed loudly and held Rufio close to my chest as we sprinted towards the van. Everyone was standing outside, either staring at the sky, smoking, or on their cell phones. Azrael ran in circles, barking loudly as he chased Gabe and Chuck. Gabe stopped dead in his tracks and stared at us as we approached the van.

"What the hell is that?" Gabe asked, pointing to Turkey, in Lamar's arms.

"This is Turkey." Lamar grinned proudly.

"Holy shit, you weren't kidding! He's huge!" he mused.

I turned to Lamar, sticking my tongue out, "I told you."

"Wow, I thought you were exaggerating," Gabe was in awe. "If a cat can be that big, that means that everything else I've ever doubted must be true."

"Yep. The dingle berry fairy and other mythical beasts truly do exist," I mused.

Gabe laughed loudly and climbed into the van, coaxing Azrael to follow him.

"Where's Mikie?" Chuck asked.

I shook my head as I turned to him, "He's staying with Lana. They're going to stay with her family."

Chuck studied our expressions and I knew he felt the same pain we felt. We weren't just leaving a friend behind, we were leaving a brother.

Everyone piled into the vans and settled in for yet another drive. This time the trip would be relatively short, as long as nothing went wrong. I decided to drive, since I knew exactly how to get to my parent's house. The mood was very somber as we all thought about what we were leaving behind. We got onto the I10 bridge and began to pick up speed. From atop the bridge we could see what was left of our city. Downtown Baton Rouge was completely destroyed. The capital building barely stood, with chunks missing from its sides. Smoke filled the air, billowing from hundreds of spots. I cringed and focused on the road in front of me. I couldn't bear to see the city any longer.

I started to think of the trek ahead and some of the landmarks. I instantly remembered the miles of Atchafalaya Basin Bridge that we were going to have to cross. Granted without many cars on the road we would be able to traverse it relatively quickly. But if anything was wrong with the elevated roadway, we were totally boned. I opted not to share my worries with the others.

As we sped towards the Atchafalaya Basin, I glanced at Elijah in the rearview mirror. He had his legs curled up, lotus style, as he munched on pieces of beef jerky and tore small pieces off for the three animals that were harassing him. He giggled to himself as they took their pieces and ate them hastily. I was glad to see he was amused and not suffering from our trip. I looked up at the sky. The clouds continued to spin and swirl with an eerie green hue. They looked like the clouds that form right before a tornado touches down.

"Don't worry, Aunt Eden. We'll be fine," Elijah said from behind me around pieces of beef jerky.

I drove silently, checking my mirrors with paranoid frequency. I glanced in the rearview mirror again and saw Elijah resting his head on Thomas' arm. He was half asleep as he pet Rufio, who was asleep in his lap. I could hear his purr over the sounds of the van, the sounds of the road and music seeping out of Riley's headphones. Rufio, much like Elijah, was truly at peace. Content. Innocent. It was hard to focus on the road ahead of me after seeing the beautiful face in the rearview mirror. There was something so amazingly *magnetic* about that child.

Looking at Elijah, it was so hard to believe that he'd lived as long as he had. He'd seen everything that's happened throughout history, first hand. Though he was well educated and well trained in the ways of the world, he was still a child. He still carried that naïve air about him. He was absolutely wonderful. I focused my thoughts on him as I drove. I also thought about what Jonah had told me, when I had barely known him. I remembered him telling me that he saw children in my future. I felt a sudden sadness as I realized he was probably seeing Elijah, or my nieces and nephews. He said he knew I wanted a family of my own, that I wanted children. He was right. I wanted a child to love, unconditionally. What I didn't expect was to find a child, that *was* family and that I *did love unconditionally.*

Never, in any of my lifetimes, had I had a child of my own. There was something between Riley and me, a curse from God, perhaps, that prohibited us from conceiving. Maybe because of who I was to God, He didn't create me with all of the proper equipment.

While the thought of Elijah warmed my heart and forced me to smile instead of filling me with sadness, a new thought sprung to mind and the anxiety flooded back into my head. What if I couldn't protect him? What if I couldn't keep him safe? He was immortal, but so were the angels that we'd defeated. I can only hope that if we were found and they noticed he's an angel that he'd be spared. I could only hope that they'd allow him to return to Heaven, to his parents. I could only hope, that if we were found, it'd be by Gabriel, or as much as I *still* hate to say it, Lilith.

We had completely crossed the Atchafalaya unscathed before I even realized it. I was so relieved. It seemed that not only was Elijah a miracle to me, he was also a lucky charm! We'd managed to stay out of harm's way since he'd been with us. That *child* could be the single greatest thing to ever happen to my life. The more I thought about him, the more past memories flashed in my mind, reminding me of the bond that we'd shared throughout time.

As we approached Lafayette, visibility began to drop until I was having a hard time seeing the road ahead of us. There was thick smoke blanketing everything. The only light visible was flames as they demolished what was left of the city. I turned on the high beams in an attempt to see through the thick smoke, but that only made it more difficult to see. I slid over to the middle lane and slowed my speed. The smoke was creeping into the van through the ventilation. I pulled my shirt over my mouth and nose and turned off the air conditioning. Everyone in the van woke up, confused and coughing.

"Are we on fire?" Gabe asked, mid-cough.

"It's okay. It's not the van," I reassured them.

"Where are we?" Riley asked, rubbing his eyes.

"We're in what used to be Lafayette," I replied. I could see a bright light piercing through the smoke off to the right of us.

Riley saw it, and pointed while shouting, "Watch out!"

I sped up and got into the far left lane, swerving around a vehicle entering the interstate. "Shit, sorry! I couldn't tell what it was." I winced and apologized to no one in particular.

Riley turned around, handing a blanket to Elijah and commanded the boy to cover his mouth and nose. Elijah coughed loudly, grabbed the blanket and did as he was told.

I sped blindly westward through the smoke. It was so thick it hung in the air and stung my lungs like slivers of glass. After what seemed an eternity, the smoke began to thin, eventually clearing out entirely. I looked in the rearview mirror, waiting to see the other vans emerge from the smokescreen. Not only did I see the two vans, but I saw the large vehicle that had merged onto the interstate, scaring the shit out of me and Riley.

We continued hastily towards Texas, and were nearly halfway there without any major incidents. I was curious about Lafayette, but not enough to stop and investigate, or to search the internet. I wasn't sure if there had really been any survivors, it appeared that the entire city was on fire. I couldn't help but wonder if that was Pestilence's doing. Or should I say his horse's doing. I looked in my side mirrors and the rearview mirror with regularity, constantly on guard for danger while trying to maintain visual contact with the other vans in the convoy at all times. Though the people I cared most about were in our van, that didn't change a thing. I was concerned about all of our wellbeing since we were all in this journey together.

The further west we drove, the more traffic began to pick up again. We passed cars stuffed to the brim, and trucks with the beds full of people. It seemed there were quite a few large groups of people that had managed to escape the wrath, wherever they were from. It didn't make a difference. Every town, city and state was being destroyed, without mercy.

It was so hard for me to wrap my head around all of this. I was once so close with God. His thoughts were my thoughts. His love was my love. It was hard for me to think of Him turning His back on anything living. I couldn't comprehend how He was able to sit on His celestial throne while all of this murder and carnage took place on the same planet He called His best masterpiece. *His magnum opus.*

I continued to drive west. The land around us was desolate. The only life I had seen for miles was the friends and family of our convoy and the survivors that speckled the roads, on their own journeys to safety. It was almost 8pm, and we were about thirty minutes from my parents' place when we reached Lake Charles. I was very surprised to see as much movement in the city as I did.

There were dozens of vehicles on the roads, merging on the bridges, turning onto or off of the loop. I felt so relieved to see others out and about, safe. It gave me hope. Not a lot, but still. In these days, any spark of hope was welcomed and cherished. As much death and destruction as I'd seen, the thought that maybe, just maybe, we'd be able to save the world made me feel slightly relieved. Maybe we'd make a difference. Maybe we'd allow children to grow up, have children of their own and recall these tragic times as just a horrific part of history. Those thoughts gave me an infinitesimal bit of hope for the future of mankind.

We were now in the home stretch. My thoughts were several miles ahead of me. I became less worried and more excited. I was going to get to see my family, the center of my universe. We blazed through Calcasieu Parish, zooming past Sulphur, Vinton and the Toomey/Starks exits. My heart began to race as I saw the bridge over the Sabine River. I drove onto the bridge and let out a loud, content sigh as we got to the top of the bridge and saw it was fully intact. As we drove down the decline of the bridge, I was happy to see that the large metal star near the welcome center was still standing.

We approached the 16th Street exit and took the sharp turn onto Meeks Drive. I sped down the road, passed the shopping center and the church. I slowed down as I reached the cemetery. It was hard to believe that my grandpa's body was buried in there, yet he was actually alive and young again in Houston. I shook the thought from my mind and passed the park. As I instinctually turned on my blinker, a smile stretched across my face.

Home.

CHAPTER THIRTY EIGHT
HELLO, MY NAME IS:

_____

We pulled into my parent's driveway and parked as the two other vans parked in the street along the curb. Looking out of the front windshield, I could see the curtains pushed aside, with little faces peeking out. I laughed to myself and stepped out of the van. Riley opened his door, stepped out, and yawned loudly as he stretched.

Everyone began to get out and move around. I waited for Gabe to follow me out the side door, then heard the front door of the house open and turned to see half of my family, running full speed towards us. I wasn't sure if I was going to get trampled or hugged to death.

"Daddy!" Lily shouted as she ran from Sara's side towards Gabe, like a bolt of lightning.

I was happy. It was great to see smiling faces, after all of the bullshit we'd been through.

"There's my babies," my mom said, walking towards us with a smile that could have lit up the sky.

"Hey, Momma," I replied, hugging her tightly.

She held me close as she spoke into my hair, "I'm so glad you guys are here. I was so worried about you."

"I'm glad we're here, too." I pulled away long enough to smile at her, then laid my head on her shoulder. I heard the familiar sound of my dad clearing his throat inconspicuously. I peeked over my shoulder and laughed, broke free of my mom's grasp and ran towards my dad.

"Hey, Daddy!" I said cheerfully as I hugged him.

"Hey, pork chop!" he replied, kissing my cheek and squeezing me tightly. "How's everything going?"

"I was hoping you'd be able to tell me that when you got here. You have a lot of explaining to do," he replied, wrapping his arm around my shoulder and turning towards the large crowd of people awkwardly standing in his driveway.

"Elijah, come here a minute." I smiled, calling him over.

He looked up from the concrete bashfully and ran to my side. He wrapped his arms around my waist and buried his shy smile in my ribs.

"Mom, Dad, this is my nephew, Elijah," I explained.

"What? One of Riley's nephews?" my dad asked, confused.

"I'm guessing you haven't told Dad everything?" I asked my mom.

My mom shook her head, "This is news to me, as well!"

"No. My *soul twin*, Gabriel's son," I elaborated.

My dad waved a hand in the air dismissively, "Oh, you know I'm not into that science fiction horse shit. Speak to me in English!"

"We need to get inside," Riley cut in as he stared intently at the sky.

"You're right," I agreed, leading Elijah towards the front door.

"Let's go, guys! Everyone inside!" Riley ordered, waving his arms in the air like a flight attendant explaining where the exits were.

"Edie, you really do have a lot to explain," my mom said, putting her hands on her hips as she watched everyone filing out of the vans and heading towards her front door.

"Look. This was the biggest place I could think to meet up. Not to mention we probably won't be here long," I said as way of an apology, looking at the sky warily.

She sighed in that aggravated tone all mothers make, "Well, that isn't what I wanted to hear, either."

"I'm sorry. I wasn't trying to upset you."

"I know, honey. I just worry, you know that." she frowned and rubbed my back.

I nodded, "I know."

I was taken aback when I stepped through the door and saw the crowded den. I watched as my family, new friends and travel companions, trickled into the living room and squeezed against the walls. I saw my other brothers, Ross, Eli and Lucas standing in the corner, smiling at me. This was all so farfetched, so hard to believe. What else could I tell them, but the truth? The alternative was even more unbelievable. *Aliens? Come on.* The only thing I could do was be upfront and honest. I realized that there was probably going to be some mockery and general sarcasm, but I accepted it and knew it was all for the best. For *their* safety, they all needed to know what we were up against.

I spoke loudly to get everyone's attention, "I realize you are all probably very tired, very confused and very troubled by the events that are unfolding. But, I ask that you please listen to us. Please, take it to heart and trust us. What we're going to be saying, is nothing but the absolute truth," I began.

"Everyone, I'd like to introduce you to some of our friends," Riley introduced each of our earthly angels with a proper game show host style presentation. They in turn each nodded or waved politely as they were pointed out.

I picked up at the end of introductions, "Though everyone here is important and special to us, this group in particular is crucial. I know some of your religious views and I'm a bit cloudy on others'. But what we're here to explain is the truth, regardless of your beliefs."

Riley and I explained the current events to the best of our ability. We had now spread our message so many times, we were able to bounce off of each other like a well-choreographed duet. Though this was not a show I'd like to see.

"You, an angel? So, how the hell does that work? I was there the day you were born. You were born in Beaumont. You were *born an infant*, Eden Quinn McDowell," Eli said, confused.

"So, if God didn't create us, what happens when *we* die?" Ross asked.

Elijah stepped forward and began softly speaking. His angelic appearance and gentle voice quieted the room as everyone listened to his words, "You have the same moment of judgment. If you prove to be a soul worthy of His good graces, you are allowed into Heaven. You then *become* an angel, as most religions believe, in their own way. Those that prove to be unworthy, are discarded. The truly evil are claimed by the dark forces, long before they even have the opportunity to be judged."

My father had a look of displeasure on his face. "Wait a minute. So, you're saying that this is it? *This is the Apocalypse?*"

"Unfortunately, that's exactly what we mean," Riley confirmed.

"I know it's very hard to believe. It was difficult for all of us to accept. But it's the truth and unless we do something about it, this entire planet is going to be annihilated, leaving only a shell, if that," I explained.

Riley spoke up, "The military seems to be involved now. I don't think they understand how big of a mistake they're making. They're challenging God's army to a battle that they cannot win."

"So what do we do? Do we just lay down and surrender? Do we beg for forgiveness and allow ourselves to be murdered?" Lucas asked.

"No, we *fight!*" I replied, fists balled and in front of my face, imitating a boxer.

"But I thought you guys just said it was a battle we can't win?" Dad asked.

"No, Riley said it was a battle that the *military* can't win. *We* are a different story," I replied. "We have things that the military doesn't. We have trick cards in our pocket that could turn the entire war in our favor. We know things that no military leader could know. We aren't *just* humans. *We* are a force to be reckoned with!" I grinned. I knew what I had up my sleeve.

"Obviously, we can't all run off to fight. What do you expect for all of us to do?" Amber, Lucas' wife asked.

"Those that opt to stay out of the battle, or just can't do it, will need to remain in hiding. The children will need protection, shelter, food and aid," Riley explained.

"We aren't here to ask for people to join our ranks. We're here to make sure that you know the truth. To assure you that this danger is real and it's imminent, unless we step forward. We're here to protect you," Jonah added.

"Fia fusu?" Gabe asked in Samoan, looking at Lucas and Eli.

"Ioe! I'm in," Lucas said with a grin.

Amber looked at Lucas and shook her head.

"Ma oe?" Lucas asked turning to Eli.

"Ioe," Eli replied with a somber nod.

"Boys, speak English. Not everyone here speaks Samoan!" Dad lectured my brothers.

Eli and Lucas mumbled to each other and laughed.

"What did Gabe say?" Riley asked me, leaning over my shoulder.

"He asked if they wanted to fight. They both said yes," I clarified.

Riley nodded, "Oh, okay. Cool."

"Fa'afetai lava." I smiled at my brothers.

"Now what did you say?" Riley whispered to me, again.

"Thank you very much."

"I'm in as well," Ross said.

Dad began to pace back and forth. "This is all way too hard to believe. I'm not saying you're lying, it's just so... intense. So insane."

The room was buzzing loudly from everyone attempting to talk over each other.

Elijah gently tugged on Riley's shirt sleeve. "You need to call them tonight."

"Is something wrong? Is something going to happen?" Riley asked, kneeling down next to Elijah. Elijah grabbed Riley's hands and leaned in, whispering in his ear.

"Alright, we need to send some people out for food, now. We also need to start boarding up the windows and getting some bedding together. Everyone will need to stay together."

Elijah clarified to the room, "It's safe to go now. The Archangels will be passing through with Famine in the early morning. If we don't act soon, there will be no food to collect by then."

Riley gathered a group and got them ready to go scavenging for food. My mom and sisters-in-law helped prepare bedding for all of us while my dad and brothers began covering the windows and securing our shelter as much as possible.

"Be careful," I ordered as Riley stepped towards the front door.

"We will. Stay out of trouble."

"What? You think I'm gonna get grounded in the couple hours you'll be gone?" I laughed.

"I'd never doubt it with you." he chuckled as he stepped outside with his group.

Now that we were actually preparing for war, it was hard to believe. We'd spent the last week running across the nation, gathering our comrades. I wasn't sure if I was glad about having my family involved or not. That just meant more people I had to worry about. Perhaps I should've told them; ordered them; *forced* them to all just stay out of it.

Yeah, right. As hardheaded as my brothers are? My brothers have always shared an amazing bond. They'd stand by each other's side until their last breath. Granted, I didn't want to test that. But I understood that to have one brother with me, I was going to have them all. It was no wonder why they were my heroes, my role models. I had a wonderful family. I had wonderful friends. I had people in my life that I treasured so very much. I couldn't imagine life without them. I couldn't imagine *this world* without them. I was fighting for everyone, for all of humanity. But the majority of the fuel, the core of my motivational, internal fire, was my family.

I want to know that my wonderful nieces and nephews, my great nephews and niece, my cousins and their children, everyone, had a chance to live a full life. I knew that rebuilding would be difficult, but that's a small price to pay if we were able to save the Earth and its inhabitants from total annihilation. I love my family more than life itself. And for them, I'd give anything, including my life. I could rest peacefully, knowing that I died to save and protect those that I love. I knew it wasn't the option *they'd* prefer, but I'd do whatever it takes to preserve their lives.

I watched my nephews Kadence and Rendon run through the living room laughing as they chased Rufio and Azrael. They were both beautiful boys, or should I have said handsome. They had the most gorgeous skin tone, chicken nugget brown, as we all refer to it. Their dazzling white smiles appeared to glow against their beautiful skin. They're the sons of my Ponapean adopted brother Lucas and his stunning wife, Amber.

I walked into the game room and found the rest of the kids playing video games, coloring, or helping each other put a puzzle together. Ian and Lily were lying on the floor, swinging their feet in the air as they colored in some coloring books. Elijah sat in the corner smiling, silently watching the kids. He looked awkward. Though the kids appeared to be the same age, his maturity outweighed even mine.

Lily's beautiful blue eyes sparkled in the bright flashes from the TV screen. Her loose blonde curls sprung and bounced as she heavily scribbled on the page, with her tongue poking out of the corner of her mouth and her nose scrunched in concentration. She stopped coloring and looked at her masterpiece. She grinned at the page then looked up at me with a huge, gapped tooth smile.

I found myself laughing. "It's beautiful, Lily bug! Good job!" I praised her with a smile.

"Yeah, I know. It's for Daddy," she stated nonchalantly.

I laughed again as I walked back out of the room and downstairs, following a hallway to the room that was once my dad's office. It had now been converted into a makeshift shelter. There were blankets, pillows, inflatable mattresses, sleeping bags, couch cushions, and throw pillows sprawled across the floor in every possible direction and position.

"What'cha doing?" Bridget, Ross' wife asked me with a grin.

"I was just coming to see if you ladies needed some extra help," I replied as I surveyed the room.

"No, ma'am! We've got this under control. We have a couple of the guys upstairs grabbing mattresses and stuff."

I fell back onto the couch. "Oh, okay. Cool. I guess I'll just hide out in here for a few minutes and enjoy the peace." I watched the wonderful women of my family as they attempted to make each sleeping pallet comfortable. I know Bridget was concerned about Ross volunteering to fight with us. I didn't blame her; I didn't really want him to get involved. I was worried about all of my brothers.

Bridget is definitely the older sister I always wished I had. Granted, she was an in-law, but it didn't matter. She was still a sister to me. I knew I could talk to her about anything and everything. And I truly valued her opinions. She was a fantastic mother, wife, sister, grandmother and woman. I was so very lucky to have her in my life and I know for a fact that Ross would wholeheartedly agree with that.

My aunts, Karla and Kristi, are my mom's older sisters. They both have the ability to warm a room with their smiles. They're both able to calm me down, even in the scariest of times. All three of them, my mom included, look very similar, carrying the distinguishing traits of both of their parents. They all have crystal blue eyes, dark brown hair and beautiful smiles that instantly warm your heart. I was so thankful that my aunt Kristi, Karla and her husband, Robert, had come. I couldn't imagine the worry and sheer panic I would've felt, wondering if they were safe. They had arrived shortly before we had and jumped straight into assisting. Though my other aunts and uncles didn't come, I hoped they were in a safe place and wished them well.

I silently watched as my aunts set up the bedding, chatting like schoolgirls. Aunt Kristi is one of the most beautiful women I've seen in my life. Her sense of humor is unrivaled. Her charm and charisma are undeniable. She soon had the room laughing as she recounted stories since the last time the sisters had seen each other.

Aunt Karla has always been like a second mother to me. She was my mentor when I went to military school as a teen. She was always a supportive shoulder to lean on, had open ears and an open mind when I needed to talk. She'd always been able to make me see the big picture, looking beyond myself, or taking the time for myself when need be. She'd been a wonderful role model ever since I was old enough to remember her. She'd always been my fairy godmother, swooping in to save me whenever I needed rescuing. This time it was my turn to do the saving.

I sat up, yawned loudly and stretched, then rose from the couch. I knew the women were going to have to put the kids to bed and I didn't want to be a distraction. I needed to head back upstairs and make sure everyone was okay and offer my assistance to anyone who may need it. I was just so exhausted and ready to relax. As I was walking down the hallway, I passed Sara. She was carrying a fast asleep Aiden in her arms.

"Hey," she whispered with a smile, stopping on the same step I was on.

"Aww," I grinned and kissed his sweet face. *He* looked like an angel.

"I'm so glad to see you guys again," she whispered.

"I'm glad we all made it here."

"I gotta get this beast to bed." Sara smiled and continued down the hall with Aiden.

Once back upstairs I grabbed my hoodie off of the table and slid my arms into the sleeves, zipping it up. I called Azrael and waited for him to come to my side. I slid the glass door in the kitchen open and stepped out onto the back deck. I admired the night air as I pulled my pack of cigarettes from a pocket and lit one, watching Azrael yawn and stretch before eventually jumping off of the deck and running out into the dark backyard. I pulled my phone from my pants pocket. It was 12:27am and I still hadn't heard from Riley. Granted, they had only been gone a few hours and perhaps they were trying to be as quiet and stealthy as possible, but I still worried. I fought with my conscience as to whether or not I should call or text him. I really didn't want to draw attention to him, if they were being sneaky or in a tough situation. I hated not knowing what was going on. I knew I was just being overly paranoid, but with all of this shit going on, how could I *not* worry?

I sat down in one of the deck chairs and pulled my knees up into my chest. It was remarkably chilly, for being a Texan autumn. Long after I exhaled smoke, I could still see my breath. The question that piqued in my mind was, was it cold because of the season, or was there death in the air? It was hard to know for sure, knowing that the avenging Archangels would be passing through with Famine in the morning.

Did Elijah say what *time*? Technically, it's morning now. Could our party have been caught while they were out? Oh, God. I was once again caught in that horrible cycle of paranoia and concern. I scanned the backyard for my furry guardian. I couldn't see him out in the darkness. I started to feel extremely uneasy, like someone was watching me. I've always hated that feeling. The small hairs on the nape of my neck began to stand on end and my jaw clenched instinctively. There was *something* in the darkness.
Déjà vu.

I stood from my seat and flicked my cigarette out into the yard. I held my hand over my eyes, trying to block the porch light. I could see movement, but didn't hear any sound. My heart began to increase its tempo as I instantly remembered the gas station incident. I slowly backed towards the glass door.

"Azrael? Come here, boy!" I waited. There was no sound. No bark in reply. No rustling of leaves as he ran to the deck.

"Azrael! Come on!" I shouted, again. This time I felt more frantic.
What did I do?

"Come on, Mutt! Get up here, now!" I shouted. I heard the glass door slide behind me, startling me. I quickly turned to see my Uncle Robert. "Holy shit! You scared me half to death!" I grabbed my chest.

He laughed and stepped outside around me. "Just getting a smoke in?" he asked, pulling his pack of cigarettes from a jacket pocket.

"Um, yeah. I was. But, something's weird. I felt like something's out there and now Azrael isn't coming when I call him," I spoke low, attempting to warn him.

"He ran around the side. He went into the garage with your dad," he explained, exhaling loudly.

"Well, that's good, kind of…" I replied.

"Should we not be out here?" he asked quietly.

"I'm thinking not," I replied in a whisper, slowly backing towards the door.

He flicked his cigarette into the yard and slid the door open. He pushed me behind him, shoving me gently through the doorway. I stepped in backwards then grabbed his jacket, pulling him inside quickly. He slammed the glass door shut and locked it. We both backed away from the door, until we bumped into a counter and cabinets. We stared out through the glass doors until the motion activated patio light turned itself off. Moments later, there was a bright flash and pop as the motion lightbulb exploded. There was a flicker of light bouncing off of two small reflective surfaces. *Pupils.* I gasped and covered my mouth.

"Who the hell's out there?" he asked me, staring into the darkness.

"I'm not exactly sure, but I'm glad we made it inside before we found out," I replied, terrified.

"We need to get these doors covered and reinforced," he suggested.

"Yeah, we do." I caught myself on the edge of the counter as my head began to spin.

"Are you okay, Edie?" he asked, looking concerned.

I tried to catch my breath, "I think I'm gonna puke."

"Can I get you anything?"

"No, I'm fine. I've just been getting sick, and I'm just a little freaked out. I'm so glad you came out there with me. I was kind of frozen with fear."

"No problem, Kid. Sorry I scared you." he grinned awkwardly. "Alright, we should get in the garage and see if there's any plywood left big enough to cover the patio doors."

We stepped into the garage and were greeted by many exhausted, yet smiling faces. I noticed Azrael lying on the ground near the garage door. He was obviously on guard duty. Ross and our father were bantering back and forth as they cut the wood for the windows.

Looking at the two of them, it was uncanny how much they looked alike. Ross' hair had turned grey rather early in life, but it suited him perfectly. It made him look even more like our father, and more distinguished. They had the same sense of humor, the same cackle when they laughed, the same wit. Both of them had a way of joking with you, making fun of you where you didn't even catch it until hours later. By then they were long gone and you could only retort to yourself, 'son of a bitch!'

It was so wonderful to have my family by my side. Of course, I wished it was under better circumstances. But, if you were faced with the Apocalypse, you'd want to spend your last remaining days with your family, as well. I wanted to laugh with them. I wanted to tell them it was going to be "alright". I wanted to lie through my teeth. But alas, I'm a terrible liar.

Chapter Thirty Nine
Riley's True Calling

God only knows how long I sat at the window, staring out of the tiny slot between the plywood and the window frame. It must have been hours, but it felt more like days. How long had Riley and the others been gone? Honestly, I didn't know. I couldn't remember what time it was when Elijah told them to move. I couldn't remember what time we arrived. I couldn't even tell you what time it was right then, even if I was staring at a clock.

I sat motionless for hours, daring not to move lest I miss something. My mind had become so numb from worrying, sleep deprivation and questioning my plan. If I failed, the world would be gone. Well, not the planet, just the inhabitants. But the inhabitants were what made it what it was. I knew they weren't perfect. Nothing is. My eyes felt as heavy as the anchors of some great ship. Once again, I knew that bastard Sandman was to blame. If I ever saw him in an alleyway, I was gonna beat the crap out of him for years of torture and torment.

Come on, Riley. Come home.

Home. What home? Everything had been destroyed. We had no home left. Well, I suppose that wasn't true. If home is in fact where the heart is, then we did have a home… and it was there, at that place in that moment. I rested my head on my folded arms and continued to stare out of the tiny hole. I watched and waited, waited and watched. When would they be back? I wanted to call Riley so terribly bad. I wanted to know that they were safe, but by doing so I knew I could draw attention to them. I'd told myself that a hundred times, talking myself out of it every time I pulled my phone out of my pocket and stared at his number.

I can't risk it.

I wanted to sleep, but I didn't want to leave my spot on the couch. I couldn't drag myself away from my self-inflicted sentry duty. I wasn't sure what was happening to my body, but it hurt. My stomach felt like it was stuck on a spin cycle. I was sure I was more *sick of* throwing up than the actual sickness causing it. The more still I sat, the easier it was to handle.

The house was silent, other than the occasional cough, or the sound of something squeaking as someone shifted in their sleep. I was happy to know that everyone was able to rest, despite the circumstances. I glanced over at the other couches and saw Erick and Corey fast asleep. The dim light from the corner lamp bounced off of their peaceful faces and made me smile. They looked like children. That thought didn't ease my mind any more; it only made me realize how much they risked, how much they were throwing away to be with us. I was glad they had stayed behind, but I knew they wouldn't sit out every time.

I looked towards the door and stared at the rifle leaning against the frame. I didn't want to use it. I shouldn't be on watch. I don't think I could kill one of the angels. And why would a rifle be lying around with kids about? Desperate times call for desperate measures and we took all precautions that we could. But everyone needed to rest. I needed to watch for Riley. I needed to wait and know that he was safe.

"Aunt Eden?" Elijah's little voice carried across the room like a soft breeze, cutting into my thoughts.

I smiled as I turned to face the beautiful child, "Why aren't you asleep, honey?" I asked him.

"I keep having really bad visions. Why aren't you asleep?" he asked, crawling into my lap.

I ran my fingers through his hair as I held him. "Well, I'm a bit worried about Riley, Gabe and the others. I haven't heard from anyone yet."

He rested his head on my chest. "You'll see them soon. I promise. I'm unable to show you, I don't have my father's gift. But I can tell you they're safe and on their way back."

"Thank you," I looked down at the child, teary eyed, and kissed his forehead.

We laid on the couch together, silently waiting for Riley and the others to return. I hoped Elijah was right, I didn't see why he would lie to me. If there was anything to be concerned about, I'm sure he would've warned me. False hope was useless in this situation. He laid his head down on my chest and placed his left hand on my stomach. He had been laying there so still that I thought he had fallen asleep. I heard a slight giggle and looked down to see Elijah smiling and drawing on my stomach with his fingers.

"What're you laughing about?" I asked with a smile.

He sat up on my lap and smiled. He opened his mouth to speak and shut it quickly. I could tell there was something he wanted to say. Maybe he was afraid of my reaction. I stared at his soft face patiently, waiting for him to spill the beans.

"What is it, Elijah?" I repeated, trying to pinpoint his expression.

"Can I tell you something, without you panicking?" he asked timidly.

I laughed awkwardly, "Don't you already know how I'll react?"

"Yes, that's why I'm asking you beforehand. It's something you need to know. And when I tell you, you're going to go ballistic. I need you to know, upfront, that you should stay calm." Elijah climbed off my lap and pulled my hands, spinning me around to face him. I set my feet on the floor and stared at my spiritual nephew.

"Is it something that is going to change things? Is it something I'm going to be afraid of, or break my heart?" I questioned him nervously.

"It's something that is both frightening and miraculous. It's something that could turn this entire war in our favor," he explained, sitting down between my feet on the floor.

"What is it, Elijah?" I asked, taking in a deep breath anxiously.

"For the first time in your life, the first time since you were created, you're with child. Or should I say, *children*." Elijah smiled and placed his hands on my stomach.

"What?" I shouted, jumping to my feet.

I stumbled over my nephew, tripped and caught myself on the edge of the coffee table. In my panic I woke up Erick and Corey, who instantly sat up and started looking around. I froze, leaning over the coffee table attempting to catch my breath and balance.

He shook his head, brows creased with concern, "Aunt Edie, I asked you to stay calm. It's something you need to know. You need to be cautious, not only for yourself now. I tried to warn you."

"What's wrong, Edie?" Corey asked, jumping to his feet.

"It all makes sense now. I've been throwing up and I couldn't heal it away. I've been hungry. I've been emotional. How did I not see this coming? After years of training and knowing the signs of pregnancy. I'm a paramedic! I'm medically trained. How was I so blind?" I attempted to rationalize everything, but only wound up making myself feel stupid.

"What's going on?" Erick asked, confused.

Corey helped me stand up straight, "You're pregnant? Oh, shit. This is bad timing."

"I need to sit down," I replied dizzily. Erick ran to my other outstretched arm.

The two of them helped me back to the couch where I slumped back down. Erick grabbed a pillow and placed it behind my head.

"I can't believe this," I said taking the pillow from behind my head and covering my face.

"Aunt Eden, I told you. This is something that could turn the war in our favor. If God finds out, your plan will work. The only threat we face is keeping you safe. You can't fight." Elijah took both of my hands and placed them on my stomach, then pulled the pillow from my face and looked at me with a grin. He rested his head gently on my stomach and sighed. After a few moments, he sat back up, looking at me. Corey and Erick were still standing by the couch, speechless.

Elijah grinned, "Aunt Eden, I'd like to introduce you to Orion and Lucian."

"Oh… my God," I gasped as my head dropped back into peaceful oblivion.

I woke up in the beautiful field. The same field I had visited during my anesthesia induced coma. The same field where I had met with Seth, Flemming and Kenneth. The same field that was once my garden. It wasn't as magical as it was then, but over time everything loses its allure.

I sat up and cradled my head in my hands. I knew I wasn't just *asleep*, I had passed out. I could remember all the words Elijah had just said, and I didn't know how to react. I placed my hands on my stomach and began to cry.

"Why are you crying?" the beautifully familiar voice of my soul twin rang in the air.

I looked up, wiped my eyes and reached my hand out to my hovering brother. He landed and sat down next to me, taking my hand and pulling me to his chest as I sobbed uncontrollably. My cheek was cold and uncomfortable. I turned and looked at him again. He was wearing his armor. Not the shadow armor, not the manipulation of light. No, he was wearing his golden armor, geared for war. His cold breastplate was chiseled like a Greek god's. Muscles and ribs intricately shaped with a glowing crest in the center. His eyes were the soft, beautiful grey that I demanded God give him. I was so happy to see Gabriel. I was so happy to see him without his shell, without his hardened lifeless eyes, without his shadow skin. I was so happy to see my soul twin, in the flesh, as he was intended to be.

"Your son," I sniffled.

"What of him?" he asked, "Is he alright?"

I wiped my eyes, "Of course, he is. We're keeping him protected at all costs. He just told me that I'm pregnant with twins!" I sobbed.

His concern turned to joy. "Oh, don't cry! This is a gift! A gift you've never been given. This is the part of your life that has always been missing. You've created life for thousands and thousands of years, yet you never were able to create it in yourself," Gabriel attempted to comfort me.

"You know just as well as I do, that I've always wanted a child. Any other time, I'd be so elated that I wouldn't be able to breathe. But have you forgotten what times we're facing? Have you forgotten what's ahead of us?"

His face became serious again, "No, I haven't forgotten."

"I've finally been given the gift I've wanted my entire existence. And now, it's going to be taken away. I won't even get to see my sons." I began sobbing again.

"Your *sons*? I'm an uncle. I'm an uncle!" he shouted merrily.

"How can you be so excited? Gabriel, we're probably going to die. These children will never *be* born. I'll never have the chance to hold them in my arms. I'll never get to brush their hair out of their eyes, or walk hand in hand with them," I said between inhalations as the tears poured from my eyes.

"Do you *not* see the possibilities? This could be our saving grace. Your sons could, in fact, be the saviors of mankind without even knowing it," he grabbed my hands and lifted me to my feet.

"How so? Are you saying I'm carrying messiahs?" I asked, confused.

He chuckled softly. "No. Do you remember when you told me to have faith in you? You were so confident that your plan was going to work. You seem to have lost faith in yourself. This could be the greatest blessing. This could be exactly what was needed to end this war."

"Elijah said the same thing. But I don't understand." I looked to the sky, trying to compose myself and dry my eyes.

"You will. In due time." he smiled.

"So, what do we do now?" I asked.

"You continue as planned. Seth has been watching you. I sent him down this evening. He's awaiting Riley's return to discuss the calling of the army. Once that is set into motion, they will begin their descent. They'll be ready to wage war by morning."

"So that's who I saw in the backyard?" I asked.

"More than likely. He's been ordered to stay back, until he's able to communicate with Riley. He hasn't informed us of any others in the area."

"Elijah said there would be others in the morning. He said they'd arrive with

Famine," I relayed the words of son to father.

"My son is far more talented than I." he smiled inwardly with pride as the sun shined down on us like a ray sent directly from God, Himself.

"What do we do about the others? What do we do about Famine? If they find us, it's over. How do we prepare ourselves? How do we protect ourselves?" I questioned.

"By the time they reach your city, you'll have your army. If you remain in hiding, you should be safe. You'll find when they return that the city is barren. The angels and Famine will find nothing to destroy but the things left behind," Gabriel explained.

"Elijah warned us earlier to get food, before Famine arrived. Will our supplies be damaged?"

Gabriel looked to the sky and sighed heavily. I couldn't tell what he was thinking, or if he was receiving some sort of message. He looked troubled, deep in thought. I wished we were still as mentally in tune as we once were. It seemed that I had lost my touch, unlike him.

Gabriel finally nodded to himself and looked at me, "I'm going to come down early."

"Are you supposed to? You aren't blowing your horn now, are you?" I asked, panicked.

"There's no more time. The war is set to begin. Father has sent everyone out of the heavens," he explained. "I'll arrive early and redirect Famine. I'll try to get them all off of your trail."

"How will you do that?"

"I'll lie. Simple as that. I'll inform them that God has ordered them to move north." he grinned wickedly. He was proud of himself. I could see it in his eyes.

"Gabriel, you're brilliant! But will they buy it? Will they believe you? How will you avoid God's attention?" I continued to batter him with questions.

He laughed mischievously, "In case you've forgotten, God has turned away from the Earth. He's left it all up to Michael. I'm to bring the announcement and orders, when and if I feel they're needed. God won't know of this."

I began to laugh with him as I shook my head in disbelief. "Wow, you're bad. Well, in a good way."

"We have much in common, don't we?" He grinned and pulled me towards him, kissing my forehead. "Now, you must wake up. Riley is there. He already has heard the news from Elijah and he's in a bit of a fog. He's been sitting at your side, with his head resting on your stomach for the past ten minutes. I'm pretty sure he's catatonic."

"Oh, shit. Poor Riley!"

"Goodbye, Eden. I'll see you in the next few hours. I'll arrive as swiftly as I'm able." he kissed my cheek.

"Bye, Gabriel. Please be careful," I replied nervously.

"You do the same. Goodbye boys, I'll see you soon!" Gabriel had his hands on both sides of my stomach, talking directly into my bellybutton like a megaphone as I laughed at his foolishness.

Gabriel was right. When I opened my eyes, Riley was laying half on the couch, half on the floor, with his head resting on my stomach. I looked down at him, attempting to read his expression. His face was blank, completely void of all emotion.

"Riley, are you okay?" I asked with a slight chuckle.

He stared blankly, turning his face slowly towards me.

I smiled, "Hi."

"Shit," Riley frowned.

"It's not as bad as you think, Uncle Riley," Elijah said.

"Are you okay? Can I get you anything? Are you hungry? Oh, shit!" Riley babbled, obviously nervous.

"I'm fine," I replied, sitting up.

"Don't move," Riley ordered, trying to adjust my pillows.

"Riley, knock it off! I'm not going to give birth in the next 2 minutes!" I yelled, frustrated.

"I don't know what the hell I'm doing! Don't forget, I've *never* been a parent." he pulled his hat off as he visibly tried to calm himself.

"Well, we may not have to worry about it much longer." I frowned.

"Don't say that," Gabe finally spoke up.

I hadn't even seen him standing by the door behind me.

"It's true."

"No, it isn't!" Elijah shouted angrily.

"I'm sorry, Kiddo. I wasn't trying to upset you. I'm just worried. You know that." I grabbed his hands and pulled him onto my lap.

"I know you're scared. But you have to trust me." Elijah pouted. For once, he truly looked like a child instead of an immortal trapped in a ten year old body.

"We need to stop talking about all of this and get back to the important stuff," I attempted to change the subject.

"This is important. This is more relevant than you realize. Without these children, the world could be over and done with. With them in the picture, you may have that bargaining chip you and Gabriel talked about," Elijah explained.

"Bargaining chip?" Riley cocked his head to the side, confused.

I cradled my head in my hands, "I *really* don't think we should talk about this now."

"No, Eden. I think it's finally time," Jonah interjected.

I looked at him and narrowed my eyes. "Thanks, guys. I really appreciate it," I said sarcastically. I was pissed that they had even opened their mouths.

Paul sat down next to me, "Apparently, you have something to tell us."

"Not really, no." I grinned innocently.

Riley shook his head, "Bullshit. Speak up."

"Look, you need to call your army. Seth's here, somewhere, waiting to talk to you," I attempted to change the subject *again*.

"This is true, Uncle Riley. But it is beside the point. Aunt Eden, it's time you discuss your plan. They need to know what your strategy is. They need to know what's going on," Elijah continued to lecture me.

Paul laughed. "Shouldn't you be asleep? You're like, eight."

"I'm far older than you are. And I didn't ask for your input, Paul. I suggest you either keep your mouth shut and listen, or leave the room." Elijah folded his little arms across his chest.

"Ah, shit!" Riley laughed loudly. We all joined him, happy for a momentary break in the tension.

"You're alright, kid," Paul laughed and leaned back.

"Thank you. Now back to the point. Aunt Eden, they deserve to know the truth. Jonah and I are the only ones here that know what's in your mind," Elijah reminded me.

"Maybe we should have a little *angels* meeting. I don't think it's a good idea to include the others," I motioned towards Gabe and Lamar.

"Yeah, fuck you, too, Eden. We haven't been through hell with you or anything. I have just as much of a right to hear your 'plan' as anyone. Seriously, we're *blood. Aiga*, remember? Family. I've been with you for all 30 years of your life. Yeah, so I haven't known you since you were an angel, but I've been your brother through this life. The life that's taking place now. The life that's threatened, for fuck's sake." Gabe shook his head, furious at my statement. I couldn't blame him.

"I agree. I haven't sided with you since the beginning just to have you leave me out now," Lamar added somberly.

I bit my lip, anxiously. "Fine!" I took in a deep breath and sat up straight, "You guys might want to sit down."

I waited until everyone was seated around me like a depressing, bad tidings campfire. I stared from face to face. All of my companions were here and awaiting my words when a knock came from the front door.

Elijah looked from Riley's face to my own, "I suppose this isn't the proper time after all. Perhaps it would be best to discuss this with Mother and Father present. They're here."

I sighed with relief.

Thank you, Gabriel. You saved my ass yet again.

There was a second knock on the door, this time much louder, much more urgent. Paul walked to the front door and peeked through the peephole. He snickered and pretended to slick his hair back, across his shaven head, then opened the door with a smile and leaned against the doorjamb seductively, "Hey, sexy. Miss me? It's okay. I missed you, too."

"I suggest you bite your tongue unless you want your fat little jaw removed," Lilith replied, pushing him aside and stepping inside.

"That's kinky! I *love* the feisty ones!" Paul grinned and rubbed his hands together, as if he had just been given an enticing invitation.

"Mother!" Elijah ran to her, wrapping his arms around her waist.

"Hello, Elijah," she smiled warmly and hugged her son. "Eden," she nodded.

"What brings you here?" Riley asked, leaning back against the arm of the couch.

"Can't a mother visit her son? Do I have to have a reason to be here?" she asked.

Riley shrugged, "Well, no. I was just curious. I wasn't sure if you had a message."

"No, that would be Gabriel's job. Seth is awaiting his arrival, then we can begin," Lilith explained. "I'm just here to help strategize."

I grinned at Lilith, "It's nice to see you again."

"Oddly enough, I have to agree. Elijah has informed me that we now have something even more so in common. Congratulations!" she smirked.

"I wish I could say 'thank you', honestly. However I'm concerned about the outcome." I placed my hands on my stomach.

"We will not allow any harm to come to either of them, nor you," Lilith spoke sincerely.

It was a side of her I had never seen. I suppose it was the mother in her. I suddenly felt horrible for my animosity. I had always held it against her that she had allowed Elijah to remain on Earth, motherless, while she was in Heaven. Then I realized that he wasn't motherless. She was there for him when she was able, but she had also sacrificed more than I had realized.

Elijah and Lilith both knew what he needed to do now. But they knew it then, thousands of years ago, as well. It was for that reason that Lilith reluctantly severed her heavenly tie to her only son, and placed him in the care of her only brother. I wished I had realized it much earlier, instead of hating her every lifetime for something I didn't understand, for something I didn't even remember. Of all of us involved, *she* had made the biggest sacrifice.

I watched silently as she sat on the floor with Elijah, sharing stories and adventures with him. He giggled like the child he appeared to be, enthralled by the vivid, enthusiastic theatrics of his mother. I smiled and chuckled to myself, as I watched his eyes glow with admiration towards her and returned with her stare of adoration towards him. They were in their own world.

Just then, I heard multiple sets of wings flapping outside the window. I peeked through my sentry hole and instantly felt my shoulders slump, relaxed. Elijah's face lit up instantly. He knew just as well as I did that his father had arrived, and with him a group of gold and white clad angels and Valkyrie.

"Father!" Elijah darted for the front door.

I got up from the couch and walked to the door to greet my brother. As he approached us, he removed his helmet and smiled brightly. He reached down, grabbing his son's face and kissed his forehead. He then walked to me, kissed my cheek and leaned down to greet his nephews once more.

"Good morning, Orion! Good morning, Lucian!" he shouted to my stomach with a chuckle.

I grinned, "Well, between you and Elijah, you saved me the trouble of coming up with names."

Elijah beamed at my side, "Those were the names you were going to pick out, regardless. And yes, I did save you the time. You were going to ponder it for many months to come."

I looked around the crowd of familiar faces standing behind Gabriel. They had all taken off their helmets or hoods and stood totally exposed to prying eyes. Flemming and Seth nervously scanned the horizon, watching for any threats. They were not only warriors, they were skilled hunters, with vision sharper than eagles.

"Please, come inside." I smiled, pointing towards the front door. We all walked inside together and crowded into the den.

"It's wonderful to see you once more, Eden," Callin said, hugging me tightly.

"The pleasure's all mine, I assure you. I've missed your beautiful face."

"The feeling is mutual." she chuckled lightly. Her voice was so melodic.

"Where's Emily?" I asked.

"She's preparing the Valkyrie. We didn't wish to draw any extra attention to ourselves, so we brought only a few, until we had Thaddeus' orders," Callin explained.

Flemming came in from watching the skies and approached me, "Hello again, Eden."

"Hey, how are you?" I asked politely.

"Fair. Much better now that we're in your company."

"Meridith!" I shouted, brushing past Flemming as I caught sight of her.

"Hello, Eden!" she chuckled, catching me before I tackled her.

"I've missed you!" I couldn't stop smiling. This was like a spiritual family reunion. All of their names and faces came back to me, in a flood of memories. I looked around the room, amazed. I hoped that my family would sleep through our commotion and allow us to speak freely without having to alter our conversation. I didn't want them to worry any more than they already were. If they heard my plan, they'd try anything in the world to stop me, and I knew I no longer had a choice. It was going to be forced out of me at our little powwow.

Gabriel's voice cut through the room, interrupting the light banter that comes from long awaited reunions, "Friends, loved ones, comrades. This is the time that we must stand together, united with a common goal, a common purpose. We must ready the shields and sharpen the swords. The horns of war will blow sooner than you'd expect. I can no longer fend off the onslaught alone." Gabriel bowed to Riley. "Now, without further ado, I'd like to reintroduce my brother-in-law, brother in battle, and hero."

As he spoke, Corey and Brooke stared in awe at Gabriel. I knew the feeling. My soul twin was an amazing being. Having my memory back and remembering his creation, I was still impressed to see him command a room. I could only imagine what it must be like to be witnessing his presence in this form for the first time.

Jeremiah, Seth, Paul, Brandon and Jonah clapped loudly. I winced nervously, worried the commotion would wake my parents.

Riley chuckled awkwardly as he gazed across the room. "Um, hello. Uh, I wish I knew what to tell you guys, exactly. I realize the *past me* had been baptized in battle and thoroughly knew what the hell he, *I*, was doing. But, I might need a bit of a refresher course."

"Well, I'm sure your memory will be refreshed soon. We don't have much time," Gabriel urged.

"Well, then. I uh, I guess... wow. Where to begin?"

"What are your orders, *Captain?*" Jeremiah smiled, waiting for the words.

Gabriel and I stared at Riley's face. It was in that moment that we finally had our mental link returned.

He's nervous, he doesn't remember how to lead this big of an army.

It's been years, we have to cut him some slack.

You have to show him some of his past.

We, have to show him his past.

"Riley, come with me a moment, please. Elijah, you as well." Gabriel motioned towards the kitchen, then taking Elijah's and my hands in each of his own.

"If you'll excuse us for a few minutes, we'll continue shortly." Gabriel smiled politely.

Riley followed the three of us into the kitchen. We all sat down at the kitchen table, Riley and I side by side, across from Gabriel and Elijah. I was nervous, but I knew what was to come. Gabriel held out his hands, offering one to Riley and one to Elijah. I grabbed Riley's free hand and stretched across the table to reach Elijah's little hand, completing the circle.

"Now, between the four of us, we're going to take a bit of a journey throughout time. I realize it's going to be hard to focus, as most of what you see will be flashes. But I've shown you some of your past before, Riley, and you had no adverse reactions. Elijah will be able to use me to show you glimpses of the future. With that being said, please close your eyes, relax, breathe slowly and deeply," Gabriel explained in a calm soothing voice.

Riley squeezed my hand tightly. I could feel his anxiety. He only had one fear in the world. He didn't fear death, demon, or even God. He laughed in the face of challengers. He was only afraid to risk my life, and now, the lives of our unborn boys.

I squeezed his hand in return, as a silent "I'm here".

I gasped as I felt the atmosphere change. The air rapidly swept through my lungs as images flashed and skittered through my mind. It was impossible to focus. It was like we were sitting in the center of a tornado. I glanced to my side and saw Riley staring upwards, intently. I slowed my breathing and turned my eyes towards the heavens. As my inhalations slowed, so too, did the visions. I saw pieces of my past interwoven with Riley's. I watched as I prepared his armor for previous battles. I watched as he rallied the troops, shouting war chants and fueling their inner fires. He was a natural leader, an amazing being. This really was Riley's true calling.

I don't know how long we sat at the table, watching Riley's vivid past and our bleak, yet hopeful future. But as we sat, Elijah shared pieces of the future, including the role he would play, the importance of my plan, and the likelihood that it would all play out accordingly. When we finished our little journey through time, the four of us sat silently, looking at each other as we all took in the reality. I could see the cogs turning in Riley's mind, as a smirk slowly stretched across his beautiful face.

"Now I know why I picked you. You're brilliant, Eden Quinn!" Riley smiled and kissed me.

"So, you agree to it?" I asked nervously.

"If anything will work, that will," he reassured me.

"But you do realize the risks, what we may have to give up?" I questioned.

He nodded, "If it spares the lives of everyone else, it'll be well worth it. We all know they'd say the same thing, as well."

Elijah grinned, "I agree."

"And you, little one. Holy crap! You're very crucial to this. I hope your visions are correct. Though some of them are very troubling," Riley looked down at the immortal child.

"Yes, well. It isn't a guarantee. It's possible that we can position them elsewhere, saving them from the encounter entirely. I knew that wasn't something you'd be happy to see. It came in my dreams and broke my heart." Elijah frowned, then buried his face in Gabriel's shoulder as his father stroked his hair.

"Well, we both know, not all is lost," Gabriel said, pulling his son's face from his shoulder and cupping it in both of his palms, reassuring him with a look. His son nodded and looked to Riley.

Gabriel grinned and nodded towards the crowd of people squeezed into the living room. "Well sir, it's about that time."

I looked into the crowded room, Tori and the ladies from our caravan were now in there, as well. I drew in a deep breath to steel my resolve, stood up from my seat and offered Riley my hand. He stood without my help, straightened his backwards hat and popped his neck. I could tell he meant business.

"Let's go, kids. We're wasting time," Riley ordered.

Gabriel and I smiled at each other and followed Riley into the den. He stepped in and cleared his throat. Everyone turned to hear what he had to say. We all waited, silently, for the orders we expected to receive.

"Alright, here's how this is going to go. We have limited time and even less resources at the moment. My group and I have scoured the city for as much food as we could gather. Seeing as how the *heavenly* angels don't need food for sustenance, it will be much easier on our reserve."

He stepped towards the coffee table and pushed everything on its surface aside, then grabbed a notepad off of my dad's stack of paper and a pink highlighter. He returned to the coffee table and began drawing out plans like a football play.

Paul tried to restrain his laughter, "Nice highlighter, Riley. It matches your purse."

"Shut up, ass. It's the only one I could find," Riley shot back with a grin.

He continued drawing out his ideas. "Okay, Seth. As soon as we're done here, I need you to return to the others. I'm officially calling you *all* down. Bring on the army. Callin and Lilith, with your permission I'd like to start having the Valkyrie arrive and position themselves. We originally thought we'd be headed elsewhere for this war. Little did we know, this war was coming to us."

"Whoa, whoa, whoa. Are you serious? The battle for the Earth is going to happen in Orange, Texas? Not Rome, or New York, or London... Tokyo. Orange?

Orange, Texas?" Gabe asked, baffled, then laughed hysterically at the irony.

Gabriel silenced Gabe with a look. "Had we gone to Rome, or London or wherever else you just said, then yes, we'd be fighting there. But the fight comes here, because we are here. The angels have assembled and they have no choice. We have no time left to move."

Riley continued, "Now, we're limited on firearms and ammunition. We're going to have to be very selective of how they're used. We'll either leave them in the hands of people trained to use them, or we'll have to divvy them out another way."

Jeremiah leaned forward, "I could teach some people how to use them."

"We may need you to do that." I nodded to him.

"That would be a waste of invaluable ammunition." Riley held up his hand.

"It's worth the sacrifice," Jeremiah retorted.

Seth interjected, "Thaddeus, I'm sorry... *Riley*, all angels will be given armor, proper equipment to protect themselves and weapons. We've been gathering enough for you. I'm sorry we're unable to provide these for the humans, they would be unable to use it, regardless."

Lamar frowned, "Well, that sucks."

Callin smiled at Lamar, "Don't worry, we will fully protect you, ourselves." I watched as their eyes connected, longer than I would've expected.
Holy shit, go Lamar!

"Well, I guess that leaves manmade weaponry for the humans and possibly a few to spare for those of us trained to use them. I'm not sure what exactly you have in your arsenal Callin and Lilith, but I assume you don't plan on doing much fighting?" Riley questioned.

"We will do whatever has to be done, to keep you all safe. Our number one concern at this point is allowing Eden to remain unscathed long enough to talk directly with God. As my son will be helping in this portion, I will more than likely be leaving the mortal plane to accompany him and assure his safety," Lilith replied gracefully, looking to Elijah.

"Eden's gonna be talking to God?" Paul asked, turning his gaze to me suspiciously.

Gabriel waved his hand for silence. "We'll discuss her plan in a minute."

"Is there anything I can do?" Corey asked.

Riley spoke up, "You will all have your part to play, whether that's fighting on the battlefield, triaging and moving the wounded, supplying food and drinks or protecting the others."

"So, when does this all begin? What kind of timetable are we looking at here?" Chuck asked.

Riley looked to Elijah and smiled. "That's your field of expertise."

"It's 6:32am, currently. My father has successfully diverted Famine and the others, so we don't have to worry about their approach, which would've taken place shortly after 10am," Elijah rambled on with his forecast of the future.

Lilith chuckled, interrupting him. "I think they were wondering more about the war, Elijah."

"Oh, I'm sorry. I knew what Aunt Eden and Miss Melanie were thinking. Forgive me. Once the army arrives, which will be in about two hours, Michael will notice the loss of angels and dispatch a scouting party to locate the others," Elijah explained.

"Will they find us here?" Tori asked.

"Yes, but they will not make it back to Michael to report their findings. Once Michael realizes he's losing more of his army to ours, or because of ours, he will send down his true wrath and all hell will break loose," Elijah continued.

"Elijah! Watch your mouth!" Lilith snapped.

"Sorry, Mother."

I chuckled and covered my mouth, nonchalantly coughing, as Gabriel elbowed my arm and winked.

Riley met the eyes of every person in the group, "Now, we need to get moving. So before we split up and everyone receives their individual orders, we'll allow Eden to divulge her sinister plan."

"It's not sinister!" I replied defensively.

"Go ahead, Edie. We're all *dying* to know," Gabe said mockingly.

I frowned at his choice of words. "Unfortunately... *you are*."

I had been dreading this moment since I came up with my decision. Sharing it with the rest of our group was going to be one of the hardest conversations I had ever been involved in. How could I tell everyone that I was going to make a major sacrifice; one that would remove me from everyone's lives? It was heart wrenching. But it had to be done.

CHAPTER FORTY
BATTLE CHANTS AND THE DRUMS OF WAR

The morning went exactly as Elijah had predicted. It wasn't long after everyone's arrival that the sun began to rise, and as it did, it glistened and glimmered off of the golden armor of the now descending angels, coming to join our ranks. We all watched in awe as twenty or so angels and Valkyrie landed and got on bended knee to Riley. It was absolutely breathtaking, and rather humbling in its austerity.

There were familiar faces mixed in with new ones. Of course, there were angels I hadn't met before The Great Divide; that I had only seen during their creation. But over the thousands of years that I had been stranded on the Earth, millions more had joined the ranks, as God allowed humans into His fold. I couldn't help but wonder how many of the angels I knew had chosen to work with us. The small group that had descended was merely the first wave. They were sent to secure our location, begin the training and strategy planning preemptively.

Within two hours of the angels' arrival, the members of my family and some of the others that had fallen asleep began to wake up and shamble outside. As introductions were made and welcomes given, we began gearing up and preparing ourselves, the best that we could, for the action to come. In the backyard, Jeremiah was instructing how to load and operate some of the guns we had in stock. Riley was in the driveway, talking to the angels about his strategy and placement of our troops. I had pulled a few aside that I felt would work best with me.

I was informed earlier by Gabriel, Riley and Elijah, that I was not allowed to fight. I would be staged for healing the wounded, with my own protection and a fleet of flying friends to transport the wounded to me. I knew it was going to be difficult. I knew I would have a hard time focusing. Not to mention, I had the nagging fear in my mind that I may not be able to heal just anyone.
What if I can only heal angels?

The more I thought about my abilities, the more I actually found humor in my life. Since I was old enough to think for myself, I've always wanted to be a doctor, or a nurse, or someone who saved lives. Before I had even gotten into emergency medicine, I played online role playing video games, and always chose the healers. Then, I find out that it's actually an ability I was able to perform, without the need of bandages, medication or needles.

The fear continued to nag my conscience. I needed to find out if I was able to heal humans. I needed to know, before they were depending on me. If this war was going to be anything like the World Wars, or any other throughout history, the wounded would be carted to me nonstop. And to think, we're maybe one hundred strong, verses God only knows how many.
I need a couple of guinea pigs.

I walked through the kitchen and out into the garage, but there wasn't anyone around. Next, I stepped out front and saw Riley speaking to a large crowd of people, angels and the majestic Valkyrie. Though they were angels themselves, the Valkyrie were far beyond something so easily defined as an angel. They were a group of women whose sole purpose was to retrieve the fallen souls. They were known as the deliverers of death, the handmaidens of Odin, a bad omen. No, they were beautiful, silver and white clad women, with enormous, brightly radiating snow white wings. Death was the Horseman, not the Valkyrie. And I hoped I wouldn't see him in this battle.

I didn't want to disturb Riley, or anyone involved in their discussion. I noticed my dad standing by Riley with his hand on his chin, deep in thought. I could tell he was blown away by all of this. I walked around the side of the house and headed towards the back. Jeremiah was explaining the proper handling techniques and etiquette when using a firearm. I was so thankful that he had joined us and was just as dedicated to the success of our side. He was one of the first to agree with my plan and because of that we had both felt a new bond we never had before. To me, he was my husband's best friend. And to him, I was his best friend's wife. Though we got along perfectly well beforehand, minus a few jabs here and there, we now shared a common goal.

"Hey, Jere, I'm sorry to interrupt, but can I ask a favor?" I spoke up as soon as there was a pause in his teaching.

"Yeah, of course, Edie. What's up?" he asked, dismissing himself from his pupils and coming over to where I stood.

"I was hoping I could borrow a volunteer or two."

"Sure, I can come help. They can wait a few," Jeremiah replied.

"No, I need a human. I need someone who's willing to deal with a little pain to try an experiment." I scratched at my head nervously.

"I can help." Chuck nodded.

"Yup," Lamar agreed.

"Yeah, me too!" Corey stood up.

"We all can, if you need us to, Edie," Erick added.

Gabe winked with a slight smile. "You're not testing shit on me."

I looked at the volunteers. "Lamar, you've been through enough with me. Corey and Chuck, if you really don't mind, come with me please."

Chuck grinned, "Sure thing."

The two followed me back around the side of the house and in through the garage door. We stepped into the kitchen, where I pulled two chairs out from the table for my test subjects and walked over to the stove, pulled a few paper towels from the holder and returned to the table. I divided the paper towels into two stacks then folded them in half, setting them in front of Corey and Chuck.

"Um, are we having an eating contest?" Corey grinned.

Chuck smirked, "Are we making macaroni art?"

"Nope. Much more painful." I looked at each of them with a mischievous smile.

"Hmm, more painful than making macaroni art… we're playing bingo?" Corey continued to question me.

I walked into the den and grabbed my backpack, then returned and set it on the table across from my two victims. I opened the front compartment and rifled through its contents, pulling out a few alcohol prep pads and two scalpels.

"Whoa, what're you doing with those?" Corey asked nervously.

"I wanted to make very small cuts, and see if I'm able to heal you," I explained timidly.

Chuck looked confused, "But you know you can heal people, why do you need to test it all of sudden? I've seen Riley and Jeremiah's backs."

"I'm concerned I may not be able to heal *humans*. I want to test this before we go into battle. Seeing as how I'm a trained paramedic, if I can't heal you directly with my hands, I'll know that I'll need my supplies and will handle the humans as I would under normal circumstances."

"Have anything smaller?" Corey asked. I could tell he wasn't a fan of the scalpels.

"Fine. Yeah, we can try it with lancets. It'll be a tiny hole, but it should give us a definitive answer either way," I replied, placing the scalpels back into my backpack and removing two lancets.

"Oh, yeah. That's much less terrifying." Chuck nodded nervously.

I ignored the sarcastic remark, "Good. Now, both of you wipe a finger down with these alcohol pads and let me know when they're dry."

I watched as they both cleaned their index fingers and waved them in the air. Chuck then blew on his finger and inspected it. Satisfied with the end product, he then presented it to me like a birthday gift. I chuckled and grabbed his hand. I squeezed the tip of his finger and poked it with the lancet. He flinched, jerking his hand back. Corey laughed, but I noticed he had hidden his hand under the table.

"Don't be a puss," Chuck chided. I grinned and motioned for Corey to give me his hand.

Corey nodded towards Chuck, "Try healing him, first." When I waved my hand impatiently, he relented and reluctantly held out his finger, allowing me to prick it. When it was finished he shrugged with exaggerated bravado, "That wasn't so bad."

"What is with you people? You have tattoos and piercings, yet a needle prick gets you all worked up?" I shook my head.

Corey laughed. "Well, I didn't choose for you to poke me."

"You volunteered to be my guinea pig!" I reminded him.

"Meh."

"Okay, now for the true test." I nervously held both of their hands.

"Is it gonna hurt?" Corey asked.

"It shouldn't," I replied with a smile.

"It's a trick!" Chuck's eyes narrowed sarcastically.

I closed my eyes and felt their warm hands in mine. I took in a deep breath and attempted to focus my energy. I felt it move from my core, through my spine, down my arms and into my hands. I tried to concentrate. I tried to see my garden, my center. But as much as I tried, I was distracted. I felt my energy slip through my fingertips like grains of sand.

"Damn it!" I shouted, frustrated.

"What's wrong?" Chuck asked with a frown.

"I can't do it. I can't heal you," I sighed, laying my head on the table.

"Why not?" Corey questioned.

I wasn't sure if I was embarrassed, ashamed, or just disappointed. "I don't know why I can't. Maybe it's because I'm not human. Maybe it's because you are human. Maybe it's because we're all spiritually connected as angels because I helped create them. I don't know the reason." I banged my forehead on the edge of the table.

"It's okay, Edie. It was only a little poke," Chuck attempted to comfort me.

"Yeah, don't worry about it. It doesn't even hurt," Corey agreed.

"I'm not worried about the pain you're dealing with right now. I'm worried about what's going to happen during the war. If I can't heal all of you, I'm going to have to treat you the old fashioned way."

Chuck laughed awkwardly. "You don't mean like, 'put us down', do you?" He was trying to lighten the mood, but it wasn't helping.

"No, I meant I am going to have to just be a paramedic to you. At least I do have quite a bit of supplies. I just don't like the fact that I won't be able to 100% fix you. At least not instantaneously."

"It's okay, Edie. Hell, just some Band-Aids and a pat on the back will be nice." Chuck smiled.

Corey nodded in agreement, "Yep. Don't stress yourself out. We'll be careful."

"Well, thanks guys. Sorry I poked you for nothing. Now I'm glad I didn't slice you with scalpels!" I laughed, finally lifting my head from the table.

"Oh, yeah. Me too!" Corey chuckled.

"Go ahead and get back to your shooting, or whatever it was you were doing. I'm sorry for wasting your time," I said.

"It wasn't a waste of time. It was important to know, we realize that. Had you had to learn that during the fighting and not had supplies with you, I'm sure you would've panicked," Chuck reassured me.

"I would've absolutely freaked out," I agreed.

"Well, if you need us again for anything, just let us know," Corey said, getting up from the table and pushing his chair in.

"Thanks, guys. I really appreciate it."

"No problem," Chuck stepped out of the kitchen, followed by Corey.

I felt bad for allowing them to feel any pain at all, without being able to alleviate the hurt. I was glad that they at least handled it well and didn't bitch about it. Those guys had turned out to be a wonderful addition to our group and I only wished to see them safely through to the other side of this awful mess.

I left the kitchen and wandered back outside, strolling from group to group, listening to the discussions that were being had. I felt guilty for not being as involved as I could've been. I hadn't gotten a chance to spend very much time with anyone.

Even Riley and I had barely spoken all day.

I ran into Lily a couple times, and she told me how excited she was about Halloween coming up. She told me that she was going to be a princess, a fairy, a doctor, and a pilot... all in one. She had the absolute certainty that comes with youth and innocence, and I couldn't help but melt listening to her. I supposed her costume was going to be fairly extravagant. All I could picture was my niece running around wearing fairy wings, a tiara, a fancy dress, and a stethoscope; with a patient's chart, bomber coat and Parajumper boots. The images in my head made me laugh. It wasn't long before Lily was following Kadence and Rendon around. She was like their miniature shadow. She pranced and skipped behind them, with her golden springs bouncing in the cool autumn breeze.

Even the day was surprisingly chilly for Texas. I couldn't recall a time in my life that I had ever been around here in anything more than a t-shirt in October. The chill in the air seemed unnatural, forced. I thought to myself it was the millions of last breaths and final sighs of the dead, chilling the land. The wind howled loudly, and my thoughts made me shiver. I pulled my hood over my head and continued to the backyard.

As I quietly stepped around the side of the house, I watched as Jeremiah explained himself to another small group of humans. I listened for a couple of minutes, then remembered I had nothing to gain from the weapons discussion. I wasn't *allowed* to fight. I wasn't going to be allowed anywhere near the actual battlefront. I returned to the front of the house and stopped short. Riley and Paul had taken a folding table outside, where they, with my father's help, had drawn out a map of the surrounding area and were holding counsel with several of the angels. They were discussing the plans and strategy for keeping the house secured, providing me with my own protection and maintaining a large enough amount of soldiers on the battlefield.

As I stood there, Kenneth approached the table and waited silently until Riley finished what he was doing and acknowledged his presence. "Riley, with your permission, we'd like to send for the next wave of angels' descent. I think it's imperative that the others are prepared and well informed."

Gabriel shook his head, "I don't know if that's a good idea."

"But, of course, it's up to Riley," Lilith interjected.

"Thanks, Lilith. And I agree with Gabriel on this one. I'm not sure if we should yet. I think we need to solidify our plan and make sure that we're completely ready before we begin to draw Michael's attention to us. As Elijah has informed us, once many of you are missing, he's going to begin looking for you. We don't need that pressure on us ill prepared," Riley explained.

Kenneth nodded, "I understand."

"Don't worry, Ken, we'll get this ball rolling soon. We don't have a choice anymore. If we don't get off of our asses, we're going to be blindsided. I don't want to take that chance," Riley reassured the angel.

Callin smiled from across the table. "Riley, you don't have to justify your reasons. We all trust your judgment."

"Absolutely," Damien spoke up.

"Well, I'm glad you guys trust me. I hope I don't let you down."

"After seeing all of your past commanding, I doubt you'll fail." Gabriel smirked.

"Let's not bet on it, just yet," Riley replied, the creases of concern evident across his face.

"Eden, what's your take on all of this?" Lilith asked me, gesturing for me to come forward and join the group.

"I don't know, honestly. I'm not one to help strategize. I'm just here to look pretty," I replied.

Damien laughed. "Yes, yes you are."

Riley raised a brow and locked eyes with the other.

"Sorry," Damien grinned sheepishly, then cleared his throat.

I threw my hands up in a sign of helplessness, "But seriously, yeah. I don't know what to tell you guys. I'm here to help in any way I can. But as of earlier this morning, we learned that I will no longer be involved in the battle. So, I'm just the bandage-bitch."

"You're more than that, Eden. You are crucial to this," Gabriel stopped me, aggravated by my cynicism.

"Very much so," Lilith confirmed.

"Stop being nice to me! It's awkward," I shot at the bird-woman. Seriously, it was creeping me the fuck out.

Lilith cackled hysterically at my discomfort. "Fine. You're completely worthless. Get out of here."

"That's more like it," I nodded.

She laughed again and shook her head.

I heard the front door open and turned to see Amber walking towards us with a smile. She walked up behind me and wrapped her arms around my neck. I grabbed her hands and embraced her hug.

"How are you, Kiddo?" she asked me.

"Good. You?" I replied with a smile.

"Pretty good. I was just hoping we could spend some time together. Is there anything I can help you take care of?" she asked me.

"Actually, if you want to help me get my gear all sorted, that would be great. It looks like I'm gonna be needing it after all," I said dejectedly.

"Wait, what?" Riley stopped mid conversation and turned to look at me.

"Well, it seems I can't heal humans. I'm hoping I can still heal angels. We might have to test that, too," I said, embarrassed.

"You can try with one of us," Gabriel suggested.

"I can handle it!" Damien flexed and kissed his bicep.

I laughed loudly. "Just for that, you're definitely going to be my lab rat."

"Yeah, get him out of here. And kick him in the nuts, while you're at it," Riley jabbed.

"Oh shit! Let's go!" I laughed and grabbed Damien's arm, pulling him towards the house.

"Am I allowed inside?" he asked nervously.

"Um, I don't know. Do angels have boundary issues like vampires? Do you have to be invited in? I mean, you can close your wings so you can fit through the doorway," I replied sarcastically.

"No, I meant more along the lines of your family freaking out," he explained.

Amber looked over my shoulder with a confused look on her face, "Why would they freak out?"

"Hmm, I don't know. Maybe because angels have been killing millions of people worldwide, then 'wow, look at that. There's an angel in my house'. I don't really want to be shot at or harpooned." he laughed half joking.

"They know there's good and bad. They know you guys are on our side. You're more than welcome in our home." I smiled.

He had a valid point, though. We had made it rather clear that we were being aided by the angels and Valkyrie, but I hadn't really seen anyone's reaction to the winged helpers. I tried to think for a moment, had I noticed any extended glances? Had there been hushed voices around them, or crying children? I supposed not.

All three of us walked into the kitchen and sat at the table. Damien refused to put his wings away, so he had to sit sideways in the chair to allow us to test my abilities. Amber sat across the table from the two of us, silently watching as we prepared. She smiled at Damien, who smiled brightly in return.

"Okay, you ready?" I asked.

"As long as you aren't actually going to kick me in the groin, then yes. By all means, let's get this show on the road," he replied sarcastically.

I turned to grab a lancet out of my bag. "Alright. Let's go with something easy. I could prick your finger," I said as I turned back. I returned my gaze to the angel and my jaw dropped.

"Done and done," he chuckled. He had sliced his palm open with his own sword.

Amber and I looked from each other to him.

"What?" he asked nonchalantly.

"I just kind of figured we'd try something small," I said, quickly wrapping his palm in a wad of paper towels to try to absorb the blood.

"I figured this was small to you," he replied with a confused look.

I shook my head in disbelief, "No, but let's try to get this shit healed."

"What do I need to do?" he asked.

"Well, I need silence so I can concentrate and center myself. So, if you don't mind, Amber, will you keep everyone out of here?"

"Absolutely," she replied. She got up from her seat and walked to both of the doors that entered the kitchen, closing and locking each in turn. I could hear people moving around upstairs, but I didn't think it was going to be too distracting. Luckily, they had stopped firing guns in the backyard shortly before we settled in the kitchen.

"Okay. Give me your hand," I said, reaching for Damien's wounded extremity.

He handed it over without hesitation, showing no pain or concern.

"Alright, give me a second to center myself and we'll be good to go." I smiled and closed my eyes. I wrapped both of my hands around his and took in a long, deep breath. I exhaled slowly and repeated the process. I thought about the beautiful flowers, the fresh smell of the life giving rain. I pictured the fresh breeze as it passed through my nose into my lungs and dispersed through my body like beams of pulsing light.

"Whoa!" Damien said, pulling his hand back with a jerk.

"What?" my eyes shot open.

"Seeing what you see. It's just bizarre."

"Did it work?" Amber asked expectantly.

Damien pulled the paper towel away from his hand and revealed a healed wound.

"I'd say, yes. You haven't lost your touch, Muse!" he said with a grin.

"I'm so glad."

"See? You have nothing to worry about." Amber smiled.

"Well, yeah, I do. I have to worry about all of you. I can't heal humans." I frowned.

There was a knock on the kitchen door. "Yeah?" I asked.

"Edie, honey, we need to get in the kitchen and start cooking," my mother stated.

"Oh, sorry!" I replied, jumping to my feet and opening the two doors.

"It's okay. I just wanted to give you time to finish up. Riley told me what was going on."

"Yeah, we're all done. I've completed my experiments for the day," I said with a wicked grin.

She laughed at my expression. "Good, I was starting to worry if I was going to walk into my kitchen and see it converted to a Frankenstein-esque lab."

I rolled my eyes, "Oh, real funny, Mom."

"Okay, kids. Hop on out of here so we can get to cooking! If for some reason the electricity gets knocked out with all of your... *fighting*, we don't want to have to cook for 100 plus people over a camp fire," she explained.

"Excuse me, Eden's earthly mother. Just to let you know, we don't eat." Damien shook his head, smiling politely.

"Oh, really? How do you stay so healthy? Oh, wait. Never mind." she chuckled to herself.

"Yeah, that whole 'divine being' thing. I forget about it too, sometimes."

"Well, just because you guys know that you're angels now, does that mean that you don't eat, either?" she asked me.

"No, we're kind of borderline. I thought I explained that. We still have to eat to survive," I explained.

"You especially, Eden!" Damien smiled and patted my stomach.

"What?" My mom's eyes narrowed, her head cocked to the side.

I bit my lip nervously, "Oh, shit. We didn't really talk about that, did we?"

"Eden Quinn, what's going on?" my mom put her hands on her hips.

"Oh, look at the time. I better head outside and share the good news... about your healing." Damien smiled awkwardly, and slipped out of the door sideways, avoiding getting his wings caught. As he was leaving he turned to me, shot me a wink, and the last thing I heard was a snicker as I heard him make his way down the hall.

Once Damien had left the room, I sat down at the table with my mother and shared the news with her. I explained what Elijah had told me, the children's names and that they may save everyone. She sat, speechless, for what felt like an eternity.

"Mom, are you okay?" I finally asked.

"Honey, you just told me last night that the world is probably going to end. We don't even know if you're going to live, which has scared me enough. And now you tell me, today, that you're pregnant with twins?" her voice trembled.

"It isn't like I planned all of this. I had no clue. I didn't know that was going to happen. I didn't know I was pregnant until this morning. I'm just as blown away by this as you are. Actually, more so."

"I know, I'm sorry. I know this is stressful. I just hope everything will work out. I'd hate for anything to happen to you. I couldn't live without you. I probably wouldn't live without you, anyway." she frowned.

"Hey, come on! You're going to be a grammy! You're finally going to get to hold my kids! Stay positive!" I smiled. It was a fake smile, but I think she needed it.

"I sure hope so."

"Alright. I need to get back to helping everyone, and I know you need to get to cooking. Do you need me to go get Aunt Kristi and Aunt Karla?" I asked.

She laughed. "No, I'm sure they were just waiting for us to finish talking."

"Yeah, we're here, honey!" Aunt Kristi laughed guiltily as she sidled through the doorway.

I turned and faced my awkwardly smiling aunts. I couldn't help but laugh. "You ladies have fun. Let me know if you need me for anything, otherwise I'm just going to be running in circles, making sure everyone is doing alright. I need to get caught up with all of the preparations," I said as I rose from the table.

"Okay. Thanks," Aunt Karla smiled and kissed my cheek as I passed.

I could hear them talking as I left the room. There were a few squeals and some "congratulations" to my mom for being a grandma, again. Under normal circumstances, I know she'd be ecstatic. I understood why this was hard for her. Her baby girl, *her only girl*, was pregnant during the Apocalypse.

I made my way outside. I didn't know where I should be, or what I should be doing to help. I was lost. I was confused. I was emotionally and mentally distracted. And it seemed the more I thought about everything, the more nauseated I became. This was going to be hellacious. But, I knew what I had to do. I knew what needed to be done in order to save the lives of my children.

I stepped around the side of the house and pulled my pack of cigarettes from a pocket. I retrieved one, staring at it in my hand. My nerves were screaming for me to light it, while my conscience and common sense forced me to slip it back into its slot and throw the whole pack as far from me as I possibly could. Of course, there was a chance that we were all going to die, and my actions now wouldn't influence their fetal development. But I wasn't willing to take the chance.

I stepped over to Riley's war council for a moment and listened to the progress. It was hard for me to tell what was going on, though it was easy to see that they were well devised. The mood was rather intense as they clustered around the table, speaking in hushed tones.

"Eden!" Jonah called me from the front door, startling me.

"Hey. What's up?"

"If it's okay with you, we're going to gather in your old bedroom for some blessings. I was wondering if you wanted to join us?" Jonah asked, polite as ever.

"Absolutely," I replied.

"Wonderful! The more the merrier!" he grinned happily.

"Well, guys, if you'll excuse me, I'm gonna go join the battle chants." I kissed Riley on the lips and walked towards the front door to join Jonah.

"Great," Riley scoffed as I was walking off.

"What?" Gabe asked.

"Here comes the battle chants and the drums of war," I heard Riley say as I slipped through the front door.

CHAPTER FORTY ONE
I PLEDGE ALLEGIANCE, TO THE FLAG
OF THE UNITED STATES OF SUBURBIA...

The day went as any day during the Apocalypse would. There was frantic running about, people feeling overwhelmed, and twisted humor that truly had no place being spoken. But, as always, that didn't stop us. Jokes had been carried on whispers, passed around a small circuit of friends who would much rather laugh than have an emotional breakdown. One of those groups in particular was charged with setting up watch posts around the neighborhood.

Gabe looked from face to face, "What do you call six humans, against one pissed off angel?"

"Fucked," Paul jeered.

"Outnumbered," I sighed as I walked through the group.

I continued walking, uninterested in the punch line. I knew it wasn't going to be any less cynical than my guess. We were all reaching a point of feeling the futility. The larger the scale of Michael's army became, the smaller our chances of survival. He had a personal vendetta and he was going to exact his revenge.

"Hey, sis, you have a second?" Eli called to me from the edge of the driveway.

"Yeah, be right there," I replied, and set down the cooler I had been carrying around. I walked towards the end of the driveway and scanned the road in either direction. It was awkwardly quiet this afternoon. It was bizarre to see my parent's neighborhood so barren. I had once been used to the sound of neighborhood kids screaming and annoying the shit out of me. Now, the only screaming I heard was full of fear, and it was in my mind.

"What's up?" I asked as I approached my brother.

"Garrett came to me earlier, with questions. I wondered what you thought I should tell him. He misses his mom, you know? He wonders why he isn't allowed outside to play, or why there's so many guys running around wearing fake wings. He's smart. He's not going to buy my shit forever." Eli looked me in the eyes.

"We don't have forever. We have barely over a week. Tell him what you think is right. But I don't think anyone here should have false hope, or think that this is some kind of family reunion." I pulled the rubber band out of my hair and let my tresses settle for a few moments, contemplating what I would say in this situation. My nephew Garrett is a brilliant kid. His preteen curiosity is fine-tuned.

The brisk wind picked up, carrying the smell of death. Eli and I both sniffed at the air, turned to each other with a knowing look, then turned our attention down the road in the direction the breeze was coming. The faint sound of whistling twisted through the distance, followed by a hearty chuckle. I looked over my shoulder at Eli, startled, then turned to see if anyone else had noticed the strange occurrence.

Everyone was busy with the tasks at hand.

"That was odd…" Eli shook his head suspiciously.

"Mmhmm," I nodded. "What the fuck was that?"

After a few silent seconds, I shrugged and returned my attention to my brother.

He returned his attention to our conversation, "As I was going to say, I know you have enough on your mind and I don't expect you to have the answers to everything. I'm not asking you to tell me how to raise my kids, or what I should and shouldn't teach him. But this is a bit different of a scenario. Do I cut his childhood short and keep him restless, in fear for the next few days? Or do I partially keep him in the dark and allow him to treasure what fleeting moments he has left?" Eli's eyes reflected pain. Pain only a father could bear. It hurt me immeasurably.

I rubbed my temples. "Let him enjoy the next week. Let him be a kid, play with his cousins, enjoy your company. Don't take that away from him."

He smiled sadly, "Yeah. That's what I thought, too."

I returned his smile. "I need to finish passing out water to the guys. We'll have to continue this conversation later."

"Yeah, I know. Get back to work," he ordered, as only a big brother could.

I turned and began walking towards the cooler I set down by the garage, "Oh, and Eli? I love you." The smile I shot him was pained, but genuine.
Please make it through this.

"Love you, too, sis." he chuckled at my softness.

I kept a very slow pace as I returned to the others. I turned once, to see where Eli was. He continued to stand at the edge of the driveway, staring out into the vast reaches of The United States of Suburbia. Memories of my childhood flashed through my mind. Sitting on the warm, tropical sand, watching my hero of a brother ride a wave into the coast, like a decorated knight on a valiant steed. I thought about his laid back surfer personality, his optimistic outlook on life, and a twinge of guilt stabbed at my stomach. When the people I loved most needed hope, needed faith, I dashed those hopes with my pessimism.
I'm such an asshole.

"Wench! Fetch me water!" Gabe shouted.

"Get it yourself, douche!" I yelled back, yet continued my stride towards the cooler as he laughed. I opened the lid of the cooler and pulled out a bottle, which I promptly threw at him with all of the force I could muster. After years of having random items thrown at him accompanied by my outbursts, he had mastered cat like reflexes. He caught the bottle, split seconds before it came in contact with his groin.

He grinned. "Your beating has been postponed."

"I spit in that," I retorted.

"Wouldn't be the first time." he chuckled and returned to his duties.

I secured the lid of the ice chest and took a seat on my throne, leaning back against the garage door and staring out into the empty neighborhood. One might ask if we were the only ones that *knew* what was on the horizon. Where had everyone run off to? The answer to that was trivial, really. I didn't know. My guess, pure speculation and assumption, of course, was that people had gathered bits and pieces from the news, and began fleeing the area in search of some safe location with their families. But realistically, that safe haven just didn't exist.

Based on news reports, the events unfolding were sketchy, at best. Reporters and the broadcasting companies had made up lie after lie to attempt to explain the recent happenings. People bought it. But the only thing that was successfully being done by these reports, was buying time. They knew that the truth would eventually rear its head, and when it did, they would try to manipulate it to fit into their falsities. Some said it was aliens. *Ha.* Others said it was terrorists. *That's more realistic.* Some even went so far as to say it was the fulfillment of religious prophecies. *Who in their right mind, other than rightwing Bible-thumpers would believe that?* The people were scared. The people were looking for answers. But the answers would not come. So they all did what any self-respecting, self-preserving human would do. They ran. They'd continue to run. And as they did, they'd run straight into the traps set in place by the Archangels. By the Horsemen. *The end is really fucking nigh.* Nine days, to be exact.

"Where's Riley?" Paul asked, standing unnoticed until that moment, directly in front of me.

"I... I don't know, offhand. I haven't seen him much today," I replied, coming out of my reverie and looking up at him.

"Are you okay?" he asked, kneeling down closely.

"What?" I was confused. "Oh, yeah. Dude, I'm just tired."

"Well, you should probably go lay down or something. Take a load off." he grinned politely.

"Yeah, not a bad idea," I nodded and rose from my seat.

As I righted myself he looked at me and winked. "We got this, don't worry."

"That's what I'm afraid of."

I took my leave and went inside. The sun was beginning to set and the mood was beginning to change again. The kids ran around the house like a pack of rabid hyenas. Their laughter was the only thing that broke up the macabre mood. It felt as if we were all gathered for a wake. I journeyed into the kitchen and watched the women of my family bustling about. My aunts and sisters-in-law strategically placed bowls and plates of various sizes around the counter tops. As dinner time drew closer, the wolves descended. Through the doorway, a little face would peek in. Around the corner of a cabinet, a little hand would be seen.

"Dinner!" Mom finally shouted from the kitchen.

The doors opened and in flooded a crowd of hungry family and friends. Mixed in the group was my angelic brother. I cocked my head, curiously. Why the hell was he in here? Angels don't eat.

"Hungry?" I questioned.

"No, I just need to talk to you when you're free," Gabriel clarified.

"Can I eat first?"

He gently patted my stomach. "Please do. I've yet to see you eat today, and the boys need their nutrients!" he smiled, "And please find Elijah. He has a bit of a mission."

"Will do," I nodded and looked for my nephew in the crowd.

Gabriel shifted through the masses, making his way back towards the garage door and safely out of the feeding frenzy taking place. I looked from face to face, smiling and scanning for Elijah. The heavenly child was nowhere to be seen. I snuck to the front of the line, fixed myself a small helping of gumbo and hurried to the living room. I sat on the floor, crossing my legs, and dug into my dinner. A few bites in, I felt a twist in my stomach and buckled forward.

"Are you okay?" Dad asked, with an anxious look on his face.

"I'm fine, Daddy." I smiled up at him awkwardly.

"Let me know if I can get you anything." he rubbed my back supportively.

I managed to finish eating before my stomach felt like it was going to erupt. The twins must've spent time building a volcano in there that was surely going to explode any minute. I made my way to the front door and was met again by Gabriel.

"You look awful," he stated.

"Thanks," I sneered. "I feel about as fantastic as I look."

"Elijah's already gone," he replied, gauging my intent.

"What? I thought I needed to speak with him?" I was confused.

"Lilith said he left shortly after everyone gathered to eat," he explained.

"Where'd he go?" I asked.

"To speak with God."

"So this is it, huh? We're finally going to know the fate of the world." I closed my eyes for a moment, envisioning a million different horrific endings at once.

He wrapped his arm around my shoulders. "Have a little faith in yourself, your Father, and your children."

I pulled away, looking up at him, "I don't know them yet. How am I supposed to invest so much stock into their character?"

"You know exactly what they will become; heroes. The likes of which this world has never seen before." he pulled me close once more. I didn't resist, just rested my head on his shoulder.

"So, now what? We wait?" I asked, changing the subject.

"We wait. He'll be back soon. He's been gone about twenty minutes now," Gabriel confirmed.

"I'm going to head back inside and try to relax. I need to spend some time with my family." I pulled away, grabbing the door knob.

"I'll let you know once he's returned," he said to my back as I reentered the house.

I entered the living room and was joined by members of my family and an assorted group of friends, both new and old. Everyone sat around the room in a circle, conversing amongst themselves. I couldn't help but feel uneasy.

The mood was far too relaxed for the occasion. There was an unspoken somber dirge in the minds, looming over everyone in the room. I looked from face to face, attempting to read the expressions like short stories. The weak tried their hand at bluffing, hiding their fear behind a facade of strength. The attempts were futile. I could see straight through the covers. I could peer into their hearts. I could smell the fear on them, like a rabid dog out for blood.

But, the truth of the matter was we were all terrified to some degree, as we had the right to be. The burden was unbearable. We carried a secret that no one else in the world knew. Well, perhaps the paranoid, the delusional, the criminally insane had pieced some of the puzzle together. But the standard person, aware of self and self alone, was clueless as to what we faced.

Also see: Death. Annihilation.

We were the world's one true hope, the last line of defense. And our hearts were faltering like weakened bridges.

I rose from the couch as my stomach turned, and walked to the boarded window. I stared out into the twilight through the small hole, wondering what the night would bring. The thought of what we faced was more sickening than the changes in the hormones occurring in my body. Of all the times for a life altering occurrence, a mosaic of emotion, it had to be during the middle of the end of the world. This was irony at its finest. This was the dictionary definition of the adjective "fucked". As in, "this is a really fucked up situation, man." Because in fact, it was.

Granted, this could be the world's saving grace. Or, it could be the final nail in the coffin, sending our Father into a tailspin of wrath and vengeance. All I could do was wait patiently for the answers. I expected hesitance, a reluctance to face me. What I didn't expect was an embrace and redemption. That farce would make me question everything. I'd become so pessimistic in my centuries of limbo. The one thing that truly tore me apart was the thought of throwing my unborn children to the wolves. Little lambs to slaughter.

I put my hoodie on and stepped out into the brisk air. It had been a very long day, full of preparations and panic. Paul and Riley had made sure the sharpened poles on the front lawn, the new home for the deceased, had been reinforced and wouldn't fall over under the weight of the fallen angels. Jeremiah had continued to train others in the short time he had to work with. The angels didn't need any help. They knew exactly how to keep us nestled under their wings, and I couldn't thank them enough for that.

Throughout centuries, brother had fought alongside brother during times of war. There had also been cases of brother versus brother. But never once had there been a battle of this magnitude. These weren't simply brothers. These were heavenly beings, bound by the soul, ready to dispatch their soul twins, ready to die at the hands of their beloved, to defend a people they weren't even akin to. This was a whole new tragedy. This was a depressing moment in time, the likes of which would never be repeated.

I stepped further out into the cold air, shivered a bit and zipped up my jacket. I pulled my hood over my head and watched my breath dance in the stagnant air. There was a heaviness that was palpable. There was death, malice, convoluted fear weighing heavily in the lungs of everyone around. I stepped around the side of the house and again joined Riley's gathered war council. Riley pointed to marks on a crudely drawn map, weighed down on one end by a battery powered lantern. Several angels stood in a semicircle around him, staring intently at their fearless leader and his treasure map of death. X marked the spot that another scarecrow, scare-*angel*, as it were, would be erected. The plan was to encircle the house, to invoke fear into the hearts of the encroaching. At this point, anything to buy us time was well worth the trouble.

Thanks to the angels that had been watching out for us, we had been spared from an attack the night before. But nevertheless, there had been casualties. We now had three carcasses positioned in the yard. One more and we were sure to be able to tell the time based on where the sun sat between the bodies. I could see it now. I'd walk outside in a robe, cup of coffee in my hand and my beloved Bruins slippers on my feet. I'd grab the newspaper and mutter under my breath, as the neighbor's dog took a dump on my lawn. On the way back in, instead of looking at my watch, I'd simply look to the bloated bodies skewered in my yard and bitch about not wanting to be awake so damned early.

I left the discussion and continued to the backyard, where I found peace in solitude. I needed time to think, to wrestle with my demons and find the bit of clarity I needed to gather strength. It wasn't just a fight of physical strength. No. It was a test of every facet of our being. We were going against God, for the right to continue life. We were defending people, the most of which, in all honesty, deserved the retribution for their self-inflicted tribulations. Society as a whole was a breeding ground of corruption and disgrace. But all life should be valued, even the braggart and the heathen.

I needed to speak with Him. Only one being, The One Being who would be able to halt this lunacy. If only I could convince Him to salvage the Earth, perhaps start a new world and turn His cheek. Only then would we be safe. My soul in exchange for millions. It hardly seemed fair, but a noble attempt nonetheless. I deserved some kind of award or gold star sticker for offering, at the very least. The thought of The All-powerful laughing in my face, shook me to the core. It was nothing short of what I deserved, at least in my opinion.

"Aunt Eden?" a low whisper questioned. "I'm back!" Elijah popped around the trunk of a tree with a smile bright enough to illuminate the darkest cave.

"How'd it go, Kiddo?" I asked nervously.

He looked as nervous as I felt, "He's willing to see you. But, there are conditions."

"And they are?" I cocked my head to the side suspiciously.

"He said only you may approach him. Anyone traveling with you will be dispatched from the heavens, and existence. He will grant you passage once, safely, of course. If you refuse His invitation now, you will not be given another chance to speak your peace." he sat at my feet and rested his head on my knee.

"When does he expect me to arrive?" I asked, already knowing the answer.
"Now."

"I should go tell Riley, and I need to..." I sorted the thoughts in my mind.

"No," the eternal child said, interrupting my thoughts. "That was also a condition. You are to tell no one of your journey. He expects secrecy and discretion."

"Is there anything else I should know about?" I questioned in a whisper.

"He told me to warn you. He said for you to avoid Michael; for your safety. As it stands, Michael is gathering his troops and preparing the next assault. He's distracted for the time being."

"Well, that's great then. Are you going with me?" I smiled hopefully.

He frowned, "No. You're on your own."

"Where do I go?" I shook my head, confused.

"Follow your heart," he replied cryptically.

"Uh. Kid? That's not a location. That's how people end up four thousand miles from their target destination. Well that and eating mushrooms, but that's a whole different story. Trust me, I know." I chuckled lightly as the boy looked up at me with a confused look painted across his face. "Don't ask. I was a stupid kid." I blushed sheepishly and scratched at my hair.

"That's probably for the best. However, I do have something I'm supposed to give you. I can't promise you that it's going to be easy, seeing as how I've never done this before." he popped his little knuckles and cricked his neck. "Then again, I've never been entrusted with a gift from God!"

I suddenly felt very sick and entirely too nervous to breathe. Elijah stood up, adjusted his shirt and exhaled deeply, staring at the darkened ground, "This may hurt a little."

A surge of agony ripped at my flesh. I tried to stifle my screams, as I felt the lashes on my spine. I bellowed louder as I noticed my muted voice, letting go of all pain. I fell forward, my head landing on Elijah's shoulders. He embraced me and lulled me to a state of catatonia. My body screamed silently as my flesh seared and sizzled.

"Shh. It's all over. It's all over," he repeated as he gently stroked my hair.

"Why? Why would He do this to me, again?" I quietly asked.

"You've been returned a gift, but not without the Earthly sacrifice of the flesh. You must remember where you came from," he stated very matter-of-fact like.

He grabbed my hands, cradling them in his own and gently nudged me to return to the moment. I composed myself as best I could and rose to my feet. They trembled beneath me like a newborn fawn's. I caught my balance on the arm of the chair and arched my back, hoping that the pain would run off of my body like beads of sweat, or rain. There was weight there. Weight that I hadn't felt in an eternity.

I reached back with a quivering hand in a breathless daze, and felt a stream of tears run down my cheeks. Whether this was a short lived gift, or a permanent addition, there were no words to describe the shear ecstasy I felt in my soul. My true beauty, the grace of God, had been restored to my body.

"How do they look?" I asked with a light chuckle as I wiped the tears from my face.

"Very fitting!" Elijah was elated by his newfound talent. He marveled at his work.

I smiled brightly, "I can't thank you enough for everything you've done."

"Aw, it was nothing." he kicked at the wooden deck bashfully.

I leaned down, kissing his forehead.

"It was everything," I whispered.

"You're welcome. Now, you need to get going before the others see," he reminded me.

I stepped out into the darkness. I could feel the light radiating from my wings, from my soul. It was a glow only humbled by the sun itself. I lightly flexed the muscles in my back, letting my wings open like sails. It was a natural feeling, as if I had never lost my appendages to begin with. It felt amazing. I suddenly longed to feel the breeze twisting through my tangled locks. The sweet air kissing my cheeks as I rode the warm currents through the sky.

I leapt into the air and hovered for a second, studying the horizon and assuring my safety as I ascended. The last thing I wanted to do was to be taken down by an archangel, like a feeble fledgling caught in the talons of a predatory bird. I heard voices as they flocked towards the backyard. Time was running short. I bolted into the air like a bottle rocket and sped towards my Father. I didn't look behind me. I didn't even think to check on Elijah. I was sure he was going to either explain our actions, or lie by omission. I climbed towards the heavens. Everything began to blur. Hues of black and blue morphed into the perfect pitch of night. Night melted into the deafening sounds of the heavens. The heavens shifted into the blinding light of my Creator. I tried to slow my speed. I put my feet forward, as to somehow build friction, but realized I hadn't been flying. I hadn't been moving on my own at all. I was as a lassoed calf, being hauled in by a burly cowboy. God had the reins as He pulled me to His side. I saw His face and sobbed.

"Father..." my voice trembled.

"My love!" He smiled warmly back.

"Father, I'm so sorry," I said as my voice broke, and I was again sobbing.

He turned to me, grabbing my hands and pulled me into His warm embrace.

"This reunion is long overdue, Eden," He shook His head and cradled me to His chest.

"I'm so sorry," These were the only words I felt I could utter.

"Come little one, converse with me, as you planned." He smiled warmly, and pulled me from his chest to take a seat at His side.

"I... I don't... I don't know what to say." I shook my head, dazzled, entranced.

"I'd suggest we start with the formalities, but time is of the essence," He mused.

"Right. I guess now isn't the time to discuss minute lifetimes and multiple deaths. We can save the small talk for later." I grinned, wiping the tears from my eyes.

He laughed lightly at my attempt at humor, "There's the smile I've dreamt of for years."

I mustered the strength to speak up, "Father, there obviously is much going on, and we both know you're the only one who can change the course of this. I've come to negotiate with you, in hopes that you'll spare the humans."

"*Spare* the humans? Eden, do you not understand the entire point of this action?" His expression flattened.

"I do. I truly do. I know that the humans were not your creation. If it were up to you, they never would've come to exist. However, *they do*. And they're alive. They're living beings, created in your image, capable of all the good that is *you*," I explained.

"Surely you do not blaspheme in front of your creator? Have you lost all sanity and reason in your exile?" His eyes narrowed sharply.

"No, you don't understand. I didn't mean..." I tried to continue.

"No, it is you that doesn't understand. Those *abominations* were created in the image you traitors so sought fit. I had no control over your actions," He reminded me brusquely.

"I had no contribution to the population, Father... Until now." I sighed and looked to my trembling feet.

"I beg your pardon?" He adjusted Himself on His throne.

"Father, I'd yet to ever conceive. I had always wanted a family of my own, regardless of your acceptance. It was a longing I had, a desire. I envied the human women, capable of unconditional love. I wanted that, but had always been punished with infertility. This is the first lifetime I've had where I *was* destined to be a mother. And now, well, now even that desire is flashing before my eyes and slipping between my fingers, like sand falling out of a broken hourglass." I felt the tears welling in my eyes once more.

"You're what?" He whispered.

"I'm pregnant... " my voice quivered as I looked up at Him, fear gripping me.

"You *dare* to defy my laws? You *breed* with one of those *monsters*, and yet you have a desire for sympathy?" His voice reverberated with anger.

"I didn't 'breed' with a human," I replied defensively.

"Then explain to me how you're with child." He folded His arms like an angry parent, awaiting my next words.

"Quite easily, Father," an angelic voice resounded.

I turned to see Gabriel landing and approaching the two of us. His wings shone brightly in the cosmic light as they gently folded towards the small of his back. He winked and smiled lovingly at me, with an unspoken "I've got your back" kind of debonair.

"My son, you've returned." God smiled, ignoring me for a moment.

"Of course, Father. As always," Gabriel grabbed God's hand and gently kissed the top.

The emotions hit me like the onslaught of a tsunami battering an unprotected coast. I felt my fears wash away in the brisk wave, unfettered by my brother and his instantly calming persona. If by chance God felt that relief as well, the answers I longed to hear might be possible. Gabriel was the one soul who could mediate this dilemma and force reason into the unswayable. Or so I hoped.

"Father, the birth of Eden's children is nothing short of a miracle. It's as if you, yourself, allowed it to happen. These children are heavenly, the perfect union of two holy souls. There are two, *twin boys*, capable of bringing a reign of peace to the world. They're the combined love of Eden and Thaddeus. Their loss would be devastating."

"Is this true, Eden?" God turned to me suspiciously.

I nodded once, "Of course. Thaddeus is the father."

"And you do realize the position you've placed me in, correct?" He stroked his beard, staring out into the cosmos.

"I'll never fully understand the pain and anguish you feel, Father. What I've done, what *we've* done, is beyond words. I know our choices and actions have hurt you. I'm so sorry. But, yes. These children have a chance to bring harmony into this bleak world. If you'll have them," my voice trembled as I bartered for my unborn children's souls.

"And it's been seen?" God asked.

Gabriel simply nodded.

"I need time to think on this. I hope you understand." God rose and turned away.

"Yes, Father," I choked on my words.

Gabriel stepped to my side and wrapped his arm around mine. He gently herded me away from our Creator and led me through the heavens. "Eden, have no fear. Everything will happen as it's supposed to. All we can do is await His decision patiently. Try to rest."

"Easier said than done," I sneered.

"It's for the best. For you, and the babies." he gently rubbed my shoulder.

"Do you know what's going to happen?"

"Goodbye, Eden. Give my love to Lilith and Elijah." he gently pushed me off the edge of the cosmos.

If ever there was something I was certain about, it was that moment in time. There, right then... *life* was on a fast track to the end and there was nothing more anyone could do but sit back and patiently await the answers. That was exactly what I was doing, at any rate. It's not like anyone out there *knew* what was going on, or knew about the conversation God and I had. Gabriel was the only other, and he had been asked to stay at our Father's side, until a decision had been made. Cheap shot. It's not hard to figure out the reasoning behind that request. I would, of course, attempt to weasel the final decision out of my unsuspecting brother.

I returned to Earth that night, anxious and extremely nervous. Riley was poised on the back deck, protective and obviously as anxious as myself. He watched me as I descended from the sky and nestled my bare feet into the cold, dewy grass.

"Any news?" he asked, reaching his hand out to me.

"Not yet." I shook my head and accepted his hand.

"When will we hear something?" he gently pulled me into his arms, held me tightly and kissed my forehead.

"I'm not sure, exactly. I'm not even entirely sure who I'll be finding it out from. None of that was clarified."

"We need to get inside. Paulie and Corey were out scouting tonight and reported back some fires and what appeared to be some rogue angels downtown." Riley grabbed my arms and spun his back towards me.

"What the hell are you doing?" I was so confused.

He bent down and motioned for me to climb onto his back. "Get on. You're barefoot... And pregnant," he snickered.

I slapped his hand away, and then walked towards the side of the house. Riley ran to my side and smiled at me. I watched his eyes shift from my face, to my shoulders. His pace slowed slightly as he lined himself up with my back. I felt the gentle caress on my back as he stroked the feathers of my wings.

"They're beautiful on you," he stated somberly.

I smiled, "Thanks. They feel nice."

"I bet so." he smiled halfheartedly.

I shrugged. My wings shrugged with my shoulders. "I figured they'd be gone by now. I figured it was like a round trip ticket only."

"Who knows? You always were His favorite. But if you are blessed with keeping them, then you better remember how to put them away," Riley suggested.

We stopped in the front yard as Erick, Gabe and Brandon pulled in and put the van in park. I watched as they silently piled out of the vehicle and strode towards us with a weary air about them. As they drew near they all stared at the wings protruding from my back, but no one said a word.

"What's up?" Riley asked, breaking the silence as though nothing were amiss.

The cold ground stung my feet as we stood motionless. I tapped Riley's shoulder and pointed to his back, accepting his offer from a few moments before. He bent down, allowing me to climb onto his back, then bucked his shoulders, getting me positioned and wrapping his arms around my thighs.

"They've completely demolished Bridge City. There was nothing there but flames, smoke and corpses." Gabe shook his head, as his voice caught in his throat.

"Did you find anything? Were there any angels still in the city?" I asked, squeezing tightly around Riley's neck.

"We didn't find anything, anyone, alive." Brandon pulled his hood over his head and walked towards the front door without another word.

Gabe and I stared intently at one another. There was something deeply troubling about this news. The complete destruction was moving closer. It was rather clear that tonight would be an eventful one.

"We need to get you inside. I need to gather the angels, discuss our plan for tonight and get everyone set up. It's not going to be quiet." Riley helped me off of his back, gently aiding me back to the ground.

Gabe looked at me, and suddenly a smile played across his lips, "Your wings are pretty fruity. I was expecting something a little bit fancier."

"You're fruity!" I gibed.

"Nice come back, kid." Gabe shook his head in mock disappointment. "Come on, we need to get you tucked into bed. Did you brush your teeth?" he patronized.

"Oh, shut up!" I stormed off towards the door.

I could hear his laugh fading behind me.

"Asshole..." I muttered under my breath as I opened the front door.

Chapter Forty Two
Dancing with the Devil

I awoke in a dark room. Faint hints of crimson swept the walls. I felt pain. Deep, dark, gut wrenching pain. It wasn't physical in the sense that I had somehow been injured. It was physical in the sense that my heart ached, to the point of angina. I sat up from a mattress on the floor and attempted to squeeze the discomfort from my chest. After a moment I rose to my feet with a stumble, and closed my eyes to try to readjust my equilibrium.

The pain isn't real. Get a hold of yourself.

I opened my eyes and began to investigate the room. There were small trinkets strewn about, broken, deteriorating. I saw a cracked picture frame lying in the corner of the room and walked towards it.

Housed in the frame was a photo of me, from my teen years. My smile was plastered from ear to ear. I was genuinely happy. I had been carefree once. I wanted to smile when I saw it, but felt the pain grow stronger in my chest. I looked at the handsome face of the man whose lap I was sitting on in the picture, and closed my eyes. It wasn't Riley, but the brilliantly breathtaking blue eyes were so very familiar. I set down the frame and cradled my head in my hands.

If I could take it all back, I would.

I looked towards the bed and saw countless pill vials, empty bottles of liquor and a note lying on the pillow next to where my head had once rested. Curiosity had gotten the better of me. I had to know who the note was from.

You never once, truly, tried to stop me.
You let this happen.
You let me go.
I know I've hurt you, but the pain of seeing
your face in my mind, has haunted me
far too long. Without you, I am nothing.
So nothing is what I will become.
A ghost of your past.
A shadow in your memories.
Forever, I will love you... just as I promised.

The words rang in my mind like a broken record, an endless cycle. The words were seared into my brain and had been for almost a lifetime. I knew this letter. I knew it like the back of my hand. My hand? I looked down to see a pen, the same used to write the note.

The pain was worse now. It traveled into my throat, constricting my airway. I buckled to the ground and gasped for air. I clawed at my chest, my throat, praying that I could clear the obstruction. I crawled towards the nearest doorway; a light shown through the crack. I pulled myself with one hand, burying my nails into the matted carpet, until reaching the door. I pushed it open and collapsed on the other side.

It felt like hours later when I regained consciousness. I was leaning against a tattered wall. The torn wallpaper reeked of musk and dust, like old tombs. The room was dark, with a sickening green tint. A single old bulb reflected the color of the dilapidated room. I was uneasy. A part of my subconscious knew exactly why I was here, and was screaming for me to run. I tried to rise, but had no strength.

The pain in my chest had now traveled peripherally. My arms stung like a thousand hornets had angrily attacked them. The burning pulsed. I tried to clasp my hands shut and realized I was unable to move them. Though the neutrons were firing, my muscles were not responding.

I looked down at my left hand as my eyes welled with tears. *What have I done?* My hands were covered with blood. It dripped from my fingertips, forming puddles on the floor. I followed the trail as it flowed in the grout of the dingy tiling until it came to rest at the toe of a small shoe. My eyes traced the outline of the shoe, up to the figure wearing it. There was a little boy, standing in the doorway, tears streaming from his eyes. He stood speechless, motionless, with his hands behind his back. My eyes betrayed his face, spotting another face behind his right shoulder. They were identical. They were my boys, roughly four years old, by the looks of them. I felt my lip quiver as I realized the severity of my actions.

"I'm so sorry," my voice cracked.

They stumbled forward, collapsing onto my lap. They held one other, each with an arm draped around my shoulders. I rested my chin on the top of their heads and closed my eyes. *I'm so sorry.* I felt myself lose consciousness again as the pain stabbed at my heart for the last time.

Now, for the eternal dance with the Devil.

I woke up gasping for air and sat straight up. I snapped into reality with a start. My hand instinctively grasped my chest then slowly moved down to my stomach. Though I couldn't feel my sons, I felt the need to connect with them. My mind was deeply troubled, obviously, but that was uncalled for. I tried to shake the thought from my mind. I stumbled to the bathroom, closed the door and collapsed to my knees. Within seconds, my face was inches away from the porcelain gods, paying homage. I wretched and heaved, then fell backwards against the wall. I couldn't help but sob. I laid on the bathroom floor, in a fetal position for what felt like an eternity.

Eventually fatigue and anguish settled in my mind and I began to fall back to sleep. I was afraid. I didn't want to end up back in that dark world. But I wasn't able to fight the sandman. I dosed off, lying on the tile floor, curled into a tight ball.

I awoke once more, sometime later to the sound of knocking.

"Yeah?" I called out.

"Edie?" the muted voice replied, "You alright?"

"I'm sorry, I'll be out in a second." I staggered to my feet, catching myself on the counter, and then opened the door. "Yeah, I'm fine. Morning sickness," my lip curled instinctively.

"Ew!" Paul stepped away from me as if it were contagious.

I stepped around him as he pat my back and walked down the hallway, towards the living room. Some of the guys were gathered around, eating breakfast and talking. Their voices were hushed, as not to wake the others.

"What're you doing up, Edie?" Riley asked.

"Can't sleep. I had a shitty dream, then got sick," I replied with a pout. I sat down on the couch next to him and laid my head on his shoulder. He turned and gently kissed my lips.

Everyone finished their breakfast and began preparing to head outside. I grabbed my hoodie, deciding that I was going to join them. Rather than sit around and dwell on the dream I had, I figured that if I were productive, I would be properly distracted from the woes of my wicked mind.

It was almost as if we had peace during the days, though we knew it was a far cry from it. So far, we had encountered the majority of the action at night. It wasn't always going to be as such, we were sure. But for now we acted as quickly as we could, in groups during the day for protection. We kept a watchful eye on the skies, on the land, and every other direction to which we were exposed.

I sat down on the front steps and watched as Riley and Paul set up more poles and assigned tasks to the others. Lamar was running back and forth between two groups, carrying orders and supplies. He had become Riley's right hand man and messenger when it came to preparing. It had been reasonably quiet last night, which made us all extremely nervous. With my unplanned trip to speak with God, we had reasons to be fearful. What if Michael was aware of my travels? What if he was speaking to God on the Archangels' behalf, convincing Him of the need for our demise? What if his next attack would be the last? My mind was everywhere all at once. I was definitely fearful, justifiably so. I was utterly horrified.

"I think we're going to need a few more of these assholes in the front," Paul stated, kicking at a lifeless shell of an angel, lying face down in the grass.

"We'll get more. They're bound to descend again soon. I can't imagine they're done with us. All we've done so far is manage to piss them off further," Riley replied, spearing the tough Earth with his shovel. "Besides, if I have to I'll get to Heaven myself, and pull Michael's punk ass down here. We're not done. I'm not done with him... not until he's dead."

"Whatever floats your boat, man!" Paul laughed as he threw his hands up.

I quietly watched as everyone went about their activities. I had been exempt from everything, and though it was nice to not feel the stress first hand, the boredom alone was stressful. Not to mention that nagging feeling of having too much time in my own mind to think of everything and how it could go horribly, horribly wrong. And just as I had hoped it wouldn't, the dream continued to haunt me.

Time had passed slowly for me, sitting on the steps. It was like watching one of those slow paced indie movies. I couldn't help but wish it would just blow up and the action would start. The suspense killed me. I was on the edge of my seat, or the stair, quite literally. But when the mood did change, I couldn't help but feel like a frightened animal, and long for the comfortable silence I just had. At least I was feeling that, at that very moment.

The breeze stood still. The smell of death penetrated the already dead air. My ears rang with a cautious white noise. Something was coming. Not just *something*, but something dangerous.

Everyone stopped what they were doing at the same time, and scanned the horizon with a collective sense of dread. A cold chill ran up my spine, leaving the small hairs on the nape of my neck standing on end. The last time I felt *this* uneasy, this panicked, I was running from a rogue angel at the gas station. This was my self-defense mechanism I had grown so weary of. Yea, the good old autonomic response; fight or flight. That *"Get the fuck up! Get the fuck out! Jesus Christ, run!"* feeling. The alarms had sounded in my mind, the exit signs were flashing, and what remained of my nerves were tripping over each other in a panic to flee.
Exit stage left.

"What the fuck?" Paul whispered, dropping his shovel to the ground.

The air instantly felt heavier, like all of the oxygen had been sucked from the world. I grasped at my throat as I watched dozens of birds suddenly take to the sky and flee, as if startled. And on the stagnant, cold breeze that began to blow, a menacing noise was carried on its back. *Whistling.*

"Who the hell *is that?*" Gabe asked, standing next to me. He placed his hand on my shoulder protectively.

"I'm not sure I want to know," I replied.

A faint silhouette approached from the east. I squinted and leaned forward, cupping my hands around my eyes like a horse's blinders. The morning sun was absurdly bright. I tried to trace the outline of the approaching being, hoping to find something familiar to run with. I didn't recognize it. It was far too small to be a horseman. There were no visible wings or bulky armor. Something very strange was going on.

I rose from the steps and walked towards Riley. He heard my approach, turned towards me for a split second, and held out his hand for me to stop. But, being the hardheaded woman that I am, I instead took his hand and stood by his side.

"Who is it?" I asked quietly.

"I can't tell yet," he replied, taking a half step in front of me, protectively. "Oh, God damn it. You've *got* to be kidding..." Riley's whisper trailed off as the figure grew closer.

"What? Who is it?" I asked urgently as Riley let go of my hand.

Riley looked to Gabe, "Get her inside, *now.*"

"What the hell's going on? Who is it?" I begged.

"Come on, let's go," Gabe said, grabbing my arm and beginning to pull me towards the house.

"No. I'm not going anywhere!" I shrugged, pulling my arm out of my brother's grasp. He didn't fight. He was more interested in what was happening outside.

We both stood, watching as Riley stepped through the small crowd of people and into the street to meet the mysterious man. It was easier to see him now. The air about him was ominous, yet extremely familiar. He wore a black suit with blood red trim and pinstriping, perfectly cut and fitted to his muscular physique. His hair was dark and curly, loosely slicked back like the churning waves of the sea before a storm. His porcelain-like complexion glowed perfectly in the morning sun as he strolled casually towards us, seemingly unaware of his surroundings. He was by far the most mesmerizing creature I had ever laid eyes on. I was instantly drawn to him. I was drawn to him the same way I had been drawn to the angel that... *it's him!*

As he neared us, he stopped about ten feet out, looked at Riley for a moment, then gave a slight bow; the seemingly perfect gentleman that he was.

"Good day to you, Thaddeus."

"What the hell do you want?" Riley asked in an angry tone, with his arms across his chest in a posture of defiance. I peeked around Gabe, staring at the curiously beautiful being.

He smiled at Riley's posture, casually measuring him for the briefest of moments, "Aw, what's wrong? Can't a fellow stop by and say hello to some old acquaintances? I'm merely here to admire your handy work, which I might say, is magnificent... and to offer my assistance, of course." the strange man's expression transitioned to a grin as he cocked his head to the side and studied the impaled carcasses like 16th century paintings, no more intimidated than a parent admiring a child's macaroni art.

Riley took a menacing step forward. "Look, Lucy. *If* we needed help, it sure as shit wouldn't be yours or your little minions' we'd be asking for. We've been just fine on our own, so far. I'd appreciate it if you'd ever so kindly, fuck right off."

Paul, Brandon and Jeremiah took the cue and stepped forward. From behind me, I heard the light footsteps of others approaching. I slowly turned to see Damien and a few other angels walking towards us, as well.

"Oh tsk, tsk, Thad the Impaler." he wagged his finger at Riley. "Well, c'est la vie, I suppose." he hung his head with mock dejection.

"We have a lot to do, so I think it would be best if you headed out," Riley repeated.

The figure raised his head slowly, that grin, once again, spread across his chiseled face. Humming what sounded like a show tune to himself, he deftly stepped around Riley with a twirl and walked directly up to me. His smoldering, crystal blue eyes pierced through me and shook me to the core, as he stared me down. Who was he, exactly? What had Riley called him? Where the hell did he find that awesome suit? And was he seriously humming a song from 'Jesus Christ, Superstar'? I looked over his tailored shoulder and saw Riley silently stepping towards us. The man stuck his arm out, catching Riley by the chest and halting him in place with one outstretched finger. Through all of this sudden action, he never missed a beat of that catchy tune.

"Ah, bonjour, mademoiselle!" His beautiful smile took my breath away, as he grabbed my hand and gently kissed the top of it.

"Good morning, Frenchy," I replied, hushed.

He laughed charmingly, "I'm not French, I'm just well-traveled. Would you prefer a different language?" he asked smugly. "Maybe Gaelic, or Latin?"

"I prefer English." I pulled my hand from his, nervously. With a smile like that, I was afraid to know what he was capable of.

"Well then, good morning, Madame *Muse*. How are you and the babies, this fine ante meridiem?"

I sniffed at the top of my hand. It smelled of bitterness and honey. "I'm fine, but who the hell are you?" I asked, "I've seen you before…"

"You need to leave, right fucking *now*!" Riley ordered more forcefully.

"Oh, Thaddeus. Always up in arms and ready to dispatch his ever-so-diabolical, ferocious foes!" he said, coldly. "I suggest you cool your head, lest you lose it." his grin fell flat and his eyes flashed brightly in Riley's direction. I mean literally. Like, they lit up. It was weird as shit.

I heard the front door open and growling ensued. Azrael stepped out and sprung to the ground below. I turned and watched as he stalked towards us, a low rumble erupting from his tightly caged chest. His head was lowered almost to the ground, and his hackles were raised in one solid mohawk that traced down the spine of his back. I could see in his narrowed eyes, he was geared and ready for war.

"I see you let your pussy cat out to play. How delightful!" he chuckled, clapping his hands with amusement.

"Azrael, come!" Riley called for my protector in a tense voice. It made me unsure if he was trying to keep Az from attacking, or trying to protect him from the stranger.

"*Azrael?* Interesting," he paused. "Azrael and I just played a game of chess a few days ago. How pleased he would be to know he was still feared and respected. Though, I can't help but feel distraught and overlooked. Here I was such a *dear* friend, and you don't even think to name your rodent after me? I'm saddened. Single tear." he pouted and traced a faux tear down his snow white cheek.

"I didn't think it was a good idea to stand out on my front lawn screaming for 'douche bag' to get in the house," Riley sneered.

"Douche bag? What is this? I must apologize. I'm not familiar with your terminology. Though I do rather enjoy what I can only assume, is a feeble attempt to insult me." Douche bag smiled.

"You guys don't have Google in Hell?" Paul asked.

Azrael stepped towards the strange man, his growl growing louder, hackles raised and teeth bared.

"You fine gentlemen will find out, soon enough." he grinned wickedly. "Well! It appears I have worn out my welcome, as it were. I'll be seeing you again, very soon." Douche bag turned his attention back to me and smiled, then gently pat my stomach. I flinched at his touch. He ignored my reaction and leaned in close to my ear, "My love, I do fear your hand belongs to the wrong devil, for now. We'll remedy that atrocity soon enough," he whispered softly. He was so close I could smell the enticingly sweet, pheromone-laced scent coming off of him, like lilies mixed with the slight hint of a campfire's smoke.

I stood speechless. His words wormed their way into my mind and set up camp in my subconscious. After a brief pause he backed away a step, turned on his heel and sauntered off. When he was a good distance from the group, he slowly turned and bowed once more. *Always* the gentleman. I watched, in awe, as he walked nonchalantly towards the rising sun, once again, whistling that *insane* melody. Curiosity had the better of me, though I was certain I probably shouldn't ask any questions.

"Who was that?" I asked, against my better judgment.

"That, my dear, was the Seraph," Paul spoke up.

"Seraph... A seraphim. Ok, an angel? So? I kinda figured that. What's the big deal?" I asked, trying to piece it together.

Paul spit on the ground in disgust. "No, no. Not 'an angel', THE Seraphim. That term isn't used anymore, thanks to one being. THE being. The one and only, Lucifer. The Dark Prince. The only bastard to get himself exiled before The Great Divide ever even happened. The Devil. Satan... whatever you choose to call him."

"You're joking, right?" I asked, confused.

"Look at Riley's face and tell me I'm still joking." he nodded, gesturing towards the towering, pissed off Riley, still staring out into the sunrise, where Lucifer made his exit.

"Shit. As if we needed anyone else thrown into the mix," I said, irritated.

It wasn't long after Lucifer left that we all went back to our duties, trying to maintain a calm that no one felt. I snuck off into the house. Mostly everyone was still asleep, which was comforting to me. It would've been difficult to explain why the Devil was standing in our front lawn. Well, I guess it wouldn't be too much of a surprise. At least not with this crowd.

A million thoughts dashed through my head concerning Lucifer. Part of me realized my curiosity probably wasn't healthy, but I couldn't help it. I wanted to know more. I remembered seeing him, *the wolf in the darkness*, but *knew* nothing about him. Nothing, other than what religious fiction had claimed, of course.

Paul said he had been exiled before The Great Divide, but what for? That explained why I hadn't seen him there. But what could he have possibly done to be sent out of the heavens? He's been feared for centuries, hailed as being the cause of every inhuman act by millions of people, since the dawn of civilization. "The Devil made me do it" became a household saying.

I decided that I wanted answers, and I wasn't going to stop asking until I got them. There was only one person who would be able to give me the truth, in all aspects. Unfortunately, he was currently playing lap dog to our Father. Fortunately, I had someone else to interrogate.

"Jonah. I need to talk to you. Are you free for a few minutes?" I asked as I entered the living room.

Jonah looked up from his silent circle, "Of course. Give me just a moment."

I stepped out of the room, moving into the hallway and leaned against the wall. He came up the couple of steps a few minutes later with a look of concern on his face. I grabbed his arm and led him to my old bedroom then closed the door behind us. I jumped onto the bed, folded my legs under me in the infamous lotus style, and patted a spot on the bed next to me.

"Is everything okay?" he asked with his head cocked suspiciously.

I smiled reassuringly, "Of course. I just was hoping you could give me a bit of a history lesson."

His eyes narrowed, "Go on?"

"Tell me about Lucifer," I said, straight faced.

"Uh, Eden? That isn't exactly my expertise. You do remember I'm Pagan, and not a Satanist, right? There is a huge difference." he stood up from the bed and walked towards the door. I could see the discomfort in his eyes.

"No, I mean like, tell me about the Seraphim version. I know what history has said. I don't buy it," I called after him.

"Where is this coming from?" He reluctantly returned to the side of the bed.

"He showed up a little bit ago. I don't remember anything about him. I want to know. Come on, you have to tell me."

Jonah shook his head, "His story is probably better left in the past, Edie. I really don't want to get into it."

"Please, Jonah. You're one of the only people I know who would be honest with me. He isn't taboo. He was favored, wasn't he?" I was trying my best to weasel more out of him.

"Of course, he was favored! He was a lot like you, in his own way. Lucifer was created last. He was the incarnation of God's sense of judgment, if that makes any sense. He was given an incredible gift. He could sway anyone, anywhere, about any matter he wished. He could see anyone's weakness, anyone's desire and play off of it, like a puppeteer. He was created as a test of our strength, once God noticed we had begun to stray. He was the serpent in the garden, so to speak. The voice in our subconscious. He was pure temptation incarnate," Jonah explained. "Or should I say, he is temptation."

"But why was he exiled? He was doing God's bidding, wasn't he?" I asked, confused.

"Let's just say, he had a way with the ladies." Jonah smirked. "His presence alone invoked jealousy, envy, and wrath in the hearts of a lot of the angels... Pretty much all of them. It's impossible to be around him, without feeling keyed up. Regardless of what that emotion is."

I leaned back, settling in for a good story.

"With those emotions came violence, pure, unrivaled malice. The reactions he saw only empowered him more. He found pleasure in knowing what he was capable of. He felt no fear. His gifts made him invincible and with that knowledge, he grew stronger."

"So, God exiled him for doing what he was created to do?" I questioned, "That's fucked up."

"You are so impatient!" he laughed and continued. "Lucifer was like Casanova, of sorts, and had eventually pushed too many buttons. Some of the angels, including your brother, got together and approached God. They understood the importance of the test of faith, but did not understand the need for some of his other antics. Lucifer had such a charismatic air about him that he could convince almost anyone into delving into their deepest, darkest passion and embracing the most carnal of pleasures."

I thought about what he had whispered in my ear, the beautiful smile, the way his eyes captivated me, and knew what Jonah spoke of was the truth.

"The group of angels had confronted him, like an angry mob, chasing a Hollywood-style monster. They hoped to scare him, to make him fear them, but all it did was amuse him. Even when faced with a dozen enraged heavenly beings, he suggested that they do exactly what felt right, what brought them pleasure. That, of course, only angered them further. But in turn, they did just that. Lucifer started a battle that tore a rift between brothers. He was the cause of The Great Divide." Jonah shook his head as he stared at the floor, as if he was stunned by his own words.

"He didn't cause it. We all did. We chose our... oh my God!" It finally made perfect sense.

"You got it! We chose those carnal pleasures over the heavens. Weeks passed, as God attempted to determine the best course of action. Gabriel summoned Lucifer one night and he never returned. His exile was unwitnessed, other than by your brother. The next day, word spread about the banishing of the beloved Lucifer. Anger rose among the future earthbound angels, those who loved him. We all felt as if we had a leader taken from us, for crimes that hadn't been committed. It was unjustified. And for that reason, we turned against the others. He had proven to be stronger than God, Himself," Jonah's voice trailed off as he concluded, then he turned to face me.

"I remember seeing him, but I never was able to talk to him," I whispered.

"He was part of the reason you were hidden away in the garden," Jonah chuckled.

"That definitely makes sense. I would've fallen for him, any day." I grinned shyly, feeling my cheeks flush.

"Bingo!"

"Thanks, Jonah. I really appreciate hearing the truth."

"No problem. I suppose it's no harm, no foul." Jonah's eyes trailed off to the corner of the room in a blank stare, deep in some thought of his own.

"You were one of the angels that liked him, weren't you?" I asked.

"Yes, very much so. I suppose he's partially to thank for my penchant for the unorthodox. I have kept a part of his methods as a part of my life, which is perhaps why I've yet to return to the fold," he replied with a sigh.

I realized that I still wanted to speak with Gabriel on the matter. Not that I didn't believe Jonah, but because I wanted to know the rest of the story. With Gabriel being at God's side, I wouldn't be able to speak with him directly. But I could always find him in my subconscious. I wanted the whole picture.

"Well, Ms. Edie. I need to get back to the group, unless you have any more uncomfortable questions for me." Jonah gave me a gentle smile as he stood from the bed and stretched.

"Nah, I'm good. I may take a nap." I smiled, looking to the old bright pink alarm clock sitting on my bedside table.

"Good. You need the rest. Tell Gabriel I said hello." he grinned knowingly and left the room.

I closed my eyes and felt my body relax. I counted each breath and felt the weight of reality leave my mind. I was drifting out of consciousness and into the world I had grown to loathe. So many times, the dream state proved to be even less desirable than the state of New Jersey. Hard to believe, I know. I focused all of my mind on finding my soul twin and waited. I knew he'd hear me calling, soon enough.

I paced the space I had arrived in. My naked toes flexed in the cold airy clouds. I shivered and rubbed my arms vigorously, trying to find some warmth. I didn't remember it ever being so cold here before. I suppose the absence of our Creator has an atmospheric effect on everything.

It wasn't long after slipping into the subconscious that I saw the winged, golden glow of my angelic twin. He had a bright smile on his face that stretched from ear to ear. As soon as he landed, I approached him. His smile fell flat as soon as he noticed my lack of enthusiasm and look of determination.

Gabriel raised a brow, "Hello, Eden."

"Hey, I have a favor to ask," I skipped the formalities.

"Okay? Nice to see you, too. What can I do for you?" he asked. "And don't ask me about God's answer. You know I can't tell you, even if I knew."

"No, no. I know you can't. I want you to show me Lucifer's exile. I want to see it for myself."

He shook his head, "I don't think that's wise. What's done is done. Why do you want to witness it, anyway?" he asked suspiciously.

"It doesn't matter. Please, just do this for me. I know you were there. I know you're able to show me the past, as you've done all too often," I reminded him. "Don't try and talk me out of this. I want to see it. I have the right to see it. Are you hiding something from me?" I placed my hands on my hips and cocked my head.

"It's not that. Don't turn this on me." his hands were raised defensively, concern etched across his face.

"Then let's get on with it." I grabbed his raised hands and looked him in the eyes. "Please. I won't ask for anything else from you, ever again."

"Lies!" he laughed, then the smile left and he let out a slow sigh, "Fine. But you better listen to me."

"Yeah, yeah!" I chuckled and ran towards the edge of the clouds.

"Give me a second. I have to retrieve the memories."

Moments later, he took my hand and we jumped into the dense air. We sped towards another towering shelf of the heavens. We softly landed and put our wings back in their resting position. Gabriel stepped ahead of me, surveying the area. I stepped into the cloudy cosmos and took a seat on the bank. I could see our Father, anxiously pacing. It was obvious that He was dreading the confrontation with His son.

Gabriel approached me and held his finger to his mouth, as if he was hushing a rambunctious kid.

"I'm not a child. Don't hush me, Gabriel. You're not my mom!" I sarcastically sassed him in a whisper.

"Eden, please. You aren't supposed to be here." he shook his head.

"I'm just kidding. But this is a flashback, remember? Don't give me that bullshit. I'm not going to change anything." I folded my arms with attitude.

"This is a memory, of God's, no less. You think He's blind to anything? No. He isn't. Don't push your luck!" he scolded me.

"I'm sorry," I said, realizing the severity of the situation.

"No, you're not," he grinned.

"You're right. I'm not," I stifled a giggle.

Gabriel turned to face God, looked out towards the distant horizon and turned to me, once more. "I must call on Luke. I'll return shortly. I highly recommend you stay quiet and out of sight!" he gently kissed my forehead and took off, disappearing from the misty shelf.

I found a spot, well hidden and a safe distance from the upcoming event. I hoped that I'd be able to hear everything from here. I leaned back, balancing my body weight on my palms behind me. I stretched my legs out in front of me and settled in. I waited, not so patiently, tapping my feet together.

After hearing everything that Jonah had just explained to me, I couldn't help but wish I had been here for the actual banishment. Maybe I could have helped. Maybe I could have kept him from ever being exiled to begin with. From everything I've heard or read about the Devil's existence, it didn't seem like he had it any worse than the rest of us cast outs. We were all God's discarded children, self-inflicted pain or not. Only time would tell if his release from the heavenly bonds had been as excruciating as what we had experienced.

Though it had only been moments, it felt like hours had passed by the time Gabriel reemerged onto the feather soft walkway. Behind him strode the breathtaking Seraphim. His pride radiated from his perfect body as he walked with a measured step, head held high, seemingly in no hurry at all. The tension in the air was palpable, yet he sauntered forward without even a glint of concern in his sky blue eyes. He was untouchable, fearless... he was absolutely perfect.

"Let the show begin," I whispered to myself with a frown.

Lucifer approached his Father, while smiling, gave a slight bow, "Good evening, my Lord."

"Lucifer," God bowed his head in return.

"Shall I leave the two of you, Father?" Gabriel asked.

"No, son. This will be handled swiftly," He replied, somberly. "Lucifer, your actions as of late have been disheartening to me, to say the very least."

"So I've heard," Lucifer replied. He began a slow pace back and forth in front of his small audience, hands clasped casually behind his back.

"Many others have come forward, concerned with your methods and your intentions. They feel as if you're trying to overthrow me. I know this is not the case, or at least I hope it is not. However, this matter must be addressed," God explained.

Lucifer stopped mid-pace and turned to face God. His words were spoken with a smug disdain, "Pardon me? I can only hope you would not take the words of envious peons over my own. I've done nothing but use the gift you entrusted in me. How I've chosen to test your *dogs* has no bearing on this conversation."

"Heed my words, son. Those 'dogs' you're referring to, are your brothers. I suggest you learn your place in my home!" God bellowed.

"I have no 'brothers', *no equals*. You and I both know I was created out of duty, suspicion and weariness. You had grown tired of questioning their loyalty. I have done nothing more than test that loyalty. I will not beg for forgiveness. I will not grovel. I have done nothing that someone else with my gift wouldn't have done themselves. The pleasure I take in my job is justifiable," Lucifer explained. His tone barely concealed his anger, but his posture remained calm, his hands never leaving their station behind his back.

"Justice is not yours to deal, Son. You are not my right hand. You are my eyes, my ears, my senses," God corrected.

Lucifer scoffed, *"Senses?* There is no sense here! There is no *reason.* These charades have gone on far too long. You've been duped by your own children."

"Watch your tongue, brother." Gabriel stepped forward defensively.

"Brother, be damned!" Lucifer shouted, his eyes never addressing Gabriel, but instead unwaveringly focused on the Lord.

God shook his head, "Damned you are, my son. When your sense has quickened, we will continue this meeting."

Lucifer's eyes narrowed. "No. This must end here and now. Do with me what you will, but know this; you *will* rue the day you created those poor excuses for 'angels'. Their hearts hold more malice and discontent than you will ever know. They are not worthy of your blessings. They are not heavenly. They are sinful souls, thriving on cheap thrills and selfish satisfactions. The time will come when you see this for yourself. Your heart will ache, and I will not be there to comfort you." his own hatred was obvious and deep. Hatred he had held for the kind he had been created to coexist with. His own kind.

"You have left me with no choice. Your heart has grown cold and bitter. Your judgment has become misguided. You cannot be trusted with the others. I truly fear the worst." God hung his head, daunted and full of doubt.

"The worst? You haven't even caught a glimpse of it. Not yet you haven't. They will disappoint you, Lord. If I were in your position, the whole lot of them would be annihilated. To be alone is far better than to be defeated by imbeciles. Your throne is, in fact, being overturned, and you are allowing it to happen without intervening. Without letting *me* intervene. This degradation is within your power to undo. Yet, you are overpowered by your 'love' for these heathens. You've become weak," Lucifer spat these last words, disgusted.

"Stand down!" Gabriel shouted, reaching for the hilt of his sword.

Lucifer finally turned to address Gabriel, the air turbulent between them. "No. I refuse! I was not created to bow like you, God fearing cretin!" he said, his voice growing in power and intensity. "I was not created as a... *play thing.* I *am* God! I am a piece of Him. You will never fathom that. I am perfection!" His rage was palpable, his disdain for Gabriel and all angels evident. His outburst finished, a smile slowly crawled across his handsome features as he continued to stare at Gabriel. Even from my distant vantage the smile and smoldering hatred behind those eyes chilled me to my core. After a long silence he turned his attention back to the Lord and simply said "Let us finish this."

God sighed and cradled His head in His hands. "What shall I do with you, Lucifer? I need a moment to think."

"You already know what you're going to do. Save us both the time and energy. I will not cower. Do what you will." Lucifer popped his neck and rolled his shoulders back, seemingly exhausted from the exchange.

"Oh, no!" I gasped and covered my mouth.

"Very well. As you will not give me the time to contemplate, you've left me with no choice but to act as I had originally planned. Bear no ill will, son, for you have brought this on yourself. You have grown unruly, and powerful beyond what I had expected. You're far too dangerous to stay." God stood from his lofty throne. "Give me but a moment to prepare your new home."

"Oh, God. I have to stop this…" I stood.

Gabriel caught my movement from the corner of his eye and dashed towards me. "Eden, don't you *dare*! There's *nothing* you can do now!" he whispered as he caught me by the shoulders.

I glanced around him, only to see Lucifer staring deep into my eyes, a quizzical expression on his face and one eyebrow raised. He looked… amused? My heart leapt from my chest. How could he see me? "You have to do something to stop him!" my brows furrowed as I pleaded with my brother.

"There's nothing any of us can do. This is the past, not the present," Gabriel reminded me.

Then how did Lucifer notice me?

"I have to return. Sit down. Stay quiet," he said, then bolted towards God and Lucifer.

God was standing, staring out into the vastness, with His back turned to the rest of us. I wished I could approach Him. If I couldn't stop this from happening, I could at least help create a world suitable for such an amazing being. I was vexed. I wanted to, but I knew I would do best by listening to my brother for once. I fought the urge and waited for the inevitable conclusion.

"Lucifer, this is your last chance. Speak with me, admit your wrong doing and be forgiven. It's your pride that has landed you in this situation. Let us handle this in a civilized manner," God attempted to reason.

"To admit fault would be lying to you. I cannot do that. I will not lie to you. You will have to deal with the consequences, much like I will," Lucifer replied, raising his chin in the air with confidence.

"Bow, and all will be forgiven." God stepped towards Lucifer, holding out His hand.

"…no," Lucifer stepped backwards.

"You refuse? Have you no sense?" Gabriel asked.

"Just do it," I whispered to myself.

"I am not a slave. *I will not bow*." Lucifer turned, looking towards me.

I hid behind my knees. My thighs were pulled to my chest in a tight, anxious coil.

"BOW!" God bellowed.

"I will do no such thing!" he returned his gaze to our Father. "That feeling you feel, that *wrath*, gives you power! You will use it, grow more powerful from it. Use it! Now! Forever..." Lucifer's fists clenched.

The fury in God's eyes grew like a flame, higher, brighter with every word Lucifer uttered. "You are a blasphemous demon. You will pay for your transgressions for the rest of eternity. You will bathe in the darkness; the flames will lap at your feet, nipping at your heels, forever. Your new home resembles your black soul, twisted, mangled, full of hate. Your pride has done you in, Prince of Darkness. And let it be known, your only company will be yourself. Your inner demons will dispense from their cage, dancing at your side and driving you mad. You'll beg for forgiveness, if it's the last words you utter. And I will tell you, 'no'. Be damned!" God grabbed Lucifer's forehead, raising him off of the ground.

For a moment, Lucifer hung in the air, limp as a rag doll. Then his back arched, his fists were balled. Though he refused to show it, it was obvious he was in pain. The corner of his mouth curled into a grin.

His beautiful, enormous, snow white wings caught fire. His skin sizzled and smoldered, yet still, he refused to show it. From his chiseled back, a large pair of red, hooked wings emerged. They glowed brightly like fresh embers, charred and disfigured. God raised His son high above His head, and tossed him over the edge of the shelf like a piece of refuse.

I sat straight up in bed with a very bothersome feeling. If God could so easily remove Lucifer from the heavens, a piece of Himself, how would we fare? Perhaps I was a bit jaded, but as I saw it, Lucifer had truly done no wrong, yet he was tossed aside, cast out for doing his duties; while we had undeniably gone against God, completely. My fear rose in my chest. I fell back onto my pillows and played with the tips of my hair, deep in thought.

We're so screwed.

Chapter Forty Three
Denial is Not a River in Hell. Styx is.

I decided to keep a journal of my last days on Earth. Not that anyone would read it, but it was therapeutic to get it off my chest. Society wouldn't be here to read the history postwar, like we have been after our earthly battles of the past.

October 25th, 7 days until the end:
Days have passed with awkward silence. I don't trust the situation. We've mulled about, nervous, anxious, waiting for the next move. It's bound to happen. It's like a high stakes game of chess between the divine and the damned. I won't say who my money is on.
I've drifted through the groups of people like a ghost in the shadows, picking up pieces of conversations and concerns. The general consensus is that the end is nearing and we're going to meet the same fate as those already fallen. Though I can't help but pray my end will be swift and my soul will be salvaged, rather than my death being drawn out by one of the Horsemen.
We've lost all sight of the horsed bastards since Famine came through, and hope we've seen the last of them. But I know, deep down, that's highly unlikely. There's a reason I experienced all of the visions of the pain, the torment, the prophecies. They WILL return, and when they do, death will be dealt.

I could only hope, for the time being. I hadn't received word of God's decision. I assumed that I'd hear something, seeing as how there was only a week until the end. Or perhaps I wouldn't hear anything and I would be swept away and killed, like the rest. I wouldn't ask for myself to be spared, personally. I couldn't imagine carrying on, knowing that everyone I knew and loved had been taken from me. I'd rather join them in the afterlife, or lack thereof, than continue on without them.
That day seemed longer than usual. The day was just dragging its feet and left me scared, for some reason. I wasn't entirely sure why I felt more uneasy than normal. There was obviously something weighing heavily on my mind and heart, and I couldn't tell what it was. I ran through my mental checklist and couldn't find the answers. I fed and loved on Rufio and Azrael, so I knew they were content. I'd eaten. I slept relatively well besides the nightmare and projectile vomiting this morning, so it was not my body. My family and friends were all safe, so far. Still, even after confirming everything with myself, I still had that feeling that something was truly out of place.

"Edie? Is everything okay?" Brooke asked me as she came up from behind, startling me.

"Huh? Oh, yeah. I'm fine." I closed my journal and turned to her with a polite smile.

"Alright, I just wanted to make sure. You looked a bit down and out," she stated bluntly.

I shook my head.

"Well, if you need anything, just let us know. We're here for you."

"I appreciate it," I replied. "Oh, come to think of it, have you seen Elijah?"

"He's in the backyard with Lilith. They were talking to someone I didn't recognize." she replied, shrugging.

"I wonder who..." I trailed off and rose from my seat at the kitchen table. I walked over to the small section of the patio door that had been left uncovered and looked out. There, standing near an old oak tree was Elijah, Lilith and Lucifer. I hurried to the door leading to the garage and ran out. I rounded the corner of the garage and checked to make sure the coast was clear. I had some questions, and I didn't want to draw attention to myself. Once I ensured that no one was watching me, I made a mad dash around the side and hurriedly came into the backyard.

"Well, look what the cat dragged out." Lilith grinned as I approached.

Elijah's eyes brightened, "Hello, Aunt Eden!"

"Hello, kiddo."

"It's a pleasure to see you again, Madame." Lucifer bowed his head, slightly, ever the makings of a smile ready on his lips.

I eyed him suspiciously, "Yes, I'm sure it is. When you guys are done, is there any chance I could speak with you a moment?" I asked the Seraphim, never shifting my gaze.

"Me? You and I, converse? Surely you jest." he grinned as his hand came up to his chest in a look of pretend surprise.

"No, I mean it. I can wait, though. I just, uh, had some questions," I replied. His intense stare and Cheshire catlike smile were beginning to unnerve me.

"I'm done with this devil." Lilith winked at me. "Luke, I'll pass on your message to Gabriel and make sure that The Lord is aware. I thank you for your hard work, despite what you've been through." Lilith wrapped her arm around Elijah's shoulder and turned away, guiding the boy as she went. Her glowing green eyes shown like emeralds in the bright midday sun as the two left us, the Devil and I.

"Now, what can I do for my queen?" Lucifer grabbed my hand and kissed the top of it in one smooth motion. "Are you here to make a deal? I'm afraid I can't negotiate with you. Your soul is far too precious to tether at the moment, and I have more souls than I can handle presently." his smile left like a feather on the breeze and was replaced by something that oddly resembled concern, but I brushed the thought away as soon as it came to me.

"No, no deals, thanks. You have some answers I'd like to hear."

"Well, I will be as honest with you as a 'devil' can be, but I make no guarantee that you will find my answers suitable for your tastes, nor that you would like to hear them."

"Why were you banished?" I asked outright.

A flash of anger momentarily sparked in his eyes, but they were immediately back to their beautiful blue color. He stared at me for a moment, then nodded once to himself. "Walk with me, Madame Muse." He gently led me away from everyone with one hand on the small of my back, like an unwitting lamb to slaughter. "Now, if you don't mind me asking, why is it that you wish to know about my banishment, when you yourself, saw the events this morning following your interrogation of Jonah?"

"How'd you know about that?" I asked with a curious grin as I looked over to him.

He looked back and chuckled. "Love, I know all. For instance, would you like me to recap your teen years? I can remind you, verbatim, of the times I gently persuaded you to…"

"No, thanks! I believe you," I cut him short as my cheeks began to flush. "I wanted to know your side. Why did you continue to push God, after He gave you an opportunity to repent?"

"I had done nothing against God's will. What happened was contemptuous and *extremely* hypocritical. I was not going to beg, I made that perfectly clear. Your soul twin had the audacity to assist in my exile, yet returns to me for news and to carry messages. Though our Father released me from His good graces, He's never released me from His bonds. We are still tied by spirit. By soul," he explained, slowly guiding us further into a field.

I stopped in place, "So He kicked you out, but you continued to do His bidding?"

"Yes. Precisely. My job will never be done. What He gave me, was my own kingdom to rule. And I would gladly give you a throne alongside of mine." he bowed politely.

I snickered at the offer. "I think I'll have to pass. Heat makes my hair curl."

"You'll change your mind," he laughed, devilishly. "Someday, you'll beg me to allow you into my sanctuary."

I cocked an eyebrow at him in utter disbelief. "I doubt it."

"Did I not already tell you, I know all? It's the truth, my queen. My blessing and curse." he gently pressed on my back and we continued deeper into the field.

I grinned to myself, "I assume your cockiness is a side effect of your powers."

"Did you come to insult me, or learn of the truth?" he asked, his smile gone.

"I'm sorry," I paused. "Yes, I want the truth." my head hung with embarrassment.

He stopped once more and gently lifted my chin with a single finger, meeting my eyes with his own. My heart stopped beating altogether. "Leave with me. I'll keep you and the children safe. I can promise you, you will never feel pain again. You will never feel fatigue, age, sickness. You will once again be immortal."

I pulled away from his touch, "What're we up against?"

"*Death*," he turned once more and walked ahead of me.

After the shock of that single word had passed, I sprinted lightly, catching up to the Seraphim. "Is there anything we can do?"

"I told you what you can do. I told you how you could save yourself, and protect your little ones. What more do you want from me?"

I raised a brow, "I want a solution that doesn't involve selling my soul to the Devil."

"Love, I will not bargain for your soul. I want my Queen, not another minion. My kingdom is large enough, but my chambers are empty." his expression saddened for the first time.

I stared at the Seraphim, unable to read his intentions. "That isn't open for discussion now, nor is it an appropriate topic of conversation. So I suggest you get over it and help me figure out how to handle this."

He laughed loudly, "Well, I'll find a new approach. I now see charm and pity will not work on you. You're a sly minx!" he winked at me from the side of his eye.

"I'm glad you see this as a game and your prey amuses you," I rolled my eyes.

"You're even more enticing when you're angry," he taunted me. "Alas, we've strayed from the point of this meeting. Where were we? Ah, what to do. There is obviously more than one way to skin a cat, or an arrogant archangel, as it were."

"I don't want to do any skinning. I'd actually hope we could complete this without any more bloodshed."

"That's impossible," he flouted. "What you wish and what will happen are two entirely different things, love. This will not be simplistic. This will be complicated. There will be death, pain, despair. Brother will kill brother. The meek shall not inherit the Earth, the bastardized 'chosen' will... unless..." he stopped dead in his tracks as his voice trailed off.

"Unless what?" I asked, curious by his obvious *eureka* moment.

"Unless, perhaps, you chose to surrender to me, and I allowed my minions to fight in your stead." he grinned wickedly.

"Oh, my God! You're such an asshole!" I slapped his arm instinctively.

He laughed maniacally. "I'm jesting, Muse. Truly, I am," he continued to press forward, urging me to follow suit. "What I meant to say, was perhaps the abominations will win this war, with a bit of assistance from the Dark Prince, himself."

"And how do we know we can trust you?" I asked.

He shrugged nonchalantly, "You don't."

"That doesn't help your argument."

"My argument isn't what needs help in this dilemma. Besides, you're certainly not the best when it comes to negotiations. Your children, as leverage? Your soul, as leverage? It isn't safe. You think trusting 'Satan' is dangerous? You seem to forget who created me. My traits originated somewhere, dear." he left me behind as he sped up slightly, head down, lost in thought.

I stood in place, contemplating what he had said. For years, we had all been told not to trust him, that he was bad for our spirituality. Life is full of checks and balances. You can never fully understand good without knowing evil. You can never see the positives, without first experiencing the negatives. I then realized the magnitude of what was happening.

"Wait!" I called out to Lucifer.

He stopped in place as he raised his head, turned, and watched me approach him once more. His bright blue eyes glowed with intensity, as if they were emitting their own light. He folded his arms across his chest and waited patiently.

"What were you and Lilith discussing?" I asked as I drew next to him.

"That business is between us," he replied, turned away and continued walking.

"You said you'd tell me the truth," I reminded him.

"That was when I thought you were willing to hear me out, rather than judge me like the others. Time is fleeting in my line of work. I will not waste it with pointless quarrels and historical lessons," he sneered.

"I don't judge you, I want to know. Prove to me, show me how you intend to help," I pleaded.

"Then come with me, let me show you the truth." he held his hand out for me to take.

I turned, facing my parents' house in the distance. My conscience was torn. I wanted to see all of our options, to see the bigger picture. But I also understood there were risks in doing so. I looked at his hand, traced his tailored suit sleeve up to his face and decided to trust him. I placed my palm in his, timidly.

"We need to hurry," I spoke low.

"I'll have you home by ten o'clock. I don't want you to be grounded." he grinned with a wink.

He arched his back, flexing his shoulder blades. His ember like wings emerged from his back gracefully, sending out little puffs of black smoke as they stretched. I followed suit and let my wings out of their muscular bonds. He leapt into the air, pulling me along with him.

We traveled at an astonishing speed, without leaving the Earth's atmosphere. I had expected to experience something otherworldly, rather than stay in our plane. I held his hand tightly as we sped towards our target location. I hadn't the slightest clue where we were going. After a short while he began to descend, slowing his pace.

We landed on a rooftop, overlooking a crumbling city. Rubble tumbled to the ground, cracking and booming in the thick air. I coughed, choking on the smoke in the atmosphere, thanks to the numerous, burning, nearby buildings. He lifted his forearm to his face, cuing for me to use my sleeve to block my mouth and protect my airway.

"Where are we?"

"Beaumont," he paused, scanning the damaged horizon. He pointed, "That, right there, is the place of your birth," he replied with a whisper, indicating a building across from us. "Six miles to the east was the first school you ever attended. Two miles south of there, is the home you spent the first few years of your life."

"Why are we here?" I asked sadly.

"When you look at your surroundings, what do you see?"

"Destruction. Hell on Earth," I choked on my words.

"And what do you feel?" he persisted.

"Anger. Sadness. Heartache."

"You say this reminds you of Hell. We did not do this. The chaos that springs from my influence is an internal battle. The destruction is a self-inflicted, spiritual destruction. I do not plant emotions, or force my will. I haven't had to lift a finger in centuries. I test the strength of those inhabiting the Earth, I do not control them." He sat on the edge of the roof top, looking down at the burning city with a somber disconnection.

"This was the Horsemen's doing, wasn't it?" I asked, confused by his statements.

"On the contrary. This city was destroyed by the Archangels themselves, under Michael's command. The *heroic* right hand of God. What he has done is inhumane. What he has done is reverse years of progress, for both myself, and God."

"And the people?" I didn't want to know the answer.

"Erased. None were spared. The good, the just, the women and children. All were executed without being tried. Without defense."

"What must we do?" I frowned as I sat next to him.

"There is one, rising to power out of all of this. One being claiming the glory, basking in the glow of all of this death and destruction. It is not your God. It is not yours truly. It is Michael. He has been given too much authority and has grown corrupt. We both know of his hatred for mankind. His grudge has never left his blood. His vengeance grows with every screaming child. He feels vindicated. He feels justified."

"And with Michael out of the picture, what will happen? Will everything return to how it's supposed to be?"

He laughed slightly at my ignorance and shook his head slowly, "No. That's impossible. Nothing will ever be as it was. The times have changed. Far too much damage has been done. The people have now seen wrath, and will never fully recover. God will most likely choose to dispatch the Earth entirely, to clean up Michael's mess." he turned and looked deep into my eyes.

I felt helpless. "Then what should we do?"

His smile grew slowly to one of defiance, a glimmer appearing in his eyes. "Fight. Stand up. Make your voice be heard."

"We're doing that. We're trying!" his cryptic messages were frustrating me.

"Your cause must be a just one. Your voices must become singular. The world has been overturned by chaos, beyond even my control. All I can do is sit back and watch as the world burns. I'm no different than the rest of you." he grabbed my hand casually. It was reassuring and yet uncomfortable.

"I'm so lost." I rubbed my temple with my free hand.

"Be the muse you were created to be. Use that creative mind, that Godsend you were blessed with." he gently poked my head with his free hand.

"I'm so beyond confused." I pulled my hand from his and cradled my head.

"You wonder why I'm able to walk freely amongst the humans after being exiled, do you not?" he rose to his feet and grabbed my hand once more, pulling me up.

"I do," I nodded, struggling for my footing.

"I was sent away from all of you, from the angels. I was sent to the darkness, the cold, burning, darkness. As the angels lost their ways and became what they are today, I came into power, fully came into my own." he released my hand and began pacing the rooftop, looking into the distance. "I tested my boundaries, stepping out further and further over the years. The more the angels failed, detached and became human, the more I was able to socialize. God felt no need to protect them any longer. My reign was soon approaching. I would be a stronger God, able to make clear decisions, without the clouded vision of love. I waited thousands of years for that moment, and it was hastily approaching."

He suddenly stopped and spun towards me, his normally stoic appearance giving way to anger as he pointed at me, "The only ones left in my way, were the twelve of you. All the others had successfully returned to the fold. Before long, I would've had you all out of the picture, either by claiming you as my own, or sending you back to the heavens. The Earth was so close to being mine. The humans would become *my* bastard children, *my* play things." he grinned at the notion.

"Michael not only bested God, he bested me. And with that being said, I have been enraged by his pomposity. He is callous, and he will always be so. His victories have always been won by the hands of those he commanded. He is a pseudo hero," he regained his composure, popped his neck slowly, and let out a short laugh.

"Then that's the answer. We need to get Michael out of the limelight?" I cocked my head. I was trying to find answers in his stories.

"Lilith and I have worked, side by side, since the dawn of time," he began again. "And to answer your question, what I told Lilith was news I hoped to have delivered to The Lord. He does not understand the troubles Michael has caused for Him. I simply showed Lilith the whole story. The prophecies that have occurred, the plagues, the wrath, the death and wars, were not God's doing, nor my own. They were conceived by a wicked mind." His wings flapped in the wind, stretching and rousing from a groggy boredom, seemingly with a mind of their own.

"Michael?" I guessed.

"None other," he stood on the ledge of the roof, teetering on the balls of his feet. "I promote pleasure. The Lord promotes love. Michael promoted pain. He is the disease, the cancer spreading, plaguing this planet. It's imperative that God sees this truth for Himself and puts an end to it, once and for all." He stretched his arms forward, as if to symbolize his own restlessness and boredom. Leaning forward, his wings sprang into action and caught him, countering his balance.

"Where are we headed now?" I asked, assuming we were preparing to depart.

"There's one other location I wish for you to see," he admitted. "It will pain you, more so than you could have thought possible."

He leapt into the air without warning and headed south. I followed, keeping pace as best I could. The cold wind ripped at my lungs, already aching from the smoke inhalation. We flew for a few minutes and touched down in front of what appeared to be an old school house.

"Where are we now?"

"Just follow me," he replied curtly and walked towards the building.

We stepped into the doorway, over shattered pieces of wood and a broken door. The entry room was scantily decorated, with hallways outstretched from each side. These corridors were also bare and branched in numerous directions of their own. I followed as he walked down the first hallway we approached.

Suddenly, Lucifer paused. I stopped short, almost running into the folded wings on his back. He turned to me and placed both of his hands on the sides of my face, covering my eyes with his snow white palms. His cold skin soothed my overheated body, and I wondered how a creature of so much fire and ash could feel so cold. I relaxed for a moment, enjoying the comfort, the silence, the momentary peace.

He removed his hands and whispered into my ear, "Madame, let us view the past, shall we?"

I opened my eyes to see dozens of children laughing and running about. They shouted names and squealed as they caught up with each other. A young boy ran by me and looked upwards, meeting my gaze. His eyes took my breath away. He had a single blue eye, and a single green. His blonde hair was combed over in a wisp.

"*Dad*?" I whispered, confused.

He nodded once, "Oui, ma cherie. This was the orphanage your father lived in."

I was speechless. I wasn't sure what he was up to, but I felt nervous. We walked the halls wordlessly. I watched the children as they ran by, playing. Some were in rooms, sitting in circles, gossiping. Some were silently reading or drawing. None of them so much as noticed us, let alone greeted us.

"Now, let us return to the present," he said abruptly. He stepped forward and placed his hands on my face once more.

I gasped as the cool air left my lungs, replaced with a stagnant, putrid stench. The pungent odor filled my nose and I bent over, heaving. Lucifer stepped to my side, placing his cold hand on the back of my neck. I inhaled deeply, comforted by the cool. When I had composed myself I stood and turned to him. He placed his hands on my chest, above my heart. I closed my eyes and slowed my breathing.

"Feeling well again, love?" he asked, removing his hands slowly and raising one brow inquisitively.

"Yes, thanks," I nodded with a halfhearted smile.

"Then let us continue." he grabbed my hand, turned, and began walking again.

We walked through the hallway, stepping over broken toys and discarded dolls, soot covered childhood treasures. I looked from room to room. It was unusually dark for the time of day, and I could barely see but something odd caught my eye and I stopped dead in my tracks. Lucifer noticed my pause and turned.

I released his hand and stepped into the doorway rubbing my eyes, attempting to focus on the curious object. It was pale, stone in appearance, almost glowing from the light sneaking in through the window. As I approached, my heart sank and my stomach rose. I gasped and covered my mouth, dropping to my knees.

"What've they done?" I cried through my fingers and reached for the bed. "Oh, my God."

"I regret that you've been forced to see the world cast in this light. Your gentle soul has seen far too much pain in these latter days. Nonetheless, I needed you to see the truth for yourself, as unpleasant as it is. Forgive me, love." he gently rested his hand on my back, remaining as still as a statue at my side.

I pulled away, rising to my feet, *"Who did this?"*

"You know, very well, who did this. There is only one capable of such an atrocity." he tried to gently turn me from the gruesome scene.

I pulled away, reaching down. I picked up the lifeless body spread across the bed top. Tears streamed down my face. I held the body close as rage filled my heart. "He's going to pay for this," I spit through my clenched jaw.

I carried the deceased child in my arms, through the doorway and walked towards the once grand entrance. My mind shrieked, begging me not to look into the other rooms. They were everywhere. Children. Their shells laid lifeless, tortured. I felt every cry deep in my soul.

"Where are you taking him?" Lucifer asked, sounding more curious than compassionate.

"Outside. He deserves to rest in peace, not in this prison," my voice cracked as I choked on my words.

"Eden, there's very little we can do now," he replied.

"Anything is better than nothing. Help me gather them up, please." I stepped through the doorway, exiting the cursed building. I found a large oak tree and set the body down beneath its branches, then leaned over the corpse and gently kissed his forehead. The child was no more than seven. His brown hair hung to the side, dancing in the bitter breeze. I closed his eyes with my middle and index fingers and wept. For a moment, he looked alive, at peace. Asleep. I knew it wasn't the case, but it was the only comfort I could afford here.

"Reverto ut Deus, meus parvulus," I cried, kissing the top of the child's head. "God, please take this little soul. *Please!*"

"Love, He cannot hear you here." Lucifer strutted up from behind, setting another young boy alongside of the first.

"Make Him hear!" I shouted and dashed to Lucifer, laying my head on his chest.

He wrapped his arms around me, gently rubbing my back, "We'll call on the Valkyrie. You can only hope they're able to save their souls," he said with a resigned sigh.

"I hate Michael," I sobbed.

"You're not alone, love." he pulled me from his chest by both of my arms and stared into my eyes. "We'll make this right as rain, you'll see."

I sniffled, "That's impossible. We can't reverse this. Any of it!"

He wiped the tears from my cheeks. "But we can prevent it from happening to the rest of the world."

"We need to get the rest of them. We need to bring them all out," I whispered, my voice trembled.

"No, we must leave. If we hurry, the Valkyrie may be able to aid them. We have far too many pressing matters to be in this bleak dwelling." he rubbed my arms, attempting to comfort me.

"But…" I frowned.

"We're wasting precious time." his expression was flat; grieved, but logical. He was planning ahead once more.

I returned my gaze to the ominous building. "I want to save them," I whispered.

"And you will, if we leave now and act with haste. If nothing else, I can handle this. But it would be better for the Valkyrie to help," he explained.

"Then let's leave." I wiped the tears from my cheek and spread my wings.

"That's my girl!" he nodded with a wicked grin.

We leapt into the air and sped towards home. Neither of us spoke a word. We flew with incomparable speed. The wind and smoke ripped at my face as we bolted towards the house.

As we descended, I saw Riley and Gabriel standing out back, searching the sky. I locked eyes with my soul twin and felt my breath catch in my chest. I landed on the ground first and watched, almost as if in slow motion, as Riley ran towards Lucifer. His fist made contact with the Seraphim's right cheek, "Stay the fuck away from her!"

Lucifer cracked a grin, his stance unbroken from the blow. "Jealousy is a canny temptress."

"Stop!" I shouted, pulling Riley back.

I could feel every one of his muscles tense. Gabriel stepped between the two of them, placing a hand on each of their chests, with arms stretched wide to hold the distance. Riley shrugged, forcing me from his side.

"You need to hear him out," Gabriel spoke to Riley.

"I don't need to hear shit! What I need is for him to get the hell out of here before I tear his ass apart! I don't have time for this!" Riley pushed Gabriel's arm off of his chest. "You act like he's trustworthy. You act like it's not a big deal that he just disappeared with Eden, your own sister," Riley hissed at Gabriel.

"He did no wrong," Gabriel replied.

Lucifer's grin had not fallen. He stood still as stone, soaking up the hatred. It was almost as if his energy was being recharged. I stepped away from Riley and walked over to Lucifer's side. Gabriel looked deep into Riley's eyes, silently reasoning with him, then dropped his arms.

"Speak, quickly," Riley's jaw clenched tightly.

Lilith walked around the side of the house with her son in tow. Behind her, strode Meridith, Callin and Kenneth. They joined us in the small, tension filled circle.

Elijah stepped forward and took Lucifer's hand. His sad face broke my heart.

"So, it's true?" Elijah asked.

"Yes," Lucifer spoke, eyes not wavering from Riley.

"There's nothing we can do. You'll have to call on Charon to collect their souls," Callin stated.

"Who the hell is Charon? What the hell's going on?" Riley continued to question.

"The Ferryman," Lucifer responded.

"As in, *ferry to hell*? Luke... how could you?" I asked angrily.

"Yes, as in the Ferryman, traveling across the Styx," Lucifer explained with a patronizing "blah, blah, blah" style hand signal, obviously annoyed. "Eden, I can keep their souls dormant for now. I can house them until God will accept them. If you want them protected, you're going to have to stop being petty and allow us to do what needs to be done."

"*Luke*? You have a little pet name for the Devil, now? What the fuck is going on?!" Riley was beyond irate.

"Riley, shut up! Would you hold on, *please*!" I screamed.

His expression changed quickly, from angry to confused and shocked.

Gabriel spoke up, "Eden, God has closed the doors. He isn't allowing anyone to enter. Not even the Archangels. His decision has been made. Everyone, including Michael, are now on Earth."

I looked to Meridith. She nodded solemnly.

"But what about the children? We can't let their souls be lost." I frowned, crushed.

"I will call on Charon. Callin, Meridith, will you be dears and gather some of the Valkyrie? Have them assist the Ferryman in harvesting souls. Kenneth, will you inform the others and gather a couple angels to secure the location? Riley, you need to prepare for lock down. Michael will act fast," Lucifer commanded, all business.

"Don't tell me how to do my job, *asshole*." Riley turned, walking away from the rest of us.

"Riley, stop!" I chased after him, leaving the others behind to arrange their affairs.

"I can't believe you!" he shook his head.

"What's *wrong* with you?" I asked, angered by his reaction.

"I've spent my entire life, no, *lives*, trying to keep you safe. I've done anything and everything to make sure that you weren't in pain, weren't sad or in danger. But, you. You go behind my back, getting all buddy-buddy with the fucking Devil? Whose side are you on, Eden? Are you *trying* to get yourself and the babies killed?" his words dug deep.

"You can be such a jerk, you know that? I'm trying to help. It's not my fault that you feel threatened. You've been face down in maps and books, running around in secrecy, making plans, strategies... You wouldn't take the time to hear him out. Heaven forbid, someone else does!" I shook my head, disgusted.

"Oh, fuck you! And what good have you done by doing that? You've basically invited Satan, himself, to the party. You've allowed him to dabble in this war, when it isn't his place. This is a holy war, remember?" he began walking towards the front of the house. "Good job, oh, noble Princess. I hope you're happy with yourself."

"Don't walk away from me!" I shouted.

"I have to go get shit done. I have to clean up your mess!" he yelled over his shoulder.

"An honorable man, a good leader, will hear everyone out! A good man will take all things into consideration before running in, guns blazing!" I frowned.

"Well, I suppose I'm no better than your little pet demon," he jabbed and walked away.

"Eden, you have to let him go," Gabriel spoke from behind me.

"I've never seen him like this." I sighed, rubbing my forehead.

"And now you see the strength of Lucifer. His presence invokes and amplifies traits. It's both a blessing and a curse for us, right now," he explained.

"What am I supposed to do? I hate this." I let my hair down and scratched at my head, attempting to fathom the situation.

"Stay with us. Give Riley time to wind down. He has a lot on his mind and is under a multitude of stress," Lucifer offered, stepping around the house with his hands folded behind his back.

"I agree," Gabriel said.

"I don't know."

"Come. Let us discuss the proceedings." Lucifer held out his hand, pointing towards the back of the house.

I followed Gabriel and Lucifer behind the house and sat with them on the ground. We were joined by Lilith and Elijah. We discussed the situation and planned our side of the fight. We would be in the background, ensuring all souls would be tended, rightfully.

Lucifer had dispatched Callin and Meridith, who had retrieved a few others and went to the site of the old orphanage. Kenneth took Damien and a handful of angels with him to keep the Valkyrie safe as they worked. They would have to act fast to return to us before nightfall and the wolves descended.

Shortly after telling Gabriel about Michael's doings, Lucifer left to summon Charon and keep him under a watchful eye. Though Charon was under Lucifer's control, Lucifer knew there would be consequences if he wasn't there to supervise the demon's presence on Earth.

"Eden, we need to talk," Gabriel said later that evening with a saddened look on his face.

That could only mean one thing. God had made his decision.

CHAPTER FORTY FOUR
(CUE DRAMATIC ACTION SCORE)

It wasn't long after Lucifer and the others left that the shit began to hit the fan. As night fell, the anxiety rose, and it was well deserved. It started with random 'boom's as the ground trembled. I could only think of two logical reasons for that to happen; A) an explosion. B) the Horsemen. And I'll be the first to announce, it was both.

"Are we going to be safe?" Mom asked, gently placing her hands on my shoulders, as we stared out of the only peephole left uncovered.

I frowned. "I don't know, Momma."

"That's reassuring," she chided.

Nothing was reassuring at this point. Gabriel had left, attempting to reason with God, once more. Lucifer still hadn't returned with the others. We were down quite a few able bodies and it was starting to take its toll.

"Eden! We need your help!" Corey screamed, busting open the front door.

"What's wrong?" I asked, coming around the edge of the couch to see Erick in his arms.

"Ah! Fuck! It hurts!" Erick shrieked through his clenched teeth.

"Get him to the kitchen. What happened?" I asked, following Corey and Gabe, carting our friend.

"Ah!" Erick continued to writhe in pain.

"Calm down. Try and relax," I said, putting gloves on.

"We were running towards Paul and Riley. One of those douche bags came down on top of him," Gabe filled me in.

"Edie, it was bad. He knocked him to the ground, face first and stabbed him in the back with some kind of golden spear," Corey continued, as I cleared everything from the table.

They laid him down as my eyes traced the trail of blood that followed behind them. Erick's eyes were closed tight. He was hyperventilating, with his fists balled tightly. Corey looked terrified. Gabe looked pissed.

"Guys, I got it from here. I'm gonna need some space, if you don't mind," I shouted, placing a hand on Erick's wrist to check his pulse.

"We'll head back outside," Gabe said, herding Corey towards the kitchen door.

"Honey, your mom said you were in here. Do you need a hand?" Aunt Kristi asked.

"Yeah, please. Get that door closed and get over here," I answered, cutting Erick's shirt from his torso with a pair of trauma shears.

"What do you need?"

"I need you to help me turn him onto his uninjured side, and then find Melanie," I ordered.

"I can do that," she nodded.

We counted to three and gently rolled him onto his left side. He cried out in pain, as the blood poured off of the table and pooled on the floor below. I watched as my new friend drifted in and out of consciousness.

I placed a compression bandage on his gaping wound, obtained a blood pressure and started an IV to replace his blood volume. I listened to his lung sounds to confirm whether the spear had entered into one of them, or if it had missed it. I was comforted to know that his lung sounds were present and clear.

"Edie, I'm here. What do you need?" Mel asked as she entered the room with my aunt.

"He's going into shock. Grab me a blanket, find my morphine and get another line set up. He's going to need a second IV," I replied.

"Gotcha!" she moved fast, grabbing everything I had asked for.

I established an IV in his arm and began to run the saline solution. As I was giving Erick a dose of morphine, there was a loud boom, and within two minutes, there was more commotion in the living room. My mom opened the kitchen door and stuck her head in. A look of terror was smeared across her face, as she turned back to us.

"Edie, honey, we need you in here." my mom's eyes welled with tears.

"You got this a second?" I asked Mel.

"Go," she nodded.

I pulled off my gloves, tossing them to the floor and followed the cries, stepping into the living room. Brandon, Paul, and Gabe were kneeling over someone I couldn't see. I pushed Gabe aside and saw Jonah lying on the floor, with the mask of death stretched across his face. My heart sank.

"Oh, God!" I covered my mouth.

"Help him, please! Oh, fuck. Bro, get up!" Paul's voice quivered, as he shook his soul brother's shoulders. "Edie, please save him. Don't let it end like this!"

"I'll do what I can." I rushed out of the room, ahead of the others.

Stepping into the kitchen, I motioned for Mel to grab the top half of Erick. We carried him down the hall and set him on a small pallet of bedding that was lying on the floor of my parents' room. I asked her to stay with him while I tended to Jonah.

"What happened?" I asked, feeling for a pulse in his neck.

"Death's here," Paul said, gently brushing the hair from Jonah's face.

"He has a pulse!" I sighed with relief. "Y'all need to get out. I need as much quiet as possible."

"Can I stay, please?" Paul asked.

"Dude, you know we need you." Brandon frowned.

Paul fell silent. "Will you at least send word?" he asked.

"Of course, now go!" I replied. My mom hurried them out of the room and closed the door behind her.

I placed my hands on Jonah's chest, inhaling deeply. I closed my eyes and focused all of my mind on the garden. Trees. Flowers. A cool breeze dancing through the soft grass. *What are his injuries?* I opened my eyes, frustrated. My concentration had been broken.

"Damn it!" I growled angrily.

I closed my eyes again, unconcerned with his bodily state. I silently stepped into the garden, imagining the dew covered grass under my bare feet. I could see Jonah seated under my tree. He turned and faced me with a gentle smile. The breeze was a bit cool, sending a shiver through my body. I shook it off and stepped towards Jonah.

"Hello, Eden." he smiled wide.

"Jonah!" I was so relieved to see him here.

"Leave, please." his smile faltered.

I shook my head, "No, we need to return."

"I'd like you to leave me, please. I don't want to return. I want to stay." he rose from the ground, stepping towards me.

"I'm sorry. I can't do that. You can't stay here."

His brows furrowed, "I don't want to go, please don't make me. This is the first time I've felt at peace for thousands of years."

"I'm so sorry, please forgive me." My brow crumbled as I grabbed his hands.

I was startled back to reality as Jonah gasped loudly and sat straight up on the kitchen table. He grasped his chest, pulling what was left of his shirt away from his body. He wiped his brow, then fell forwards onto his raised knees.

"Why did you pull me away?" his voice was deep, raspy and pained.

"I had to. I.."

"No, you didn't," he cut me short, swinging his legs around and off of the table.

"Jonah, that isn't the Kingdom. That's only a memory. If I hadn't aided you, you would've died. There's no place for us right now. Your soul would've been lost," I explained finally.

"My soul is none of your concern." he stood, throwing his shredded shirt to the floor. "I need to get back out there."

"No, you need to rest for the night."

"I will do no such thing." he attempted to walk, falling forward.

There was a knock on the door. "Come in!" I shouted, holding Jonah upright in my arms.

"Sorry, I'm fashionably late, love." Lucifer grinned as he entered the doorway. "What happened here?"

"Oh, thank God!"

"You know He has nothing to do with my wondrous presence... well not presently, at any rate." he winked and walked towards me.

"We need to get him in the bedroom with Erick. Will you help me?" I asked, throwing one of Jonah's arms around my shoulder.

He smirked as he lifted Jonah lightly, by himself, "Anything for you."

Jonah hadn't put up a fight, once he realized he was weakened. I was surprised by his suddenly sharp tongue. It wasn't long before I realized the link between his reaction and the arrival of Lucifer. Gabriel had spoken the truth. He had a way of bringing out the hidden traits of everyone. But what had he done to me?

I checked on Erick while I was in the bedroom. He was resting comfortably. Melanie sat by his side and told me that his vital signs had remained stable and without significant changes. Lucifer and I left the bedroom and returned to the kitchen. I cleaned up the mess as he reported the day's events from the old orphanage.

"So you guys managed to save all of the souls? That's amazing." I smiled warmly.

"Yes, ma'am. I gave you my word." he bowed his head slightly from his spot leaning against the wall.

"I appreciate everything you've done for us." I threw the remainder of the trash into the trashcan and closed the lid.

"Charon was all but pleased by my orders." he rolled his piercing blue eyes.

"I'm sorry." I frowned and hung my head.

He lifted my chin with a single finger, "Do not apologize for caring, love. That's what makes you a good being."

I felt my cheeks flush with heat. "Thanks," I grinned sheepishly, pulling away from his touch. "And where are the others?"

"They're outside, assisting your pawns," he replied, moving slightly to stare into my eyes.

I felt my heart stop, then race. "I should go check on them."

"They're fine. Death has finished his game here, for the night. Most of the Archangels are retreating. I anticipated that you would want a full report. I touched base with the others, before finding your beautiful, welcoming smile." he grinned softly.

I tried to ignore his charm. "Thanks. I appreciate the news."

"May I ask you something?" he sidestepped once more to block my path and peer into my eyes.

"Sure." I looked away.

"Have you received word from God?" he asked.

"Somewhat. But apparently, He forced everyone from the heavens and sent them to Earth. I can only assume, knowing Michael, that God's decision was not in our favor. If He is allowing him to come here, then death will be dealt," I replied with a frown.

"And if this is the case, if you are all doomed to death…" he began, and then stopped short.

"What?" I asked, curious. I was fairly sure of what he was going to ask, and for once I would welcome the option.

"If that is to happen, will you continue to fight? Or will you succumb to Him?"

"Oh." That wasn't what I was expecting. "I don't really know. I'm not one to just walk away from anything."

"So, if God has refused you, and you are to die, that would mean that your precious soul would be lost," he surmised.

I shrugged. "I suppose."

"Then would it be safe to assume that perhaps then, you'd accept my offer? Contemplate it carefully, Love. I would save your beautiful soul, your children's, your family's. All for a very low cost to you."

"I'll think about it," I chuckled lightly. "But what is this 'low cost'?" I asked suspiciously.

"Why, your hand, of course." he smiled brightly.

I laughed loudly. I didn't know how to reply. I'm sure my eyes answered more than he expected to hear in return. Preservation; my reliable civil service instincts had kicked in. I could save all of those that I cared about. The thought was tempting. He was tempting. Or was he simply *temptation*?

He winked. "Well, I suspect this negotiation will continue at a later date."

"Maybe. Don't press your luck." I raised a brow. "I should go check on everyone. I'm really worried."

"They're fine, love. You should go relax. I don't anticipate there being any more danger for the remainder of the night. And if there is, you'd do more good well rested." he gently kissed my cheek. "Do take a moment for yourself. All will be quiet."

He disappeared into the chaotic night. The sweet honey smell lingered around my face, long after his kiss. I sat at the kitchen table for a few minutes thinking about everything he had said. For being the Devil, he wasn't such a bad guy. He seemed just as protective of me as the others that I've trusted for years. He cared just as much about my wellbeing as the angels we were siding with. The true question was, what were his motives? It couldn't be compassion.

I made my rounds. While I had been kept company by Lucifer, two more walking wounded had arrived in the living room and were being treated by Mel. Corey had hurt his ankle somehow, though neither of us noticed any deformity. He was given an ice pack and some ibuprofen for the swelling.

Paul had been grazed by a sword, and had a gash on his arm. The bleeding had been controlled before I even found him sitting there. He was more angered that he was sitting inside, instead of seeking revenge for his new "bad ass scar".

"Chick's dig scars, Edie," he joked.

I chuckled. "Corey, how are you feeling?" I asked our other patient.

"I'm golden. As soon as I'm good to walk on it again I'm headed back out." he nodded.

"Nah, I hate to tell you this, but you're out for at least the night. We'll check the swelling and mobility tomorrow," I replied. "Go rest near Erick."

"I'm good. I'd rather him get some solid sleep. I'd be tossing and turning all night."

I snuck into my parents' bedroom to check on Erick and Jonah. They were both resting soundly. I was very comforted to know that they were okay, for now. As hectic as tonight had been, I was oddly elated to know we had been attacked and only had four people injured. Two saves. Those were very good odds, considering the presence of Death, himself.

I walked back out into the living room and saw my mom and Aunt Kristi helping Mel getting our freshly injured guys comfortable. I know some amazing women. I stood in the doorway smiling, admiring the wonderful women as they cared for others in need.

"Do you ladies mind if I go take a shower?" I looked down at the dried blood stains on my shirt and forearms. "You can come get me if you need me."
My mother paused, staring at me covered in blood. "Uh, yeah. Go get yourself cleaned off. We've got this, honey."

I went upstairs and gathered some clothes, then stepped into the bathroom, turned on the shower and stripped. I looked at myself in the mirror, studying my body. I didn't look pregnant, or feel pregnant for that matter. It was hard to believe that I was. Maybe this was all a hoax, to try and convince God to save us.

I stepped into the shower, let my hair down and stood under the warm water. I closed my eyes and took the warmth in, letting my anxiety, my anger, and my fear run off of my body with the free flowing water. I completely relaxed and let myself go.

When finished, I turned off the water and stepped out of the shower, wrapping a towel around my body. I started to dry off my hair when there was another loud boom. The lights flickered, and then turned off completely. The sound of panic filled the house.

I stumbled to the sink counter, feeling around for the large candle I knew was there. The little bit of moonlight seeping in through the small window was not enough to light the room. Finding the candle, I then fumbled around for the bottom drawer, looking for a lighter. I had one hidden in the back of the drawer, under the clutter, from my teen years when I snuck a smoke break. Upon finding it, I lit the candle and pressed my ear to the door. My heart was pounding so loudly it was all I could hear reverberating in my head. My mind journeyed to the orphanage; I saw images of my family, my friends, lying on the ground lifeless like so many small children.

The anxiety crept up my throat and I turned to the toilet. I coached myself to calm down. Now wasn't the time to get sick, I was needed. I wiped my mouth, slipped my legs into my pajama pants and pulled my t-shirt over my head. I pressed my ear to the door again, hearing nothing but a few muffled cries.

I blew the candle out and stood in the bathroom for a moment, allowing my eyes to adjust to the darkness. Once I was able to fully see, I turned the door knob as silently as I was able and crept around the doorway, positioning myself against the hallway wall. The cries coming from the end of the hall were the children's. The soft hushes of the women of my family comforted me, as if they were meant for my racing heart. Outside, the sounds of fighting continued. Was there something in here, or was the power loss due to the war erupting outdoors? I trusted my instincts. I needed to stay alert.

The hardwood floors beneath my feet creaked. I stopped, nervous. My heart replied to the noise, shouting for the floors to be silent. It did no good. Every tiptoed step I took, the floor groaned. I felt a little breeze brush my cheek, and once more, my heart was in my throat. I tried to swallow, to force it back down to its respective position with no luck.

I heard a sigh in the quiet, an unfamiliar breath, and felt the hairs on the nape of my neck stand at attention. *Someone* was *definitely* here. I attempted my best rendition of a ninja, stealthily creeping towards the small staircase that led down into the living room. I reached the edge, cringing every time the wood barked. This house is beautiful, but not very helpful when it comes to moving about in silence.

I scanned the living room, looking for anyone, anything familiar that would put my mind at ease, but found none. Streaks of fading moonlight, sneaking through the tiny hole in the plywood, bounced off of glossy surfaces, confusing my vision. I tried to focus, there was someone here. Someone who made me wary.

I felt the sigh again, hot on my neck. I turned quickly, seeing nothing. I swung my arm, expecting to come in contact with something, anything. I was being toyed with, like defenseless prey. I felt helpless and angry. "Stop fucking with me, and just get it over with!" I shouted, scanning the darkness.

A light chuckle broke the silence in the living room. My breath halted, choking me. *Oh, God.* The soft light glistening off of the coffee table that I had been concentrating my attention on was broken. Something was now blocking that light. Standing directly in front of me; no more than twenty feet away.

My eyes attempted to trace the outline of the darkness. I couldn't tell who or what it was, but my subconscious was well aware of the likelihood. *Run. RUN!* What was the point?

"I'm not afraid of you," my voice trembled.

"Your racing heart and uneven breath say otherwise," the raspy voice taunted.

My breath caught in my throat. Whoever he was, he smelled my fear, like something feral. Like a dog. A dog…Where's Azrael?

The brief sound of movement was broken by the gut wrenching sound of my head hitting the floor, a sharp pain shooting through my head and neck. The weight squeezed the air from my lungs and silenced my scream. I struggled for a moment, trying to break free of the black mass' tight grip on my throat. My trachea closed, begging for air.

"Eden!" a familiar voice shouted from the living room, right before my ears rang loudly, then fell silent.

I awoke to an unexpected face. The memories were cloudy at best. I sat up, rubbed my eyes and balanced myself on my elbows. Riley was perched on the edge of the bed, waiting for me to rouse from my coma.

"Good morning, sleepyhead." he grinned pleasantly.

"Howdy," I frowned. "What time is it?"

"7am. You slept through the night." he kissed my forehead.

I raised myself up further, to stretch the sleep from my muscles and felt a sharp pain shoot down my back. I flinched and turned to Riley. He had a saddened look on his face. Something was wrong. I twisted my arm behind me, touching my back. There was thick padding there, and an unspeakable pain.

"What happened last night? I don't remember." I cringed.

"We need to keep someone with you at all times. This is my fault. I thought you were safe. Had I been inside with you, none of this would've happened."

"And what is it that happened, exactly?" I asked again, readjusting myself for comfort.

"One of the archangels got inside the house, knocked out the power and took you down. By the time Az and I got to you, you were already passed out and your wings.." his words trailed off into silence.

"Are you serious?" I scoffed angrily. "What the hell? I just got them back!"

"Azrael and I took care of him, but it was too late. I'm so sorry. Mel didn't know what else to do, so she had Lucy heal you up as best as he could. She tried her best with an IV, which took a few tries." he grinned, sheepishly.

I uncovered my arms to find half a dozen cartoon bandages crisscrossed from wrist to elbow.

"She loaded you up with some morphine and you slept it off," he continued.

"Well, she gets an 'A' for effort." I smirked.

"Can you heal yourself the rest of the way?" he asked nervously.

"Hopefully. I'm really tired and weak. I'm not sure what I'll be able to do." I shrugged. "What else happened last night?"

"Lilith was injured. The Valkyrie are tending to her still. Death got a hold of her, hell bent on some kind of revenge. Gabe was involved in a little, uh, scuffle, with a few from our side. But he's alright."

"What do you mean? What happened with Gabe? How's Erick and Jonah?" I asked.

"They're fine. Erick is still resting. Jonah is up and about already. And Gabe, well, he's fine, but I can't say the same for Damien. After we found you hurt, he went a bit ape shit. Damien tried to stop him, and is now a little black and blue." he chuckled lightly.

"Sounds a lot like my brother."

"Exactly." Riley laughed. "Look, I'm really sorry about yesterday. I'm not sure what got into me."

"It's alright. I know exactly what did. Don't worry about it." I smiled.

"I need to head back downstairs and make sure everyone's doing something. You should try to rest." Riley kissed my forehead and disappeared.

The last thing from last night that I could recall, was speaking with Lucifer before my shower. He told me all would be calm. He specifically told me that there would be nothing else to worry about. Was it a trick? Did he know I was going to be attacked? I wanted the truth.

I struggled to get out of bed, but the pain was unbearable. I fell backwards onto the pillows with a groan and a wince. I closed my eyes and concentrated on my body. It was impossible for me to heal myself. All I could think about was the wind in my face as I flew for the first time since The Great Divide. The pain burned deeper in my soul than in my flesh. The healing was going to have to wait.

After a few moments, I eased myself onto the edge of the bed and sat up, holding the side for stability. I dug my fingers into the mattress as I thought about yesterday. The muscles in my back twitched; burning, fueling me with a new fire. I was enraged. I thought about trying to heal myself again, but I needed the strength.

"Fuck it," I whispered, rising to my feet.

I was in pain. But not as much pain as they would feel. I was emotionally damaged. But not as damaged as they would be, seeing their brothers strewn about the lawn. I felt vengeance. I wanted vindication. There would be retribution. And that was *exactly* what I was going to get.

Chapter Forty Five
Cockfights and Cat Scratches

"Nary a word to soothe the wave,
Of inconsolable pain.
Nary a breath to comfort death,
Or lull the trifle and vain.
The crimson daughters, leave their Father,
Circling the sky above.
Feathered, the forms lead sheep to slaughter,
With sweet lips and lies of love.
Follow, we will, through ash and sand,
Through forgotten times and distant lands,
The history runs from our hands,
As the end finally encroaches.
Beat the drums and ready the fields,
With weary hearts and battered shields,
The end is nigh!
The truth is revealed.
As the Four Horsemen approacheth."

Lilith spoke loud and rhythmically, as she stepped through the crowd in the front yard. Chills swarmed my body as I envisioned her dark words.

I stared at the bloodstained ground and felt the chills leave my body as quickly as they had arrived, replaced with a fire. For the first time in my life, I was out for blood. I felt the anger, the hatred, welling in my soul. My heart beat like the drum from Lilith's foreshadowing poetry, riling me, pumping me up.

I left the warmongers and strode hastily towards the backyard. I was on a mission and no one would get in my way. The fields came into view, as I turned around the back corner of the house.

Lucifer was in the dead field, working with angels and some of our human companions. Gabriel was standing on the sidelines, watching the action with his arms crossed in front of him. Rested at his side was his bulky golden armor and weaponry. His pale, naked torso shone brightly, despite the overcast morning. I came up behind him and with my finger, traced the wing markings on his back.

"Good morning, sister." he grinned, turning his beautiful face to me.

"Hello," I replied.

He followed my eyes from his face to his back, as I continued to trace his brands. "I'm very sorry to hear about your evening. I wish I would've been able to stop it."

"Apparently, there was nothing anyone could do. I guess it was just meant to be." I dropped my hands to my sides, shoving them deeply into my pants pockets.

"I know it's painful to you. If it brings you any ease at all, the favor was returned. Though you have the upper hand. At least your life was spared," he offered. "Daniel cannot say the same thing."

"It was *Daniel*?" I asked.

"Yes. I suppose it was a bit of retaliation for his brother's death. 'An eye for an eye' of sorts." Gabriel nodded, returning his gaze back to the field.

"I thought he understood? I thought he knew what his brother did was wrong?" I stared at the ground, dumbfounded and pained.

"If your brothers, or I, had made a mistake, and our lives were taken without regard, would you not avenge us?" he lifted my chin to see my expression.

I nodded. "I would."

"Then you see where he was coming from." he dropped his hand from my chin. "I'm only sorry to see that it was you who paid for David's death."

I watched silently as Lucifer rose into the air, grabbing Gabe by the arm and tossing him face first onto the ground below. Gabe arose with a roar and leapt, reaching for Lucifer's feet. Lucifer sprung higher with a patronizing chuckle.

"Get back down here, you pussy!" Gabe shouted. "Fight me like a fucking *man!*"

"And why would I give up my advantage?" Lucifer called down smarmily. "I'm no man. Nor should I choose to fight like one, weak and afraid."

"Get down here so I can bash your skull in!" Gabe replied, leaning down to the ground suspiciously.

"If they will not face you valiantly, neither shall I." Lucifer grinned.

Gabe grabbed a weighted net and flung it into the air with a roar. The netting snared Lucifer's feet, pulling him down low enough for Gabe to grab his leg. I was awestruck, as my brother bowed his chest and threw the Seraphim to the ground with a loud thud. Dust circled in the air like a sandstorm.

I stepped forward, startled.

"Leave them be." Gabriel reached his arm out, stopping me.

Gabe ran to Lucifer as he raised himself on his elbows with a laugh. He doubled behind him, pulling two knifes from his belt. He held one to Lucifer's wings, and the other to his throat. Lucifer began to clap loudly, then stopped and in a move too fast to fully appreciate, twisted his body, disarmed my brother and appeared on his feet at Gabe's side.

"Very good. Very good, indeed," Lucifer praised, dropping the two knives point first into the cold ground casually.

Gabe grinned triumphantly. "I know. I'm bad ass." he bent down, retrieving his weapons.

"Eden," Lucifer called to me. "Did you see your brother's display?"

I nodded.

"He will be able to hold his own," he replied, turning his gaze back to Gabe.

Just as Lucifer turned to face him, Gabe threw an elbow into his chest, catching him off guard. Lucifer buckled backwards, popped his neck, and sprung forward, knocking Gabe to the ground once more. Lucifer laughed maniacally then held his hand out to help Gabe to his feet.

"I don't recommend using that trick again, lest you wish to break your arm on golden breastplates." Lucifer grinned and pat Gabe on the back.

"Meh, I was just going for a free shot," Gabe shrugged.

"Touché," Lucifer chuckled. "Well played, sir."

Gabe returned to a small group of our friends seated on the cold ground. He fell backwards in the dead grass and laid there. Lamar punched him in the stomach and laughed. Lucifer strode towards me, with a warm smile and open arms.

"Why did you lie to me?" I asked, denying his embrace.

"I did nothing of the sort." Lucifer folded his arms across his chest, obviously annoyed by the accusation.

"You said I'd be safe," I argued.

"And here you are, safe and sound."

"What do you call the missing wings?" I asked, eyes narrowed.

"A sacrifice." he shrugged. "A casualty of war."

"A sacrifice? That's all? Oh, I'm *so glad* that's the worst I've endured!" I mused sarcastically.

"Had he not wasted his time with your feathery accessories, you'd be dead right now. It was a small price to pay," he reminded me.

"Why didn't you tell me it would happen?" I asked.

"Because I didn't know it would," he answered without hesitation.

"You said you *see* everything."

He laughed. "You don't think a devil has tricks up his sleeve? Come on now. You're smarter than the average mutt. Haven't boys been pulling wool over the eyes of damsels for generations?"

"You're not funny. I trusted you. I thought I was safe!" I replied angrily.

"Turn your bite on those who deserve it," he sneered. "Would you have allowed me in the room with you while you bathed? I could've kept you safe. I could've also washed your back. Though my hands may not have stopped there." he grinned.

"You're such an asshole."

He chuckled softly and returned to his group.

"I can't believe him," I whispered to Gabriel.

"Yes, you can. I see it in your eyes. I see the way you look at him. You respect him." he nudged my arm with his bony elbow. "He's stolen a bit of your heart and you know it."

"I guess." I shrugged and sat on the ground, letting the implication drop.

Lucifer motioned for Brandon to approach. Brandon jumped to his feet and took off his jacket. He stepped towards Lucifer and began hopping in place with his hands out in front of him in a fighter's stance. Tori turned around and grinned in the direction of myself and Gabriel.

"This'll be good. Brandon's into martial arts." she smiled proudly.

I laughed loudly, waiting for the sparring to begin. I kicked my feet out in front of me and leaned back on my palms. The cold, prickly ground stabbed at my naked hands. I ignored the pain and sat attentively.

"How is your back?" Gabriel asked, lowering himself to the ground beside me.

"It's fine, now. It took some time, but I managed to heal myself before I came out."

"Well, that's good." he nodded and returned his gaze to the impending brawl.

"I wasn't going to heal myself. I was going to keep the pain as a reminder. But it weakened me," I explained unnecessarily.

"Better safe than sorry," he stated. "And how are the boys?"

"They're fine. I found Elijah after healing myself. I asked him if they were alright. He said they're doing well. He also said I'm fourteen weeks along." I grinned.

"Wow, and you didn't even know!" he replied, amazed.

"Neither did you!" I reminded him. "Everything has been so chaotic."

The two of us fell silent as the fight began. I watched as Lucifer and Brandon danced around each other, waiting for the first strike. I couldn't help but wonder who was going to make the first move, or whether they were going to continue the charade like little girls afraid to get hurt. But that thought was cut short.

Brandon leapt forward, wrapping his arm around Lucifer's neck, taking them both to the ground. Lucifer rolled himself onto his stomach and firmly planted his hands into the desolate field. He shot into the air, breaking free of Brandon's grasp. Brandon flipped backwards onto his hands, and then sprang to his feet. Lucifer speared towards him, kicking him in the chest and knocking him back to the cold ground.

Lucifer looked down at his opponent with a blank stare. "Never choose flash over necessity. It leaves you off balance."

He waited for Brandon to get himself up and secure his footing. Brandon dusted off his backside and adjusted his shoulders. He motioned for Lucifer to come forward then ducked low to the ground. Lucifer lunged for him, accepting his challenge. Brandon connected with his torso, gripping him around his waist, and throwing him backwards over his shoulder. Lucifer tumbled to the ground and slid a good distance.

"Good throw," Lucifer said, easing himself off of the ground. "Your talents would best suit you with a companion."

Lucifer motioned for Gabe to step forward again and walked over to a group of angels seated on the far side of the fighting circle. He leaned down, speaking to them. A few moments later, two angels stepped forward and removed their armor.

"Now, I want the two of you to practice with what you'll be up against. Use whatever trickery and skill it takes to obtain victory," he spoke to Brandon and Gabe, then turned to the other two combatants. "I expect you both to challenge them. But remember, you can be healed fully, they cannot. Do not inflict any mortal wounds or ailments that will prevent them from reaching their full potential later. These pups could be the ones to save your wings in the future."

Lucifer took the angels' weapons and handed them to Brandon and Gabe. They stared at the dazzling swords in their hands. They both got into position, as

Lucifer left the circle and returned to my side. He sat down next to me and grinned.

"Begin!" he shouted.

I spaced out as the fighting began. I followed the movement with my eyes, but my mind strayed from the action. I pulled my knees tight to my chest and rested my chin on them. I thought about the visions of the future I saw, what Elijah had shown us, and I felt very ill.

"He'll be fine," Gabriel stated as he stared ahead.

"You know he won't be." I buried my face in my knees.

"Who?" Lucifer questioned.

"Gabe," I replied shortly, muffled by my blue jean covered legs.

"He has remarkable skill for a human," Lucifer attempted to assure me.

"It won't be enough to save him." I looked at my brother as he threw an angel to the ground.

"And you know this for sure?" Lucifer asked.

"Elijah showed us his visions of the battle. It's fragmented, but Gabe will be lost. We're unsure how, but it's been foretold," Gabriel confirmed.

"Maybe it's for the best. Kill one to save a thousand." Lucifer shrugged nonchalantly.

"The one I'm terrified to lose." I rose to my feet testily and turned away from the fight.

I left the field and returned to the house. I had spent far too much time watching the helpless attempt to battle the divine. I knew it was needed, preparatory, but it didn't help to ease my mind. The visions were set in stone. It was not a possibility, it was an inevitability. I was going to lose my brother.

I walked through the garage and into the kitchen, grabbing a sandwich off of a tray on the counter and sat at the table. Lily was already at the table with Sara, drawing.

"What's that?" I asked, pointing to crudely smeared crayon lines.

"It's Daddy!" she smiled, looking up from the mess.

"And what's that?" I asked again, pointing to the blur of colors positioned behind the awkward portrait of her father.

"Those... would be his wings." Sara laughed and rolled her eyes.

"Oh. Well they're beautiful, Lilybug." I smiled.

"Yeah, I know." Her assurance reminded me of my brother. He had passed on some of his less than appealing traits. I laughed and rose from the table.

Her artwork hit me like lightning. I had an epiphany. I choked down the rest of my sandwich and stole a sip from Sarah's glass of water, and then washed my hands hastily.

"Where are you off to in such a hurry?" Sara asked.

"I need to talk to Luke," I replied, hurrying out to the garage.

I ran to the field and saw Lucifer seated next to Gabriel where I had left them. They were watching as Damien and Paul fought with Seth and Tobias. The air was filled with a dust cloud as the four of them were intensely locked in a Battle Royale.

Lucifer heard me approaching and called without turning, "Welcome back, love."

"If it does happen, can you save him?" I asked.

"Who?"

"Gabe. If his death is unavoidable, will you save his soul?" I clarified.

Gabe heard his name and rose from the ground to approach us. "What're you talking about?"

"Nothing. Go back to the group."

"I suppose arrangements could be made," Lucifer nodded, still not looking up.

"An arrangement for what?" Gabe continued to question.

"Don't worry about it," I said, annoyed.

"Don't worry about *my soul being lost*?" he raised a brow. "Nah, I'm not worried about that. Who gives a shit about something so miniscule?"

"I'll do what I can, when the time arrives. That's all I can promise," Lucifer reassured us both from the ground.

"Oh. Well then. I suppose that's good enough!" Gabe shrugged sarcastically and returned to the group.

"You need to remain calm, love. You worry needlessly about things you cannot change. And the things you *can* change, you turn your back on. Relax, take this wave in stride and see what unfolds." Lucifer finally cocked his head back to look up into my face, a devilish smile painted across his lips.

"I don't want to lose him."

"Then you won't."

Paul and Damien howled loudly as they claimed their victory over Seth and Tobias. I couldn't help but laugh as Paul danced and humped the back of Seth's head. He covered his face with his hands, ashamed, as his pride was violated. Our group of friends erupted into laughter over Paul's antics.

"He's a bit on the insane side, but a stronger brute there is none," Lucifer nodded towards Paul.

I grinned. "You nailed it!"

The day slowly transitioned into evening, as we all sat around and watched the sparring continue. Everyone eventually made it out back, minus the women and children of my family.

Each of my brothers teamed up with angels and went against another group. Riley had even joined in the fun, going against Flemming. Save a few cuts and bruises, everyone made it through the fights unscathed.

As dusk approached, an eerie chill rode in on the winds. I tried to stifle the anxiety, but it rose in my chest. Night brought fear, and it was moving in fast. I looked to the east as darkness began to settle in the distance.

"Your fears are sound, for once," Lilith said, bumping into my arm with her own as way of a greeting.

"How are you feeling?" I changed the subject.

She grinned. "Much better. The Valkyrie returned me to tip-top shape, no thanks to you."

"I'm sorry I missed it. You know I would've done what I could."

"I do know, thank you. I'm still a little tender and I'm not sure if I can transform again yet, but we'll find out soon enough," she replied, looking to the sky.

"Would you like me to fully heal you now?" I asked.

"No, I wouldn't want to inconvenience you," she shook her head.

"Bullshit! You're just cocky and don't want to ask," I jeered.

"Pride is *her* weakness." Lucifer winked.

"And gossip is yours, you devil," she sassed.

"Come on, let's get you healed up." I stood and turned towards the house.

She followed me wordlessly back towards the makeshift shelter. I glanced behind me and saw everyone trailing back to the house, other than a few stragglers, with Lucifer trailing behind the rest. It was an unspoken rule that no one was to be out after dark without orders.

Lilith and I stood in the doorway of the garage, waiting for all of the people to file inside. The angels remained out front, securing their armor to their bodies and gearing up for tonight's action. Riley shuffled past me, with Elijah on his shoulders and gently kissed my cheek as he passed.

Once everyone had made it through the garage and into the kitchen, Lilith and I secured the garage door and pulled two folding chairs to the center of the space. She sat directly across from me and held out her hands. I took them in mine. She flinched instinctively, but relaxed quickly.

Time warped swiftly as we stepped into an old world. Conversation seemed out of place, so we opted for silence as I repaired her wounds. She was far more injured than she led me to believe. I looked deep into her body, her soul, and tinkered with her gears and cogs.

The silhouette of a caged bird hopped around in her soul, waiting to be freed. It was interesting to see the way she coexisted with her feathered form. A symbiotic union. Curiosity had the better of me, as I reached into her spirit and touched the crow. She gasped loudly, startling me back to reality, then rose from the chair quickly and lifted the garage door. She stepped out, looked at me once more, and pulled the door closed behind her. I suppose playing with her soul like a broken toy wasn't the best idea.

Two whole hours of silence was what we were given. To be honest, I was surprised it lasted that long. It started out much like it did the night before. Booming in the distance, growing closer until it surrounded us.

Tonight, I was to be staged in the garage for healing, rather than inside the house. We figured it made for easier access, and everyone would be able to keep a better eye on me. Gabriel and Lucifer returned to me frequently, informing me of the action. Meridith, Haley and Emily ware staged right inside the garage door, with me and Melanie completing our small group.

"Don't worry, girls. Christopher and Jared are just outside. They're first on duty and will keep anyone from breeching the entrance," Meridith confirmed.

"I know, I trust you." I nodded, kicking my dangling feet as they hung over my perch on the edge of the deep freezer.

Haley snapped to attention, resting her hand on the hilt of her gleaming sword.

"Death has returned," she hissed.

"Death, the noun? Or death, the verb?" I asked nervously.

"The Horseman. He's approaching from the North," she replied.

"How do you know?" Mel asked.

"I feel him," she stated, stepping slowly back towards us.

I jumped down from the freezer and stepped behind Haley. Melanie ran to Meridith's side and looked at me nervously. The Valkyrie looked to one another and nodded, then turned to me.

"We're needed outside. Humans have fallen, there is no saving them," Haley said somberly.

"Oh, my God," I gasped, covering my mouth. "Who was it?"

"I don't know, but we need to get their souls to Charon for safekeeping. We need to hurry," Meridith replied.

Fear raced through my mind. Who could it have been? Had Gabe been killed? It could've been anyone. They were all my friends, my brothers. They were all important to me. I paced the garage until the door flew open. I stood, staring out into the carnage. I felt the blood leave my face, unable to move, like a deer caught in headlights. I saw bodies, lying everywhere.

As Meridith and Haley stepped out and flew into the mayhem, Corey and Gabe stepped in. They were both out of breath, panting and wiping the blood from their foreheads. I stared at them blankly, wondering who of the remainder had been killed.

"Fuck that shit," Gabe groaned, as he pulled the garage door closed.

"You ain't kidding, dude." Corey pulled his shirt over his head and wiped the blood and sweat from his face.

"Who died?" I finally asked, choking on my words.

"Couple of theirs, why?" Gabe shook his head, confused.

"Meridith and Haley said there were *people* dead," I clarified.

"Oooh. *Them*." Corey nodded. "None of ours."

Emily placed her sword back into her sheath and lowered her guard.

"What?" I asked, baffled. "What other people are there, other than 'ours'?"

"You see, what had happened was…" Gabe laughed nonchalantly. "They started catapulting corpses at us. It's no big deal, Edie, they were already dead."

"I was worried it was one of y'all." I suddenly relaxed a little.

Gabe shook his head, "Nah, it's just some 12th century scare tactics."

"It's still fucked up, but we're alright." Corey nodded.

"Well, that's a bit of a relief." I sat down. "So, what're you two doing in here?"

"We needed a break. It's been relentless and we're exhausted," Gabe replied.

"Get inside, relax for a bit." I motioned towards the kitchen door.

The two of them went inside. Melanie and I returned to our wait, wondering what was next to happen. A few minutes later, the garage door opened once more and Paul stepped in.

"It's like a metaphorical salad toss out there. We're getting bent over!" he dug into the ice chest filled with water bottles.

"Paulie, how's Jere? Is he okay?" Mel asked.

Paul nodded, as he swigged from a bottle. "Ahhh…" he paused to answer her question. "He's good. Him and Riley are tearing shit up." There was a loud 'thud' on the roof top. "I better head back outside." Paul threw his empty bottle at me.

Gabe and Corey emerged from the kitchen door, startled. They noticed Paul leaving the garage and followed suit. I watched as the three of them disappeared into the night once more. I tried to steal a glance at the battle, knowing that my friends and loved ones were safe, but the garage door shut before my eyes could adjust to the darkness beyond. *Bah.*

"I need to go inside for a few minutes. I'll be right back. If you need me, don't hesitate to find me," I instructed Mel.

She gave me a thumbs-up, "Gotcha."

I stepped into the kitchen and greeted my mom, sisters-in-law and aunts seated at the table. They seemed uncomfortable and anxious, but smiled nonetheless. I stepped into the living room and found Erick on a couch, sleeping off his injuries. I checked his IV site and made sure it was still running smoothly. I flicked the drip chamber and lowered the flow, then squeezed the bag. He stirred for a moment, then settled back down.

"Brooke checks on him frequently," my mom confirmed, standing in the doorway to the kitchen. "She rarely leaves his side."

"Good. Where are the others?"

"Last I knew, Thomas was with Elijah, Paige and Brooke, upstairs in your bedroom," she replied.

"Thanks," I responded, then climbed the few steps into the hallway. I walked past the game room, waving. The kids were wrapped up in art projects, led by Amber. Now that I knew that everyone was safe, I was able to relax a little. I stepped into my dad's office and flipped on the lights. No one was in there. I turned to the steps and stopped. I could hear voices coming from my bedroom at the top, none of which were in distress.

I returned to the living room and sat on the opposite end of the couch from Erick. He had woken up briefly and was staring at the TV, attempting to gather some form of information from one of the last remaining news sources. He could obviously tell something was on my mind, but returned his attention to the TV screen. I flipped around, moved the curtain and peeked out of the small hole in the plywood.

Besides the occasional update I received from the battle outside, I had no clue what was going on. I wanted to be out there, but I knew the risks. I stared out of the tiny hole, viewing the action as it passed by.

It was like watching a movie, except I knew the actors, and the dangers were real. There weren't stunt doubles. The blood on the ground was genuine. The bodies were not plastic; they had once belonged to the living. And the anxiety wouldn't end with a scene cut away. My breath caught in my throat as my eyes fell on Death for the first time. So far, the only Horseman I had seen in the flesh, in this world, was Pestilence. I had seen some of the destruction each had created, but never in action.

Death's skeletal warhorse was much larger than that of Pestilence. His large, bright eyes glowed in the darkness, like embers embedded in his etched steel mask and barding. His bare bones gleamed brightly in the fading moonlight. He stamped his hooves impatiently, and as he did, the house quaked.

Atop the undead equidae, was Death himself. His silver armor glinted light where his black robe was tattered and torn. His head was covered with a large helmet, adorned with two horns, resembling those of a bull. In his gauntlet covered hands, he held a huge scythe, as he had in renaissance art and nightmares.

I watched helplessly as our angels swooped down attacking the Horseman. He swatted them out of the skies like pesky insects and stared intently at something across the yard. I moved to the side, attempting to view what had his attention, but was unable to see.

"Damn!" I muttered. "This hole's too small."

The fighting continued, as a few of the Archangels descended into the yard. Marcus touched down, and in a single step, morphed from his brightly glowing skin, into a shadow covered deathtrap. Behind him others landed, ready to spill blood.

CHAPTER FORTY SIX
WHEN LIFE HANDS YOU LEMONS, USE THEM AS AMMO.

Death wasn't the only Horseman to pay us a little visit that night. Too bad neither he nor Pestilence RSVP'd for the party. Nevertheless, a good time was had by all. There was cake, ice cream, streamers and laughs...
Bullshit.

There was exactly what trails behind them; carnage.

Around midnight, Pestilence reared his ugly mug and set the neighborhood ablaze. Thankfully, our home was spared, but only by the grace of Lady Luck. Everything else had been laid to waste.

Gabriel made an executive decision forcing all of the humans to seek shelter inside. Pestilence was far too dangerous to cross without the risk of catching his deadly plague. I was grateful to know that my family and friends were safe, though the same cannot be said for our winged comrades. The death toll was heartbreaking by the time morning approached.

Once we were allowed to return outside, the world seemed much bleaker. Our hopes were dashed. The cries rang in the air, as we and the angels mourned the loss of our fallen friends. Michael's forces had finally managed to dent our defenses and we felt it, like a thousand swords pressed firmly in our hearts.

Though we had managed to take down four more of their army, seven were lost in the fight from our side. Had I been allowed to intervene, perhaps we would've lost less. But Gabriel chose not to risk my life to save those that had perished. Their deaths were noble and their lives would not be lost in vain.

I stepped out into the cold morning, escorted by Meridith and Seth. I surveyed the damage left in the wake of the Horsemen. The ground still hissed and steamed from Pestilence's blaze. No homes were left standing on the street. We were now nestled, in the wide open field of destruction and waste. I could only guess what the house looked like from the sky.
Bullseye. X marks the spot. Strike here.

The field behind the house, which had just yesterday been the location of games and laughter, was now the humble resting place of our deceased. The grave of Damien was being dug as I approached the disheartening, makeshift cemetery. A small group of angels strode from graveside to graveside, leaving final words and prayers of safe passage for the departed souls.

Lucifer had managed to get six of the seven souls to Charon over the course of the night. The only soul unable to be salvaged was that of Gwendolyn. Her soul had been taken by Death himself, as a trophy. This was the first time that a Valkyrie had been slain in battle. She died defending Paul, as he made his escape into the house.

He sat by her grave, silently. Of all the emotions I had seen Paul reflect, heartache was not one of them. I knew it was best to leave him alone. Their love was a story that only he could tell, that spanned the course of history. What I knew of Gwendolyn was bittersweet. I knew she was the only being to have ever held Paul's heart. All the others had just been play things for his carnal appetite. Even Paige. She had just arrived and now she was gone.

The sadness was overwhelming. The tears that fell stained the burnt land with a somber darkness. This was the first of our losses, but I was certain it wouldn't be the last. The cries echoed in my mind like a broken record. I returned to the battered shelter and sat on the damp concrete of the driveway. Meridith and Seth noticed my unease and left me alone for the time being. They never strayed far enough to risk my life, but gave me the space I desperately needed.

"*Fear no more the frown o' the great; Thou art past the tyrant's stroke: Care no more to clothe and eat; To thee the reed is as the oak: The sceptre, learning, physic, must: All follow this, and come to dust,*" Lucifer spoke, as he sat beside me on the wet ground.

"You didn't strike me as the Shakespearean type," I replied, staring out into the destruction.

"His talents were undeniable." he grinned. "He was a pretty swell old chap."

We sat together, without speaking another word for longer than I would've anticipated. I could've said *thank you* for saving the souls of the fallen angels, but that would've required me to admit our loss. He could've said for me *not to worry*, but that would've required him to offer me false hope. By the time he did speak, the words exiting his mouth caught me off guard.

"What was it like in the house last night?" he asked.

"Terrifying."

"I can only imagine. I've never been faced with the kind of situation that you're in. Never have I been fragile. Never have I had loved ones to worry for." he turned to focus his attention on me.

"It must be nice to not give a shit about anyone but yourself," I replied, looking deep into his bright blue eyes.

"I care about many things, even more so, as of late," he defended.

"The kids were screaming. Every sound shook the house, reminding us that we were both alive, and able to die at any given moment. I felt like an animal, caught in a trap. I couldn't see out. I couldn't tell what direction the onslaught was coming from. I've never been so scared before in my life."

"I'm very sorry," he stated somberly.

"I wished to live through the night. I wished to die, just to get this over with. My mind couldn't make itself up," I continued.

"Alas, here you are. It seems as though your mind was made up for you." he smiled, leaning back on his palms and looking into the distance once more.

"But was it the right decision? Seven were lost, fighting to protect us. Had we not been here to defend, they would still be alive." I shook my head. "The events that play out can no longer be called 'God's will'. He's stepped out of the way."

"They are *my* will. They are *yours*." he gently rubbed my back with one hand. "I realize you're frightened, you're in mourning. But you cannot lose sight of our goal. This isn't simply self-preservation. This is for the *world*. This is for humanity, as a whole."

"I'm being selfish."

He smirked softly, "No, you're being *human*."

I laughed. "The rest is still new to me. I don't know anything else to *be*."

"Rein in your emotions, love, or they will be your undoing. You need to focus. Have the strength you were graced with. Wings do not make you heavenly, it is still your birthright," he said.

My *birthright*.

His words rekindled that fire in my soul. I rose from the ground and offered him my hand. He accepted and rose to his feet. Meridith and Seth noticed our movement and came to my side. I waved them away and began walking towards the street.

"There's nowhere left to hide," I stated.

"No, there isn't. Pestilence and his steed made sure of that."

"If we moved to a safer location, could we maybe funnel them into a trap?" I asked.

"This isn't Thermopylae. We're not engaging a manmade army. Suspicion would grow, they'd be cautious. Not to mention, the Horsemen..." he stretched, allowing his wings to break free of their skin-tethered bonds. They stretched and shook, with the animalistic traits resembling that of a wild cat. "And there is no 'safer' location."

"Luke. I need to speak with you," Gabriel said as he approached us from behind.

"Very well." Lucifer waved him forward casually.

"Alone." Gabriel nodded towards the house.

"I bid you adieu, love." Lucifer grinned and left me standing in the driveway. He motioned for Meridith and Seth to return to me.

I watched curiously as Gabriel and Lucifer strode to the western side of the desolate yard. They continued to walk, until they were far enough out of range to discuss their matters in privacy. What could Gabriel possibly have to say that he couldn't say in front of me? And where the hell had he been all morning?

"Where's Elijah?" I asked Seth.

"He left with his mother and Gabriel earlier this morning. I'm not sure where they had gone, but obviously your brother is back with a message," Seth replied, pointing to the private discussion.

Lucifer looked to me for a long moment, then opened his wings entirely and shot into the air. Gabriel watched as he ascended through the clouds then began walking towards me. His expression was blank, impossible to read.

"Now, you and I must speak." he offered me his hand.

We walked down the barren street as he explained our current dilemma. He told me about the two conversations he had now had with God concerning our situation. God was no longer turning a blind eye to the Earth. His mind had been altered in a single night.

God had sent for Lucifer, to converse with Him and explain what he knew. Gabriel was confident that Lucifer would be the very being to save us, based on his knowledge and powers of persuasion. If God was suddenly concerned with our outcome, and Lucifer explained everything that Michael had done, did we now stand the chance of survival?

"This is good news, then. We can do this." I grinned excitedly.

"It isn't over yet," he stated very matter-of-factly. "We still have to hold out until God has made a decision. Every day the fighting gets more intense. Elijah has seen far worse for the next few days. Peace is not yet in sight."

"We have to do something. We can't just sit back and watch as more lives are lost," I said, digging deeply for the answers.

"We're biding time." Gabriel wrapped his arm around my shoulder. "Have faith in the Ever-Forgiving."

We were about a block away from the house when we noticed darkness approaching on the horizon.
Shadows.

"We have to leave," Gabriel said, bending down and lifting me over his shoulder.

"What the hell?" I asked.

"Damn them! We don't have time," he hissed, pulling his horn from his hip.

He hopped into the air, blasting his trumpet twice loudly. I kept my ears covered as he raised the alarm for the others. He sped towards the house and lowered me to the ground upon our arrival. I watched as the angels assembled in the front yard, joined by Riley and the others.

"What's going on?" Riley asked, stepping forward with Azrael.

"We have to act quickly. They're here," Gabriel explained, gently pushing me towards Paul.

"Get everyone inside!" Riley shouted, removing Azrael's leash.

Before we could react, the battle had begun. Our forces attempted to ready themselves as quickly as possible. Gabe ran to my side and pulled me towards the house. I struggled, turning to see the attack.

"Gabriel!" I shouted, trying to warn my twin.

A shadow-clad angel rushed behind Gabriel like a bullet, grabbing him by his throat and lifting him into the air. He drew his sword in a flash and held it to my brother's throat. Gabriel morphed into his shadow form quickly. Kicking a leg out behind him, he knocked himself and the angel to the ground.

As the angel leapt into the air towards Gabriel, Lilith descended with her son in tow. She planted her foot square in the middle of the archangel's back, easing Elijah to the ground. She unsheathed her sword and removed his wings. The angel let out an ear piercing shriek, as the darkness surrounding him dissipated.

Gabriel darted forward, and in one fell swoop removed the angels head with his sword. Lilith kicked aside the head and grabbed the ring of light lying underneath. She picked it up, pulled her tunic aside and sucked the halo into her core. I had never seen the actual death of an angel. I was both terrified and intrigued.

"Elijah!" Thomas shouted, running towards our nephew.

"Thomas, no!" I screamed.

An angel was positioned above Thomas, with his bow trained on Elijah. As Thomas dove in front of the angelic child, wrapping his arms around him like a shield, an arrow pierced his back. He fell forward, resting his head on Elijah's shoulder for a moment before falling to the ground. I looked towards the sky just as Callin attacked the bowman.

"Get him inside!" Gabriel said, pushing Elijah into my arms.

I wrapped myself around his body and ran with him and Gabe to the front door. As we reached the entrance, Gabe beat on the door. At that moment a blood curdling scream erupted from the field. I turned to see Lilith cradling her brother's dead body in her arms. The front door opened and we were pulled inside. I turned and saw Eli and Lucas. I pushed my brothers aside and ran to the hole in the plywood covering the living room window.

I watched as Lilith sprung to her feet. Smoke and feathers billowed out of her, in all directions as she struggled with her emotions. It was clear that she had lost focus. Seeing Lilith in her current form was horrifying.

She stood, half woman, half beast. Her chest expanded rapidly as her breath kept rhythm with her raging heart. Feathers molted from her shadow covered skin, dripping like blood from untellable wounds. She wailed ferociously, as the giant beak retracted, revealing razor sharp teeth. Her emerald green eyes quivered and sparked to a piercing red. The war goddess was now on the prowl.

She ran on all fours, building speed, then barreled into the chest of an opposing angel. She knocked him to the ground and began slashing at his body with her talon-like hands. She unsheathed her sword and ended the squabble with the slightest of ease. Lilith moved about the yard with fluid grace and morbid efficiency. It was like watching a dance, twisted with death and beauty. Every move was precise. Every slash of her blade was deadly. She was unstoppable.

My attention was broken by Elijah's sobbing. He sat, cradled in Gabe's arms, with his face buried in my brother's chest. I hesitated for a second. I didn't want to leave my window to the war, but I knew he needed me. I reluctantly stepped across the living room and sat down next to Elijah and Gabe.

"Honey, don't cry. He had to protect you."

"That bolt was meant for *me*," he sniffled.

"He did what any of us would've done, kiddo," Gabe said, brushing the hair from Elijah's face.

"I'm so sorry." I gently kissed his forehead.

"Three will be lost, today alone. Five tonight," he foretold.

"Is there anything we can do to keep it from happening?" I asked.

"No," he sobbed loudly.

Gabe and I looked at each other. There was a loud crash, and the sound of breaking glass coming from the kitchen. The children screamed loudly and huddled together. Gabe and I ran to the kitchen door and saw an angel rising to his feet. Gabe pulled the kitchen door closed and stepped to the side, shielding the view of the angel as the children escaped.

"Hurry, get the kids into the office. Keep them quiet," he ordered to Lucas.

"Will do," Lucas began herding them down the hallway.

I ran to the front door and flung it open. I looked around, trying to focus on one of our own. Shadows and light bounced around everywhere. It was impossible to tell who was who.

"What's wrong?" Riley asked, noticing my expression and running to my side.

"One of them. They're in the house!" I panicked.

"Kenneth! Christopher! Come," he shouted and stepped in the front door.

Azrael barked loudly and bolted in after him, followed by Kenneth and Christopher. The four of them turned to Gabe, who pointed at the kitchen door. Riley grabbed my hand and guided me towards my brother, coaxing both of us down the hallway.

Riley turned the door knob quietly, then rolled across the floor, out of the way as Azrael leapt into the kitchen snarling, hackles raised. Kenneth sped in behind him, as Christopher drew his sword and protected us in the hall.

A few moments later, Azrael emerged from the kitchen wary, but wagging his stubby tail. He ran to me and began licking me. Riley stepped into the doorway to survey the damage.

"We're going to need to get that window covered again. We also need to keep more of us inside to protect the humans," Riley observed. "These kids do not need to see one of these bastards up close and personal."

"I'm on it." Kenneth nodded, and then stepped out of the room.

"How are you?" Riley asked, turning to me.

"Scared," I replied. "And you?"

"Having the time of my life." he rolled his eyes. "Where's Lucy?"

"Gabriel sent him to talk to God earlier."

"Lovely. Perfect timing," Riley jabbed.

The front door flew open, "Edie, help!" Jonah shouted.

Jonah and Flemming carted in a bloodied Paul. They carried him to the kitchen as Riley and I brushed the broken glass off of the table, then set him down and stepped back. Jonah's eyes welled with tears as Flemming explained what had happened. I put on a fresh pair of gloves and listened.

"Paul had been inconsolable, he would not listen to reason," Flemming spoke, pulling Paul's torn shirt aside. "The Horsemen have returned."

"He wanted revenge for Gwen," Jonah's voice trembled.

"Oh, Paulie, no!" Riley shook his head. "Damn it!" he slammed his fist on the counter and ran out of the kitchen.

I inspected the cauterized wound across his torso. "What happened?"

"As soon as Death approached the grounds, Paul began running towards him. I stepped in front of him, tried to stop him... he head butted me! He took my sword and ran after the Horseman," Flemming explained.

I leaned in towards Paul, listening to his shallow breathing. I feared the worst.

"It was horrible, Edie. Paulie demanded Gwen's soul back and pierced Flemming's sword into the side of Death," Jonah sniffled.

Flemming continued, "Death pulled the sword from his ribs. It was glowing, like it had been in a blacksmith's forge for hours. He slashed at Paul, catching him across the chest and impaling the blade into his abdomen."

"Please, save him," Jonah pleaded.

"I'll do my best. But I need to know we'll be safe while I attempt to heal him. Flemming, can you secure this door while I help him?" I asked, pointing to the broken patio entrance.

"Of course."

I took off my gloves, pulled my hair back into a tight ponytail and stood above Paul's head. I took in a deep breath and leaned in over Paul's face. His breathing was getting much shallower, more uneven. I placed my hands on his clavicles and closed my eyes. I expected to see my welcoming garden. I expected a cocky grin strewn across Paul's face. Neither of which were there. The land reminded me of the dreams I had for so very long. The crimson sky, the wispy black clouds swarming and swirling into ominous points, like thorns on a blighted rose.

Paul was lying on the ground, curled into a fetal position and staring out beyond the cliffs. I sat down behind him and placed my hand on his side. He turned slightly, looked me in the eyes, and then returned his gaze forward.

"It's over, Edie."

"No, it's not. You have to come back with me," I replied, trying to squeeze my arm under his torso to help him off the ground.

"I can't." he struggled, raising himself onto his hands and knees.

He stopped in place, coughing repeatedly and covered his mouth. Black tinged blood oozed from between his fingers, falling to the dry earth beneath him. He wiped his mouth, then fell over. I tried to catch him, to ease him back to a comfortable position.

"Paulie, you can't…" I cried.

"You can't save me this time," he coughed. His breathing slowed.

"Yes, I can. You have to let me try!" I argued, and laid my head on his chest.

"It's too late," he struggled to speak. "Tell Jonah I love him."

"You can't do this to me! We need you, you idiot!" I sobbed uncontrollably. *I have to control my emotions. I have to focus.*

"Look at what he did. There's no coming back from this." he pulled his shirt aside. His wound was glowing red, with a black substance seeping out, moving across his abdomen like a necrotic plague. Each time his heart beat, more oozed out, spreading further, climbing up his ribs. I pulled away from him, afraid to be touched by the toxic fluid.

"You have to leave." he winced, pushing me away.

"No, I won't leave you!" I sobbed.

"You *have* to," he clenched his jaw tightly and closed his eyes, then turned on his side and roared loudly, writhing in pain. It hurt me to know there wasn't a thing I could do. I knew I couldn't heal him. I knew I couldn't even ease his torment. And worst of all, he was going to die, alone.

"Goodbye, Paulie," I sniffled and wiped the tears from my cheeks.

I stepped backwards away from the brute. I tried to think of him as he once was, not as I was seeing him now. His tortured body twisted as the blackness enveloped him. I turned away and ran as fast as I could. The tears streamed down my face as I raced to safety. I stopped when the silence set in, and collapsed to the ground and cradled my knees in my arms. I pressed my face against my legs and cried. I wanted to leave this place. The sound of sobbing broke through the silence, startling me from my trance.

Jonah was leaning over Paul, crying into his chest. Flemming attempted to pull him away. I staggered backwards, falling into a chair. I didn't know what to say. I couldn't make this right.

"Why didn't you save him?" Jonah asked, looking me in the eyes.

I dropped my head, staring at the glass covered floor. "I couldn't. Death's wound was incurable."

"Did he suffer?" Jonah asked, closing Paul's eyes with his fingers.

Lie.

"... Yes," I couldn't lie to him.

Jonah dropped to his knees at Paul's side. He buried his face in his soul brother's hand. I felt horrible. Not only could I not bring peace to Paul, I brought no peace to Jonah, either. I should've lied. I should've told him that he died happily.

"He wanted me to tell you that he loved you." I placed my hands on Jonah's shoulders. He said nothing in reply, only sobbed harder.

News traveled swiftly about Paul's death. Brooke and Paige came into the kitchen. Brooke ran to Jonah's side, to comfort her mate. Paige buckled in the doorway, heartbroken. It had been obvious that she cared for Paul, but the pain in her eyes reflected the intensity of that emotion.

"It should've been me. It was supposed to be me." Jonah shook his head.

I stood, helpless and hardened. We knew death was a risk we were taking. We also knew that we wouldn't all be spared from the deed. But to lose two of us in less than an hour, knowing the pain and torment that both Lilith and Jonah were feeling, made this all the more real.

We were on the doorstep of annihilation. We had one foot in the grave already. Paul had once told me, "When life hands you lemons, use them as ammo," and that was exactly what I intended to do.

CHAPTER FORTY SEVEN
OVER MY DEAD BODY!

Sadness filled the space where Paul once stood, and anger filled in Thomas' stead. Riley had returned to battle with a vengeance. His pained motivation scared me worse than the Horseman being present. There were now three out of the four in the area, and Riley wasn't fighting with a clear head. He was hell bent on avenging Paul.

Lilith was still in a blood thirst, following her brother's passing. Thankfully, she had successfully managed to retrieve his soul as he passed. Gabriel was concerned that she had completely come off her perch and would become reckless. An unhinged war goddess assured death, though not necessarily on the right side.

Jonah was still catatonic and would not leave Paul's side. We had moved his body to the garage, as it wasn't safe to travel to the field to give him a proper burial yet. Jonah continuously told stories about some of their past adventures, mainly to Paul, but really to anyone who would listen to his incoherent babble. It was sad to see him like that. Brooke and Paige remained close by, listening to Jonah's tall tales. He had become completely despondent and emotionally disconnected. They were obviously very worried about him, but tried to be as supportive as they could. I only hoped he wouldn't do something stupid. Seeing his reaction after I healed him, then seeing his reaction after Paul's death, I was certain that in this instance, stupid was his nom de plume.

Erick was now fully awake and talking again. He was still weak and would need to recover, but I was comforted to know that he had survived. Corey was resting by his side, after keeping an eye on him all morning. Ross, Eli and Flemming had secured the plywood over the patio door in the kitchen and had now set up another guard post close by. I was so thankful to have my brothers with me and helping. I was glad to know they were safe, and felt guilty for not being able to spend time with them. But I knew they understood. Lucas was in the game room with his boys and the other kids, while Amber and Bridget attempted to prepare some food for everyone. The rest of my family was here and there, making sure that the house was fully secured and everyone was well tended to.

Shortly after 3pm, I received word from Callin and Emily that Michael had been seen in the vicinity and that he had brought more angels with him. So far, today alone we had dispatched seven of his army, while losing three. The words Elijah had spoken replayed in the back of my mind. I knew five more of ours would be lost over the course of the day. I wondered if they would be friends, people I loved, or some of the nameless faces in our winged arsenal.

It sounded like bombs were being dropped outside. Loud crashes reverberated through the house, as the angels and horsemen raged their war. As the sounds got closer, we gathered together in the office and huddled in the corner. My Aunt Karla began saying The Lord's Prayer to comfort the children. Listening to her words, hearing the loud cadence of war outside, reminded me of the prophetic dream I had. I pictured myself, holding the pistol to my mouth and pulling the trigger. I shook the thought from my mind and stared at my family.

My mind instantly flashed to the next dream of the sequence. The calming tan walls of my dad's office were warped into the horrific cages of the concentration camp. My family huddled together for protection reminded me of the children, hopeless and left for dead. I couldn't take it anymore. I felt my mind buckle under the pressure. I had to do something. I had to help somehow. Hiding in the corner like a caged animal wasn't doing a single thing to save those I cared about most.

"Where are you going?" Lucas asked me as I rose from the group.

"I have to go," I replied shaking my head.

"Where?"

"I... I'll be back," I answered, closing the door.

"Edie!" he shouted as I walked away.

I hurried down the hallway as the walls quaked. I could hear the screams echoing from the office, as my nieces and nephews feared for their lives. The shaking was getting more violent, knocking family photos and mementos from the walls. I stepped over the broken glass, picking up a portrait of my brothers and me. I stared at the picture for a moment and laughed. I distinctly remembered the moment the picture was taken. We wouldn't cooperate. There had been four takes prior to the final. In each, at least one of us would either make a stupid expression, or say something to get the others laughing. "Seriously, guys. Someday we're going to want to have at least one picture of us together, civil, and sane. Can we please cooperate?" I had asked. And they had... for one picture, and I mean one picture alone. From that day forward, every other one was smeared with ridiculous poses.

I pulled the picture from its broken frame and folded it, then shoved it into my back pocket and returned to reality. I ran through the living room as the ground trembled, knocking me to my knees. I rose, running through the kitchen and into the garage.

Jonah was still seated next to Paul as Brooke and Paige pulled on his arm, pleading or him to go inside with them.

"Please, Jonah. It isn't safe out here!" Brooke begged, then kissed his cheek.

"I'm not leaving my brother," he replied coldly.

"What about me? What about Paige?" Brooke asked, pained.

He looked at her, emotionless.

I helped Brooke lift him from the ground. "Jonah. You have to. You can't stay out here."

The three of us pulled him forcefully out of the garage as he screamed and reached for Paul. He fought our grasp as we got him into the kitchen and helped him into the office where everyone else was hiding. He sat on the floor, pulled his knees to his chest and hid his face.

"Thank you," Brooke said to me, wrapping her arm around Jonah's shoulders.

I nodded and left the room once more. I returned to the garage and found Mel tending to Riley. His arm was covered with blood as he cursed and fought for her to let him leave. Lucifer was standing behind him, holding him in place as she tended to his wounds.

"What happened?" I asked, pulling a pair of gloves from my pocket.

"Nothing. Let me up," he argued.

Lucifer tried to hide a pleased smile, "He was grazed by a sword. I thought it was a good idea to get the wound wrapped."

"I'm fine. Let me go," Riley continued to argue. "It's just a flesh wound."

"Alright, calm down. Let me see it," I ordered, pushing Lucifer aside. I inspected his wound and wrapped it in gauze.

"Are you okay?" I asked, securing the gauze.

"I'm fine, like I said. Can I go now?" Riley replied.

"Get out of here," I sighed, stepping aside and letting him dash out of the garage.

"Kids," Lucifer said as he watched Riley leave.

"You're not funny," I stated, pulling off my gloves and throwing them in the trash. I pulled up a chair and sat near Lucifer as Melanie disappeared into the house.

"So what's the verdict?" I asked, avoiding any potential for small talk.

"I believe it's in our favor. God has sent for Gabriel to ascend. I suppose he's receiving the orders to halt the war."

"Really? You think so?" I smiled ever so slightly, relieved.

"I think so. I'm not certain." he shrugged, his smoke spewing wings shrugged with him. "God was very upset by the news of what Michael has done. He's deeply troubled with the rising war in the East. His attention has been drawn to it, leaving this side of the globe untended. I can only hope that He'll be more assertive with Michael."

"But if He gives Gabriel the orders to stop the war, then that's it?" I cocked my head, confused. "I mean, God's word is final. Michael would have to stop, right?"

"I fear that he wouldn't, immediately. Not until he feels his job has been done," Lucifer stated bluntly.

"But, he *has* to. 'Thy will be done', remember? He has to follow God's orders," I said.

"I'm afraid not. You see, as God explained to me... How do I put this gently?" he searched for the proper words. "God had given up hope, which you already knew. God had also given Michael the authority to do what he felt was just. Michael was vested with the final word, in this case."

"That isn't the case anymore. If God has said to stop, they have to. This isn't a toy that He has given to Michael, then taken away. This isn't a game." I shook my head, dumbfounded.

"Eden, love. Michael takes his orders from God, only. Michael knows that God will not step foot on this wretched planet. Therefore, even if Gabriel commands the forces to stop, Michael will surely dispute the account, saying that Gabriel is lying." Lucifer sat on the ground next to me. "His army is loyal."

"What about the Horsemen? Can you stop them?" I asked.

"Not exactly, no. They're controlled only by God's will and emotions. Once His mind has been made in concrete determination, they will do His bidding," he explained.

"So they'll be gone soon. Wouldn't that convince the angels to leave?" I continued to bombard him with questions.

"I'm doubtful. Michael has a firm grasp on his troops," Lucifer replied.

"What do we do?" I asked, concerned with the news.

"We continue, business as usual, until Michael backs down," he said, voice barely above a whisper.

"If we live through this, if Michael does, in fact, stop, will our lives remain as they are?" I swallowed hard and winced.

He looked me in the eyes. His expression saddened. "No."

"That's what I was afraid of," I said, resting my head on my knees.

"He expects you to follow through with your offer. You will have to say goodbye to those you love," he replied with little reserve.

"That's going to be hard." I buried my head in my hands.

His voice deepened, gravely. "There's worse, love."

"What? What do you mean?" I asked, terrified.

"It'll tear you apart, destroy you. I don't know if I can say it." he shook his head, distraught.

"Oh, no. What? Just tell me." I frowned, scared.

He took in a deep breath and let it out slowly. He looked to the ground, then deeply into my eyes. My breath caught in my throat anxiously. Would I have to give up my children? Was my family going to be taken as a sacrifice?

"You'll…" he stood and turned away from me. "You'll have to say goodbye to me."

I watched his shoulders jerk as he laughed to himself. I felt my jaw drop as I realized what he was saying.

"You're such an *asshole*!" I shouted with a laugh.

He turned to face me, laughing hysterically. "You will lose sleep over the concept."

"I doubt it," I chuckled.

"Before long, you'll be waging a war with God, Himself, to descend to my kingdom." he grinned smugly.

"You are so full of shit," I guffawed.

Thunder rumbled in the distance as lightning cracked the sky. Our laughs were cut short, as we listened to the ominous sound. They were the first sounds to overpower the fighting. The only sounds heard, besides the battle cries and mournful wails.

"And God will send a flood to end the savage battle," Lucifer stated. "Or at least, halt it for the time being."

The minutes dragged on like days as the thunder grew louder, closer and more aggressive. I could've sworn I heard words of warning, echoing from the doom laden clouds. I only hoped that everyone else heard them, as well. Hours passed, as evening approached and all of our Earthly companions migrated inside. The storm had rolled in, full force and was making it too hard for them to fight. The angels remained outside, led by a relentless Lilith and the headstrong Kenneth.

Michael had not been seen since Emily and Callin had spotted him, while his army continued their onslaught. I can only guess the coward was riding out the storm somewhere safe, as his troops suffered. So typical of the arrogant bastard.

Riley was restless. He paced the living room, chewing his fingernails to the quick and checking through the peep hole frequently. I wasn't sure what he was looking for, but I assumed he was waiting for the rain to let up enough to head back outside.

Azrael was curled up with Rufio on the floor, licking his feline buddy. Rufio, of course, didn't enjoy his bath much, and continuously whined and swiped at Azrael's muzzle. It was nice to see my guardian getting to be a dog again, rather than a warrior. He was too young for such a serious duty.

Gabe seemed to be enjoying his time with his kids. They were curled up on the couch reading a book. Well, Gabe was listening, as Lily read him the story. He would begin to fall asleep, and she would gently nudge him in the ribs and tell him to pay attention.

Jonah had secluded himself in my bedroom, now claiming that he was fine, but that he needed time to think. I was genuinely concerned that he would do something irrational, and sent his group up to him to keep him company and keep him safe.

Elijah was taking Thomas' death much better now. I wasn't sure if he knew something I didn't, or if he was just really good at faking smiles. He was resting peacefully on my parents' bed, curled up with some of my old stuffed animals.

Brandon was impatiently bouncing his knee sitting at the kitchen table. Tori was attempting to calm him, but only managing to annoy him further. I opted to stay out of that little tiff.

As the winds and rain battered the roof, I thought about the storm we had once endured. Luckily we didn't have nineteen days to suffer through, though the heartache was very similar. The pain was different, but it still permeated the statically charged air. I fixed myself a sandwich and stood against the kitchen counter, rubbing my stomach. I hadn't had much time today to think for myself, let alone my children. If God hadn't actually forbid the killing to continue, we were down to a little over four days. And if He had, well, it was just a matter of getting Michael to stop. That could take a while.

I just wanted the death and destruction to be over with. Every loud noise, every thunder crash, every cry of a child, scared the shit out of me. This isn't a life anyone should have to live, especially not children. These memories would cause permanent damage, nightmares for years, and a lack of faith, despite the need to believe it that much more. The floorboards quivered under the deafening thunder. The rain sounded like thousands of bolts breaking through the roof at once. *Poor Thomas.* The thought made my skin crawl. The only good things arising from this storm were that the humans had been forced inside and the gruesome weather drowned out the sounds of the fighting. It was as if, for a moment, we could forget it was happening.

I walked into the living room and looked from face to face. These people had been my motivation to press on. They were the whole reason I was there fighting, thriving. Regardless of how these events played out, I was going to have to say goodbye. Whether it was as Michael's vengeful sword fell, or by the grace of God, there was no way around it. How could you say *farewell* to those you love, for good? *There aren't words.*
There's only pain.

I left the room and ran upstairs. I grabbed my journal, checked on Jonah and the others, and then left the room. I went into my parents' room, where Elijah was resting peacefully. I needed privacy. I laid down on the bed, next to Elijah and stared at his beautiful face. I turned to a blank page and pulled a pen from my pocket. This was going to be impossible. These would be the hardest words I've ever attempted to compile.

Mom,
You've always been my best friend.
You've always been the woman that inspired me.
For 30 years, you've been my sounding board,
my strength, my conscience and my guidance.
No words can describe how much you mean to me.
No amount of time will ever be enough to spend with you.
I will never be far. I will never be out of reach.
Continue to pray, I will hear your words.
Continue to be strong; I will be at your side.
I love you. Forever.

I couldn't bring myself to say it. Perhaps I didn't need to. Maybe I would see them, either by visiting, or in dreams. Though my ties with Riley were sure to be cut as punishment, maybe my connection to my family would remain intact.

Daddy,
You have always been my hero.
There isn't a man in existence that I respect more.
You've always been a wonderful husband, an amazing
father, and a great man. The things you've taught me will
never be forgotten. You've helped to make me a strong woman.
I love you more than I could ever describe, and I will, always.

I closed the book and cried, burying my face in the pillows. I sobbed heavily, as I let go of the pain and torment stabbing at my heart. I felt a gentle hand rested on my back and turned to see Elijah's soft smile.

"I know it's hard, Aunt Edie. But it must be done." he frowned.

"I'm sorry, kiddo. I didn't mean to wake you." I wiped the tears from my cheek.

"It's okay. I needed to get up. I've had a vision. I know what will come," he replied, sitting up with a loud yawn.

I sat up with him. The thunder shook the house, knocking out the electricity. I reached into my pocket and pulled out my lighter, using the small flame to locate a nearby candle and light it. I then walked to the doorway and cracked it open.

"It's okay, it was just the storm. We're fine," he reassured me. "Come sit back down, we have much to discuss." I sat down on the bed next to him, curling my legs underneath me.

"The Horsemen are retreating. God has made His decision," he stated.

"And Michael?"

He shook his head. "He will not be stopping his assault. Not yet."

I cradled my head in the palms of my hands. "Tell me everything."

"Father will return soon, sounding his horn to end the war. Michael will demand that his troops continue to carry out his orders. The onslaught will continue. Under Michael's orders, not those of God. Two more days of fighting are ahead. The death toll will be incomparable, as Michael fills with rage," he explained.

"How many more will we lose, do you know? And will Gabe's death still happen?" I asked, afraid of the answers.

"The siege will be worldwide. He's keeping some of his forces here, but some are being sent to other parts of Earth. As for your brother, his death has been predestined. Fear not, however, he will die a hero, a martyr," he replied, attempting to comfort me.

"That brings me no peace, whatsoever." I looked to the floor.

"God is allowing souls back into the Kingdom. Though his judgment is much harsher now. He feels betrayed. He is hurt. He will not allow these atrocities to go unpunished." Elijah grabbed my hands. "And you know that applies to you, as well."

"You mean with Riley?" I asked, wincing.

"Yes. You have three days. You will be called upon to return to the fold. Yes, you will be allowed to keep your children. Yes, your family will be spared. But you will no longer have a connection to Riley. You will remain at God's side."

"And what will happen to Riley?" I asked as the tears filled my eyes.

"A decision has not yet been made, so I'm unable to answer that."

"And the other earthbound angels?" I asked.

"All but one will be returning to the heavens. God has sent word to the Ferryman, by way of the Valkyrie. The souls that he possesses will be allowed into Heaven, as well as Paul and Thomas'. They will be reborn in Heaven." he smiled.

"Oh, that's wonderful." I smiled widely. "This is great news!"

"It isn't over yet, but the end is in sight. We were blessed that God has seen the truth and has not yet given up hope, entirely. There will come a day that the world will be brought to its knees. But this is not that day," he reminded me.

"So, what's the next step?" I asked.

"I must speak to Riley. You must rest," he stated.

"But I..." I was cut short.

"You have to. For your health and the health of the boys. Our little heroes deserve a break." he smiled. "Had it not been for them, God would've continued to turn His back to the world. They saved us, Aunt Eden."

I grinned and pat my stomach.

"Now, rest up. The shelter will have extra security tonight. There will be a final attack, then peace for a little while. You're safe. Tomorrow we will bury the dead." he kissed my cheek, and left the room.

I stared at the flickering flame, thinking about the news I had just been given. I had mixed emotions. I was thankful to know that this would be coming to an end, but there was still a price to pay. Lives would still be lost. Love would still be lost... *Riley*.

Love was one of the greatest gifts that God had given us. It was infallible. It was perfect. And it was being taken from me. Part of me was glad to know that I would be saved and able to raise my children in the sanctity of the Kingdom. But how would I be able to raise two boys on my own, without their father? Why would God allow something like that to happen? The questions continued to fester in my mind. If Gabe will be considered a "hero", what does that mean for his soul? Surely, he wouldn't be lost or turned away. *Over my dead body!* I wouldn't allow that to happen. He was a good man. He deserved a spot in the Kingdom, more so than I did.

The flame began to tremble, as the wick was smothered by molten wax. As the room began to dim, I fought my heavy eyelids. When was the last time I had slept? I readjusted myself, trying to concentrate and stay awake. The flame went out, as darkness crept into my mind.

Chapter Forty Eight
While Visions of Sug... What the Hell is a Sugarplum, Anyway?

The lighthearted giggles bounced from side to side, as the boys chased each other through the clouds. I couldn't help but laugh as Lucian sprung out of a cloud bank and landed on top of his brother.

"En garde!" Orion shouted, swinging a wooden sword at his identical twin.

"You'll have to catch me first!" Lucian laughed and bolted into the air.

I watched as the two raced through the bright sunlight; their long, auburn hair flowing behind them. Their pale skin glowed with almost as much intensity as their small golden breastplates, refracting the beams of the midday sun.

"Boys, you need to find your uncle and return to your studies," I lectured.

"Aw, Mom. Can't we stay today? We can return tomorrow. He'll understand," they spoke in unison.

"That's between the three of you. I'm not getting involved." I leaned back in the enveloping clouds.

"But it's our *birthday*!" they whined.

"And so it will be next year, and the year after that, and the year after that." I laughed. "And guess what? It will *still* be your birthday after your lesson."

"You're no fun at all," Orion pouted.

"That's not the first time I've heard that." I raised a brow.

"Uncle Gabriel would let us play." Lucian threw his wooden sword down.

"Well, he isn't here right now, and Gabe is far scarier than either of us." I sat up with a chuckle.

"True." Orion grinned. "*Very true.*"

"Bye, Mom. We'll be back soon." Lucian kissed my cheek and shot into the air.

"Be careful." I said, pulling Orion's face down so that I could kiss him.

They disappeared into the heavens, leaving their small wooden swords and other toys behind for me to clean up. I smiled as I held the two swords Gabriel had brought back from Earth. They loved to play fight, yet complained about the combat lessons they had to endure with Gabe. I laughed at the irony.

Gabriel's horn sounded in the distance, startling me. Why was he back so soon? Something was wrong. I set the toys down and turned towards the direction they had flown. Gabriel's horn sounded again, but I couldn't pinpoint the direction. By the third horn blast, I awoke and realized it had come from the present. I looked over at the clock on my dad's nightstand. It was 6:45am. I stumbled to my feet and went into the bathroom. I looked in the mirror for a second and smiled, as I thought about the dream I had just had. My boys were beautiful. Their bright eyes looked just like my own. Their beautiful smiles reminded me of a certain devil though, not my own or their father's. I chuckled to myself and finished getting ready for the day.

When I finished I left the room and walked past the office where most of my family was still sound asleep. I closed the door quietly and continued down the hallway; stopped in the game room, turned off the TV and threw a blanket on top of Aiden and Gabe, who were curled up together on a couch.

In the living room there wasn't a soul in sight, so I peeked into the kitchen and found Corey and Erick joking and shoving pieces of muffins into their mouths between chortles. They stopped, looked at me and laughed loudly. Corey choked for a second, coughing a chunk of muffin onto the counter.

I left them to their own devices and went into the garage. There was no one there, even Paul's body was gone. The garage door sat open, exposing a soaked world outside of our haven. I zipped up my hoodie and stepped out into the damp morning, watching as my breath clouded in front of me.

I looked around the front lawn, expecting to see *someone*, but no one was around. I scanned the neighborhood, the horizon, the skies. When I felt reasonably sure that it was safe, I tucked around the side of the house and made my way into the backyard.

I entered the backyard and saw everyone else gathered together in the field. Some of the angels speared the wet ground with shovels while the others stood, or hovered, mourning and conversing. A large blue tarp was spread out on the ground, with multiple bodies wrapped in white sheets and secured with golden rope.

I counted the pile of corpses. There were eight. Elijah's prophecy had come true. I scanned the faces present, fearing the worst, looking for those I cared most about, silently praying that they had survived the night. Riley noticed me and smiled faintly. He was safe, thankfully.

"I was worried about you," I whispered, wrapping my arms around his neck.

"I'm fine." he kissed my cheek. "How did you sleep?"

"Really well, actually." I pulled away and turned my gaze to the graves being dug. "When did they back down?"

"They've been gone about an hour. I don't expect it to stay silent very long though," he sneered.

"So, they *will* be back?"

Gabriel turned in our direction, "Michael's army is confused. They heard my orders, but Michael has them convinced that it's a lie. He's probably talking to them once more, ensuring that they believe him and will carry out his final command." I watched as a body was lifted and set into the first grave. "Who didn't make it through the night? Anyone I know?"

"No." Riley shook his head. "I don't think so."

I tried not to show my relief. I wanted to be excited, knowing that those I cared about were safe. But this was not the time to celebrate a victory. Others had lost brothers, friends and close comrades. I kept my emotions tightly wrangled and wrapped my arms around Riley.

"Can we talk? Do you have a minute?" I asked, looking up at his saddened face.

"Sure," he answered, grabbing my hand and walking back towards the house.

As we strode back to the patio, I stared at him. He didn't look well. His eyes were encircled with darkness, lack of sleep. His face was covered with a dark tint, as he hadn't shaved in God only knows how long. He looked disheveled. He looked weary and worn.

"How are you?" I asked, concerned.

"I'm alright. It's been rough, but you already knew that." he smirked.

"And how's your arm?" I continued the small talk, avoiding the important questions.

"It's fine. Nothing I'm worried about."

I laughed. "Of course not."

"I know about God's demands," he stated somberly.

"And what do you think of it?" I asked.

"It's for the best."

"You're willing to make the sacrifice?" my brow crumpled.

"We don't have a choice. To save you, the boys and everyone else..." he paused for a second, composing himself. "It has to be done."

"Elijah said that I had three days," I reminded him.

"I have much longer, I think," he gibed.

"Won't you be returning with the rest of us?" I shook my head, confused.

"No, I'll be left behind to keep an eye on things around here. Once it's safe for me to ascend, I will. If that day ever comes." he looked me in the eyes.

"So you're the one that stays. Elijah said all but one return." I pieced the words together in my mind.

"Yup," he looked out into the field.

"Maybe when you return..." I searched for the words to lighten the mood.

"Edie, it's never going to be as it was. Not again. And maybe that's for the best. We made a mistake that day. We've lived with that mistake, hundreds of times over. The best thing about mistakes is learning from them and making the right decision the next time you're offered the chance," he spoke. "I won't let you make that mistake again."

I felt the tears building in my eyes and turned away.

"I love you. I always have, and I always will. But this isn't for us anymore. We've suffered enough. You have to do the right thing for the boys. And that means returning to Heaven, raising them without the dangers that we experienced. They'll have a chance to be happy. They won't struggle like we have, or feel heartache, or hunger. They'll never have to worry about stupid *girls*, or high school drama." he smiled.

I had to laugh. "But they'll also miss out on the things we loved most." my smile fell flat.

"They'll never know the difference."

"So, you really think this is for the best?" I questioned.

"Of course," he replied, kissing my lips.

"And I *will* see you again?" I frowned.

"I'm sure you'll see me stalking you from a distance," he chuckled loudly.

I laid my head on his chest and stared out into the graveyard. Jonah was now sitting by Paul's wet graveside. He had been buried right next to Gwendolyn. This was the only reunion they would have. Paul was to be reborn, but not with his long lost love. Jonah, on the other hand, would be with his brother once more. I wondered if he was aware of the news, or had seen it for himself.

Corey and Erick came around the back of the house and sat down on the patio with us. This was the first time Erick had ventured outside in days. His expression was rather confusing, as he looked around. I could tell he was startled by the changes and was bothered by seeing Jonah in mourning. Corey seemed rather upbeat, despite the current conditions. He rocked back and forth on the edge of the wooden deck and looked up to the sky, then leaned forward as he stared out in the distance.

"Will we get to see it for ourselves?" Corey asked.

"What do you mean?" Riley questioned.

"The grand finale."

"No," Riley stated simply.

"I didn't think so." Corey frowned, leaning back.

I looked at Riley, confused.

"Of course you will, ass hat!" Riley laughed to himself.

Corey laughed and continued rocking.

"Hopefully, no time soon," I interjected.

Erick rose from the deck and walked out into the dismal field. He sat down next to Jonah and wrapped his arm around his shoulder. They sat, silently observing the others and staring at Paul's resting place.

Gabriel walked towards us, staring at the ground. He stopped, looked to the sky, then returned his gaze to the ground and continued his march. He climbed onto the patio and stared out at the crowd.

"Where's Lilith?" I asked.

"Gone," he replied.

"Gone as in?" I asked nervously.

"She's in the Middle East attempting to end the war," Riley explained.

Gabriel's expression didn't change. "It's been far too quiet for too long. You know that they will return soon."

"Fuck!" Riley shouted and rose from the deck.

He disappeared around the corner of the house, returning to the front. Gabriel whistled sharply, drawing the attention of some of the angels. He motioned for them to head our way and stepped off of the deck. He turned to me and kissed my forehead.

"You need to get inside," he ordered.

"I'll head in, in a few," I replied, jumping off of the deck.

I saw Lamar and waited for him to approach, "Hey, Llama."

"Hey," he replied shortly.

"How are you?" I asked, nonchalantly.

"I've seen much better days," he replied, waiting for Chuck to catch up.

I figured they needed some time together and that I would only get in the way. Corey stepped off of the deck and strode towards me. He walked at my side as we returned to the house. My parents were standing outside watching everyone get geared and ready for the probable attack.

"How's everything going?" Dad asked.

"Good, kind of. Everything should be over with in about two days," I replied.

"And then what?" Mom asked.

"I don't know," I lied well, for once.

"So, will you stick around here for a little while, or head back to Baton Rouge?" she pressed.

"Um, not sure really," I lied again. "I hadn't given it much thought, I suppose."

"Well, you know you're welcome to stay as long as you want," Dad smiled. "I expect you to get this all cleaned up, anyway." he pointed out to his destroyed yard.

"We'll see," I laughed. "We need to get inside. This isn't quite over yet."

The three of us walked into the garage with the others and secured the door. We stepped into the kitchen and were met by my aunts, uncle and some of our travel companions. I sat at the table while my mother and aunts fixed all of us some breakfast. I told them what I knew from Elijah, leaving out the parts that would cause my mother to break down. Like the idea of her losing both of her children, for example.

My dad explained that we were going to need more gas for the generator. At the rate we were going, we would be out by nightfall and didn't want to spend another night in the dark. He recommended that we discuss it with Riley and get a search party to go out and gather some fuel.

We brought the generator problem to Riley's attention. He agreed that we didn't need to risk another night of darkness, with angels that could easily stealth their way through the shadows and into the rooms of sleeping children. He decided that it was worth the risk to send some of us out to gather gas. We were both concerned about the outcome, but knew it needed to be done.

We gathered in the garage, eating breakfast and discussing what was to come of the day ahead. Lamar and Gabe volunteered to lead the hunt for gas. Gabe still remembered his way around the area, for the most part, including some of the back roads and sneaky ways. I wasn't very comforted by them volunteering, but knew they were best for the job.

Corey wanted to sit this field trip out. He stated very simply that he didn't feel comfortable leaving me, Jonah and Erick here as each of us were vulnerable at the moment. He, of course, joked about my "fragile state" referring to my pregnancy, which led to him getting slapped.

Tobias and Seth would follow the van from the air, with Flemming scouting ahead. I was at least glad to know that we would have some eyes in the sky to accompany my brother and friends. We didn't know what our time table was, or when things would get sketchy again. The sooner they left and returned, the better.

Everyone filed out of the garage and stood in the driveway to see the group off. Gabe sent me a text message to see if the phone towers were still operational. I didn't receive his message. We realized that we were dealing with much more tech savvy bastards than we had thought. We would have to go about this the old fashioned way, the way of our founding fathers. Sans cellphones. Truly a terrifying thought.

Gabe hugged me and hopped into the driver's seat as Lamar climbed into the passenger side. Chuck and Jeremiah got into the back while Flemming, Seth and Tobias got into position circling above the van and looked around for anyone approaching. Flemming gave Gabe the "all clear" nod, and he backed out of the driveway.

"Be careful!" I shouted as they pulled back and peeled out, speeding down the desolate road.

"Don't worry," Riley rubbed my back. "They'll be fine."

"I hope you're right," I replied, turning back to the house.

I went inside and found Sara who was now up and about. She asked where Gabe was, so I explained the situation. She wasn't very happy that he had once again volunteered himself for a dangerous task, but knew I didn't like the idea of it, either. We went into the game room and spent some time with Lily and Ian before the other kids woke up. She asked me how I had been lately and wanted to know if I had heard anything else about the twins. I explained to her what Elijah had told me, about how God had decided our fate, partially in their favor. I told her about my dream and described exactly what they looked like, from their auburn locks to their flat bare feet. She laughed, enjoying the story about her nephews. I was fairly certain that she knew she wouldn't watch them grow up. She was very careful not to ask about anything that would force me to drop my smile. She's smart, very smart.

I was comforted by the fact that Lily would be raised by such an amazing woman. I was also distraught knowing that Gabe would be leaving her, but at least Sara would be there. I could only hope that Lily would never forget her dad; that she would hold on to her memories fondly.

Chapter Forty Nine
Is That Your Professional Opinion, Master of Deceit?

Hours had passed without a word from our fuel retrieving party. I'd been worried, of course. Shortly after they left, some of Michael's army had attacked us. And rather stealthily, I might add. Two of them busted through my window upstairs, while Jonah and the others said blessings of protection around their circle. They took Paige and left the rest, terrified.

Riley had not been able to locate them, or Paige, but I believe their plan was a success. They managed to break Jonah from his morose trance and fill him with anger and purpose. He was now back in the game and geared for war. They were toying with us, and we knew it.

Kenneth left to scout the local area, looking for the two angels and their hostage. I spoke with Jonah, asking if he could see anything. He explained that he hadn't been able to focus at all since Paul's death. He was unable to see any glimpses of the future, leaving him blinded and just as scared as we were.

Brandon and Tori offered to take one of the remaining vans and search for the others. I reminded them that the more we split up, the more danger we were inviting in. Michael's troops would have a field day, picking us off in small groups. Erick agreed that splitting up wasn't a good idea and joined Riley once more in the yard.

The area was silent at the moment. It felt like the eye of a hurricane. The quiet was completely unnatural, and I knew something was amiss. I stood outside with Brandon and Riley, scanning the skies and wondering when the action would stir up again.

"I believe they're becoming more clever," Lucifer said as he approached us.

"Is that your professional opinion, Master of Deceit?" Riley folded his arms across his chest.

"Why, yes it is, *O brave warrior of the Heavens*," Lucifer grinned.

"Yeah, I'm sure it is. I'd even bet that you gave them the brilliant idea to ambush us." Riley turned, staring at the Seraphim with disdain.

"A chance to be done with you would be a reprieve, indeed. But risking Eden's life wouldn't be worth the chicanery. So for now, I'll just endure your *presence*." Lucifer curled his lip as he spoke.

"I bet you can't wait until God separates us," Riley sneered.

Lucifer grinned. "I'm counting down the days!"

"Okay, enough! You two are worse than kids," I scoffed. "Get the fuck over yourselves. Now isn't the time for this!"

"Thanks." Brandon elbowed my arm. "I was about to kick them both in the taint."

Brandon and I laughed as Riley and Lucifer walked off in opposite directions.

"Will they ever get along?" he asked.

I shook my head, "Not likely."

"That's nice," he mused. "There's more tension between the two of them, than there is between our side and Michael's."

"It seems that way, sometimes."

I noticed movement in the sky, in my peripheral vision. I turned to the east nervously and stepped back slowly, inching towards the garage. The approaching angel dropped his shadowy armor and descended to the ground. He had a body tightly curled to his chest.

"Eden, I need your help," Kenneth stated, laying the body on the ground.

"Oh, shit, Paige!" I gasped and turned to Brandon. "Find Jonah, keep him occupied for the time being."

"I found her a few miles from here. It looked as if she had been tortured. I'm not exactly sure if they were leaving her for dead, or if it was a trap," Kenneth explained, as I put on a pair of gloves.

"Has she been conscious at all since you found her?" I asked, checking for a pulse.

"No."

I couldn't feel a pulse. I leaned down close to her mouth, listening for a breath, but heard nothing. "Oh, no. No, no, no. Paige... no!"

"Is she..." Kenneth took her hand in his, as I pressed my stethoscope to her chest.

I nodded, distraught. "Yes, unfortunately. Poor Jonah." I removed my stethoscope and rose to my feet.

Kenneth lifted her body off of the ground, moving it to the same spot Paul had been laying just this morning. I kneeled next to her and began cleaning her face, making her presentable for Jonah. I gently wiped the dried blood off of her cold cheek. I couldn't imagine what she had just gone through, or what Jonah would be feeling as soon as he received the news. She was so young.

It wasn't long before Jonah overheard that Kenneth had found her. He entered the garage and saw her, with false hope in his heart, expecting her to still be alive. I watched his expression change from relieved, to grief-stricken in less than a second. Every range of emotions flooded the room as he broke down and wept at her side. Kenneth approached him, explaining everything that he had seen. Of course, the truth hurt him, but it was the least that he deserved. Kenneth spared the gruesome details of her body's condition when he found her.

Jonah was beyond saving at this point. Just yesterday, he lost the only being he knew as a brother. Today, he had lost the girl he had raised as his own daughter. All ties he considered family had been cut. Everyone that he loved was being taken from him. I couldn't imagine the torment he was enduring. He silently lifted Paige in his arms and carried her through the open garage door.

"Jonah, don't," Kenneth said, attempting to stop him.

"Let him go. He needs this." I placed my hand on Kenneth's shoulder. "Just go with him, keep him safe."

Kenneth followed Jonah out of the yard and into the field behind my parents' land. I sat alone in the garage, thinking about everything that was happening around us. Had Jonah been targeted for the attacks, or was it just coincidental? Would each of us be brought to our knees? The awkward silence was broken by the sound of a speeding vehicle approaching. I arose from my seat in the garage and walked out onto the driveway. Gabe started honking the horn as he pulled in, screaming "get back" from his window. Flemming swooped down in front of the van and led me back into the garage quickly.

"What's going on?" I asked.

"We've been followed. Get inside," he replied.

I watched as Flemming shot out of the garage once more, cloaking himself in shadow. He landed on top of the van and surveyed the area, then stamped his foot twice on the roof of the van, informing the others that it was now clear. They exited the van with gas cans and bags full of supplies and ran towards the open garage door.

Warning cries and angry screams filled the air, as the angels that had followed them back to the house approached the area. Gabe slammed the garage door closed and sighed with relief. They had all made it back, unharmed.

"Have you seen Seth or Toby?" Gabe asked me, as he unloaded the goods he had returned with.

"No," I shook my head.

"Shit, I knew we shouldn't have separated!" Lamar stated with a growl.

"What do you mean? *They were your lookouts.*" I was confused by his statement.

"As we were wrapping up, we were ambushed. They stayed behind to keep the angels at bay. There were only a few of them," Gabe explained.

"How long ago was that?"

"Maybe fifteen minutes," Jeremiah estimated.

"Well, hopefully they'll be back soon. But we can't risk sending anyone out right now, I don't think. We can talk to Riley about it, but I'm doubtful. We've already gotten screwed today," I justified.

I explained everything that had happened since they left. I told them all about the two angels' attack, Paige being kidnapped, and being found dead. As I filled them in with what they had missed, the sounds of fighting began.

Corey helped carry things inside and then disappeared to find Erick and the others. Lamar and Chuck took off for their newly acquired guard post. Jeremiah ran off to find Riley. Gabe kissed Sara and Lily goodbye and gallivanted off to war. I was once again left alone and fearful, so I snuck upstairs to my bedroom. The room was empty. Splinters of broken wood and shattered glass blanketed the floors and bed. I dropped to my hands and knees and crawled to the uncovered window, trying to stay out of sight. My hands stung as slivers of glass embedded themselves in my palms. When I got to the window I inched my way to the ledge until I could see out.

I had a full view of the backyard and field, from this side of the house. I spotted Jonah, as he dug a grave for Paige on the opposite side of Paul's. It was like a love triangle in death. I could only imagine what that tension would be like, if they were able to tell what the hell was going on. Poor Paul, stuck in the middle.

Kenneth and two others hovered above, as Jonah and Brandon dug the grave as hastily as they could. I heard the flapping of wings nearby and ducked low, pressing my body firmly against the windowed wall. I felt my heart race as I envisioned myself being snatched from the room. I closed my eyes and silently prayed.

"Retrieve John and Noah. We can flank them from the west," the gruff voice ordered.

John and Noah? I hadn't heard either of these names associated with anyone from our side. *Oh shit. These weren't our own.* I fought my racing heart. I was going to have to make a decision, and fast. I stared at the door, wondering how quickly I could make it there. I peeked my head up, slightly, judging the distance between me and the others in the field. They could surely hear me if I shouted loud enough.

I sat against the wall, building my courage, attempting to muster my voice. I was going to have to warn them, one way or another. The sound of flapping continued as the angel hovering above my window continued to survey the battle, unaware of my presence. His shadow bobbed on the window frame, as the sunlight filtered around his massive body.

I repositioned myself next to the window and crouched. I looked to the door one more time. *This is it. I have to do this.* I peeked out once more, ensuring that the angel was out of view, then took in a deep breath and prepared myself to make the mad dash to the open door.

One.

Two.

Three.

"Kenneth! They're coming!" I shouted out the window and raced to the doorway.

"You!" the angel shouted in return, staring in through the open window.

I struggled to close the door behind me and ran as fast as I could down the stairs. I tripped halfway down and slid to the bottom, catching myself as I hit the hallway floor. I looked in and saw some of my family together in the makeshift bedroom that was once my dad's office, and slammed the door closed as I ran by and darted into the living room.

"Run!" I shouted to Lucas and the others seated on the couches.

"What's going on?" Amber asked as I ran by.

Moments later, I was in the kitchen and heard the crash as my door was shattered upstairs. Aiden and the others shrieked and ran into the kitchen behind me. I held the door open as they filed out into the garage.

"Kadence! Get the door open, get someone's attention!" I ordered.

"Finally! Something to do!" he threw the garage door open as I pushed out into the room and closed the door. The sounds of breaking glass and an angry roar emerged from the house. The attacking Archangel would surely be out here in a matter of moments.

Riley, Jeremiah and three angels piled into the garage and sprinted towards the kitchen door. Riley counted to three and threw the door open, as the others stormed the house. He stayed behind.

"What happened?" Riley asked.

I explained.

"Eden, you could've been *killed!*" he lectured.

"Yeah, well, I wasn't. I needed to warn the others," I defended myself.

"This isn't the time for this. Once this asshole's dealt with, we'll get the window covered," he replied. "Where are the others he was with?"

I shook my head. "I don't know. I shouted and ran."

He peeked into the kitchen to make sure the angel was being handled, then ran to the open garage door where two angels stood guard. He whistled sharply, gaining the attention of Flemming, who descended to his side.

"Get out back, make sure Kenneth and the others are safe," Riley ordered.

"Yes, sir," Flemming replied and darted around the side of the house.

A few moments later, there was a loud explosion from within the house. My family and friends who had been sent to the garage for protection, screamed loudly and huddled together. Riley ran into the kitchen, closing the door behind him.

I paced the garage, worried. The minutes dragged on, as I wondered what had happened and whether they were safe inside. My parents, my family was in there. Riley, the other angels… Had I just unwittingly forced everyone into a trap?

Riley emerged from the kitchen door, coughing and covered in soot. He wiped his face off on his bicep and staggered out into the garage. Behind him, Jeremiah was carried out in the arms of a shadow clad angel. The other two angels were nowhere in sight. A trail of blood followed behind them.

"Jere!" Mel shouted and ran to our friend.

The angel set him on the ground and returned inside. I ran to Jeremiah's side and put on gloves. Melanie cried hysterically as I tried to work around her. I knew my partner wouldn't be able to help at this point. I motioned for Riley to pull her back as I tried to help Jeremiah. Melanie and Jeremiah were the best of friends. She was in obvious pain.

Between Mel's crying and the fighting outside, I wasn't able to focus. I needed silence. I couldn't center myself. I couldn't meditate. I became frustrated as I felt Jeremiah slipping from my grasp. My hands shook as I lost focus and struggled. *I can't heal him.*

I opened my eyes and stepped to his side. I knelt down with a pair of trauma sheers and began removing his shirt. I inspected his body, from his head down, searching for all of his injuries. If I wasn't able to heal him, I was going to have to treat him, for now.

"Nix," he spoke gruffly, opening his eyes.

"Jere!" Riley shouted, running to Jeremiah's opposite side.

I tried to listen to his lung sounds and find the source of the pooling blood at his side. I asked Riley for an explanation, but he stated he had missed the explosion.

All that he knew was a chunk of the living room was now missing, and that Jeremiah and two of the angels had been caught in the blast.

The blood continued to pool as I tried to stop it. Jeremiah had a large gash on the inside of his left arm, and a small slash across his chest, caused by debris flying in the explosion. I was concerned his brachial artery had been severed. I used a piece of his shirt, tying it around his arm and using it as a tourniquet, attempting to stop the bleeding. His trachea was shifting to the right side of his throat, indicating a collapsed left lung. Before I could perform a decompression to Jeremiah's chest, he lost his color and went flaccid. I slumped at his side, as Mel and Riley approached. I checked for a pulse, listened to his heart with my stethoscope and felt all hope leave my body. I had just assisted in the murder of Riley and Melanie's best friend.

I did everything that I could think of, to attempt to reverse his condition. I did a pleural decompression, releasing a slight hiss as his left lung reinflated. I started an IV, attempting to replenish fluids in his body, hoping that would help to maintain a heartbeat. But I never got one back. I tried CPR. I pounded on his chest, between crying and begging for God to bring him back. All for naught.

"This is my fault," I whispered, pulling off my gloves.

"You were only trying to help," Mel said, placing her hand on my shoulder.

I snapped out of my remorse when I heard my dad cussing in the kitchen and ran to the door. He was standing in the doorway, examining his ruined living room. I went to his side and surveyed the destruction. The front wall was now missing, exposing the inside of the house to the elements. The wall that was behind the former TV, adjacent to the game room, was now missing, as well. I pulled my dad back, keeping him out of sight of the angels outside. I saw the legs of one of the angels poking out from underneath charred rubble and got Riley's attention. He and two other angels accompanied him inside, retrieved the two bodies and dragged them out into the garage.

Elijah emerged from the office and ran into the kitchen. He wrapped his arms around my waist, turning his head away from the destruction. He explained to me that this had been the work of Michael, himself. That Michael had been the angel who saw me, entered our home, and destroyed the living room, killing the three allied angels.

"How did he do this? Where is he now?" Riley asked Elijah, jaw clenched.

"He realized that the destructive ways of humans were far more productive. He found some explosives and set them off, knowing that he could take out two birds with one stone. He managed to kill Jeremiah and the two uncloaked angels, and destroy the shelter in one act," Elijah explained. "And I'm not sure exactly where he is. He fled to safety, somewhere nearby."

Riley ordered the evacuation of my family and our friends from inside the house to the garage. Meridith collected Jeremiah's soul, and then stood guard in the garage with everyone. Jared and Christopher were once more posted outside, as some of the other angels and Riley secured the living room.

I stayed in the kitchen, with both doors open, keeping an eye on everyone at once. Riley and I knew there was no way we were going to be able to repair the wall.

We were left with an open window to the outside world, and an inviting welcome to the avenging angels. The room would now become another guard outpost, leaving the house cut in half and unsafe to travel through without an escort.

My father turned off the circuit to that part of the house, ensuring that there were no electrical hazards. Both sides of the split home were still receiving power from the generator, thankfully. There was at least some minor relief with all of this.

Kenneth and the others returned from the field after fighting off the attackers. They thanked me for the warning, but felt the guilty pangs of the repercussions. They helped us try to get the room secure, and assisted with security for those out in the garage. Riley kept himself occupied, keeping his mind off of his now deceased best friend. I knew he was hurting, but he had to remain as focused as possible. We both knew, deep down, that Jeremiah was a good person. He would definitely be reborn by God's gracious hand.

As evening approached, fear settled in all of our hearts. Gabriel had disappeared shortly after warning us about the upcoming attack this afternoon. Lilith still hadn't returned since being called to the Middle East. Some of the Valkyrie had been sent to aid her. And now, Lucifer had come up missing. I wondered if constantly turning down his advances had finally pushed him away.

This was not the time to be without such helpful beings. We were becoming shorthanded and short on spirit. The death toll was rising and there was nothing we could do, but continue to send out more sheep to slaughter. The end was approaching, much quicker than I was prepared for.

Chapter Fifty
Huff My Taint, Chief.

Riley opted to leave my window uncovered and was now using it as a sniper's nest. He hid upstairs in the darkness, watching the skies and the fields. The exposed living room was now a roost for angels, as well. When we would need to pass through, we'd be heavily guarded for the twelve feet we had to travel. It was a bit of overkill, but we couldn't put it past the others.

Since Jeremiah's death, we had been attacked three times. It was starting to feel as if we were injured animals, being pecked at by vultures. They never quite sunk their talons in. They just continued the cat and mouse game; scaring us, toying with us. I stayed in the garage, treating the injured as they arrived. Gabe had been brought in by Flemming, after being stabbed in his butt cheek. He wasn't too pleased with the injury, but was rather proud of the reaction he had gotten.

"I'm telling you, it's worth it," Gabe stated, dropping his pants slightly.

"What the hell did you do?" I asked, laughing to myself and trying to avert my eyes.

"One of them was gunning for Gabe, so I snuck up behind him for a killing blow," Flemming explained.

"I told him, 'huff my taint, Chief'. He didn't like that very much and stabbed me in the ass. Hurt like hell, but I'd do it again." Gabe laughed. "In fact, I may. It may become my tag line. It'll go down in the history books as the new war taunt. And I still have another ass cheek to flash."

"You're such a dork," I jabbed, applying a trauma pad to his wound and securing it with tape.

"This is really awkward, I'll admit that," he sneered.

I chuckled, "Yeah, it is."

"I used to change your diapers, give me a break." he frowned.

"Get out of here!" I laughed, pulling off my gloves and popping him in his injured glute.

Gabe laughed, guarded his injury from further trauma and disappeared back into the night. If that was the worst I'd be dealing with, it would be a good night, indeed. But let's be realistic. We were in the middle of a war. That's impossible.

I stepped into the kitchen and grabbed a plate of food that my mom and aunts had prepared. I got the attention of one of the angels posted in the living room, letting him know that I needed to pass. As they came together like a shadowy wall, I ducked low and ran towards the damaged hallway, then crept up the stairs with the plate in my hand and stopped just below the top. I pulled the penlight from my back pocket and flashed it twice, then dropped to the ground. Riley noticed my signal and snuck over to the door.

He stepped over the rubble that was once the entryway into my room. "What're you doing up here?" he whispered to me. "Get back downstairs."

"I wanted to bring you some food," I whispered in reply.

"Edie," he paused, "Thanks." He decided against arguing and took the plate appreciatively.

"You haven't been eating enough. You know you need it for strength," I whispered.

"I know. I appreciate you watching out for me." he kissed my forehead. "Now, get back downstairs before you get hurt."

I left him to his rat killing, and returned downstairs. I opened the office door and checked on the group inside. I sat down for a moment, conversed with Ross and Bridget, then left the room, returning to the edge of the living room and ensuring my safe passage to the kitchen.

I made my way to the garage and sat silently with Melanie for a while. Since Jeremiah's death, she hadn't said much of anything, but had gotten much more involved with the current events. I believe that reality had struck her, leaving her to realize just how fragile we really were. I worried about her safety, but appreciated having her to help me, when the time came.

Jonah had gone missing shortly after we returned from burying Paige. I wasn't sure where he was, or what he was up to. Elijah couldn't see him, as he had now taken a path that hadn't been mapped out for him. I felt as though he had done this on purpose, knowing that we would be blind to his actions.

We still had not received word from Seth and Tobias. I was starting to fear the worst. They were both skilled hunters, and wouldn't be taken down easily. Which only made me that much more concerned. If they had been captured or killed, it was by angels even more skilled than they were. That put us in a very unsafe position.

As the evening turned into night, I was given some rather encouraging news. Callin had returned to inform us that the war in the Middle East was now under control. Lilith's group would soon be headed back to assist us with our endeavors. She told me that Gabriel and Lucifer had both made their way to the battlegrounds and would be coming back shortly to aid us, as well. That was a huge relief.

I told her about what had happened since they left and asked her to carry a message back to Lilith and Gabriel that Elijah was safe. I explained the situation with the explosion, and passed on the word that Michael was now involved with the attacks. I knew if anything would get the two of them back quickly, the concern of having Michael picking off the earthbound angels, personally, would light a fire under them. Callin left as swiftly as she had arrived.

The hours passed by slowly. I began to feel the toll the day had placed on me. I was weary, fatigued and troubled. Mel noticed my disposition and offered me a chance to nap, telling me that she'd be sure to get me if I was needed. I left her with Corey and Erick and snuck off to my parents' bedroom to sleep.

I curled up in bed with Rufio and Azrael, just like old times. With Riley upstairs, he needed to remain as quiet and hidden as possible. A rowdy dog would more than likely blow his cover, and there was no way that Azrael would listen to anyone else the way he did with Riley.

I gently stroked Rufio's soft fur, as he laid against my chest and purred. I envisioned my own bed, in my own home, before any of this mess had begun. I wished I could go back in time and just enjoy it once more. I wished there was some way just to undo all of this. I wished it had all just been a nightmare.

I felt my eyelids become heavy and my strokes became fewer and farther between. I heard Azrael's content sigh as he nodded off to sleep. I smiled, pat his head and followed suit.

I awoke in an unfamiliar land. I rose from the ground and brushed the wet sand from my side, noticing the river bed, nestled in the crook of twilight. In the distance ahead, I saw the bright unmistakable red glow of Lucifer's demonic wings and followed the waterline towards him. He stopped what he was doing when he noticed my approach and turned to me with the most dazzling smile.

"Bonsoir, love!" he shouted from a distance, standing along the shoreline.

"Hello, Frenchy." I grinned as I approached. "What're you doing?"

He shrugged casually, "Fishing."

I cocked my head to the side, confused by his answer, then looked down to the dark water. He didn't have a rod and reel, but simply a stick. I looked out into the pitch black waters. It was hard to see anything in the fading light, but there was movement, bobbing. I was unable to focus on the objects.

There was a splash in the distance, as something large landed in the water. I peeked around the Seraphim, attempting to locate the source. He leaned forward, blocking my view and handed me a stick. I looked at the stick, curiously, and then turned my gaze upwards to his breathtaking face.

"Care to join me?" he asked with a childlike smile.

"What're we fishing *for*?" I asked suspiciously.

"Whatever catches your fancy," he chuckled. "Dreams, lost hopes, nightmares... but the catch of the day is *souls*."

I lowered the stick into the water, "And how many have you caught already?"

"Only a few," he frowned. "The demons haven't been very productive tonight."

His words settled in my mind. I realized that something wasn't right.

"Wait, what?" I asked, pulling my stick from the water.

"Hold on! Don't move. You've got one!" he exclaimed excitedly.

He set down his stick and stepped behind me. He wrapped his arms around the outside of mine and helped me pull back on the stick. With one quick jerk, we fell backwards into the wet sand. He laughed and helped me to my feet. I looked to the bank, wondering what it was that I had caught.

I leaned down over the black mass and poked it with my stick. Lucifer kicked at it with disappointment. My stomach turned as the putrid smell of death overpowered my senses. I staggered back as Lucifer rolled the object over.

"Oh, shit!" I shrieked and covered my mouth.

Lying only a few feet from me, was the decomposing body of Jonah. I struggled to my feet and stepped away. I didn't know what to say, or what to think.

Jonah? Are you in trouble?

"I was hoping you caught something *worthwhile*," Lucifer sneered.

"What happened to him?"

"The same thing that will happen to them all. All but you, love." he smiled fondly.

"What the hell's going on?" I asked, confused.

"Oh, let's just throw him back. He's not worth the hassle. I'm sure the boys are waiting in the throne room," he replied, rolling Jonah into the tar-like waters.

I looked down at my bloodied hands. "What have I done?"

My vision panned upwards, as I watched the ferry floating by in front of my eyes. Charon rowed by slowly, reaching down with his bony arms and retrieving corpses from the river. The single lantern on the mast of his vessel reflected faintly on the black waters. I watched as he passed into the distance, and darkness set in.

I awoke with a gasp and sat up in bed. The room was as dark as the River Styx. I felt around for my pets, but found an empty bed. My groggy hands fumbled with my back pocket, as I attempted to find my small push button flashlight. I retrieved my penlight and pushed the button, scanning the room. It was completely empty. No light was coming from the doorway. No sounds could be heard. Something was wrong. I turned off the light and closed my eyes as my heart raced.

Please be a dream.

Please be a dream.

Please be a dream.

I opened my eyes once more and tiptoed towards the door. I rested my head against the doorjamb and listened to the rest of the house. Silence rang in my ears as I held my breath. Leaving the bedroom I slid along the hallway wall and crossed over, right before the office door. I felt for the doorknob. Realizing the door was open, I flashed my penlight. A few bodies lay in place, covered.

Please be sleeping.

Oh, God. Please be asleep.

Images of the orphanage, children lying dead on their beds, crept into my mind. I turned off my light and continued down the hallway. A faint light glinted off a wall in the hallway, reflecting from the kitchen. I edged down towards the living room. A shadow darted towards me and stopped short. I clenched my eyes closed and choked on my breath.

"Eden, where are you going?" the masked angel asked.

"I need to pass," I replied, opening my eyes.

"Hurry. They're close by," the angel ordered.

I looked to the exposed sky, and ran into the kitchen. There was no one around. I could hear hushed voices resonating from the garage. Flickers of pale light bounced in and out of sight. I walked to the garage door and grabbed my chest, relieved.

"What's going on?" I asked as I approached.

"Those *bastards* sabotaged the generator," my dad explained.

"Everyone's fine," Riley reassured me.

"Thank God. I glimpsed into the office and saw everyone lying around. I was worried that…" I shook my head. "Never mind. Is it fixable?"

"I don't know. I don't have enough damned light to see what the hell they did to it," my dad swore.

"I'll go get some lanterns," Riley offered. "Edie, stay in here."

"10-4."

I used my penlight to pan around the room. Familiar faces were scattered throughout, huddled in groups. Everyone looked terrified, worried. I saw my mom and ran to her side.

"Are you okay?"

"We're fine. How are you?" she questioned as though nothing was amiss.

"I'm alright. Where's Rufio and Az?" I asked.

"I put them in the bathroom together, so that they wouldn't get hurt or lost. Don't worry, your boys are safe," she comforted me.

I smiled, "Thanks."

Riley returned to my dad's side with two battery powered lanterns. The two of them scoured over the generator, trying to find the damage the saboteurs had caused. I stood over them, with one of Riley's lanterns in each hand.

"Any word on Jonah?" I asked Riley.

"No," he replied, removing the side panel.

"I had a really bad dream about him. I'm starting to worry." I leaned over the generator, attempting to see into the machine.

"That's great, Edie," he stopped and stared up at me for a moment. "Could you hold the lantern still so we could actually see shit?"

"Oh, sorry," I adjusted myself. "Heard from Gabriel or Luke yet?"

"No," he replied shortly.

"Damn it!" Dad shouted, standing up.

"What's wrong?" Riley and I asked simultaneously.

"The gas line's been cut!"

"Can you fix it?" Riley asked.

"Not right now, I can't. I'll have to look at it in the morning, when I can actually *see* what the hell I'm doing," he replied.

"Awesome," Riley scoffed. "Son of a bitch got us again."

I heard a low beep, followed by my brother's voice coming across a speaker. "Hey, uh… Riley? You might want to get up here. Looks like we have some douche-baggery afoot." Gabe went silent.

Riley pulled the walkie-talkie from his hip and hit the button, "I'll be right there. Stay low."

"Where'd you get that?" I asked with a grin.

"Your brilliant brother found them when they went out for gas." he smirked, then kissed my cheek.

"Nice." I nodded. "Be careful, please."

"Always am!" he replied as he dashed out of the garage and into the kitchen.

I returned to my mom's side and curled up next to her on the floor, laying my head on her lap. She stroked my hair as she spoke to her sisters. They talked about their childhood and what Orange had once been like. I closed my eyes and pictured all of the things they described. I felt myself dozing, as I fought to stay awake. My mom's methodical movements lulled me to sleep.

I awoke again to the sounds of water. I sighed and threw my head back. *Not again.* I scanned my surroundings, looking out into the vast reaches. This was nothing like before. Laid out before me, miles in each direction, a creek wound through the picturesque woods.
Much better.

The sound of the babbling brook soothed my soul. The tranquility relaxed me, allowing me to let my guard down. I heard the soft giggles coming from the distant tree line and I turned expecting to see my two boys, but didn't. I rose to my feet, as they sunk into the soft, wet Earth and walked to the edge of the woods, listening. The two distinct laughs bounced through the wooded land, accompanied by the whistles and chirps of birds. A cool breeze danced around me, sending gooseflesh up my skin. The soft rays of the sun on my back warmed me in response to the wind.

I pressed forward, following the laughter and the tree line. I came to a bend in the creek, and followed it around. There were my two boys, facing the water with their backs to me. I called to them, but they didn't answer. They bent over, playing with something in the water.

"What're you two doing?" I asked as I approached them.

They turned to me simultaneously. They're eyes were as black and empty as the river water now below them. I gasped and staggered backwards, away from them. I looked from the water to their faces. They weren't my boys. It was the faces of Seth and Tobias. Grins spread across their faces as they stabbed below them with their swords.

I looked down as I stepped backwards, Jonah was lying half in the water, half out on the bank. I shook my head. *What the hell's going on?* I looked back at the two, as they morphed into their shadow form and dropped to all fours. I backpedaled hastily, trying to get away from the scene.

Seth sprang forward, landing on me and knocking me to the ground. I struggled to breath beneath his weight. Tobias threw his head back, laughing loudly. He popped his neck, and sauntered towards me like a wolf about to strike. My breath was becoming impossible to catch as Tobias approached. I closed my eyes and prayed silently.

The weight was lifted. I opened my eyes, nervously. Standing before me were my twins. I sat up slightly, allowing myself to calm down. I looked from Orion's face to Lucian's. They both looked concerned, deeply troubled. Orion offered me his hand. I took it in mine and began to rise to my feet.

"Jump," he said, as he let go of my hand.

"What? No!" I shouted.

I began to fall backwards. I closed my eyes, bracing for the impact of the ground right below me. I winced, then opened them when I realized I hadn't hit. The crimson sky enveloped me as I fell backwards. I was right back where I started, falling. The first memory of this entire ordeal.

I glanced behind me as I sped towards the sharply twisted ground. My eyes darted back up, to see both of my boys, standing on the edge of the cliff, peering down. I closed my eyes once more and awaited the impact...
Again.

The loud crash startled me awake. I sat up, as my head spun and I attempted to catch my breath. Lucas lunged forward, covering my mouth. He held his finger to his own mouth, indicating for me to be quiet. I felt my brow crumple, confused by the commotion.

Another loud 'thud' was heard, directly above us. *Something* was on the roof of the garage. I stifled a scream behind my brother's warm hand. I felt myself panting, as my heart raced.

And then there was a third, closer to the edge of the garage, near the door. The sound continued, rolling, then stopped. Whatever it was, had hit the roof, then rolled off onto the pavement below it. Muffled screams were heard as the objects were discovered by our men outside. The garage door rattled.

I stood, pulling Lucas' hand from my mouth and began herding them in through the kitchen door. Aiden began to cry, as Sara rose and attempted to hush him. I pushed the kitchen door closed behind them, climbed next to the deep freezer and turned off the lantern. I watched, waiting in the silence, for the garage door to open.

Chapter Fifty One
Hell Hath No Fury Like a War Goddess Scorned.

When the garage door opened, my heart sank into the pit of my stomach. Carried in by Kenneth, Flemming and Brandon, were the bodies of our missing friends. I ran to the angels, hoping it wasn't too late. But it was. Tobias, Seth and Jonah had been killed.

"It's worse than I thought," Kenneth stated as he set Jonah down next to a lantern I brought forward. He took it and held the light high to reveal the battered face of our friend.

"An eye for an eye." Kenneth removed the note fixed to his chest with a small dagger.

"I don't get it." I shook my head, distraught. I looked at his face, noticing the sunken sockets around his eye lids. "Oh, my God. Why?" I covered my mouth and fell to my knees.

"Jonah could see the future, so they took his eyes," Flemming surmised.

"That's fucked up," Brandon said, setting Seth on the ground with care.

"What'll they do to Elijah if they get hold of him? Jonah only saw flashes, small fragments. Elijah knows exactly what's to come," I cried.

"We can't allow that to happen. This has to end," Kenneth stated, setting down the lantern and rising to his feet. "We are being killed just because we are in the way. It seems that you earthbound are their main objectives."

Brandon and I stared at each other.

"Tori. Where is she?" he asked anxiously.

"She's inside with Elijah and the others," I replied.

He darted in through the kitchen door without another word.

Kenneth, Flemming and I sat around the bodies helplessly, wondering what the next move would be. I couldn't help but think about my dreams. Had they been foreshadowing? Was it just that I had been concerned about my friends? At this stage in the game, it was hard to tell. Kenneth reaped their souls and paced the garage as he awaited orders from Riley.

It was 2am by the time things started to piece together. Gabriel and Lucifer returned, and sent word to Riley. Kenneth and I filled them in on everything that had happened. Gabriel was deeply troubled by the deaths of the earthbound. He felt somewhat responsible, because he hadn't been here to assist. Lucifer didn't seem troubled, as usual. In fact if anything, this meant less beings in his way, getting him closer to taking over. Or so I surmised.

Gabe came downstairs and into the garage. He was to give Gabriel the other walkie-talkie and Riley's orders. As far as we were aware, we only had one more day of fighting ahead of us. But we had suffered such a devastating loss in numbers, it wasn't likely that we'd be able to fend them off much longer. If they continued to attack us with brute strength and cunning, we may not make it to the end. Riley wondered if we could receive help from God; divine intervention, either by way of His interjection, or more troops to keep them at bay.

Gabriel was convinced that neither of those were likely, as God does not condone war and violence. As we argued, we were merely trying to stop the battle He had initially started by giving Michael power. We were only trying to survive, at the moment. Self-preservation in light of defense. Drastic times called for drastic measures. Blah, blah, blah.

"Where is your overprotective, trigger-happy lover?" Lucifer asked me snidely.

"Upstairs, why?" I asked in reply.

"Just curious," he shrugged. "So, we have time to ourselves... yes?"

"You really don't like him much, do you?" Melanie asked.

"It's a loathe/hate relationship," he nodded.

"You mean *love*. It's *love and hate*, if you weren't aware of the saying," she corrected him.

"Oh, no, mademoiselle. I meant exactly as I said. I loathe him. He hates me. It's as simple as that," he clarified.

"That's exactly what we need right now. Two little boys, butting heads," I mused.

"I don't see him here," he looked around cockily. "In fact, I'm having a hard time remembering the last time he was around to keep you safe. When was your last loving embrace? When was the last time that he satisfied you?"

I stared at the Seraphim as he eased his way under my skin.

"I know. I know. I'm such an asshole, correct?" he chuckled. "Ah, you already have a pet name for me. I'm slowly but surely winning you over, love." he winked. I had to get away from him. "Come on." I wrapped my arm around Melanie's neck and walked with her into the kitchen.

"Where are we going?" she asked, as I dragged her along side of me.

"We need to talk to Elijah," I said.

With the watchful eyes of *our* angels on us, we passed through the living room and into the hallway. I pulled my penlight from my pocket and used the dim light to safely traverse the path to my parents' bedroom. We stepped into the room and found Elijah seated on the bed next to a lantern, meditating.

"Hey, kiddo. Do you have a minute?" I asked softly.

He opened his eyes and smiled faintly, "Yes, ma'am. What can I do for you ladies?"

"I, *we*, need to know what to expect for today," I stated.

He sat up straight, and pat the bed next to him. We took our seats and got comfortable. Mel hadn't spent much time around him and seemed slightly hesitant. I reassured her that despite his looks, he was our window into the future.

He foretold the morning as if it were written in a daily planner. The schedule was laid out, almost down to the minute. Mel questioned how he *knew* such things when even God, apparently, had no control over free will. He explained the difference between freewill and destined paths, and returned to his prophesizing.

The day was mapped out, and it looked rather bothersome, to say the least. We were to expect more ambushes, and even more deaths. The house would be attacked directly, so we were advised to discuss the conditions of security with Riley, and give him Elijah's recommendations regarding fortification.

I acted as if the question hadn't ever been posed to Gabriel, and asked Elijah what he thought about asking God for assistance to aid the ending of the war here. He informed me that, though he wasn't sure of the exact circumstances since it was God's actions, our Father would be intervening.

He mentioned the arrival of several other angels and Valkyrie. Bethany, one of the head Valkyrie, would be bringing more of their forces. They would be geared and ready for battle, not just soul retrieval. Lilith would soon be returning, and with her, her insatiable need for revenge on her brother's behalf.

Hell hath no fury like a war goddess scorned.

Elijah explained that the ending was masked, as if he were blindfolded, due to God's decisions. He expressed Gabe's need to say his farewells to Sara, his kids and our family. He also explained that this was both Riley and Lucifer's moment of truth, earning their places among history and legend.

Elijah concluded his foreshadowing and hugged me tightly around the neck. He thanked me for everything that I had done, both in this world and the heavens. My eyes clouded as they filled with tears. I couldn't believe everything that we had been through, together and separate. I kissed his sweet forehead, then Mel and I left him to his thoughts.

We snuck up the staircase, towards what was left of my bedroom. I signaled to Riley with my penlight and stepped back a few steps to stay out of sight. He emerged from the rubble and followed us into the hallway. I passed on all of the knowledge Elijah had given to me and left him with a kiss. We returned to the steps just before the living room and asked for coverage as we crossed. Jared informed me that he would need a few moments, as he had seen shadows darting above the rooftop. He didn't trust the situation, and I trusted his gut. We sat down in the hallway, settling in until we were able to cross.

"This is insane, you do realize that, right?" Melanie asked, cradling her head in her hands.

"I've kind of given up on sanity. Well, not recently. It was a while ago," I grinned.

"I miss Jere," her voice quivered. "I want him to tell me everything will be alright."

"I know. I'm so sorry."

"It's not your fault. I know you've done everything you can. And I just want you to know that I'm going to miss you." she frowned.

"What?" I asked, nervously.

"Jere told me what was going to happen. He told me about your plan," she explained. "I wish it wasn't like that. But I understand why you're doing it. Thank you."

I didn't know how to respond. "You're... welcome?"

"If I ever decide to have a kid, I'll name it after you," she chuckled with a sniffle.

I laughed, "I wouldn't recommend that."

"Yep, I will. We'll go with Quinn." she wiped her eyes.

"I'm sure your kids would be awesome." I wrapped my arm around her shoulder.

I sat silently, as Mel cried into my shoulder. We waited patiently for the all clear from Jared. The sounds of fighting broke through the silence and echoed through the house, as they finally caught the intruders.

"Ladies, hurry. Pass while they're distracted," Jared ordered.

Finally.

I helped Mel to her feet as she wiped away her tears. We darted through the living room, into the kitchen and stopped. We both grabbed a snack and entered the garage, where Gabriel was conversing with Riley over the walkie-talkies. Lucifer chimed in occasionally, throwing in his opinion.

I looked around the room at the dimly lit faces. Everyone was listening intently as the plans for the day were formulated. It wouldn't be long before the first major attack took place. We had to prepare ourselves.

By 0630, we were about as organized as a group of people expecting an ambush from celestial beings could be. Most of our family and friends were positioned in the office with three angelic guards. Melanie and I were in the garage with two new additions at our side as protection. Zachariah and Ty were none too thrilled with their assignment, feeling more like babysitters and less like warriors.

Gabe had woken up Sara and the kids early, and was spending time with them, rather than fighting with the others. Riley was in the garage with us for the time being, but wouldn't remain long. He and Lucifer were discussing the probability of survival, based on our new additions, versus the amount Elijah predicted of Michael's troops. The odds were looking much more in our favor, for once.

I stepped over to Lucifer and Riley. The tension was palpable as I approached. "Is there any getting through to Michael? I mean, really. We're about to return to God's side and walk away from the Earth."

"No," they answered simultaneously.

"He doesn't care. This is a personal vendetta, not a negotiation," Lucifer explained as Riley nodded in agreement.

"Michael doesn't honestly think he's going to get away with this, does he?" I asked.

"I don't know exactly what he's thinking, or what will happen to him for his transgressions," Riley said, shrugging his shoulders.

"God was definitely infuriated, but I'm not certain how He will punish Michael. I think we all know what *should* become of him," Lucifer stated.

"Yeah, well, He didn't handle the situation with *you* any better. I wouldn't have let you live." Riley grinned smugly.

"If you have yet to realize, it's nigh impossible to kill an extension of God. Hence, the reason the Horsemen were still standing. It wasn't from lack of effort," Lucifer replied with bravado. "I'm fairly certain even God couldn't kill me. It would be suicide. Besides, I'm actually a very loveable individual when you get to know me," he said with a wink in my direction.

"I'll find a way to take you out," Riley sneered.

"Oh, I'm trembling in fear! How ever will I survive the attack of a mortal?" Lucifer pretended to cower. "Get over yourself, *boy*. The day you 'take me out' will be the day you destroy God. Oh, wait, that's impossible." he grinned wickedly.

"Is this really productive?" I asked, arms crossed.

Lucifer shrugged, "I didn't start this, love. I merely ended it."

Riley's jaw was clenched.

"Riley, they're here," Gabriel called over the walkie talkie.

"I'm on my way," Riley answered Gabriel, then turned to Lucifer. "Go get your prettiest panties on, Lucy. It's your turn to dance."

"Eden, may I borrow that lingerie you wore for me?" Lucifer looked at me with a smug grin.

I felt my jaw drop.

"In your dreams, sweetie. She's into men, not flaming Goth girls like yourself," Riley mused and slapped Lucifer on the ass. "Though I must say, good game."

Lucifer chuckled heartily. "Let's go."

I felt my jaw dangle further. For once, they seemed to be enjoying the verbal sparring. I was speechless.

Riley hugged me tightly and kissed my cheek. He reassured me that everything would be alright, told Zachariah and Ty to keep a tight rein on me and hugged Melanie as he left. Lucifer grinned, kissed my other cheek and dashed out of the garage like a caped crusader. It was strange watching him. While everyone else was serious and stoic in preparation for the attack, he seemed almost childlike in his excitement. It was disconcerting.

I shrugged off the feeling, pulled a chair over by Mel and sat down. My mind was everywhere at once. I started to think back to the beginning. Everything, *all* of this, had started with a dream. Not a chain of events, *a dream*. That dream will never leave my mind. I could remember every detail.

Everything is red... Miles of crimson swept with wisps of black and grey. The clouds swirl and dance to a rhythm only heard by the gods. The trees are black, twisted, screaming in agony. Every thought is crystal clear. Every sense is piqued. The air is as stagnant as death...

I waited for my hero. I waited for that valiant steed. Little did I know that my hero *did* arrive. I saw him as a monster, a demon-like creature. He was there to save me. A piece of my soul... my knight in shining armor. *I'm sorry, Gabriel.* He tried, countless times, but I ran.
I ran as I always have.

One way or another, I've always run. I've taken the easy way out, not necessarily the high road. *This will all be over soon,* I thought, so many months ago. I was right, just not in the same sense that I was assuming. I thought *this dream* will all be over soon.

This is not a dream.

This is not a nightmare.

This is not a test. I repeat, this is not a test.

Now that I'm here, at the end of the rope, the questions are raised again. Would I take this all back? Would I, if I could, go back to being "just Eden"? Would I give up the knowledge of the origins, the creation, the Creator? Would I, if I could, wake from this, like a dream, running from the truth? The answer is, no. Not at all.

I will never run again. I will never back down, or betray my honor. Before long, the world, as I knew it, would no longer exist. The world I both feared and respected, the life I both loved and hated, will be over.

Eden Quinn McDowell-Nixon, a resident of Baton Rouge and wherever the hell else she's been throughout the past few thousands of years, has shuffled off this mortal coil and ascended to the heavens. Survived by her furry sons, Rufio and Azrael, residents of wherever Riley winds up; loving parents, Kurt and Kim McDowell, of the freshly demolished Orange, Texas, which her father isn't pleased with, by the way; brothers, Ross, Eli, Lucas and Gabe; her husband, Riley, who was totally screwed and stuck on this crap-ass planet, left to clean up everyone's mess; aunts; uncles; cousins; nieces; nephews; and last, but not least, oddly enough, her final douche bag glass.

Yes, it managed to outlast her.

Thanks a lot, Apocalypse. That was a real bitch slap in the face, right there.

Chapter Fifty Two
Sic Semper Tyrannis

"Honey, those were my good sheets!" my mom exclaimed, staring at her ruined 1500 thread count Egyptian cotton sheets, now covered in red paint.

"Um, yeah, well, that was also your 'good car' that was thrown through the roof of the garage. I don't see you bitching at Michael about that one," I replied, staring up from the kitchen floor.

"Well, you both could've asked first," she jeered.

"*I'm* sorry. And I'll let him know that not consulting you first was very rude," I joked and continued splattering Dad's paint onto the flat sheet.

"What exactly are you writing, anyway?" she asked, head cocked to the side, attempting to read my cryptic message.

"You'll see," I replied, then returned to my art.

"That isn't very reassuring." her eyes narrowed. "Do me a favor and at least *tell me* before you destroy something else." she turned on her heel and left the room.

Here's a little history lesson, folks. *Supposedly*, the phrase was coined and trademarked, signifying the downfall of tyranny, through the art of assassination. So it's been said, that Marcus Junius Brutus was the contributing dude. The guy that killed Julius "I like little boys" Caesar. And anyone aware of American history should know that John Wilkes Booth shouted it when he shot up Mr. Honest Abe. *Sic Semper Tyrannis*, or "Thus always to tyrants", if you're not fluent in Latin.

I finished scrawling my war cry on the sheet and stood above, admiring my work proudly... and also hoped it didn't bleed through to the kitchen tiles. I didn't want to explain that one to Mom. I gathered my cheaply made, yet still rather expensive sign and carried it to the living room.

"Jared?" I whispered, waiting for his attention.

"Yes?" he replied.

"Can you hang this on the front of the house somehow?" I asked.

"What is it, exactly?" he asked, eyes narrowed.

"A victory speech."

He took the sheet in his hands and unfolded it to read it, "You're a woman of few words, I see."

"Not really, but in this case, three words say more than a novel could." I grinned.

"I'll get it taken care of. Get back to safety," he replied.

"Thanks!" I shouted as I darted through the living room and hopped to the hallway.

It was now 1400 and this morning had been all but kind to us. As previously stated, but not explained, Michael had lodged my parents' car in the roof of their garage. From what I'd heard, he had thrown it at Gabriel, calling him a "traitor". It seemed rather juvenile, if you ask me. Is "wittle man" so upset that he's having a temper tantrum? *Aw, poor baby.*

The mood hadn't been this light all morning. At this point, I've just thrown my hands in the air and said "this, too, shall pass". We'd lost more friends and comrades, but I've had to tell myself it'll be okay. I'll see them in the cosmos soon. Their souls have been reaped and will be delivered from this darkness.

It was the circumstances of *how* that bothered me, more so than the *who.* Two men that had protected me, even until death. I hated to know that they had died, but I knew where they'd be, and I was forever in their debt.

I was in the garage, removing an arrow from Corey's leg, when Michael had his conniption fit and heaved the vehicle at Gabriel. Erick had just arrived in the garage, bringing me supplies. He lunged forward, pushing me out of the way, as the car crashed through the roof and pinned them both. Had it not been for Erick, I wouldn't be here. He died almost instantly. The same cannot be said for Corey, who drew the attention of Michael just long enough for me to get completely inside the house. I owed them my life, my boys' lives. I don't know what would've happened, had it not been for them. The next time I see them, I owed them both a huge hug.

I thought about the fact that we now had three more bodies to bury in the makeshift cemetery. It hadn't really crossed my mind until now. If for some reason those bodies were found later, would my parents be suspected serial killers? At any other point in time, it would've been smarter to bury them somewhere else, but with all of this going on, I'm pretty sure there was bodies buried everywhere on Earth. Last respects must be paid. It's a way of life. It must be done, even when your foot is balancing on the edge of your own grave.

I didn't really know him, since he had only just arrived, but Joel had also lost his life today. He was like one of those nameless henchmen that fell into a shark tank, or were accidentally gunned down while tying his shoe. "Wrong place, wrong time" red shirt, type of circumstances. I only knew his name because I had asked it. I didn't like having someone I didn't know "protecting" me. So sorry, Joel. Tough break, man.

Lilith had returned a few hours before. I had yet to speak with her, but I had seen her numerous times. She had come back from the Middle East war in a frenzy. Between Thomas' death and the human bloodshed she witnessed, she was a wreck. A beautiful wreck. This was only the second time that I could recall seeing her in her three forms. Well, I should be more specific. I've seen her as Lilith, the bitch, Lilith, the torn war goddess, and Lilith, the wiry flea ridden bird. But I mean Lilith, the three sisters, *the Mórrígna.* And to see her, outside of a dream, was mesmerizing.

She moved with such grace. Her body flowed like a soft cloth blowing in the wind; silent; deadly. The two "sisters" passed behind her with mimicking movement, lagging seconds after, like tracers from drug consumption. Where her sword fell, theirs fell after a brief pause, finishing the deed. Where she climbed into the air, they swept behind her, like haunting visions of a schizophrenic. It was amazing. It was creepy. Had I not known what was going on, I would've thought that I had finally lost my mind, for sure.

Lucifer had shed his formal jacket and donned a blackened breastplate. I was sure Michael was none too thrilled to see that. The Devil was not only siding with us, but wearing divine armor. It wasn't like he needed it. And I'm not even sure when or where he got it. But I was sure it was more for dramatic flair. I couldn't blame him. If I was untouchable, and hell bent on taking out a tyrannical jerk, I'd use whatever tactics played to my advantage, as well. Especially if those tactics meant looking incredibly dapper, and Lucifer did have a flair for the dramatic.

Though Riley couldn't split into three beings at once, he might as well have been. He was juggling so many different tasks. I knew I had less than 24 hours with him, and wanted to be at his side, but I knew that was impossible. As Elijah had explained to me, it was for the best to start detaching anyway. It hurt. It truly did. But we knew it was coming.

Gabe had spent most of the morning with Sara and the kids. Every time I saw him, my stomach turned. *Knowing* that your brother was going to perish was a horrible burden to bear, even when you *knew* where he'd be afterwards. I'd still spent my life with him. I still had to worry about whether or not he'd change. He was going to be so pissed if he lost all of his tattoos. Well, I should say when. I didn't foresee God letting him keep them. And I *was going to* rub it in his face for the shit he said when I lost mine.

Brooke had been completely broken since the death of Corey and Erick. I knew losing Paige was hard. Then, she lost the love of her life. Then, she lost a good friend. But then, to top it all off, she also lost her brother. There was no one left for her to lean on. I figured she needed space, so I left her alone. I knew she was a strong woman, but no amount of courage can get you through that much devastation, sane.

Melanie, luckily, had not been in the garage when Erick and Corey had died. I was very thankful for that. She had been asleep in the office with the others. I knew she'd be awake soon and hoped that she and Brooke would start to bond. They could be assets to each other, once this was all over. They would both be left to fend for themselves, alone.

My mom and dad were in their bedroom, praying. I tried to tell them that faith was great. Praying was a wonderful catalyst for recovery, but it wouldn't change a thing. What was to come could not be changed. No amount of wishful thinking, or offering their life in our stead, would sway the outcome. I was to return to the Fold. Gabe was to sacrifice himself for the world. Gabe and I sat down with them and broke the news. It didn't go very well, to say the least. My dad was speechless. I wasn't sure if he was choosing not to believe it, or if he was in shock. My mom cried, uncontrollably. I knew it was hard for her to fathom, losing both of her children at once. But, we knew, they would never give up their Faith.

I reassured them both that they *would* see us again. It wasn't a lie, though I knew I wouldn't be allowed back down to Earth. I could learn how to pass through dreams. I would be there for them as much as I possibly could. We both spent time with them, allowing them the chance to grieve and say their goodbyes.

But as with the sheet thing, my family has a tendency to deal with pain and fear of the unknown, through laughter. It's an admirable trait, and we all have my dad to thank for that one. By the time my dad opened his mouth, it was to inform me that he wouldn't allow God to take me, until I had "cleaned this shit up". Though his words didn't express it, I knew deep down inside he was heartbroken.

I found Elijah shortly after conversing with my parents. He seemed down about something. I pulled him to the stairs and talked with him. He handed me the silver trinket that had once belonged to me. It had been dear to him for so long, but he knew it was now time to return it to me. I turned the trinket in my hands, looking at the delicately etched filigree. I popped the beautiful locket open and looked inside. There was a picture of me on the left hand side, and a picture of Riley on the right. I smiled fondly as my eyes filled with tears.

Though the photos were aged, from a life so very long ago, they reflected the same love that we had shared in this lifetime. Between the two pictures, where the hinges were, sat a small hollow tube. I twisted the mechanism and removed the tiny scroll placed inside.

I read the note and began to cry. It was a short message I had written to Elijah, dated May 4th, 1866. I had informed him that I wouldn't be around much longer, due to an illness I had been enduring. I asked that he treasure the locket and keep it safe, that one day I would need it. That day, it would be the only reminder that I had existed on this Earth. And that day would be the day I returned to Heaven.

He had done just as I had asked, and treasured it for almost 150 years. We both knew, this was that day I had described. I would have to pass the trinket on to Riley. And he would know that when he was returning to Heaven, he would have to pass it on to my parents.

While speaking with Elijah, I remembered that we had never contacted Mary or Anthony. I asked him what would become of their souls. He reminded me that as he had explained, *all but one* would be returning to the Fold. They would be offered the chance, and would take it. Even Matthew, who had done something horrific, had the opportunity for redemption.

As the afternoon dredged on, my anxiety rose. Gabe returned to the fighting, leaving me to question when his end would come. Tori stayed with me for a while, helping me mentally prepare for our ascension and the end of the war.

Riley took some time away from the action to spend with me. He laid his head gently on my stomach and talked to my bellybutton. He told the boys some of our stories, and how he would always love them. He explained that even though he would not always be there with them, they would forever be in his heart and on his mind. He promised that he would see them again, and hoped that, someday, we could reunite as a family.

I gave him the locket and cried in his arms. This was one of the hardest moments I had ever experienced in my life. I couldn't help but wonder if death would've been easier to grieve for, rather than knowingly walking away from the man I loved. So many years, so many lives, stories, adventures, fights, so many memories, and I was letting them go. But as he reminded me, it was for our sons. It was for the rest of the world. It was for the best. Sometimes, knowing an action is in the best interest of everyone doesn't necessarily make it any easier to do.

He returned to the battle and I found my brothers. I gathered Eli, Lucas and Ross together and explained what was ahead. I can't imagine how hard it was to hear that their youngest siblings would be the ones lost. Ross, being the extremely spiritual man that he is, accepted the news much better than anyone else in my family. He was saddened, yet supportive. He admitted that he would do the exact same, if placed in either of our positions.

Lucas and Eli were more reluctant to let go of us. I had never seen my brothers show emotion so blatantly. Not only were they losing their brother, their sister; but they were also losing the nephews that they had only days ago found out about. I understood the pain that inflicted on them, but I didn't have a choice. I asked all three of them to explain the situation as delicately as they could to their families.

I returned to the hallway just before the living room. The sunlight filtered through the room, throwing shadows against the remaining walls. I looked to the sky, but found it blocked by my message. Jared had secured the sheet over the gaping hole where the roof once was. Though this wasn't protective, and the front side was still exposed, it put my message in plain sight. I smiled to myself. *Sic semper tyrannis, indeed.*

I passed into the kitchen and stopped near the doorway. From a safe distance, I watched the action taking place in the front yard. Lilith continued to dance through the crowd, as the blade of her sword destroyed all that it touched. I saw Riley run by, followed by a shadowy being, then race back by screaming "shit!" I couldn't help but laugh sadly by the cartoon-esque sequence that had just taken place.

Tori was the first to notice and got my attention, as Chuck and Lamar approached. Chuck stumbled through the rubble of the living room, with an injured Lamar in his arms. I felt my breath pause as I watched Chuck enter the house. He carried Lamar into the kitchen and set him down on the table. He explained that they had been attacked at their guard post and Lamar had been stabbed in his stomach.

I asked Tori to retrieve Melanie for me, then stepped to the garage door, scoping around for my jump bag. I found it near the steps and snuck back inside without drawing the attention of Michael or his forces. I returned to Lamar's side as I put on a new pair of gloves and began gathering supplies.

"Where's Turkey?" he asked with a groan and a wince.

"You were just stabbed, and you're asking about Fat-ass?" Chuck scoffed.

"He's in the office, with Rufio," I replied, tearing open a package of trauma dressings.

I inspected the wound. I was relieved to see, based on where it was, it had more than likely missed anything vital. It wasn't a wound to leave untreated, and I knew he was in an enormous amount of pain, but it wouldn't be the death of him. I was grateful for that. There were no organs exposed and the bleeding was easily controlled. When Mel arrived, I asked that she get the wound dressed, while I established an IV and gave him medication for pain. She placed numerous pads around the wound and secured it in place with a bandage, wrapped around his torso.

I loaded Lamar up with morphine and watched as he drifted off into a drug-induced sleep. I explained to Chuck that as soon as he was able to, he would need to get the wound sutured shut, but that we'd keep an eye on Lamar as long as we could. We carried him into the office and got him comfortable on a pallet. Chuck stayed by his side while he rested.

I wasn't happy to know that Lamar had gotten hurt, but I was incredibly thankful to know that was the worst of it. It wasn't an injury anyone would want to endure, but I was sure that he was going to live. They were both now out of the fight, relatively safe, and would have long lives in front of them.

The fighting continued outside well into the evening, with several casualties. The angels that had once been guarding the house, inside the living room, had now moved into the office to cover as extra protection for our family and friends, or had relocated outside to assist with the war. I was standing in the doorway of the kitchen, eating a sandwich, when I noticed Elijah peek around the corner of the hallway. His expression was unreadable.

"It's time," he stated simply.

Moments after his words were muttered, Gabriel's horn sounded outside, startling me. I grasped my chest in response. He blew it twice more and he landed right in front of the house. He peeked in, grinned at Elijah, then turned to me. He motioned for me to come to his side.

I was nervous. I felt very hesitant. For days, they had made it abundantly clear that I wasn't allowed outside, *especially* with Michael now out and about. Yet, all of a sudden, I was being told to come outside? This could only mean one thing. As Elijah had said, it *was* time.

I shoved the remainder of my sandwich in my mouth and gulped down the last of my water. I pulled the rubber band from my hair and secured my tangled tresses in a somewhat presentable ponytail. I took in an excruciatingly deep breath and let it out slower than molasses on a cold, winter day. I was stalling. I was terrified.

"Eden, Father is here. Are you not coming?" Gabriel peeked around the kitchen door.

I lifted my head to meet his eyes, "I don't know."

"It's okay. He's here to end this." he grinned, offering me his hand.

As I emerged from the kitchen, I noticed the hallway, lined with my family and friends. Lucas, Amber, Kadence and Rendon were at the front of the line, and each hugged me as I passed them. Gabriel reached for Elijah, taking his son's hand in his free one.

"You are not to witness this, I'm afraid," Gabriel said, turning to the group of friends and family. "I ask that you either return to the room, or stay well hidden. This is not best for your eyes, or your hearts."

Sara let go of Ian's hand, stepped forward, teary eyed and picked Aiden up. She grabbed Lily's hand and stared at me. I knew I needed to talk to her for a moment.

"Gabriel, I'll be right there. Give me a minute." I let go of his hand and turned to Sara.

"So, this is it? I lose you both now?" she cried.

"Sara... it's not like you think." I shook my head, turning my gaze to the beautiful blue eyes of my niece, and the handsome faces of my nephews.

"Oh, really? 'Cause I'm pretty sure both of you assholes are leaving me. Which would mean I'm losing you both," she sniffled.

"He'll be back." I grinned, uncomfortably.

"You're the worst liar I've ever met, Eden Quinn," she said as she wiped her tears.

I frowned, "I'm sorry. I love you. You know this."

Gabriel tapped my shoulder, and then, grabbed my hand again. I wrapped my free arm around Sara, hugging her, then kissed Lily, Ian and Aiden. I followed my soul twin as he led me through the rubble, out into the evening. I looked around the yard in awe.

Every angel, both our side and Michael's, were bowed on one knee. I turned towards the driveway and saw God, standing less than 100 yards away. I gasped and dropped to my knee, bowing my head. He stepped forward with a deep sigh.

"Why is it, that all of you did not heed my words, as given to you by Gabriel?" He asked, stepping through the crowd of kneeling angels. "Why did you continue to attack these beings, after I had clearly stated that you must cease?"

The group was silent. I looked around, waiting for some kind of answer.

"Why are you silent now? Why did you end the bloodshed once I had arrived?" He placed His hand on top of my head as he walked by. "Ah, yes. Because you *knew* it was against my will. *You knew!* Yet, you continued to do Michael's bidding, after hearing the words from my son, *my voice!*"

"Father, we were only following orders from..." one angel stood, defending their actions.

"SILENCE!" God bellowed angrily. "These questions were rhetorical. Do not think me a fool. I *know* your reasons. I *know* why you did as you have done. I *know* who is to blame and *I know* who the heroes are."

I looked around the crowd. I was startled to see Gabe, the only fighting human left, out in the crowd of angels. As earthbound, we were human, too, but we were still of the heavenly variety. We were here for the exact same reason the other angels were.

"What the hell are you doing?" I mouthed to Gabe from across the yard.

He curled his lip in a smile and shrugged. He looked nervous.

"Thaddeus, come forward," God ordered.

Riley stood and dusted off his knee. He adjusted his shirt and cleared his throat, biding time. He slowly began walking towards our Creator. I could see the gears spinning in his mind as he weighed his options, his words, his actions.

"What is it that you wish to speak to me about?" God asked.

Riley nervously approached our Creator. "I, uh. I realize that I pissed you off pretty good in the past. I know that I've never successfully redeemed myself for what happened, and I may never be able to do so." he raised his head with pride. "But I wanted to thank you for sparing Eden and the twins. And I would like to serve you, by remaining on Earth for the time being and correcting these atrocities that *Michael* has caused." he shot a glare at Michael.

"I have *caused* nothing! I was curing the disease you cretins have created!" Michael shouted, rising to his feet.

"Michael, calm yourself. We'll get to you shortly," God ordered.

"*Calm myself?* I'm being placed on trial for something I was commanded to do. I did no wrong. Yet I should stand in front of my '*peers*' and be judged as a criminal?" Michael gibed.

"I suggest you bite your tongue, Michael." Lucifer stood up, stepping towards the archangel with his black sword drawn.

"Shut your devilish mouth, *Satan*," he hissed in reply. "*Traitors! You're all traitors!* You couldn't stand by your convictions if your measly lives depended on it!" he looked around, shouting at everyone.

God stepped forward, pushing Riley aside. "*You will be punished* for your deeds, Michael."

"My deeds were justified!" he argued.

God shook His head, ashamed, "Cruelty and malice are not justifiable. Ever."

"I showed no ill will." Michael grinned, smugly.

"Bullshit! You *heartlessly murdered* innocent people, you lying asshole!" Gabe shouted, rising from the ground and pointing at Michael.

"Daddy!" Lily shouted from the hallway and dashed towards him.

"Lily, no!" Gabe and I shouted simultaneously.

I rose from the ground running towards my niece to stop her.

"Lily, stop!" Sara shouted as she sprinted towards her daughter.

I felt myself fall forward as Michael pushed me to the ground and snatched Lily up in his hands. He held her by the back of her shirt, as she squealed loudly. He grinned wickedly, turning towards us.

"Heartless, you say? Heartless would be stealing the soul of this child right in front of her helpless parents, right in front of the very beings that tried to protect her," he stated gravely.

Lucifer dashed forward, grabbing Michael by the throat and raising him into the air. "Let her down, *now!*" his voice was unrecognizably deep, terrifying. It sent chills down my spine as it reverberated in the air. I had never seen such utter ferocity and anger from the typically suave, arrogant creature. His ember coated wings flapped, his eyes flashed like flame.

Michael cackled loudly and held his hand to her chest, "Or what, *Devil?*"

"I'll kill you!" Gabe let out an ear piercing cry as he ran forward and slashed the wings from Michael's back with a sword.

Michael roared as he let go of Lily. He was dropped to the ground by Lucifer. Lucifer grabbed Lily, handing her to me. I wrapped my body around her, attempting to shield her eyes as Michael writhed in pain. He was feeling the same pain that we felt during The Great Divide. Gabe and Lucifer stood above him, swords drawn and awaiting the word. They were both filled to the brim with anger, with hatred.

"Lord, he deserves nothing less than death," Lucifer stated. "Let me deliver it."

"Death would be a release for him," God replied somberly. "I will grant him no such pardon."

"Please, please Father. You are the Ever-Forgiving," Michael groveled at His feet.

"Let me end this, once and for all," Lucifer offered. "Let me spill his blood."

"No!" God shouted.

Gabe dropped his sword to the ground and ran to my side. He pulled Lily from my arms and held her tightly to his chest. He kissed her forehead and whispered into her ear. She pulled away, kissing her hand and shoving it down his shirt.

A kiss for later.

"Michael... As you've believed that this world has become more of a prison cell than hell itself, this is where you will stay," God stated.

"No..." Michael shook his head.

"You will age, just as the humans age. You will feel sickness, pain, hunger, just as the humans have felt," God continued.

"No... You can't do this to me." Michael's voice trembled with anger. "I have done nothing wrong!"

"You will suffer for every life you've taken. You will feel every emotion, every last ounce of heartache possibly known to man or angel."

"No!" Michael grabbed the sword Gabe had left on the ground and rose to his feet.

"You will die, alone and without redemption," God stated somberly.

"No! No! No! No! No!" Michael shouted and ran towards us.

"Gabe, watch out!" I shouted.

Michael raced towards Gabe with his sword held high. In one fluid movement, Michael pulled Gabe's head back and slashed his throat. Lily screamed in his arms as Gabe's body fell backwards.

"Gabe!" I shouted. I cried and cradled his body in my arms.

Faster than a lightning bolt, so fast I could not track it with my eyes, Lucifer was by our side, Michael's arm was broken, and his sword was on the ground. Lucifer wrapped his hands around Michael's throat and began to squeeze tightly.

Sara ran to my side, sobbing and grabbed Lily. She tried to keep Lily's face turned away from her dying father. Lily continuously turned her head towards us, whispering "Daddy". I cradled Gabe's head in my hands, wailing loudly. God stepped forward and placed his hand on my shoulder.

"Put Michael down, son," God ordered to Lucifer. "Bethany, Lilith, get this traitor out of here, now. Take him as far from this place as possible and leave him to his demise."

"Of course, Father." Lilith yanked him from Lucifer's grip.

"And I meant what I said, Lilith. Leave him alive," God commanded.

"He deserves nothing less," she grinned.

"Eden, my child, I need you to move." God frowned.

"I can't. I can't leave him," I sobbed.

Riley walked to my side and helped me to my feet. I buried my face in his chest, as God knelt down over my brother. I turned as I heard Sara gasp. God held His hand to Gabe's chest and held his brightly glowing soul.

I watched, amazed, as the blood and ink ran off of his skin like beads of water. God stood up, grabbing my hand and pulling me forward. He knelt down to my brother once more, cradling him in the crook of His arm. I stood next to them both as my lip quivered. Riley placed his hands on my shoulders, reassuringly.

"Eden, do you wish to give part of yourself to your brother? Do you wish to complete his soul and make him a part of you, as you had with Gabriel?" God asked.

"Yes!" I cried and laughed at the same time. "Please. Yes."

"Then it shall be done." God eased Gabe to the ground.

He held His hand to both our chests. I felt my head fall backwards, as part of my soul was removed from my body. Images of my brother and I playing as children, fighting, laughing, crying, flashed through my mind, as a piece of him was nestled in my body.

"Oh, my God," Sara gasped, dropping to her knees.

"What the fuck just happened?" Gabe asked, as he opened his eyes and sat up.

"Gabe!" I laughed and wrapped my arms around his neck.

"Edie?" he asked, eyes narrowed.

"Welcome back, my son." God grinned.

"Whoa. Oh, holy shit." Gabe shook his head. "I mean, divine shit. Shit, I mean. Whoa."

God chuckled heartily, "I will forgive your reactions. I realize that this is much to take in."

Gabe rose to his feet and spread his newly acquired wings for the first time. "Holy shit," he whispered. He looked at Sara and grinned. He looked at me and smiled widely, laughed to himself, then looked at his hands and arms. "Are you kidding me?!"

I laughed loudly and wrapped my arms around his chest, "What was that shit you said about me being jealous of your tattoos? Eat it."

"Huff my heavenly taint, shit head!" Gabe laughed and hugged me tightly.

EPILOGUE

As dusk settled into night, our hearts and minds began to settle as well. The fighting had ended, only by the grace of God. The peace was awkward, after the torture and turmoil we had endured for so long. It was hard to grasp. Every noise made us jump out of habit. It was going to take a while to fully recover from everything that had happened, but the healing process had begun.

Goodbyes were whispered, and tears were shed, as we all began to part ways. After restoring him to his heavenly form, God had agreed to allow Riley to stay on Earth. He would be in charge of the Earth's restoration project, leading a group of Michael's angels seeking redemption and a few others who refused to leave his side. It would be a burden, but it was only fitting.

Most of those who had joined us from the heavens returned to their lofty home and left all of us to our farewells. It was hard to say goodbye, even though we knew we'd be reunited again very soon. The following day, to be exact. The angels had risked so much by aiding us. One could only hope that the people of Earth would show them gratitude for their actions, but that wouldn't happen. People didn't know of those sacrifices they had made. People were completely unaware of the war that raged in the little suburb in Orange, Texas.

The family members, friends and companions that had once taken shelter together, were now making plans to return to their homes and do their parts to enlighten the world. It would be a heartfelt endeavor, but wouldn't necessarily make a difference. Humanity had become so jaded, so selfish, that their voices would go unheard. Pathetic? Of course. But that's the way of our world.

Lucifer had disappeared behind the scenes, once more. As he strode off into the sunset like a villainous, yet heroic cowboy, he left us all with a newfound respect for his work. Oddly enough, it was very hard to say goodbye to him. He had done so much for us, despite his intentions. Whether he had done what he had to ensure his reign on Earth or not, he had aided us beyond what we could've imagined. In typical Lucifer fashion, his last words to me as he departed were "see you soon, Love", with a wink and that dazzling smile. I'm not sure if it was a warning or a promise, but it was unnerving.

Gabe had a chance to say goodbye to Sara and the kids in a much more positive manner. Though Lily was not handling any of it very well, she at least could kiss her father, without the mask of death covering his face. We feared that what she had witnessed would have permanent repercussions, but at that point, there was nothing we could do about that.

Lilith and Gabriel returned to the cosmos with Elijah. This was the first time ever that he would be a part of the Fold. This was also the first time they had been reunited as a functioning family, since The Great Divide. After thousands of years of separation and heartache, they all deserved the peace and stability.

God gave me back my wings, talents, and peace of mind. Gabe and I would get to spend the rest of the night with our family and friends, but had to join everyone the following day in Heaven. It was like Cinderella, except our pumpkin coach involved the wrath of God if we missed our curfew. Needless to say, that wouldn't be happening... not this time.

To appease my father, I did clean up... some. Granted, I couldn't do a damned thing about the house, but I could at least give them some pretty awesome flowers. I knew it wasn't exactly a fair trade, and couldn't help but laugh seeing the house in shambles with a yard worthy of a spot in a gardening magazine.

So, what happened to Michael, the twins, and the rest of the world, you ask? Oh, honey, that's a whole other story altogether...

My unending, heartfelt thanks go out to many, but more specifically, to a select group of amazing individuals:

To my wonderful mother, hugest supporter, and most loyal fan, Kim. She painstakingly read this atrocity countless times with nary a complaint, other than the damned vulgarity. Ha ha! Just kidding... kind of. Thanks, Momma!

To my immeasurably adorable, devilish muse, Ryan, for thoughtfully luring me out of my hiatus and forcing me back to the writing, rewriting and marketing sweatshop. Without you, this project would still be sitting in fifty folders, collecting pixilated dust. You successfully managed to give me hope, helped me see my goals and were more supportive through this process than I could've dreamt possible. You have my heart, kind sir. Thank you, so very much. I love you, more than anything in the universe.

To my role model and gift from God, my dad, Kurt. You helped create this twisted mind and without your guidance through life and never ending support, I'd never have amounted to anything. I still may not, but it wouldn't make a difference to you; I'd still be your pork chop/ princess. Thank you, Daddy. I love you.

To all of my awesome brothers, who... Well, they influenced a lot of things in my life, up to and including my harsh humor, my horrible tendency to handicap my locutions, but most importantly, my fervent love and pride for my family. Ross, Eli, Lucas, and Gabe; you're all amazing. Gabe, in particular for being forced to drag me around like your annoying puppy for most of your childhood, thanks. I owe y'all the world, which is what I intend to give you in return.

Thank you very much, Aidan Boyd! She absolutely nailed the cover! She tirelessly worked on the text and design to get it exactly as I wanted and did an amazing job! Kudos, ma'am! You're phenomenal.

To Rufio, my old furry bundle of joy, I miss you so and hope you are still a happy boy. To Turkey, you sexy beast. To my friends and family who patiently waited for the finished product and didn't outright shun me in public for my heresies. To anyone and everyone who contributed to Descension's publication, thank you for being a part of this beast's birth! To Lamar, Mike, Chuck, and Paul for inspiring some of my favorite characters ever written. Y'all are some of the coolest people on this planet and I will always be thankful for the friendship you have given me.

And most importantly, to my new meaning(s) of life, Quinn and Connell. When you popped up unexpectedly, you scared the crap out of me, twice! In an amazing way, of course. Little did I know, I was meant for more; to be a mother. It was like I had predicted it with writing?! It was fortuitous that I'd not only write about the future saviors of the world, but I would one day create them in reality, as well. Though you won't read this until you're old enough, probably not interested, no longer grounded for giving me stretch marks during pregnancy and putting me on bed rest twice, I'm forever thankful to have you both. You've inspired me to see unconditional love, without skepticism or cynicism. I love you both, more than you will ever fathom.

To everyone else who read this and enjoyed it, thank you! On to the next!

ASCENSION:
Book Two of the Legacy Series

"They gather in secrecy; completely undetectable by both Heaven and Hell, my lord," the scout reported.

"And what of Azrael? Has he been seen?" I readjusted myself on my throne.

"Not that I've been informed of, my lord. As far as our troops are aware, he's currently in Russia, cleaning up a bit of a mess."

"I somehow find that hard to believe, given some of his past antics. I foresee him sticking his boney little fingers in this soup as often as possible. You know as well as I do, his fascination with meddling in the most chaotic of affairs." I leaned forward, allowing my wings to flex and stretch. I was feeling restless. "Thank you, Andras. Keep me informed of all of your findings, including all of the muttering you hear as you mull about."

"Yes, my lord." he bowed and exited the throne room.

It's been nineteen years since the event known as "The End of Days" occurred. Strange title for a moment that never exactly took place. There were cities and countries destroyed, yes; millions upon millions of people lost their lives. Yet, how can you call something 'the end' when you are, in fact, still around to see the aftermath? It's all malarkey to me. It was merely a minor scuffle, of a sort. I would say I've seen worse, but nothing quite stuck in my craw like that little fiasco with Michael.

After almost two decades, you would only assume that emotions would have toned themselves down, ever so slightly. Not a chance. Life has been lived as if everyone was teetering on the edge of a samurai's blade. Any day, God could return and say, "Just kidding, I want it back." In everyone's defense, that was perfectly feasible. I wouldn't have put it past him. He's like a selfish, little brat. And I can say that, because I am a part of Him.

The throne room was bleak, beyond the scarce torches illuminating the Renaissance art clung to the sooty, singed walls. The black marble flooring scattered light about, reminiscent of the cosmos, themselves. It was both my sanctuary and my cell. The perfect fit for the king of temptation and self-gratification. Punishment? I think not. Solitude was my solace. An eternity of this life was simply heaven sent. Quite literally, to be exact.

I still made my journey to the heavens, quite frequently. Especially when I'd decided to stir up a little action, or merely to visit Madame Muse. After all of this time, she still refused to join me in my chambers. But, I was fairly certain that her will would bend one day. Until then, I wouldn't stop turning on the suave and debonair demeanor. She's a stone cold minx.

Speaking of the muse, Eden had spent every day by God's side, since returning to the heavens; raising her boys to be the *heroes* they were intended to be... *Self-righteous, little twats.*

She had lost a bit of her sparkle. But, I suppose that was to be expected as she became more heavenly. She was still a perfect specimen. Beautiful on the inside and out... and in no distress without what's-his-face, I might add.

Ah, yes, *Thaddeus.* Where to begin with that imbecile? What a waste of divine grace. Though he always was, he'd proven himself to be even more worthless since "Judgement Day". He was like a child with a wooden sword against the hellions, and had yet to get the whole Michael situation under control. In fact, he'd yet to get his drinking problem under control, either. As far as I could tell, he hadn't given up hope that his soul would be redeemed and he'd someday be granted a return to the heavens and his sweet love. He wasn't going anywhere... Especially not with his actions, as of late.

Of which, left me with more work to handle myself, and more conversations than could be avoided with God and Gabriel, who I simply got sick of seeing. It's like I went from being the right hand, to being the bastard stepchild perched adeptly below the golden boy. Damn him and his perfection. Damn him and his bond with Eden. I hold the reins of the world in my hand, but it was still, not quite enough. I wanted what he had. *I wanted her.*

Enough about Eden. There had been far too many events in the last nineteen years to dwell like a love struck boy. That was not what this story was ever intended to be about. It was merely a side note, that shouldn't have even crept into my mind. Alas, women worm their ways in with much skill and grace. And try as you might to avoid the mere thought of them, their intoxicating smell, the very sway of their hips as they walk, the silkiness of their voice as they fall head over heels for a devil's chicanery, is enough to send me into a tailspin of wickedness.

But, don't I have the right to that? I do, of course, hold the key to both Hell and humanity, right in the palm of my hand. It's as if I'm in charge of the world. In a sense, I *was.* And it was the threat against that world that caught my soul aglow, once more. I was filled with rage, renewed like a phoenix, born again and more than ready to seek vengeance.

I arose from my throne and poured myself a crystal goblet of Pinot Noir. I sloshed it around for a second, took a sip and spit it to the floor. I never understood my obsession with wine that was hundreds of years old. Not only did it taste putrid, but it did absolutely nothing for me. I didn't eat. I didn't drink. It was pointless. Yet, someone out there, was dreaming of owning that very bottle. Losing sleep over that exact bottle. The very bottle that I poured out into the hellhound's dish.

"Drink up, Bauchan."

He sniffed at the red wine and backed away. It seemed his tastes were no better than my own.

"That's what I thought. Humans are such vile creatures; filling themselves with such heinous toxins, for sheer enjoyment." I scratched at my hellhound's hackles. "Oh, the debauchery! I *love* it!"

I traversed the hallways. It was another sleepless night. No rest for the wicked, one might say. Though I didn't physically need sleep, sometimes I craved it. It was a chance to delve into the hearts and minds of man. It was a chance to lure the weak into caving, giving into their most carnal of pleasures. And sometimes, every so often, it was a way to communicate with Eden. Though she pretended to not be excited to see me, her racing heart and lip biting told me a different story.

I stepped out onto the balcony, overlooking an abyss of restless souls. The mournful wails reminded me of banshees serenading me with sweet nothings. I could hear a symphony, playing in my head; beautiful and blithe. The story was painful, of love lost; of life ill-lived. It rang in my ears like a siren's call, helping me to regain my composure and shake the present thoughts from my mind.

Far below my balcony, the cold blue flames licked at the withered trees, long since dead and never to see sunlight again. This world was barren and bleak, just as I loved it. It was a reflection of my mind, my soul, my dark heart. For you may call this place Hell, but I call it home. It is my kingdom. And I am its rightful ruler.
I am, Lucifer.

Layla Reddoch is a paramedic, currently working in an emergency room at a hospital in Washington, DC. She spent the majority of her life rather nomadic and has since settled down in a small suburb outside of the Washington, DC area, in neighboring Maryland, with her fiancé and two small children. She is currently working on the remaining books of the Legacy Series, as well as an art project revolving around DESCENSION, called REPENT! She uses humor and raw emotion to address complex, sensitive material, making it more lighthearted and contemplative.

Contact her at descensionbook@gmail.com, on Twitter @descensionbook or on Facebook.

DESCENSION

First Printing: August, 2015
Printed in the United States of America

First Edition: August, 2015